EDITED BY

EDITED BY

Ellen Datlow

Subterranean Press 2020

First Edition

ISBN
978-1-59606-967-1

See pages 629-632 for individual story credits.

Subterranean Press
PO Box 190106
Burton, MI 48519

subterraneanpress.com

Manufactured in the United States of America.

This book is dedicated to all the writers
I've been working with over the years.
You, my dears, have given me a joyous career.

Acknowledgments

Thanks to Betsy Mitchell and Open Road Media for getting me manuscript files for some of my anthologies that were published in the stone ages, before the existence of electronic files.

Thanks to William Schafer of Subterranean, who came up with the idea—I thought/think he's crazy, but hey, what do *I* know?

Thanks to all my authors who provided me with electronic copies of their stories, whether I used those stories or not.

Finally, a special thanks to those who run the Internet Speculative Fiction Database (ISFDB) for its invaluable help not only in writing story notes for this book, but for being such a useful reference tool.

Table of Contents

Introduction:
The Fiction Editor

Gary K. Wolfe

Fantasy, science fiction, and horror writers love their editors.
Well, maybe not all editors, and maybe not all the time, and there might be a certain number of writers who view rejection notes or requests for revisions as though they were challenges to the dueling field. But by and large writers recognize that their genres were shaped, and in some cases nearly invented, by the short fiction editors—first in the pulp magazines, later in their digest-sized inheritors and anthologies, and in a few cases in the handful of mainstream magazines which were receptive to genre fiction. (Book and novel editors specializing in genre didn't really become a force in the field until the 1950s for science fiction, and even later for genre fantasy and horror.) When the first big science fiction and horror anthologies appeared in the 1940s, they were a way of preserving in book form stories which had originally appeared in ephemeral magazines, but by the early 1950s editors like Frederik Pohl and Raymond Healy were introducing anthologies of all original stories. Today, building an anthology of original stories—or a mix of originals and reprints, as Ellen Datlow has sometimes done—can be seen as an art form in itself, an almost musical one. A good anthology has a shape and a rhythm (even though, as Datlow notes, not every reader follows the order of stories as presented), with a mix of counterpoint, harmony, and occasional dissonance, and almost always with a few surprises.

A generation of readers in the 1950s learned to appreciate short fiction not only from the magazines, but from anthologists like Groff Conklin, August Derleth, or Judith Merril; in the 1960s it might have been Terry Carr or Robert Silverberg or Harlan Ellison, in the 1970s Damon Knight or Harry Harrison, in the 1980s (for horror in particular) Charles M. Grant. By the 1980s, Gardner Dozois had come to dominate the "year's best science fiction field," while an equally influential companion volume, *The Year's Best Fantasy and Horror*, was co-edited by Terri Windling and Ellen Datlow. Nowadays, of course, editors may buy fiction for online magazines or websites as well as print magazines, but the anthology remains a crucial part of the field, and to a great extent *Edited By* is a celebration of—well, of anthologies in general, and in particular of the work of one of the most prolific and widely honored anthologists the field has ever seen.

Those honors which Datlow has received are another indication of the degree to which the fantastic genres recognize and celebrate their editors. (To my knowledge, this is not generally true of genres like mysteries or romance.) With the exception of the Nebula Award (which is specifically designated for writers), nearly every major award in the field includes categories for editors and/or anthologies—and in fact the most prominent science fiction award, the Hugo, is even named after the field's first prominent editor, Hugo Gernsback, even though by modern (or even not-modern) literary standards, he wasn't really very good as an editor. Datlow has won, so far, eight Hugo Awards out of twenty nominations since 1990. She's also won ten World Fantasy Awards out of an astonishing 46 nominations, five Bram Stoker Awards for horror out of 18 nominations, 14 Locus Awards out of a ridiculous 98 nominations, three Shirley Jackson Awards out of 11 nominations, and two British Fantasy Awards out of nine nominations. This is in addition to lifetime achievement honors from World Fantasy and the Bram Stoker Awards and a special Karl Edward Wagner Award from the British Fantasy Society. The awards won by authors and stories she has published, dating all the way back to her fiction editing of *Omni* magazine in 1981, would be daunting to even begin to calculate—but, as Datlow herself would be the first to point out, awards aren't really the issue.

What is an issue, perhaps, is the sheer variety of *kinds* of anthologies represented in this volume. Note that the litany above includes awards for fantasy, for science fiction, and for horror—genres which have sometimes been given collective labels like supergenre, metagenre, or (in critic John Clute's term) fantastika, but which can also eye each other warily across the room, as though someone might be hogging the sweets table. Each genre has its devoted readers who want little to do with their alleged sister genres, and each has its dedicated awards and conventions. But since the beginning of her career, Datlow has helped to shape the tastes of readers in each of these fields, and probably to help broaden those tastes as well. She first came to prominence as the fiction editor of the slick science-and-fiction magazine *Omni* (and its online successor) from 1981 to 1998, during which time the magazine published not only classic SF stories by virtually every major writer in the field, but work by widely-known "mainstream" authors such as Joyce Carol Oates and T. C. Boyle, and stories which sometimes blurred the boundaries of the fantastic genres. After *Omni* folded, Datlow went on to edit fiction for the online venues *Event Horizon* and *Sci Fiction*, and since 2013 has acquired fiction for *Tor.com*.

While still at *Omni*, Datlow began a two-decade stint co-editing *The Year's Best Fantasy and Horror*, with Terri Windling choosing the fantasy selections and Datlow separately responsible for horror—although occasionally a particular story would be chosen by both in tandem, again reinforcing the notion that the line between fantasy and horror could often be arbitrary. About the same time, and while she was also editing a well-received series of anthologies drawn from *Omni* (but including original fiction as well), Datlow assembled *Blood is Not Enough: 17 Stories of Vampirism*, a collection of mostly original poems and stories, which began a long series of themed anthologies including *Alien Sex* (1990), *A Whisper of Blood* (1991), and many others, including another series of collaborations with Terri Windling. These various anthologies ranged from stories based on fairytales, folk legends, and trickster tales to tributes to authors like H.P. Lovecraft, Edgar Allan Poe, and Lewis Carroll and even collections focused on such particular themes as birds and dolls. As many of the stories which follow demonstrate, Datlow's (or Datlow and Windling's) ideas for such anthologies prompted some very distinguished writers to come up with some very distinguished work that might not have been written at all otherwise. See in particular the stories by Kij Johnson, Howard Waldrop, Catherynne Valente, Pat Cadigan, Carol Emshwiller, Ted Chiang, Nalo Hopkinson, Priya Sharma, John Langan, Jane Yolen, Jeffrey Ford, and Richard Bowes.

Datlow also has an impressive track record of spotting and inviting into her anthologies new or relatively new talent, such as Caitlín R. Kiernan (who had yet to publish her first novel when "Anamorphosis" appeared), Nalo Hopkinson (whose second story appeared in a Datlow/Windling anthology), and Ted Chiang. The Chiang story included here, "Seventy-Two Letters," was only his fifth published story—but Datlow had also bought his first, "Tower of Babylon," for *Omni* in 1990. Similarly, Nathan Ballingrud had published only a handful of stories prior to "The Monsters of Heaven," and much the same is true of Glen Hirshberg, whose second published story had been sold to Datlow when she was editing *Sci Fiction*. For two decades, many aspiring writers regarded an appearance in *The Year's Best Fantasy and Horror*—or even an "honorable mention"—as a sign of having arrived, or at least of having made it onto the genre's radar.

On Datlow's website, *ellendatlow.com,* she simply identifies herself as "Fiction Editor," which sounds pretty unprepossessing until you realize what it means for a career now in its fourth decade. "Anthologist" would be far too limiting, since another equally impressive anthology could be compiled from stories she has acquired for magazines or online venues (and I, for one, would like to see it). Few editors, even the legendary ones, have had careers as durable and wide-ranging: Hugo Gernsback's tenure as an editor of any real influence barely lasted a decade past the founding of *Amazing Stories* in 1926, and while John W. Campbell, Jr. lasted 34 years as editor of *Astounding/Analog*, arguably his influence had begun to wane by the 1960s. Groff Conklin, one of the few anthologists to work in horror as well as science fiction, edited volumes from 1946 until his death in 1968 (with a couple of posthumous titles later), while Judith Merril's active career lasted 20 years, mostly of "year's best" volumes. With the 40th anniversary of her career approaching, probably faster than she would like to think, Datlow shows no signs of flagging, remaining as open as ever to new voices and new directions in fantastic fiction, and as inventive in finding new themes to explore (birds! dolls! carnivals! Mad Hatters!). But as the stories that follow demonstrate, there's far more to Datlow's career than a record-breaking run and an almost unprecedented string of honors: there is, above all, the fiction, much of which we would never have seen except for the exceptional taste, the ingenious ideas—and occasionally the tireless nudging and cajoling—of the Fiction Editor.

Home by the Sea

by Pat Cadigan

(From *A Whisper of Blood,* 1991)

There was no horizon line out on the water.

"Limbo ocean. Man, did we hate this when I was a commercial fisherman," said a man sitting at the table to my left. "Worse than fog. You never knew where you were."

I sneaked a look at him and his companions. The genial voice came from a face you'd have expected to find on a wanted poster of a Middle Eastern terrorist, but the intonations were vaguely Germanic. The three American women with him were all of a type, possibly related. A very normal-looking group, with no unusual piercings or marks. I wondered how long they'd been in Scheveningen.

I slumped down in my chair, closed my eyes, and lifted my face to where I thought the sun should be. It was so overcast, there wasn't even a hot spot in the sky. Nonetheless, the promenade was crowded, people wandering up and down aimlessly, perhaps pretending, as I was, that they were on vacation. It was equally crowded at night, when everyone came to watch the stars go out.

Of course *we're on vacation,* a woman had said last night at another of the strange parties that kept congealing in ruined hotel lobbies and galleries. This had been one of the fancier places, ceilings in the stratosphere and lots of great, big ornate windows so we could look out anytime and see the stars die. *It's an* enforced *vacation. Actually, it's the world that's gone on vacation.*

No, that's not it, someone else had said in an impeccable British accent. It always surprised me to hear one, though I don't know why; England wasn't that far away. *What it is, is that the universe has quit its job.*

Best description yet, I'd decided. *The universe has quit its job.*

"Hey, Jess." I heard Jim plop down in the chair next to me. "Look what I found."

I opened my eyes. He was holding a fan of glossy postcards like a winning poker hand. Scheveningen and The Hague as they had been. I took them from him, looked carefully at each one. If you didn't know any better, you'd have thought it had been a happy world, just from looking at these.

"Where'd you find them?"

"Up a ways," he said, gesturing vaguely over his shoulder. He went *up a ways* a lot now, scavenging bits of this and that, bringing them to me as if they were small, priceless treasures. Perhaps they were—souvenirs of a lost civilization. Being of the why-bother school now, myself, I preferred to vegetate in a chair. "Kid with a whole pile of them. I traded him that can of beer I found." He stroked his beard with splayed fingers. "Maybe he can trade it for something useful. And if he can't, maybe he can fill a water pistol with it."

What would be useful, now that the universe had quit its job? I thought of making a list on the back of one of the postcards. Clothing. Shelter. Something to keep you occupied while you waited for the last star to go out—a jigsaw puzzle, perhaps. But Jim never showed up with one of those, and I wasn't ambitious enough to go looking myself.

My old hard-driving career persona would have viewed that with some irony. But now I could finally appreciate that being so driven could not have changed anything. Ultimately, you pounded your fist against the universe and then found you hadn't made so much as a dent, let alone reshaped it. Oddly enough, that knowledge gave me peace.

Peace seemed to have settled all around me. Holland, or at least this part of Holland, was quiet. All radio and TV communications seemed to be permanently disrupted—the rest of the world might have been burning, for all we knew, and we'd just happened to end up in a trouble-free zone. Sheerly by accident, thanks to a special our travel agency had been running at the time. We joked about it: *How did you happen to come to Holland? Oh, we had a coupon.*

A kid walked by with a boombox blaring an all-too-familiar song about the end of the world as we know it and feeling fine. The reaction from the people sitting at the tables was spontaneous and unanimous. They began throwing things at him, fragments of bricks, cups, cans, plastic bottles, whatever was handy, yelling in a multitude of languages for him to beat it.

The kid laughed loudly, yelled an obscenity in Dutch, and ran away up the promenade, clutching his boombox to his front. Mission accomplished, the tourists had been cheesed off again. The man at the next table had half risen out of his chair and now sat down again, grinning sheepishly. "All I was gonna do was ask him where he found batteries that work. I'd really like to listen to my CD player." He caught my eye and shrugged. "It's not like I could hurt him, right?"

Jim was paying no attention. He had his left hand on the table, palm up, studiously drawing the edge of one of the postcards across the pad below his thumb, making deep, slanted cuts.

"I wish you wouldn't do that," I said.

"Fascinating. Really fascinating." He traced each cut with a finger. "No pain, no pain at all. No blood and no pain. I just can't get over that."

I looked toward the horizonless ocean. From where I was sitting, I had a clear view of the tower on the circular pier several hundred feet from the beach, and of the woman who had hanged herself from the railing near the top. Her nude body rotated in a leisurely way, testifying to the planet's own continuing rotation. As I watched, she raised one arm and waved to someone on the shore.

"Well," I said, "what did you expect at the end of the world?"

"You really shouldn't deface yourself," I said as we strolled back to the hotel where we were squatting. If you could really call it a hotel—there was no charge to stay there, no service, and no amenities. "I know it doesn't hurt, but it doesn't heal, either. Now you've got permanent hash marks, and besides not being terribly attractive, they'll probably catch on everything."

Jim sighed. "I know. I get bored."

"Right." I laughed. "For the last twenty years, you've been telling me I should learn how to stop and smell the roses and now *you're* the one who's complaining about having nothing to do."

"After you've smelled a rose for long enough, it loses its scent. Then you have to find a different flower."

"Well, self-mutilation *is* different, I'll give you that." We passed a young guy dressed in leather with an irregular-shaped fragment of mirror embedded in his forehead. "Though maybe not as different as it used to be, since it seems to be catching on. What do you suppose *he's* smelling?"

Jim didn't answer. We reached the circular drive that dead-ended the street in front of our hotel, which had gone from motorcycle parking lot to motorcycle graveyard. On impulse, I took Jim's hand in my own as we crossed the drive. "I suppose it's the nature of the end of time or whatever this is, and the world never was a terribly orderly place. But nothing makes sense anymore. Why do we still have day and night? Why does the earth keep turning?"

"Winding down," Jim said absently. "No reason why the whole thing should go at once." He stopped short in the middle of the sidewalk in front of the hotel. "Listen."

There was a distant metallic crashing noise, heavy wheels on rails. "Just the trams running again. That's something else—why does the power work in some places and not in others?"

"What?" Jim blinked at me, then glanced in the general direction of the tram yard. "Oh, that. Not what I meant. Something I've been wondering lately"—there was a clatter as a tram went by on the cross street "—why we never got married."

Speaking of things that didn't seem important anymore—it wasn't the first time the subject had come up. We'd talked about it on and off through the years, but after eighteen years together, the matter had lost any urgency it might have had, if it had ever had any. Now, under a blank sky in front of a luxury hotel where the guests had become squatters, it seemed to be the least of the shadow-things my life had been full of, like status and career and material comforts. I could have been a primitive tribeswoman hoarding shiny stones for all the real difference those things had ever made. They'd given me nothing beyond some momentary delight; if anything, they'd actually taken more from me, in terms of the effort I'd had to put into acquiring them, caring for them, keeping them tidy and intact. Especially the status and the career. And they sure hadn't stopped the world from ending, no more than our being married would have.

But I was so certain of what Jim wanted to hear that I could practically feel the words arranging themselves in the air between us, just waiting for me to provide the voice. *Well, dear, let's just hunt up a cleric and get married right now.* Add sound and stir till thickened. Then—

Then what? It wasn't like we actually had a future anymore, together or singly. The ocean didn't even have a horizon.

"I think we *are* married," I said. "I think any two people seeing the world to its conclusion together are married in a way that didn't exist until now."

It should have been the right thing to say. Instead, I sounded like a politician explaining how a tax increase wasn't really a tax increase after all. After two decades, I could do better than some saccharine weasel words, end of the world or no.

Say it, then. The other thing, what he's waiting for. What difference does it make? The question I had to answer first, maybe the question Jim was really asking.

The edges of the cuts he'd made in his hand moved against my skin. They felt like the gills of an underwater creature out of its element, seeking to be put back in.

No pain at all. No blood and no pain.

It's not like I could hurt him, right?

Right. It's the end of the world as we know it, and I feel nothing. So we can go ahead now, do all those things that used to be so dangerous. Self-mutilation, bonding rituals, any old hazard at all.

Jim's eyes were like glass.

"Better get into the lobby now if you want to see it."

It was the Ghost of Lifetimes Past; that was what Jim and I had been calling her. She stood a respectful distance from us, a painfully thin blond woman in a dirty white tutu and pink satin ballet shoes. The most jarring thing about her was not her silly outfit, or the way she kept popping up anywhere and everywhere, but that face—she had the deep creases of someone who had lived seventy very difficult years. Around the edge of her chin and jawbone, the skin had a peculiar strained look, as if it were being tightened and stretched somehow.

"The crucifixion," she said, and gave a small, lilting giggle. "They're probably going to take him down soon, so if you want a look, you'd better hurry." Her gaze drifted past us and she moved off, as if she'd heard someone calling her.

"You in the mood for a crucifixion?" I said lightly. It was a relief to have anything as a distraction.

"Not if we can possibly avoid it."

But there was no way we could. Pushing our way through the small crowd in the lobby, we couldn't help seeing it. I vaguely recognized the man nailed directly to the wall—one of the erstwhile millionaires from the suites on the top floor. He was naked except for a wide silk scarf around his hips and a studded collar or belt cinched wrong side out around his head in lieu of a crown of thorns. No blood, of course, but he was doing his best to look as if he were in pain.

"God," I whispered to Jim, "I hope it's not a trend."

He blew out a short, disgusted breath. "I'm going upstairs."

Somehow, I had the feeling that it wasn't really the crucifixion he was so disgusted with. I meant to follow him but suddenly I felt as nailed in place as the would-be Christ. Not that I had any real desire to stand there and stare at this freak show, but it held me all the same. All that Catholic schooling in my youth, I thought, finally catching up with me after all these years, activating a dormant taste for human sacrifice.

Ersatz-Christ looked around, gritting his teeth. "You're supposed to mock me," he said, the matter-of-fact tone more shocking than the spikes in his forearms. "It won't work unless you mock me."

"You're a day late and a few quarts low," someone in the crowd said. "It won't work unless you shed blood, either."

The crucified man winced. "Shit."

There was a roar of laughter.

"For some reason, that never occurs to them. About the blood."

I looked up at the man who had spoken. He smiled down at me, his angular face cheerfully apologetic. I couldn't remember having seen him around before.

"This is the third one I've seen," he said, jerking his head at the man on the wall. The straight black hair fell briefly over one eye and he tossed it back. "A grand gesture that ultimately means nothing. Don't you find it rather annoying, people who suddenly make those grand risky gestures only after there isn't a hope in the hell of it mattering? Banning the aerosol can after there's already a hole in the ozone layer, seeking alternate sources of power after nuclear reactors have already gone into operation. It's humanity's fatal flaw—locking the barn after the horse has fled. The only creature in the universe who displays such behavior."

I couldn't place his accent or, for that matter, determine if he actually had an accent—I was getting tone-deaf in that respect. He didn't look American, but that meant nothing. All the Americans were getting a European cast as they adopted the local face.

"The universe?" I said. "You must be exceptionally well traveled."

He laughed heartily, annoying ersatz-Christ and what sympathizers he had left. We moved out of the group, toward the unoccupied front desk. "The universe we know of, then. Which, for all intents and purposes, might as well be all the universe there is."

I shrugged. "There's something wrong with that statement, but I'm no longer compulsive enough to pick out what it is. But it might be comforting to know that if there is a more intelligent species somewhere, its foibles are greater than ours, too."

"Comforting?" He laughed again. "It would seem that in the absence of pain, no comfort is necessary." He paused, as if waiting for me to challenge him on that, and then stuck out his hand. "I'm Sandor."

"Jess." The warmth of his unmarked, uncut hand was a mild shock. Fluctuations in body temperatures were as nonexistent as blood in these nontimes. Which would only stand to reason, since blood flow governed skin temperature. Everyone was the same temperature now, but whether that was something feverish or as cold as a tomb was impossible to tell with no variation. Perhaps I just hadn't been touching the right people.

"Odd, isn't it," he said, politely disengaging his hand from mine. I felt a rush of embarrassment. "They wanted to investigate it at the hospital, but I wouldn't let them. Do you know, at the hospital, people are offering themselves for exploratory surgery and vivisection? And the doctors who have a stomach for such things take them willingly. Yes. They cut them open, these people, and explore their insides. Sometimes they remove internal organs and sew the people up again to see how they manage without them. They manage fine. And there is no blood, no blood anywhere, just a peculiar watery substance that pools in the body cavity.

"And hidden away in the hospital, there is a doctor who has removed a woman's head. Her body is inactive, of course, but it does not rot. The head functions, though without air to blow through the vocal cords, it's silent. It watches him, they say, and he talks to it. They say he is trying to get the head to communicate with him in tongue-clicks, but it won't cooperate. *She* won't cooperate, if you prefer. And then there's the children's ward and the nursery where they keep the babies. These babies—"

"*Stop* it," I said.

He looked dazed, as if I'd slapped him.

"Are you insane?"

Now he gave me a wary smile. "Does sanity even come into it?"

"I mean…well, we just met."

"Ah, how thoughtless of me."

I started to turn away.

That strangely warm hand was on my arm. "I do mean it. It *was* thoughtless, pouring all that out on someone I don't know. And a stranger here as well. It must be hard for you, all this and so far from home."

"Oh, I don't know." I glanced at the crucified man. "It's all so weird, I think maybe I'd just as soon not see it happen anyplace familiar. I don't really like to think about what it must be like back home." I jerked my thumb at the man nailed to the wall. "Like, I'd rather that be some total stranger than one of my neighbors."

"Yes, I can see that. Though it must be a little easier to be with someone you're close to, as well." He looked down for a moment. "I saw you come in with your companion."

I gave him points for perception—most people assumed Jim was my husband. "Are you from here?" I asked.

"No. As I'm sure you could tell."

"Not really. Is Sandor a Polish name?"

He shrugged. "Could be. But I'm not from there, either."

There was a minor commotion as the police came in, or rather, some people dressed in police uniforms. Scheveningen was maintaining a loose local government—God knew why, force of habit, perhaps—with a volunteer uniformed cadre that seemed to work primarily as moderators or referees, mostly for the foreigners. They pushed easily through the thinning crowd and started to remove the crucified man from the wall, ignoring his protests that he wasn't finished, or it wasn't finished, or something.

"Ite missa est," I said, watching. "Go, the Mass is over. Or something like that."

"You remember the Latin rite. I'm impressed."

"Some things hang on." I winced at the sound of ersatz-Christ's forearm breaking. "That sounded awful, even if it didn't hurt."

"It won't heal, either. Just goes on looking terrible. Inconvenient, too. At the hospital, they have—" He stopped. "Sorry. As you said, some things hang on."

"What do you suppose they'll do with him?" I asked as they took him out. "It's not like it's worth putting him in jail or anything."

"The hospital. It's where they take all the mutilation cases bad enough that they can't move around on their own. If they want mutilation, they can have plenty there, under better conditions, for better reasons, where no one has to see them."

Finally, I understood. "Did you work there long?"

"Volunteered," he said, after a moment of hesitation. "There are no employees anymore, just volunteers. A way to keep busy. I left—" He shrugged. "Sitting ducks."

"Pardon?"

"That's the expression in English, isn't it? For people who leave themselves open to harm? In this case, literally open."

"If it doesn't hurt and it doesn't kill them, and this is the end of it all as we know it," I said slowly, "how can they be leaving themselves open to harm?"

"A matter of differing cultural perspectives." He smiled.

I smiled back. "You never told me what culture you were from."

"I think you could say that we're all from here now. Or might as well be. There's an old saying that you are from the place where you die, not where you were born."

"I've never heard that one. And nobody's dying at the moment."

"But nothing happens. No matter what happens, nothing happens. Isn't that a description of a dying world? But perhaps you don't see it that way. And if you don't, then perhaps *you* aren't dying yet. Do you think if you cut yourself, you might bleed? Is it that belief that keeps *you* from mutilating yourself, or someone else? Do you even wonder about that?"

I looked from side to side. "I feel like I'm under siege here."

He laughed. "But *don't* you wonder? Why there aren't people running through the streets in an orgy of destruction, smashing windows and cars and each other? And themselves."

"Offhand, I'd say there just doesn't seem to be much point to it." I took a step back from him.

"Exactly. No point. No reward, no punishment, no pleasure, no pain. The family of humanity has stopped bickering, world peace at last. Do you think if humans had known what it would take to bring about world peace, that they'd have worked a lot harder for it?"

"Do you really think it's like this everywhere in the world?" I said, casually moving back another step.

"Don't you?" He spread his hands. "Can't you feel it?"

"Actually, I don't feel much." I shrugged. "Excuse me, I'm going to go catch up on my reading."

"Wait." He grabbed my arm and I jumped. "I'm sorry," he said, letting go almost immediately. "I suppose I'm wrong about there being no pleasure and pain. I'd forgotten about the pleasure of being able to talk to someone. Of sharing thoughts, if you'll pardon the expression."

I smiled. "Yeah. See you around." I shook his hand again, more to confirm what I'd felt when he'd grabbed my arm than out of courtesy, and found I'd been right. His skin definitely felt cooler. Maybe *he* was the one who wasn't dying and I had sucked whatever real life he had out of him.

Only the weird survive, I thought, and went upstairs.

No matter what happens, nothing happens. Jim was curled up on the bed, motionless. The silence in the room was darkening. Sleep canceled the breathing habit, if "sleep" it actually was. There were no dreams, nothing much like rest—more like being a machine that had been switched off. Another end-of-the-world absurdity.

At least I hadn't walked in to find him slicing himself up with a razor, I thought, going over to the pile of books on the nightstand. Whatever had possessed me to think that I would wait out the end of the world by catching up with my reading had drained away with my ambition. If I touched any of the books now, it was just to shift them around. Sometimes, when I looked at the covers, the words on them didn't always make sense right away, as if my ability to read was doing a slow fade along with everything else.

I didn't touch the books now as I stretched out on the bed next to Jim. He still didn't move. On the day—if "day" is the word for it—the world had ended, we'd be in this room, in this bed, lying side by side the way we were now. I am certain that we both came awake at the same moment, or came to might be a better way to put it. Went from unconscious to conscious was the way it felt, because I didn't wake up the way I usually did, slowly, groggily, and wanting nothing more than to roll over and go back to sleep for several more hours. I had never woken up well, as if my body had always been fighting the busy life my mind had imposed on it. But that "day," I was abruptly awake without transition, staring at the ceiling, and deep down I just *knew*.

There was no surprise in me, no regret, and no resistance. It was that certainty: *Time's up.* More than something I knew, it was something I *was*. Over, finished, done, used up...but not quite gone, as a bottle is not gone though emptied of its contents. I thought of Jim Morrison singing "The End," and felt some slight amusement that in the real end, it hadn't been anywhere near so dramatic. Just…*time's up.*

And when I'd finally said, "Jim…?" he'd answered, "Uh-huh. I've got it, too." And so had everyone else.

I raised up on one elbow and looked at him without thinking anything. After awhile, still not thinking anything, I pulled at his shirt and rolled him over.

Sex at the end of the world was as pointless as anything else, or as impossible as bleeding, depending on your point of view, I guess. The bodies didn't function; the minds didn't care. I felt some mild regret about that, and about the fact that all I *could* feel was mild regret.

But it was still possible to show affection—or to engage in pointless foreplay—and take a certain comfort in the contact. We hadn't been much for that in this no-time winding-down. Maybe passion had only been some long, pleasant dream that had ended with everything else. I slipped my hand under Jim's shirt.

His unmoving chest was cadaver-cold.

That's it, I thought, *now we're dying for real.* There was a fearful relief in the idea that I wouldn't have to worry about him mutilating himself any further.

Jim's eyes snapped open and he stared down at my hand still splayed on his stomach, as if it were some kind of alien, deformed starfish that had crawled out of the woodwork onto his torso.

"You're warm," he said, frowning.

And like that, I was lost in the memory of what it was to feel passion for another human being. What it was to *want*, emotions become physical reactions, flesh waking from calm to a level of response where the edge between pleasure and pain thinned to the wisp of a nerve ending.

I rolled off the bed and went into the bathroom. Behind me, I heard Jim rolling over again. Evidently he didn't want to know about my sudden change in temperature if I didn't want to tell him. A disposable razor sat abandoned on the counter near the sink. If I took it and ran my fingertip along the blade, would I see the blood well up in a bright, uneven bead? I didn't want to know, either.

The exploding star was a fiery blue-white flower against the black sky. Its light fell on the upturned faces of the crowd on the promenade, turning them milky for a few moments before it faded.

"Better than fireworks," I heard someone say.

"Ridiculous," said someone else. "Some kind of trick. The stars are thousands and millions of light-years away from us. If we see them exploding now, it means the universe actually ended millions of years ago and we're just now catching up with it."

"Then no wonder we never made any contact with life on other planets," said the first voice. "Doesn't *that* make sense? If the universe has been unraveling for the last million years, all extraterrestrial life was gone by the time we got the technology to search for it."

I looked around to see who was speaking and saw her immediately. The Ghost of Lifetimes Past was standing just outside the group, alone as usual, watching the people instead of the stars. She caught my eye before I could look away and put her fingertips to her mouth in a coy way, as if to stifle a discreet giggle. Then she turned and went up the promenade, tutu flouncing a little, as an orange starburst blossomed in the west.

If Jim had come out with me, I thought, weaving my way through the crowd, I probably wouldn't have been doing something as stupid as following this obviously loony woman. But he had remained on the bed, unmoving, long after it had gotten dark, and I hadn't disturbed him again. I had sat near the window with a book in my lap and told myself I was reading, not just staring until I got tired of seeing the same arrangement of words and turning a page, while I felt myself fade. It had been a very distinct sensation, what I might have felt if I had been awake when the world had ended.

The Ghost of Lifetimes Past didn't look back once but I was sure she knew I was following her, just as I knew she had meant for me to follow her, all the way to the Kurhaus. Even from a distance, I could see that the lights were on. Another party; what was it about the end of the world that seemed to cry out for parties? Perhaps it was some kind of misplaced huddling instinct.

I passed a man sitting on a broken brick wall, boredly hammering four-inch nails into his chest; if we hung notes on them, I thought, and sent him strolling up and down the promenade, we could have a sort of postal service-cum-newspaper. Hear ye, hear ye, the world is still dead. Or undead. Nondead. Universe still unemployed after quitting old job. Or was it, really?

The Ghost flounced across the rear courtyard of the Kurhaus without pausing, her ballet shoes going scritch-scritch on the pavement. Light spilled out from the tall windows, making giant, elongated lozenges of brightness on the stone. One level up, I could see people peering out the galleria windows at the sky. When the sun went, I thought suddenly, would we all finally go with it, or would it just leave us to watch cosmic fireworks in endless night?

They made me think of birds on a nature preserve, the people wandering around in the lobby. Birds in their best plumage and their best wounds. A young, black-haired guy in a pricey designer gown moved across the scuffed dusty floor several yards ahead of me, the two chandelier crystals stuck into his forehead above the eyebrows, catching the light. Diaphanous scarves fluttered from holes in his shoulder blades. Trick or treat, I thought. Or maybe it was All Souls' Day, every day.

At the bar island, someone had used the bottles on the surrounding shelves for target practice and the broken glass still lay everywhere like a scattering of jewels. I saw a woman idly pick up a shard lying on the bar and take a bite out of it, as if it were a potato chip. A man in white tie and tails was stretched out on the floor on his stomach, looking around and making notes on a stenographer's pad. I wandered over to see what he was writing, but it was all unreadable symbols, part shorthand, part hieroglyphics.

There was a clatter behind me. Some people were righting one of the overturned cocktail tables and pulling up what undamaged chairs they could find. It was the group that had been sitting near me on the promenade that day, the man and his three women companions, all of them chattering away to each other as if nothing was out of the ordinary. They were still unmarked and seemed oblivious to the freak show going on around them—I half expected the man to go to the bar and try to order. Or maybe someone would sweep up some broken glass and bring it to them on a tray. Happy Hour is here, complimentary hors d'oeuvres.

The Ghost reappeared on the other side of the bar. She looked worse, if that were possible, as if walking through the place had depleted her. A tall man on her left was speaking to her as he ran a finger along the wasted line of her chin while a man on her right was displaying the filigree of cuts he'd made all over his stomach, pulling the skin out and displaying it like a lace bib. The skin was losing its elasticity; it sagged over the waistband of his white satin pajama pants. The layer of muscle underneath showed through in dark brown.

I turned back to the group I'd seen on the promenade, still in their invisible bubble of normalcy. The man caught sight of me and smiled a greeting without a pause in what he was saying. Maybe I was supposed to choose, I thought suddenly; join the freaks or join the normalcy. And yet I had the feeling that if I chose the latter, I'd get wedged in among them somehow and never get back to Jim.

They were all staring at me questioningly now and something in those mild gazes made me think I was being measured. One of the women leaned into the group and said something; it was the signal for their intangible boundary to go back up again. Either I'd kept them waiting too long, or they didn't like what they saw, but the rejection was as obvious as if there had been a sign over their heads.

I started for the side door, intending to get out as fast as I could, and stopped short. The boy standing near the entrance to the casino might have been the same one who'd had the boombox, or not—it was hard to tell, there were so many good-looking blond boys here—but the man he was talking to was unmistakably Jim. He hadn't bothered to change his rumpled clothes or even to comb his hair, which was still flat on one side from the way he'd been lying on the bed.

Jim was doing most of the talking. The kid's expression was all studied diffidence, but he was listening carefully all the same. Jim showed him his hand and the kid took it, touching the cuts and nodding. After a few moments, he put his arm around Jim's shoulders and, still holding his hand, led him around the front of the closed, silent elevator doors to the stairs. I watched them go up together.

"Do you wonder what that was all about?"

I didn't turn around to look at him. "Well. Sandor Whoever from Wherever. The man who can still raise the mercury on a thermometer while the rest of us have settled at room temperature. If you start talking about interesting things people are doing in the hospital, I might take a swing at you."

He chuckled. "That's the spirit. Next question: Do you wonder how they get the power on in some places when it won't work in others?"

"In a way."

"Do you want to find out?"

I nodded.

He didn't touch me even in a casual way until we reached his room on the fourth floor. It was the first time I'd ever been higher than the galleria level. The lights in the hallway shone dimly, glowing with what little power was left from whatever was keeping the lobby lit up, and his hand was like fire as he pulled me out of the hallway and into the room.

His body was a layer of softness over hard muscle. I tore his clothing to get at it; he didn't mind. Bursts of light from the outside gave me fleeting snapshots of his face. No matter what I did, he had the same expression of calm acceptance. Perhaps out of habit, covering the secret of his warmth—if the rest of us pod creatures knew he was the last (?) living thing on earth, what might we not do for this feeling of life he could arouse?

Already, his flesh wasn't as warm as it had been. That was me, I thought, pushing him down on the bed. I was taking it from him and I couldn't help it. Or perhaps it was just something inherent in the nature of being alive, that it would migrate to anyplace it was not.

Even so, even as he went from hot to cool, he lost nothing. Receptive, responsive, accommodating—in the silent lightning of dying stars, calm and accepting, but not passive. I was leading in this pas de deux, but he seemed to know how and where almost before I did, and was ready for it.

And now I could feel *how* it was happening, the way the life in his body was leached away into my own un-alive flesh. I was taking it from him. The act of *taking* is a distinctive one; no one who had ever taken anything had taken it quite like I took Sandor.

He gave himself up without resistance, and yet *give up* was not what he was doing, unless it was possible to surrender aggressively. It was as if I wanted him because his purpose was to be wanted, and he had been waiting for me, for someone to provide the wanting, to want him to death. Ersatz-Christ in the lobby had had it wrong, it never could have worked. Humans didn't sacrifice themselves, they were sacrificed to; they didn't give, they were alive only in the act of taking—

Somehow, even with my head on fire, I pulled away from him. He flowed with the movement like a storm tide. I fought the tangle of sheets and cold flesh against warm, and the violence felt almost as good as the sex. If I couldn't fuck him to death, I'd settle for beating his head in, I thought dimly. We rolled off the bed onto the carpet and I scrambled away to the bathroom and slammed the door.

"Is there something wrong?" The puzzlement in his voice was so sincere I wanted to vomit.

"Stop it."

"Stop what?"

"Why did you let me do that to you?"

He might have laughed. "Did *you* do something to me?"

A weak pain fluttered through my belly. There was a wetness on my thighs.

"Turn on the light," he said. "You can now, you know. It'll work for you, now that you're living."

I flipped the switch. The sudden brightness was blinding. Turning away from the lights over the sink, I saw myself in the full-length mirror on the door. The wetness on my thighs was blood.

My blood? Or his?

The pain in my belly came again.

"Jess?"

"Get away. Let me get dressed and get out of here. I don't want this."

"Let me in."

"No. If you come near me, I'll take more from you."

Now he did laugh. "What is it you think *you* took?"

"Life. Whatever's left. You're alive and I'm one of the fading ones. I'll make you fade, too."

"That's an interesting theory. Is that what you think happened?"

"Somehow you're still really alive. Like the earth still turns, like there are still stars. Figures we wouldn't all fade away at once, us people. Some of us would still be alive. Maybe as long as there are still stars, there'll still be some people alive." The sound of my laughter in the small room was harsh and ugly. "So romantic. As long as there are stars in the sky, that's how long you'll be here for me. Go away. I don't want to hurt you."

"And what *will* you do?" he asked. "Go back to your bloodless room and your bloodless man, resume your bloodless wait to see what the end will be? It's all nothing without the risk, isn't it? When there's nothing to lose, there's really nothing at all. Isn't that right?"

The lock snapped and the door swung open. He stood there holding on to either side of the doorway. The stark hunger in the angular features had made his face into a predator's mask, intent, voracious, without mercy. I backed up a step, but there was nowhere to go.

He lunged at me and caught me under the arms, lifting me to eye level. "You silly cow," he whispered, and his breath smelled like meat. "*I didn't get cooler, you* just got *warmer.*"

He shoved me away. I hit the wall and slid down. The pain in my shoulders and back was exquisite, not really pain but pure sensation, the un-alive, undead nerve endings frenzied with it. I wanted him to do it again, I wanted him to hit me, or caress me, or cut me, or do anything that would make me *feel*. Pain or pleasure, whatever there was, I wanted to live through it, get lost in it, die of it, and, if I had to die of it, take him with me.

He stood over me with the barest of smiles. "Starting to understand now?"

I pushed myself up, my hands slipping and sticking on the tiled wall.

"Yeah." He nodded. "I think maybe you are. I think you're definitely starting to get it." He backed to the sink and slid a razor blade off the counter. "How about this?" He held the blade between two fingers, moving it back and forth so it caught the light. "Always good for a thrill. Your bloodless man understands that well enough already. Like so many others. Where do you think he goes when he takes his little walks up the promenade, what do you think he does when he leaves you to sit watching the hanging woman twist and turn on the end of her rope?" He laughed and popped the blade into his mouth, closing his eyes with ecstasy. Then he bared his teeth; the blood ran over his lower lip onto his chin and dripped down onto his chest.

"Come on," he said, the razor blade showing between his teeth. "Come *kiss* me."

I wasn't sure that I leaped at him as much as the life in him pulled me by that hunger for sensation. He caught me easily, holding me away for a few teasing seconds before letting our bodies collide.

The feeling was an explosion that rushed outward from me, and as it did, I finally did understand, mostly that I hadn't had it right at all, but it was too late to do anything about it. The only mercy he showed was to let the light go out again.

Or maybe that wasn't mercy. Maybe that was only what happened when he drained it all out of me and back into himself, every bit of pain and pleasure and being alive.

He kept the razor blade between his teeth for the whole time. It went everywhere, but he never did kiss me.

The room was so quiet, I thought he'd left. I got up from where I'd been lying, half in and half out of the bathroom, thinking I'd find my clothes and go away now, wondering how long I'd be able to hide the damage from Jim— if damage it was, since I no longer felt anything—wondering if I would end up in the hospital, if there was already a bed with my name on it, or whether I'd be just another exotic for nightly sessions at the Kurhaus.

"Just one more thing," he said quietly. I froze in the act of taking a step toward the bed. He was standing by the open window, looking out at the street.

"What's the matter?" I said. "Aren't I dead enough yet?"

He laughed, and now it was a soft, almost compassionate sound, the predator pitying the prey. "I just want to show you something."

"No."

He dragged me to the window and forced my head out. "See it anyway, this one time. A favor, because I'm so well pleased." He pulled my head back to make me look up at the sky. A night sky, very flat, very black, featureless, without a cloud and with no stars, none at all.

"A magic lantern show, yes," he said, as though I'd spoken. "*We* put the signs and wonders in the sky for you. So you wouldn't see *this*."

He forced my head down, digging his fingers more deeply into my hair. Below, in the courtyard, people wandered among a random arrangement of cylindrical things without seeing them. They were pale things, silent, unmoving; long, ropy extensions stretched out from the base of each one, sinking into the pavement like cables, except even in the dim light, I could see how they pulsed.

While I watched, a split appeared in the nearest one. The creature that pushed its way out to stand and stretch itself in the courtyard was naked, vaguely female-looking, but not quite human. It rubbed its hands over the surface of the cylinder, and then over itself. I pulled away.

"You see, that's the other thing about your kind besides your tendency toward too little, too late," he said conversationally as I dressed. If I tucked my shirt into my pants I could keep myself together a little better. "You miss things. You're blind. All of you. Otherwise, you'd have seen us before now. We've always been here, waiting for our time with you. If even one of you had seen us, you might have escaped us. Perhaps even destroyed us. Instead, you all went on with your lives. And now we're going on with them." He paused, maybe waiting for me to say something. I didn't even look at him as I wrapped my shirt around the ruin of my torso. "Don't worry. What I just showed you, you'll never see again. Perhaps by the time you get home, you'll even have forgotten that you saw anything."

He turned back to the window. "See you around the promenade."

"First time's the worst."

The Ghost of Lifetimes Past fell into step beside me as I walked back along the promenade. She was definitely looking worse, wilted and eaten away. "After that," she added, "it's the natural order of things."

"I don't know you," I said.

"I know you. We all know each other, after. Go home to your husband now and he'll know you, too."

"I'm not married."

"Sure." She smiled at me, her face breaking into a mass of lines and seams. "It could be worse, you know. They like to watch it waste me, they like to watch it creep through me and eat me alive. They pour life into us, they loan it to us, you could say, and then they take it back with a great deal of interest. And fascination. They feed on us, and we feed on them, but considering what they are, we're actually feeding on ourselves. And maybe a time will come that will really be the end. After all, how long can we make ourselves last?"

She veered away suddenly, disappearing down a staircase that led to one of the abandoned restaurants closer to the waterline.

As I passed the tower, the hanging woman waved a greeting. There would be no horizon line on the ocean again today.

I had thought Jim would know as soon as he saw me, but I didn't know what I expected him to do. He watched me from where he lay on the bed with his arms behind his head. Through the thin material of his shirt, I could see how he'd been split from below his collarbone down to his navel. It seems to be a favorite pattern of incision with them, or maybe they really have no imagination to speak of.

He still said nothing as I took a book from the stack on the nightstand and sat down in the chair by the window, positioning myself with my back to the room. The words on the pages looked funny, symbols for something I no longer knew anything about.

The mattress creaked as Jim got up and I heard him changing his clothes. I didn't want to look—after all, it wouldn't matter what I saw—and still not wanting to, I put the unreadable book aside and turned around.

The incision was actually very crude, as if it had been done with a jagged shard of glass. I wanted to feel bad at the sight, I wanted to feel sorry and sad and angry at the destruction, I wanted of feel the urge to rush to him and offer comfort. But as Sandor had pointed out, in the absence of pain, no comfort was necessary.

Abruptly, Jim shrugged and finished dressing, and I realized he'd been waiting for something, maybe for me to show him my own. But I had no desire to do that yet.

"I'm going for a walk up the promenade," he said, heading for the door. "You can come if you want." He didn't look back for a response.

"Do you think," I heard myself say just before he stepped out into the hall, "they're everywhere? Or if we could just get home somehow…"

"Jess." He almost smiled. "We *are* home."

I followed him at a distance. He didn't wait for me, walking along briskly but unhurriedly, and I didn't try to catch up with him. The sky seemed darker and duller, the sounds of the people on the promenade quieter, more muffled. The trams didn't run.

I stayed out until dark. The dying-stars show was especially spectacular, and I watched it until Sandor finally got around to coming back for me.

HOME BY THE SEA

Some history about how I got into the anthology editing game: I had been fiction at *Omni* Magazine for several years, when an editor at our sister magazine *Penthouse*, approached me for some ideas for theme anthologies he wanted to pitch to an interested book publisher. I came up with four or five. The pitches went nowhere.

However, I realized I'd like to work on anthologies because I was only publishing two or three stories a month at *Omni*, and I was eager to edit more. An agent friend promptly sold what became *Blood Is Not Enough* to David G. Hartwell at William Morrow.

Half the book consisted of classics that I loved, and recent stories that I was forced to turn down for *Omni* at the time (horror). The other half would be stories I commissioned. At the time, I was concerned that my bosses at *Omni* not see my editing of non-*Omni* anthologies as a conflict of interest, which is why I entered the horror field. Until well into my fiction editorship of *Omni* I was told, no horror, despite the fact that Ben Bova had acquired and published the Hugo and Nebula Award winning sf/horror novelette "Sandkings" by George R.R. Martin in the first year of *Omni*'s existence.

In both books (and my most recent vampire anthology *Blood and Other Cravings*) I was intent on expanding the trope of vampires, that is, to play with the possibilities of a larger view of vampirism, not just the draining of blood, but the theft of something psychological or emotional—the essence of what makes us human.

I was hoping to reprint Pat Cadigan's long novelette "Dirty Work" here but it was just too long. Instead, I've chosen "Home by the Sea," a vivid story about the end of the world, from *A Whisper of Blood*, the second volume in my so-called "blood" series of anthologies.

The Evolution of Trickster Stories Among the Dogs of North Park After the Change

by Kij Johnson

(From *The Coyote Road: Trickster Tales,* 2007)

North Park is a backwater tucked into a loop of the Kaw River: pale dirt and baked grass, aging playground equipment, silver-leafed cottonwoods, underbrush—mosquitoes and gnats blackening the air at dusk. To the south is a busy street. Engine noise and the hissing of tires on pavement mean it's no retreat. By late afternoon the air smells of hot tar and summertime river-bottoms. There are two entrances to North Park: the formal one, of silvered railroad ties framing an arch of sorts; and an accidental little gap in the fence, back where Second Street dead-ends into the park's west side, just by the river.

A few stray dogs have always lived here, too clever or shy or easily hidden to be caught and taken to the shelter. On nice days (and this is a nice day, a smell like boiling sweet corn easing in on the south wind to blunt the sharper scents), Linna sits at one of the faded picnic tables with a reading assignment from her summer class and a paper bag full of fast food, the remains of her lunch. She waits to see who visits her.

The squirrels come first, and she ignores them. At last she sees the little dust-colored dog, the one she calls Gold.

"What'd you bring?" he says. His voice, like all dogs' voices, is hoarse and rasping. He has trouble making certain sounds. Linna understands him the way one understands a bad lisp or someone speaking with a harelip.

(It's a universal fantasy, isn't it?—that the animals learn to speak, and at last we learn what they're thinking, our cats and dogs and horses: a new era in cross-species understanding. But nothing ever works out quite as we imagine. When the Change happened, it affected all the mammals we have shaped to meet our own needs. They all could talk a little, and they all could frame their thoughts well enough to talk. Cattle, horses, goats, llamas; rats, too. Pigs. Minks. And dogs and cats. And we found that, really, we prefer our slaves mute.

(The cats mostly leave, even ones who love their owners. Their pragmatic sociopathy makes us uncomfortable, and we bore them; and they leave. They slip out between our legs and lope into summer dusks. We hear them at night, fighting as they sort out ranges, mates, boundaries. The savage sounds frighten us, a fear that does not ease when our cat Klio returns home for a single night, asking to be fed and to sleep on the bed. A lot of cats die in fights or under car wheels, but they seem to prefer that to living under our roofs; and as I said, we fear them.

(Some dogs run away. Others are thrown out by the owners who loved them. Some were always free.)

"Chicken and French fries," Linna tells the dog, Gold. Linna has a summer cold that ruins her appetite, and in any case it's too hot to eat. She brought her lunch leftovers, hours-old but still lukewarm: half of a Chik-fil-A and some French fries. He never takes anything from her hand, so she tosses the food onto the ground just beyond kicking range. Gold likes French fries, so he eats them first.

Linna tips her head toward the two dogs she sees peeking from the bushes. (She knows better than to lift her hand suddenly, even to point or wave.) "Who are these two?"

"Hope and Maggie."

"Hi, Hope," Linna says. "Hi, Maggie." The dogs dip their heads nervously as if bowing. They don't meet her eyes. She recognizes their expressions, the hurt wariness: she's seen it a few times, on the recent strays of North Park, the ones whose owners threw them out after the Change. There are five North Park dogs she's seen so far: these two are new.

"Story," says the collie, Hope.

2. One Dog Loses Her Collar.

This is the same dog. She lives in a little room with her master. She has a collar that itches, so she claws at it. When her master comes home, he ties a rope to the collar and takes her outside to the sidewalk. There's a busy street outside. The dog wants to play on the street with the cars, which smell strong and move very fast. When her master tries to take her back inside, she sits down and won't move. He pulls on the rope and her collar slips over her ears and falls to the ground. When she sees this, she runs into the street. She gets hit by a car and dies.

This is not the first story Linna has heard the dogs tell. The first one was about a dog who's been inside all day and rushes outside with his master to urinate against a tree. When he's done, his master hits him, because his master was standing too close and his shoe is covered with urine. *One Dog Pisses on a Person.* The dog in the story has no name, but the dogs all call him (or her: she changes sex with each telling) One Dog. Each story starts: "This is the same dog."

The little dust-colored dog, Gold, is the storyteller. As the sky dims and the mosquitoes swarm, the strays of North Park ease from the underbrush and sit or lie belly-down in the dirt to listen to Gold. Linna listens, as well.

(Perhaps the dogs always told these stories and we could not understand them. Now they tell their stories here in North Park, as does the pack in Cruz Park a little to the south, and so across the world. The tales are not all the same, though there are similarities. There is no possibility of gathering them all. The dogs do not welcome eager anthropologists with their tape recorders and their agendas.)

(The cats after the Change tell stories as well, but no one will ever know what they are.)

When the story is done, and the last of the French fries eaten, Linna asks Hope, "Why are you here?" The collie turns her face away, and it is Maggie, the little Jack Russell, who answers: "Our mother made us leave. She has a baby." Maggie's tone is matter-of-fact: it is Hope who mourns for the woman and child she loved, who compulsively licks her paw as if she were dirty and cannot be cleaned.

Linna knows this story. She's heard it from the other new strays of North Park: all but Gold, who has been feral all his life.

(Sometimes we think we want to know what our dogs think. We don't, not really. Someone who watches us with unclouded eyes and sees who we really are is more frightening than a man with a gun. We can fight or flee or avoid the man, but the truth sticks like pine sap. After the Change, some dog owners feel a cold place in the pit of their stomachs when they meet their pets' eyes. Sooner or later, they ask their dogs to find new homes, or they forget to latch the gate, or they force the dogs out with curses and the ends of brooms. Or the dogs leave, unable to bear the look in their masters' eyes.

(The dogs gather in parks and gardens, anywhere close to food and water where they can stay out of people's way. Cruz Park ten blocks away is big, fifteen acres in the middle of town, and sixty or more dogs already have gathered there. They raid trash or beg from their former owners or strangers. They sleep under the bushes and bandstand and the inexpensive civic sculptures. No one goes to Cruz Park on their lunch breaks any more.

(In contrast North Park is a little dead-end. No one ever did go there, and so no one really worries much about the dogs there. Not yet.)

3. *One Dog Tries to Mate.*
This is the same dog. There is a female he very much wants to mate with. All the other dogs want to mate with her, too, but her master keeps her in a yard surrounded by a chain-link fence. She whines and rubs against the fence. All the dogs try to dig under the fence, but its base is buried too deep to find. They try to jump over, but it is too tall for even the biggest or most agile dogs.

One Dog has an idea. He finds a cigarette butt on the street and tucks it in his mouth. He finds a shirt in a dumpster and pulls it on. We walks right up to the master's front door and presses the bell-button. When the master answers the door, One Dog says, "I'm from the men with white trucks. I have to check your electrical statico-pressure. Can you let me into your yard?"

The man nods and lets him go in back. One Dog takes off his shirt and drops the cigarette and mates with the female. It feels very nice, but when he is done and they are still linked together, he starts to whine.

The Evolution of Trickster Stories Among the Dogs of North Park After the Change

The man hears and comes out. He's very angry. He shoots One Dog and kills him. The female tells One Dog, "You would have been better off if you had found another female."

The next day after classes (hot again, and heavy with the smell of cut grass), Linna finds a dog. She hears crying and crouches to peek under a hydrangea, its blue-gray flowers as fragile as paper. It's a Maltese with filthy fur matted with twigs and burrs. There are stains under her eyes and she is moaning, the terrible sound of an injured animal.

The Maltese comes nervous to Linna's outstretched fingers and the murmur of her voice. "I won't hurt you," Linna says. "It's okay."

Linna picks the dog up carefully, feeling the dog flinch under her hand as she checks for injuries. Linna knows already that the pain is not physical; she knows the dog's story before she hears it.

The house nearby is massive, a graceful collection of Edwardian gingerbread-work and oriel windows and dark-green roof tiles. The garden is large, with a low fence just tall enough to keep a Maltese in. Or out. A woman answers the doorbell: Linna can feel the Maltese vibrate in her arms at the sight of the woman: excitement, not fear.

"Is this your dog?" Linna asks with a smile. "I found her outside, scared."

The woman's eyes flicker to the dog and away, back to Linna's face. "We don't have a dog," she says.

(We like our slaves mute. We like to imagine they love us, and they do. But they are also with us because freedom and security war in each of us, and sometimes security wins out. They do love us. But.)

In those words Linna has already seen how this conversation will go, the denials and the tangled fear and anguish and self-loathing of the woman. Linna turns away in the middle of the woman's words and walks down the stairs, the brick walkway, through the gate and north, toward North Park.

The dog's name is Sophie. The other dogs are kind to her.

(When George Washington died, his will promised freedom for his slaves, but only after his wife had also passed on. A terrified Martha freed them within hours of his death. Though the dogs love us, thoughtful owners can't help but wonder what they think when they sit on the floor beside our beds as we sleep, teeth slightly bared as they pant in the heat. Do the dogs realize that their freedom hangs by the thread of our lives? The curse of speech—the things they could say and yet choose not to say—makes that thread seem very thin.

(Some people keep their dogs, even after the Change. Some people have the strength to love, no matter what. But many of us only learn the limits of our love when they have been breached. Some people keep their dogs; many do not.

(The dogs who stay seem to tell no stories.)

4. One Dog Catches Possums.

This is the same dog. She is very hungry because her master forgot to feed her, and there's no good trash because the possums have eaten it all. "If I catch the possums," she says, "I can eat them now and then the trash later, because the they won't be getting it all."

She knows that possums are very hard to catch, so she lies down next to a trash bin and starts moaning. Sure enough, when the possums come to eat trash, they hear her and waddle over.

"Oh, oh oh," moans the dog. "I told the rats a great secret and now they won't let me rest."

The possums look around but they don't see any rats. "Where are they?" the oldest possum asks.

One Dog says, "Everything I eat ends up in a place inside me like a giant garbage heap. I told the rats and they snuck in, and they've been there ever since." And she let out a great howl. "Their cold feet are horrible!"

The possums think for a time and then the oldest says, "This garbage heap, is it large?"

"Huge," One Dog says.

"Are the rats fierce?" says the youngest.

"Not at all," One Dog tells the possums. "If they weren't inside me, they wouldn't be any trouble, even for a possum. Ow! I can feel one dragging bits of bacon around."

*After whispering among themselves for a time, the possums say, "We can go in
and chase out the rats, but you must promise not to hunt us ever again."*

"If you catch any rats, I'll never eat another possum," she promises.

*One by one the possums crawl into her mouth. She eats all but the oldest,
because she's too full to eat any more.*

"This is much better than dog food or trash," she says.

(Dogs love us. We have bred them to do this for ten thousand, a hundred
thousand, a million years. It's hard to make a dog hate people, though we
have at times tried, with our junkyard guards and our attack dogs.

(It's hard to make dogs hate people, but it is possible.)

Another day, just at dusk, the sky an indescribable violet. Linna has a
hard time telling how many dogs there are now: ten or twelve, perhaps. The
dogs around her snuffle, yip, bark. One moans, the sound of a sled dog trying
to howl. Words float up: *dry, bite, food, piss.*

The sled dog continues its moaning howl, and one by one the others join
in with drawn-out barks and moans. They are trying to howl as a pack, but
none of them know how to do this, nor what it is supposed to sound like. It's
a wolf-secret, and they do not know any of those.

Sitting on a picnic table, Linna closes her eyes to listen. The dogs outyell
the trees' restless whispers, the river's wet sliding, even the hissing roaring
street. Ten dogs, or fifteen. Or more: Linna can't tell, because they are all
around her now, in the brush, down by the Kaw's muddy bank, behind the
cottonwoods, beside the tall fence that separates the park from the street.

The misformed howl, the hint of killing animals gathered to work
efficiently together—it awakens a monkey-place somewhere in her corpus
callosum, or even deeper, stained into her genes. Adrenaline hits hot as panic.
Her heart beats so hard that it feels as though she's torn it. Her monkey-self
opens her eyes to watch the dogs through pupils constricted enough to dim
the twilight; it clasps her arms tight over her soft belly to protect the intestines and liver that are the first parts eaten; it tucks her head between her
shoulders to protect her neck and throat. She pants through bared teeth,
fighting a keening noise.

Several of the dogs don't even try to howl. Gold is one of them. (The howling would have defined them before the poisoned gift of speech; but the dogs have words now. They will never be free of stories, though their stories may free them. Gold may understand this.

(They were wolves once, ten thousand, twenty thousand, a hundred thousand years ago. Or more. And before we were men and women, we were monkeys and fair game for them. After a time we grew taller and stronger and smarter: human, eventually. We learned about fire and weapons. If you can tame it, a wolf is an effective weapon, a useful tool. If you can keep it. We learned how to keep wolves close.

(But we were monkeys first, and they were wolves. Blood doesn't forget.)

After a thousand heartbeats fast as birds', long after the howl has decayed into snuffling and play-barks and speech, Linna eases back into her forebrain. Alive and safe. But not untouched. Gold tells a tale.

5. One Dog Tries to Become Like Men.

This is the same dog. There is a party, and people are eating and drinking and using their clever fingers to do things. The dog wants to do everything they do, so he says, "Look, I'm human," and he starts barking and dancing about.

The people say, "You're not human. You're just a dog pretending. If you wanted to be human, you have to be bare, with just a little hair here and there."

One Dog goes off and bites his hairs out and rubs the places he can't reach against the sidewalk until there are bloody patches where he scraped off his skin, as well.

He returns to the people and says, "Now I am human," and he shows his bare skin.

"That's not human," the people say. "We stand on our hind legs and sleep on our backs. First you must do these things."

One Dog goes off and practices standing on his hind legs until he no longer cries out loud when he does it. He leans against a wall to sleep on his back, but it hurts and he does not sleep much. He returns and says, "Now I am human," and he walks on his hind legs from place to place.

"That's not human," the people say. "Look at these, we have fingers. First you must have fingers."

One Dog goes off and he bites at his front paws until his toes are separated. They bleed and hurt and do not work well, but he returns and says, "Now I am human," and he tries to take food from a plate.

"That's not human," say the people. "First you must dream, as we do."

"What do you dream of?" the dog asks.

"Work and failure and shame and fear," the people say.

"I will try," the dog says. He rolls onto his back and sleeps. Soon he is crying out loud and his bloody paws beat at the air. He is dreaming of all they told him.

"That dog is making too much noise," the people say and they kill him.

Linna calls the Humane Society the next day, though she feels like a traitor to the dogs for doing this. The sky is sullen with the promise of rainstorms, and even though she knows that rain is not such a big problem in the life of a dog, she worries a little, remembering her own dog when she was a little girl, who had been terrified of thunder.

So she calls. The phone rings fourteen times before someone picks it up. Linna tells the woman about the dogs of North Park. "Is there anything we can do?"

The woman barks a single unamused laugh. "I wish. People beep bringing them—been doing that since right after the Change. We're packed to the rafters—and they keep bringing them in, or just dumping them in the parking lot, too chickenshit to come in and tell anyone."

"So—" Linna begins, but she has no idea what to ask. She can see the scene in her mind, a hundred or more terrified angry confused grieving hungry thirsty dogs. At least the dogs of North Park have some food and water, and the shelter of the underbrush at night.

The woman has continued "—they can't take care of themselves—"

"Do you know that?" Linna asks, but the woman talks on.

"—and we don't have the resources—"

"So what do you do?" Linna interrupts. "Put them to sleep?"

"If we have to," the woman says, and her voice is so weary that Linna wants suddenly to comfort her. "They're in the runs, four and five in each one because we don't have anywhere to put them, and we can't get them outside because the paddocks are full; it smells like you wouldn't believe. And they tell these stories—"

"What's going to happen to them?" Linna means all the dogs, now that they have speech, now that they are equals.

"Oh, hon, I don't know." The woman's voice trembles. "But I know we can't save them all."

(Why do we fear them when they learn speech? They are still dogs, still subordinate. It doesn't change who they are or their loyalty.

(It is not always fear we run from. Sometimes it is shame.)

6. One Dog Invents Death.

This is the same dog. She lives in a nice house with people. They do not let her run outside a fence and they did things to her so that she can't have puppies, but they feed her well and are kind, and they rub places on her back that she can't reach.

At this time, there is no death for dogs, they live forever. After a while, One Dog becomes bored with her fence and her food and even the people's pats. But she can't convince the people to allow her outside the fence.

"There should be death," she decides. "Then there will be no need for boredom."

(How do the dogs know things? How do they frame an abstract like *thank you* or a collective concept like chicken? Since the Change, everyone has been asking that question. If awareness is dependent on linguistics, an answer is that the dogs have learned to use words, so the words themselves are the frame they use. But it is still *our* frame, *our* language. They are still not free.

(Any more than we are.)

It is a moonless night, and the hot wet air blurs the streetlights so that they illuminate nothing except their own glass globes. Linna is there, though it is very late. She no longer attends her classes and has switched to the dogs' schedule, sleeping the afternoons away in the safety of her apartment. She cannot bring herself to sleep in the dogs' presence. In the park, she is taut as a strung wire, a single monkey among wolves; but she returns each dusk, and listens, and sometimes speaks. There are maybe fifteen dogs now, though she's sure more hide in the bushes, or doze, or prowl for food.

"I remember," a voice says hesitantly. (*Remember* is a frame; they did not "remember" before the word, only lived in a series of nows longer or shorter in duration. Memory breeds resentment. Or so we fear.) "I had a home, food, a warm place, something I chewed—a, a blanket. A woman and a man and she gave me all these things, patted me." Voices in assent: pats remembered. "But she wasn't always nice. She yelled sometimes. She took the blanket away. And she'd drag at my collar until it hurt sometimes. But when she made food she'd put a piece on the floor for me to eat. Beef, it was. That was nice again."

Another voice in the darkness: "Beef. That is a hamburger." The dogs are trying out the concept of *beef* and the concept of *hamburger* and they are connecting them.

"*Nice* is not being hurt," a dog says.

"Not-nice is collars and leashes."

"And rules."

"Being inside and only coming out to shit and piss."

"People are nice and not nice," says the first voice. Linna finally sees that it belongs to a small dusty black dog sitting near the roots of an immense oak. Its enormous fringed ears look like radar dishes. "I learned to think and the woman brought me here. She was sad, but she hit me with stones until I ran away, and then she left. A person is nice and not nice."

The dogs are silent, digesting this. "Linna?" Hope says. "How can people be nice and then not nice?"

"I don't know," she says, because she knows the real question is, *How can they stop loving us?*

(The answer even Linna has trouble seeing is that *nice* and *not-nice* have nothing to do with love. And even loving someone doesn't always mean you can share your house and the fine thread of your life, or sleep safely in the same place.)

7. One Dog Tricks the White-Truck Man.

This is the same dog. He is very hungry and looking through the alleys for something to eat. He sees a man with a white truck coming toward him. One Dog knows that the white-truck men catch dogs sometimes, so he's afraid. He drags some old bones out of the trash and heaps them up and settles on top of them. He pretends not to see the white-truck man but says loudly, "Boy that was a delicious man I just killed, but I'm still starved. I hope I can catch another one."

Well, that white-truck man runs right away. But someone was watching all this from her kitchen window and she runs out to the man and tells him, "One Dog never killed a man! That's just a pile of bones from my barbeque last week, and he's making a mess out of my backyard. Come catch him."

The white-truck man and the person run back to where One Dog is still gnawing on one of the bones in his pile. He sees them and guesses what has happened, so he's afraid. But he pretends not to see them and says loudly, "I'm still starved! I hope that human comes back soon with that white-truck man I asked her to get for me."

The white-truck man and the woman both run away, and he does not see them again that day.

"Why is she here?"

It's one of the new dogs, a lean Lab-cross with a limp. He doesn't talk to her but to Gold, and Linna sees his anger in his liquid-brown eyes, feels it like a hot scent rising from his back. He's one of the half-strays, an outdoor dog who lived on a chain. It was no effort at all for his owner to unhook the chain and let him go; no effort for the Lab-cross to leave his owner's yard and drift across town killing cats and raiding trash cans, and end up in North Park.

There are thirty dogs now and maybe more. The newcomers are warier around her than the earlier dogs. Some, the ones who have taken several days to end up here, dodging police cruisers and pedestrians' Mace, are actively hostile.

"She's no threat," Gold says.

The Lab-cross says nothing but approaches with head lowered and hackles raised. Linna sits on the picnic table's bench and tries not to screech, to bare her teeth and scratch and run. The situation is as charged as the air before a thunderstorm. Gold is no longer the pack's leader—there's a German Shepherd dog who holds his tail higher—but he still has status as the one who tells the stories. The German Shepherd doesn't care whether Linna's there or not; he won't stop another dog from attacking if it wishes. Linna spends much of her time with her hands flexed to bare claws she doesn't have.

"She listens, that's all," says Hope: frightened Hope standing up for her. "And brings food sometimes." Others speak up: *she got rid of my collar when it got burrs under it. She took the tick off me. She stroked my head.*

The Lab-cross's breath on her ankles is hot, his nose wet and surprisingly warm. Dogs were once wolves; right now this burns in her mind. She tries not to shiver. "You're sick," the dog says at last.

"I'm well enough," Linna says through clenched teeth.

Just like that the dog loses interest and turns back to the others.

(Why does Linna come here at all? Her parents had a dog when she was a little girl. Ruthie was so obviously grateful for Linna's love and the home she was offered, the old quilt on the floor, the dog food that fell from the sky twice a day like manna. Linna wondered even then whether Ruthie dreamt of a Holy Land, and what that place would have looked like. Linna's parents were kind and generous, denied Ruthie's needs only when they couldn't help it; paid for her medical bills without too much complaining; didn't put her to sleep until she became incontinent and messed on the living-room floor.

(Even we dog-lovers wrestle with our consciences. We promised to keep our pets forever until they died; but that was from a comfortable height, when we were the masters and they the slaves. Some Inuit tribes believe all animals have souls—except for dogs. This is a convenient stance. They could not use their dogs as they do—beat them, work them, starve them, eat them, feed them one to the other—if dog's were men's equals.

(Or perhaps they could. Our record with our own species is not so exemplary.)

8. *One Dog and the Eating Man.*

This is the same dog. She lives with the Eating Man, who eats only good things while One Dog has only dry kibble. The Eating Man is always hungry. He orders a pizza but he is still hungry, so he eats all the meat and vegetables he finds in the refrigerator. But he's still hungry, so he opens all the cupboards and eats the cereal and noodles and flour and sugar in there. And he's still hungry. There is nothing left, so he eats all One Dog's dry kibble, leaving nothing for One Dog.

So One Dog kills the Eating Man. "It was him or me," One Dog says. The Eating Man is the best thing One Dog has ever eaten.

Linna has been sleeping the days away so that she can be with the dogs at night, when they feel safest out on the streets looking for food. So now it's hot dusk, a day later, and she's just awakened in tangled sheets in a bedroom with flaking walls: the sky a hard haze, air warm and wet as laundry. Linna is walking past Cruz Park, on her way to North Park. She has a bag with a loaf of day-old bread, some cheap sandwich meat, and an extra order of French fries. The fatty smell of the fries sticks in her nostrils. Gold never gets them any more, unless she saves them from the other dogs and gives them to him specially.

She thinks nothing of the blue and red and strobing white lights ahead of her on Mass street until she gets close enough to see that this is no traffic stop. There's no wrecked car, no distraught student who turned left across traffic because she was late for her job and was T-boned. Half a dozen police cars perch on the sidewalks around the park, and she can see reflected lights from others otherwise hidden by the park's shrubs. Fifteen or twenty policemen stand around in clumps, like dead leaves caught for a moment in an eddy and freed by some unseen current.

Everyone knows Cruz Park is full of dogs—sixty or seventy according to today's editorial in the local paper, each one a health and safety risk—but very few dogs are visible at the moment, and none look familiar to her, either as neighbors' ex-pets or wanderers from the North Park pack.

Linna approaches an eddy of policemen; its elements drift apart, rejoin other groups.

"Cruz Park is closed," the remaining officer says to Linna. He's a tall man with a military cut that makes him look older than he is.

It's no surprise that the flashing lights, the cars, the yellow CAUTION tape, and the policemen are about the dogs. There've been complaints from the people neighboring the park—overturned trashcans, feces on the sidewalks, even one attack when a man tried to grab a stray's collar and the stray fought to get away. Today's editorial merely crystalized what everyone already felt.

Linna thinks of Gold, Sophie, Hope. "They're just dogs."

The officer looks a little uncomfortable. "The park is closed until we can address current health and safety concerns." Linna can practically hear the quote marks from the official statement.

"What are you going to do?" she asks.

He relaxes a little. "Right now we're waiting for Animal Control. Any dogs they capture will go to Douglas County Humane Society, they'll try to track down the owners—"

"The ones who kicked the dogs out in the first place?" Linna asks. "No one's gonna want these dogs back, you know that."

"That's the procedure," he says, his back stiff again, tone harsh. "If the Humane—"

"Do you have a dog?" Linna interrupts him. "I mean, did you? Before this started?"

He turns and walks away without a world.

Linna runs the rest of the way to North Park, slowing to a lumbering trot when she gets a cramp in her side. There are no police cars up here, but yellow plastic police tape stretches across the entry: CAUTION. She walks around to the side entrance, off Second Street. The police don't seem to know about the break in the fence.

9. One Dog Meets Tame Dogs.

This is the same dog. He lives in a park, and eats at the restaurants across the street. On his way to the restaurants one day, he walks past a yard with two dogs. They laugh at him and say, "We get dog food every day and our master lets us sleep in the kitchen, which is cool in the summer and warm in the winter. And you have to cross Sixth Street to get food where you might get run over, and you have to sleep in the heat and the cold."

The dog walks past them to get to the restaurants, and he eats the fallen tacos and French fries and burgers around the dumpster. When he sits by the restaurant doors, many people give him bits of food; one person gives him chicken in a paper dish. He walks back to the yard and lets the two dogs smell the chicken and grease on his breath through the fence. "Ha on you," he says, and then goes back to his park and sleeps on a pile of dry rubbish under the bridge, where the breeze is cool. When night comes, he goes looking for a mate and no one stops him.

(Whatever else it is, the Change of the animals—mute to speaking, dumb to dreaming—is a test for us. We pass the test when we accept that their dreams and desires and goals may not be ours. Many people fail this test. But we don't have to, and even failing we can try again. And again. And pass at last.

(A slave is trapped, choiceless and voiceless; but so is her owner. Those we have injured may forgive us, but how can we know? Can we trust them with our homes, our lives, our hearts? Animals did not forgive before the Change; mostly they forgot. But the Change brought memory, and memory requires forgiveness, and how can we trust them to forgive us?

(And how do we forgive ourselves? Mostly we don't. Mostly we pretend to forget, and hope it becomes true.)

At noon the next day, Linna jerks awake, monkey-self already dragging her to her feet. Even before she's fully awake, she knows that what woke her wasn't a car's backfire. It was a shotgun blast, and it was only a couple of blocks away, and she already knows why.

She drags on clothes and runs to Cruz Park, no stitch in her side this time. The flashing police cars and CAUTION tape and men are all still there, but now she sees dogs everywhere, twenty or more laid flat near the sidewalk, the way dogs sleep on hot summer days. Too many of the ribcages are still; too many of the eyes open, dust and pollen already gathering.

Linna has no words, can only watch speechless; but the men say enough. First thing in the morning, the Animal Control people went to Dillon's grocery store and bought fifty one-pound packages of cheap hamburger on sale, and they poisoned them all, and then scattered them around the park. Linna can see little blue styrene squares from the packaging scattered here and there, among the dogs.

The dying dogs don't say much. Most have fallen back on the ancient language of pain, wordless yelps and keening. Men walk among them, shooting the suffering dogs, jabbing poles into the underbrush looking for any who might have slipped away.

People come in cars and trucks and on bicycles and scooters and on their feet. The police officers around Cruz Park keep sending them away—"a health risk" says one officer: "safety," says another, but the people keep coming back, or new people.

Linna's eyes are blind with tears; she blinks and they slide down her face, oddly cool and thick.

"Killing them is the answer?" says a woman beside her. Her face is wet as well, but her voice is even, as if they are debating this in a class, she and Linna. The woman holds her baby in her arms, a white cloth thrown over its face so that it can't see. "I have three dogs at home, and they've never hurt anything. Words don't change that."

"What if they change?" Linna asks. "What if they ask for real food and a bed soft as yours, the chance to dream their own dreams?"

"I'll try to give it to them," the woman says, but her attention is focused on the park, the dogs. "They can't do this!"

"Try and stop them." Linna turns away tasting her tears. She should feel comforted by the woman's words, the fact that not everyone has forgotten how to love animals when they are no longer slaves, but she feels nothing. And she walks north, carved hollow.

10. *One Dog Goes to the Place of Pieces.*
This is the same dog. She is hit by a car and part of her flies off and runs into a dark culvert. She does not know what the piece is, so she chases it. The culvert is long and it gets so cold that her breath puffs out in front of her. When she gets to the end, there's no light and the world smells like cold metal. She walks along a road. Cold cars rush past but they don't slow down. None of them hit her.

One Dog comes to a parking lot which has nothing in it but the legs of dogs. The legs walk from place to place, but they cannot see or smell or eat. None of them is her leg, so she walks on. After this she finds a parking lot filled with the ears of dogs, and then one filled with the assholes of dogs, and the eyes of dogs and the bodies of dogs; but none of the ears and assholes and eyes and bodies are hers, so she walks on.

The last parking lot she comes to has nothing at all in it except for little smells, like puppies. She can tell one of the little smells is hers, so she calls to it and it comes to her. She doesn't know where the little smell belongs on her body, so she carries it in her mouth and walks back past the parking lots and through the culvert.

One Dog cannot leave the culvert because a man stands in the way. She puts the little smell down carefully and says, "I want to go back."

The man says, "You can't unless all your parts are where they belong."

One Dog can't think of where to the little smell belongs. She picks up the little smell and tries to sneak past the man, but the man catches her and hits her. One Dog tries to hide it under a hamburger wrapper and pretend it's not there, but the man catches that, too.

One Dog thinks some more and finally says, "Where does the little smell belong?"

The man says, "Inside you."

So One Dog swallows the little smell. She realizes that the man has been trying to keep her from returning home but that the man cannot lie about the little smell. One Dog growls and runs past him, and returns to our world.

There are two police cars pulled onto the sidewalk before North Park's main entrance. Linna takes in the sight of them in three stages: first, she has seen police everywhere today, so they are no shock; second, they are *here*, at *her* park, threatening *her* dogs, and this is like being kicked in the stomach; and third, she thinks: *I have to get past them.*

North Park has two entrances, but one isn't used much. Linna walks around to the little narrow dirt path from Second Street.

The park is never quiet. There's busy Sixth Street just south, and the river and its noises to the north and east and west; trees and bushes hissing with the hot wind; the hum of insects.

But the dogs are quiet. She's never seen them all in the daylight, but they're gathered now, silent and loll-tongued in the bright daylight. There are forty or more. Everyone is dirty, now. Any long fur is matted; anything white is dust-colored. Most of them are thinner than they were when they arrived. The dogs face one of the tables, as orderly as the audience at a string quartet; but the tension in the air is so obvious that Linna stops short.

Gold stands on the table. There are a couple of dogs she doesn't recognize in the dust nearby: flopped flat with their sides heaving, tongues long and flecked with white foam. One is hunched over; he drools onto the ground and retches helplessly. The other dog has a scratch along her flank. The blood is the brightest thing Linna can see in the sunlight, a red so strong it hurts her eyes.

The Cruz Park cordon was permeable, of course. These two managed to slip past the police cars. The vomiting one is dying.

She realizes suddenly that every dog's muzzle is swiveled toward her. The air snaps with something that makes her back-brain bare its teeth and scream, her hackles rise. The monkey-self looks for escape, but the trees are not close enough to climb (and she is no climber), the road and river too far away. She is a spy in a gulag; the prisoners have little to lose by killing her.

"You shouldn't have come back." Gold says.

"I came to tell you—warn you." Even through her monkey-self's defiance, Linna weeps helplessly.

"We already know." The pack's leader, the German Shepherd dog, says. "They're killing us all. We're leaving the park."

She shakes her head, fighting for breath. "They'll kill you. There are police cars on Sixth—they'll shoot you however you get out. They're *waiting*."

"Will it be better here?" Gold asks. "They'll kill us anyway, with their poisoned meat. We *know*. You're afraid, all of you—"

"I'm not—" Linna starts, but he breaks in.

"We smell it on everyone, even the people who take care of us or feed us. We have to get out of here."

"They'll *kill* you," Linna says again.

"Some of us might make it."

"Wait! Maybe there's a way," Linna says, and then: "I have stories."

In the stifling air, Linna can hear the dogs pant, even over the street noises. "People have their own stories," Gold says at last. "Why should we listen to yours?"

"We made you into what we wanted; we *owned* you. Now you are becoming what *you* want. You belong to yourselves. But we have stories, too, and we learned from them. Will you listen?"

The air shifts, but whether it is the first movement of the still air or the shifting of the dogs, she can't tell.

"Tell your story," says the German Shepherd.

Linna struggles to remember half-read textbooks from a sophomore course on folklore, framing her thoughts as she speaks them. "We used to tell a lot of stories about Coyote. The animals were here before humans were, and Coyote was one of them. He did a lot of stuff, got in a lot of trouble. Fooled everyone."

"I know about coyotes," a dog says. "There were some by where I used to live. They eat puppies sometimes."

"I bet they do," Linna says. "Coyotes eat everything. But this wasn't *a* coyote, it's *Coyote*. The one and only."

The dogs murmur. She hears them work it out: *coyote* is the same as *this is the same dog.*

"So. Coyote disguised himself as a female so that he could hang out with a bunch of females, just so he could mate with them. He pretended to be dead, and then when the crows came down to eat him, he snatched them up and ate every one! When a greedy man was keeping all the animals for himself, Coyote pretended to be a very rich person and then freed them all, so that everyone could eat. He—" She pauses to think, looks down at the dogs all around her. The monkey-fear is gone: she is the storyteller, the maker of thoughts. They will not kill her, she knows. "Coyote did all these things, and a lot more things. I bet you'll think of some, too.

"I have an idea of how to save you," she says. "Some of you might die, but some chance is better than no chance."

"Why would we trust you?" says the lab-cross who has never liked her, but the other dogs are with her. She feels it, and answers.

"Because this trick, maybe it's even good enough for Coyote. Will you let me show you?"

We people are so proud of our intelligence, but that makes it easier to trick us. We see the white-truck men and we believe they're whatever we're expecting to see. Linna goes to U-Haul and rents a pickup truck for the afternoon. She digs out a white shirt she used to wear when she ushered at the concert hall. She knows *clipboard with printout* means *official responsibilities,* so she throws one on the dashboard of the truck.

She backs the pickup to the little entrance on Second Street. The dogs slip through the gap in the fence and scramble into the pickup's bed. She lifts the ones that are too small to jump so high. And then they arrange themselves carefully, flat on their sides. There's a certain amount of snapping and snarling as later dogs step on the ears and ribcages on the earlier dogs, but eventually everyone is settled, everyone able to breathe a little, every eye tight shut.

She pulls onto Sixth Street with a truck heaped with dogs. When the police stop her, she tells them a little story. Animal Control has too many calls these days: cattle loose on the highways, horses leaping fences that are too high and breaking their legs; and the dogs, the scores and scores of dogs at Cruz Park. Animal Control is renting trucks now, whatever they can find. The dogs of North Park were slated for poisoning this morning.

"I didn't hear about this in briefing," one of the policemen says. He pokes at the heap of dogs with a black club; they shift like dead meat. They reek; an inexperienced observer might not recognize the stench as mingled dog-breath and shit.

Linna smiles, baring her teeth. "I'm on my way back to the shelter," she says. "They have an incinerator." She waves an open cell phone at him, and hopes he does not ask to talk to whoever's on the line, because there is no one.

But people believe stories, and then they make them real: the officer pokes at the dogs one more time and then wrinkles his nose and waves her on.

Clinton Lake is a vast place, trees and bushes and impenetrable brambles ringing a big lake, open country in every direction. When Linna unlatches the pickup's bed, the dogs drop stiffly to the ground, and stretch. Three died of overheating, stifled beneath the weight of so many others. Gold is one of them, but Linna does not cry. She knew she couldn't save them all, but she has saved some of them. That has to be enough. And the stories will continue: stories do not easily die.

The dogs can go wherever they wish from here, and they will. They and all the other dogs who have tricked or slipped or stumbled to safety will spread across the Midwest, the world. Some will find homes with men and women who treat them not as slaves but as friends, freeing themselves, as well. Linna herself returns home with little shivering Sophie and sad Hope.

Some will die, killed by men and cougars and cars and even other dogs. Others will raise litters. The fathers of some of those litters will be coyotes. Eventually the Changed dogs will find their place in the changed world.

(When we first fashioned animals to suit our needs, we treated them as if they were stories and we the authors, and we clung desperately to an imagined copyright that would permit us to change them, sell them, even delete them. But some stories cannot be controlled. A wise author or dog owner listens, and learns, and says at last, "I never knew that.")

11. *One Dog Creates the World.*

This is the same dog. There wasn't any world when this happens, just a man and a dog. They lived in a house that didn't have any windows to look out of. Nothing had any smells. The dog shit and pissed on a paper in the bathroom, but not even this had a smell. Her food had no taste, either. The man suppressed all these things. This was because the man didn't want One Dog to create the universe and he knew it would be done by smell.

One night One Dog was sleeping and she felt the strangest thing that any dog has ever felt. It was the smells of the world pouring from her nose. When the smell of grass came out, there was grass outside. When the smell of shit came out, there was shit outside. She made the whole world that way. And when the smell of other dogs came out, there were dogs everywhere, big ones and little ones all over the world.

"I think I'm done," she said, and she left.

THE EVOLUTION OF TRICKSTER STORIES AMONG THE DOGS OF NORTH PARK AFTER THE CHANGE

"The Evolution of Trickster Stories Among the Dogs of North Park After the Change" by Kij Johnson was originally published in 2007 in Terri Windling and my *The Coyote Road: Trickster Tales*, the third of our "mythic series" of young adult anthologies published by Viking. Here is where you find out that I'm a sucker for animal stories, especially bittersweet ones.

The Bedroom Light

by Jeffrey Ford

(From *Inferno*, 2007)

They each decided, separately, that they wouldn't discuss it that night. The autumn breeze sounded in the tree outside the open kitchen window and traveled all through the second story apartment of the old Victorian house. It twirled the hanging plant over the sink, flapped the ancient magazine photo of Veronica Lake tacked to his office door, spun the clown mobile in the empty bedroom, and, beneath it, set the wicker rocker to life. In their bedroom it tilted the fabric shade of the antique floor lamp that stood in the corner by the front window. Allison looked at the reflection of them lying beneath the covers in the mirror set into the top of the armoire while Bill looked at their reflection in the glass of the hand colored print, "Moon Over Miami," that hung on the wall above her. The huge gray cat, Mama, her belly skimming the floor, padded quietly into the room and snuck through the partially open door of the armoire.

Bill rolled over to face Allison and ran his hand softly down the length of her arm. "Today, while I was writing," he said, "I heard, coming up through the grate beneath my desk, Tana, getting yelled at by her mother."

"Demon seed?" said Allison.

He laughed quietly. "Yeah." He stopped rubbing her arm. "I got out of my chair, got down on the floor, and turned my ear to the grate."

She smiled.

"So the mom's telling Tana, 'You'll listen to me, I'm the mother. I'm in charge and you'll do what I say.' Then there was a pause, and I hear this voice. Man, this was like no kid's voice, but it *was* Tana, and she says, 'No, Mommy, I'm in charge and you will listen to me.'"

"Get outa here," Allison said and pushed him gently in the chest.

"God's honest truth. So then Cindy makes a feeble attempt to get back in power. 'I'm the Mommy,' she yells, but I could tell she meant to say it with more force, and it came out cracked and weak. And then there's a pause, and Tana comes back with, 'You're wrong, Mommy. I am in charge and you will listen to me.'"

"Creep show," Allison said.

"It got really quiet then, so I put my ear down closer. My head was on the damn floor. That's when I heard Cindy weeping."

Allison gave a shiver, half fake, and handed Bill one of her pillows. He put it behind his head with the rest of his stack. "Did I tell you what Phil told me?" she said.

"No," he said.

"He told me that when he's walking down the street and he sees her on one side of the road, he crosses over to the opposite side."

"I don't blame him," he said, laughing.

"He told you about the dog, right?" she said, pulling the covers up over her shoulder.

Bill shook his head.

"He said the people who live in the apartment on the second floor next door—the young guy with the limp and his wife, Rhoda—they used to have a beagle that they kept on their porch all day while they were at work."

"Over here," he said and pointed at the wall.

"Yeah. They gave it water and food, the whole thing, and had a long leash attached to its collar. Anyway, one day Phil's walking down to the Busy-Bee to get coffee and cigarettes and he sees Tana standing under the porch, looking up at the dog. She was talking to it. Phil said that the dog was getting worked up, so he told Tana to leave it alone. She shot him a 'don't fuck with me' stare. He was worried how it might look, him talking to the kid, so he went on his way. That afternoon the dog was discovered strangled, hanging by the leash off the second story porch."

"He never told me that. Shit. And come to think about it, I never told *you* this... I was sitting in my office just the other day, writing, and all of a sudden I feel something on my back, like it's tingling. I turn around, and there she is, standing in the doorway to the office, holding Mama like a baby doll, just staring at me. I jumped out of my chair, and I said, like, 'I didn't hear you knock.' I was a little scared actually, so I asked her if she wanted a cookie. At first she didn't say anything, but just looked at me with that… if I was writing a story about her I'd describe her face as *dour*—an old lady face minus the wrinkles… Then, get this, she says in that low, flat voice, 'Do you Lambada?'"

"What the fuck?" Allison said and laughed. "She didn't say that."

"No," he said, "that's what she said, she asked me if I *Lambada*. What the hell is it anyway? I told her no, and then she turned and split."

"Lambada, I think…" she said and broke out laughing again, "I think it's some kind of South American Dance."

"What would have happened if I said yes?" he asked.

"Lambada," she whispered, shaking her head.

"Phil's got the right strategy with her," he said.

"But I don't like her coming up here in the middle of the day uninvited," said Allison.

"I'll have to start locking the door after you go to work," said Bill.

"This place…there's something very… I don't know." She sighed. "Like you ever lean against a wall? It kind of gives like flesh," she said.

"That's just the lathing…it's separating away from the sheet rock cause the place is so old. I know what you mean, though, with that egg shell smoothness and the pliancy when you touch it—spongy-weird."

"I'm talking there's a sinister factor to this place. The oriental carpets, the lion's paw tub, the old heavy furniture—the gravity of the past that was here when we moved in. I can't put my finger on it. At first I thought it was quaint, but then I realized it didn't stop there."

"Like melancholy?" he asked.

"Yeah, exactly—a sadness."

"Just think about it. You've got Corky and Cindy down there, hitting the sauce and each other almost every night. They must have had to buy a whole new set of dishes after last weekend. Then you got the kid…nuff said there.

What about next door, over here on this side, the guy who washes his underwear on the fucking clothes line with the hose? That guy's also classically deranged."

"I forgot about him," she said.

"Well," he said, "let's not forget about him. I watch him from the kitchen window. I can see right down through the tree branches and across the yard into his dining room. He sits there every night for hours, reading that big fat book."

"I've seen him down there," she said. "Sometimes when I wake up at three am and go into the kitchen for a glass of water, I notice him down there reading. Is it the Bible?"

"Could be the fucking phone book for all I know."

"Cindy told me that when they got Tana that yippie little dog... Shotzy, Potzy...whatever, the kid was walking on that side of the house over by the old guy's property, and he came out his backdoor, and yelled at her, 'If I find your dog in my yard, I'll kill it.' Now, I know Tana's demon seed and all, but she's still a little kid... Cindy didn't tell Corky because she was afraid he'd Cork off and kick the crap out of the old guy."

"What, instead of her for once? Hey, you never know, maybe the old man's just trying to protect himself from Tana's...*animal magic.*" said Bill. "You know, Cindy swears the kid brought a dead bird back to life. She just kind of slips that in in the middle of a "hey, the weather's nice" kind of conversation."

"Yeah, I've caught that tale," said Allison. There was a pause. "But do you get my overall point here?" She opened her hands to illustrate the broadness of the concept. "Like we're talking some kind of hovering, negative funk."

"Amorphous and pungent," he said.

"I've felt it ever since the first week we moved in here," she said.

"Does it have anything to do with the old woman who answered the door with her pants around her ankles?"

"Olive Harker?" she said, "Corky's illustrious mom?"

"Remember, Olive hada get shipped out for us to move in. Maybe she cursed the joint...you, know, put the Lambada on it."

"It wasn't her so much," said Allison. "I first felt it the day the cat pissed in the sugar bowl."

He stopped rubbing her forehead. "Right in front of me—between bites of French toast," he said. "That cat sucks."

"Don't talk about Mama that way," she said.

"It baahhhs like a lamb and eats flies. I hate it," he said.

"She's good. Three whole weeks gone and she still came back, didn't she? You shouldn't have thrown her out."

"I didn't throw her, I drop kicked her. She made a perfect arc, right over the back fence. But the question is, or at least the point is, if I follow you, is how strange is it that she pissed right in the sugar bowl—jumped up on the table, made a bee line for it, parked right over it and pissed like there was no tomorrow?"

"That's what I'm getting at," said Allison. "It fulfills no evolutionary need. It's just grim."

"Maybe it's us," he said. "Maybe we're haunting ourselves."

"I saw Corky digging a big hole out in the yard the other day," she said. "His back's full of ink—an angel being torn apart by demons… I was more interested in the hole he was digging cause I haven't heard any yipping out of Potzy for a few days."

"Don't worry," he said. "I'm ready for him."

"How?" she asked.

"Last Thursday, when I went out garbage picking and found Veronica's picture, I brought back a busted off rake handle. I wound duct tape around one end for a grip. It's in the kitchen behind the door for when Corky gets shit faced and starts up the stairs. Then I'm gonna grab that thing and beat his ass."

"Hey, do you remember that guy Keith back in college?" she asked.

"McCurly, yeah," he said. "He did the apple dance. What made you think of him?"

She nodded. "Every time he flapped his arms the apple rolled off his head, remember?"

"He danced to Steve Miller's 'Fly Like An Eagle'," Bill said. "What a fuckin fruitcake. I remember Oshea telling me that he ended up working for the government."

"Well, remember that time he was telling us he was reading *The Amityville Horror?*"

"Yeah," he said.

"McCurly said that one of the pieces of proof that the author used in the book to nail down his case that the house was really haunted was that they found an evil shit in the toilet bowl. Remember that?"

"Yeah."

"You said to him, 'What do you mean by an *evil* shit?' And McCurley looked like he didn't get your question."

"But what he eventually said was, 'It was heinous.' I asked him if he could explain that and he said, 'Really gross.'"

They laughed.

She touched his face as if to make him quiet, and said, "That's the point. We paint the unknown with the Devil's shit to make it make sense."

"Heavy," said Bill. A few seconds passed in silence.

"Right…?" she said.

"That Amityville House was only like two towns over from where I grew up," he told her. "New people were in there and it was all fixed up. I'd go out drinking with my friends all night. You know, the Callahans, and Wolfy, and Angelo, and Benny the Bear, and at the end of the night we'd have these cases of empty beer bottles in the car. So around that time the movie of Amityville Horror came out. We went to see it and laughed our asses off—come on, Brolin? Steiger we're talking. One of the things that cracked us up big time was the voice saying, 'Get out. For god's sake get the hell out.' I don't want to get into it now but Steiger and the flies…baby, well worth the price of admission. So we decided we're gonna drive to the Amityville Horror House and scream, "Get the hell out," and throw our empties on the lawn."

"That's retarded," she said.

"We did it, but then we kept doing it, and not just to the Amityville Horror House. Every time we did it, I'd crack like hell. It was so fucking stupid it made me laugh. Plus we were high as kites. We did it to people we knew and didn't know and we did it a lot to the high school coaches we'd had for different sports. There was this one guy, though, we did it to the most—Coach Pinhead. Crew cut, face as smooth as an ass, goggly eyes, and his favorite joke was to say "How Long is a Chinaman." He was a soccer coach, a real douche bag, but we swung by his house every weekend night for like three months, dropped the empties and yelled 'Pinhead!!!' before peeling out on his lawn. We called the whole thing a 'Piercing Pinhead.'

"Could you imagine how pissed off you'd be today if some kids did that to you," she said.

"Yeah," he said "I know. But get this. I was talking to Mike Callahan about five years later. When he was working selling furniture and married to that rich girl. I saw him at my mother's funeral. He told me that he found out later on that Pinhead died of pancreatic cancer. All that time we were doing the Piercing Pinheads, screaming in the middle of the night outside his house, tormenting him, the poor guy was in there, in his bedroom, dying by inches."

"That's haunted," said Allison.

"Tell me about it," he said and then rolled closer to kiss her.

They kissed and then lay quiet, both listening to the sound of the leaves blowing outside. She began to dose off, but before her eyes closed all the way, she said, "Who's getting the light?"

"You," said Bill.

"Come on," she said, "I've got an early shift tomorrow."

"Come on? I've gotten the damn light every night for the past two weeks."

"That's cause it's your job," she said.

"Fuck that," he said but started to get up. Just then the light went out.

She opened her eyes slightly, grinning. "Sometimes it pays to be haunted," she said.

Bill looked around the darkened room and said, as if to everywhere at once, "Thank you."

The light blinked on and then off.

"Maybe the bulb's loose," he said.

The light blinked repeatedly on and off and then died again.

"That's freaky," she said, but freaky wasn't going to stop her from falling asleep. Her eyes slowly closed and before he could kiss her again on the forehead, she was lightly snoring.

Bill lay there in the dark, wide awake, thinking about their conversation and about the lamp. He thought about ghosts in Miami, beneath swaying palm trees, doing the Lambada by moonlight. Finally, he whispered, "Light, are you really haunted?"

Nothing.

A long time passed, and then he asked, "Are you Olive?"

The light stayed off.

"Are you Pinhead?"

Just darkness.

"Are you Tana?" he said. He waited for a sign, but nothing. Eventually he closed his eyes and thought about work. He worked at Nescron, a book store housed in the bottom floor of a block long, four story warehouse—timbers and stone—built in the 1800's. All used books. The owner, Stan, had started, decades earlier, in the scrap paper business and over time had amassed tons of old books. The upper three floors of the warehouse were packed with unopened boxes and crates from everywhere in the world. Bill's job was to crawl in amid the piles of boxes, slit them open and mine their cargo, picking out volumes for the Literature section in the store down stairs. Days would pass at work and he'd see no one. He'd penetrated so deeply into the morass of the third floor that sometimes he'd get scared, having the same feeling he'd had when he and Allison had gone to Montana three months earlier to recuperate and they were way up in the mountains and came upon a freshly killed and half-eaten antelope beside a water hole. Amidst the piles of books, he felt for the second time in his life that he was really "out there."

"I expect some day to find a pine box up on the third floor holding the corpse of Henry Miller," he'd told Allison at dinner one night.

"Who's Henry Miller?" she'd asked.

He'd found troves of classics and first editions and even signed volumes for the store down below, and Stan had praised his efforts at excavating the upper floors. As the months went on, Bill was making a neat little stack of goodies for himself, planning to shove them in a paper sac and spirit them home with him when he closed up some Monday night. An early edition of Longfellow's translation of Dante, an actual illuminated manuscript with gold leaf, a signed, first edition of *Call of the Wild*, an 1885 edition of *The Scarlet Letter*, were just some of the treasures.

Recently at work he'd begun to get an odd feeling when he was deep within the wilderness of books, not the usual fear of loneliness, but the opposite, that he was not alone. Twice in the last week, he'd thought he'd heard whispering, and once, the sudden quiet tumult of a distant avalanche of books. He'd asked down below in the store if anyone else was working the third floor, and he was told that he was the only one. Then, only the previous day, he couldn't locate his cache of horded books. It was possible that he was disoriented, but in the very spot he'd thought they'd be, he instead found one tall slim volume. It was a book of fairy tales illustrated by an artist named Segur. The animals depicted in the illustrations walked upright with personality, and the children, in powder-blue snowscapes surrounded by Christmas mice, were pale, staring zombies. The colors were odd, slightly washed out and the sizes of the creatures and people were haphazard.

Without realizing it, Bill fell asleep and his thoughts of work melted into a dream of the writer Henry Miller. He woke suddenly a little while later to the sound of Allison's voice, the room still in darkness. "Bill," she said again and pushed his shoulder, "you awake?"

"Yeah," he said.

"I had a dream," said Allison. "Oh my god…"

"Sounds like a good one," he said.

"Maybe, maybe," she said.

He could tell she was waiting for him to ask what it was about. Finally he asked her, "So what happened?"

She drew close to him and he put his arm around her. She whispered, "Lothianne."

"Lothianne?" said Bill

"A woman with three arms," said Allison. "She had an arm coming out of the upper part of her back, and the hand on it had two thumbs instead of a pinky and a thumb, so it wouldn't be either righty or lefty. The elbow only bent up and down, not side to side."

"Yow," said Bill.

"Her complexion was light blue, and her hair was dark and wild, but not long. And she wore this dress with an extra arm hole in the back. This dress was plain, like something out of the Dust Bowl, gray and reached to the ankles, and I remembered my fifth grade teacher, Mrs. Donnelly, the mean old bitch, having worn the exact one back in grade school when we spent a whole year reading *The Last Days of Pompeii*."

"Did the three arm woman look like your teacher?" asked Bill.

"No but she was stupid and mean like her. She had a dour face, familiar and frightening. Anyway, Lothianne wandered the woods with a pet jay that flew above her and sometimes perched in that tangled hair. I think she might have been a cannibal. She lived underground in like a woman-size rabbit warren."

"Charming," he said.

"I was a little girl and my sister and I were running hard toward this house in the distance, away from the woods, just in front of a wave of night time. I knew we had to reach the house before the darkness swept over us. The blue jay swooped down and, as I tried to catch my breath, it spit into my mouth. It tasted like fire and spread to my arms and legs. My running went dream slow, my legs dream heavy. My sister screamed toward the house. Then, like a rusty engine, I seized altogether and fell over."

"You know, in China, they eat Bird Spit Soup..." he said.

"Shut up," she said. "The next thing I know, I come to and Lothianne and me are on a raft, in a swiftly moving stream, tethered to a giant willow tree that's growing right in the middle of the flow. Lothianne has a lantern in one hand, and in the other she's holding the end of a long vine that's tied in a noose around my neck. The moon's out, shining through the willow whips and reflecting off the running water, and I'm so scared.

"She says, 'Time to practice drowning' and kicks me in the back. I fall into the water. Under the surface I'm looking up and the moonlight allows me to see the stones and plants around me. There are speckled fish swimming by. Just before I'm out of air, she reels me in. This happens three times, and on the last time, when she reels me in, she vanishes, and I'm flying above the stream and surrounding hills and woods, and I'm watching things growing—huge plants like asparagus, sprouting leaves and twining and twirling and growing in the moonlight. Even in night, it was so perfectly clear."

"Jeez," said Bill.

Allison was silent for a while. Eventually she propped herself up on her elbow and said, "It was frightening but it struck me as a "creative" dream cause of the end."

"A three armed woman," said Bill. "Rembrandt once did an etching of a three armed woman having sex with a guy."

"I was wondering if the noose around my neck was symbolic of an umbilical cord..."

He stared at her. "Why?" he finally said.

She was about to answer but the bedroom light blinked on and off, on and off, on and off, without stopping, like a strobe light, and from somewhere or everywhere in the room came the sound of low moaning.

Bill threw the covers off, sat straight up and said, "What the fuck?"

Allison, wide eyed, her glance darting here and there, said, "Bill..."

The light show finally ended in darkness, but the sound grew louder, more strange, like a high pitched growling that seemed to make the glass of the windows vibrate. She grabbed his shoulder and pointed to the armoire. He turned, and as he did, Mama the cat came bursting out of the standing closet, the door swinging wildly. She screeched and spun in incredibly fast circles on the rug next to the bed.

"Jesus Christ," yelled Bill, and lifted his feet, afraid the cat might claw him. "Get the fuck outa here!" he yelled at it.

Mama took off out of the bedroom, still screeching. Allison jumped out of the bed and took off after the cat. Bill cautiously brought up the rear. They found Mama in the bathroom, on the floor next to the lion paw tub, writhing.

"Look," said Bill, peering over Allison's shoulder, "she's attacking her own ass. What the hell..."

"Oh, man," said Allison. "Check it out," She pointed as Mama pulled this long furry lump out of herself with her teeth."

"That's it for me," he said, backing away from the bathroom doorway.

"Bill, here comes another. It's alive."

"Alive?" he said, sitting down on a chair in the kitchen. "I thought it was a mohair turd."

"No, you ass, she's having a kitten. I never realized she was pregnant. Must be from the time you kicked her out."

Bill sat there staring at Allison's figure illuminated by the bulb she'd switched on in the bathroom.

"This is amazing, you should come see it," she called over her shoulder to him.

"I'll pass," he said. He turned then and looked through the open kitchen window, down across the yard toward the old man's house. For the first time he could remember, his neighbor wasn't there, reading the big book. The usual rectangle of light was now a dark empty space.

Later, he found Allison sitting in the wicker rocker, beneath the clown mobile, in the otherwise empty bedroom. The light was on, and she rocked, slowly, a rolled up towel cradled in her arms. "Come see," she said to him, smiling. "The first was stillborn, and this is the only other one, but it lived. It's a little girl."

He didn't want to, but she seemed so pleased. He took a step closer. She pulled back a corner of the towel, and there was a small, wet, face with blue eyes.

"We have to think of a name," she said.

THE BEDROOM LIGHT

Inferno was published in 2007 and won the final International Horror Guild Award, the World Fantasy Award, and the inaugural Shirley Jackson Award. It's one of two un-themed horror anthologies I've edited. And looking back at them both, (the other is *Fearful Symmetries*) it turns out that many of my favorite stories are from these two books. Readers complain about theme anthologies and say they want un-themed anthologies. But they just don't sell as well.

I love "The Bedroom Light" by Jeffrey Ford because of its intimacy. It's a lovely (and ultimately creepy) tale of a marriage.

The Carrion Gods in Their Heaven

by Laird Barron

(From *Supernatural Noir*, 2011)

The leaves were turning.

Lorna fueled the car at a mom and pop gas station in the town of Poger Rock, population 190. Poger Rock comprised a forgotten, moribund collection of buildings tucked into the base of a wooded valley a stone's throw south of Olympia. The station's marquee was badly peeled and she couldn't decipher its title. A tavern called Mooney's occupied a gravel island half a block down and across the two lane street from the post office and the grange. Next to a dumpster, a pair of mongrel dogs were locked in coitus, patiently facing opposite directions, Dr. Doolittle's Pushmi-pullyu for the twenty-first century. Other than vacant lots overrun by bushes and alder trees, and a lone antiquated traffic light at the intersection that led out of town, either toward Olympia, or deeper into cow country, there wasn't much else to look at. She hobbled in to pay and ended up grabbing a few extra supplies—canned peaches and fruit cocktail, as there wasn't any refrigeration at the cabin. She snagged three bottles of bourbon gathering dust on a low shelf.

The clerk noticed her folding crutch, and the soft cast on her left leg. She declined his offer to carry her bags. After she loaded the Subaru, she ventured into the tavern and ordered a couple rounds of tequila. The tavern was dim and smoky and possessed a frontier vibe with antique flintlocks over the bar, and stuffed and mounted deer heads staring from the walls. A great black wolf snarled atop a dais near the entrance. The bartender watched her drain the shots raw. He poured her another on the house and said, "You're staying at the Haugstad place, eh?"

She hesitated, the glass partially raised, then set the drink on the counter and limped away without answering. She assayed the long, treacherous drive up to the cabin, chewing over the man's question, the morbid implication of his smirk. She got the drift. Horror movies and pulp novels made the conversational gambit infamous; life imitating art. Was she staying at the Haugstad place indeed. Like hell she'd take *that* bait. The townsfolk were strangers to her and she wondered how the bartender knew where she lived. Obviously, the hills had eyes.

Two weeks prior, Lorna had fled into the wilderness to an old hunting cabin, the so-called "Haugstad place," with her lover Miranda. Miranda was the reason she'd discovered the courage to leave her husband Bruce, the reason he grabbed a fistful of Lorna's hair and threw her down a flight of concrete stairs in the parking garage of SeaTac airport. That was the second time Lorna had tried to escape with their daughter Orillia. Sweet Orillia, eleven years old next month, was safe in Florida with relatives. Lorna missed her daughter, but slept better knowing she was far from Bruce's reach. He wasn't interested in going after the child; at least not as his first order of business.

Bruce was a vengeful man, and Lorna feared him the way she might fear a hurricane, a volcano, a flood. His rages overwhelmed and obliterated his impulse control. Bruce was a force of nature, all right, and capable of far worse than breaking her leg. He owned a gun and a collection of knives, had done time years ago for stabbing somebody during a fight over a gambling debt. He often got drunk and sat in his easy chair, cleaning his pistol or sharpening a large cruel-looking blade he called an Arkansas Toothpick.

So, it came to this: Lorna and Miranda shacked up in the mountains while Lorna's estranged husband, free on bail, awaited trial back in Seattle. Money wasn't a problem—Bruce made plenty as a manager at a lumber company, and Lorna helped herself to a healthy portion of it when she headed for the hills.

Both women were loners by necessity or device, as the case might be, who'd met at a cocktail party thrown by one of Bruce's colleagues and clicked on contact. Lorna hadn't worked since her stint as a movie theater clerk during college—Bruce insisted she stay home and raise Orillia, and when Orillia grew older, he dropped his pretenses and punched Lorna in the jaw after she pressed the subject of getting a job, beginning a career. She'd dreamed of going to grad school for a degree in social work.

Miranda was a semi-retired artist; acclaimed in certain quarters and much in demand for her wax sculptures. She cheerfully set up a mini studio in the spare bedroom, strictly to keep her hand in. Photography was her passion of late and she'd brought along several complicated and expensive cameras. She was also the widow of a once famous sculptor. Between her work and her husband's royalties, she wasn't exactly rich, but not exactly poor either. They'd survive a couple of months "roughing it." Miranda suggested they consider it a vacation, an advance celebration of "Brucifer's" (her pet name for Lorna's soon to be ex) impending stint as a guest of King County Jail.

She'd secured the cabin through a labyrinthine network of connections. Miranda's second (or was it a third?) cousin gave them a ring of keys and a map to find the property. It sat in the mountains, ten miles from civilization amid high timber and a tangle of abandoned logging roads. The driveway was cut into a steep hillside; a hundred-yard-long dirt track hidden by masses of brush and trees. The perfect bolt-hole.

Bruce wouldn't find them here in the catbird's seat overlooking nowhere.

Lorna arrived home a few minutes before nightfall. Miranda came to the porch and waved. She was tall; her hair long and burnished auburn, her skin dusky and unblemished. Lorna thought her beautiful; lush and ripe, vaguely Rubenesque. A contrast to Lorna's own paleness, her angular, sinewy build. She thought it amusing that their personalities reflected their physiognomies—Miranda tended to be placid and yielding and sweetly melancholy, while Lorna was all sharp edges.

Miranda helped bring in the groceries—she'd volunteered to drive into town and fetch them herself, but Lorna refused and the reason why went unspoken, although it loomed large. A lot more than her leg needed healing. Bruce had done the shopping, paid the bills, made every decision for thirteen, tortuous years. Not all at once, but gradually, until he crushed her, smothered her, with his so-called love. That was over. A little more pain and suffering in the service of emancipation—figuratively and literally—following a lost decade seemed appropriate.

The Haugstad Cabin was practically a fossil and possessed of a dark history that Miranda hinted at, but coyly refused to disclose. It was in solid repair for a building constructed in the 1920s; even on the cozy side: thick, slab walls and a mossy shake roof. Two bedrooms, a pantry, a loft, a cramped toilet and bath, and a living room with a kitchenette tucked in the corner. The cellar's trapdoor was concealed inside the pantry. She had no intention of going down there. She hated spiders and all the other creepy-crawlies sure to infest that wet and lightless space. Nor did she like the tattered bearskin rug before the fireplace, nor the oil painting of a hunter in buckskins stalking along a ridge beneath a twilit sky, nor a smaller portrait of a stag with jagged horns in menacing silhouette atop a cliff, also at sunset. Lorna detested the idea of hunting, preferred not to ponder where the chicken in chicken soup came from, much less the fate of cattle. These artifacts of minds and philosophies so divergent from her own were disquieting.

There were a few modern renovations—a portable generator provided electricity to power the plumbing and lights. No phone, however. Not that it mattered as her cell reception was passable despite the rugged terrain. The elevation and eastern exposure also enabled the transistor radio to capture a decent signal.

Miranda raised an eyebrow when she came across the bottles of Old Crow. She stuck them in a cabinet without comment. They made a simple pasta together with peaches on the side and a glass or three of wine for dessert. Later, they relaxed near the fire. Conversation lapsed into a comfortable silence until Lorna chuckled upon recalling the bartender's portentous question, which seemed inane rather than sinister now that she was half-drunk and drowsing in her lover's arms. Miranda asked what was so funny and Lorna told her about the tavern incident.

"Man alive, I found something weird today," Miranda said. She'd stiffened when Lorna described shooting tequila. Lorna's drinking was a bone of contention. She'd hit the bottle when Orillia went into first grade, leaving her alone at the house for the majority of too many lonely days. At first it'd been innocent enough: A nip or two of cooking sherry, the occasional glass of wine during the soaps, then the occasional bottle of wine, then the occasional bottle of Maker's Mark or Johnny Walker, and finally, the bottle was open and in her hand five minutes after Orillia skipped to the bus and the cork didn't go back in until five minutes before her little girl came home. Since she and Miranda became an item, she'd striven to restrict her boozing to social occasions, dinner, and the like. But sweet Jesus, fuck. At least she hadn't broken down and started smoking again.

"Where'd you go?" Lorna said.

"That trail behind the woodshed. I wanted some photographs. Being cooped up in here is driving me a teensy bit bonkers."

"So, how weird was it?"

"Maybe weird isn't quite the word. Gross. Gross is more accurate."

"You're killing me."

"That trail goes a long way. I think deer use it as a path because it's really narrow but well-beaten. We should hike to the end one of these days, see how far it goes. I'm curious where it ends."

"Trails don't end; they just peter out. We'll get lost and spend the winter gnawing bark like the Donners."

"You're so morbid!" Miranda laughed and kissed Lorna's ear. She described crossing a small clearing about a quarter mile along the trail. At the far end was a stand of Douglas Fir and she didn't notice the tree house until she stopped to snap a few pictures. The tree house was probably as old as the cabin; its wooden planks were bone yellow where they peeked through moss and branches. The platform perched about fifteen feet off the ground, and a ladder was nailed to the backside of tree…

"You didn't climb the tree," Lorna said.

Miranda flexed her scraped and bruised knuckles. "Yes, I climbed that tree, all right." The ladder was very precarious and the platform itself so rotted, sections of it had fallen away. Apparently, for no stronger reason than boredom, she risked life and limb to clamber atop the platform and investigate.

"It's not a tree house," Lorna said. "You found a hunter's blind. The hunter sits on the platform, camouflaged by the branches. Eventually, some poor hapless critter comes by, and blammo! Sadly, I've learned a lot from Bruce's favorite cable television shows. What in the heck compelled you to scamper around in a deathtrap in the middle of the woods? You could've gotten yourself in a real fix."

"That occurred to me. My foot went through in one spot and I almost crapped my pants. If I got stuck I could scream all day and nobody would hear me. The danger was worth it, though."

"Well, what did you find? Some moonshine in mason jars? D.B. Cooper's skeleton?"

"Time for the reveal!" Miranda extricated herself from Lorna and went and opened the door, letting in a rush of cold night air. She returned with what appeared to be a bundle of filthy rags and proceeded to unroll them.

Lorna realized her girlfriend was presenting an animal hide. The fur had been sewn into a crude cape or cloak; beaten and weathered from great age, and shriveled along the hem. The head was that of some indeterminate predator—possibly a wolf or coyote. Whatever the species, the creature was a prize specimen. Despite the cloak's deteriorated condition, she could imagine it draped across the broad shoulders of a Viking berserker or an Indian warrior. She said, "You realize that you just introduced several colonies of fleas, ticks, and lice into our habitat with that wretched thing."

"Way ahead of you, baby. I sprayed it with bleach. Cooties were crawling all over. Isn't it neat?"

"It's horrifying," Lorna said. Yet, she couldn't look away as Miranda held it at arm's length so the pelt gleamed dully in the firelight. What was it? Who'd worn it and why? Was it a garment to provide mere warmth, or to blend with the surroundings? The painting of the hunter was obscured by shadows, but she thought of the man in buckskin sneaking along, looking for something to kill, a throat to slice. Her hand went to her own throat.

"This was hanging from a peg. I'm kinda surprised it's not completely ruined, what with the elements. Funky, huh? A Daniel Boone era accessory."

"Gives me the creeps."

"The creeps? It's just a fur."

"I don't dig fur. Fur is dead. Man."

"You're a riot. I wonder if it's worth money."

"I really doubt that. Who cares? It's not ours."

"Finders keepers," Miranda said. She held the cloak against her bosom as if she were measuring a dress. "Rowr! I'm a wild-woman. Better watch yourself tonight!" She'd drunk enough wine to be in the mood for theater. "Scandinavian legends say to wear the skin of a beast is to become the beast. Haugstad fled to America in 1910, cast out from his community. There was a series of unexplained murders back in the homeland, and other unsavory deeds, all of which pointed to his doorstep. People in his village swore he kept a bundle of hides in a storehouse, that he donned them and became something other than a man, that it was he who tore apart a family's cattle, that it was he who slaughtered a couple of boys hunting rabbits in the field, that it was he who desecrated graves and ate of the flesh of the dead during lean times. So, he left just ahead of a pitchfork-wielding mob. He built this cabin and lived a hermit's life. Alas, his dark past followed. Some of the locals in Poger Rock got wind of the old scandals. One of the town drunks claimed he saw the trapper turn into a wolf and nobody laughed as hard as one might expect. Haugstad got blamed whenever a cow disappeared, when the milk went sour, you name it. Then, over the course of ten years or so a long string of loggers and ranchers vanished. The natives grew restless and it was the scene in Norway all over again."

"What happened to him?"

"He wandered into the mountains one winter and never returned. Distant kin took over this place, lived here off and on the last thirty or forty years. Folks still remember, though." Miranda made an exaggerated face and waggled her fingers. "Booga-booga!"

Lorna smiled, but she was repulsed by the hide, and unsettled by Miranda's flushed cheeks, her loopy grin. Her lover's playfulness wasn't amusing her as it might've on another night. She said, "Toss that wretched skin outside, would you? Let's hit the sack. I'm exhausted."

"Exhausted, eh? Now is my chance to take full advantage of you." Miranda winked as she stroked the hide. Instead of heading for the front door she took her prize to the spare bedroom and left it there. She came back and embraced Lorna. Her eyes were too bright. The wine was strong on her breath. "Told you it was cool. God knows what else we'll find if we look sharp."

They made fierce love. Miranda was much more aggressive than her custom. The pain in Lorna's knee built from a small flame to a white blaze of agony and her orgasm only registered as spasms in her thighs and shortness of breath, pleasure eclipsed entirely by suffering. Miranda didn't notice the tears on Lorna's cheeks, the frantic nature of her moans. When it ended, she kissed Lorna on the mouth, tasting of musk and salt, and something indefinably bitter. She collapsed and was asleep within seconds.

Lorna lay propped by pillows, her hand tangled in Miranda's hair. The faint yellow shine of a three-quarter moon peeked over the ridgeline across the valley and beamed through the window at the foot of the bed. She could tell it was cold because their breaths misted the glass. A wolf howled and she flinched, the cry arousing a flutter of primordial dread in her breast. She waited until Miranda's breathing steadied, then crept away. She put on Miranda's robe and grabbed a bottle of Old Crow and a glass and poured herself a dose and sipped it before the main window in the living room.

Thin, fast moving clouds occasionally crossed the face of the moon and its light pulsed and shadows reached like claws across the silvery landscape of rocky hillocks and canyons, and stands of firs and pine. The stars burned a finger-width above the crowns of the adjacent peaks. The land fell away into deeper shadow, a rift of darkness uninterrupted by a solitary flicker of manmade light. She and Miranda weren't welcome; the cabin and its former inhabitants hadn't been either, despite persisting like ticks bored into the flank of a dog. The immensity of the void intimidated her, and for a moment she almost missed Bruce and the comparative safety of her suburban home, the gilded cage, even the bondage. She blinked, angry at this lapse into the bad old way of thinking, and drank the whiskey. "I'm not a damned whipped dog." She didn't bother pouring, but had another pull directly from the bottle.

The wolf howled again and another answered. The beasts sounded close and she wondered if they were circling the cabin, wondered if they smelled her and Miranda, or whether their night vision was so acute they could see her in the window—she half in the bag, a bottle dangling from her hand, favoring her left leg, weak and cut from the herd. She considered the cautionary tale of Sven Haugstad and drank some more. Her head spun. She waited for another howl, determined to answer with her own.

Miranda's arms encircled her. She cupped Lorna's breasts and licked her earlobe, nibbled her neck. Lorna cried out and grabbed Miranda's wrist before she registered who it was, and relaxed. "Holy crap, you almost gave me a heart attack!" The floor creaked horribly, they'd even played a game of chopsticks by rhythmically pressing alternating sections with their shoes, but she hadn't heard her lover cross the room. Not a whisper.

Something metallic snicked and an orange flame reflected in the window and sweet, sharp smoke filled Lorna's nostrils. Miranda gently pressed a cigarette to Lorna's lips. Miranda said, "I needed this earlier, except I was too damned lazy to leave the covers. Better late than never."

"Gawd, you read my mind." Lorna took a drag, then exhaled contentedly. The nicotine mixed with the alcohol did its magic. Her fear of the night land and its creatures receded. "I guess I can forgive you for sneaking up on me since you've offered me the peace pipe. Ahhh, I've fallen off the wagon. You're evil. Did you hear the wolves?"

"Those aren't wolves," Miranda said. She reclaimed the cigarette. She inhaled and the cigarette's cherry floated in the window as her face floated in the window, a blur over Lorna's shoulder. "Those are coyotes."

"No shit?"

"Is that why you're so jumpy? You thought the *wolves* were gonna get you?"

"I'm not jumpy. Well, sheesh—an almost full moon, wolves howling on the moor, er, in the woods. Gotta admit it's all kinda spooky."

"Not wolves. Coyotes. Come to bed… It's chilly."

"Right. Coyotes," Lorna said. "I'm embarrassed. That's like peeing myself over dingoes or raccoons."

Snug under a pile of blankets, Lorna was drifting off to sleep when Miranda said in a dreamy voice, "Actually, coyotes are much scarier than wolves. Sneaky, sneaky little suckers. Eat you up. Lick the blood all up."

"What?" Lorna said. Miranda didn't answer. She snored.

One morning, a woman who resembled Vivian Leigh at the flowering of her glory knocked on the door. She wore a green jacket and a green and yellow kerchief and yellow sunglasses. Her purse was shiny red plastic with a red plastic strap. Her gloves were white. Her skirt was black and her shoes were also black. She smiled when Lorna opened the door and her lipstick was blood red like the leaves. "Oh, I'm very sorry to disturb you, Ma'am. I seem to be a trifle lost." The woman introduced herself as Beth. She'd gone for a drive in the hills, searching for the Muskrat Creek Campground. "Apparently, I zigged when I should've zagged," she said, and laughed a laugh worthy of the stage. "Speaking of zigzags, do you mind?" She opened an enamel case and extracted a cigarette and inserted it into a silver holder and lighted up with a stick match. It was all very mesmerizing.

Lorna had nearly panicked upon hearing the knock, convinced Bruce had tracked her down. She invited the woman inside and gave her a cup of coffee. Miranda had gone on her morning walk, which left Lorna with the task of entertaining the stranger while deflecting any awkward questions. She unpacked the road map from her Subaru and spread it across the table. She used a pencil to mark the campgrounds, which were twenty-odd miles from the cabin. Beth had wandered far off course, indeed.

"Thank goodness I came across you. These roads go on forever." Beth sipped her coffee and puffed on her fancy cigarette. She slipped her sunglasses into her purse and glanced around the cabin. Her gaze traveled slowly, weighing everything it crossed. "You are certainly off the beaten path."

"We're private people," Lorna said. "Where's your car?"

Beth gestured toward the road. "Parked around the corner. I didn't know if I could turn around in here, so I walked. Silly me, I broke a heel." She raised her calf to show that indeed yes, the heel of her left pump was wobbly.

"Are you alone?"

"Yes. I was supposed to meet friends at the campgrounds, but I can't reach anybody. No bars. I'm rather cross with them and their directions."

Lorna blinked, taking a moment to realize the woman meant she couldn't get proper phone reception. "Mine works fine. I'd be happy to let you place a call—"

"Thanks anyway, sweetie." Beth had sketched directions inside a notebook. "It'll be a cinch now that I've got my bearings." She finished her coffee, said thanks and goodbye, waving jauntily as she picked her way down the rutted lane.

Lorna started the generator to get hot water for a quick shower. After the shower she made toast and more coffee and sat at the table relaxing with a nice paperback romance, one of several she'd had the foresight to bring along. Out the window, she glimpsed movement among the trees, a low and heavy shape that she recognized as a large dog—no, not a dog, a wolf. The animal almost blended with the rotten leaves and wet brush, and it nosed the earth, moving disjointedly, as if crippled. When it reared on its hind legs, Lorna gasped. Miranda pulled back the cowl of the hide cloak, and leaned against a tree. Her expression was strange; she did not quite appear to be herself. She shuddered in the manner of a person emerging from a trance and walked to where the driveway curved and left three paper plates pressed into the bank. She spaced the plates about three feet apart. Each bore a bull's-eye drawn in magic marker.

Miranda came inside. She'd removed the hide. Her hair was messy and tangled with twigs and leaves. "Who was here?" Her voice rasped like she'd been shouting.

"Some woman looking for a campground." Lorna recounted the brief visit, too unnerved to mention what she'd witnessed. Her heart raced and she was overcome by dizziness that turned the floor to a trampoline. Miranda didn't say anything. She opened a duffel bag and brandished a revolver. She examined the pistol, snapping its cylinder open, then shut. Lorna wasn't particularly conversant with guns, but she'd watched Bruce enough to know this one was loaded. "I thought we were going to discuss it before you bought one," she said.

Miranda rattled a small box of shells and slipped them into the pocket of her vest. "I didn't buy one. A friend gave it to me when I told him about Brucifer. An ex cop. This sucker doesn't have a serial number."

"There's no reason to be upset. She was lost. That's all."

"Of course she was."

Lorna watched her put the gun in her other pocket. "What's wrong?"

"You've only paid cash, right? No debit card, no credit card?"

"You mean in town?"

"I mean anywhere. Like we agreed. No credit cards."

"Tell me what's wrong. She was lost. People get lost. It's not unheard of, you know. And it doesn't matter. I didn't tell her my name. I didn't tell her anything. She was lost. What was I supposed to do? Not answer the door? Maybe stick that gun in her face and demand some ID?"

"The campgrounds are closed," Miranda said. "I was outside the door while she gave you her shuck and jive. She came in a panel van. A guy with a beard and sunglasses was driving. Didn't get a good look at him."

Lorna covered her face. "I think I'm gonna be sick."

Miranda's boots made loud clomping sounds as she walked to the door. She hesitated for a few moments, then said, "It's okay. You handled her fine. Bruce has got entirely too much money."

Lorna nodded and wiped her eyes on her sleeve. "We'll see how much money he has after my lawyer gets through with him."

Miranda smiled. It was thin and pained, but a smile. She shut the door behind her. Lorna curled into a ball on the bed. The revolver fired, its report muffled by the thick walls of the cabin. She imagined the black holes in the white paper. She imagined black holes drilling through Bruce's white face. Pop, pop, pop.

Miranda brought Lorna to a stand of trees on the edge of a clearing and showed her the hunting blind. The bloody sun fell into the earth and the only slightly less bloody moon swung, like a pendulum, to replace it in the lower black of the sky. "That is one big, bad moon," Miranda said.

"It's beautiful," Lorna said. "Like an iceberg sliding through space." She thought the fullness of the moon, its astral radiance, presaged some kind of cosmic shift. Her blood sang and the hairs on her arms prickled. It was too dark to see the platform in the branches, but she felt it there, heard its timbers squeak in the breeze.

"Been having strange dreams," Miranda said. "Most of them are blurry. Last one I remember was about the people who used to live around here, a long time ago. They weren't gentle folks, that's for sure."

"Well, of course not," Lorna said. "They stuck a deer head over the fireplace and skinned poor hapless woodland critters and hung them in the trees."

"Yeah," Miranda said. She lighted a cigarette. "Want one?"

"No."

Miranda smoked most of her cigarette before she spoke again. "In the latest dream it was winter, frost thick on the windows. I sat on the bearskin rug. Late at night, a big fire crackling away, and an old man, I mean old as dirt, was kicked back in a rocker, talking to me, telling me stuff. I couldn't see his face because he sat in the shadows. He wore old-timey clothes and a fur jacket, and a hat made out of an animal head. Coyote or wolf. He explained how to set a snare for rabbits, how to skin a deer. The dream changed and jumped around, like dreams do, and we were kneeling on the floor by the carcass of, I dunno what. A possum, I think. The meat was green and soft; it had been dead a while. The old man told me a survivor eats what's around. Then he stuck his face into that mess of stinking meat and took a bite."

"That's a message," Lorna said. "The great universal consciousness is trying to tell you, us, to adapt. Adapt or die."

"Or it could be a dream, full stop."

"Is that what you think?"

"I think it's time to get our minds right. Face the inevitable."

"The inevitable?"

"We're never going to get away," Miranda said.

"Well, that's a hell of an attitude."

"I saw that van again. Parked in that gravel pit just down the road. They're watching us, Lorna."

"Oh, Jesus."

"Don't worry about those bastards. They'll be dealt with."

"Dealt with? Dealt with how?" Lorna's mind flashed to the revolver. The notion of Miranda shooting anyone in cold blood was ridiculous. Yet, here in the dark beyond the reach of rule or reason, such far-fetched notions bore weight. "Don't get any crazy ideas."

"I mean, don't worry yourself sick over the help. Nah, the bigger problem is your husband. How much time is Bruce going to get? A few months? A year? Talk about your lawyer. *Bruce's* lawyer is slick. He might not get anything. Community service, a stern admonition from the judge to go forth and sin no more."

Lorna winced. Stress caused her leg to throb. The cigarette smoke drove her mad with desire. She stifled a sharp response and regarded the moon instead. Her frustration dissolved in the presence of its cold, implacable majesty. She said, "I know. It's the way of the world. People like Bruce always win." She'd called Orillia earlier that evening, asked her how things were going at the new school. Orillia didn't want to talk about school; she wanted to know when she could see Daddy again, worried that he was lonely. Lorna had tried to keep emotion from her voice when she answered that Mom and Dad were working through some issues and everything would soon be sorted. Bruce was careful to not hit Lorna in front of their daughter, and though Orillia witnessed the bruises and the breaks, the sobbing aftermath, she seemed to disassociate these from her father's actions.

"There are other ways to win." Miranda was a black shadow against the dead silver grass. "Like you said—adapt or die. The old man showed me. In the beginning you need a prop, but it gets easier when you realize it's all in your head."

It was a long walk back through the woods. Dry leaves crunched beneath their shoes. They locked themselves into the cabin and got ready for bed.

Lorna's dreams had been strange as well, but she'd kept quiet. She wasn't open about such things, not even with Miranda. The ghost of old man Haugstad didn't speak to Lorna; instead, her dreams transported her to the barren slopes above the tree line of the valley. The moon fumed and boiled. She was a passenger in another's body, a body that seethed with profound vitality. The moon's yellow glow stirred her blood and she raced down the slope and into the trees. She smelled the land, tasted it on her lolling tongue, drawing in the scent of every green deer spoor, every droplet of coyote musk, every spackling of piss on rock or shrub. She smelled fresh blood and meat-blacked bone. There were many, many bones scattered across the mountainside. Generational heaps of them—ribs, thighs, horns, skulls. These graveyards were secret places, scattered for miles across deep, hidden caches and among the high rocks.

Lorna stroked Miranda's belly. Miranda's excess had melted away in recent days. She was lean from day-long hikes and skipped meals and her scent was different, almost gamey, her hair lank and coarse. She was restless and she whined in her sleep. She bit too hard when they made love.

Miranda took Lorna's hand and said, "What is it?"

"I'm afraid you're going to leave."

"Oh, where the fuck is this coming from?"

"Something's different. Something's changed. You weren't honest about where you found the coat. The skin."

Miranda chuckled without humor. "Let sleeping dogs lie."

"I'm not in the mood for cute," Lorna said.

"My sweet one. I left out the part that might…frighten you. You're skittish enough."

"I'm also not in the mood for Twenty Questions. What did you mean earlier—the old man showed you?"

"Old man Haugstad told me where to look, what I needed to do."

"In a dream."

"Not in a dream. The day I discovered the blind, a coyote skulked out of the bushes and led me along the path. It was the size of a mastiff, blizzard white on the muzzle and crisscrossed with scars."

"I don't understand," Lorna said, but was afraid she might.

"We're here for a reason. Can't you feel the power all around us? After I lost Jack, after I finally accepted he was gone, I pretty much decided to off myself. If I hadn't met you at that party I probably would've died within a few days. I'd picked out the pills, the clothes I intended to wear, knew exactly where it was going to happen. When was the only question."

Lorna began to cry.

"I won't leave you. But it's possible you might decide not to come with me." Miranda rolled to her opposite side and said nothing more. Lorna slowly drifted to sleep. She woke later while it was still dark. Miranda's side of the bed was a cold blank space. Her clothes were still piled on the floor. In a moment of sublimely morbid intuition, Lorna clicked on a flashlight and checked the spare bedroom where Miranda had taken to hanging the fur cloak from a hook on the door. Of course the cloak was missing.

She gathered her robe tightly, sparing a moment to reflect upon her resemblance to the doomed heroines on any number of lurid gothic horror novel covers and went outdoors into the freezing night. Her teeth chattered and her fear became indistinguishable from the chill. She poked around the cabin, occasionally calling her lover's name, although in a soft tone, afraid to attract the attention of the wolves, the coyotes, or whatever else might roam the forest at night.

Eventually she approached the woodshed and saw that the door was cracked open by several inches. She stepped inside. Miranda crouched on the dirt floor. The flashlight was weak and its flickering cone only hinted and suggested. The pelt covered Miranda, concealed her so she was scarcely more than a lump. She whined and shuddered and took notice of the pallid light, and as she stirred, Lorna was convinced that the pelt was not a loose cloak, not an ill-fitted garment, but something else entirely for the manner in which it flexed with each twitch and shiver of Miranda's musculature.

The flashlight glass cracked and imploded. The shed lay in utter darkness except for a thin sliver of moonlight that burned yellow in Miranda's eyes. Lorna's mouth was dry. She said, "Sweetheart?"

Miranda said in a voice rusty and drugged, "Why don't you…go on to bed. I'll be along. I'll come see you real soon." She stood, a ponderous yet lithe, uncoiling motion, and her head scraped the low ceiling.

Lorna got out fast and stumbled toward the cabin. She didn't look over her shoulder even though she felt hot breath on the back of her neck.

They didn't speak of the incident. For a couple of days they hardly spoke at all. Miranda drifted in and out of the cabin like a ghost and Lorna dreaded to ask where she went in the dead of night, why she wore the hide and nothing else. Evening temperatures dipped below freezing, yet Miranda didn't appear to suffer, on the contrary, she thrived. She hadn't eaten a bite from their store of canned goods, hadn't taken a meal all week. Lorna lay awake staring at the ceiling as the autumn rains rattled the windows.

One afternoon she sat alone at the kitchen table downing the last of the Old Crow. The previous evening she'd experienced two visceral and disturbing dreams. In the first she was serving drinks at a barbeque. There were dozens of guests. Bruce flipped burgers and hob-knobbed with his office chums. Orillia darted through the crowd with a water pistol, zapping hapless adults before dashing away. The mystery woman Beth, and a bearded man in a track suit she introduced as her husband, came over and told her what a lovely party, what a lovely house, what a lovely family, and Lorna handed them drinks and smiled a big dumb smile as Miranda stood to the side and winked, nodding toward a panel van parked nearby on the grass. The van rocked and a coyote emerged from beneath the vehicle, growling and slobbering and snapping at the air. Grease slicked the animal's fur black, made its yellow eyes bright as flames.

A moment later, Lorna was in the woods, chasing the bearded man from the party. His track suit flapped in shreds, stained with blood and dirt. The man tripped and fell over a cliff. He crashed in a sprawl of broken limbs, his mouth full of shattered teeth and black gore. He raised a mutilated hand toward her in supplication. She bounded down and mounted him, licked the blood from him, then chewed off his face. She'd awakened with a cry, bile in her throat.

Lorna set aside the empty bottle. She put on her coat and got the revolver from the dresser where Miranda had stashed it for safekeeping. Lorna hadn't fired the gun despite Miranda's offer to practice. However, she'd seen her lover go through the routine—cock the hammer, pull the trigger, click, no real trick. She didn't need the gun, wouldn't use the gun, but somehow its weight in her pocket felt good. She walked down the driveway, moving gingerly to protect her bum knee, then followed the road to the gravel pit where the van was allegedly parked. The rain slackened to drizzle. Patches of mist swirled in the hollows and the canyons and crept along fern beds at the edges of the road. The valley lay hushed, a brooding giant.

The gravel pit was empty. A handful of charred wood and some squashed beer cans confirmed someone had definitely camped there in the not so distant past. She breathed heavily, partially from the incessant throb in her knee, partially from relief. What the hell would she have done if the assholes her husband sent were on the spot roasting wienies? Did she really think people like that would evaporate upon being subjected to harsh language? Did she really have the backbone to flash the gun and send them packing John Wayne style?

She thought the first muffled cry was the screech of a bird, but the second shout got her attention. Her heart was pounding when she finally located the source about a hundred yards farther along the road. Tire tracks veered from the narrow lane toward a forty foot drop into a gulch of trees and boulders. The van had landed on its side. The rear doors were sprung, the glass busted. She wouldn't have noticed it all the way down there if not for the woman crying for help. Her voice sounded weak. But that made sense—Beth had been trapped in the wreck for several days, hadn't she? One snip of the brake line and on these hills it'd be all over but the crying. Miranda surely didn't fuck around, did she? Lorna bit the palm of her hand to stifle a scream.

"Hey," Miranda said. She'd come along as stealthily as the mist and lurked a few paces away near a thicket of brambles. She wore the mangy cloak with the predator's skull covering her own, rendering her features inscrutable. Her feet were bare. She was naked beneath the pelt, her lovely flesh streaked with dirt and blood. Her mouth was stained wine-dark. "Sorry, honeybunch. I really thought they'd have given up the ghost by now. Alas, alack. Don't worry. It won't be long. The birds are here."

Crows hopped among the limbs and drifted in looping patterns above the ruined van. They squawked and squabbled. The woman yelled something unintelligible. She wailed and fell silent. Lorna's lip trembled and her nose ran with snot. She swept her arm to indicate their surroundings. "Why did you bring me here?"

Miranda tilted her misshapen head and smiled a sad, cruel smile. "I want to save you, baby. You're weak."

Lorna stared into the gulch. The mist thickened and began to fill in the cracks and crevices and covered the van and its occupants. There was no way she could navigate the steep bank, not with her injury. Her cell was at the cabin on the table. She could almost hear the clockwork gears of the universe clicking into alignment, a great dark spotlight shifting across the cosmic stage to center upon her at this moment in time. She said, "I don't know how to do what you've done. To change. Unless that hide is built for two."

Miranda took her hand and led her back to the cabin and tenderly undressed her. She smiled faintly when she retrieved the revolver and set it on the table. She kissed Lorna and her breath was hot and foul. Then she stepped back and began to pull the hide away from her body and as it lifted so did the underlying skin, peeling like a scab. Blood poured down Miranda's chest and belly and pattered on the floorboards. The muscles of her cheeks and jaw bunched and she hissed, eyes rolling, and then it was done and the dripping bundle was free of her red-slicked flesh. Lorna was paralyzed with horror and awe, but finally stirred and tried to resist what her lover proffered. Miranda cuffed her temple, stunning her. She said, "Hold still, baby. You're gonna thank me," and draped the cloak across Lorna's shoulders and pulled the skullcap of the beast over Lorna's eyes.

"You came here for this?" Lorna said as the slimy and overheated pelt cupped her and enclosed her. The room went in and out of focus.

"No, babe. I just followed the trail and here were are. And it's good. You'll see how good it is, how it changes everything. We've been living in a cage, but that's over now.

"My god, I loved you." Lorna blinked the blood from her eyes. She glanced over and saw the revolver on the table, blunt and deadly and glowing with the dwindling light, a beacon. She grabbed the weapon without thought and pressed it under Miranda's chin and thumbed the hammer just as she'd seen it done. Her entire body shook. "You thought I'd just leave my daughter behind and slink off to Never-Never Land without a word? Are you out of your fucking mind?"

"Give it a minute," Miranda said. The fingers of her left hand stroked the pelt. "One minute. Let it work its magic. You'll see everything in a whole new way. Come on, sweetie." She reached for the revolver and it barked and twisted in Lorna's hands.

Lorna didn't weep. Her insides were stone. She dropped the gun and swayed in place, not focusing on anything. The light began to fade. She stumbled outside. She could smell everything and strange thoughts rushed through her head.

There was a moment between twilight and darkness when she almost managed to tear free of the hide and begin making the calls that would return her to the world, her daughter, the apocalyptic showdown with the man who'd oppressed her for too long. The moment passed, was usurped by an older and much more powerful impulse. Her thoughts turned to the woods, the hills, a universe of dark, sweet scent. The hunt.

Two weeks later, a hiker spotted a murder of crows in a raucous celebration as they roosted around the wrecked van. He called emergency services. Men and dogs and choppers swarmed the mountainside. The case made all of the papers and ran on the local networks for days.

Investigators found two corpses—an adult male and an adult female—in the van. The cause of death was blunt force trauma and prolonged exposure to the elements. Further examination revealed that the brake lines of the van were sawed through, indicative of homicide. The homicide theory was supported by the discovery of a deceased adult female on the floor of a nearby cabin. She'd died of a single bullet wound to the head. A fourth individual who'd also lived on the premises remained missing and was later presumed dead. Tremendous scrutiny was directed at the missing woman's estranged husband. He professed his innocence throughout the subsequent trial. That he'd hired the deceased couple to spy on his wife didn't help his case.

Years later, a homicide detective wrote a bestseller detailing the investigation of the killings. Tucked away as a footnote, the author included a few esoteric quotes and bits of trivia; among these were comments by the Chief Medical Examiner who'd overseen the autopsies. According to the ME, it was fortunate picture ID was present on scene for the deceased. By the time the authorities arrived, animals had gotten to the bodies in the van. The examiner said she'd been tempted to note in her report that in thirty years she'd never seen anything so bizarre or savage as these particular bites, but wisely reconsidered.

THE CARRION GODS IN THEIR HEAVEN

I'm often asked which are my favorites of my anthologies. I used to have difficulty responding. It felt disloyal to name some and not others. But I got over it.

So, *Supernatural Noir*, published by Dark Horse Books in 2011—which is about exactly what it sounds like—is one of my favorites. I love the theme and I love the mix of stories in it. I enjoyed editing it so much that I'd be very happy to edit a second volume one of these days.

In any case, here's a sampling from that volume: Laird Barron's "The Carrion Gods in Their Heaven." I've been publishing Laird's work since 2004, when I first noticed his work, picking up "Old Virginia" for *The Year's Best Fantasy and Horror: Seventeenth Annual Collection*. I've been commissioning and/or reprinting a good deal of his short fiction ever since.

The Crow Palace

By Priya Sharma

(From *Black Feathers: Dark Avian Tales,* 2017)

Birds are tricksters. Being small necessitates all kinds of wiles to survive but Corvidae, in all their glory as the raven, rook, jay, magpie, jackdaw, and crow have greater ambitions than that.

They have a plan.

$\mathscr{H}\!\!\mathscr{p}$

I used to go into the garden with Dad and Pippa every morning, rain or shine, even on school days.

We lived in a house called The Beeches. Its three acre garden had been parcelled off and flogged to developers before I was born, so it became one of a cluster of houses on an unadopted cul de sac.

Mature rhododendrons that flowered purple and red in spring lined the drive. The house was sheltered from prying eyes by tall hedges and the eponymous beech trees. Dad refused to cut them back despite neighbours' pleas for more light and less leaf fall in the autumn. *Dense foliage is perfect for nesting*, he'd say.

Our garden was an avian haven. Elsa, who lived opposite, would bring over hanging feeders full of fat balls and teach us about the blue tits and cheeky sparrows who hung from them as they gorged. Stone nymphs held up bowls that Dad kept filled. Starlings splashed about in them. When they took flight they shed drops of water that shone like discarded diamonds. The green and gold on their wings caught the sun.

Pippa and I played while Dad dug over his vegetable patch at the weekends. The bloody chested robin followed him, seeking the soft bodied and spineless in the freshly turned earth.

Dad had built a bird table, of all things, to celebrate our birth. It was a complex construction with different tiers. Our job was to lay out daily offerings of nuts and meal worms. At eight I could reach its lower levels but Pippa, my twin, needed a footstool and for Dad to hold her steady so that she didn't fall.

Elsa taught me to recognise our visitors and all their peculiarities and folklore. Sometimes there were jackdaws, rooks, and ravens but it was monopolised by crows, which is why I dubbed it the crow palace. Though not the largest of the corvidae, they were strong and stout. I watched them see off interlopers, such as squirrels, who hoped to dine.

After leaving our offerings we'd withdraw to the sun room to watch them gather.

"Birdies," Pippa would clap.

The patio doors bore the brunt of her excitement; fogged breath and palm prints. Snot, if she had a cold. She touched my arm when she wanted to get my attention, which came out as a clumsy thump.

"I can see."

Hearing my tone, Pippa inched away, looking chastised.

Dad closed in on the other side with a forced, jovial, "You're quiet, what's up?"

It was always the same. *How are you feeling? What can I get you? Are you hungry? Did you have a bad dream last night?*

"I'm fine." Not a child's answer. I sounded uptight. I didn't have the emotional vocabulary to say, *Go away. Your anxiety's stifling me.*

I put my forehead against the glass. In the far corner of the garden was the pond, which Dad had covered with safety mesh, unfortunately too late to stop Mum drowning herself in it. That's where I found her, a jay perched on her back. It looked like it had pushed her in. That day the crow palace had been covered with carrion crows; bruisers whose shiny eyes were full of plots.

I sit in a traffic queue, radio on, but all I hear is Elsa's voice.

"Julie, it's Elsa. From Fenby."

As if I could forget the woman who brought us birthday presents, collected us from school, and who told me about bras, periods, and contraception (albeit in the sketchiest terms) when Dad was too squeamish for the task.

"Julie, you need to come home. I don't know how to say this, so I'll just come out with it. Your dad's dead." She paused. "He collapsed in the garden this morning. I'll stay with Pippa until you get here."

"Thank you."

"You will come, won't you?"

"Yes."

Ten years and they jerk me back with one phone call.

The journey takes an hour longer than I expected. Oh, England, my sceptred and congested isle. I'm not sure if I'm glad of the delay or it's making my dread worse.

The lane is in dire need of resurfacing so I have to slow down to navigate the potholes. I turn into the drive. It's lined by overgrown bushes. I stop out of view of the house and walk the rest of the way. I'm not ready for Pip and Elsa yet.

The Beeches should be handsome. It's crying out for love. Someone should chip off the salmon pink stucco and take it back to its original red brick. The garden wraps around it on three sides, widest at the rear. I head there first.

The crow palace is the altar of the childhood rituals that bound us. It looks like Dad's lavished more love on it than the house. New levels have been added and parts of it replaced.

I stoop to pick something up from the ground. I frown as I turn it over and read the label. It's an empty syringe wrapper. Evidence of the paramedics labours. The grass, which needs mowing is trampled down. I think I can see where Dad lay.

A crow lands on the palace at my eye level. It struts back and forth with a long, confident stride as it inspects me. Its back is all the colours of the night. It raises its head and opens its beak wide.

Caw caw caw.

It's only then that the patio doors open and Elsa runs out, arms outstretched.

Job done, the crow takes flight.

Elsa fusses and clucks over me, fetching sweet tea, "For shock."

"What happened to him?"

"They think it was a heart attack. The coroner's officer wants to speak to you. I've left the number by the phone."

"How can they be sure? Don't they need to do a post mortem?"

"They think it's likely. He's had two in the last three years."

"I didn't know."

"He wouldn't let me phone you." I don't know if I'm annoyed that she didn't call or relieved that she doesn't say *Perhaps, if you'd bothered to call him he might have told you himself.* "Your dad was a terrible patient. They told him he should have an operation to clear his arteries but he refused."

Elsa opens one of the kitchen cupboards. "Look."

I take out some of the boxes, shake them, read the leaflets. There's twelve months of medication here. Dad never took any of it. Aspirin, statins, nitrates, ace-inhibitors. Wonder drugs to unblock his stodgy arteries and keep his blood flowing through them.

I slam the door shut, making Elsa jump. It's the gesture of a petulant teenager. I can't help it. Dad's self neglect is a good excuse to be angry at him for dying.

"We used to have terrible rows over it. I think it was his way of punishing himself." Elsa doesn't need to say *guilt over your mother.* She looks washed out. Her pale eyes, once arresting, look aged. "I don't think Pippa understands. Don't be hurt. She'll come out when she's ready."

Pippa had looked at me as I put my bag down in the hall and said, "Julieee," prolonging the last syllable as she always did when she was excited. Then she slid from the room, leaving me alone with Elsa.

Elsa's the one who doesn't understand, despite how long she's known Pippa.

Pip's cerebral palsy has damaged the parts of her brain that controls her speech. It's impaired her balance and muscle tone. It's robbed her of parts of her intellect but she's attuned to the world in other ways.

She understands what I feel. *She's* waiting for *me* to be ready, not the other way around.

Perhaps it's a twin thing.

Pippa stopped speaking for several years when she was a child. It was when she realised that she didn't sound like other children. That she couldn't find and shape the words as I did. Her development wasn't as arrested as everyone supposed. Dad, Elsa and her teachers all underestimated her.

I could've tried to help her. I could have acted as an interpreter as I've always understood her but I didn't. Instead, I watched her struggle.

And here she is, as if I've called out to her.

Pippa's small and twisted, muscle spasticity contorting her left side. That she's grey at the temples shocks me, despite the fact mine's the same but covered with dye. She's wearing leggings and a colourful sweatshirt; the sort of clothes Dad always bought for her. That she's unchanged yet older causes a pang in my chest, which I resent.

Pip looks at the world obliquely, as if scared to face it straight on. She stands in the doorway, weighing me up and then smiles, her pleasure at seeing me plain on her narrow face.

That's what makes me cry. For her. For myself. I've abandoned her again and again. As soon as I could walk, I walked away from her. As we grew older, my greatest unkindness towards her was my coldness. As a teenager, I never wanted to be seen with her. After our twenty-third birthday, I never came back.

"Julieee."

I put my arms around her. I've not asked Elsa if Pip was with Dad when he collapsed, if she sat beside him, if she saw the paramedics at work.

The onslaught of my tears and sudden embrace frighten her and I'm the one who feels abandoned when Pip pulls away.

Ten years since my last visit to The Beeches. Ten years since Dad and I argued. I drove home after spending the weekend here for our birthday. Elsa had made a cake, a sugary creation piled up with candles that was more suitable for children.

Dad rang me when I got back to my flat in London.

"I'm disappointed, Julie."

"What?" I wasn't used to him speaking to me like that.

"You come down once in a blue moon and spend the whole time on the phone."

"I have to work." I was setting up my own recruitment agency. I was angry at Dad for not understanding that. I was angry that he thought I owed him an explanation. "I'm still getting things off the ground."

"Yes, I know your work's more important than we are."

"It's how I make a living. You sound like you want me to fail."

"Don't be preposterous. All I'm saying is that it would be nice for you to be *here* when you're actually here."

"I drove all the way to be there. It's my birthday too."

"You act like coming home is a chore. Pippa's your sister. You have a responsibility towards her."

"Yes, I'm her *sister*, not her mother. Aren't I allowed a life of my own? I thought you'd be happier that you've only got *one* dependent now."

"Don't talk about Pip like that."

"Like what?"

"Like you're angry at her. It's not her fault that your mother killed herself."

"No? Whose was it then? Yours?"

Those were my final words to him. I don't know why I said them now.

The following morning's a quiet relief. I wake long before Pippa. The house is familiar. The cups are where they've always lived. The spoons in the same drawer, the coffee kept in a red enamel canister as it always had been when I lived here. It's like returning to another country after years away. Even though I recognise its geography, customs, and language, I'll never again be intrinsic to its rhythms.

My mobile rings.

"Ju, it's me." Christopher.

"Hi."

I'm never sure what to call him. Boyfriend sounds childish, partner business-like and lover illicit.

"The new Moroccan place has opened. I wondered if you fancied coming with me tonight."

Not: Shall *we* go? There's *him* and *me* with all the freedom between *us* that I need.

"I can't. Take Cassie." There's no jealousy in that remark. Over the two years I've been seeing Chris, seeing other people too has worked well for us. It's precisely why I picked a man with form. A player won't want to cage me but Chris keeps coming back to me, just when I expect him to drift off with someone new.

"I stopped seeing her months ago. I told you."

I don't care. It makes no difference to me.

"My Dad's dead," I say, just to try and change the subject.

"Oh God, Julie I'm so sorry. I'd just presumed he was already dead from the way you talked about him. What happened?"

"Heart attack."

"Where are you? I'll come and help."

"No need."

"I want to."

"And I don't want you to."

"I'm not trying to crowd you, but may I call you? Just to see if you're okay."

"Sure. Of course." He can call. I may not answer.

I hang up.

"Julie."

Pippa sidles up to me. We're both still in our pyjamas. It's an effort but I manage a smile for her.

"Do you want breakfast, Pippa? Cereal?"

I'm not sure what she eats now. It used to be raspberry jam spread thickly on toast. She tugs on my sleeve and pulls me up.

A trio of swallows hang from her bedroom ceiling. It was sent one Christmas, like all my presents to her for the last ten years, chosen for being flat packed and easy to post. Pippa reaches up and sets the birds in motion as she passes.

It's the bedroom of a child. No, it's the bedroom of an innocent. It needs repainting. The realisation makes me wonder what I feel. Our future's a knife.

"Look," Pippa beams.

Her childhood collection has grown to dominate the room. It's housed in plastic craft drawers that are stacked on shelves to a height that Pippa can reach. Her models are lined up above the drawers, on higher shelves.

She used to make them in plasticine. They were crude lumps at first. Now she's graduated to clay. They must fire them at the day centre. Her years of practice are in the suggestive details. A square tail. The shape of the head with a pinched beak.

They're crows, over and over again.

Pippa opens one of the drawers and picks out buttons, one at a time, and drops them into my open hand. Each one's unique, only their colour in common. They're white plastic, mother of pearl, enamel, stained fabric, and horn. She laughs as they spill through my fingers. The rest of that block of drawers contains buttons, each separated by compartment for the rainbow.

"Pippa, are all these from the crow palace?"

"Yes, birdies." She mangles some of the syllables but she's definite.

She shows me more. Her collection is sorted by type of object, or by shape where Pippa was unsure. Coins and bottle tops. Odd earrings. Screws. Watch parts. The tiny bones of rodents, picked clean and bleached by time.

I used to have a collection of my own, the crows left us treasures on the crow palace in return for food. They came with presents every day. I threw mine out when I started high school.

I regret it now, as I sit here with Pippa.

"Here." She thrusts one of the drawers into my hands.

Something lonely rattles around inside. I tip it out. I hold it up between my fore finger and thumb. A ring designed as a feather that wraps around the finger. Despite the tarnish, its lovely—the hard line of the shaft, the movement of the hundreds of vanes and downy barbs.

It's impossible that it's here because I'm sure Mum was buried with it. I watched Dad lay out the things for the undertaker: a silk blue dress, tights, a pair of leather heels, a lipstick, and this ring. He put her wedding band and diamond engagement ring in a box and placed it in his bedside drawer. *For you, when you get married*, as if this was given.

The feather ring was kept to go with her into the grave. *We were on holiday when she realised she was expecting. She chose this from an antique shop in France the same day that she told me. I was thrilled. I think she'd want to wear this.*

I close my eyes. Had I imagined that? As I do, the ring finds its way onto the ring finger of my left hand, which goes cold. I can feel the blood in my wrist freezing. I yank it off before ice reaches my heart.

"Where did you get this?" My voice is shrill. "Pippa?"

"Crows," she says.

I force myself to go into Dad's room. It's stifling. Being north facing and a dull day, the poor quality light brings out the green undertones in the patterned gold wallpaper. The dark, heavy furniture makes the room crowded and drab.

Everything's an effort. There's something about being back here that's put me in a stupor. I'm procrastinating about everything.

Looking through Dad's things should hurt but it doesn't. It's like rifling through a stranger's personal effects for clues. He was an unknown entity to me because I didn't care enough to want to find out who he was. Shouldn't blood call out to blood? Mine didn't. I felt more for Pip, my dead mother, and for Elsa. Dad's love was smothering and distant all at once as if I was something to be feared and guarded closely.

I pile his clothes in bin bags to take to the charity shop. I pause when I find box files full of football programmes. I never knew he was a fan. It looks like he went regularly before we were born. It crosses my mind that they might be worth something, but then I chuck them on the pile to get rid of.

It's only when I'm clearing out the second wardrobe that I find something that piques my interest. There's a steel box at the back with his initials on it, under a pile of moth eaten scarves. It's locked. I spend the next hour gathering together every key I can find, searching drawers and cupboards for them. Nothing fits.

I carry the box downstairs and put it on the kitchen table. It's too late in the day to take it to a locksmith. I'll go tomorrow.

Who knew that death is so bureaucratic? I'm relieved there won't be a post mortem but there's still the registering of Dad's death and meetings with the undertaker, bank and solicitors. Elsa's a brick, taking Pip to the day centre or over to her place if I have things to arrange.

The future leaves me in a stupor of indecision. I stare out of the kitchen window at where the pond used to be. Now it's a rockery in the same kidney shape.

What sort of people would have a pond with young children in the house?

The pond was where I found Mum's body, looking boneless as it slumped over the stones at the water's edge. I was four. I thought she'd just fallen over. I ran out to help her get up. A jay sat on her back. The bird is the shyest of all Corvids, flamboyant by comparison to its family, in pink, brown, and striped blue. It normally confines itself to the shelter of the woods.

I paused as the wind blew up her skirt, revealing the back of her thighs. Her head was turned to one side. The jay hopped down to look at her face, then pecked at one of her open, staring eyes.

The jay turned as I approached and let out a screech, blood on its beak. Or maybe I was the one screaming. I'd put my hands over my ears.

A shriek comes from the sun room, next door. I drop my coffee cup, imagining Pippa has conjured the same image. She'd followed me out that day and seen Mum too. By the time my cup smashes on the floor and sends hot coffee up my legs and the cabinets I realise something's actually wrong.

Pippa's pressed against the window, shouting and banging with her fists. "What is it?"

I grab her shoulders but she twists around to look outside again. From here we have an uninterrupted view of the back garden.

A magpie deposits something on the crow palace, then starts to make a racket. Its blue-black-white colouring reveals its affinities for the living and the dead.

Only then does the sudden whirring motion draw my gaze down to the lawn. The cat's bright pink collar contrasts with its grey fur. A second magpie is pinned by the cat's paw on its spread wing. Its other wing is a blur as it struggles. The magpie's mate flies down and the cat breaks its gaze with its prey and hisses.

I know it's the natural order of things but I'm sickened and trembling. I open the patio door and clap my hands as if such a banal gesture can end this life and death struggle. Pippa's more decisive, stumbling out and I hold her back for fear she'll be scratched.

Flat black shapes with ragged wings darken the sky. Ravens. One swoops, catching the cat's ear with its bill as fierce as pruning shears as it passes over. The cat contorts, blood on its fur, releasing the magpie which makes an attempt at broken flight.

The cat crouches, a growl in its throat. Its ears are flat to its head, its fur on end, doubling its size. The birds are coming down in black jets, from all directions. The cat raises a paw, claws unsheathed, to swipe at its assailants. The ravens take it by surprise with a group attack. One lands, talons clutching the nape of the cat's neck. It writhes and screams. The sound cuts through me. The birds are like streaks of rain. I can't see the cat anymore. It's been mobbed by darkness.

Pippa and I clutch one another. The cat's silent now. The ravens lift together into the sky and all that remains on the grass are steaks of blood and tufts of fur.

I remember later that the magpies left us a gift, a task which made them careless of their long collective memory of their past persecutions by game-keepers and farmers.

The key they left on the crow palace shines as if calling to me. The metal's so cold that it hurts to hold it, as if it's just come out of a freezer.

I have the queasy feeling that I know what it's for. It slides into the pad-lock on the steel box with ease and I feel its teeth catch as I turn it.

Everything I know about Mum is distilled from scant memories. I'm shaking at the prospect of something concrete. I open the lid. Here's where Dad buried her significant remains.

It contains a random assortment. A lady's dress watch. A pair of pearl earrings. A silk patterned scarf. An empty perfume bottle. I open it and the stale fragrance brings Mum back to me on a drift of bluebells. I wipe my eyes. I'd forgotten she always wore that. There's a birthday card signed *With more than love, Karen.*

What is there that's more than love?

We weren't a photographed family. There aren't any happy snaps that feature Pip and me. This pile of photographs are of Mum and Dad when they were young, before we were born. I shuffle through them. Mum and Dad at the beach, on bicycles, another in formal dress. Their happiness grates. Why couldn't they saved some of it for us?

The last thing out of the box is a handkerchief. Whatever's knotted within clinks as I lift it out. It's a pair of eggs. They're unnaturally heavy, as if made of stone. And they're warm.

I can't resist the impulse to crack one of them open. Fluid runs over my fingers. I sniff it. Fresh egg white.

A baby's curled up within, foetal like, her tender soles and toes, her gen-itals displayed. She's perfect. I don't know what she's made of. Something between rubber and wax that's the colour of putty.

I break open the second one. Another girl. This one's different. She has massive, dark eyes that are too wide set to be normal. There are sparse, matted feathers on her back. Faint scale cover her feet.

I carefully rewrap the pair, trying not to touch them, and put them back in the box.

My phone rings. Then stops. Starts again. There's nothing for it. I answer it.

"Chris." I try not to sound irritated.

"How are you?"

"Busy. You know."

"No, I don't. Tell me."

"Stuff to sort out. Dad and for my sister."

"You have a sister? What's her name?"

"Phillipa. We call her Pippa."

"What's she like?"

Pippa? She likes birds, me, the colour turquoise, chocolate, having a routine, crow gifts, sunshine. She gets frustrated when she can't make herself understood. Her eyes are hazel brown and she has eczema.

"She has cerebral palsy. My Dad took care of her."

"Will I meet her at the funeral?"

I'm about to say *Of course she'll be at the funeral* but then I realise that Chris is assuming he's invited.

"Why do you want to come? You never met him."

"Not for him, for you. Tell me your address."

"I don't need you here."

I don't understand. It feels like an argument, full of unspoken baggage that I didn't even know we were carrying.

"Julie, what are we doing?"

His tone sets off an alarm bell in my head.

"You must know that I—" Don't say it. Don't say *I love you*. He falters, "You must know how much I care about you."

I feel sick. I thought we were alike. Just my luck to find a man who falls in love with the one woman who's not chasing him.

"I'm not talking about marriage or children."

Children. For all the carelessness of my affections there's never been a child.

"I told you at the start that I'm not like other people. You promised me that you understood completely."

"There's more to us than just sex."

I can't believe he's doing this.

"Don't you get it?" I should be angry but a column of coldness is solidifying inside me. "There *is* no more. I'm not broken, so you can't fix me. I don't love you because I can't love anyone."

"Julie, please..."

I hang up and bar his number.

There's never been so many people in the house. I don't like it. I wanted it to be just us, but Elsa went on so much that I relented. I wish I hadn't now.

I forgot to pack a black dress so I had to buy one in a hurry. I took Pippa with me, there being nothing suitable in her wardrobe either. The shop assistant stared at her while she touched the expensive silks. The woman's tune changed when it was clear that I didn't have to look at the price tags.

I picked out a neat black dress for myself and a black tunic, leggings and ankle boots for Pippa. On impulse, I took her to a salon to get her hair dyed and styled. She was more patient than I expected. She liked being somewhere new. My favourite part was Pippa's smile when the shampoo was massaged into her scalp.

It was a nice day.

Today isn't. When we went out to the funeral car, Elsa said, "Look at the two of you. Pippa, you look so grown up. And Julie, wonderful. Black suits you more than any other colour. You should wear it more."

Grief fucks people up.

The mourners come in, folding up their umbrellas like wings, dripping rain on the parquet floor.

"Elsa, are any of the neighbour's coming?"

"God, no. All the one's you'd know are dead or moved away."

I don't know the people here. Some used to work with Dad, apparently, others knew him from Pippa's day centre or through Elsa. They all greet her like she's long lost family.

It's unnerving that they line up to speak to me, something more suited to a wedding than a funeral.

The first is a tall, broad man, dressed in a shiny tight suit and winkle pickers. Spiv's clothes but he's gentle, paternal even. He takes my hand and looks right into my eyes, searching for something.

"My name's Charlie."

"Thank you for coming."

"I'm so very pleased to meet you, my dear. You're as lovely as I thought you'd be. I understand you're a smart lady, too." Then as if he's just recalled why we're here, "I'm sorry for your loss."

A pair of elderly ladies are next. They're twins. Both have the same bob, cut into a bowl shape at the front, hooked noses and dowager's humps that marks their identically crumbling spines.

"Do you have children?" says the first one, which isn't the opener I expected.

The second one tuts and pushes her sister along. They're followed by a couple who call themselves Arthur and Megan. A first I think they're brother and sister as they're so alike, but the way he hovers around her suggests their relationship is more than familial. Her arm's in plaster.

"How did you know Dad?"

"Through my father." The man waves his hand in a vague gesture that he seems to think explains everything.

Young men, a few years younger than I am, come next. They're all in designer suits. Each is striking in his own way. They stand close to me as they introduce themselves. One even kisses my hand. The last one interests me the most. He's not the tallest or best looking but I like his quiet confidence and lively face. There's a yearning in his voice when he says my name that tugs at me. To smile at him seems weak, so I nod.

"My name is Ash."

"Ash." The word coats my tongue with want.

A woman edges him along.

"I'm Rosalie."

She has the manner of entitlement that only certain hard, beautiful women have. Her fingernails are painted black. The lacquer's like glass. She looks me up and down as she passes.

I sip my drink as more people introduce themselves, then go off to decimate the buffet and the wine boxes. I try not to look at Ash's every movement. It's a lovely agony. I close my eyes, the tannin in the red wine shrinking the inside of my mouth.

"How is Julie settling back in here?" It's Charlie.

"Well, she's here for now." I don't like Elsa's tone. She must be drunk too.

I open my eyes. Charlie's suit can't settle on a single shade of black.

"I'm sorry Elsa. You must be missing Michael."

I turn away a fraction, not wanting them to know I'm listening. From the periphery of my vision I see him embrace Elsa.

The young men congregate by the hearth. Rosalie's berating them for something. I catch her final words: "I don't see what's so special about her anyway."

I know she's talking about me because Ash looks over and keeps on looking even though he's caught me eavesdropping. "Don't you?" he replies with a smirk.

"I'm Stephanie." A woman gets in the way, just when I think he's going to walk over and join me. "You're Julie, yes?"

"Hello."

There's a long pause. I sigh inwardly. I'm going to have to try and make conversation with her. She's in her fifties. She's only wearing one earring and most of her hair's escaped from her bun.

"Where are you from?"

"From?" she says.

"Your accent…" Her pronunciation's off kilter, her phrasing odd.

"I've lived in lots of different places." She glances around the room. "I think Elsa would rather I hadn't come."

She reaches out and swipes a sandwich from a plate, gobbling it down in two mouthfuls. "These are delicious."

The volume of the chattering around us bothers me. I've drunk too much on an empty stomach.

"This place hasn't changed since your mother's funeral."

"You met her?"

"Tennis club."

Tennis. How little I knew about her.

"Such a gracious, joyous woman." Stephanie twitters on. "Want and need. How they undo us."

"Pardon?"

Stephanie blinks.

"There are so many crows in Fenby now. They've quite pushed out the cuckoos." She speaks in a comedy whisper, getting louder with each word. "Your mother guessed that they'd double crossed her."

The chatter's dying. Everyone's watching us now.

"You know how it works, don't you? They laid one of their own in your mother's nest…"

Charlie comes over and puts an arm around her.

"Stephanie, what are you taking about? Julie doesn't want to hear this rubbish." He pulls a face at me. "It's time for you to go home."

"You can't push me around. I have a right to be here. We had a deal." She breaks away from him and seizes me in a hug.

"I'm sorry. For all of it," she whispers in my ear. "It's true. Look under the crow palace."

I want to ask her how she knows that's what we call the bird table but Ash comes and takes her arm.

"Aunt Steph, I'll see you home."

"I'm not your aunt."

"No, Ash, you should stay." Elsa joins us.

"It's fine." Ash kisses my cheek. My flesh ignites. "May I come and see you again? Tomorrow?"

"Yes." It's as easy at that.

"Until then." He steers Stephanie towards the door.

The noise starts up again in increments. Ash's departure has soured my mood.

Pippa can't settle. As the mourners gathered around Dad's grave she cringed and started to wail as if finally understanding that he's gone. Now she's wandering about, refusing to go to her room but flinching when any of our guests come near her. She stands, shifting her weight from foot to foot, in front of the twins who are perched in her favourite armchair.

"Oh for God's sake, just sit somewhere will you?" I snap.

Pippa's chin trembles. The room's silent again.

Elsa rushes over to her but Pippa shoves her away. Elsa grabs her wrist.

"Look at me, Pippa. It's just me. Just Elsa." She persists until Pippa stops, shaking. "Better? See? Let's go outside for a little walk."

Pippa's face is screwed up but she lets Elsa take her out onto the patio.

I lock myself in the bathroom and cry, staying there until everyone leaves. I've no idea what I'm crying for.

I wish this humidity would break. It' sticky, despite yesterday's rain. I feel hungover. Lack of sleep doesn't help.

I wave goodbye to Elsa and Pippa as they go out. Elsa's keen to be helpful. *I'll drop Pippa off, I'll be going that way to the shops. Why don't you go and get some fresh air on the lawn? You'll feel better.*

I can't face sorting out the last of Dad's clothes. The thought of the hideous green-gold wallpaper in there makes me want to heave. Instead, I take boxes of papers out to a blanket I've laid out on the lawn. It's prevarication. I'm pretending that I'm doing something useful when I should be sorting out our future.

All the ridiculous talk of swapped babies and symbolic eggs seems stupid now that I'm out in the fresh air.

I imagined it would be cut and dried when Dad died. Sell the house. Find somewhere residential for Pippa or pay Elsa to take care of her. Now I hate myself. I have all along, and have taken it out on Pip. She's the purest soul I know. There's such sweetness in her. How can I leave her to the mercy of others?

How can I love her so much yet can't bear to be near her sometimes? I fought everyone who tried to bully her at school. I became a terror, sniffing out weakness and reducing other children to tears. I started doing it just because I could. They hated me and in return and I felt nothing for them, not anger, not contempt. That's how damaged I am.

I'm afraid that everything people think of me is true, but I'm not afraid enough to change. I *am* selfish. I like my own silence and space. I hated Dad for saying, "You will look after Pippa won't you? The world's a terrible place."

Need. Nothing scares me more.

Then I look at Pippa, who is far more complete a human being than I am. She's no trouble, not really. I could work from here and go to London for meetings. All I need to run my business is a phone. It would only need a bit of will to make it work.

I pull papers from the box. It's an accumulation of crap. Receipts from electrical appliances, their warranties long outdated, bills, invitations and old business diaries.

It's so quiet. I lie back. There's not even the slightest breath of a breeze. I shield my eyes as I look up. The trees are full of corvidae.

Birds don't roost at eleven in the morning, yet the rookeries are full. Sunlight reveals them as oil on water creatures with amethyst green on their foreheads and purple garnets on their cheeks.

Rooks, weather diviners with voices full of grit who sat on Odin's shoulders whispering of mind and memory in his ears.

How Elsa's lessons come back to me.

She taught me long ago to distinguish rooks from crows by their diamond shaped tails and the bushy feathers on their legs. I find these the strangest of all corvidae, with their clumsy waddles and the warty, great patch around the base of their beaks. It's reptilian, Jurassic, even. A reminder that birds are flying dinosaurs, miniaturised and left to feed on insects and carrion.

I turn my head. Crows have gathered too, on the patio furniture, the bird baths, the roof and, of course, the crow palace. The washing line sags under their weight.

I daren't move for fear of scaring them. Perhaps *I'm* scared.

Ash walks through their silence. They're not unsettled by his presence. He's still wearing the same suit. His stride is long and unhurried.

He doesn't pay attention to social niceties. He falls to his knees. I lean up, but I'm not sure if it's in protest or welcome. It's as if he's summed me with a single glance when I'm not sure what I want myself. He presses his mouth against mine.

He pushes my hair out of the way so he can kiss the spot beneath my ear and then my throat. The directness of his desire is exhilarating, unlike Chris' tentative, questioning gestures.

He pulls open my dress. I unbutton his shirt. He pulls down my knickers with an intensity that borders on reverence.

His body on mine feels lighter than I expect, as if he's hollow boned.

When he's about to enter me he says, "Yes?"

I nod.

"Say it. I need to hear you say it. You have to agree."

"Yes, please, yes."

I'll die if he stops now. The friction of our flesh is delicious. It's as necessary as breathing.

When Ash shudders to a climax, he opens his mouth and *Caw,caw,caw* comes out.

I wake, fully dressed, lying on a heaped up blanket beneath the crow palace. There's a dampness between my legs. I feel unsteady when I get up. The shadows have crept around to this side of the house. It must be late afternoon.

When I go in, Elsa's in the kitchen. She's cleaned up after yesterday.

"I'm sorry. I was going to do that…"

"It's okay." She doesn't turn to greet me.

"Where's Pippa?"

"Having a nap. We're all quite done in, aren't we?"

She turns to wipe down the worktops. She looks so at ease, here in Dad's kitchen.

"What happened to my mother?"

I have to take the damp cloth from her hand to make her stop and look at me.

"It's all on record."

"I want to hear what's not on record."

"Then why didn't you ask Michael while he was still alive?"

I've been expecting this but the anger and resentment in Elsa's voice still surprises me. I take a deep breath. Retaliation won't help my cause.

"Because he hated taking about her."

"Then it's not my place to tell you, is it?"

"Of course it's your place. You're the closest thing to a mother that either of us have ever had." I should've said it long ago, without strings. The tendons at Elsa's neck are taut. She's trying not to cry. I didn't just leave Dad and Pip. I left her too.

"You were born in this house. The midwife didn't come in time. Your father smoked cigarettes in the garden. Men didn't get involved in those days. I helped bring you both into the world. I love you both so much. Children fly away, it's expected. I just didn't realise it would take you so long to come back."

"I know you loved Dad too. Did he love you back?"

"He never loved me like he loved your mother." Poor Elsa. Always at hand when he needed her.

"You sacrificed a lot to be with him." Marriage. A family of her own.

"You've no idea." Her voice is thick with anger. "It's utterly changed me."

Then she bows her head. The right thing to do would be to comfort her. To hold her and let her weep on my shoulder. I don't though. It's a crucial moment when Elsa's emotions are wide open.

"The papers said Mum had postnatal depression and psychosis."

An illness that follows childbirth. A depression so deep that it produces bizarre beliefs.

"They were desperate for children. They would've done anything."

"Anything?"

Fertility treatments weren't up to much back then."

"So what happened?"

"Well, you happened. A surprise, they told everyone. I remember holding you in my arms. It was such a precious moment."

"When did she get ill?"

"When it became clear that Pip wasn't doing so well. You were a thriving, healthy baby but Pippa was in and out of hospital because she was struggling to feed. She slept all the time. She never cried. You were smiling, then rolling over, then walking and she was falling further and further behind."

"And Mum couldn't cope?"

"The doctors became worried as she had all these strange ideas. And you were a real handful."

"Me?"

"I'm sorry, maybe I shouldn't say this."

"Tell me."

"You were just a little girl, trying to get their attention. You'd bite Pippa, steal her food. When you we big enough, you'd try and tip her from her high chair."

"And what exactly was it that Mum believed?"

"She insisted she'd been tricked by the birds. They'd helped her to conceive and then they went and swapped one of you for one of their own."

I wake in the hours when the night turns from black to grey to something pale and cold. My mind's full. It's been working while I sleep.

Mum's insistence that she'd been tricked by birds. That they'd helped her to conceive.

They laid one of their own in your mother's nest...

Cuckoo tactics. Mimic the host's eggs and push out one of their own. Equip your chick for warfare. Once hatched, the hooks on its legs will help it to heave its rivals from the nest.

Look under the crow palace.

I pull on jeans and a sweatshirt. Dad kept his tools in his shed. I pull the shovel from the rack, fork and a trowel for more delicate work.

It's chilly. I leave footprints on the damp lawn. It takes a while because I go slowly. First I take up turf around the crow palace. Then I dig around the base. The post goes deep into the rich, dark soil. My arms ache.

I lean on the post, then pull it back and forth, trying to loosen it. It topples with a crash. I expect the neighbours to come running out but nobody does.

I have to be more careful with the next part of my excavation. I use the trowel, working slowly until I feel it scrape something. Then I use my hands.

I uncover a hard, white dome. Soil's stuck in the zigzag sutures and packed into the fontanelle. The skull eyes me with black orbits full of dirt that crawl with worms.

I clean off the skeleton, bit by bit. Its arms are folded over the delicate ribcage. Such tiny hands and feet. It's small. She's smaller than a newborn, pushed out into the cold far too early.

Mum and Stephanie were right. Here is my real sister, not the creature called Pippa.

Oh my God, you poor baby girl. What did they do to you?

"Are you okay?" Elsa ushers me into the kitchen. It's eight in the morning. She has her own key.

I can't bring myself to ask whether Pippa, my crow sister, is awake. How was the exchange made? Was it monstrous Pippa that heaved my real sister from my mother's womb? Was she strangled with her own umbilical cord? And who buried my blood sister? Was it Mum and Dad? No wonder they were undone.

"What happened to you?"

Elsa opens a cupboard and pulls out a bag of seed mix, rips it open and tips out a handful. When she eats, some of it spills down her front. She doesn't bother to brush it off. When she offers me some I'm hit by a wave of nausea that sends me across the room on rubbery legs to vomit in the bin.

"You've got yourself in a right old state." Elsa holds back my hair.

I take a deep breath and wipe my nose.

"Elsa, there's a baby buried in the garden."

She goes very still.

"You knew about it, didn't you?" I sit down.

She pulls a chair alongside mine, its legs scraping on the tiles. She grasps my hands.

"I didn't want you to know about it yet. I wish that cuckoo-brained Stephanie hadn't come to the funeral. And Arthur and Megan hadn't interfered with that damn key. You found the eggs, didn't you?"

I think I'm going to faint so I put my head on the table until it passes. Elsa rubs my back and carries on talking. When I sit up, Elsa's smiling, her head tilted at an odd angle. A gesture I don't recognise. "I'm actually relieved. It's easier that you know now you're staying."

"Elsa, I can't stay here."

"It's best for everyone. You've others to consider now."

I press my fists to my closed eyes. I can't consider anything. My mind's full of tiny bones.

"Mum knew that Pippa wasn't hers, didn't she?" I'm thinking of the human-bird-baby in its shell.

"Pippa?" Elsa's eyes are yellow in this light. "No, she knew that it was you that wasn't hers. She had to watch you like a hawk around Pip."

I vomit again. Clumps of semi digested food gets caught in my hair. Elsa dabs at my mouth with a tea towel. Her colours are the jay's—brown, pink and blue. Was it her, stood at Mum's back and pecking at her eye?

Pippa stands in the doorway looking from my face to Elsa's and back again. I've never seen Pip's gaze so direct.

Now I know why my heart's loveless. Pip's not the aberration, I am. I'm the daughter of crows, smuggled into the nest. Pippa is how she is because of my failed murder attempt. I affected her development when I tried to foist her from the womb.

It's all my fault.

Pippa edges around the room, giving the woman who raised her a wide berth. She tucks herself under my arm and puts a hand low down on my abdomen. She peers into my face, concerned, and says, "Birdies".

THE CROW PALACE

Priya Sharma has been publishing short fiction since 2005, but I only began to notice her work in 2010, when a story from *Albedo One* caught my eye and made my Best of the Year recommended list. The next year I reprinted one of her stories in *The Best of the Year Volume Eleven*, and then again in the next two volumes. I also began to acquire new work from her for Tor.com and various anthologies, including the provocative novelette "Fabulous Beasts," which won the British Fantasy Award and made the final ballot of the Shirley Jackson Awards.

"The Crow Palace" by Priya Sharma is from my 2017 anthology, *Black Feathers: Dark Avian Tales*, which was commissioned by the publisher of Pegasus Books.

Some Strange Desire

By Ian McDonald

(From *Omni Science Fiction Three,* 1993)

19th November, 10:30 P.M.

The *hru-tesh* is a beautiful piece of craftsmanship. Mother says he can remember Grandmother taking him, while still very small, to watch Josias Cunningham, Gunsmith by Appointment, of Fleet Street at work on it. In that small shop, in those small hours when the city slept, Josias Cunningham worked away while the spires and domes of Wren's dream of London rose from the ashes of the Great Fire, chasing and filing and boring and inlaying. It was a work of love, I suppose. A masterpiece he could never disclose to another living soul, for it was the work of demons. On the bone-handled stock is a filigreed silver plate on a pivot-pin. Underneath, an inscription: *Diabolus me Fecit.* The Devil Made Me.

He was *ul-goi* of course, Josias Cunningham, Gunsmith by Appointment, of Fleet Street.

After three hundred years, the firing mechanism is still strong and precise. It gives a definite, elegant click as I draw back the bolt and lock it.

Lights are burning in the apartment across the street. The white BMW sits rain-spattered under its private cone of yellow light. Have you ever known anyone who drives a white *BMW* to do anything or anyone of any significance? I cannot say that I have, either. I blow on my fingers. I cannot let them become chilled. I cannot let their grip on *hru-tesh* slacken and weaken. Hurry up and go about your business *goi,* so I can go about mine and get back into the dry and the warm. Cold rain finds me in my bolt-hole on the roof, penetrates my quilted jacket like needles. None so cold as the needle I have waiting for you, *goi*. I touch the thermos flask beside me, for luck, for reassurance, for the blessing of the *hahndahvi*.

Come on, goi, when are you going to finish what you are doing and go out to collect the day's takings from your boys? Voices are raised in the lighted apartment across the yellow-lit cobbled street. Male voices I cannot make out the words, only the voices.

Even on my rooftop across the street, the blow is almost palpable, and then the weeping. A door slams. I uncap the thermos, shake a tiny sliver of ice into the breech of the *hru-tesh*. The street door opens. He is dressed in expensive leather sports gear. In the dark I cannot read the labels. He turns to swear one last time at the youth at the top of the stairs. I let a drop of saliva fall from my tongue onto the needle of ice resting in the chamber. Slide the breech shut. Move from my cover. Take aim, double-handed, over the fire-escape rail.

Coptic crosses and peace medallions catch the yellow street light as he bends to unlock the car door. The silver filigree-work of the *hru-tesh* crafted by the three-hundred-year-dead hand of Josias Cunningham, Gunsmith by Appointment, glitters in that same light. I squeeze the trigger.

There is only the faintest *tok*.

He starts, stands up, clasps hand to neck. Puzzlement on his meat-like face. Puzzlement under that so-cool baseball cap at that ideologically correct angle. And it hits him. He keels straight over against the car. His head rests at a quizzical angle on the rain-wet metal. Complete motor paralysis.

I am already halfway down the fire escape. Flat shoes. No heels. I have it all planned. As I had thought, bundling him into the passenger seat is the hardest part of the operation. I think I may have broken a finger wresting the keys from him. It will be academic, soon enough. As I drive up through Bethnal Green and Hackney to Epping Forest I pass at least twenty other white BMWs. I sample his *CD* selection, then scan across the *am* wavebands until I find some anonymous Benelux station playing hits from the forties. Childhood tunes stay with you all your life. I chat to him as we drive along. It is a rather one-sided conversation. But I do not think he would have been much of a conversationalist anyway. It is really coming down, the wipers are on high speed by the time we arrive at the car park. I shall get very wet. Another crime against you, *goi*.

It is wonderful how much can be expressed by eyes alone. Anger, incomprehension, helplessness. And, as I pull the syringe out of my belt-pouch, *terror*. I tap the cylinder a couple of times. I can tell from his eyes he has never seen so much in one needle before. He may consider himself honoured. We have our own discreet sources, but we, like you, pay a price. I squat over him. He will take the image of who I am into the dark with him. Such is my intention.

"Hear these words: you do not touch us, you do not harass us, you do not try to recruit us or bully us into your stable. We are *tesh*, we are older and more powerful than you could possibly imagine. We have been surviving for centuries. Centuries."

He cannot even flinch from the needle.

I find a sheltered spot among the bushes and crushed flat lager cans, away from the steamed-up hatchbacks, and go into *tletchen*. I strip. I dress in the denims and shell-suit top I brought in my backpack. I stuff the rain soaked clothes in around the *hru-tesh*. I go to the cardphone half a mile down the road and call a minicab to pick me up at the pub nearby and take me back to Shantallow Mews. The driver is pleased at the generosity of the tip. It is easy to be generous with the money of people who have no further use for it.

The *hru-tesh* goes back to its place under the hall floor-boards. Rest there for a long time, beautiful device. The unused needles go into the kitchen sink to melt and run and lose themselves in the sewers of London town. The soaked clothes go into the machine, the jacket will need dry cleaning. I make tea for my sister, bring it to him on the Harrods tray with the shelduck on it.

The only light in the room is from the portable television at the foot of the bed. The remote control has slipped from his hand. His fingers rest near the "mute" button. Late-night/early morning horror. Vampires, werewolves, Freddies. A little saliva has leaked from his lips onto the pillow. So peaceful. On the pale blue screen, blood is drunk, limbs dismembered, bodies chainsawn apart. I want that peace to last a little longer before I wake him. By the light of the screen I move around the room setting the watches and wards, the little shrines and votives to the Five Lords of the *tesh* that keep spiritual watch around my sister. Pere Teakbois the Balancer, Tulashwayo Who Discriminates, Filé Legbe Prince of the Changing Ways, Jean Tombibie with his bulging eyes and hands crossed over replete belly, Saint Semillia of the Mercies: the five *hahndahvi*. I trim wicks, tap ash from long curls of burned incense, pour small libations of beer and urine. I may not believe that the *hahndahvi* are the literal embodiments of the character of the Universe, I have lived long enough among the *goi* to know the Universe is characterless, faceless. But I do believe power resides in symbol and ritual.

He is awake. The brightness in his eyes is only the reflection of the television screen. Awake now, he seems a thing of horror himself. Shrunken, shrivelled, transparent skin drawn taut over bird bones, fingers quivering spastically as they grip the edge of the duvet. Trapped in that final *tletchen*, too weak to complete the transformation. His breasts are slack and withered like the dugs of old bitches.

"I've made tea, but it's probably cold now." I pour a cup, milk and sugar it, hold it steady as he lifts it to his lips. The tea is cold, but he seems glad of it.

"You were out." His voice is a grotesque whisper.

"Business." He understands. Our clients, both *ul-goi* and *goi*, are never *business*.

"That pimp?"

"He won't trouble you again. I can promise that."

"This isn't forty years ago. They've got computers, genetic finger printing."

"The people in the car park, if any of them even noticed, will tell them it was a woman got out of the car. The taxi driver will swear he drove a man."

"Still..."

I take his hand in mine; modulate my pheromone patterns to convey calm, assurance, necessity. It was more than just a pimp harassing us to join his stable, more than him breaking into this apartment, terrorizing my sick sister, overturning the furniture, desecrating the shrines of the *hahndahvi*. It was *security, tesh* security, which is *more* powerful and paranoid than any *goi* conception of the word, for it has its roots in ten thousand years of secrecy.

I offer him a Penguin biscuit. He shakes his head. Too weak. Too tired. I pull the stand from its position behind the headboard close *by* the side of the mattress. From the fridge in the kitchen I take the next-to-last bag of blood. As I run a line in, he says,

"There was a call for you. I couldn't get to it. Sorry. It's on the answering machine."

I am back in the kitchen, filling a basin with water. I test the temperature with my elbow.

"Vinyl Lionel?"

I fetch the natural sponge I bought from the almost-all-night chemist around the corner, whip the water to froth with Johnson's baby-bath.

"A new one," my sister Cassiopia says.

I pull back the duvet. The smell of the sickroom, the terrible smell of prolonged, ingrained sickness, is overpowering. As the blood, my blood that I pumped out of myself into plastic bags yesterday, runs into him, drip by drip, I wash my sister's body. Gently. Lovingly. With the soft natural sponge and the gentle baby-bath; neck and arms and sagging, flat breasts, the small triangle of pubic hair and the tiny, wrinkled penis and testicles, smaller even than a child's, and the shrivelled labia.

15–16 November

Only four days. It seems like a small forever, since the afternoon Cassiopia came back from the pitch at Somerville Road with twenty pounds in his pocket.

"He insisted on paying. One of the lace-G-string-and-stocking brigade. Took me back to his place. Why do they always have posters of racing cyclists on their walls?"

Though we do not do it for money—genetic material is the price we ask for our services—cash in hand is never refused. I had taken the twenty down to the off-license for a bottle of Californian Chardonnay and a sweet-and-sour pork while Cassiopia changed for the evening client, an *ul-goi* who liked to tie our wrists to the ceiling hooks while he slipped rubber bands around our breasts, more and more and more of them, tighter and tighter and tighter. Thank God once every six weeks seemed to satisfy him. Vinyl Lionel had Word he was Something in the Foreign Office. Whatever, he had taste in tailoring. We made sure he paid for his game with the rubber bands.

When I returned Cassiopia had *tletched*. He is very beautiful as a woman. When he *tletches*, it is like a flower blossoming. Yet there was a subtle change in the atmosphere, something in his personal aroma that smelled not right.

"It hurts," he said. "Here. Here. Here. And here." He touched breasts, loins, neck and, on the final *here*, pressed fingers into belly in the way that says *deep within, everywhere.*

Of course, you never think it can be you. Your lover. Your partner . Your sibling. I gave him two paracetamol and a cup of corner-store Chardonnay to wash them down with.

He scratched all night. I could not sleep for his scratching, scratching, scratching. In the shower he was covered in yellow crusted spots. The sting of hot water made him wince. Even then I pretended not to know. I convinced myself he had picked up some venereal bug from one of the *goi*. Despite the fact that our immune systems make us almost invulnerable to *goi* infections. Such was my self-deception, I even bought some under-the-counter antibiotics from the Almost-All-Night Pharmacy.

You can imagine the smell of sickness. It is not hard, even for your limited senses. Imagine, then, a whole street, a whole town, terminally sick, dying at once. That is what I smelled when I came home after an afternoon with a first-timer who had passed furtive notes: *what are you into, I'm into, I got a place,* under the partitions of the cubicles in the gents' toilets.

I found him lying on the carpet, hands opening and closing spastically into tight, futile fists. He had failed halfway in *tletchen*, caught between like something half-melted and twisted by flame. I cleaned thin, sour, vomited-up coffee and slimmer's soup from his clothes. Over and over and over and over and over and over, he whispered, *Oh my God oh my God oh my God oh my God.* I got him into bed and a fistful of Valium down him, then sat by his side in the room that was filling with the perfume of poisoned earth, looking at everything and seeing only the shadow my thoughts cast as they circled beneath my skull.

We have a word for it in our language. *Jhash.* There is no direct translation into your languages. But you know it. You know it very well. It haunts your pubs and clubs and Saturday night scores. It is the unspoken sermon behind every mint-scented condom machine on the toilet wall. Like ours, yours is a little word too. When I was small and ran in gray flannel shorts wild and heedless over the bomb-sites of Hackney Marshes, my grandmother, who was keeper of the mysteries, taught me that *jhash* was the price Pere Teakbois the Balancer with his plumb-bob in his hand demanded of the *tesh* in return for their talents. I think that was the point at which my long, slow slide from faith began: Grandmother had been a gifted spinner of tales and his graphic descriptions of the terrible, enduring agony of *jhash* left me nightmarish and seriously doubting the goodness of a god who would deliberately balance the good gifts he had given us with such dreadfulness.

The bomb-sites have given way to the tower-blocks of the post-war dream and those in turn to the dereliction and disillusionment of monetarist dogma and I no longer need faith for now I have biology. It is not the will of Pere Teakbois, Pere Teakbois himself is no more than the product of ten thousand years of institutionalized paranoia: *jhash* is a catastrophic failure of the endocrinal, hormonal, and immune systems brought on by the biological mayhem of *tletchen.*

It can take you down into the dark in a single night. It can endure for weeks. None are immune.

Let me tell you the true test of caring. We may be different species, you and I, but we both understand the cold panic that overcomes us when we first realize that we are going to die. We understand that *there* is an end, an absolute end, when this selfness will stop and never *br* again. And it terrifies us. Horrifies us. Paralyzes us, in the warmth of our beds, in the dark of the night with our loved ones beside us. There is no appeal, no repeal, no exceptions.

You are *goi* and I am *tesh* and both love and life are different things between us but this we both understand, that when we contemplate 1 hr death of the one we love and it strikes that same paralyzing, cold panic into us as if it were we ourselves, that is caring. That is love. Isn't it?

20th NOVEMBER, 9:15 P.M.

Vinyl Lionel's Law: Everyone is either someone's pimp or someone's prostitute.

By that definition, Vinyl Lionel is our pimp, though he would be quite scandalized to think that the word could be applied to himself.

Vinyl Lionel subscribes to the roller-and-tray school of cosmetics and wears a studded leather collar. Studs, in one form or another, characterize Vinyl Lionel's personal style. Studded wristbands, studded peak to his black leather SS cap, studded motorbike boots pulled up over his zip-up *PVC* one-piece with studded thighs and shoulders.

I remember *PVC* from the Swinging Sixties. You sweated like shit in those boots and raincoats. Vinyl Lionel maintains they are trying to remix the Sixties for the Nineties. Vinyl Lionel should know about the Sixties. He has an old-age pensioner's free bus pass, but he won't show it to anyone. If the Nineties are anything like the Sixties, it will be that whatever is happening is always happening somewhere else. My memory of the Swinging Sixties is that they may have been swinging in the next street or the party next door, but never swinging in your street, at your party.

Strangefella's is the kind of place where advertising copywriters and the editors of those instantly disposable street-culture magazines like to convince people they party all night when in fact they are at home, in bed, exhausted by their workloads, every night by ten-thirty. If the Nineties are swinging, it is somewhere else than Strangefella's. Vinyl Lionel has a customary pitch as far as the architecture will permit from the AV show and the white boys with the deeply serious haircuts doing things to record decks. He is always pleased to see me. The pleasure is mutual. When he has a couple of gin slings down him he can be a delightfully effervescent conversationalist.

"Darling heart, you're looking especially radiant tonight!" He kisses me, on the cheek, not the mouth-to-mouth soul kiss of *tesh* meeting. He calls for cocktails. "Your mother is well, dismal suburbia notwithstanding?"

I reply that business is booming, and tell him about the pimp.

"I heard about that on *News at Ten*. That was you? A gangland killing, they said, made to look like an overdose." He takes a Turkish from his silver cigarette case, taps it once, twice, three times. "That was bit of a bloody risk, wasn't it, dear heart?"

"He'd broken in. Credit him with some intelligence, he could have worked out something was going on."

"Still, Orion darling, you could have left him to us. It's our *job to* look after you, and yours to provide us with what we want. Yon people have a vicious streak a mile wide. One of your less endearing traits. Smoke?" I take the proffered cheroot.

"So, this new client."

Vinyl Lionel examines his chrome-polished nails. "Well, there's not a lot to say about him. Nice enough boy. You wouldn't think to look at him, but then you never do, do you? Fat Willy recruited him, you know, the usual way." He moistens a finger in his Singapore sling, draws a yin-yang symbol on the marble table top.

"How much does he know?"

"The bare minimum. He'll talk the leg off you, dear heart. One of those confessional types. Well, fiddle-dee-dee, if that isn't him now..." Vinyl Lionel waves flamboyantly, trying to attract the attention of the lost boy by the door, fidgeting and conspicuous in a chain-store gent's ready-made suit. "Oh God, I told him don't dress up, Strangefella's isn't that kind of place, and what does he do? Well, don't blame me if the gorillas bounce him."

"Nerves, Lionel," I say. "You were as bad the first time."

"Bitch," says Vinyl Lionel. He resents any overt reminder of his fall from youth and beauty while we remain changeless, ageless, ever-young. He beckons the young man between the tables and the smokes in the back-beat and the bass. "I'll bet you fifty he drives a Ford." One bet I won't be taking, Lionel. A Ford Sierra, metallic gray, F-registration, the odd rust spot. Something to do with metallic finishes, I always think. Garfield crucified upside-down on the back window. Open the glove compartment and cassettes fall out. Home bootlegs, all of them, apart from the mandatory copy of *Graceland*. Nothing more recent than three years ago.

He is nervous. I can smell it over his Heathrow Duty-Free aftershave. Nerves, and something I cannot quite place, but seems familiar. I do not much like being driven by someone who is so nervous. Gaily lit buses swing past headed down across the river South London way; girls in smog masks, denim cut-offs over cycling shorts and ski-goggles weave past on clunking MTBs like the outriders of some totalitarian, body-fascist invasion. I light up a cheroot Vinyl Lionel gave me as a keepsake as we surge and stop, surge and stop along Shaftesbury Avenue. Lionel, the outrageous old *ul-goi*, was right. This one seems to want to talk but is afraid of me. I weave pheromones, draw him into a chemical web of confidence. On New Oxford Street, he opens.

"I cannot believe this happening," he says. "It's incredible; that something so, so, *huge*, could have been secret for so long."

"It has several thousand years of pedigree as a working relationship," I say. "As long there have been *tesh*, there have been *ul-goi*. And our mutual need for secrecy from the *goi*."

"Goi?"

"Humans." I wave a lace-gloved hand at the rain-wet people huddling along Holborn. "Those. The ignorant mass."

"And *tesh?*"

I draw a circle on the misted-up quarter-light, bisect it with a curving s-shape. Yin and yang. Male and female in one. From time before time the symbol of the *tesh*.

"And *ul-goi?*"

"Those who can only achieve sexual satisfaction with a *tesh*."

The word seems to release him. He closes his eyes for a reckless moment, sighs. "It's funny. No, it's not funny, it's tragic, it's frightening. It's only recently I've found where it started. When I was a kid I read this comic, the *Eagle* or the *Lion* or the *Victor*. There was one story, one scene, where this diver is trying to find out who's been sabotaging North Sea drilling rigs and the bad guys catch him and tie him to the leg of the rig until his air runs out. That was where it started for me, with the guy in the rubber suit tied and helpless, with death inevitable. It was such an anti-climax when he got rescued in the next issue. I used to fantasize about wetsuits. I must have been Jacques Cousteau's number one fan." He laughs. Beneath folding umbrellas, girls in Sixties-revival PVC raincoats and Gerry-Anderson-puppet hair-dos dart between the slowly grinding cars, giggling and swearing at the drivers.

"You don't know what it is at that age. But it was a major motive turn in my childhood: tight clothing. Superheroes, of course, were a real turn-on. I remember one, where the Mighty Thor was being turned into a tree. Jesus! I nearly creamed myself. I was addicted to downhill skiing. If there was ever anything in the Sunday color supplements about downhill skiing, or ballet, I would cut it out, sneak it up to my room and stare at it under the sheets by the light from my electric blanket switch.

"Jane Fonda was, like, the answer to my prayers. I used to borrow my sister's leotard and tights and dress up, just to feel that head to toeness. Sometimes...sometimes, when the evenings were dark, I'd pass on late-night shopping with the family so I could dress up, nip over the back fence onto our local sports field and walk about. Just walk about. It was good, but it wasn't enough. There was something in there, in my head, that wanted something more but couldn't tell me what it was.

"When I was about seventeen I discovered sex shops. The number of times I would just walk past because I never had the nerve to push that door and go in. Then one day I decided it couldn't be any harder going in than just walking past. It was like Wonderland. I spent the fifty pounds I'd been saving in one pig-out. There was one magazine, *Mr. S.M....* I'd never seen anything like it before, I didn't know people could do that sort of thing to each other. Then, after I'd read them all twenty, fifty, a hundred times, I realized it wasn't doing it anymore. I bought new mags, but they were the same: there were things going on in my head that were far, far more exciting than what was going on in those photographs. In my best fantasies, there were things like no one had ever thought of before."

"This happens," I say. They all think they are the only ones. They start so differently, men and women, back among the sand castles and Dinky toys and Cindy dolls of childhood; they think there cannot be anyone else like them. But already they are being drawn toward us, and each other. They realize that what excites frenzies of passion in others leaves them cold and uncomprehending, and everything falls apart: friends, lovers, jobs, careers, hopes, dreams, everything except the search for that something that will fulfill the fantasy in their heads. Can anyone be as tormented, as depraved, as they? I do not disillusion them: fantasies and confessions, and the small absolutions and justifications I can offer; these are treasures held close to the heart. Tell me your story, then, *ul-goi* boy in your best suit, and I will listen, for, though it is a story I have heard ten thousand times before, it is a story that deserves to be heard. You have had the courage that so many lack, the courage to reach for what you truly want.

For the *ul-goi*, it is the frustration of desiring to be what they *are* and what they *are not* simultaneously.

Where have all the fluorescent re-spray Volkswagen Beetles started to come from?

What is he saying now? About some 0898 Sexline he used to dial "Cycle Club Lust"; how he sat hanging on the line running up obscene bills waiting for the payoff that never came. How Telecom regulations compel them to use words like "penis" and "buttocks" and "breasts." How can you get off on words like that? he says.

And I sense it again. A scent... Almost totally masked by my own pheromone patterns; that certain uncertainty. I know it. I know it...lower cranes decked out with aircraft warning lights like Christmas decorations move through the upper air. Towers of London. Close to home now. I show him a place to park the car where it will be fairly safe. In this area, you do not buy car stereos, you merely rent them from the local pub. On the street, with his coat collar turned up against the drizzle, he looks desperately vulnerable and uncertain. The merest waft of pheromones is enough to firm that wavering resolution. Gentle musks carry him through the front door, past the rooms when we cater for the particular tastes of our *goi* clients, up the stairs and along the landing past Cassiopia's room, up another flight of stairs to the room at the top. The room where the *ul-goi* go.

18 NOVEMBER

On the third day of the *jhash*, I went to see Mother, a forty-five-minute train journey past red-brick palazzo-style hypermarkets under Heathrow's sound-footprint.

When the great wave of early-Fifties slum clearance swept the old East End out into the satellite New Towns, it swept Mother and his little empire with it. Three years after the bombing stopped, the Blitz really began, he says. After three hundred years of metropolis, he felt a change of environment would do him good. He is quite the born-again suburbanite; he cannot imagine why we choose to remain in the city. With his two sisters, our aunts, he runs a discreet and lucrative brothel from a detached house on a large estate. The desires of suburbia differ from, but are no less desires than, the desires of the city, and are equally exploitable.

As Mother opened the door to me an elderly man in a saggy black latex suit wandered down from upstairs, saw me, apologized and vanished into the back bedroom.

"It's all right dear, he's part of the family," Mother shouted up "Really, you know, I should stop charging him. He's been coming twenty years, boy and man. Every Tuesday, same thing. Happily married; he's invited us to his silver wedding anniversary party; it's a nice thought but I don't think it's really us, do you?"

To the eye they were three fortysomething slightly-but-not too tarty women, the kind you see pushing shopping trolleys around palazzo-style hypermarkets, or in hatchbacks arriving at yoga classes in the local leisure centre rather than the kind that congregate at the farthest table in bars to drink vodka and laugh boorishly.

My mother was born the same year that Charles II was restored to the monarchy.

We kissed on the mouth, exchanging chemical identifications, tongue to tongue. I made no attempt to mask my feelings; anxiety has a flavour that cannot be concealed.

"Love, what is it? Is it that pimp again? Is he giving bother?" He sniffed deeply. "No. It's Cassiopia, isn't it? Something's happened to him. The Law? Darling, we've High Court judges in our pockets. No, something else. Worse. Oh no. Oh dear God no."

Chemical communication is surer and less ambiguous than verbal. Within minutes my aunts, smelling the alarm on the air, had cut short their appointments with their clients and congregated in the back room where no non-*tesh* was ever permitted. In the deep wing-chair drawn close to the gas heater sat my grandmother, seven hundred years old and almost totally submerged into the dark, mind wandering interminably and with death the only hope of release from the labyrinth of his vast rememberings. His fingers moved in his lap like the legs of stricken spiders. We spoke in our own language, sharp-edged whispers beneath the eyes of the *hahndahvi* in their five Cardinal Points up on the picture rail.

Jhash. It was made to be whispered, that word. I suggested medical assistance. There were prominent doctors among the *ul-goi*. Sexual inclinations do not discriminate. What with the advances *goi* medicine had made, and the finest doctors in the country, surely something...

"It must be concern for your sister has temporarily clouded your judgment," whispered Aunt Lyra, "otherwise I cannot imagine you could be so stupid as to consider delivering one of us into the hands of *ul-goi*."

My mother hushed him with a touch to his arm.

"He could have put it a bit more subtly, love, but he's right. It would be no problem to recruit an *ul-goi* doctor, but doctors don't work in isolation. They rely upon a massive edifice of researchers, technicians, laboratories, consultants: how long do you think it would be before some *goi* discovered the truth about Cassiopia?"

"You would let my sister, your daughter die, rather than compromise security?"

"Do not ask me to answer questions like that. Listen up. One of our regulars here is an *ul-goi* lawyer. Just to make conversation I asked him once what our legal position was. This is what he told me: we may think and talk and look like humans, but we are not human. And, as non-humans, we are therefore the same as animals—less than animals; most animals enjoy some protection under the law, but not us. They could do what they liked to us, they could strip us of all our possessions, jail us indefinitely, use us to experiment on, gas us, hunt us down one by one for sport, burn us in the street, and in the eyes of the law it would be no different from killing rats. We are not human; we are not under the protection of the law. To compromise our secrecy is to threaten us all."

"He is dying and I want to know what to do."

"You know what to do." The voice startled me. It was like the voice of an old, corroded mechanism returning to life after long inactivity. "You know what to do," repeated my grandmother, stepping through a moment of lucidity into this last decade of the millennium. "Can I have taught you so badly, or is it you were such poor pupils? Pere Teakbois the Balancer demanded *jhash* of us in return for our enormously long lives, but Saint Semillia of the Mercies bargained a ransom price. Blood. The life is in the blood; that life may buy back a life."

Of course I knew the story. I even understood the biological principle behind the spurious theology. A massive blood transfusion might stimulate the disrupted immune system into regenerating itself, in a similar sense to the way our bodies rebuild themselves by using *goi* sex cells as a template. I had known the answer to *jhash* for as long as I had known of *jhash* itself: why had I refused to accept it and looked instead for, yes, ludicrous, yes, dangerous alternatives that could not possibly work?

Because Saint Semillia of the Mercies sells his dispensations dear.

Mother had given me a shoeboxful of equipment, most of it obsolete stuff from the last century when the last case of *jhash* had occurred. She did not tell me the outcome. Either way, I was not certain I wanted to know. In the house on Shantallow Mews I ran a line into my arm and watched the *Six o'clock News* while I pumped out two plastic bags. Internecine warfare in the Tory party. Some of the faces I knew, intimately. The blood seemed to revive Cassiopia but

I knew it could only be temporary. I could never supply enough: after only two pints I was weak and trembling. All I could do was hold the sickness at bay. I took the icon of Saint Semillia of the Mercies down from the wall, asked it what I should do. His silence told me nothing I did not already know myself. *Out there. They are few, they are not perfect, but they exist, and you must find them.* I *tletched*, dressed in black leotard, black tights, black mini, black heels, wrapped it all under a duster coat and went down to the Cardboard Cities.

What is it your philosophers teach? That we live in the best of all possible worlds? Tell that to the damned souls of the cardboard cities in the tunnels under your railway stations and underpasses. *Tesh* have no such illusions. It has never been a tenet of our faith that the world should be a good place. Merely survivable.

Cloaked in a nimbus of hormonal *awe,* I went down. You would smell the piss and the beer and the smoke and the dampness and something faint and semi-perceived you cannot quite recognize. To me that thing you cannot recognize is what is communicated most strongly to me. It is despair. Derelicts, burned out like the hulls of Falklands' warships, waved hallucinatory greetings to me as I swirled past, coat billowing in the warm wet wind that blew across the wastelands. Eyes moved in cardboard shelters, cardboard coffins, heads turned, angered by the violation of their degradation by one who manifestly did not share it. When it is all you possess, you treasure even degradation. Figures gathered around smudge fires, red-eyed from the smoke, handing round hand-rolled cigarettes. Where someone had scraped enough money for batteries there was dance music from boom boxes. They would not trouble me. My pheromones made me a shadowy, godlike figure moving on the edge of the darkness.

Where should I go? I had asked.

Where no one will be missed, my mother had replied.

I went to the viaduct arches, the motorway flyovers, the shop doorways, the all-nite burger-shops, the parking lots and playgrounds. I went down into the tunnels under the stations.

Trains ground overhead, carrying the double-breasted suit men and telephone women back to suburbs ending in "ng" or "wich," to executive ghettos with names like Elmwood Grove and Manor Grange. The tunnels boomed and rang, drops of condensation fell sparkling in the electric light from stalactites seeping from the expansion joints in the roof. I paused at the junction of two tunnels. Something in the air, a few vagrant lipid molecules carried in the air currents beneath the station.

How will I know them? I had asked.

You will know them, my mother had said.

The trail of pheromones was fickle, more absent than present. It required the utmost exercise of my senses to follow it. It led me down clattering concrete stairways and ramps, under strip lights and dead incandescent bulbs, down, underground. As I was drawn deeper, I dissolved my aura of *awe* and wove a new spell: *allure*. Certain now. Certain. The lost children in their cribs barely acknowledged my presence, the air smelled of shit and *ganja*.

She had found a sheltered corner under a vent that carried warmth and the smell of frying food from some far distant point of the concourse. An outsize Aran sweater—much grimed and stretched—was pulled down over her hunched-up knees. She had swaddled herself in plastic refuse sacks, pulled flattened cardboard boxes that had held washing machines and CD midi-systems in around her.

I enveloped her in a shroud of pheromones. I tried to imagine what she might see, the tall woman in the long coat, more vision than reality, demon, angel, standing over her like judgment. How could she know it was my pheromones, and not her own free will, that made her suddenly want more than anything, anything she had ever wanted in her life, to bury her face between my nylon-smooth thighs? I knelt down, took her chin in my hand. She looked into my eyes, tried to lick my fingers. Her face was filthy. I bent toward her and she opened her mouth to me. She ran her tongue around the inside of my lips; whimpering, she tried to ram it down my throat.

And I was certain. Truth is in the molecules. I had tasted it.

I extended a hand and she took it with luminous glee. She would have done anything, anything for me, anything, if I would only take her away from these tunnels and the stink of piss and desperation, back to my apartment: I could do whatever I wanted, anything.

The corridors shook to the iron tread of a train.

She loved me. Loved me.

With a cry, I snatched my hand from the touch of her fingers, turned, walked away, coat flapping behind me, heels ringing like shots. Faster. Faster. I broke into a run. Her calls pursued me through the tunnels, *come back come back, I love you, why did you go, I love you.*

I rode the underground into the take-away-curry-and-tins-of-lager hours. *We are not human*, my mother told me from every poster and advertisement, *we cannot afford the luxuries of human morality.* Saint Semillia of the Mercies smiled upon me. I rode the trains until the lights went out, one by one, in the stations behind me, and came home at last to Shantallow Mews.

The house looked and smelled normal. There was nothing to see. From the outside. He had broken in through a rear window and trashed a path through the rooms where we entertained the *goi.* Finding the locked door, he had kicked his way into Cassiopia's room.

The pimp had done a thorough and professional job of terror. Empty glasses and cups of cold tea shattered, a half-completed jigsaw of the Royal Family a thousand die-cut pieces scattered across the floor, magazines torn in two, the radio-cassette smashed in by a heel. Shredded cassette tape hung in swaths from the lights and stirred in the draft from the open door where I stood. The metal stand by the bedside was overturned; the blood, my blood, was splashed and daubed across the walls.

Cassiopia was in the corner by the window, shivering and dangerously pale from shock. Under the duvet he clutched the icons of the five *hahndahvi* and a kitchen knife. Bruises purpled down the side of his face, he flinched from my gentlest touch.

"He said he'd be back," my sister whispered. "He said unless we worked for him, he'd be back again. And again. And again. Until we got wise."

I made him comfortable on the sofa, cleaned the blood from the walls, made good the damage. Then I went to the never-quite-forgotten place under the floorboards and unearthed the *hru-tesh.*

Saint Semillia, the price of your mercies!

20th November, 10:30 p.m.

But for the insistence of my perfumes urging him through the door at the top of the stairs, I think he would run in terror from what he is about to do. Often they do. But they are always drawn back to this door, by the sign of the yin-yang drawn in spilled vodka on a table top, by addresses on matchbooks or slipped under toilet partitions. They come back because nothing else can satisfy them.

The *hahndahvi* placed at their five cardinal points about the room fascinate him. He turns the icon of Filé Legbe over and over in his hands.

"This is old," he says.

"Early medieval," I say, offering him a drink from the cocktail bar. He takes a tequila in one nervous swallow. "The *hahndahvi*. The Five Lords of the *tesh*. We have our own private religion, a kind of urban witchcraft, you could call it. Our own gods and demons and magics. They've taken a bit of theological bashing with the advent of molecular biology, when we realized we weren't the demonic lovers, the incubi and succubi of medieval legend. Just a variant of humanity. A sub-species. Two chromosomes separate me from you." As I am talking he is undressing. He looks for a wardrobe where he can hang his smart suit and shirt and jazz-coloured silk tie. I slide open one of the mirror-robes at the end of the room. His fastidiousness is cute. I pour him another tequila so that he will not be self-conscious in his nakedness and guide him to the Lloyd-loom chair at the opposite end side of the room. As I seat him I smell it again, that uncertain something, masked and musked in a cocktail of his own sweat, aftershave and José Cuervo. Familiar.

He sips his drink; small, tight fearful sips, as I strip down to my underwear. I slowly peel off panties, stockings, suspenders, kick them away. His penis comes up hard, sudden, taking him by surprise. The glass falls to the floor. The tequila spreads across the carpet. He begins to masturbate slowly, ecstatically. Standing naked before him, I slip into *tletchen*. I feel familiar warmth behind my eyes as waves of endocrines and hormones surge through my body. I will them into every part of me, every empty space, every cell, every molecule of me. I am on fire; burning up from inside with chemical fire.

"Do you know about mitosis and meiosis?" I ask him as the hormones burn through me, changing me. *Moses supposes mitosis are roses, Moses supposes erroneously.* "The old legend was that incubi and succubi visited humans to steal sexual fluids. Sperm, eggs. It's true, insofar as we need haploid cells to self-impregnate every cell of our bodies and, in a sense, continually give birth to ourselves. That's how we live five, six, seven hundred years; world events permitting. Though, of course, our reproductive rate is very low." I have found over the years that many of them find the talking as exciting as the physical act. It is the thrill of abandoning themselves to the implacably alien. As I speak my breasts, so full and beautiful, dwindle and contract to flat nipples; the pads of flesh on my hips and ass are redistributed to my shoulders and belly; muscles contract my pelvis, my entire body profile changes from wide-hipped narrow-shouldered hourglass feminity to broad-shouldered, flat-chested narrow-waisted triangular masculinity. My genitals swell and contract and jut and fold themselves into new configurations. It excited me enormously, that first time when Mother guided me into *tletchen*, the ebb and swell of my genitals. Now what I sense is an incompleteness, a loss, when I change from female to male. But I can see what a shock of excitement it is to my client. I come to him, let him savour my new masculinity. He runs his fingers over my flat chest, twists my flat nipples between thumb and finger, caresses my buttocks, thighs, genitals. As he thrills to me, I continue, my voice an octave lower.

"We're essentially an urban phenomenon. We were there in the cities of the Nile and Indus, of Mesopotamia, of Classical Greece and Rome—some lesser members of their respective pantheons are *tesh* in disguise. We need a large population to draw genetic material from without becoming too obvious—in rural communities we have rather too high a profile for our liking. Hence the medieval legends, when the country was almost entirely rural, which died out with urbanization when we could become anonymous in the cities. My particular family came with the Norman invasion;

but we're comparative new kids on the block; the branch we bred into one hundred and fifty years back up in Edinburgh has been here since the end of the Ice Age."

There are tears in his eyes. Pressed close within his embrace, I smell it again. Intimate. Familiar. Too familiar.

I know what it is, and where I have smelled it before. But I am not finished with him yet. I step backward, out of the reach of his imploring fingers and summon up the *tletchen* energy again. Contours, profiles, genders melt and run in the heat of my hormonal fire. My body, my identity, my *teshness*, my Orion-ness dissolve into a multiplicity of possible genders. I blossom out of genderlessness into full hermaphroditism. Male and female, yin and yang in one. He is sobbing now, milking his penis in long, slow, joyous strokes. He is close now to complete sexual satisfaction for the first time in his life. I let him touch me, explore the mystery of my two-in-oneness. He stands, presses his body to mine, shuddering, moaning; long keening, dying moans. Exposed. Truly naked. From every pore of his body, every gland and mucous membrane and erogenous tissue, it pours out. The room whirls with his giddy perfume, the storm of chemicals is overpowering. *Yes! Yes! Yes!*

I look into his eyes.

"Do you know how we get our names?" I tell him. "We have public, *goi*, names, but among ourselves we use our *tesh* names. We are named after whatever constellation is in the ascendant on the night of our birth. My name is Orion. My sister is Cassiopia." I tell him, because I want him to know. I owe him at least a name. I open my mouth to kiss him, he opens to receive me. Thin ropes of drool stretch and break. I taste him. And he is right. It is the work of a moment for my saliva glands to work the chemical changes. A drop of toxin falls from my tongue onto his. It runs like chain lightning from neuron to neuron. Even as the thought to react, the awareness that he may have been betrayed, is upon him, it locks him into rigidity.

He is easy to lift. In hermaphrodite gender we have the benefit of the musculature of both sexes, and the hormonal violence of *tletchen* gives us a supernatural strength. I carry him down the stairs and along the little landing into Cassiopia's room. I can feel his heart beating against my shoulder. He fits comfortably into the bedside chair.

Cassiopia is suspended in a fever dream between sleep and waking; muttering, crying out, twitching, eyeballs rolled up in his head, crazy with hallucinations. I fetch the equipment from the Reebok box under the bed, run a line into Cassiopia's right arm, and let the blue, burned poison drip from his arm into a basin on the floor.

Only his eyes can move. He sees the needle I have for him. Have I said elsewhere it is remarkable how much can be expressed by the eyes alone? Say a thing once, and you are sure to have to say it again, soon he does not flinch as I run a line into his right arm and connect him to Cassiopia. As I pump his blood along the old rubber tubes, I tell him the tale my grandmother told me, of Pere Teakbois' bargain and the price of St. Semillia's mercy. At the very end, he deserves to know. And at the very end, I think he does begin to understand. Vinyl Lionel's Law. Everyone is someone's pimp, someone's prostitute. Everyone is user or used. Down in the tunnels, she had loved me. You had desired me. She had not loved me of her own free will. You did. I made her love me. I did not make you desire me. Understand, *goi* why I could kill the pimp without a moment's moral uncertainty, why now it is your blood pulsing down the rubber tube. We were both used. she and I. You and he, the users. Believe me, *goi* boy, I bear you no malice, I do what I do because an older, harder mercy demands it.

When the last drop is gone, I close the tubes. Cassiopia has lapsed into a quiet and tranquil sleep. Already the *jhash* pallor is gone from his skin, he is warm to my kiss.

I look at the boy, the rigor of my neurotoxins glazed over now with the serenity of death. When you went to those clubs and bars and made those contacts, did they never tell you the unwritten law of the user?

Every prostitute has his price.

In *tesh*, the words for *love* and *passion* are antonyms. It is not so different, I think, with you.

SOME STRANGE DESIRE

I edited my very first anthologies at *Omni*. They were reprints of stories I'd picked from the magazine and Zebra, a mass market house, published several volumes. Later, when GMI (OMNI's parent company) bought *Compute!* and changed its name to *COMPUTE* a decision was made to use their facilities to publishing some *Omni* titles in trade paperback. A few of the books were all reprints. A few were all or mostly originals, the originals mostly chosen from my overbought inventory (with the permission of the writers). "Some Strange Desire" by Ian McDonald was originally published in *Omni Science Fiction 3*, in 1993.

The Lepidopterist

by Lucius Shepard

(From *Salon Fantastique,* 2006)

I **found** this in a box of microcassettes recorded almost thirty years ago; on it I had written, "J. A. McCrae—the bar at Sandy Bay, Roatan." All I recall of the night was the wind off the water tearing the thatch, the generator thudding, people walking the moonless beach, their flashlights sawing the dark, and a wicked-looking barman with stilletto sideburns. McCrae himself was short, in his sixties, as wizened and brown as an apricot seed, and he was very drunk, his voice veering between a feeble whisper and a dramatic growl:

I'm **goin to** tell you bout a storm, cause it please me to do so. You cotch me in the tellin mood, and when John Anderson McCrae get in the tellin mood, ain't nobody on this little island better suited for the job. I been foolin with storms one way or the other since time first came to town, and this storm I goin to speak of, it ain't the biggest, it don't have the stiffest winds, but it bring a strange cargo to our shores.

Fetch me another Salvavida, Clifton…if the gentleman's willing. Thank you, sir. Thank you.

Now Mitch and Fifi were the worst of the hurricanes round these parts. And the worst of them come after the wind and rain. Ain't that right, Clifton? Ain't that always the case? Worst t'ing bout any storm is what come along afterwards. Mitch flattened this poor island. Must have kill four, five hundred people, and the most of them die in the weeks followin. Coxen Hole come t'rough all right, but there weren't scarcely a tree standing on this side.

And Fifi…after Fifi there's people livin in nests, a few boards piled around them to keep out the crabs and a scrap of tin over they head. Millions of dollars in relief is just settin over in Teguz. There's warehouses full, but don't none of it get to the island. Word have it this fella work for Wal-Mart bought it off the military for ten cent on the dollar. I don't know what for sure he do with it, but I spect there be some Yankees payin for the same blankets and T-shirts and bottled water that they government givin away for free. I ain't blamin nothin on America, now. God Bless America! That's what I say. God Bless America! They gots the good intention to be sending aid in the first place. But the way t'ings look to some, these storms ain't nothin but an excuse to slip the generals a nice paycheck.

The mon don't want to hear bout your business, Clifton! Slide me down that bottle. I needs somet'ing to wash down with this beer. That's right, he payin! Don't you t'ink he can afford it? Well, then, Slide me that bottle.

Many of these Yankees that go rushing in on the heels of disaster, these so-called do-gooders, they all tryin to find something cheap enough they can steal it. Land, mostly. But rarely do it bode well for them. You take this mon bought up twenty thousand acres of jungle down around Trujillo right after Mitch. He cotching animals on it. Iguana, parrots, jaguar. Snakes. Whatever he cotch, he export to Europe. My nephew Jacob work for him, and he say the mon doing real good business, but he act like he the king of creation. Yellin and cursin everybody. Jacob tell him, you keep cursin these boys, one night they get to drinkin and come see you with they machete. The mon laugh at that. He ain't worry bout no machetes. He gots a big gun. Huh! We been havin funerals for big Yankee guns in Honduras since before I were born.

This storm I'm talkin about, it were in the back time. 1925, '26. Somewhere long in there. Round the time United Fruit and Standard Fruit fight the Banana War over on the mainland. And it weren't no hurricane, it were a norther. Northers be worse than a hurricane in some ways. They can hang round a week and more, and they always starts with fog. The fog roll in like a ledge of gray smoke and sets til it almost solid. That's how you know a big norther's due. My daddy, he were what we call down here a wrecker. He out in the fury of the storm with he friends, and they be swingin they lanterns on the shore, trying to lure a ship onto the reef so they can grab the cargo. You don't want to be on the water durin a norther ceptin you got somet'ing the size of the Queen Mary under you. Many's the gun runner or tourist boat, or a turtler headin home from the Chinchorro Bank, gets heself lost in bad weather. And when they see the lantern, they makes for it in a hurry. Cause they desperate, you know. They bout to lose their lives. A light is hope to them, and they bear straight in onto the reef.

That night, the night of the storm, were the first time my daddy took me wreckin. I had no wish to be with him, but the mon fierce. He say, John, I needs you tonight and I hops to it or he lay me out cold. Times he drinkin and he feel a rage comin, he say, John, get under the table. I gets under the table quick, cause I know and he spy me when the rage upon him, nothin good can happen. So I stays low and out of he sight. I too little to stand with him. I born in the summer and never get no bigger than what you seein now.

We took our stand round St. Ant'ony's Key. There wasn't no resort back then. No dive shop, no bungalows. Just cashew trees, sea grape, palm. It were a good spot cause the reef close in to shore, and that old motor launch we use for boarding, it ain't goin to get too far in rough water. My daddy, he keep checkin' he pistol. That were how he did when t'ings were pressin him. He check he pistol and yell at ever'body to swing they lanterns. We only have the one pistol mongst the five of us. You might t'ink we needs more to take on an entire crew, but no matter how tough that crew be, they been t'rough hell, and if they any left alive, they ain't got much left in them, they can barely stand. One pistol more than enough to do the job. If it ain't, we gots our machetes.

The night wild, mon. Lord, that night wild. The bushes lashing and the palms tearin and the waves crashin so loud, you t'ink the world must have gone to spinnin faster. And dark… We can't see nothin cept what the lantern shine up. A piece of a wave, a frond slashin at your face. Even t'ough I wearin a poncho, I wet to the bone. I hear my daddy cry, Hold your lantern high, Bynum! Over to the left! He hollerin at Bynum Saint John, who were a fisherman fore he take up wreckin. Bynum the tallest of us. Six foot seven if he an inch. So when he hold he lantern high, it seem to me like a star fell low in the heavens. With the wind howlin and blood to come, I were afraid. I fix on that lantern, cause it the only steady t'ing in all that uncertainty, and it give me some comfort. Then my daddy shout again and I look to where the light shinin and that's when I see there's a yacht stuck on the reef.

Everybody's scramblin for the launch. They eager to get out to the reef fore the yacht start breakin up. But I were stricken. I don't want to see no killin and the yacht have a duppy look, way half its keel is ridin out of the water and its sails furled neat and not a soul on deck. Like it were set down on the rocks and have not come to this fate by ordinary means…

You t'ink you can tell this story better than me, Clifton? Then you can damn well quit interruptin! I don't care you heared Devlin Walker tell a story sound just like it. If Devlin tellin this story, he heared it from me. Devlin's daddy never were a wrecker. And even if dat de case, what a boy born with two left feet goin to do in the middle of a norther? He can't hardly get around and it dry.

Yes, sir! Two left feet. The mon born that way. Now Devlin, I admit, he good with a tale, but that due to the fact that he never done a day's work in he life. All he gots to do is set around collectin other folks' stories.

The Santa Caterina, that were the name on the yacht's bow…it were still sittin pretty by the time we reached it. But big waves is breakin over the stern, and it just a matter of minutes fore they get to chewin it up. I were the first over the rail, t'ough it were not of my doin. I t'ought I would stay with the launch, but my daddy lift me by the waist and I had no choice but to climb aboard. The yacht were tipped to starboard, the deck so wet, I go slidin across and fetch up against the opposite rail. I could feel the keel startin to slip. Then Bynum come over the rail, and Deaver Ebanks follow him. The sight of them steady me and I has a look around…and that's when I spy this white mon standing in the stern. He not swayin or nothin, and it were all I could do to keep my feet. He wearing a suit and tie, and a funny kind of hat with a round top were jammed down so low, all I could see of he face were he smile. That's right. The boat on the rocks and wreckers has boarded her, and he smilin. It were like a razor, that smile, all teeth and no good wishes. Cut the heart right out of me. The roar of the storm dwindle and I hear a ringin in my ears and it like I'm lookin at the world t'rough the wrong end of a telescope.

I'm t'inking he no a natural mon, that he have hexed me, but maybe I just scared, for Bynum run at him, waving he machete. The mon whip a pistol from he waist and shoot him dead. And he do the same for Deaver Ebanks. The shots don't hardly make a sound in all that wind. Now there's a box resting on deck beside the mon. I were lookin at it end-on, and I judged it to be a coffin. It were made of mahogany and carved up right pretty. It resemble the coffin the McNabbs send that Yankee who try to cut in on they business. What were he name, Clifton? I can't recollect. It were an Italian name.

Who the McNabbs? Hear that, Clifton? Who the McNabbs? Wellsir, you stay on the island for any time and you goin to know the McNabbs. The worst of them, White Man McNabb, he in jail up in Alabama, but the ones that remain is bad enough. They own that big resort out toward the east end, Pirate Cove. But most of they money derived from smugglin. Ain't an ounce of heroin or cocaine passes t'rough Roatan don't bear they mark. They don't appreciate people messin in their business, and when that Italian Yankee… Antonelli. That's he name. When this Antonelli move down from New York and gets to messin, they send him that coffin and not long after, he back in New York.

So this box I'm tellin you about, I realize it ain't much bigger than a hatbox when the man pick it up, and it can't weigh much—he totin it with the one hand. He step to the port rail and fire two shots toward the launch. I can't see where they strike. He beckon to me and t'ough I'm still scared I walk to him like he got me on a string. There's only my daddy in the launch.

He gots a hand on the tiller and the other hand in the air, and he gun lyin in the bilge. Ain't no sign of Jerry Worthing—he the other man in our party. I'm guessin he gone under the water. The mon pass me the box and tell me to hold on tight with both hands. He lift me up and lower me into the launch, then scramble down after me. Then he gesture with he pistol and my daddy unhook us from the Santa Caterina and turn the launch toward shore. It look like he can't get over bein surprised at what have happened.

My daddy were a talker. Always gots somet'ing to say about nothin. But he don't say a word til after we home. Even then, he don't say much. We had us a shotgun shack back from the water, with coco palms and bananas all around, and once de mon have settled us in the front room, he ask me if I good with knots. I say, I'm all right. So he tell me to lash my daddy to the chair. I goes to it, with him checkin the ropes now and again, and when I finish he pat me on the head. My daddy starin hateful at me, and I gots to admit I weren't all that unhappy with him being tied up. What you goin to do with us? he ask, and the mon tell him he ain't in no position to be askin nothin, considerin what he done.

The mon proceed to remove he hat and he coat, cause they wet t'rough. Shirt, shoes, and socks, too. He head shaved and he torso white as a fish belly, but he all muscle. Thick arms and chest. He take a chair, restin the pistol on his knee, and ask how old I am. I don't exactly know, I tell him, and my daddy say, He bout ten. Bout ten? the mon say. This boy's no more than eight! He actin' horrified, like he t'ink the worst t'ing a man can not know about heself is how old he is. He tell my daddy to shut up, cause he must not be no kind of father and he don't want to hear another peep out of him. I goes to fiddlin with the mon's hat. It hard, you know. Like it made of horn. The mon tell me it's a pith helmet and he would give it to me, cause I such a brave boy, but he need it to keep he head from burnin.

By the next morning, the storm have passed. Daddy's asleep in the chair when I wakes and the mon sitting at the table, eating salt pork and bananas. He offer me some and I joins him at the table. When Daddy come round, the mon don't offer him none, and that wake me to the fact that t'ings might not go good for us. See, I been t'inkin with a child's mind. The mon peared to have taken a shine to me and that somet'ing my daddy never done. So him takin a shine to me outweigh the killin he done. But the cool style he had of doing it… A mon that good at killin weren't nobody to trust.

After breakfast, he carry my daddy some water, then he gag him. He pick up that box and tell me to come with him, we goin for a walk. We head off into the hills, with him draggin me along. The box, I'm noticing, ain't solid. It gots tiny holes drilled into the wood. Pinholes. Must be a thousand of them. I ask what he keepin inside it, but he don't answer. That were his custom. Times he seem like an ordinary Yankee, but other times it like he in a trance and the most you goin to get out of him is dat dead mon's smile.

Twenty minutes after we set out, we arrives at this glade. A real pretty place, roofed with banana fronds and wild hisbicus everywhere. The mon cast he eye up and around, and make a satisfied noise. Then he kneel down and open the box. Out come fluttering dozens of moths…least I t'ink they moths, Later, when he in a talking mood, he tells me they's butterflies. Gray butterflies. And he a butterfly scientist. What you calls a lepidopterist.

The butterflies, now, they flutterin around he head, like they fraid to leave him. He sit cross-legged on the ground and pull out from he trousers a wood flute and start tootlin on it. That were a curious sight, he shirtless and piping away, wearin that pith helmet, and the butterflies fluttering round in the green shade. It were a curious melody he were playin, too. Thin, twistin in and out, never goin nowhere. The kind of t'ing you liable to hear over in Puerto Morales, where all them Hindus livin.

That's what I sayin. Hindus. The English brung them over last century to work the sugar plantations. They's settled along the Rio Dulce, most of them. But there some in Puerto Morales, too. That's how they always do, the English. When they go from a place, they always leavin t'ings behind they got no more use for. Remember after Fifi, Clifton? They left them bulldozers so we can rebuild the airport? And the Sponnish soldiers drive them into the hills and shoot at them for sport, then leave them to rust. Yeah, mon. Them Sponnish have the right idea. Damn airport, when they finally builds it, been the ruin of this island. The money it bring in don't never sift down to the poor folks, that for sure. We still poor and now we polluted with tourists and gots people like the McNabbs runnin t'ings.

By the time the mon finish playing, the butterflies has vanished into the canopy, and I gots that same feelin I have the night previous on the deck of the Santa Caterina. My ears ringing, everyt'ing have a distant look, and the mon have to steer me some on the walk back. We strop my daddy to the bed in the back room, so he more comfortable, and the mon sit in he chair, and I foolin with a ball I find on the beach. And that's how the days pass. Mornin, noon, and night we walks out to the glade and the mon play some more on he flute. But mainly we just sittin in the front room and doin nothin. I learn he name is Arthur Jessup and that he have carried the butterflies up from

Panama and were on the way to La Ceiba when the storm cotch him. He tell me he have to allow the butterflies to spin their cocoons here on the island, cause he can't reach he place in Ceiba soon enough.

I t'ought it was caterpillars turned into butterflies, I says. Not the other way round.

These be unusual butterflies, he say. I don't know what else they be. Whether they the Devil's work or one of God's miracles, I cannot tell you. But it for certain they unusual butterflies.

My daddy didn't have no friends to speak of, now he men been shot dead, but there's this old woman, Maud Green, that look in on us now and then, cause she t'ink it the Christian t'ing to do. Daddy hate the sight of her, and he always hustle her out quick. But Mister Jessup invite her in and make over her like she a queen. He tell her he a missionary doctor and he after curin Daddy of a contagious disease. Butterfly fever, he call it, and gives me a wink. It a terrible affliction, he say. Your hair fall out, like mine, and it don't never come back. The eye grow dim, and the pain… The pain excrutiatin. Maud Green cock her ear and hear Daddy strainin against the gag in the back room, moanin. He at heaven's gate, Mister Jessup say, but I believe, with the Lord's help, we can pull the mon back. He ask Maud to join him in prayin over Daddy and Maud say, I needs to carry this cashew fruit to my daughter, so I be pushing along, and we don't see no more of her after that. We has a couple of visitors the followin day who heared about the missionary doctor and wants some curin done. Mister Jessup tell them to bide they time. Won't be long, he say, fore my daddy back on he feet, and then he goin to take care of they ills. It occur to me, when these folks visitin, that I might say somet'ing bout my predicament or steal away, but I remembers Mister Jessup's skill with the pistol. It take a dead shot to pick a man off a launch when the sea bouncin her round like it were. And I fears for my daddy, too. He may not be no kind of father, but he all the parent I gots, what with my mama dying directly after I were born.

Must be the ninth, tenth day since Mister Jessup come to the island, and on that mornin, after he play he flute in the glade, he cut a long piece of bamboo and go to pokin the banana fronds overhead. He beat the fronds back and I see four cocoons hangin from the limbs of an aguacaste tree. They big, these cocoons. Each one big as a hammock. And they not white, but gray, with gray threads fraying off dem. Mister Jessup act real excited and, after we returned home, he say, Pears I'll be out of your hair in a day or two, son. I spect you be glad to see my backside goin down the road.

I don't know what to say, so I keeps quiet.

Yes sir, he say. You not goin to believe your eyes and you see what busts out of them cocoons. That subject been pressin on my mind, so I ask him what were goin to happen.

Just you wait, he say. But I tell you this much. The man ain't born can stand against what's in those cocoons. You goin to hear the name Arthur Jessup again, son. Mark my words. A few years from now, you be hearin that name mentioned in the same breath with presidents and kings.

I takes that to mean Mister Jessup believe he goin to have some power in the world. He a smart mon…least he do a fine job pretendin he smart. Still, I ain't too sure I hold with that. Bout half the time he act like somet'ing have power over him. Grinnin like a skull. Sittin and starin for hours, with a blink every now and then to let you know he alive. Pears to me somebody gots they hand on him. A garifuna witch, maybe. Maybe the butterfly duppy.

You want to hear duppy stories, Clifton be your man. When he a boy, he mama cotch sight of the hummingbird duppy hovering in a cashew tree, and ever after there's hummingbirds all around he house. Whether that a curse or a blessing, I leave for Clifton to say, but…

Oh, yeah. Everyt'ing gots a duppy. Sun gots a duppy. The moon, the wind, the coconut, the ant. Even Yankees gots they duppy. They gots a fierce duppy, a real big shot, but since they never lay eyes on it, it difficult for them to understand they ain't always in control.

Where you hail from in America, sir?

Florida? I been to Miami twice, and I here to testify that even Florida gots a duppy.

Evenin of the next day and we proceed to the glade. The cocoons, they busted open. There's gray strings spillin out of dem…remind me of old dried-up fish guts. But there's nothin to show what have come forth. It don't seem to bother Mister Jessup none. He sit down in the weeds and get to playin he flute. He play for a while with no result, but long about twilight, a mon with long black hair slip from the margins of the glade and stand before us. He the palest mon I ever seen, and the prettiest. Prettier than most girls. Not much bigger than a girl, neither. He staring at us with these gray eyes, and he make a whispery sound with he mouth and step toward me, but Mister Jessup hold up a hand to stay him. Then he goes to pipin on the flute again. Time he done, there three more of them standin in the glade. Two womens and one mon. All with black hair and pale skin. The mon look kind of sickly, and he skin gray in patches. They all of them has gray silky stuff clinging to their bodies, which they washes off once we back home. But you could see everyt'ing there were to see, and watchin that silky stuff slide about on the women's skin, it give me a tingle even t'ough I not old enough to be interested. And they faces… You live a thousand years, you never come across no faces like them. Little pointy chins and pouty lips and eyes bout to drink you up. Delicate faces. Wise faces. And yet I has the idea they ain't faces at all, but patterns like you finds on a butterfly's wing.

Mister Jessup herds them toward the shack at a rapid pace, cause he don't want nobody else seein them. They talking this whispery talk to one another, cept for the sickly mon. The others glidin along, they have this snaky style of walkin, but it all he can do to stagger and stumble. When we reach the shack, he slump down against a wall, while the rest go to pokin around the front room, touchin and liftin pots and glasses, knifes and forks, the cow skull that prop open the window. I seen Japanese tourists do less pokin. Mister Jessup install heself in a chair and he watchin over them like a mon prideful of he children.

Few months in La Ceiba, little spit and polish, he say, and they be ready. What you t'ink, boy? Well, I don't know what to t'ink, but I allow they some right pretty girls.

Pretty? he say, and chuckle. Oh, yeah. They pretty and a piece more. They pretty like the Hope Diamond, like the Taj Mahal. They pretty all right.

I ask what he goin to do for the sick one and he say, Nothin I can do cept hope he improve. But I doubt he goin to come t'rough.

He had the right of that. Weren't a half-hour fore the mon slump over dead and straightaway we buries him out in back. There weren't hardly nothin to him. Judgin from the way Mister Jessup toss him about, he can't weigh ten pounds, and when I dig he up a few days later, all I finds is some strands of silk.

We watches the butterfly girls and the mon a bit longer, then Mister Jessup start braggin about what a clever mon he be, but I suspect he anxious about somet'ing. An anxious mon tend to lose control of he mouth, to take comfort from the sound of he voice. He say six months under he lamps, with the nutrients he goin to provide, and won't nobody be able to tell the difference between the butterflies and real folks. He say the world ain't ready for these three. They goin to cut a swath, they are. Can you imagine, he ask, these little ladies walkin in the halls of power on the arm of a senator or the president of a company? Or the mon in a queen's bedchamber? The secrets they'll come to know. They hands on the reigns of power. I can imagine it, boy. I know you can't. You a brave little soldier, but you ain't got the imagination God give a tick.

He run on in that vein, buildin heself a fancy future, sayin he might just take me along and show me how sweet the world be when you occupies a grand position in it. While he talkin, the women and the man keeps circulatin, movin round the shack, whispering and touchin, like they findin our world all strange and new. When they pass behind Mister Jessup, sometimes they touch the back of he neck and he freeze up for a moment and that peculiar smile flicker on; but then he go right on talking as if he don't notice. And I'm t'inkin these ain't no kind of butterflies. Mister Jessup may believe they is, he may think he know all about them. And maybe they like he say, a freak of nature. I ain't disallowin that be true in part. Yet when I recall he playin that flute, playing like them Hindus in Puerto Morales does when they sits on a satin pillow and summons colors from the air, I know, whether he do or not, that he be summonin somet'ing, too. He callin spirits to be born inside them cocoons. Cause, you see, these butterfly people, they ain't no babies been alive a few hours. That not how they act. They ware of too much. They hears a dog barkin in the distance, a coconut thumpin on the sand, and they alert to it. When they put they eye on you... I can't say how I knows this, but there somet'ing old about them, somet'ing older than the years of Mister Jessup and me and my daddy all added up together.

Eventually Mister Jessup reach a point in he fancifyin where he standin atop the world, decidin whether or not to let it spin, and that pear to satisfy him. He lead me back to where my daddy stropped down. Daddy he starin at me like he get loose, the island not goin to be big enough for me to hide in.

Don't you worry, boy, Mister Jessup say. He ain't goin to harm you none.

He slip Daddy's gag and inquire of him if the launch can make it to La Ceiba and the weather calm. Daddy reckon it can. Take most of a day, he figures.

Well, that's how we'll go, say Mister Jessup.

He puts a match to the kerosene lamp by the bed and brings the butterfly people in. Daddy gets to strugglin when he spies them. He callin on Jesus to save him from these devils, but Jesus must be havin the night off.

The light lend the butterfly people some color and that make them look more regular. But maybe I just accustomed to seein them, cause Daddy he thrash about harder and goes to yellin fierce. Then the one woman touch a hand gainst he cheek, and that calm him of an instant. Mister Jessup push me away from the bed, so I can't see much, just the three of them gatherin round my daddy and his legs stiffening and then relaxin as they touch he face.

I goes out in the front room and sits on the stoop, not knowin what else to do. There weren't no spirit in me to run. Where I goin to run to? Stay or go, it the same story. I either winds up beggin in Coxxen Hole or gettin pounded by my daddy. The lights of Wilton James' shack shining t'rough the palms, not a hundred feet away, but Wilton a drunk and he can't cure he own troubles, so what he goin to do for mine? I sits and toes the sand, and the world come to seem an easy place. Waves sloppin on the shingle, and the moon, ridin almost full over a palm crown, look like it taken a faceful of buckshot. The wind carry a fresh smell and stir the sea grape growin beside the stoop.

Soon Mister Jessup call me in and direct me to a chair. Flanked by the butterfly people, my daddy leanin by the bedroom door. He keep passin a hand before his eyes, rubbin he brow. He don't say nothin, and that tell me they done somet'ing to him with they touches, cause a few minutes earlier he been dyin to curse me. Mister Jessup kneel beside the chair and say, We goin off to La Ceiba, boy. I know I say I'm takin you with me, but I can't be doin that. I gots too much to deal with and I havin to worry bout you on top of it. But you showed me somet'ing, you did. Boy young as you, faced with all this, you never shed a tear. Not one. So I'm goin to give you a present.

A present sound like a fine idea, and I don't let on that my daddy have beat the weepin out of me, or that I small for my age. I can't be certain, but I pretty sure I goin on eleven, t'ough I could not have told him the day I were born. But eleven or eight, either way I too young to recognize that any present given with that kind of misunderstandin ain't likely to please.

You a brave boy, say Mister Jessup. That's not always a good t'ing, not in these parts. I fraid you gonna wind up a wrecker like your daddy…or worse. You be gettin yourself killed fore you old enough to realize what livin is worth. So I'm goin to take away some of your courage.

He beckon to one of the women and she come forward with that glidin walk. I shrinks from her, but she smile and that smile smooth out my fear. It have an effect similar to Mister Jessup's pats-on-the-head. She swayin before me. It almost a dance she doin. And she hummin deep in she throat, the sound some of Daddy's girlfriends make after he climb atop them. Then she bendin close, bringin with her a sweet, dry scent, and she touch a finger to my cheek. The touch leave a little electric trail, like my cheek sparklin and sparkin both. Cept for that, I all over numb. She eye draw me in til that gray crystal all I seein. I so far in, pear the eye enormous and I floatin in front of it, bout the size of a mite. And what lookin back at me ain't no buttterfly. The woman she may have a pleasin shape, but behind she eye there's another shape pressin forward, peekin into the world and yearnin to bust out the way the butterfly people busted out of they cocoon. I feels a pulse that ain't the measure of a beatin heart. It registerin an unnatural rhythm. And yet for all that, I drawn in deeper. I wants her to touch me again, I wants to see the true evil shape of her, and I reckon I'm smiling like Mister Jessup, with that same mixture of terror and delight.

When I rouse myself, the shack empty. I runs down to the beach and I spies the launch passin t'rough a break in the reef. Ain't no use yellin after them. They too far off, but I yells anyway, t'hough who I yellin to, my daddy or the butterfly girl, be a matter for conjecture. And then they swallowed up in the night. I stand there a time, hopin they turn back. It thirty miles and more to La Ceiba, and crossin that much water at night in a leaky launch, that a fearsome t'ing. I falls asleep on the sand waitin for them and in the mornin Fredo Jolly wake me when he drive his cows long the shore to they pasture.

My daddy return to the island a couple weeks later, but by then I over in Coxxen Hole, doin odd jobs and beggin, and he don't have the hold on me that once he did. He beat me, but I can tell he heart ain't in it, and he take up wreckin again, but he heart ain't in that, neither. He say he can't find no decent mens to help, but Sandy Bay and Punta Palmetto full of men do that kind of work. Pretty soon, three or four years, it were, I lose track of him, and I never hear of him again, not even on the day he die.

Mister Jessup have predicted I be hearin bout him in a few years, but it weren't a week after they leave, word come that a Yankee name of Jessup been found dead in La Ceiba, the top half of he head chopped off by a machete. There ain't no news of the butterfly people, but the feelin I gots, then and now, they still in the world, and maybe that's one reason the world how it is. Could be they bust out of they shapes and acquire another, one more reflectin of they nature. There no way of knowin. But one t'ing I do know. All my days, I never show a lick of ambition. I never took no risks, always playin it safe. If there a fight in an alley or riot in a bar, I gone, I out the door. The John Anderson McCrae you sees before you is the same I been every day of my life. Doin odd jobs and beggin. And once the years fill me up sufficient, tellin stories for the tourists. So if Mister Jessup make me a present, it were like most Yankee presents and take away more than it give. But that's a story been told a thousand times and it be told a thousand more. You won't cotch me blamin he for my troubles. God Bless America is what I say. Yankees gots they own brand of troubles, and who can say which is the worse.

Yes, sir. I believe I will have another.

Naw, that ain't what makin me sad. God knows, I been livin almost seventy years. That more than a mon can expect. Ain't no good in regrettin or wishin I had a million dollars or that I been to China and Brazil. One way or another, the world whittle a mon down to he proper size. That's what it done for Mister Jessup, that's what it done for me. It just tellin that story set me to rememberin the butterfly girl. How she look in the lantern light, pale and glowin, with hair so black, where it lie across she shoulder, it like an absence in the flesh. How it feel when she touch me and what that say to a mon, even to a boy. It say I knows you, the heart of you, and soon you goin to know bout me. It say I never stray from you, and I going to show you t'ings whose shadows are the glories of this world. Now here it is, all these years later, and I still longin for that touch.

THE LEPIDOPTERIST

Salon Fantastique, edited by me and Terri Windling, and published in 2006, was commissioned by John Oakes, who is a passionate publisher of political books. I was friendly with him for several years, and soon after divesting himself of Four Walls, Eight Windows, the publishing house he and Dan Simon started, and during his brief time as publisher of Thunder Mouth Press he took me to lunch and asked if I'd like to edit an anthology for him. I told him that I'd love to do a non-themed, all original fantasy anthology— but that it had to be with Terri Windling.

Unfortunately, he resigned while the book was in production, so by the time it came out, it was orphaned, one of the worst things that can happen to a book. Sad and frustrating, it usually means there is no one to champion it, help in the marketing/publicity, etc that's crucial to getting a book into the consciousness and hands of readers. Despite this, the book won the World Fantasy Award.

One story was "The Lepidopterist" by Lucius Shepard. I personally feel that Lucius's best work was at novella length, but most of those I published were on SCIFICTION, where I had unlimited space.

He was an underrated writer who had a lot of more great work in him when he died.

Bird Count

By Jane Yolen

(From *Sirens and Other Daemon Lovers,* 1998)

It was his wings I fell in love with first: feathers soft, wimpling; the strong pinions flexing. They weren't white or yellow, but somewhere in between, like piano keys after years in a dark room. I dreamed those wings around me. I dreamed them against my breasts.

I dreamed them between my legs. But I never dreamed they could hurt so, the shafts scraping against my shoulders and back, leaving a deep imprint on my skin, as if I—and not he—had worn the wings.

When I saw him first, he was only a speck against the sky. I was by the fire tower at Mount Tom, one of the early risers for the annual hawk watch. I was there because my lover, Lewis, was an obsessive birder who thought nothing of spending hours in the field making lists that only he would ever care about or actually see.

Trying to hold on to a relationship that had nothing to recommend it but inertia and obsession, I had bought myself a pair of vastly-too-expensive field glasses. I would rise each weekend morning before dawn to accompany Lewis on his passionate activity—he saved his passion for birds alone. I had become a martyr to ornithology, a bird widow, even though I knew little about the birds we watched and cared less. I only wanted to get Lewis's attention. He wasn't much, but he was all I had at the time. And at thirty-two, *time* was the operative word.

My biologic clock wasn't just ticking; it was sounding like a Geiger counter in an old sci-fi movie.

The thing about Lewis was that even when we were together I was alone. Or rather Lewis was alone and I was just some *thing* that happened to be occupying space near him. It wasn't that he didn't notice me; he didn't notice anyone. If he was hungry, he ate whatever food appeared before him. If his laundry needed doing, he knew that the universe would somehow, mysteriously and wonderfully, get it cleaned. Before me there had been Lewis's mother to deal with the mundane world.

I was the intern on call when his mother had coughed gently, said "Take care of my boy," and died. Thinking she was talking about a minor child, I worried as I went out to the waiting room, afraid who I would find there. I was quite unprepared for Lewis, but relieved to find him an adult.

"Mr. Snowden," I said, "I am afraid that your mother has just passed away."

He seemed less shocked then confused, saying simply "She can't have." But his tone was not one of denial; rather he seemed put out with her, as if she had just gone on a trip without telling him.

And then he smiled a dazzling smile at me, and in all seriousness added, "I'll need a white shirt for the funeral and I don't know how to iron."

So when my shift was over, I went home with him, did his shirts, and stayed. He was quite simply the most beautiful man I had ever seen and I, while not technically a virgin, was so focused on my medical career I hadn't had much experience with men. Beauty in a man shook me, entangled me in a way for which I was unprepared.

When I say beautiful, there is no other word for it. He had a shock of dark hair that fell uncut—unless I cut it—over a clear, broad forehead. His eyes were like dark almonds and about as readable. He had a straight, perfect nose, skin that had the kind of ermine edging that is on a blackberry leaf—soft and slightly fuzzy to the touch. His ears, shell-like, were velvety and made to be touched, caressed, blown into. He was lean and well-muscled, but never had to work at it, so he did not have that false sculpting that men have who only develop their tone in a gym. And most important, he was totally unaware of his beauty. It was like his clothing—there for covering. I must have tried to write dozens of poems about him those first weeks with him, which was odd because I had never written anything before other than critical essays for school.

Even when his beauty lost its power over me, I stayed—and this will sound bizarre and slightly shocking, but is true nonetheless—because he smelled like summer, moist and hot and beckoning. He was not in fact any of those things. He was more winter than summer, arctic really. But he smelled as if he could be cultivated and might even blossom in time if only I could find the right tools.

So I stayed.

Which is how I found myself frequently on birding expeditions: tracking down errant wheatears along the stone abutments at the Quabbin Reservoir, chasing after odd rarities at feeders in Hadley and Montague, looking through snowstorms for an elusive snowy owl, spending a whole day and night driving Lewis around the Northampton meadows on the Christmas bird count. Of course he did not know how to drive. The universe supplied drivers.

As for why he stayed with me, there is no mystery in that. I was as comfortable for him as his furniture. He did not expect his furniture to up and move away. Nor did I.

Until.

Until the hawk watch when something extraordinary happened. And only I seemed to have noticed it.

A bird as big as a man, a man with wings, came down from the sky and took me in a feathery embrace. And only then, after I had been well and truly fucked by some otherworldly fowl, did I begin to understand real beauty.

I do not expect you to believe me. I expect you will say I had been drinking. Or smoking funny cigarettes. I expect you to say I was hallucinating or dreaming or having an out of body experience. I expect you to say the words "alien abduction" with a breathy laugh, and suggest I was having a breakdown.

I was not. I was awake that day as I am at this moment. The morning was still and chill. I had dressed warmly, but evidently not warmly enough for I could feel the cold through my chinos, like a light coating of ice on my thighs. My earlobes were numb.

Lewis was with the ardent birders high up on the fire tower. I was down below, my field glasses in my hand, thinking about my caseload and praying that my beeper would signal me to make an early and unanticipated visit to the hospital. My relationship with Lewis had reached the point where I could not just leave without a summons, but I spent a lot of time praying that one thing or another would demand my time away from his side.

I heard a noise. Not my beeper, but a kind of insistent high pitched cry. When I looked up, I saw this speck in the sky hurtling toward me. I put my glasses to my eyes, twisted the focus, and then dropped the glasses on the ground. $2,500 worth of Zeiss and I simply let it fall from my hand without thinking. But I was too shocked to notice. What I had seen was not possible. How quickly it moved was not possible. I scarcely had time to raise my hands to ward off the thing when it was hovering over me, the wind from its wings literally taking my breath away so that I could not have screamed if I wanted to.

No one else seemed to have noticed anything wrong and I, even as I was stunned by the quickness of the bird-thing, wondered how that could be. The best birders in Western Mass were crowding the high platform of the fire tower: Gagnon and Greene and Stemple and the rest. They were taking notes and talking hawks and comparing counts from the year before. At any one moment, eight or nine pairs of eyes were scanning the skies over the valley. Those birders missed nothing. *Nothing!* Yet not a one of them had seen what now landed in front of me, scarcely a yard away.

For a long moment I stared into the bird-thing's eyes. No, not a thing. A man. He had the fierce beaked nose of a hawk and a feathery brow, white and black and brown intermixed. His eyes were yellow; his mouth a generous gash. He was naked except for the feathers that curled around his genitals, that encircled his nipples, that streaked across his flat stomach and bare chest like ritual scars. His wings arched and beat back and forth and we were both caught in the swirling winds from them. I could scarcely stand up to those winds, even thought for a minute I might be swept off the mountain, even hoped I might so that he could rescue me and take me off into the air with him. I felt drunk with the thought.

He stood still for another long minute, with only those wings beating. Then he moved his shoulders, up and down, turned away from me and opened his wings even wider, then turned back. The feather-scars on his chest rippled like little waves, the white feathers like foam on top of the dark.

His long, black hair stuck straight up in front like a cock's comb and he was deadly serious as he stared at me. Then suddenly he threw his head back and crowed. Not like a rooster or any other bird I could name. But it was certainly some kind of triumphant cry.

Then he pumped those wings again and took off into the air and was gone.

I was stunned. It took me a while to realize that he had been doing a mating display. And by the heat in my face, by the burning between my legs, by that odd sensation in my stomach that was part nausea and part longing, I know I had responded to it as he had meant.

There was a sudden odd clatter above me as the birders descended the iron stairs. I reached out to one of the railings. *Cold iron,* I thought. *Proof against fairies.* I tore off my glove, touched the icy metal. But it did nothing to banish the picture in my head of that glorious creature—man, bird, whatever. It did nothing to discourage the flush on my face, the weakness in my groin.

"We're going for coffee," Lewis told me, "You can go on to the hospital. Dave will get me home." And they walked on by me without another word, going down the path, leaving me to follow as best I could with shaky knees and a head full of odd ideas.

I did not go out birding with Lewis the next morning before hospital rounds because I did not dare. And, quite frankly, because I thought it would mean being disloyal to Lewis. I had spent the night dreaming of the bird man, the hawk king. I had even fantasized about him while Lewis and I made love. Normally I just kept my eyes open and watched Lewis who goes through the mechanics of love-making with his eyes closed, without a single change on his beautiful face. This time I closed my eyes—not that Lewis would have noticed the difference—and fancied he had wings and feathers on his chest. It made my breath come quicker, and I climaxed as soon as he entered me, which was unusual enough for him to open his eyes and say, "Something's different." Lewis likes things to be the same.

"Pre-menstrual," I said.

"Oh," he answered. And that was all.

He went off birding with his friends and I lay in bed thinking about nothing. Or trying to think about nothing. Burying my face in the feather pillow. Trying to remember if any of my close relatives had recently gone mad. Then I got up, took a long, leisurely shower, and dried myself in front of the window. Not that anyone could see me. The bathroom overlooked an old abandoned tobacco field. The house was surrounded by trees.

I saw many specks in the sky, some easy to identify, some too far away for casual naming. But nothing that fell to earth like a feathered star.

So I put on my terry-cloth robe and made myself a cup of coffee, went out onto the deck to drink it, though the morning was even colder than it had been the day before. I was hoping, you see, for something. I was trying to keep alive the belief that I was *not* crazy. I was afire, giving off signals I suppose. Pheromones, they're called. I put my head back and tried to imitate the sound the hawk man had made right before diving to earth. "Kreeeeeeee!" I cried. But I was embarrassed to call out very loudly even though the nearest house was about a quarter mile away. "Kreeeeee!"

I turned to go back into the house when I heard something above me, looked up, and saw the speck, my feathered hallucination, falling out of the sky to my feet. I opened my arms to him and, without more foreplay than that, he embraced me with his wings, the shafts scraping my back, and then thrust himself in me. First from the front, a hot searing pinning, leaving me still weak with desire. Then he turned me around, pushed my robe up, and mounted me from behind. The feathers of his breast emblazoned themselves on my back, sticking into the raw scrapings his wings had made. I felt the pain and yet it was sweet, too, as if I were growing wings.

Then he lay me down on the cold boards and did it twice more, front and back, and I was hot and wet with him and cried, a sound more like the call of a loon than a hawk, throaty and low. He gave me love bites on the neck and shoulder and buttocks.

Then he stood, shook himself all over, pumped his wings, which covered me with wind, and fled into the sky with that defiant, triumphant cry.

I lay on my back, my robe half around my waist, till I shivered with the cold. When I got up at last, I found a feather he had dropped on the deck. Whether it was from our love making or after, when he had gave that odd shaking, I didn't know. I held the feather so tight, the shaft made a mark on my palm.

I went back inside and took another long shower, called in sick to the hospital, and went to bed. I dreamed the hawk man fucked me over and over and over, and as I dreamed, I ran the feather across my breasts and over my stomach and between my legs. The dreams were so real, I had an orgasm each time.

When Lewis came home, he didn't seem to notice anything, not my flushed face, not the marks on my back and neck and arms. He heard me when I said I thought I was pregnant. He insisted he wanted to marry me. He did not understand when I moved out.

I live now on the top floor of the highest building in Springfield. An aerie, I call it. I have made a bassinet and lined it with down. I am a doctor, I will know how to attend to my own delivery. I do not trust anyone else, for my child might look like his father. I am not certain that the attending physicians at Cooley Dickinson are ready for a baby born with pin feathers. I have practiced lullabies, especially the one about the baby in the tree tops. It seems right, some how.

I am alone now. But that does not matter. I am sure the hawk man will come back next season. One thing Lewis taught me: The big hawks mate for life.

And so do I.

So do I.

BIRD COUNT

Sirens and Other Daemon Lovers, fantasy anthology edited by Terri Windling and me was the recipient of what Terri dubbed the drowned mermaids cover. The book, published in 1998 contains a choice assortment of erotic stories.

Jane Yolen, a prolific national treasure, is not known for writing erotic fiction, yet here is "Bird Count."

Anamorphosis

by Caitlín R. Kiernan

(From *Lethal Kisses*, 1996)

Deacon was walking, ragged boots slapping concrete, not even noticing cracks or a quarter someone dropped. *Just keep walking,* marching, letting the red shit behind his eyes bleed off with the Atlanta April heat, *and what's that Mr. Eliot? Sorry, man, no lilacs,* just bus-fart diesel and the shitty, sweet stink of kudzu. In the east, the sky had bruised down to dull indigo, and there was still orange towards downtown, and Deacon, pressed in twilight.

He didn't want to go back to his apartment, one sweaty room and a thriftstore Zenith, always the same snowy channel because the knob broke off. Didn't want to stop walking and have a beer, two beers, even though he still had the twenty Hammond had shoved into his hand when no one was looking. No way he wanted to eat. Might never want to eat again.

"Yeah, well, Lieutenant Hammond says this one's different," the greasy cop with the neck like a dead chicken had said as they climbed the fire stairs, seven flights because the elevator was busted. And the stairwell choking black because the lights must have been busted, too, and Deacon had just kept his hand on the rail and followed the cop's voice and the tattoo of his shiny policeman shoes.

This one's different, and he almost stepped in front of a big ugly Pontiac, Bondo and some paint on its shark snout the color of pus. The horn blared, and behind the wheel the driver jabbed one brown finger at heaven. And Deacon stepped back up onto the curb, *This one's different, Deke, okay?*

They had stood in the long hall, yellowy incandescence and scrubby green carpet, Hammond looking old and sick, hatchet-faced and yesterday's stubble sandpapering his cheeks. Deacon had shaken his head, *yeah, man, whatever,* didn't know what else he was supposed to do, what he was supposed to say, but Hammond really looked like cold turds, and he'd said, almost whispered, *Just be cool, man, it's real rough in there, but just be cool.*

Deacon watched the Pontiac until it turned and headed down Edgewood. The streetlights along Hilliard buzzed like giant bugs and faded on.

Hammond had opened the door, and then there'd been other voices inside, other cops, muttering navy shapes past the detective's wide shoulders. The air that spilled out into the hall had been cool and smelled the way hands do after handling pennies or old keys, meat and metal, and Deacon had known that there weren't going to be any handkerchiefs or dog-eared snapshots this time, no pacing back and forth over a weedy, glass-crunchy vacant lot where someone had said the missing husband or girlfriend or daughter had last been seen. Once Hammond had even made him hold a tongue some old lady had found in her garbage can, a dried, shriveled tongue like beef jerky or some Viet Cong's misplaced trophy, and *Aren't you getting anything, Deke?*

but this one was going to be different.

Just stay cool, Deke,

He was alone on the street now, except for the sound of cars on other roads, and low voices through the opened door of a bar with its rusty sign that read Parliament Club, Ladies Always Welcome. Deacon walked on past the bar, dark in there with little pools of neon, and someone laughed, deep and threatening enough that he didn't turn his head to look.

Hammond had looked at him one more time, apologetic, before they'd stepped through the unnumbered door, and Deacon had slipped, skidded and would have gone down on his ass if chicken neck hadn't been back there, caught him under the arms. *Christ, man, what the*—but by then he could see for himself. The carpet had ended at the threshold, and the floor was just hardwood and something on it that looked like Karo syrup. Except that it wasn't, and *what the hell, Hammond. I don't need this kind of shit.* But the door had clicked shut behind them, safety bar snug down across his lap and the rickety little train was already rattling into the fun house.

The apartment had been bigger than his, cavernous studio and a kitchen off to one side, a hallway that probably led to a bedroom. One wall entirely of dirty awning windows, handcranked open, like that was gonna help the smell. He'd wanted to cross the room and stand there, stare out at the city rooftops and catch mouthfuls of clean air, not look at the syrupy maroon floors or the brighter smears down the plaster walls. But instead he had just stood, staring, tasting the acid ghost of the diner eggs and hash browns from breakfast hanging at the back of his throat and waiting for Hammond to say something, anything that would make sense of this.

You okay, Deke? I know, Christ I know, man, but

Deacon had done his hangover morning counting trick, backwards from twenty-five, and the room, impossible Jackson Pollock nightmare, shreds and things hanging, draped from furniture and lampshades. Disemboweled sofa cushions and crisp slivers of shattered glass.

just tell me if you feel anything, anything at all.

I feel sick. And he'd gagged, covering his mouth with the back of his hand.

Hammond's frown had deepened, careless thumb gouges in wet clay, and to chicken neck—*Cummins, why don't you see if you can find Mr. Silvey a glass of water?* But Deacon had raised one hand and shook his head to stop Cummins, hadn't dared open his mouth again to speak. Breakfast and bitter bile tang and the room, getting in past clenched lips, slipping through his nostrils.

Deacon had closed his eyes, swallowed, and when he opened them it had all still been there, and Hammond, running fingers through his thinning hair.

He looked up from the sidewalk, disoriented, no street signs in sight and for a moment the buildings, the billboards, meant nothing. And the unreliable certainty that if this amnesia could be generalized, made complete, but then the world tilted back; vicious recognition, a derelict beauty salon, windows and door plywood scabbed and bandaged with movie ads and election bullshit. Almost full dark, and there were better neighborhoods.

What do you want me to do? as he'd taken one step towards the center of the room, the gutted sofa and belly-up coffee table, shoes smacking like cola-sticky theater floors.

Anything you got, Deke, as he'd lit a cigarette, one of his stinking menthol Kools, exhaled gray-white smoke, but even that hadn't disguised the red smell. *Do that voodoo you do,* and to chicken-necked Cummins, lingering somewhere too close, *I want to know the second forensics shows up down there. You understand? The absolute second.*

Deacon had looked up at the high ceilings, just bare concrete and exposed plumbing, hovering fluorescent fixtures on taut chains. Jagged butt-ends of shattered tubes. And ropy garland loops dripping thick blood and shit spatterings below. The video tape, glossy brown in the morning sun and shadows, had reached down to the floor like streamers.

Who was this, Hammond?

He hadn't felt the breeze through the open windows, but the lights had swayed a little, rust creak and whine, and the tape had rustled like dead leaves.

Small-time porn operator, and the detective had sucked at his cigarette, *guy named Grambs.* Pause as the smoke whistled out of him, and Hammond had inhaled loudly, chewed at his lower lip; eyes cloudy with the familiar indecision that Deacon knew meant he was weighing how much to say.

Anyway, looks like Mr. Grambs had bigger enemies than us, so that was all he was getting today, but really Deacon hadn't given a crap. His head had begun to throb, rubber band winding itself up at the base of his skull and dull sinus burn. And hadn't he read something somewhere about poison fumes from broken fluorescent bulbs? Mercury gas. Neurotoxins. Mad as a fucking hatter.

Deacon sat down on the metal bench inside the plexiglas bus stop shelter, alone, and here the tubes were shielded behind dirty plastic and hummed like a drowsy memory of wasps, electrons danced, and he blinked in the ugly greenish light.

I don't want this one, he'd said to the detective, but that had been later, after he'd stepped over or around crimson rags and the expensive-looking chair toppled over on its side, after he'd noticed all the mean little gouges in the dark wood. And there behind the sofa, hiding in plain sight, such perfect circumference, an architect's anal-retentive circle traced in tattletale gray and argent feathers, eggshell, sharp teeth, and the pencil shafts of small, bleached bones. And the mushroom clumps, fish-belly toadstools and fleshy orange caps, sprouting from the varnished floor. Maybe five feet across, and nothing inside except the fat pinkish slug of the penis, the scrotal lump, a crinkly bit of blonde pubic hair.

Slow seconds had passed, time seep, and no sound but a garbage truck loud down on the street and the cellophane crackle of a police walkie-talkie.

I don't want this one, Hammond. Go find yourself another skull monkey, but maybe he hadn't said the words aloud, because no one had seemed to hear, and his mouth had been so dry, tongue and palate snagging at each other like worn-out velcro.

In the bus stop, Deacon closed his eyes, shut out the shitty light and the translucent reflection of himself in the plexiglas, tried to swallow, and his throat felt twice as dry as it had in the dead man's apartment. But, hey kiddies, we got a cure for that, yes sir, that's something we can most definitely fix.

Hammond had been suddenly swearing at everyone then, for not having seen, for not being able to find their assholes with a flashlight and a roll of Charmin, and Deacon had sat down on the edge of the sofa, not minding the stains, the wet that had soaked right through his threadbare jeans.

Nobody fuckin' touch it! Hammond had growled, *Don't even fuckin' breathe on it!* He'd shouted for Cummins, but Cummins had already been talking, had stopped and started over again. *Forensics is downstairs, sir. They're probably already on their way...*

But Hammond had interrupted, *Take Mr. Silvey out the way you brought him in.* And then, *If I need to talk, Deke, I want to be able to find you.* He hadn't taken his eyes off the thing on the floor, the thing within a thing. And he'd pushed the sweaty, crumpled bill into Deacon's hand.

And try to stay halfway sober.

Then Cummins had led him back across the room to the door, ride over, this way, please, and watch your step, hadn't said a word as they'd followed the darkened spiral of the stairwell back down to the sun-bright street.

Deacon had the job at the laundromat thanks to Hammond, and Tuesdays and Thursdays and weekends he sat on the wobbly bar stool behind the counter, watched street lunatics and traffic through the flyspecked windows.

Read the paperbacks he picked up at the Salvation Army or Goodwill for a quarter apiece and tried to ignore the incessant drone of washers and dryers. Just make sure no one steals anything or writes on the walls or craps on the floor. Sometimes, the machine that sold detergent and bleach would break down, or one of the Maytags would stop running and he'd have to make an out-of-order sign, red Magic Marker on ripped-up Tide boxes or pages torn from the phone book.

Late Saturday morning, and the hangover had faded to the dimmest brown pulse of pain in his head, but things could be worse, he thought, the handy credo of the damned, but true, nonetheless. The laundromat could have been full of the fat ladies in their dust-stained pink house shoes, every dryer roaring, tumbling loads of towels and boxer shorts like cotton-blend agates. The hangover could have had a little more backbone, could have done the dead soldiers proud.

There was a Ben Bova space opera beneath the counter, and a coverless collection of Faulkner short stories, but the eleven-thirty sun hurt his eyes too much for reading. Deacon pushed his sunglasses tight against his face and sipped at a warming can of 7-Up.

When the pay phone began to ring, he moaned, glared through his tinted drugstore lenses at the shrill metal box stuck up below the sign that read "The Management Assumes No Responsibility…" Thought about slipping out until it stopped, maybe going across the street for a fresh soda. Or perhaps he could just stay put and stare the fucker down.

Fifth ring, and the only customer in the laundromat, a Cuban girl in overalls and a Braves cap, looked at him. "You gonna get your phone," she said, not quite a question and before he could answer it rang again. She shook her head and went back to her magazine.

Deacon lifted the receiver halfway through the next ring, held the cool plastic to his ear. "Yeah," he said, and realized that he was actually sweating, had all but crossed his fingers.

"Jesus, Deke. Does Hennessey know you answer his phone like that?" The detective's voice was too big, too friendly; behind Hammond, Deacon could hear the station-house mutter, the clatter of tongues and typewriter keys.

"Hey," and Deacon wanted to sit down, but knew that the cord wasn't long enough for him to reach his stool. He leaned against the wall, trying not to notice that the Cuban girl was watching him.

"We gotta talk, bubba," Hammond said, and Deacon could hear him lighting a cigarette, hear the smoke exhaled and hanging thick around the detective's head.

"I think," pause, and so quick then that the words seemed to come from someone else, "I think I'm gonna sit this one out. Yeah, man, I think I'd rather sit this one out."

Heavy silence pushing through the phone and a woman's faint laughter, Deacon's heart and sweat and the dark eyes of the girl across the laundromat. And when Hammond spoke again, his voice had lost its big, crayonyellow sun cheeriness.

"I thought we had an understanding, Deke," then more silence, skillfully measured and strung like glinting loops of razor wire against his resolve. And he wanted to ask when there'd ever been an understanding, what Hammond could possibly think he understood, how much understanding you could buy for the odd twenty bucks and this shitty job.

Instead, he stared back at the Cuban girl, and waited for the silence to end.

"Well look. I don't want to get into this over the phone, bubba, so how about we meet up after your shift, somewhere we can talk."

The girl looked away and Deacon closed his eyes, focused on the not-quite dark, the afterimages swimming there like phosphorescent fish.

"Yeah, sure," he said, finally, "whatever," imagined the cautious edges of Hammond's smile slinking back. "I'm here until six, unless Wendel's late again." And of course, the first bar he named was okay with the cop, and certainly, six-thirty was perfectly fine, calculated concessions now that any pretense at resistance had been put down.

Deacon set the receiver back in its cradle, and when he opened his eyes the girl was gone.

He wanted more than the beer he'd nursed since six thirty-five, wanted more than anything else, even the amber burn of the scotch and crystal clarity of the vodka lined up pretty behind the bar, to just get up and walk out. Almost half an hour and no sign of Hammond, and he was still sitting in the smoky gloom, obedient, sober. He sipped at his flat beer and watched the glowing Budweiser clock over the door, tiny Clydesdales poised forever in mid trot, and promised himself that at seven he was out of there.

Just what exactly is it that's got you so fucking spooked anyway, Deke? the purling, sexless voice inside his head asked again, something he pictured from a cartoon, angel-white wings and a barracuda grin perched on his shoulder. *A little goo and a couple of 'shrooms? Afraid whatever chewed up poor ol' Mr. Grambs and sprayed him back out is gonna come lookin' for you?* Deacon watched the clock and the door, and concentrated on tearing his cocktail napkin into soggy confetti.

Think the boogeyman wants your balls, too, Deke?

And the door opened, still so much brighter out there, and for a moment the street sounds were louder than the jukebox disco, for a moment Hammond stood framed in the fading day, silhouetted absurdly like some Hollywood bad ass. Then the door eased itself so slowly shut behind him, and Deacon was blinking past the light trapped inside his eyes, the detective moving through the murmuring happy-hour crowd towards the corner booth.

"I'm late," he said, like Deacon wouldn't have noticed on his own. And the waitress, swooping in like a harpy with a tray and a soppy bar rag; Hammond pointed at Deacon's almost empty mug, held up two fingers for her to see. She took the mug away, left Deacon staring at the ring of condensation on the table between them, the wet rim raised around something scratched into the wood.

"Look, before you even say a word, I gotta apologize for dragging you up there the other day," and he fished the green pack of cigarettes from his coat pocket, tapped it hard against his wrist, and a single filtered-tip slid smoothly out; the Kools made Deacon think of burning cough drops, and he wondered if there was a word for that, for being reminded of an odor you'd never actually smelled.

"Sick fuckin' shit, Deke, but I just wanted you to see it, you know. I needed you to be there, stand there and—"

"It's all right," but he didn't look up, didn't dare meet Hammond's eyes when he said that. "I'm all right."

"Yeah, well, you had me worried, bubba. On the phone, you had me thinking I'd scared you off." And before Deacon could respond, the big kraft envelope was lying in front of him, nothing on the outside but a coffee stain, and he really didn't want to know what might be inside.

"There's some stuff in there I need you to take a look at, Deke," and then the waitress was back with their beers, set them roughly down and was gone again. "Just tell me if you get anything. And then we'll talk."

Deacon picked up the envelope, carefully folded back the brass-colored clasps, reached inside and pulled out several sheets of heavy paper; a child's drawings in colored pencils, one done in the sort of pastels that smear and stain your fingers if you touch the finished page. Stiffer, slick paper underneath, and he knew without looking that those would be glossy black and whites. He put it all back on the table, took a long swallow from the fresh beer, dry cold, and Hammond sipped at his own, watching every move.

"Just the drawings for now," the detective said, "and then we'll go over the photographs, afterwards."

Deacon studied each piece, each as unremarkable as the last, depthless stick figures outside stick houses, an animal that might have been a horse or a brown dragon, another that he was pretty sure was supposed to be a giraffe. Simple green and blue and red, violet, and everything traced in heavy black lines that bracketed the primaries. The last was actually a page torn from a coloring book, and he recognized Winnie-the-Pooh and Eeyore. Lots of messy smudges, as if someone had handled these with dirty hands, but even the smudges held inside dark borders.

He chose the giraffe, random pick or maybe it seemed like the one that must have taken the most work, the most time, each brown spot divided from yellow with that bold black. Deacon followed the outlining with his fingertips and waited for the gentle vertigo, for the taste like licorice, and the first twinge of the migraine that would swell and dog him for days. Index finger past indistinct shoulders and up the long neck, and here was another of the smudges, hovering to the left of the giraffe's head.

Glasses clinked loud behind the bar, and stitched into the din of voices, an old Rolling Stones song blaring from the jukebox, people talking louder to be heard. Deacon tried to shut it out, tried to focus on the rough grain of the paper beneath the whorl of his fingerprint. He lingered a moment longer on the head, goblin parody of a giraffe's head, both eyes on the same side and the knobby little horns looking more like a television antenna, rabbit ears. Long tongue lolling from the corner of its mouth.

But like sitting on the john, five days and no BM, or the maddening name or word or thought just out of reach, tip of your tongue but nothing, grasping at shadows at the corner of your vision. Nothing.

Almost ten minutes spent staring before, finally, "I'm sorry," although Deacon didn't *feel* sorry, felt vague relief and reluctant embarrassment, a need to escape the smell of stale beer and the detective's smoke, the pounding mesh of conversation and rock and roll. To escape this thing that was being asked and the memories of that eighth-floor abattoir, fungus and copper, the growing certainty that Thursday morning had only been window dressing.

"Shit," and Hammond crushed out his cigarette, gray wisp curling from the ashtray, and drained his glass. "Then that's all she wrote, hmmm?"

"Maybe if I knew something, man, if I knew *anything,* maybe then—"

"Maybe then you could just tell me what I want to hear, right, Deke? Maybe then you could be wrong, and I'd go the fuck away, get out of your face and let you get back to the booze, right?"

Deacon didn't answer, stared at the giraffe, the smudge carefully bordered. Waited for Hammond to be finished.

"Look, you think I like getting messed up in all this hocus-pocus? Christ, Deacon, you know how much flak I caught over the Broder case? And if IA finds out I had you up there the other day, my ass is gonna sizzle for a month."

The waitress rushed past, balancing empty mugs and cocktail glasses, stopped long enough to ask them if there'd be anything else.

"No ma'am, I think we're finished," cold, slamming finality in the statement, words like fishhooks, and Hammond took out his wallet, laid down money for them both, and a fat tip, besides.

Deacon returned the giraffe drawing to the stack, pulled the photos from underneath. On top, surprise, not crime-scene *noir,* but a color portrait of a small girl, seven or maybe eight, cheesy K-Mart pose in front of a flat winter backdrop. Red and spruce-green dress, and she'd smiled for the camera, wide and gap-toothed, plastic holly in her gingery hair.

"Did she do the drawings?"

"Yeah, she did them."

"And Grambs, he was into children."

"Yeah, Kreskin, Mr. Freddie Grambs was a grade-A, first-class sicko," exhaustion, exasperation thinning his voice, sharpening its edges. "And he liked to take dirty pictures of little girls. Made a lot of money selling them to other sickos."

"And she's missing, isn't she." *Or dead,* and he knew, more than ever, that he didn't want any part of this, but the hot barbs, Hammond's twisting guilt needles, were in his flesh now. Flensing resolve, backing him into submission, lightless cul-de-sac, and the barracuda jaws laughed and yammered, *So close, Deke, so goddamned close, and you don't even give a shit, just too fucking yellow to say no.*

The detective said nothing out loud, nodded slowly.

Deacon laid the smiling child on top of the giraffe, her giraffe, and there was the thing from behind the couch, the methodical arrangement of bone and feather, and the corpulent fungi, spongy organs from ruptured floorboards, *but, something's different, what?* And *yes,* the next shot, wider angle this time, and it wasn't Grambs' apartment at all, someplace smaller, seedier, one room and no evidence of a window. Ruined walls that might have been papered, pinstripe ghosts of darker and lighter grays within the splatter.

"Those were taken the day before, over in Midtown," a pause, then "Grambs had a partner."

Deacon didn't look at the lump inside the ring, been there, seen that shit. He rubbed his smokesore eyes, began to put the drawings, the photos, back the way he'd found them, stuffing it all back into the envelope.

"Look, bubba, do you see now? Do you see *why* I'm going outside the department for help on this?" Hammond was speaking quietly, calmly measuring his words, his tone, making Deacon feel like a fish straining at the end of an invisible line, the big one, easy does it, a little slack, don't let him get away.

"*Two* of these, and we're stumping around with our thumbs up our butts. Forensics has been over both scenes with tweezers and goddamned microscopes, and they don't have a fuckin' clue what happened to those SOBs."

Deacon closed his eyes, smoothing the envelope flat with the palms of both hands.

"What do you want from me?" he asked, and that was the white flag, wasn't it, "I tried, honestly. I tried, and I didn't get anything."

"Those things on the floor, the circles, is that some sort of cult symbol or what?"

"I don't have any idea," and the basement smell, musty cloy, rushed suddenly back at him. "Sometimes mushrooms grow like that, you know, toadstools, in the woods. Fairy rings."

Hammond sighed, rapped the table once with his knuckles.

"Well, hang onto the pictures, Deke. Keep trying. Maybe something will come to you later."

Deacon opened his eyes and Hammond was standing now, straightening his tie, rubbing at wrinkles in his white shirt.

"You think she might still be alive, don't you, the girl who did the drawings."

"Hell, bubba, I can hope, right?" and he laid a twenty and a crumpled ten on the table. "Eat something, okay. Call if you come up with anything."

After the detective had gone, Deacon signaled the waitress, ordered a pitcher and a double shot of oily bar-brand vodka. When she brought the drinks, he gave her the ten, pretty much wasted the bill, crammed his change and the twenty into the front pocket of his jeans. And then he sat for a while, breathing other people's cigarettes, and watched the yellow-brown envelope.

Deacon woke up, dragged slowly, by degrees, back to fuzzy consciousness by the noise next door, men shouting and the hot smack of flesh against flesh. He'd dozed off sitting on the old army hospital bed, his back against the cast-iron headboard and wall, sheetrock washed the blue of swimming-pool concrete. Rumpled blanket and the lost girl's art scattered carelessly across his lap like fallen leaves. His bladder ached and his back hurt, a dull drum between his shoulder blades, neck stiff and slime on his lips, his stubbled chin, coagulating slug trail of his own saliva. Dark outside, eleven-fourteen by the clock radio on the floor, still playing public radio jazz.

Through the thin plasterboard, androgynous weeping, and "You suck dick like a woman, sissy," the man said. "You suck dick just like a goddamned lousy fish." Deacon brushed the drawings aside and stood, waited out the vertigo before risking the long walk across the room to the toilet.

His urine was dark, the color of apple juice or rum, and after he'd flushed it away, he went back to sit on the squeaky edge of the bed. His mouth still tasted like stale beer and the greasy fried egg and sausage sandwich he'd picked up on his way home from the bar, keeping promises. He briefly considered another trip to the bathroom to brush his teeth, but picked up the envelope, instead, and dumped its contents across the foot of the bed.

And there was the girl, Sarah M. in black felt tip on the back, and so she had a name, and a birthday beneath, 2/23/87, so it was eight after all.

"Sarah," he said, and turned the Kodak paper back over. Next door, something hit the wall and shattered, and the crying faded down to ragged sobs. A door slammed, and Deacon listened to heavy footsteps pass his door.

And then she came, no effort, swept inside him in a choking swirl of orange peels and dirty river water, and Deacon dug his fingers into the mattress, gripping cotton-swathed springs like a lover's flesh,

and Sarah's on another bed, green pencil in her hand making grass for a giraffe that floats in construction-paper nothingness until she lays her streaky lawn beneath its bulbous feet the scalding chills and nausea, the sinking, folding himself into her, into himself; Deacon held onto the bedding, held onto her.

the pencil scratches the paper like a claw, and something moves, flutters past her face and she smiles, more teeth than in the portrait, swats it playfully away, but it's right back, a whirlwind around her head, whipping curls and shimmering strands of blackness, glimpses of mockingbird-gray wings and a dry clatter like jackstraws falling

"Oh," that single, empty syllable drawn out of him again and again, "*Oh*," and Deacon knew better, knew to stay put and ride it out, but the pain at the base of his skull leapfrogged past migraine, past anything he'd ever imagined, and he tried to stand, panic and legs like taffy, blind to everything now but Sarah, Sarah M. and her goddamned mutant giraffe and the whirlwind racing itself around her red hair.

As he fell, feet tangling in lamp cord and old magazines, as gravity sucked him towards the floor, his perspective shifted, falling past the girl, past the edge of her bed and its gaudy pink Barbie bedspread

and the whirling thing settles on her shoulder, snuggles itself into her hair, and from this fleeting vantage the blur solidifies, light curdling into substance,

as Deacon landed hard, hard enough to knock the wind out of him, leave him gasping, tasting blood,

wings spread wide, kite-boned and iridescent butterfly scales, gristle twigs,

clinging madly to the floor, sensing there was farther to fall. He opened his mouth to scream and felt the warm rise, the indisputable acid gush from his lips,

leering jaws, lipless, eyes like indigo berries sunk deep in puckered skin, and it sees him, then hides its impossible face in her hair.

Sarah laughs. And the sunlight through her window, the tempera sky, goes out, and here it is cold, slime dank, and beneath his fingers, bare stone. A dark past the simple absence of light, can't see, but he can hear, metal clink and scrape and her breath, labored; the sweet-sour ammonia stink of piss, shitty-rich pungence, mold. Distant traffic and the steady drip of water from somewhere high overhead. Wet hiss, air drawn hard across clenched teeth, or escaping steam, and

she was gone, and nothing left under him but the floor of his own apartment, his face cushioned in cooling vomit and umber shag. He did not open his eyes, already strained painfully wide, but the darkness had begun to pale, thinning itself to a pasty, transparent charcoal as the world faded leisurely in, neat Polaroid trick.

Deacon blinked at the huge and somber dust bunnies massed beneath his bed, an old Schlitz can back there just out of reach. And then the straggling headache caught him, slammed home, and he turned over onto his back and stared helplessly into the electric white sun screwed inside its bug-filled globe, crisped little Icaruses; he knew that feeling, passing too fucking close to something hot enough, black enough, to boil your blood and brains and leave behind a hollow parchment husk.

Deacon Silvey lay very still, hands fisted, and waited for the pain to ease off enough that he could move without puking again or passing out, until the phantom smells faded and finally there was only the vomit reek, the kinder mustiness of his room. And then he crawled the five feet to the telephone and dialed Hammond's number.

Hammond had sent a car for him, and the two officers had complained about the Olympics while Deacon stared silently out at the lighted, empty streets, at the bright cluster of office towers and high-rise real estate like a talisman against the night sky. If there'd been stars out, they'd been hidden safely behind the soft Dreamsicle-orange curtain, the combined glow of ten thousand sodium-vapor bulbs. The envelope with Sarah M.'s drawings and the photos had ridden on the seat next to him.

Now it sat marooned in the wild clutter of the detective's desk, concealing the art history textbook he'd spent fifteen minutes rummaging for in cardboard boxes and on the sagging shelves he'd built out of alley-found boards and concrete blocks. Deacon sipped scalding, sugary coffee from a styro-foam cup and waited for Hammond, waited to say words that sounded just as insane no matter how many times he pulled them apart and stuck them back together, polished absurdities, arranged and rearranged in his head like worn and finger-worried Scrabble tiles.

Just show him everything, let him connect the dots for himself. If he can see this on his own—

The office door slammed open, banged loud against the wall, and Hammond seemed pulled through by the slipstream, threaded into the disorder. More than exhaustion on his face, haggard; around his guarded eyes not sleep, but sleep forestalled, sleep purposefully misplaced. The eyes of someone who might not want to sleep ever again. For a moment, Hammond stared at him, as if he hadn't expected to find Deacon sitting there, anyone else, either; as if he'd been escaping, fleeing into this sanctuary of manila folders and overflowing ashtrays and had encountered an obstacle, had been caught.

"Deacon," he said, shutting the door more carefully behind him, but the *way* he said it, Deacon hardly recognized his own name. "So what you got for me, bubba," and the words sighed out, hushed of their intended tone, sieved raw. Deacon chewed at his lower lip, toying with a ragged piece of skin there, his eyes drawn past the impatient envelope to the dusty gray streaking the detective's suit, unwashed hands stained with rust and dirt.

"C'mon Deke. You even look sober, man. Something's up," and still that brittleness, picture-perfect likeness of Hammond's bluster, but cold porcelain cast and maybe already broken. Sharp and scattered edges waiting to slice. Deacon set down his coffee cup, no clear spot on the desk, so he put it on the floor a safe distance from his feet. And then he slid the big green book from beneath the envelope, *Art Through The Ages* and Matisse's five dancing maidens on the cover, imperfect ring, left hand to right to left; began to flip through dog-eared pages as he spoke fast, nearly stuttering, before he lost his nerve.

"Remember when you said that it didn't matter whether or not you believed, if *I* even believed, that the only thing that mattered to you was whether or not it worked? You said that, the first time—"

"I remember what I said, Deacon."

"It's important this time," and he wandered past Hieronymus Bosch and the St. Anne altarpiece and into pages of baroque architecture; couldn't recall the page number, but this was certainly too far, and so he began to search more slowly backwards. "It's important, or else you're gonna throw me out on my ass before I'm finished."

And there, the top two-thirds of page 691, and he turned the book around so Hammond could see, bent across the desk; caught the fusty smell clinging to the detective beneath ubiquitous stale menthol, faint dampness, mold and iron rot.

"This was done by a Sixteenth Century German painter named Hans Holbein," and he pointed at the two men in the painting, standing, neat-trimmed beards and somber faces, before an emerald curtain, arms resting on the tall side table between them.

"They were ambassadors to England. You have to understand, this thing is fucking meticulous. Look at the stuff on the table," and he jabbed his finger, first at a globe, then a compass, astronomical and navigational instruments he knew no names for. "The realism is incredible. He got every detail, the numbers on the sundial, the broken string on the lute, and the perspective is flawless. But here," and Deacon moved his finger down towards the men's shadowed feet. "There," and the gray-black slash across the bottom of the painting. "What do you see there?" Hammond took the book from him, shrugged, stared a moment longer before shaking his head. "Now," Deacon said, "Move your face a little closer to the book, and look *across* the painting from an angle, towards the upper right-hand corner."

Hammond hesitated, mouth drawn taut and sincerest I-have-no-intention-of-humoring-you-much-longer cast in his eyes, but then he obeyed, leaned close and tilted his head, stared at *The French Ambassadors*, eyes narrowed, almost squinting.

"Do you see it?" Deacon said, nearly a whisper.

Hammond shook his head again, his cheek almost touching the paper now. "Yeah, okay, it's a skull," he said, "but it's still distorted, all stretched out."

"That's because Holbein meant it to be viewed through a special cylinder shaped mirror. Now," and he reached for the envelope, noticed how his hands had begun to tremble, "look at this." Deacon pulled out the giraffe drawing and laid it inside the open book. "The smudge up next to the head. Try the same thing, except this time, look out of the corner of your eye, straight down from the top edge of the paper."

Hammond paused, then set aside the textbook and lifted the draw-ing, flat across both palms, to eye level. He turned his head away so that he seemed to be watching a row of file cabinets across the office, instead. Then, lips parted slightly and not exactly a sigh, but lungs emptying, breath across ivory-yellowed teeth and nothing drawn in to replace the expelled air.

"It's there on every one of them, more than once on some," Deacon said, and waited for a response. Hammond said nothing, laid the drawing on the desk and continued to stare at the file cabinets.

But Deacon knew what he'd seen, knew what Sarah M. had carefully scrawled there in the same deliberate hand as she'd decorated the giraffe. Knobby arc of wings and the ridiculous, needle-toothed grin, the spidery arms and legs, too many joints, ending in the stiletto intimation of claws. Pupiless eyes like poisonous blue-black berries.

"Okay, bubba," Hammond said quietly, sometime later, after he'd finally returned the giraffe to the envelope and closed *Art Through The Ages,* "now it's my turn."

Deacon and the detective sat alone in the darkened conference room, their faces lit by a shifting salt-and-pepper blizzard of electronic snow; Hammond had hit the mute button even before the tape began, and now, past the three and a half minutes salvaged from Gramb's apartment, the voiceless storm raged across the screen.

"The optics guys thought maybe it was a flaw in the camera lens," Hammond said; he made no move to turn the lights back up or shut off the television.

Deacon concentrated furiously on the writhing static, but saw nothing past the last seconds, the last scratched frames of tape. Final, brutal close-up of Sarah's face, harsh light and tears and something indistinct moving rapidly across the shot. And then the VCR had clicked itself off, rewind whir, and this, white and gray and black and him talking, the things he'd seen in his apart-ment when he'd held the giraffe, the darting blur and the piss-stinking place.

Playing the proper psychic and describing every sound, the traffic, the dripping water, every vague, half-assed excuse for an impression he could recall.

And Hammond nodded, took out a Kool, but didn't light it, held the cigarette tight between his fingers and stared down at the dull glimmer from the television reflected in his shoes.

"Yeah, bubba," he said. "Well, we've been there. We tracked down a realtor friend of Mr. Grambs this evening, and he was nice enough to show us a basement over on Butler," and Hammond coughed, clearing his throat, too loud in the dark room. "Shit, Deke, those guys had their own little Hollywood crammed into a hole about the size of the men's crapper down the hall."

"No," Deacon said. "The place I saw was nothing like that."

"They were keeping her in a subbasement, Deke. Christ, there are old cellars and tunnels down there that go all the way back to the friggin' Civil War. Nobody has any fucking idea..." and Deacon turned, his chair grating on the tile; the detective looked like an old man, timesick, every line, every wrinkle deepened, and bleeding shadow.

"We found the trapdoor under a throw rug, right there in the middle of the basement. Brand new Yale padlock on it, big enough to choke a goddamn horse," and he held up his fist to demonstrate.

"I climbed down first, this rickety-shit ladder, you know. Guess it went down twenty or twenty-five feet, and the floor was just cobblestones. It was like crawling into the sewers, man, the smell..." Deacon looked away, didn't care for the sudden age masking Hammond's face, clouding his eyes.

"That kid's been missing since *February,* Deke."

"She was dead?"

"Dead? Hell, she wasn't even *there*. I stepped off that ladder right into a bunch of those goddamn mushrooms, *huge* things, high as my ankle and big around as dinner plates. I shined a flashlight around, hardly ten feet square, and it was just like before. Not a soul, just this perfect circle of those things. And the bones, pokin' up out of all those toadstools. And this."

Hammond removed something from the pocket of his jacket, handed it to Deacon. Slippery, cool plastic, an evidence bag, already numbered, and inside, something he had to hold up into the flickering light to see clearly. Four, maybe five ginger strands of hair.

"Listen, bubba. I'm telling you this because if I don't tell someone…but it doesn't leave this room. Do you understand?"

"Who would I tell, Hammond?"

"I picked those up right at the center, before anyone else came down the ladder. And I swear before the saints and angels and Holy Jesus, they weren't just lying there, Deke, they were sticking up *out* of those old cobbles. I had to *break* them off."

Deacon passed the bag back to the detective, and for a little while they sat, not speaking, only their breathing and footsteps coming and going in the hallway outside, muffled conversation from other rooms.

"I'm not going to be able to help you anymore," Deacon said, and he stood up. Hammond remained seated, had gone back to staring at his shoes.

"I'm sorry," he said. "I truly am sorry about that, bubba, but after this shit, I guess it's fair enough. You take care of yourself, Deacon Silvey."

"Yeah, you too," and then Deacon walked to the door, slow, stepping cautiously around other chairs, invisible in the dark and the flittering afterimages from the television screen. The doorknob was cold, almost as cold as the fluorescent light that flooded in through the open door, keen and sterile light that could cut like scalpel steel if you looked directly at it long enough.

He shut the door behind him.

Come away, O human child!
To the waters and the wild
With a faery, hand in hand,
For the world's more full of weeping than you can
understand.

W. B. Yeats, "The Stolen Child" (1886)

ANAMORPHOSIS

Lethal Kisses, published in 1996, was intended as a follow-up to *Little Deaths*, which was a sexual horror anthology, but with the theme of revenge and vengeance. The book was commissioned by Caroline Oakley of Millennium. Publisher Anthony Cheetham changed our title *Wild Justice* to *Lethal Kisses: 19 Stories of Sex, Horror and Revenge*, with the cover art showing a sexily dressed woman standing with her back to us, holding a knife behind that back—and a guy with no shirt seated next to her. Few, if any of the stories, are at all sexual.

"Anamorphosis" by Caitlín R. Kiernan, a harrowing, early story by the author.

The Hortlak

by Kelly Link

(From *The Dark: New Ghost Stories,* 2003)

Eric was night, and Batu was day. The girl, Charley, was the moon. Every night, she drove past the All-Night in her long, noisy, green Chevy, a dog hanging out the passenger window. It wasn't ever the same dog, although they all had the same blissful expression. They were doomed, but they didn't know it.

Bız buradan çok hoslandık.
We like it here very much.

The All-Night Convenience was a fully stocked, self-sufficient organism, like the *Starship Enterprise,* or the *Kon-Tiki.* Batu went on and on about this. They didn't work retail anymore. They were on a voyage of discovery, one in which they had no need to leave the All-Night, not even to do laundry. Batu washed his pajamas and the extra uniforms in the sink in the back. He even washed Eric's clothes. That was the kind of friend Batu was.

Burada tatil için mi bulunuyorsunuz?
Are you here on holiday?

All during his shift, Eric listened for Charley's car. First she went by on her way to the shelter and then, during her shift, she took the dogs out driving, past the store first in one direction and then back again, two or three times in one night, the lights of her headlights picking out the long, black gap of the Ausible Chasm, a bright slap across the windows of the All-Night. Eric's heart lifted whenever a car went past.

The zombies came in, and he was polite to them, and failed to understand what they wanted, and sometimes real people came in and bought candy or cigarettes or beer. The zombies were never around when the real people were around, and Charley never showed up when the zombies were there.

Charley looked like someone from a Greek play, Electra, or Cassandra. She looked like someone had just set her favorite city on fire. Eric had thought that, even before he knew about the dogs.

Sometimes, when she didn't have a dog in the Chevy, Charley came into the All-Night Convenience to buy a Mountain Dew, and then she and Batu would go outside to sit on the curb. Batu was teaching her Turkish. Sometimes Eric went outside as well, to smoke a cigarette. He didn't really smoke, but it meant he got to look at Charley, the way the moonlight sat on her like a hand. Sometimes she looked back. Wind would rise up, out of the Ausible Chasm, across Ausible Chasm Road, into the parking lot of the All-Night, tugging at Batu's pajama bottoms, pulling away the cigarette smoke that hung out of Eric's mouth. Charley's bangs would float up off her forehead, until she clamped them down with her fingers.

Batu said he was not flirting. He didn't have a thing for Charley. He was interested in her because Eric was interested. Batu wanted to know what Charley's story was: he said he needed to know if she was good enough for Eric, for the All-Night Convenience. There was a lot at stake.

What Eric wanted to know was, why did Batu have so many pajamas? But Eric didn't want to seem nosy. There wasn't a lot of space in the All-Night. If Batu wanted Eric to know about the pajamas, then one day he'd tell him. It was as simple as that.

Erkek arkadasınız var mı?
Do you have a boyfriend?

Recently Batu had evolved past the need for more than two or three hours sleep, which was good in some ways and bad in others. Eric had a suspicion he might figure out how to talk to Charley if Batu were tucked away, back in the storage closet, dreaming his own sweet dreams, and not scheming schemes, doing all the flirting on Eric's behalf, so that Eric never had to say a thing.

Eric had even rehearsed the start of a conversation. Charley would say, "Where's Batu?" and Eric would say, "Asleep." Or even, "Sleeping in the closet."

Charley's story: she worked night shifts at the animal shelter. Every night, when Charley got to work, she checked the list to see which dogs were on the schedule. She took the dogs—any that weren't too ill, or too mean—out for one last drive around town. Then she drove them back and she put them to sleep. She did this with an injection. She sat on the floor and petted them until they weren't breathing anymore.

When she was telling Batu this, Batu sitting far too close to her, Eric not close enough, Eric had this thought, which was what it would be like to lie down and put his head on Charley's leg. But the longest conversation that he'd ever managed with Charley was with Charley on one side of the counter, him on the other, when he'd explained that they weren't taking money anymore, at least not unless people wanted to give them money.

"I want a Mountain Dew," Charley had said, making sure Eric understood that part.

"I know," Eric said. He tried to show with his eyes how much he knew, and how much he didn't know, but wanted to know.

"But you don't want me to pay you for it."

"I'm supposed to give you what you want," Eric said, "and then you give me what you want to give me. It doesn't have to be about money. It doesn't even have to be something, you know, tangible. Sometimes people tell Batu their dreams if they don't have anything interesting in their wallets."

"All I want is a Mountain Dew," Charley said. But she must have seen the panic on Eric's face, and she dug in her pocket. Instead of change, she pulled out a set of dog tags and plunked it down on the counter.

"This dog is no longer alive," she said. "It wasn't a very big dog, and I think it was part Chihuahua and part collie, and how pitiful is that. You should have seen it. Its owner brought it in because it would jump up on her bed in the morning, lick her face, and get so excited that it would pee. I don't know, maybe she thought someone else would want to adopt an ugly little bedwetting dog, but nobody did, and so now it's not alive anymore. I killed it."

"I'm sorry," Eric said. Charley leaned her elbows against the counter. She was so close, he could smell her smell: chemical, burnt, doggy. There were dog hairs on her clothes.

"I killed it," Charley said. She sounded angry at him. "Not you."

When Eric looked at her, he saw that that city was still on fire. It was still burning down, and Charley was watching it burn. She was still holding the dog tags. She let go and they lay there on the counter until Eric picked them up and put them in the register.

"This is all Batu's idea," Charley said. "Right?" She went outside and sat on the curb, and in a while Batu came out of the storage closet and went outside as well. Batu's pajama bottoms were silk. There were smiling hydrocephalic cartoon cats on them, and the cats carried children in their mouths. Either the children were mouse-sized, or the cats were bear-sized. The children were either screaming or laughing. Batu's pajama top was red flannel, faded, with guillotines, and heads in baskets.

Eric stayed inside. He leaned his face against the window every once in a while, as if he could hear what they were saying. But even if he could have heard them, he guessed he wouldn't have understood. The shapes their mouths made were shaped like Turkish words. Eric hoped they were talking about retail.

Kar yagacak.
It's going to snow.

The way the All-Night worked at the moment was Batu's idea. They sized up the customers before they got to the counter—that had always been part of retail. If the customer was the right sort, then Batu or Eric gave the customer what they said they needed, and the customer paid with money sometimes, and sometimes with other things: pot, books on tape, souvenir maple syrup tins. They were near the border. They got a lot of Canadians. Eric suspected someone, maybe a traveling Canadian pajama salesman, was supplying Batu with novelty pajamas.

Siz de mi bekliyorsunuz?
Are you waiting too?

What Batu thought Eric should say to Charley, if he really liked her: "Come live with me. Come live at the All-Night."

What Eric thought about saying to Charley: "If you're going away, take me with you. I'm about to be twenty years old, and I've never been to college. I sleep days in a storage closet, wearing someone else's pajamas. I've worked retail jobs since I was sixteen. I know people are hateful. If you need to bite someone, you can bite me."

Baska bir yere gidelim mi?
Shall we go somewhere else?

Charley drives by. There is a little black dog in the passenger window, leaning out to swallow the fast air. There is a yellow dog. An Irish setter. A Doberman. Akitas. Charley has rolled the window so far down that these dogs could jump out, if they wanted, when she stops the car at a light. But the dogs don't jump. So Charley drives them back again.

Batu said it was clear Charley had a great capacity for hating, and also a great capacity for love. Charley's hatred was seasonal: in the months after

Christmas, Christmas puppies started growing up. People got tired of trying to house-train them. All February, all March, Charley hated people. She hated people in December too, just for practice.

Being in love, Batu said, like working retail, meant that you had to settle for being hated, at least part of the year. That was what the months after Christmas were all about. Neither system—not love, not retail—was perfect. When you looked at dogs, you saw this, that love didn't work.

Batu said it was likely that Charley, both her person and her Chevy, were infested with dog ghosts. These ghosts were different from the zombies. Nonhuman ghosts, he said, were the most difficult of all ghosts to dislodge, and dogs were worst of all. There is nothing as persistent, as loyal, as *clingy* as a dog.

"So can you see these ghosts?" Eric said.

"Don't be ridiculous," Batu said. "You can't see that kind of ghost. You smell them."

Civarda turistik yerler var mı, acaba?

Are there any tourist attractions around here, I wonder?

Eric woke up and found it was dark. It was always dark when he woke up, and this was always a surprise. There was a little window on the back wall of the storage closet, which framed the dark like a picture. You could feel the cold night air propping up the walls of the All-Night, thick and wet as glue.

Batu had let him sleep in. Batu was considerate of other people's sleep.

All day long, in Eric's dreams, store managers had arrived, one after another, announced themselves, expressed dismay at the way Batu had re-invented—*compromised*—convenience retail. In Eric's dream, Batu had put his large, handsome arm over the shoulder of the store managers, promised to explain everything in a satisfactory manner, if they would only come and see. The store managers had all gone, in a docile, trusting way, trotting after Batu, across the road, looking both ways, to the edge of the Ausible Chasm. They stood there, in Eric's dream, peering down into the Chasm, and then Batu had given them a little push, a small push, and that was the end of that store manager, and Batu walked back across the road to wait for the next store manager.

Eric bathed standing up at the sink and put on his uniform. He brushed his teeth. The closet smelled like sleep.

It was the middle of February, and there was snow in the All-Night parking lot. Batu was clearing the parking lot, carrying shovelfuls of snow across the road, dumping the snow into the Ausible Chasm. Eric went outside for a smoke and watched. He didn't offer to help. He was still upset about the way Batu had behaved in his dream.

There was no moon, but the snow was lit by its own whiteness. There was the shadowy figure of Batu, carrying in front of him the shadowy scoop of the shovel, full of snow, like an enormous spoon full of falling light, which was still falling all around them. The snow came down, and Eric's smoke went up and up.

He walked across the road to where Batu stood, peering down into the Ausible Chasm. Down in the Chasm, it was no darker than the kind of dark the rest of the world, including Eric, especially Eric, was used to. Snow fell into the Chasm, the way snow fell on the rest of the world. And yet there was a wind coming out of the Chasm that worried Eric.

"What do you think is down there?" Batu said.

"Zombie Land," Eric said. He could almost taste it. "Zomburbia. They have everything down there. There's even supposed to be a drive-in movie theater down there, somewhere, that shows old black-and-white horror movies, all night long. Zombie churches with AA meetings for zombies, down in the basements, every Thursday night."

"Yeah?" Batu said. "Zombie bars too? Where they serve zombies Zombies?"

Eric said, "My friend Dave went down once, when we were in high school, on a dare. He used to tell us all kinds of stories."

"You ever go?" Batu said, pointing with his empty shovel at the narrow, crumbly path that went down into the Chasm.

"I never went to college. I've never even been to Canada," Eric said. "Not even when I was in high school, to buy beer."

All night the zombies came out of the Chasm, holding handfuls of snow. They carried the snow across the road, and into the parking lot, and left it there. Batu was back in the closet, sending off faxes, and Eric was glad about this, that Batu couldn't see what the zombies were up to.

Zombies came into the store, tracking in salt and melting snow. Eric hated mopping up after the zombies.

He sat on the counter, facing the road, hoping Charley would drive by soon. Two weeks ago, Charley had bitten a man who'd brought his dog to the animal shelter to be put down.

The man was bringing his dog because it had bit him, he said, but Charley said you knew when you saw this guy, and when you saw the dog, that the dog had had a very good reason.

This man had a tattoo of a mermaid coiled around his meaty forearm, and even this mermaid had an unpleasant look to her: scaly, corseted bottom; tiny black dot eyes; a sour, fangy smile. Charley said it was as if even the mermaid were telling her to bite the arm, and so she did. When she did, the dog went nuts. The guy dropped its leash. He was trying to get Charley off his arm. The dog, misunderstanding the situation, or rather, understanding the situation, but not the larger situation, had grabbed Charley by her leg, sticking its teeth into her calf.

Both Charley and the dog's owner had needed stitches. But it was the dog who was doomed. Nothing had changed that.

Charley's boss at the shelter was going to fire her, anytime soon—in fact, he had fired her. But they hadn't found someone to take her shift yet, and so she was working there, for a few more days, under a different name. Everyone at the shelter understood why she'd had to bite the man.

Charley said she was going to drive all the way across Canada. Maybe keep on going, up into Alaska. Go watch bears pick through garbage.

"When a bear hibernates," she told Batu and Eric, "it sleeps all winter and never goes to the bathroom. So when she wakes up in spring, she's really constipated. The first thing she does is take this really painful shit. And then she goes and jumps in a river. She's really pissed off now, about everything. When she comes out of the river, she's covered in ice. It's like armor. She goes on a rampage and she's wearing armor. Isn't that great? That bear can take a bite out of anything it wants."

Uykum geldi.
My sleep has come.

The snow kept falling. Sometimes it stopped. Charley came by. Eric had bad dreams. Batu did not go to bed. When the zombies came in, he followed them around the store, taking notes. The zombies didn't care at all. They were done with all that.

Batu was wearing Eric's favorite pajamas. These were blue, and had towering Hokusai-style white-blue waves, and up on the waves, there were boats with owls looking owlish. If you looked closely, you could see that the owls were gripping newspapers in their wings, and if you looked even closer, you could read the date and the headline:

"Tsunami Tsweeps Pussy
Overboard, All is Lots."

Batu had spent a lot of time reorganizing the candy aisle according to chewiness and meltiness. The week before, he had arranged it so that if you took the first letter of every candy, reading across from left to right, and then down, it had spelled out the first sentence of *To Kill a Mockingbird*, and then also a line of Turkish poetry. Something about the moon.

The zombies came and went, and Batu put his notebook away. He said, "I'm going to go ahead and put jerky with Sugar Daddies. It's almost a candy. It's very chewy. About as chewy as you can get. Chewy Meat gum."

"Frothy Meat Drink," Eric said automatically. They were always thinking of products that no one would ever want to buy, and that no one would ever try to sell.

"Squeezable Pork. *It's on your mind, it's in your mouth, it's pork.* Remember that ad campaign? She can come live with us," Batu said. It was the same old speech, only a little more urgent each time he gave it. "The All-Night needs women, especially women like Charley. She falls in love with you, I don't mind one bit."

"What about you?" Eric said.

"What about me?" Batu said. "Charley and I have the Turkish language. That's enough. Tell me something I need. I don't even need sleep!"

"What are you talking about?" Eric said. He hated when Batu talked about Charley, except that he loved hearing her name.

Batu said, "The All-Night is a great place to raise a family. Everything you need, right here. Diapers, Vienna sausages, grape-scented Magic Markers, Moon Pies—kids like Moon Pies—and then one day, when they're tall enough, we teach them how to operate the register."

"There are laws against that," Eric said. "Mars needs women. Not the All-Night. And we're running out of Moon Pies." He turned his back on Batu.

Some of Batu's pajamas worry Eric. He won't wear these, although Batu has told him that he may wear any pajamas he likes.

For example, ocean liners navigating icebergs on a pair of pajama bottoms. A man with an enormous pair of scissors, running after women whose long hair whips out behind them like red and yellow flags, they are moving so fast. Spiderwebs with houses stuck to them.

A few nights ago, about two or three in the morning, a woman came into the store. Batu was over by the magazines, and the woman went and stood next to Batu.

Batu's eyes were closed, although that doesn't necessarily mean he was asleep. The woman stood and flicked through magazines, and then at some point she realized that the man standing there with his eyes closed was wearing pajamas. She stopped reading through *People* magazine and started reading Batu's pajamas instead. Then she gasped, and poked Batu with a skinny finger.

"Where did you get those?" she said. "How on earth did you get those?"

Batu opened his eyes. "Excuse me," he said. "May I help you find something?"

"You're wearing my diary," the woman said. Her voice went up and up in a wail. "That's my handwriting! That's the diary that I kept when I was fourteen! But it had a lock on it, and I hid it under my mattress, and I never let anyone read it. Nobody ever read it!"

Batu held out his arm. "That's not true," he said. "I've read it. You have very nice handwriting. Very distinctive. My favorite part is when—"

The woman screamed. She put her hands over her ears and walked backwards, down the aisle, and still screaming, turned around and ran out of the store.

"What was that about?" Eric said. "What was up with her?"

"I don't know," Batu said. "The thing is, I thought she looked familiar! And I was right. Hah! What are the odds, you think, the woman who kept that diary coming in the store like that?"

"Maybe you shouldn't wear those anymore," Eric said. "Just in case she comes back."

Gelebilirmiyim?

Can I come?

Batu had originally worked Tuesday through Saturday, second shift. Now he was all day, every day. Eric worked all night, all nights. They didn't need anyone else, except maybe Charley.

What had happened was this. One of the managers had left, supposedly to have a baby, although she had not looked in the least bit pregnant, Batu said, and besides, it was clearly not Batu's kid, because of the vasectomy. Then, shortly after the incident with the man in the trench coat, the other manager had quit, claiming to be sick of that kind of shit. No one was sent to replace him, so Batu had stepped in.

The door rang and a customer came into the store. Canadian. Not a zombie. Eric turned around in time to see Batu duck down, slipping around the corner of the candy aisle, and heading towards the storage closet.

The customer bought a Mountain Dew, Eric too disheartened to explain that cash was no longer necessary. He could feel Batu, fretting, in the storage closet, listening to this old-style retail transaction. When the customer was gone, Batu came out again.

"Do you ever wonder," Eric said, "if the company will ever send another manager?" He saw again the dream-Batu, the dream-managers, the cartoonish, unbridgeable gape of the Ausible Chasm.

"They won't," Batu said.

"They might," Eric said.

"They won't," Batu said.

"How do you know for sure?" Eric said. "What if they do?"

"It was a bad idea in the first place," Batu said. He gestured towards the parking lot and the Ausible Chasm. "Not enough steady business."

"So why do we stay here?" Eric said. "How do we change the face of retail if nobody ever comes in here except joggers and truckers and zombies and Canadians? I mean, I tried to explain about how new-style retail worked, the other night—to this woman—and she told me to fuck off. She acted like I was insane."

"The customer isn't always right. Sometimes the customer is an asshole. That's the first rule of retail," Batu said. "But it's not like anywhere else is better. I used to work for the CIA. Believe me, this is better."

"Were you really in the CIA?" Eric said.

"We used to go to this bar, sometimes, me and the people I worked with," Batu said. "Only we have to pretend that we don't know each other. No fraternizing. So we all sit there, along the bar, and don't say a word to each other. All these guys, all of us, we could speak maybe five hundred languages, dialects, whatever, between us. But we don't talk in this bar. Just sit and drink and sit and drink. Used to drive the bartender crazy. We used to leave nice tips. Didn't matter to him."

"So did you ever kill people?" Eric said. He never knew whether or not Batu was joking about the CIA thing.

"Do I look like a killer?" Batu said, standing there in his pajamas, rumpled and red-eyed. When Eric burst out laughing, he smiled and yawned and scratched his head.

When other employees had quit the All-Night, for various reasons of their own, Batu had not replaced them.

Around this same time, Batu's girlfriend had kicked him out, and with Eric's permission, he had moved into the storage closet. That had been just *before* Christmas, and it was a few days *after* Christmas when Eric's mother lost her job as a security guard at the mall and decided she was going to go find Eric's father. She'd gone hunting online, and made a list of names she thought he might be going under. She had addresses as well.

Eric wasn't sure what she was going to do if she found his father, and he didn't think she knew, either. She said she just wanted to talk, but Eric knew she kept a gun in the glove compartment of her car. Before she left, Eric had copied down her list of names and addresses, and sent out Christmas cards to all of them. It was the first time he'd ever had a reason to send out Christmas cards, and it had been difficult, finding the right things to say in them, especially since they probably weren't his father, no matter what his mother thought. Not all of them, anyway.

Before she left, Eric's mother had put most of the furniture in storage. She'd sold everything else, including Eric's guitar and his books, at a yard sale one Saturday morning while Eric was working an extra shift at the All-Night.

The rent was still paid through the end of January, but after his mother left, Eric had worked longer and longer hours at the store, and then, one morning, he didn't bother going home. The All-Night, and Batu, they needed him. Batu said this attitude showed Eric was destined for great things at the All-Night.

Every night Batu sent off faxes to the *World Weekly News*, and to the *National Enquirer*, and to the *New York Times*. These faxes concerned the Ausible Chasm and the zombies. Someday someone would send reporters. It was all part of the plan, which was going to change the way retail worked. It was going to be a whole different world, and Eric and Batu were going to be right there at the beginning. They were going to be famous heroes.

Revolutionaries. Heroes of the revolution. Batu said that Eric didn't need to understand that part of the plan yet. It was essential to the plan that Eric didn't ask questions.

Ne zaman geri geleceksiniz?
When will you come back?

The zombies were like Canadians, in that they looked enough like real people at first, to fool you. But when you looked closer, you saw they were from some other place, where things were different: where even the same things, the things that went on everywhere, were just a little bit different.

The zombies didn't talk at all, or they said things that didn't make sense. "Wooden hat," one zombie said to Eric, "Glass leg. Drove around all day in my wife. Did you ever hear me on the radio?" They tried to pay Eric for things that the All-Night didn't sell.

Real people, the ones who weren't heading towards Canada or away from Canada, mostly had better things to do than drive out to the All-Night at three a.m. So real people, in a way, were even weirder, when they came in. Eric kept a close eye on the real people. Once a guy had pulled a gun on him—there was no way to understand that, but, on the other hand, you knew exactly what was going on. With the zombies, who knew?

Not even Batu knew what the zombies were up to. Sometimes he said that they were just another thing you had to deal with in retail. They were the kind of customer that you couldn't ever satisfy, the kind of customer who wanted something you couldn't give them, who had no other currency, except currency that was sinister, unwholesome, confusing, and probably dangerous.

Meanwhile, the things that the zombies tried to purchase were plainly things that they had brought with them into the store—things that had fallen, or been thrown into the Ausible Chasm, like pieces of safety glass. Rocks from the bottom of Ausible Chasm. Beetles. The zombies liked shiny things, broken things, trash like empty soda bottles, handfuls of leaves, sticky dirt, dirty sticks.

Eric thought maybe Batu had it wrong. Maybe it wasn't supposed to be a transaction. Maybe the zombies just wanted to give Eric something. But what was he going to do with their leaves? Why him? What was he supposed to give them in return?

Eventually, when it was clear Eric didn't understand, the zombies drifted off, away from the counter and around the aisles again, or out the doors, making their way like raccoons, scuttling back across the road, still clutching their leaves. Batu would put away his notebook, go into the storage closet, and send off his faxes.

The zombie customers made Eric feel guilty. He hadn't been trying hard enough. The zombies were never rude, or impatient, or tried to shoplift things. He hoped that they found what they were looking for. After all, he would be dead someday too, and on the other side of the counter.

Maybe his friend Dave had been telling the truth and there was a country down there that you could visit, just like Canada. Maybe when the zombies got all the way to the bottom, they got into zippy zombie cars and drove off to their zombie jobs, or back home again, to their sexy zombie wives, or maybe they went off to the zombie bank to make their deposits of stones, leaves, linty, birdsnesty tangles, all the other debris real people didn't know the value of.

It wasn't just the zombies. Weird stuff happened in the middle of the day too. When there were still managers and other employees, once, on Batu's shift, a guy had come in wearing a trench coat and a hat. Outside, it must have been ninety degrees, and Batu admitted he had felt a little spooked about the trench coat thing, but there was another customer, a jogger, poking at the bottled waters to see which were coldest. Trench-coat guy walked around the store, putting candy bars and safety razors in his pockets, like he was getting ready for Halloween. Batu had thought about punching the alarm. "Sir?" he said. "Excuse me, sir?"

The man walked up and stood in front of the counter. Batu couldn't take his eyes off the trench coat. It was like the guy was wearing an electric fan strapped to his chest, under the trench coat, and the fan was blowing things around underneath. You could hear the fan buzzing. It made sense, Batu had thought: this guy had his own air-conditioning unit under there. Pretty neat, although you still wouldn't want to go trick-or-treating at this guy's house.

"Hot enough for you?" the man said, and Batu saw that this guy was sweating. He twitched, and a bee flew out of the gray trench coat sleeve. Batu and the man both watched it fly away. Then the man opened his trench coat, flapped his arms, gently, gently, and the bees inside his trench coat began to leave the man in long, clotted, furious trails, until the whole store was vibrating with clouds of bees. Batu ducked under the counter. Trench-coat man, bee guy, reached over the counter, dinged the register in a calm and experienced way so that the drawer popped open, and scooped all the bills out of the till.

Then he walked back out again and left all his bees. He got in his car and drove away. That's the way that all All-Night stories end, with someone driving away.

But they had to get a beekeeper to come in, to smoke the bees out. Batu got stung three times, once on the lip, once on his stomach, and once when he put his hand into the register and found no money, only a bee. The jogger sued the All-Night parent company for a lot of money, and Batu and Eric didn't know what had happened with that.

Karanlık ne zaman basar?
When does it get dark?

Eric has been having this dream recently. In the dream, he's up behind the counter in the All-Night, and then his father is walking down the aisle of the All-Night, past the racks of magazines and towards the counter, his father's hands full of stones from the Ausible Chasm. Which is ridiculous: his father is alive, and not only that, but living in another state, maybe in a different time zone, probably under a different name.

When he told Batu about it, Batu said, "Oh, that dream. I've had it too."

"About your father?" Eric said.

"About your father," Batu said. "Who do you think I meant, *my* father?"

"You haven't ever met my father," Eric said.

"I'm sorry if it upsets you, but it was definitely your father," Batu said. "You look just like him. If I dream about him again, what do you want me to do? Ignore him? Pretend he isn't there?"

Eric never knew when Batu was pulling his leg. Dreams could be a touchy subject. Eric thought maybe Batu was nostalgic about sleeping, maybe Batu collected pajamas in the way that people nostalgic about their childhoods collected toys.

Another dream, one that Eric hasn't told Batu about. In this dream, Charley comes in. She wants to buy a Mountain Dew, but then Eric realizes that all the Mountain Dews have little drowned dogs floating in them. You can win a prize if you drink one of the dog sodas. When Charley gets up to the counter with an armful of doggy Mountain Dews, Eric realizes that he's got one of Batu's pajama tops on, one of the inside-out ones. Things are rubbing against his arms, his back, his stomach, transferring themselves like tattoos to his skin.

And he hasn't got any pants on.

Batık gemilerle ilgileniyorum.
I'm interested in sunken ships.

"You need to make your move," Batu said. He said it over and over, day after day, until Eric was sick of hearing it. "Any day now, the shelter is going to find someone to replace her, and Charley will split. Tell you what you should do, you tell her you want to adopt a dog. Give it a home. We've got room here. Dogs are good practice for when you and Charley are parents."

"How do you know?" Eric said. He knew he sounded exasperated. He couldn't help it. "That makes no sense at all. If dogs are good practice, then what kind of mother is Charley going to be? What are you saying? So say Charley has a kid, you're saying she's going to put it down if it cries at night or wets the bed?"

"That's not what I'm saying at all," Batu said. "The only thing I'm worried about, Eric, really, is whether or not Charley may be too old. It takes longer to have kids when you're her age. Things can go wrong."

"What are you talking about?" Eric said. "Charley's not old."

"How old do you think she is?" Batu said. "So what do you think? Should the toothpaste and the condiments go next to the Elmer's glue and the hair gel and lubricants? Make a shelf of sticky things? Or should I put it with the chewing tobacco and the mouthwash, and make a little display of things that you spit?"

"Sure," Eric said. "Make a little display. I don't know how old Charley is, maybe she's my age? Nineteen? A little older?"

Batu laughed. "A little older? So how old do you think I am?"

"I don't know," Eric said. He squinted at Batu. "Thirty-five? Forty?"

Batu looked pleased. "You know, since I started sleeping less, I think I've stopped getting older. I may be getting younger. You keep on getting a good night's sleep, and we're going to be the same age pretty soon. Come take a look at this and tell me what you think."

"Not bad," Eric said. "We could put watermelons with this stuff too, if we had watermelons. The kind with seeds. What's the point of seedless watermelons?"

"It's not such a big deal," Batu said. He knelt down in the aisle, marking off inventory on his clipboard. "No big thing if Charley's older than you think. Nothing wrong with older women. And it's good you're not bothered about the ghost dogs or the biting thing. Everyone's got problems. The only real concern I have is about her car."

"What about her car?" Eric said.

"Well," Batu said. "It isn't a problem if she's going to live here. She can park it here for as long as she wants. That's what the parking lot is for. But whatever you do: if she invites you to go for a ride, don't go for a ride."

"Why not?" Eric said. "What are you talking about?"

"Think about it," Batu said. "All those dog ghosts." He scooted down the aisle on his butt. Eric followed. "Every time she drives by here with some poor dog, that dog is doomed. That car is bad luck. The passenger side especially. You want to stay out of that car. I'd rather climb down into the Ausible Chasm."

Something cleared its throat; a zombie had come into the store. It stood behind Batu, looking down at him. Batu looked up. Eric retreated down the aisle, towards the counter.

"Stay out of her car," Batu said, ignoring the zombie.

"And who will be fired out of the cannon?" the zombie said. It was wearing a suit and tie. "My brother will be fired out of the cannon."

"Why can't you talk like sensible people?" Batu said, turning around and looking up. Sitting on the floor, he sounded as if he were about to cry. He swatted at the zombie.

The zombie coughed again, yawning. It grimaced at them. Something was snagged on its gray lips now, and the zombie put up its hand. It tugged, dragging at the thing in its mouth, coughing out a black, glistening, wadded rope. The zombie's mouth stayed open, as if to show that there was nothing else in there, even as it held the wet black rope out to Batu. The wet thing hung down from its hands and became pajamas. Batu looked back at Eric. "I don't want them," he said. He looked shy.

"What should I do?" Eric said. He hovered by the magazines. Charlize Theron was grinning at him, as if she knew something he didn't.

"You shouldn't be here." It wasn't clear to Eric whether Batu was speaking to the zombie. "I have all the pajamas I need."

The zombie said nothing. It dropped the pajamas into Batu's lap.

"Stay out of Charley's car!" Batu said to Eric. He closed his eyes and began to snore.

"Shit," Eric said to the zombie. "How did you do that?"

There was another zombie in the store now. The first zombie took Batu's arms and the second zombie took Batu's feet. They dragged him down the aisle and toward the storage closet. Eric came out from behind the counter.

"What are you doing?" he said. "You're not going to eat him, are you?"

But the zombies had Batu in the closet. They put the black pajamas on him, yanking them over the other pair of pajamas. They lifted Batu up onto the mattress, and pulled the blanket over him, up to his chin.

Eric followed the zombies out of the storage closet. He shut the door behind him. "So I guess he's going to sleep for a while," he said. "That's a good thing, right? He needed to get some sleep. So how did you do that with the pajamas? Is there some kind of freaky pajama factory down there?"

The zombies ignored Eric. They held hands and went down the aisles, stopping to consider candy bars and Tampax and toilet paper and all the things that you spit. They wouldn't buy anything. They never did.

Eric went back to the counter. He wished, very badly, that his mother still lived in their apartment. He would have liked to call someone. He sat behind the register for a while, looking through the phone book, just in case he came across someone's name and it seemed like a good idea to call them. Then he went back to the storage closet and looked at Batu. Batu was snoring. His eyelids twitched, and there was a tiny, knowing smile on his face, as if he were dreaming, and everything was being explained to him, at last, in this dream. It was hard to feel worried about someone who looked like that. Eric would have been jealous, except he knew that no one ever managed to hold on to those explanations, once you woke up. Not even Batu.

Hangi yol daha kısa?
Which is the shorter route?

Hangi yol daha kolay?
Which is the easier route?

Charley came by at the beginning of her shift. She didn't come inside the All-Night. Instead she stood out in the parking lot, beside her car, looking out across the road, at the Ausible Chasm. The car hung low to the ground, as if the trunk were full of things. When Eric went outside, he saw that there was a suitcase in the backseat. If there were ghost dogs, Eric couldn't see them, but there were doggy smudges on the windows.

"Where's Batu?" Charley said.

"Asleep," Eric said. He realized that he'd never figured out how the conversation would go, after that.

He said, "Are you going someplace?"

"I'm going to work," Charley said. "Like normal."

"Good," Eric said. "Normal is good." He stood and looked at his feet. A zombie wandered into the parking lot. It nodded at them, and went into the All-Night.

"Aren't you going to go back inside?" Charley said.

"In a bit," Eric said. "It's not like they ever buy anything." But he kept an eye on the All-Night, and the zombie, in case it headed towards the storage closet.

"So how old are you?" Eric said. "I mean, can I ask you that? How old you are?"

"How old are you?" Charley said right back.

"I'm almost twenty," Eric said. "I know I look older."

"No you don't," Charley said. "You look exactly like you're almost twenty."

"So how old are you?" Eric said again.

"How old do you think I am?" Charley said.

"About my age?" Eric said.

"Are you flirting with me?" Charley said. "Yes? No? How about in dog years? How old would you say I am in dog years?"

The zombie finished looking for whatever it was looking for inside the All-Night. It came outside and nodded to Charley and Eric. "Beautiful people," it said. "Why won't you ever visit my hand?"

"I'm sorry," Eric said.

The zombie turned its back on them. It tottered across the road, looking neither to the left, nor to the right, and went down the footpath into the Ausible Chasm.

"Have you?" Charley said. She pointed at the path.

"No," Eric said. "I mean, someday I will, I guess."

"Do you think they have pets down there? Dogs?" Charley said.

"I don't know," Eric said. "Regular dogs?"

"The thing I think about sometimes," Charley said, "is whether or not they have animal shelters, and if someone has to look after the dogs. If someone has to have a job where they put down dogs down there. And if you do put dogs to sleep, down there, then where do they wake up?"

"Batu says that if you need another job, you can come live with us at the All-Night," Eric said. His lips felt so cold that it was hard to talk.

"Is *that* what Batu says?" Charley said. She started to laugh.

"Batu likes you," Eric said.

"I like him too," Charley said. "But I don't want to live in a convenience store. No offense. I'm sure it's nice."

"It's okay," Eric said. "I don't want to work retail my whole life."

"There are worse jobs," Charley said. She leaned against her Chevy. "Maybe I'll stop by later tonight. We could always go for a long ride, go somewhere else, and talk about retail."

"Like where? Where are you going?" Eric said. "Are you thinking about going to Turkey? Is that why Batu is teaching you Turkish?" He wanted to stand there and ask Charley questions all night long.

"I want to learn Turkish so that when I go somewhere else I can pretend to be Turkish. I can pretend I *only* speak Turkish. That way no one will bother me," Charley said.

"Oh," Eric said. "Good plan. We could always go somewhere and not talk, if you want to practice. Or I could talk to you, and you could pretend you don't understand what I'm saying. We don't have to go for a ride. We could just go across the road, go down into the Chasm. I've never been down there."

"It's not a big deal," Charley said. "We can do it some other time." Suddenly she looked much older.

"No, wait," Eric said. "I do want to come with you. We can go for a ride. It's just that Batu's asleep. Someone has to look after him. Someone has to be awake to sell stuff."

"So are you going to work there your whole life?" Charley said. "Take care of Batu? Figure out how to rip off dead people?"

"What do you mean?" Eric said.

"Batu says the All-Night is thinking about opening up another store, down there," Charley said, waving across the road. "You and he are this big experiment in retail, according to him. Once the All-Night figures out what dead people want to buy, it's going to be like the discovery of America all over again."

"It's not like that," Eric said. He could feel his voice going up at the end, as if it were a question. He could almost smell what Batu meant about Charley's car. The ghosts, those dogs, were getting impatient. You could tell that. They were tired of the parking lot, they wanted to be going for a ride. "You don't understand. I don't think you understand?"

"Batu said that you have a real way with dead people," Charley said. "Most retail clerks flip out. Of course, you're from around here. Plus you're young. You probably don't even understand about death yet. You're just like my dogs."

"I don't know what they want," Eric said. "The zombies."

"Nobody ever really knows what they want," Charley said. "Why should that change after you die?"

"Good point," Eric said.

"You shouldn't let Batu mess you around so much," Charley said. "I shouldn't be saying all this, I know. Batu and I are friends. But we could be friends too, you and me. You're sweet. It's okay that you don't talk much, although this is okay too, us talking. Why don't you come for a drive with me?" If there had been dogs inside her car, or the ghosts of dogs, then Eric would have heard them howling. Eric heard them howling. The dogs were telling him to get lost. They were telling him to fuck off. Charley belonged to them. She was *their* murderer.

"I can't," Eric said, longing for Charley to ask again. "Not right now."

"Well, that's okay. I'll stop by later," Charley said. She smiled at him and for a moment he was standing in that city where no one ever figured out how to put out that fire, and all the dead dogs howled again, and scratched at the smeary windows. "For a Mountain Dew. So you can think about it for a while."

She reached out and took Eric's hand in her hand. "Your hands are cold," she said. Her hands were hot. "You should go back inside."

Rengi begenmiyorum.
I don't like the color.

It was already 4 a.m. and there still wasn't any sign of Charley when Batu came out of the back room. He was rubbing his eyes. The black pajamas were gone. Now Batu was wearing pajama bottoms with foxes running across a field towards a tree with a circle of foxes sitting on their haunches around it. The outstretched tails of the running foxes were fat as zeppelins, with commas of flame hovering over them. Each little flame had a Hindenburg inside it, with a second littler flame above it, and so on. Some fires you just can't put out.

The pajama top was a color that Eric could not name. Dreary, creeping shapes lay upon it. Eric had read Lovecraft. He felt queasy when he looked at the pajama top.

"I just had the best dream," Batu said.

"You've been asleep for almost six hours," Eric said. When Charley came, he would go with her. He would stay with Batu. Batu needed him. He would go with Charley. He would go and come back. He wouldn't ever come back. He would send Batu postcards with bears on them. "So what was all that about? With the zombies."

"I don't know what you're talking about," Batu said. He took an apple from the fruit display and polished it on his non-Euclidean pajama top. The apple took on a horrid, whispery sheen. "Has Charley come by?"

"Yeah," Eric said. He and Charley would go to Las Vegas. They would buy Batu gold lamé pajamas. "I think you're right. I think she's about to leave town."

"Well, she can't!" Batu said. "That's not the plan. Here, I tell you what we'll do. You go outside and wait for her. Make sure she doesn't get away."

"She's not wanted by the police, Batu," Eric said. "She doesn't belong to us. She can leave town if she wants to."

"And you're okay with that?" Batu said. He yawned ferociously, and yawned again, and stretched, so that the pajama top heaved up in an eldritch manner. Eric closed his eyes.

"Not really," Eric said. He had already picked out a toothbrush, some toothpaste, and some novelty teeth, left over from Halloween, which he could give to Charley, maybe. "Are you okay? Are you going to fall asleep again? Can I ask you some questions?"

"What kind of questions?" Batu said, lowering his eyelids in a way that seemed both sleepy and cunning.

"Questions about our mission," Eric said. "About the All-Night and what we're doing here next to the Ausible Chasm. I need to understand what just happened with the zombies and the pajamas, and whether or not what happened is part of the plan, and whether or not the plan belongs to us, or whether the plan was planned by someone else, and we're just somebody else's big experiment in retail. Are we brand-new, or are we just the same old thing?"

"This isn't a good time for questions," Batu said. "In all the time that we've worked here, have I lied to you? Have I led you astray?"

"Well," Eric said. "That's what I need to know."

"Perhaps I haven't told you everything," Batu said. "But that's part of the plan. When I said that we were going to make everything new again, that we were going to reinvent retail, I was telling the truth. The plan is still the plan, and you are still part of that plan, and so is Charley."

"What about the pajamas?" Eric said. "What about the Canadians and the maple syrup and the people who come in to buy Mountain Dew?"

"You need to know this?" Batu said.

"Yes," Eric said. "Absolutely."

"Okay, then. My pajamas are *experimental CIA pajamas,*" Batu said. "Like batteries. You've been charging them for me when you sleep. That's all I can say right now. Forget about the Canadians. These pajamas the zombies just gave me—do you have any idea what this means?"

Eric shook his head no.

Batu said, "Never mind. Do you know what we need now?"

"What do we need?" Eric said.

"We need you to go outside and wait for Charley," Batu said. "We don't have time for this. It's getting early. Charley gets off work any time now."

"Explain all of that again," Eric said. "What you just said. Explain the plan to me one more time."

"Look," Batu said. "Listen. Everybody is alive at first, right?"

"Right," Eric said.

"And everybody dies," Batu said. "Right?"

"Right," Eric said. A car drove by, but it still wasn't Charley.

"So everybody starts here," Batu said. "Not here, in the All-Night, but somewhere *here*, where we are. Where we live now. Where we live is here. The world. Right?"

"Right," Eric said. "Okay."

"And where we go is there," Batu said, flicking a finger towards the road. "Out there, down into the Ausible Chasm. Everybody goes there. And here we are, *here*, the All-Night, which is on the way to *there*."

"Right," Eric said.

"So it's like the Canadians," Batu said. "People are going someplace, and if they need something, they can stop here, to get it. But we need to know what they need. This is a whole new unexplored demographic. So they stuck the All-Night right here, lit it up like a Christmas tree, and waited to see who stopped in and what they bought. I shouldn't be telling you this. This is all need-to-know information only."

"You mean the All-Night or the CIA or whoever needs us to figure out how to sell things to zombies," Eric said.

"Forget about the CIA," Batu said. "Now will you go outside?"

"But is it our plan? Or are we just following someone else's plan?"

"Why does that matter to you?" Batu said. He put his hands on his head and tugged at his hair until it stood straight up, but Eric refused to be intimidated.

"I thought we were on a mission," Eric said, "to help mankind. Womankind too. Like the *Starship Enterprise*. But how are we helping anybody? What's new-style retail about this?"

"*Eric*," Batu said. "Did you see those pajamas? Look. On second thought, forget about the pajamas. You never saw them. Like I said, this is bigger than the All-Night. There are bigger fish that are fishing, if you know what I mean."

"No," Eric said. "I don't."

"Excellent," Batu said. His experimental CIA pajama top writhed and boiled. "Your job is to be helpful and polite. Be patient. Be *careful*. Wait for the zombies to make the next move. I'll send off some faxes. Meanwhile, we still need Charley. Charley is a natural-born saleswoman. She's been selling death for years. And she's got a real gift for languages—she'll be speaking zombie in no time. Think what kind of work she could do here! Go outside. When she drives by, you flag her down. Talk to her. Explain why she needs to come live here. But whatever you do, don't get in the car with her. That car is full of ghosts. The wrong kind of ghosts. The kind who are never going to understand the least little thing about meaningful transactions."

"I know," Eric said. "I could smell them."

"So are we clear on all this?" Batu said. "Or maybe you think I'm still lying to you?"

"I don't think you'd lie to me, exactly," Eric said. He put on his jacket.

"You better put on a hat too," Batu said. "It's cold out there. You know you're like a son to me, which is why I tell you to put on your hat. And if I lied to you, it would be for your own good, because I love you like a son. One day, Eric, all of this will be yours. Just trust me and do what I tell you. Trust the plan."

Eric said nothing. Batu patted him on the shoulder, pulled an All-Night shirt over his pajama top, and grabbed a banana and a Snapple. He settled in behind the counter. His hair was still standing straight up, but at four a.m., who was going to complain? Not Eric, not the zombies. Eric put on his hat, gave a little wave to Batu, which was either, Glad we cleared all *that* up at last, or else, So long!, he wasn't sure which, and walked out of the All-Night. This is the last time, he thought, I will ever walk through this door. He didn't know how he felt about that.

Eric stood outside in the parking lot for a long time. Out in the bushes, on the other side of the road, he could hear the zombies hunting for the things that were valuable to other zombies.

Some woman, a real person, but not Charley, drove into the parking lot. She went inside, and Eric thought he knew what Batu would say to her when she went to the counter. Batu would explain when she tried to make her purchase that he didn't want money. That wasn't what retail was really about. What Batu would want to know was what this woman really wanted. It was that simple, that complicated. Batu might try to recruit this woman, if she didn't seem litigious, and maybe that was a good thing. Maybe the All-Night really did need women.

Eric walked backwards, away and then even farther away from the All-Night. The farther he got, the more beautiful he saw it all was—it was all lit up like the moon. Was this what the zombies saw? What Charley saw, when she drove by? He couldn't imagine how anyone could leave it behind and never come back.

Maybe Batu had a pair of pajamas in his collection with All-Night Convenience Stores and light spilling out; the Ausible Chasm; a road with zombies, and Charleys in Chevys, a different dog hanging out of every passenger window, driving down that road. Down on one leg of those pajamas, down the road a long ways, there would be bears dressed up in ice; Canadians; CIA operatives and tabloid reporters and All-Night executives. Las Vegas showgirls. G-men and bee men in trench coats. His mother's car, always getting farther and farther away. He wondered if zombies wore zombie pajamas, or if they'd just invented them for Batu. He tried to picture Charley wearing silk pajamas and a flannel bathrobe, but she didn't look comfortable in them. She still looked miserable and angry and hopeless, much older than Eric had ever realized.

He jumped up and down in the parking lot, trying to keep warm. The woman, when she came out of the store, gave him a funny look. He couldn't see Batu behind the counter. Maybe he'd fallen asleep again, or maybe he was sending off more faxes. But Eric didn't go back inside the store. He was afraid of Batu's pajamas.

He was afraid of Batu.

He stayed outside, waiting for Charley.

But a few hours later, when Charley drove by—he was standing on the curb, keeping an eye out for her, she wasn't going to just slip away, he was determined to see her, not to miss her, to make sure that she saw him, to make her take him with her, wherever she was going—there was a Labrador in the passenger seat. The backseat of her car was full of dogs, real dogs and ghost dogs, and all of the dogs poking their doggy noses out of the windows at him. There wouldn't have been room for him, even if he'd been able to make her stop. But he ran out in the road anyway, like a damn dog, chasing after her car for as long as he could.

THE HORTLAK

The Dark: New Ghost Stories is an all original ghost story anthology published in 2003. It won the International Horror Guild Award. Kelly Link's "The Hortlak" is about zombies and dogs and it was nominated for the World Fantasy Award, as was the entire anthology.

In the Month of Athyr

by Elizabeth Hand

(From *OMNI Best SF Two,* 1992)

In the month of Athyr Leucis fell asleep.

—*C.P. Cavafy, "In the Month of Athyr"*

T he argala came to live with them on the last day of Mestris, when Paul was fifteen. High summer, it would have been by the old Solar calendar; but in the HORUS station it was dusk, as it always was. The older boys were poring over an illustrated manual of sexual positions by the sputtering light of a lumière filched from Father Dorothy's cache behind the galley refrigerator. Since Paul was the youngest he had been appointed to act as guard. He crouched beside the refrigerator, shivering in his pajamas, and cursed under his breath. He had always been the youngest, always would be the youngest. There had been no children born on the station since Father Dorothy arrived to be the new tutor. In a few months, Father Dorothy had converted Teichman Station's few remaining women to the Mysteries of Lysis. Father Dorothy was a *galli,* a eunuch who had made the ultimate sacrifice to the Great Mother during one of the high holy days Below. The Mysteries of Lysis was a relatively new cult. Its adherents believed that only by reversing traditional gender roles could the sexes make peace after their long centuries of open hostility. These reversals were enacted literally, often to the consternation of non-believing children and parents.

On the stations, it was easier for such unusual sects and controversial ideas to gain a toehold. The current ruling Ascendancy embraced a cult of rather recent vintage, a form of religious fundamentalism that was a cunning synthesis of the more extreme elements of several popular and ancient faiths. For instance, the Ascendants encouraged female infanticide among certain populations, including the easily monitored network of facilities that comprised the Human Orbital Research Units in Space, or HORUS. Because of recent advances in bioengineering, the Ascendants believed that women, long known to be psychologically mutable and physically unstable, might also soon be unnecessary. Thus were the heavily reviled feminist visionaries of earlier centuries unhappily vindicated. Thus the absence of girl children on Teichman, as well as the rift between the few remaining women and their husbands.

To the five young boys who were his students, Father Dorothy's devotion to the Mysteries was inspiring in its intensity. Their parents were also affected; Father Dorothy believed in encouraging discussions of certain controversial gender policies. Since his arrival, relations between men and women had grown even more strained. Paul's mother was now a man, and his father had taken to spending most of his days in the station's neural sauna, letting its wash of endorphins slowly erode his once-fine intellect to a soft soppy blur. The argala was to change all that.

"Pathori," hissed Claude Illo, tossing an empty salt-pod at Paul's head. "Pathori, come here!"

Paul rubbed his nose and squinted. A few feet away Claude and the others, the twins Reuben and Romulus and the beautiful Ira Claire, crouched over the box of exotic poses.

"Pathori, come *here!*"

Claude's voice cracked. Ira giggled; a moment later Paul winced as he heard Claude smack him.

"I *mean* it," Claude warned. Paul sighed, flicked the salt-pod in Ira's direction and scuttled after it.

"Look at this," Claude whispered. He grabbed Paul by the neck and forced his head down until his nose was a scant inch away from the hologravures. The top image was of a woman, strictly forbidden. She was naked, which made it doubly forbidden; and with a man, and smiling. It was that smile that made the picture particularly damning; according to Father Dorothy, a woman in such a posture would never enjoy being there. The woman in the gravure turned her face, tossing back hair that was long and impossibly blonde. For an instant Paul glimpsed the man sitting next to her. He was smiling too, but wearing the crimson leathers of an Ascendant Aviator. Like the woman, he had the ruddy cheeks and even teeth Paul associated with antique photographs or tapes. The figures began to move suggestively. Paul's head really *should* explode, now, just like Father Dorothy had warned. He started to look away, embarrassed and aroused, when behind him Claude swore—

"—move, damn it, it's Dorothy!—"

But it was too late.

"Boys…"

Father Dorothy's voice rang out, a hoarse tenor. Paul looked up and saw him, clad as always in salt-and-pepper tweeds, his long grey hair pulled back through a copper loop. "It's late, you shouldn't be here."

They were safe: their tutor was distracted. Paul looked beyond him, past the long sweep of the galley's gleaming equipment to where a tall figure stood in the shadows. Claude swept the box of hologravures beneath a stove and stood, kicking Paul and Ira and gesturing for the twins to follow him.

"Sorry, Father," he grunted, gazing at his feet. Beside him Paul tried not to stare at whoever it was that stood at the end of the narrow corridor.

"Go along, then," said Father Dorothy, waving his hands in the direction of the boys' dormitory. As they hurried past him, Paul could smell the sandalwood soap Father Dorothy had specially imported from his home Below, the only luxury he allowed himself. And Paul smelled something else, something strange. The scent made him stop. He looked over his shoulder and saw the figure still standing at the end of the galley, as though afraid to enter while the boys were there. Now that they seemed to be gone the figure began to walk towards Father Dorothy, picking its feet up with exaggerated delicacy. Paul stared, entranced.

"Move it, Pathori," Claude called to him; but Paul shook his head and stayed where he was. Father Dorothy had his back to them. One hand was outstretched to the figure. Despite its size—it was taller than Paul, taller than Father Dorothy—there was something fragile and childlike about it. Thin and slightly stooped, with wispy yellow hair like feathers falling onto curved thin shoulders, frail arms crossed across its chest and legs that were so long and frail that he could see why it walked in that awkward tippy-toe manner:

if it fell its legs would snap like chopsticks. It smelled like nothing else on Teichman Station, sweet and powdery and warm. Once, Paul thought, his mother had smelled like that, before she went to stay in the women's quarters. But this thing looked nothing like his mother. As he stared, it slowly lifted its face, until he could see its enormous eyes fixed on him: caramel-colored eyes threaded with gold and black, staring at him with a gaze that was utterly adoring and absolutely witless.

"Paul, come *on!*"

Ira tugged at him until he turned away and stumbled after the others to the dormitory. For a long time afterwards he lay awake, trying to ignore the laughter and muffled sounds coming from the other beds; recalling the creature's golden eyes, its walk, its smell.

At tutorial the next day Father Dorothy said nothing of finding the boys in the galley, nor did he mention his strange companion. Paul yawned behind the time-softened covers of an ancient linguistics text, waiting for Romulus to finish with the monitor so he could begin his lesson. In the front of the room, beneath flickering lamps that cast grey shadows on the dusty floor, Father Dorothy patiently went over a hermeneutics lesson with Ira, who was too stupid to follow his father into the bio-engineering corps, but whose beauty and placid nature guaranteed him a place in the Izakowa priesthood on Miyako Station. Paul stared over his textbook at Ira with his corkscrew curls and dusky skin. He thought of the creature in the galley—its awkwardness, its pallor; the way it had stared at him. But mostly he tried to remember how it smelled. Because on Teichman Station—where they had been breathing the same air for seventeen years, and where even the most common herbs and spices, cinnamon, garlic, pepper, were no longer imported because of the expense to the station's dwindling group of researchers—on Teichman Station everything smelled the same. Everything smelled of despair.

"Father Dorothy."

Paul looked up. A server, one of the few that remained in working order, lurched into the little room, its wheels scraping against the door. Claude snickered and glanced sideways at Paul: the server belonged to Paul's mother, although after her conversion she had declared it shared property amongst all the station women. "Father Dorothy, KlausMaria Dalven asks that her son be sent to her quarters. She wishes to speak with him."

Father Dorothy looked up from the monitor cradled in his hand. He smiled wryly at the ancient server and looked back at Paul.

"Go ahead," he said. Ira gazed enviously as Paul shut his book and slid it into his desk, then followed the server to the women's quarters.

His mother and the other women lived at the far end of the Solar Walk, the only part of Teichman where one could see outside into space and realize that they were, indeed, orbiting the moon and not stuck in some cramped Airbus outside of New Delhi or one of the other quarantined areas Below. The server rolled along a few feet ahead of him, murmuring to itself in an earnest monotone. Paul followed, staring at his feet as a woman passed him. When he heard her leave the Walk he lifted his head and looked outside. A pale glowing smear above one end of the Walk was possibly the moon, more likely one of the station's malfunctioning satellite beacons. The windows were so streaked with dirt that for all Paul knew he might be looking at Earth, or some dingy canister of waste deployed from the galley. He paused to step over to one of the windows. A year before Claude had drawn an obscene figure in the dust along the edge, facing the men's side of the Walk. Paul grinned to himself: it was still there.

"Paul, KlausMaria Dalven asks that you come to her quarters. She wishes to speak with you," the server repeated in its droning voice. Paul sighed and turned from the window. A minute later he crossed the invisible line that separated the rest of Teichman from the women's quarters.

The air was much fresher here—his mother said that came from thinking peaceful thoughts—and the walls were painted a very deep green, which seemed an odd choice of colors but had a soothing effect nonetheless. Someone had painted stars and a crescent moon upon the arched ceiling. Paul had never seen the moon look like that, or stars. His mother explained they were images of power and not meant to resemble the dull shapes one saw on the navgrids.

"Hello, Paul," a woman called softly. Marija Kerényi, who had briefly consorted with his father after Paul's mother had left him. Then, she had been small and pretty, soft-spoken but laughing easily. Just the sort of pliant woman Fritz Pathori liked. But in the space of a few years she had had two children, both girls. This was during an earlier phase of his father's work on the partho-genetic breeders, when human reproductive tissue was too costly to import from Below. Marija never forgave Paul's father for what happened to her daughters. She was still small and pretty, but her expression had sharpened almost to the point of cunning, her hair had grown very long and was pulled back in the same manner as Father Dorothy's. "Your mother is in the Attis Arcade."

"Um, thanks," Paul mumbled. He had half-turned to leave when his mother's throaty voice echoed down the hallway. "Marija, is that him? Send him back—"

"Go ahead, Paul," Marija urged. She laughed as he hurried past her. For an instant her hand touched the top of his thigh, and he nearly stumbled as she stroked him. Her fingers flicked at his trousers and she turned away disdainfully.

His mother stood in a doorway. "Paul, darling. Are you thirsty? Would you like some tea?"

Her voice was deeper than it had been before, *when she was really my mother,* he thought; before the hormonal injections and implants; before Father Dorothy. He still could not help but think of her as *she,* despite her masculine appearance, her throaty voice. "Or—you don't like tea, how about betel?"

"No, thanks."

She looked down at him. Her face was sharper than it had been. Her chin seemed too strong, with its blue shadows fading into her unshaven jaw. She still looked like a woman, but a distinctly mannish one. Seeing her Paul wanted to cry.

"Nothing?" she said, then shrugged and walked inside. He followed her into the arcade.

She didn't look out of place here, as she so often had back in the family chambers. The arcade was a circular room, with a very high ceiling; his mother was very tall. Below, her family had been descended from aristocratic

North Africans whose women prided themselves on their exaggerated height and the purity of their yellow eyes and ebony skin. Paul took after his father, small and fair-skinned, but with his mother's long-fingered hands and a shyness that in KlausMaria was often mistaken for *hauteur*. In their family chambers she had had to stoop, so as not to seem taller than her husband. Here she flopped back comfortably on the sand-covered floor, motioning for Paul to join her.

"Well, *I'm* having some tea. Mawu—"

That was the name she'd given the server after they'd moved to the women's quarters. While he was growing up, Paul had called it Bunny. The robot rolled into the arcade, grinding against the wall and sending up a little puff of rust. "Tea for me and my boy. Sweetened, please."

Paul stood awkwardly, looking around in vain for a chair. Finally he sat down on the floor near his mother, stretching out his legs and brushing sand from his trousers.

"So," he said, clearing his throat. "Hi."

KlausMaria smiled. *"Hi."*

They said nothing else for several minutes. Paul squirmed, trying to keep sand from seeping into his clothes. His mother sat calmly, smiling, until the server returned with tea in small soggy cups already starting to disintegrate. It hadn't been properly mixed. Sipping his, bits of powder got stuck between Paul's teeth.

"Your father has brought an argala here," KlausMaria announced. Her voice was so loud that Paul started, choking on a mouthful of tea and coughing until his eyes watered. His mother only stared at him coolly. "Yesterday. There wasn't supposed to be a drop until Athyr, god knows how he arranged it. Father Dorothy told me. They had him escort it on board, afraid of what would happen if one of the men got hold of it. A sex slave. Absolutely disgusting."

She leaned forward, her long beautiful fingers drumming on the floor. Specks of sand flew in all directions, stinging Paul's cheeks. "Oh," he said, trying to give the sound a rounded adult tone, regretful or disapproving. *So that's what it was,* he thought, and his heart beat faster.

"I wish to god I'd never come here," KlausMaria whispered. "I wish—"

She stopped, her voice rasping into the breathy drone of the air filters. Paul nodded, staring at the floor, letting sand run between his fingers. They sat again in silence. Finally he mumbled, "I didn't know."

His mother let her breath out in a long wheeze; it smelled of betel and bergamot-scented tea powder. "I know." She leaned close to him, her hand on his knee. For a moment it was like when he was younger, before his father had begun working on the Breeders, before Father Dorothy came. "That's why I wanted to tell you, before you heard from—well, from anyone else. Because—well, shit."

She gave a sharp laugh—a real laugh—and Paul smiled, relieved. "It's pathetic, really," she said. Her hand dropped, from his knee to the floor and scooped up fistfuls of fine powder. "Here he was, this brilliant beautiful man. It's destroyed him, the work he's done. I wish you could have known him before, Below—"

She sighed again and reached for her tea, sipped it silently. "But that was before the last Ascension. Those bastards. Too late now. For your father, at least. But Paul," and she leaned forward again and took his hand. "I've made arrangements for you to go to school Below. In Tangier. My mother will pay for it, it's all taken care of. In a few months. It'll be fall then, in Tangier, it will be exciting for you…"

Her voice drifted off, as though she spoke to herself or a server. "An argala. I will go mad."

She sighed and seemed to lose interest in her son, instead staring fixedly at the sand running between her fingers. Paul waited for several more minutes, to see if anything else was forthcoming, but his mother said nothing more. Finally the boy stood, inclined his head to kiss her cheek, and turned to go.

"Paul," his mother called as he hesitated in the doorway.

He turned back: she made the gesture of blessing that the followers of Lysis affected, drawing an exaggerated *S* in the air and blinking rapidly. "Promise me you won't go near it. If he wants you to. Promise."

Paul shrugged. "Sure."

She stared at him, tight-lipped. Then, "Goodbye," she said, and returned to her meditations in the Arcade.

That night in the dormitory he crept to Claude's bunk while the older boy was asleep and carefully felt beneath his mattress, until he found the stack of pamphlets hidden there. The second one he pulled out was the one he wanted. He shoved the others back and fled to his bunk.

He had a nearly new lumiere hidden under his pillow. He withdrew it and shook it until watery yellow light spilled across the pages in front of him. Poor-quality color images, but definitely taken from life. They showed creatures much like the one he had seen the night before. Some were no bigger than children, with tiny pointed breasts and enormous eyes and brilliant red mouths. Others were as tall and slender as the one he had glimpsed. In one of the pictures an argala actually coupled with a naked man, but the rest showed them posing provocatively. They all had the same feathery yellow hair, the same wide mindless eyes and air of utter passivity. In some of the pictures Paul could see their wings, bedraggled and straw-colored. There was nothing even remotely sexually exciting about them.

Paul could only assume this was something he might feel differently about, someday. After all, his father had been happy with his mother once, although that of course was before Paul was born, before his father began his work on the Breeders Project. The first generations of geneslaves had been developed a century earlier on Earth. Originally they had been designed to toil in the lunar colonies and on Earth's vast hydrofarms. But the reactionary gender policies of the current Ascendant administration suggested that there were other uses to which the geneslaves might be put.

Fritz Pathori had been a brilliant geneticist, with impressive ties to the present administration. Below, he had developed the prototype for the argala, a gormless creature that the Ascendants hoped would make human prostitution obsolete—though it was not the act itself the Ascendants objected to, so much as the active involvement of women. And at first the women had welcomed the argalæ. But that was before the femicides; before the success of the argalæ led Fritz Pathori to develop the first Breeders.

He had been an ethical man, once. Even now, Paul knew that it was the pressures of conscience that drove his father to the neural sauna. Because now, of course, his father could not stop the course of his research. He had tried, years before. That was how they had ended up exiled to Teichman Station, where Pathori and his staff had for many years lived in a state of house arrest, part of the dismal constellation of space stations drifting through the heavens and falling wearily and irretrievably into madness and decay.

A shaft of light flicked through the dormitory and settled upon Paul's head. The boy dove beneath the covers, shoving the pamphlet into the crack between bedstand and mattress.

"Paul." Father Dorothy's whispered voice was surprised, shaming without being angry. The boy let his breath out and peered up at his tutor, clad in an elegant grey kimono, his long iron-colored hair unbound and falling to his shoulders. "What are you doing? What do you have there—"

His hand went unerringly to where Paul had hidden the pamphlet. The shaft of light danced across the yellowed pages, and the pamphlet disappeared into a kimono pocket.

"Mmm." His tutor sounded upset. "Tomorrow I want to see you before class. Don't forget."

His face burning, Paul listened as the man's footsteps padded away again. A minute later he gave a muffled cry as someone jumped on top of him.

"You idiot! Now he *knows*—"

And much of the rest of the night was given over to the plebeian torments of Claude.

He knew he looked terrible the next morning, when, still rubbing his eyes, he shuffled into Father Dorothy's chamber.

"Oh dear." The tutor shook his head and smiled ruefully. "Not much sleep, I would imagine. Claude?"

Paul nodded.

"Would you like some coffee?"

Paul started to refuse politely, then saw that Father Dorothy had what looked like real coffee, in a small metal tin stamped with Arabic letters in gold and brown. "Yes, please," he nodded, and watched entranced as the tutor scooped it into a silver salver and poured boiling water over it.

"Now then," Father Dorothy said a few minutes later. He indicated a chair, its cushions ballooning over its metal arms, and Paul sank gratefully into it, cupping his bowl of coffee. "This is all about the argala, isn't it?"

Paul sighed. "Yes."

"I thought so." Father Dorothy sipped his coffee and glanced at the gravure of Father Sofia, founder of the Mysteries, staring myopically from the curved wall. "I imagine your mother is rather distressed—?"

"I guess so. I mean, she seems angry, but she always seems angry."

Father Dorothy sighed. "This exile is particularly difficult for a person as brilliant as your mother. And this—" he pointed delicately at the pamphlet, sitting like an uninvited guest on a chair of its own. "This argala must be very hard for KlausMaria to take. I find it disturbing and rather sad, but considering your father's part in developing these—things—my guess would be that your mother finds it, um, *repellent*—?"

Paul was still staring at the pamphlet; it lay open at one of the pages he hadn't yet gotten to the night before. "Uh—um, oh yes, yes, she's pretty mad," he mumbled hastily, when he saw Father Dorothy staring at him.

The tutor swallowed the rest of his coffee. Then he stood and paced to the chair where the pamphlet lay, picked it up and thumbed through it dismissively, though not without a certain curiosity.

"You know it's not a real woman, right? That's part of what's *wrong* with it, Paul—not what's wrong with the thing itself, but with the act, with—well, *everything*. It's a geneslave, it can't enter into any sort of—relations—with anyone of its own free will. It's a—well, it's like a machine, except of course it's *alive*. But it has no thoughts of its own. They're like children, you see, only incapable of thought, or language. Although of course we have no idea what other things they *can* do—strangle us in our sleep or drive us mad.

They're incapable of ever learning, or loving. They can't suffer or feel pain or, well, *anything*—"

Father Dorothy's face had grown red, not from embarrassment, as Paul first thought, but from anger—real fury, the boy saw, and he sank back into his chair, a little afraid himself now.

"—institutionalized rape, it's exactly what Sofia said would happen, why she said we should start to protect ourselves—"

Paul shook his head. "But—wouldn't it, I mean wouldn't it be easier? For women: if they used the geneslaves, then they'd leave the women alone..."

Father Dorothy held the pamphlet open, to a picture showing an argala with its head thrown back. His face as he turned to Paul was still angry, but disappointed now as well. And Paul realized there was something he had missed, some lesson he had failed to learn during all these years of Father Dorothy's tutelage.

"That's right," his tutor said softly. He looked down at the pamphlet between his fingers, the slightly soiled image with its gasping mouth and huge, empty eyes. He looked sad, and Paul's eyes flickered down from Father Dorothy's face to that of the argala in the picture. It looked very little like the one he had seen, really; but suddenly he was flooded with yearning, an overwhelming desire to see it again, to touch it and breathe again that warm scent, that smell of blue water and real sand and warm flesh pressed against cool cotton. The thought of seeing it excited him, and even though he knew Father Dorothy couldn't see anything (Paul was wearing one of his father's old robes, much too too big for him), Father Dorothy must have understood, because in the next instant the pamphlet was out of sight, squirrelled into a cubbyhole of his ancient steel desk.

"That's enough, then," he said roughly. And gazing at his tormented face Paul thought of what the man had done, to become an initiate into the Mysteries; and he knew then that he would never be able to understand anything his tutor wanted him to learn.

"It's in there now, with your father! I saw it go in—"

Ira's face was flushed, his hair tangled from running. Claude and Paul sat together on Claude's bunk poring over another pamphlet, a temporary truce having been effected by this new shared interest.

"My father?" Paul said stupidly. He felt flushed, and cross at Ira for interrupting his reverie.

"The argala! It's in there with him now. If we go we can listen at the door—everyone else is still at dinner."

Claude closed the pamphlet and slipped it beneath his pillow. He nodded, slowly, then reached out and touched Ira's curls. "Let's go, then," he said.

Fritz Pathori's quarters were on the research deck. The boys reached them by climbing the spiral stairs leading up to the second level, speaking in whispers even though there was little chance of anyone seeing them there, or caring if they did. Midway up the steps Paul could see his father's chambers, across the open area that had once held several anaglyphic sculptures. The sculptures had long since been destroyed, in one of the nearly ritualized bouts of violence that periodically swept through the station. Now his father's balcony commanded a view of a narrow concrete space, swept clean of rubble but nonetheless hung about with a vague odor of neglect and disrepair.

When they reached the hallway leading to the chief geneticist's room the boys grew quiet.

"You never come up here?" Claude asked. For once there was no mockery in his voice.

Paul shrugged. "Sometimes. Not in a while, though."

"I'd be here all the time," Ira whispered. He looked the most impressed, stooping to rub the worn but still lush carpeting and then tilting his head to flash a quick smile at himself in the polished metal walls.

"My father is always busy," said Paul. He stopped in front of the door to his father's chambers, smooth and polished as the walls, marked only by the small onyx inlay with his father's name engraved upon it. He tried to remember the last time he'd been here—early autime, or perhaps it had been as long ago as last Mestris.

"Can you hear anything?" Claude pushed Ira aside and pressed close to the door. Paul felt a dart of alarm.

"I do," whispered Ira excitedly. "I hear them—listen—"

They crouched at the door, Paul in the middle. He *could* hear something, very faintly. Voices: his father's, and something like an echo of it, soft and soothing. His father was groaning—Paul's heart clenched in his chest but he felt no embarrassment, nothing but a kind of icy disdain—and the other voice was cooing, an almost perfect echo of the deeper tone, but two octaves higher. Paul pressed closer to the wall, feeling the cool metal against his cheek.

For several more minutes they listened, Paul silent and impassive, Claude snickering and making jerking motions with his hands, Ira with pale blue eyes growing wide. Then suddenly it was quiet behind the door. Paul looked up, startled: there had been no terminal cries, none of the effusive sounds he had heard were associated with this sort of thing. Only a silence that was oddly furtive and sad, falling as it did upon three pairs of disappointed ears.

"What happened?" Ira looked distressed. "Are they all right?"

"Of course they're all right," Claude hissed. He started to his feet, tugging Ira after him. "They're finished, is all—come on, let's get out of here—"

Claude ran down the hall with Ira behind him. Paul remained crouched beside the door, ignoring the other boys as they waved for him to follow.

And then before he could move the door opened. He looked up and through it and saw his father at the far end of the room, standing with his back to the door. From the spiral stairs Claude's voice echoed furiously.

Paul staggered to his feet. He was just turning to flee when something moved from the room into the hall, cutting off his view of his father; something that stood teetering on absurdly long legs, a confused expression on its face. The door slid closed behind it, and he was alone with the argala.

"Oh," he whispered, and shrank against the wall.

"O," the argala murmured.

Its voice was like its scent, warm yet somehow diffuse. If the hallway had been dark, it would have been difficult to tell where the sound came from. But it was not dark, and Paul couldn't take his eyes from it.

"It's all right," he whispered. Tentatively he reached for it. The argala stepped towards him, its frail arms raised in an embrace. He started, then slowly let it enfold him. Its voice echoed his own, childlike and trusting.

It was irresistible, the smell and shape of it, the touch of its wispy hair upon his cheeks. He opened his eyes and for the first time got a good look at its face, so close to his that he drew back a little to see it better. A face that was somehow, indefinably, female. Like a child's drawing of a woman: enormous eyes surrounded by lashes that were spare but thick and straight. A round mouth, tangerine-colored, like something one would want to eat. Hair that was more like feathers curled about its face. Paul took a tendril between his fingers, pulled it to his cheek and stroked his chin with agonizing slowness.

His mother had told him once that the argalæ were engineered from human women and birds, storks or cranes the boy thought, or maybe some kind of white duck. Paul had thought this absurd, but now it seemed it could be true—the creature's hair looked and felt more like long downy filaments than human hair, or fur. And there was something birdlike about the way it felt in his arms: fragile but at the same time tensile, and strong, as though its bones were lighter than human bones, filled with air or even some other element. Paul had never seen a real bird. He knew they were supposed to be lovely, avatars of physical beauty of a certain type, and that their power of flight imbued them with a kind of miraculous appeal, at least to people Below. His mother said people thought that way about women once. Perhaps some of them still did.

He could not imagine any bird, anything at all, more beautiful or miraculous than this geneslave.

Even as he held it to his breast, its presence woke in him a terrible longing, a yearning for something he could scarcely fathom—open skies, the feel of running water beneath his bare feet. Images flooded his mind, things he had only ever seen in files of old movies. Small houses made of wood, clouds skidding across a sky the color of Ira Claire's eyes, cream-colored flowers climbing a trellis beside a green field. As the pictures fled across his mind's eye his heart pounded: *where did they come from?* Sensations spilled into him, as though they had been contained in too shallow a vessel and had nowhere else to pour but into whomever the thing touched. And then those first images slid away, the white porch and cracked concrete and saline taste—bitter yet comforting—of tears running into his mouth. Instead he felt dizzy. He reached out and his hands struck at the air feebly. Something seemed to move at his feet. He looked down and saw ripples like water, and something tiny and bright moving there. A feeling stabbed at him, a hunger so sharp it was like love; and suddenly he saw clearly what the thing was—a tiny creature like a scarlet salamander, creeping across a mossy bank. But before he could stoop to savage it with his beak *(his beak?)*, with a sickening rush the floor beneath him dropped, and there was only sky, white and grey, and wind raking at his face; and above all else that smell, filling his nostrils like pollen: the smell of water, of freedom.

Then it was gone. He fell back against the wall, gasping. When he opened his eyes he felt nauseated, but that passed almost immediately. He focused on the argala staring at him, its eyes wide and golden and with the same adoring gaze it had fixed on him before. Behind it his father stood in the open doorway to his room.

"Paul," he exclaimed brightly. He skinned a hand across his forehead and smiled, showing where he'd lost a tooth since the last time they'd met. "You found it—I wondered where it went. Come on, you!—"

He reached for the argala and it went to him, easily. "Turned around and it was gone!" His father shook his head, still grinning, and hugged the argala to his side. He was naked, not even a towel draped around him. Paul looked away. From his father's even, somewhat muffled, tone he could tell that he'd recently come from the neural sauna. "They told me not to let it out of my sight, said it would go sniffing after anyone, and they were right…"

As suddenly as he'd appeared he was gone, the metal door flowing shut behind him. For one last instant Paul could see the argala, turning its glowing eyes from his father to himself and back again, lovely and gormless as one of those simulacrums that directed travellers in the HORUS by-ports. Then it was only his own reflection that he stared at, and Claude's voice that he heard calling softly but insistently from the foot of the spiral stairs.

He had planned to wait after class the following morning, to ask Father Dorothy what he knew about it, how a mindless creature could project such a powerful and seemingly effortless torrent of images and sensations; but he could tell from his tutor's cool smile that somehow he had gotten word of their spying. Ira, probably. He was well-meaning but tactless, and Father Dorothy's favorite. Some whispered conference during their private session; and now Father Dorothy's usual expression, of perpetual disappointment tempered with ennui, was shaded with a sharper anger.

So *that* was pointless. Paul could scarcely keep still during class, fidgeting behind his desiccated textbooks, hardly glancing at the monitor's ruby scroll of words and numerals when his turn came to use it. He did take a few minutes to sneak to the back of the room. There a huge and indescribably ancient wooden bookcase held a very few, mostly useless volumes—*Reader's Digest Complete Do-It-Yourself Manual, Robert's Rules of Order, The Ascent of Woman.* He pulled out a natural history text so old that its contents had long since acquired the status of myth.

Argala, Paul read, after flipping past *Aptéryx, Aquilegia, Archer, Areca,* each page releasing its whiff of Earth, mildew and silverfish and trees turned to dust. *Adjutant bird: Giant Indian Stork, living primarily in wetlands and feeding upon crustaceans and small amphibians. Status, endangered; perhaps extinct.* There was no illustration.

"Hey, Pathori." Claude bent over his shoulder, pretending to ask a question. Paul ignored him and turned the pages, skipping *Boreal Squid* and *(Bruijn's) Echidna,* pausing to glance at the garishly colored Nebalia Shrimp and the shining damp skin of the Newt, *Amphibian: A kind of eft (Juvenile salamander).* Finally he found the Stork, a simple illustration beside it.

Tall stately wading bird of family Ciconiidae, *the best-known species pure white except for black wing tips, long reddish bill, and red feet, and in the nursery the pretended bringer of babies and good fortune.*

"...you *hear* me?" Claude whispered hoarsely, pinching his ear. Paul closed the book and pushed it away. Without a word he returned to his desk, Claude following him. Father Dorothy raised his head, then went back to explaining the subtleties of written poetry to Ira Claire. Paul settled into his seat. Behind him Claude stood and waited for their tutor to resume his recitation. In a moment Father Dorothy's boyish voice echoed back to them—

"'...I make out a few words—

then again "TEARS,"

It seems to me that Leucis

..."SORROW,"

and "WE HIS FRIENDS MOURN."

must have been dearly beloved...'."

Paul started as Claude shook him, and the older boy repeated, "I have an idea—I bet he just leaves it alone, when he's not in the room. We could get in there, maybe, and sneak it out..."

Paul shrugged. He had been thinking the same thing himself; thinking how he would never have the nerve to do it alone. He glanced up at Father Dorothy.

If he looks at me now, he thought, *I won't do it; I'll talk to him later and figure out something else...*

Behind him Claude hissed and elbowed him sharply. Paul waited, willing their tutor to look up; but the man's head pressed closer to his lovely student as he recited yet another elegiac fragment, wasted on the hopeless Ira—

"'A poet said, "That music is beloved that cannot be sounded."

And I think that the choicest life

is the life that cannot be lived.'"

"*Paul!*"

Paul turned and looked at Claude. "We could go when the rest are at dinner again," the older boy said. He too gazed at Ira and Father Dorothy, but with loathing. "All right?"

"All right," Paul agreed miserably, and lowered his head when Father Dorothy cast him a disapproving stare.

Trudging up the steps behind Claude, Paul looked back at the narrow plaza where the sculptures had been. They had passed three people on their way here, a man and two women; the women striding in that defiant way they had, almost swaggering, Paul thought. It was not until they turned the corner that he realized the man had been his mother, and she had not acknowledged him, had not seen him at all.

He sighed and looked down into the abandoned courtyard. Something glittered there, like a fleck of bright dust swimming across his vision. He paused, his hand sliding along the cool brass banister.

On the concrete floor he thought he saw something red, like a discarded blossom. But there were no flowers on Teichman. He felt again that rush of emotion that had come when he embraced the argala, a desire somehow tangled with the smell of brackish water and the sight of a tiny salamander squirming on a mossy bank. But when he leaned over the banister there was nothing there. It must have been a trick of the light, or perhaps a scrap of paper or other debris blow by the air filters. He straightened and started back up the stairs.

That was when he saw the argala. Framed on the open balcony in his father's room, looking down upon the little courtyard. It looked strange from this distance and this angle: less like a woman and more like the somber figure that had illustrated the Stork in the natural history book. Its foot rested on the edge of the balcony, so it seemed that it had only one leg, and the way its head was tilted he saw only the narrow raised crown, nearly bald because its wispy hair had been pulled back. From here it looked too bony, hardly female at all. A small flood of nausea raced through him. For the first time it struck him that this really *was* an alien creature. Another of the Ascendants' monstrous toys, like the mouthless hydrapithecenes that tended the Pacific hydrofarms, or the pallid bloated forms floating in vats on the research deck of Teichman Station, countless fetuses tethered to them by transparent umbilical cords. And now he had seen and touched one of those monsters. He shuddered and turned away, hurrying after Claude.

But once he stood in the hallway his nausea and anger faded. There was that scent again, lulling him into seeing calm blue water and myriad shapes, garnet salamanders and frogs like candied fruit drifting across the floor. He stumbled into Claude, the older boy swearing and drawing a hand across his face.

"Shit! What's that smell?—" But the older boy's tone was not unpleasant, only befuddled and slightly dreamy.

"The thing," said Paul. They stood before the door to his father's room. "The argala..."

Claude nodded, swaying a little, his dark hair hiding his face. Paul had an awful flash of his father opening the door and Claude seeing him as Paul had, naked and doped, with that idiot smile and a tooth missing. But then surely the argala would not have been out on the balcony by itself? He reached for the door and very gently pushed it.

"Here we go," Claude announced as the door slid open. In a moment they stood safely inside.

"God, this is a mess." Claude looked around admiringly. He flicked at a stack of 'files teetering on the edge of a table, grimaced at the puff of dust that rose around his finger. "Ugh. Doesn't he have a server?"

"I guess not." Paul stepped gingerly around heaps of clothes, clean and filthy piled separately, and eyed with distaste a clutter of empty morpha tubes and wine jellies in a corner. A monitor flickered on a table, rows of numerals and gravid shapes tracing the progress of the Breeders Project.

"*Not*," a voice trilled. On the balcony the argala did not turn, but its bright tone, the way its vestigial wings shivered, seemed to indicate some kind of greeting.

"All right. Let's see it—"

Claude shoved past him, grinning. Paul looked over and for a second the argala's expression was not so much idiotic as tranquil; as though instead of a gritty balcony overlooking shattered concrete, it saw what he had imagined before, water and wriggling live things.

"*Unh.*"

Claude's tone abruptly changed. Paul couldn't help but look: the tenor of the other boy's lust was so intense it sounded like pain. He had his arms around the argala and was thrusting at it, his trousers askew. In his embrace the creature stood with its head thrown back, its cries so rhapsodic that Paul groaned himself and turned away.

In a minute it was over. Claude staggered back, pulling at his clothes and looking around almost frantically for Paul.

"God, that was incredible, that was the *best*—"

Like what could you compare it to, you idiot? Paul leaned against the table with the monitor and tapped a few keys angrily, hoping he'd screw up something; but the scroll continued uninterrupted. Claude walked, dazed, to a chair and slouched into it, scooped up a half-full wine jelly from the floor and sucked at it hungrily.

"Go on, Pathori, you don't want to miss *that!*" Claude laughed delightedly, and looked at the argala. "God, it's amazing, isn't it? What a beauty." His eyes were dewy as he shook his head. "What a fucking thing."

Without answering Paul crossed the room to the balcony. The argala seemed to have forgotten all about them. It stood with one leg drawn up, staring down at the empty courtyard, its topaz eyes glittering. As he drew near to it its smell overwhelmed him, a muskier scent now, almost fetid, like water that had stood too long in an open storage vessel. He felt infuriated by its utter passivity, but somehow excited, too. Before he knew what he was doing he had grabbed it, just as Claude had, and pulled it to him so that its bland child's face looked up at him rapturously.

Afterwards he wept, and beside him the argala crooned, mimicking his sobs. He could dimly hear Claude saying something about leaving, then his friend's voice rising and finally the *snick* of the door sliding open and shut. He grit his teeth and willed his tears to stop. The argala nestled against him, silent now. His fingers drifted through its thin hair, ran down its back to feel its wings, the bones like metal struts beneath the breath of down. What could a bird possibly know about what he was feeling? he thought fiercely. Let alone a monster like this. A real woman would talk to you, afterwards.

To *complain,* he imagined his father saying.

...never enjoyed it, ever, his mother's voice echoed back, and Father Dorothy's intoned, *That's what's wrong with it, it's like a machine.*

He pulled the argala closer to him and shut his eyes, inhaling deeply. A wash of yellow that he knew must be sunlight: then he saw that ghostly image of a house again, heard faint cries of laughter. Because it was a woman, too, of course; otherwise how could it recall a house, and children? but then the house broke up into motes of light without color, and he felt the touch of that other, alien mind, delicate and keen as a bird's long bill, probing at his own.

"Well! Good afternoon, good afternoon…"

He jumped. His father swayed in the doorway, grinning. "Found my little friend again. Well, come in, come in."

Paul let go of the argala and took a few unsteady steps. "Dad—I'm sorry, I—"

"God, no. Stop." His father waved, knocking a bottle to the floor. "Stay, why don't you. A minute."

But Paul had a horrible flash, saw the argala taken again, the third time in what, half an hour? He shook his head and hurried to the door, face down.

"I can't, Dad. I'm sorry—I was just going by, that's all—"

"Sure, Sure." His father beamed. Without looking he pulled a wine jelly from a shelf and squeezed it into his mouth. "Come by when you have more time, Paul. Glad to see you."

He started to cross to where the argala gazed at him, its huge eyes glowing. Paul ran from the room, the door closing behind him with a muted sigh.

At breakfast the next morning he was surprised to find his mother and Father Dorothy sitting in the twins' usual seats.

"We were talking about your going to school in Tangier," his mother announced, her deep voice a little too loud for the cramped dining hall as she turned back to Father Dorothy. "We could never meet the quotas, of course, but Mother pulled some strings, and—"

Paul sat next to her. Across the table, Claude and Ira and the twins were gulping down the rest of their breakfast. Claude mumbled a goodbye and stood to leave, Ira behind him.

"See you later, Father," Ira said, smiling. Father Dorothy waved.

"When?" said Paul.

"In a few weeks. It's nearly Athyr now"—that was what they called this cycle—"…which means it's July down there. The next drop is on the Fortieth."

He didn't pay much attention to the rest of it. There was no point: his mother and Father Dorothy had already decided everything, as they always did. He wondered how his father had ever been able to get the argala here at all.

A hand clamped his shoulder and Paul looked up.

"—must go now," Father Dorothy was saying as he motioned for a server to clean up. "Class starts in a few minutes. Walk with me, Paul?"

He shook his mother's hand and left her nodding politely as the next shift of diners filed into the little room.

"You've been with it," the tutor said after a few minutes. They took the long way to the classroom, past the cylinders where vats of nutriment were stored and wastewater recycled, past the spiral stairs that led to his father's chamber. Where the hallway forked Father Dorothy hesitated, then went to the left, towards the women's quarters. "I could tell, you know—it has a—"

He inhaled, then made a delicate grimace. "It has a smell."

They turned and entered the Solar Walk. Paul remained at his side, biting his lip and feeling an unexpected anger churning inside him.

"I like the way it smells," he said, and waited for Father Dorothy to look grim. Instead his tutor paused in front of the window. "I love it."

He thought Father Dorothy would retort sharply; but instead he only raised his hands and pressed them against the window. Outside two of the HORUS repair units floated past, on their interminable and futile rounds. When it seemed the silence would go on forever, his tutor said, "It can't love you. You know that. It's an abomination—an animal—"

"Not really," Paul replied, but weakly.

Father Dorothy flexed his hands dismissively. "It can't love you. It's a geneslave. How could it love anything?"

His tone was not angry but questioning, as though he really thought Paul might have an answer. And for a moment Paul thought of explaining to him: about how it felt, how it seemed like it was showing him things—the sky, the house, the little creatures crawling in the moss—things that perhaps it *did* feel something for. But before he could say anything Father Dorothy turned and began striding back in the direction they'd come. Paul hurried after him in silence.

As they turned down the last hallway, Father Dorothy said, "It's an ethical matter, really. Like having intercourse with a child, or someone who's mentally deficient. It can't respond, it's incapable of anything—"

"But I love it," Paul repeated stubbornly.

"Aren't you listening to me?" Father Dorothy did sound angry, now. "*It* can't love *you*." His voice rose shrilly. "How could something like *that* tell you that it *loved* you!? And *you* can't love it—god, how could you love *anything,* you're only a boy!" He stopped in the doorway and looked down at him, then shook his head, in pity or disgust Paul couldn't tell. "Get in there," Father Dorothy said at last, and gently pushed him through the door.

He waited until the others were asleep before slipping from his bunk and heading back to his father's quarters. The lights had dimmed to simulate night; other than that there was no difference, in the way anything looked or smelled or sounded. He walked through the violet corridors with one hand on the cool metal wall, as though he was afraid of falling.

They were leaving just as he reached the top of the spiral stairs. He saw his father first, then two others, other researchers from the Breeders Project. They were laughing softly, and his father threw his arms around one man's shoulders and murmured something that made the other man shake his head and grin. They wore loose robes open in the front and headed in the opposite direction, towards the neural sauna. They didn't see the boy pressed against the wall, watching as they turned the corner and disappeared.

He waited for a long time. He wanted to cry, tried to make himself cry; but he couldn't. Beneath his anger and shame and sadness there was still too much of that other feeling, the anticipation and arousal and inchoate tenderness that he only knew one word for, and Father Dorothy thought that was absurd. So he waited until he couldn't stand it anymore, and went inside.

His father had made some feeble attempt to clean the place up. The clothing had been put away, and table tops and chairs cleared of papers. Fine white ash sifted across the floor, and there was a musty smell of tobacco beneath the stronger odors of semen and wine jelly. The argala's scent ran through all of it like a fresh wind.

He left the door open behind him, no longer caring if someone found him there or not. He ran his hands across his eyes and looked around for the argala.

It was standing where it usually did, poised on the balcony with its back to him. He took a step, stopped. He thought he could hear something, a very faint sound like humming; but then it was gone. He craned his neck to see what it was the creature looked at but saw nothing; only that phantom flicker of red in the corner of his eye, like a mote of ruby dust. He began walking again, softly, when the argala turned to look at him.

Its eyes were wide and fervent as ever, its tangerine mouth spun into that same adoring smile; but even as he started for it, his arms reaching to embrace it, it turned from him and jumped.

For an instant it hung in the air and he could imagine it flying, could almost imagine that perhaps it thought its wings would carry it across the courtyard or safely to the ground. But in that instant he caught sight of its eyes, and they were not a bird's eyes but a woman's; and she was not flying but falling.

He must have cried out, screamed for help. Then he just hung over the balcony, staring down at where it lay motionless. He kept hoping that maybe it would move again but it did not, only lay there twisted and still.

But as he stared at it it changed. It had been a pale creature to begin with. Now what little color it had was leached away, as though it were bleeding into the concrete; but really there was hardly any blood. Its feathers grew limp, like fronds plucked from the water, their gold fading to a grey that was all but colorless. Its head was turned sideways, its great wide eye open and staring up. As he watched the golden orb slowly dulled to yellow and then a dirty white. When someone finally came to drag it away its feathers trailed behind it in the dust. Then nothing remained of it at all except for the faintest breath of ancient summers hanging in the stale air.

For several days he wouldn't speak to anyone, not even responding to Claude's cruelties or his father's ineffectual attempts at kindness. His mother made a few calls to Tangier and, somehow, the drop was changed to an earlier date in Athyr. On the afternoon he was to leave they all gathered, awkwardly, in the dormitory. Father Dorothy seemed sad that he was going, but also relieved. The twins tried to get him to promise to write, and Ira cried. But, still without speaking, Paul left the room and walked down to the courtyard.

No one had even bothered to clean it. A tiny curl of blood stained the concrete a rusty color, and he found a feather, more like a furry yellowish thread than anything else, stuck to the wall. He took the feather and stared at it, brought it to his face and inhaled. There was nothing.

He turned to leave, then halted. At the corner of his eye something moved. He looked back and saw a spot on the ground directly beneath his father's balcony. Shoving the feather into his pocket he walked slowly to investigate.

In the dust something tiny wriggled, a fluid arabesque as long as his finger. Crouching on his heels, he bent over and cupped it in his palm. A shape like an elongated tear of blood, only with two bright black dots that were its eyes and, beside each of those, two perfect flecks of gold.

An eft, he thought, recognizing it from the natural history book and from the argala's vision. A juvenile salamander.

Giant Indian stork, feeding upon crustaceans and small amphibians.

He raised it to his face, feeling it like a drop of water slithering through his fingers. When he sniffed it it smelled, very faintly, of mud.

There was no way it could have gotten here. Animals never got through by-port customs, and besides, were there even things like this still alive, Below? He didn't know.

But then how did it get here?

A miracle, he thought, and heard Father Dorothy's derisive voice— *How could something like that tell you that it loved you?* For the first time since the argala's death, the rage and despair that had clenched inside him uncoiled. He moved his hand, to see it better, and with one finger stroked its back. Beneath its skin, scarlet and translucent, its ribs moved rapidly in and out, in and out, so fine and frail they might have been drawn with a hair.

An eft.

He knew it would not live for very long—what could he feed it, how could he keep it?—but somehow the argala had survived, for a little while at least, and even then the manner of its dying had been a miracle of sorts. Paul stood, his hands folding over the tiny creature, and with his head bowed—though none of them would really see, or understand, what it was he carried—he walked up the stairs and through the hallway and back into the dormitory where his bags waited, past the other boys, past his mother and father and Father Dorothy, not saying anything, not even looking at them; holding close against his chest a secret, a miracle, a salamander.

Note by Elizabeth Hand about the story:

I wrote this amidst my first three novels and wanted to use their milieu as a backdrop. Connie Willis's "All My Darling Daughters" has a nice space station setting, which also seemed like a good idea: I liked the notion of an insular culture giving birth to its own sexual depravities, which over time would come to be considered normal. The rest was just spun out of the fictional history of my novels' Ascendants and their geneslaves.

Cavafy's work has seen me through four novels, now, and innumerable stories; the title of this one was taken from his poem of the same name. In the ancient Egyptian calendar, Athyr is the month which corresponds roughly to our October, the traditional time to honor the dead.

IN THE MONTH OF ATHYR

Elizabeth Hand's "In the Month of Athyr" has always been one of my favorite of her stories. Alien and sexual and disturbing, it's not for nothing I drifted into editing horror, as even my science fiction choices are often downbeat. Liz's story is one of those. The novelette was originally in *Omni Best Science Fiction Two* and was published in 1992. Check out her afterword for influences.

Precious

by Nalo Hopkinson

(From *Silver Birch, Blood Moon,* 1999)

I stopped singing in the shower. I kept having to call the plumber to remove flakes of gold and rotted lilies from the clogged drain. On the phone I would say that I was calling for my poor darling cousin, the one struck dumb by a stroke at an early age. As I spoke, I would hold a cup to my chin to catch the pennies that rolled off my tongue. I would give my own address. If the plumber thought it odd that anyone could manage to spill her jewelry box into the bathtub, and not just once, he was too embarrassed to try to speak to the mute lady. I'm not sure what he thought about the lilies. When he was done, I would scribble my thanks onto a scrap of paper and tip him with a gold nugget.

I used to talk to myself when I was alone, until the day I slipped on an opal that had tumbled from my lips and fractured my elbow in the fall. At the impact, my cry of pain spat a diamond the size of an egg across the room, where it rolled under the couch. I pulled myself to my feet and called an ambulance. My sobs fell as bitter milkweed blossoms. I hated to let the flowers die. Holding my injured arm close to my body, I clumsily filled a drinking glass with water from the kitchen and stuck the pink clusters into it.

The pain in my elbow made me whimper. Quartz crystals formed on my tongue with each sound, soft as pudding in the first instance, but gems always hardened before I could spit them out. The facets abraded my gums as they slipped past my teeth. By the time the ambulance arrived, I had collected hundreds of agonized whimpers into a bowl I had fetched from the kitchen. During the jolting ride to the hospital, I nearly bit through my lip with the effort of making no sound. The few grunts that escaped me rolled onto the pillow as silver coins. "Ma'am," said a paramedic, "you've dropped your change. I'll just put it into your purse for you." The anesthetic in the emergency room was a greater mercy than the doctors could imagine. I went home as soon as they would allow.

My father often told me that a soft answer would turn away wrath. As a young woman I took his words to heart, tried to lull my stepmother with agreeableness, dull the edge of her taunts with a soft reply. I went cheerfully about my chores and smiled till my teeth ached when she had me do her daughter, Cass's, work too. I pretended that it didn't burn at my gut to see mother and daughter smirking as I scrubbed. I always tried to be pleasant, and so of course I was pleasant when Cass and I met the old woman while we were shopping that day. She was thirsty, she said, so I fetched her the drink of water, although she seemed spry enough to run her own errands. Cass told her as much, scorn in her voice as she derided my instant obedience.

Sometimes I wonder whether that old woman wasn't having a cruel game with both of us, my sister and me. I got a blessing in return for a kind word, Cassie a curse as payment for a harsh one. That's how it seemed then, but did the old lady know that I would come to fear attention almost as much as Cass feared slithering things? I believe I would rather taste the muscled length and cool scales of a snake in my mouth, sliding headfirst from my lips, than look once more into the greedy gaze of my banker when I bring him another shoebox crammed with jeweled phrases, silver sentences, and the rare pearl of laughter.

Jude used to make a game of surprising different sounds from me, to see what wealth would leap from my mouth. He was playful then, and kind, the husband who rescued me from my stepmother's greed and wrath. My father's eyes were sad when we drove away, but he only waved.

Jude could make me smile, but he preferred it when I laughed out loud, raining him with wealth. A game of tickle would summon strings of pearls that gleamed as they fell at our feet. Once, a pinch on my bottom rewarded him with a turquoise nugget. He had it strung on a leather thong, which he wore around his neck.

But it was the cries and groans of our lovemaking that he liked best. He would stroke and tongue me for hours, lick and kiss me where I enjoyed it most, thrust into me deeper with each wail of pleasure until, covered in the fragrance of crushed lily petals, we had no strength for more. Afterward he would collect sapphires and jade, silver love knots and gold doubloons, from the folds of the sheets. "I don't even need to bring you flowers," he would joke. "You speak better blossoms for yourself than I can ever buy."

Soon, however, my marriage began to sour. Jude's love-bites became painful nips that broke my skin and forced diamonds past my teeth. He often tried to scare me, hiding in the closet so that I shrieked when he leapt out, grains of white gold spilling from my mouth. One night he put a dead rat in the kitchen sink. I found it in the morning, and platinum rods clattered to the ground as I screamed. I begged him to be kind, but he only growled that we needed more money, that our investments weren't doing well. I could hear him on the phone late at night, pleading for more time to pay his debts. Often he came home with the smell of liquor on his breath. I grew nervous and quiet. Once he chided me for keeping silent, not holding up my part of the marriage, and I began to sob, withered tulips plummeting down.

"Bitch!" he shouted. "I need more gold, not your damned flowers!" The backhand across my mouth drew blood, but along with two cracked teeth, I spat out sapphires.

From then on, such beatings happened often. It was eight months later—when Jude broke my arm—that I left, taking nothing with me. I moved to a different city. My phone number is unlisted now. I pay all my bills at my bank, not through the mail. A high fence surrounds my house, and the gate is always locked.

Since I have no need to work, my time is my own. I search the folklore databases of libraries all over the world, looking for a spell that will reach the old woman. When I find her, I will beg her to take back her gift, her curse.

My stepmother will not say it, but Cassie is mad, driven to it by the bats and spiders wriggling from her mouth. It's good that her mother loves and cares for her out on that farm, because all she does is sit and rock and mutter curses, birthing an endless stream of lizards and greasy toads. "It keeps the snakes fed," my stepmother sighs when she calls with sour thanks for her monthly check. "That way they're not biting us." The mother and father who loved me are both long dead, but my stepmother still lives.

When the phone rang, I thought it was her, calling to complain about slugs in her lettuce.

"Hello?" I spat out a nasturtium.

"Precious. It is you." Jude's voice was honey dripped over steel. "Why have you been hiding, love?"

I clamped my lips together. I would not give him my words. I listened, though. I always listened to Jude.

"You don't have to answer, Princess. I can see you quite clearly from here. You must have wanted me to find you, leaving the back curtains open like that. And the lock on that gate wouldn't keep an imbecile out."

"Jude, go away, or I'll call the police." Deadly nightshade fell from my lips. I paused to spit out the poisonous sap. There was a crash in the living room as Jude came through the sliding back doors. He dropped the cell phone and the heavy mallet he carried when he stepped through the ruined glass. Petrified, struck dumb as a stone, I made it to the front door before he slammed me against the wall, wrenching my arm behind my back. From years of habitual silence, my only sound was a hiss of pain. A copper coin rolled over my tongue, a metallic taste of fear.

"You won't call anyone, my treasure. You know it would ruin your life if people found out. Think of the kidnapping attempts, the tabloid media following you everywhere. You'd have every bleeding-heart charity in the book breathing down your neck for donations. Let me protect you from all that, jewel. I'm your husband, and I love you, except when you anger me. I only want my fair share."

Pressed against mine, Jude's body was as tall as I remembered, cruelly thin, and driven by the strength of his rage. I thought perhaps I could talk my way out by being agreeable. "Let me go, Jude. I won't fight you anymore. I had to mouth the words around the petals of a dead rose. I carefully tongued the thorny stem past my teeth.

"You're sure?" He pushed my elbow higher up along my back until I whimpered, grinding my teeth on more dry thorns. I had almost fainted with relief from the pain, when he finally let me go. He grabbed my sore shoulder and pushed me ahead of him into the living room. Then he stopped and turned me to face him. "Okay, darling, you owe me. Left me in one hell of a financial mess back there. So come on, make the magic. Spit it out."

"Jude, I'm sorry I ran away like that, but I was frightened." Two silver coins rolled to the ground.

"You can do better than that, Precious." Jude raised his fist level with my face. My jaw still ached where he had dislocated it the first time he ever hit me. I forced a rush of words from my mouth:

"I mean, I love you, darling, and I hope that we can work this out, because I know you were the one who rescued me from my stepmother, and I'm grateful that you took care of me so I didn't have to worry about anything…" A rain of silver was piling up around Jude's feet: bars, sheets, rods, wire. He grinned, reaching down to touch the gleaming pile. I felt a little nudge of an emotion I didn't recognize. I kept talking.

"It was so wonderful living with you, not like at my stepmother's, where I had to do all the cooking and cleaning, and my father never spoke up for me…" Semiprecious stones started piling up with the silver: rose quartz, jade, hematite. The mound reached Jude's knees, and the delight on his face made him look like the playful man I had married. He sat on the hillock of treasure, shoveling it up over his lap. My words kept flowing:

"If Daddy were a fair man, if he really loved me, he could have said something, and wouldn't it have been easier if the four of us had split the chores?" I couldn't stop. All those years of resentment gouted forth: emeralds green with jealousy; seething red garnets; cold blue chunks of lapis. The stones were larger now, the size of plums. I ejected them from my mouth with the force of thrown rocks. They struck Jude's chest, his chin. He tried to stand, but the bounty piled up over his shoulders, slamming him back down to the floor. "Hey!" he cried. But my words flew even faster.

"So I fetched and I carried and I smiled and I simpered, while Daddy let it all wash over him and told me to be nicer, even nicer, and now he's dead and I can't tell him how much he hurt me, and the only thanks I got was that jealous, lazy hussy telling me it's my fault her daughter's spitting slugs, and then you come riding to my rescue so that I can spend the next year of my life trying to make you happy too, and you have the gall to lay hands on me, and to tell me that you have the right? Well, just listen to me, Jude: I am not your treasure trove, and I will not run anymore, and I shall be nice if and when it pleases me, and stop calling me Precious; my name is Isobel!"

As I shouted my name, a final stone formed on my tongue, soft at first, as a hen's egg forms in her body. It swelled, pushing my jaws apart until I gagged. I forced it out. It flew from my mouth, a ruby as big as a human heart that struck Jude sharply on the head, then fell onto the pile of treasure. He collapsed unconscious amidst the bounty, blood trickling from a dent in his temple. The red ruby gleamed as though a coal lit its core. I felt lightheaded, exhilarated. Jude might still have been breathing, but I didn't bother to check. I stepped around him to the phone and dialed Emergency. "Police? There's an intruder in my home."

It wasn't until I went outside to wait for the police that I realized that nothing had fallen from my mouth when I made the telephone call. I chuckled first, then I laughed.

Just sounds, only sounds.

PRECIOUS

Silver Birch, Blood Moon is the fifth volume in the retold, adult fairy tale series Terri Windling and I co-edited. It was published in 1999 and won the World Fantasy Award for Best Anthology.

Nalo Hopkinson's tale "Precious" was the second story of hers that appeared in our series. "Riding the Red," Nalo's second published story was in *Black Swan, White Raven* two years previous, recommended to Terri and me by Chip Delany, her Clarion East instructor.

Daniel's Theory About Dolls

by Stephen Graham Jones

(From *The Doll Collection*, 2015)

I'm twelve when this all starts, and Daniel's about to be five. And I thought he was like the rest of us, then. I thought he was like I had been, at his age. But he wasn't. It could be he had been born different, of course. Or maybe one day, walking down the hall on his short legs there had been a click in his head, a deep, wet shift in his chest that made him roll his right shoulder, look at all of us in a colder way. Not just me and Mom and Dad. After that click, he looked at *people* in a colder way. I should have been watching him the whole time. I should have never slept. Then I could have seen him in his twin bed across from mine one night, when he coughed up a shiny black accretion, studied it in the moonlight sifting through our bedroom window, then wrapped it in a tissue, leaving it on the nightstand for Mom to throw away.

It was his soul.

None of us would know for years.

For our whole childhood he was just Daniel, always the full name. My little brother seven years younger, the accident that almost killed my mom, being born, like he'd been picking at the walls of her womb, latching his mouth onto places not made for feeding. He didn't talk until he was four. The doctors said not to worry, that some kids just took their time.

This isn't about him getting all the attention, either. This isn't about me growing up off to the side, taping and gluing my action figures and trucks back together and starting them on another adventure I was going to have to make up alone.

I'm good with the alone part. Really.

Those first four years when Daniel wasn't talking, the house was always buzzing anyway. New wallpaper, the trim painted over and over, slightly different shades each time, like a bird's egg fading in the sun, its inside baked rotten.

Our mom and dad were preparing for our little sister. Trying to make her room at the end of the hall so perfect that she couldn't help being born. Perfect enough that she wouldn't listen to the doctors, who told Mom there was no way, that Daniel had messed her up too bad, too forever.

Dad wanted a little princess, see. And our mom would kill herself to give him that princess, if she had to.

So, when the baseboards finally matched the color of the new knobs on the cabinets, when the corners had been sanded off all the coffee table and footboards, when Dad had parked all the tractors in a line by the barn, then reparked them again, it finally happened: Janine.

Our mom and dad named her early so they could coo to her through the tight wall of skin my mom's stomach became. They named her so they could lure her out, so they could talk her through.

To explain it to us, what was happening, my dad got a black marker with a sharp point and drew the outline of a sideways baby onto Mom, like a curled over bean with fingers and toes and an open eye watching us. If we'd been a family that already had a daughter, we might have had a left over doll to use, to explain this process with, but what we had instead was Dad's strong bold lines on our mom's belly.

Years later, at a movie theater, I would see the outline of a person taped off on the street, where they'd died their dramatic movie death, and I would lean forward, away from my date. I would lean forward and turn my head sideways, to see if I could hear that person under the asphalt, whispering.

Daniel told us it's how he learned to talk: hours on the couch with Mom in her seventh month, his head pressed flat to her bared stomach, Janine whispering to him.

When she died just like the doctors had said she would, Dad had to break down the bathroom door to keep Mom from eating all the soap from the towel cabinet. I remember him carrying her down the hall, bellowing at us to get out of the way. How her mouth was foaming, how her eyes were so blank.

I don't know if she was trying to choke herself to death or if she thought she was dirty on the inside.

After she was sedated on the couch, and Dad was pouring me cereal at the formal dining room table we never used, I heard Daniel speaking words for the first time.

I stood from my chair, peered over the back of the couch.

Daniel had rolled Mom's shirt up, had the side of his head pressed to her stomach.

He was talking to Janine.

It was the only time I ever hit him.

Mom's theory when she checked back into the world, it was that some people are born for a reason. That they're born to do a specific thing. And, in teaching Daniel to talk, Janine had done that specific thing. It released her from having to be born at all.

We held a private service for her in the woods behind our house. I got dressed up and combed my hair flat and everything.

We walked single-file out to where we'd used to have picnics, under the big tree. It was maybe five minutes past the edge of the pasture. Our dad was trying not to cry. Our mom was squeezing his hand. Daniel was standing on the other side of the hole from me. I guess our dad had dug the hole the night before, or early that morning.

"Will the ants get her?" Daniel asked.

Because they always found our watermelon as soon as we cut it.

My mom shook her head no, not to worry.

The box they had for her was cardboard and waxy and as long as Dad's arm. It smelled like flowers, and, because Mom's stomach was still big, that box made less sense than anything else in the history of the world, ever.

They didn't explain it to us.

We raised our voices, sang one of the children's songs Mom had been humming down to Janine since the first month.

It was nice, it was pretty, it was good.

Except for that box.

It fit into the hole perfectly, and all four of us used our hands to clump the dirt back in over it. Then my dad pulled a little sharpshooter shovel from behind some tree and scooped a little more on, and tamped it all down into a proper mound.

"No marker," our mom said, her hand over her own heart, like cupping it. "We'll be the marker, okay?"

This is how families survive.

"Okay," Daniel said, trying the sounds out.

Dad rustled Daniel's mop of hair. It was like a hug, I guess.

"I think he's had the words in there the whole time," Dad said.

"My big boys," Mom said, and lowered herself to her knees, pulled Daniel and me to her and held on, her belly between us, a hard, dead lump.

"Okay," Daniel said again, quieter.

He wasn't talking to us.

Three nights later I woke softly, my eyes open for moments before I could see through them, I think.

They were fixed on Daniel's bed.

It was empty.

I trailed my fingers on the walls, felt my way through the darkened house. Living room, kitchen, utility. Dad's study, Mom's sewing room. Their bedroom, the two of them breathing evenly in their musty covers.

Then Janine's room at the dead end of the hall.

I would get in trouble if the sound woke my parents—Janine's room was already in the process of becoming a shrine—but I clicked the light on.

It was like stepping into a cupcake. Everything was lace and pink and white-edged, like a thousand doilies had exploded, fell into an arrangement that before had only existed in our dad's head.

Daniel wasn't there either.

I turned the light off, trying to muffle the sound in the warmth of my palm, and in that new darkness I saw a firefly bobbing outside the window.

Except it was a yellowy flashlight, moving through the trees.

Daniel.

I pulled my shoes on without tying the laces and crept out the front door, left it open a crack behind me.

Five minutes later, I caught up with him.

He'd seen where Dad put that little sharpshooter shovel. It was just his size.

By the time I got to Janine's grave, he'd already dug down to the waxy cardboard-box center.

I reached out to stop him—he didn't know I was there—but it was too late.

He'd already stepped down into the open grave, the box not supporting his weight, the sound of a jumbo staple popping loud in the night.

And then I didn't say anything.

What he pulled up from that box, holding it under the armpits like a real baby, was the doll Dad had bought for Janine, the doll he hadn't had to demonstrate the baby in Mom's stomach.

She'd been stripped naked, of course.

If her eyes rolled open, it was too far for me to see, and too dark.

Because I'd left the door open, when I got back to the house there was something turning in slow deliberate circles on the couch.

A possum. It was following its rat tail around and around, like it had lost something, or was patting down a bed for itself.

It hissed at me, showed its rows of teeth, sharp all the way back to the hinge of its jaw.

I fell back, clutching for the coat rack, to pull it down in front of me, maybe, to hide what was going to be my screaming escape, but what my fingers dug into, it was the shirt of Daniel's pajamas.

He didn't even look over at me as he crossed the living room, the shovel held over his shoulder like a barbarian axe.

The possum screamed when he swung the blade into it, and by the time our mom and dad had clambered into the living room, my dad with his pistol held high like a torch, my mom's silk sleep mask pushed up on her forehead like a visor, the possum was biting at its own opened side, and rasping.

Daniel looked up to Dad, then to Mom.

The shovel was twice as tall as he was.

"*Daniel,*" our dad said, his voice trying to be stern, I think.

It didn't work.

"Oh," Mom said then, and stepped back from the bloody couch. From the dying possum.

The possum's babies were calving off. They'd been hidden under the dark back fur on her back. They looked like malformed mice.

I clapped my hand to my mouth, threw up between my fingers.

Daniel brought the flat of the shovel down on the fastest of the babies, was, as our dad said later, too young to know better, too young to understand.

Dad wasn't standing where I was, though. He wasn't close enough to hear Daniel.

Daniel was whispering to someone.

I'm thirty-eight now, and that night under the tree, The Night of the Possum, as we came to call it, it's still as clear in my mind as if it just happened.

Daniel would be thirty, I guess.

And, I wish I could trace a line from the year Janine died to now, and put hashmarks on it. This is Daniels' first date. This is the neighbor's new colt. This is when he figured out the bus lines—when he figured out he could go into the city by himself. This is him in the guidance counselor's office, the counselor not finding an explanation for him in any of the college textbooks she'd saved.

This is Mom and Dad, watching him return again and again back into the trees.

This is me, growing up to the side.

My first date was with Chrissy Walmacher. The neighbor's new colt is hers. I sat with her while it was dying, for horse reasons I never really understood. This is me and Chrissy, riding the bus to a concert in the city. This is the guidance counselor, veering her to this school, for that life, and veering me to a different school, for a different life.

This is me at thirty-four, standing at my dad's funeral, my mom there, Daniel pulling up at the last moment, his suit perfect, his face set to "mourning," his eyes drinking the scene in for cues.

We had had the same grades, played the same sports.

Without me providing the model of what to do, I think Daniel would have had to reveal himself. As it was, he could just step into my shoes, follow my lead, fit in, attract zero attention.

What Dad died of, it wasn't anything. Just cigarettes. Just too many years.

Standing there, I was only on my second job of the year. I'd tried normal jobs, offices, even manual labor, but indexing books in the privacy of my apartment on the second floor was finally the only thing that fit. It was work that made sense.

Contracts were getting fewer and farther between, though. There's software that can do what I do, more or less. With a little fine-tuning afterward, even I have a hard time telling any substantial difference.

Dad dying, it wasn't a windfall for me, or for Mom or Daniel either, but it was going to help. My grief was a little bit of a mask as well.

After the funeral, to escape the house, I drove Daniel down to the bar my dad had been loyal to, the years after Janine—before he cut drinking off altogether, at my mom's request.

This was the real funeral. Walking through a space he had walked through, at our age. Moving as he moved, our reflections in the smoky mirror perhaps vague enough to fall into step with his. We were trying his life on, and, before we'd even sat down, we were finding his life not that interesting.

Saying goodbye, it's complicated.

Daniel ordered the same beer I did. He'd never cared about beer, probably wasn't even going to drink this one to the bottom.

"So what's what these days?" I asked.

I'd seen actors on TV open conversations exactly like that, in places like this.

"You know," he said.

He'd bloomed into an electrical engineer. In his senior year, when I was first getting on the job market, I remember him building model intersections on Dad's shop table, and wiring stoplights, giving them this or that trigger, this or that safety. The traffic was imaginary, but the lights always clicked through their cycles perfectly.

Mom and Dad would stand in the doorway, Mom's hands balled at her throat with pride.

Everything they'd been saving for Janine, they heaped it onto Daniel.

My one-time girlfriend Chrissy Walmacher's second wedding had been two weeks ago. She'd invited me, and it had put a picture in my head of me standing at a white fence, looking over. Just another sad postcard I sent to myself in a weak moment. One of many.

"Any girls to speak of?" I asked.

Daniel leaned back, shrugged his right shoulder in that way he had, like he was about to shove his right hand deep into his pocket for the perfect amount of change. He wasn't looking at me anymore, but at a college girl with hair so metallic red it had to have just been dyed, or colored, however that happens. She was sliding darts from the dartboard, one booted foot pulled up behind her like she was kissing someone in a movie.

"Stay single," I told him, raising my glass. "These are your good years."

He came back to me, his fingers circling his own mug.

What he didn't say, what he didn't ask, was How would I know this gospel I was preaching?

Big brothers are required to say certain things, though. To give advice, whether it's from experience or from a book of celebrity interviews that now has a comprehensive index.

"You going to miss him?" Daniel said then, watching my eyes for the lie.

"He's Dad," I said, taking another long drink.

"But still."

Behind me a dart struck home, and the red head tittered.

"I miss him for Mom," I said.

"Yeah," Daniel said, nodding like this was true. Like this was something he hadn't thought of.

"I saw you that night," I said then, trying to spring it on him. "Did you ever know?"

I'd been saving it for more than half my life.

Daniel looked to me, his head turned sideways, like for clarification.

"Night of the Possum," I said, in our family way.

"Oh, yeah," Daniel said. "The possum. Man. I'd nearly forget her."

Until just that exact moment, I'd never once thought of that possum as having a sex. But of course it had been a mom. It had had babies. Of course.

Her.

The way he said it was so personal, though. So intimate.

"*What* did you see?" he said, setting his mug down after touching the beer to his lips again. He wasn't drinking it, I didn't think. He was just doing what I did. He was fitting in. He was looking like one of us.

He wasn't, though.

Not even close.

According to Daniel, he'd been out to Janine's grave in private in the weeks since her funeral—a behavior learned from Mom and Dad, he claimed, from following them on the sly, making their little pilgrimage of grief before dinner two or three times a week, if it was just a casserole cooking. He'd been there, sure, but never with a shovel. Never to dig that little cardboard coffin up. What did I think he was, a ghoul? Can a kindergartner even *be* a ghoul?

"That's what I'm saying," I told him, a beer deeper into this night of nights. "You were just, like, curious, I think. As to what we'd actually buried."

"Janine," he said.

I stared at him about this, waiting for him to see it.

I'm an indexer, Daniel an electrical engineer, but still, we'd both figured out long ago that what happens with Mom's kind of miscarriage is that the body either reabsorbs the fetus or the body chunks it up, delivers it bit by bit, to be assembled never.

Not pleasant to think about, but the human body's crawly and gross when you look too close.

Each of us figuring that out about Janine, it was probably why we'd gone into comparatively sterile work settings: desks, drafting tables.

Nothing with blood.

"It would have messed me up, though, right?" Daniel said, touching that warm beer to his lips again. "Given me a unique perspective on—on *life*."

I took a real drink, waited for him to say the rest.

I didn't want to disturb this moment.

He was watching the red head behind me again, talking to the two girls she was with. It was like he was taking a series of still shots with his mind. With his heart.

The reason he was dismissing my question about girls was because girls were all there was for him. I could tell by the way he watched her. But it would cruel for him to flaunt it in front of his big brother. In front of his practically celibate big brother.

"If I'd dug her up like you say, I mean," Daniel said, coming back to me for a moment. Holding my eyes with his, probably so he could gauge how I was taking this: as hypothetical, or as confession.

"You did dig her up," I said. "That's why you had that little shovel. For the possum."

"It was right there on the porch," Daniel said, his voice falling into that little-brother whine I hated. "I was on my way back from the bathroom and I heard you, came to see. The door was open behind you, man. The shovel was right there where Dad left it. It's where he always left it, for snakes. Remember?"

I studied the grain of the table-top, trying to track this version.

Mom *had* had an encounter with a king snake. That little sharpshooter shovel *did* have a handle at top, perfect for holding the shovel blade steady over a snake's head.

But I'd seen.

"So, *if* you'd dug her up," I finally said. Because there had to be *some* ground he would cede.

Daniel pushed air out his nose in a sort of one-blow laugh, a version of the way Dad used to dismiss our pleas for money or keys or permission, and said, "Then…she would have been dug up?"

"We should go out there," I told him.

He wiped his mouth with the back of his hand. "There wouldn't be anything," he said. "Not after all these years. Maybe an eyeball. Those are hard plastic, right?"

"You're talking about Janine," I said.

"We're talking about a doll," Daniel said. Obviously. "And, say we go out there, and that doll's still there," Daniel said, leaning over his beer. "Would that somehow prove that I dug up the…the surrogate of Janine, and then put her *back* exactly as she'd been?"

He was right.

"Or it would prove that nobody'd ever dug her up at all," he said, lifting his beer and setting it down, for emphasis.

"I thought—" I said then, looking behind to the group of college girls as well, "I guess I just thought that…you were a kid, man. I thought that, that you might really think that stupid doll *was* Janine. Whether you dug her up or not."

"It. Whether I dug *it* up or not."

"I thought you'd think that that was what Mom had had inside her all along. That, I don't know, she would have grown up into a mannequin or something. That everybody was always walking around with these dolls lodged in them, waiting to get out."

"The women at least," Daniel added, in his playing-along voice.

"It's your theory," I said. "Or, I mean, it would have been."

Daniel wasn't watching the college girls anymore. Just me.

"I was five," he said, finally. "Not stupid. But thanks, big brother."

I nodded like I deserved that, and kept nodding, drank another beer, talked about nothing, and left him there with the college girls, didn't talk to him for two years, I think it was. And that was just for Mom's funeral.

Her granite headstone came in two months later.

Carved into it was that she'd been mother to three beautiful children.

I ran my fingers over the jagged valleys of those letters, and watched cars pass on Route 2.

"Guess you can die of being alone," Daniel had said to me earlier that day, about Mom.

Or, not about Mom, but *because* of Mom.

He was talking about me, though.

I was becoming the male version of a spinster.

It can happen when you grow up without enough light.

Ask anybody.

For the next year and a half or two years, Daniel was a ghost. He lived in the city, I even knew where, but the life he led—it wasn't even a mystery to me, really. I assumed it would be a follow-through of who he'd been before. And I was happy for him. One of us deserved that.

I was out at the farm, sleeping in the same bedroom I'd slept in as a boy.

Someday I'd move into Mom and Dad's room, I told myself. Someday.

The lacy drapes in Janine's room were so fragile now that touching them made them crumble. Nearly three decades of sunsets can do that.

At night, crossing to my desk for another round of pages, I would find myself watching the window over the kitchen sink. For fireflies. For Janine. She never came, though. She'd never even been born. Finally, as I'd known all along was going to happen, I walked out into the trees with a new shovel, to settle this argument.

Our big tree was the same as it had always been. In tree-years, the intervening decades hadn't even been a blink.

The grave mound was long gone, of course. Now there were beer bottles and old magazines scattered around, meaning teenagers had discovered our idyllic spot. The models in the magazines were wearing clothes from years ago, staring up at me from the past.

I pushed the blade of the shovel into the ground, leaned over it, gave it my meager weight and dug deeper than my dad had, just to be sure.

Nothing.

That night I dug two holes.

The next night, three.

On the fourth night, angry, I raised the shovel before me formally, like a cross I was about to plant once and for all, and sliced down through a long slender root. I closed my eyes, sure this had been the tap root. That this tree had lived two hundred years just to have me kill it by accident. Kill it to settle a debate that was only happening in my head.

If it had been the taproot, and if my dim recollection that this was a good way to kill a tree was accurate, it would be a week or more before the leaves wilted at the edges, anyway.

I didn't know if I could force myself to watch. Meaning this tree was either going to be alive or dead to me for the next few decades. When I'd think about it, the picture of it in my mind would shudder between possibilities, and that clutch in my gut would either be guilt or relief. Either absolution or condemnation.

And Daniel was right: the waxy cardboard box, it had long since been reclaimed. I kept hoping for at least a rusted staple to prove the burial, the coffin, the funeral we'd all been complicit in staging, but even staples would have turned back to earth, this long after.

It was about this time that something started going wrong with my stomach. With my digestion. The doctor my plan allowed told me it was nerves, it was stress, that I would push through, get better. Not to worry. Then he clapped my shoulder, guided me back out into the daylight of the city.

I stood in the parking lot by my car for longer than the attendant understood. He watched me the whole way past his little guard booth, perhaps trying to gauge for himself the news I'd just received. It would be a game you would come up with just to stay sane, sitting in that guard booth day after day.

I was dying, I didn't tell him.

It was that house. Living there, it was killing me the same way it had Dad, the same way it had Mom. Because I had no real connections to the world, no fibers or tendrils reaching out from me, connecting me to people, the world was letting me go. Letting me slip through. Maybe it was even mercy.

And the house was the mechanism. My stomach had been fine before, my digestion nothing I'd ever had to think about.

Radon, lead paint, asbestos, contaminated water, treated lumber sighing its treatment back out: it could be anything poisoning me.

I had to warn Daniel. Sell the house after my funeral, I would tell him. After I'm gone, get rid of it. Don't keep it because of Janine. She was never even real, man. And she's not there anymore, either. I looked. I looked and I looked. She's gone. And it's for the best.

Driving to the address I had lodged in my head like a tumor, the townhouse listed under Daniel's name for years in our shared legal documents and invoices, I indexed in my head the talk I was going to give him. It made it more real, having an index. Being able to turn to this page for that part, another page for a different part.

It calmed me, kept me between the lines the whole way over.

I parked behind his garage, blocking him in if he was there—the visitor slots were all taken—knocked on his door. No answer. I didn't knock again, just sat on his patio and studied the sides of my hands, my stomach groaning in its new way. After twenty or thirty minutes, the super or maintenance man came by, greeted me by Daniel's name.

"Brother," I corrected, stopping him, waving off the apology already coming together on his face.

"Oh, yeah," the super or maintenance man said, close enough now to see. "Mr. Robbins not home yet?"

"Guess not," I said. "I can wait. He didn't know I was coming by. Kind of a surprise reunion."

"Here," the maintenance man said, and stepped past, and, just on the authority of family resemblance, opened the door with the master key, pushed it open before me as if to prove this was really happening.

It was an indication of how little of a threat I looked to be. An indication of how frail I must appear, that sitting on patio furniture in the sunlight could be considered cruel, could be something he would want to save me from.

"You can die of being alone," I said to myself, once I had Daniel's door pulled shut behind me.

Daniel's place was much as I guess I'd imagined it: black and white prints bought as a set—some national park, and the sky above it—a sectional leather couch, a large television set rimed with dust. An immaculate kitchen. Ice-cold refrigerated air.

I called Daniel's name just to be sure.

Nothing.

I settled into the couch, couldn't figure out his remote control.

I felt like an intruder. Like one of those people who break into vacation homes and move through them like ghosts, running their palms over the statuettes, over the worn arms of the dining room chairs.

I almost left, to do this right, to call him, arrange a proper visit.

For all I knew, when he came home, there would a girl under his arm, fresh from happy hour, him having to guide her shoulders so she could find the couch. So she could find the couch occupied by her date's pale reflection.

I stood, breathing harder than made sense for somebody alone in a room, and told myself just the bathroom, and that I was to leave it exactly as it was, no splashes, no drops, no towels hung obviously crooked, no smudges on the mirror. And then I would leave.

Except, on the back of the toilet was a mason jar, one of those kinds with the lids that have wire cages on them, to trap all the air. Behind the thick glass was what I assumed to be potpourri, or some sort of collection of dried moss strands. I picked it up gingerly, turned it to the side.

It was hair. Long winds of dry hair.

I rolled the jar in my hand, studying it. The hair was in sedimentary layers. Like a curio from a gift shop.

I shook the jar timidly. All the hair stayed the same. And it really was hair. I set it down, zipped up, and was going to leave it there, had told myself it was the only sensible thing to do. It wasn't sensible to interrogate stranger's decorations. And that's what my brother was, by now, a stranger.

Still. I came back to the jar, tried to twist the top off to smell—this *had* to be something decorative, something all other single men knew about as a matter of course—but the lever had rusted shut, from the steam of a thousand showers.

"Good," I said out loud. This wasn't my business anyway. This wasn't my life.

When I saw the metallic red hair a few layers up from the bottom, though, my fingers opened of their own accord.

The jar shattered on the side of the toilet, the hair unwinding on the tile floor, taking up the space of a human head, and still writhing, looking for its eventual shape.

I could still hear that red head's dart sucking into the dartboard. Could still see her standing at the line painted onto the floor of that bar. But I couldn't see the rest of her life.

She hadn't been the first, and she hadn't been the last.

The way I made it make sense was that Daniel had become a hair stylist instead of an electrical engineer. That, when he'd hit thirty, he'd changed professions, gone with his heart instead of a paycheck. He got more interested in the people in the crosswalk than in the traffic cueing up at the lights.

Daniel who was just as indifferent with his wardrobe and appearance as I'd always been. He'd be no better a hair stylist than I would.

Still, this couldn't be what it seemed.

I felt my way out of the bathroom, made myself walk not into his bedroom—smelling where he slept would be too intimate—and not back down the stairs like I'd promised myself, but to the only other door on this floor I hadn't been through. The only door that was closed.

I told myself I was just going to reach in, turn the light on in there long enough to catalog it as storage or living space—I might need to stay here one night someday, brother—but then, the door open just enough for my forearm, my hand patting the wall for a light switch, something scurried behind me.

I turned, didn't catch it.

The sense the sound left in my head, though, it was an armadillo, somehow. No: a possum.

I clutched the door frame, my heart slapping the inside walls of my chest, a sweet, grainy smell assaulted the inside of my head, and looked into what was neither living space nor storage, exactly.

This was an operating room.

On the table, tied down at all four corners, was the latest woman.

All Daniel's attention had been focused on her stomach.

He'd been looking for something, I could tell.

Above the table, on the ceiling, was a large mirror. Meaning the girl had been alive when this started.

I shivered, hugged my arms to my side, and felt my chin about to tremble.

On one of the flaps of skin that had been folded back from her middle, there was still a black line.

Daniel was drawing that baby shape on the body before he cut in. And he was cutting in to free the doll, the doll he knew had to be there, the doll Mom and Dad had practically promised was going to be there.

Janine was still whispering to him.

I shook my head no, no, please, and when I turned to leave, there they were on the wall. All the dolls he'd—not *found*, that was impossible, that was wrong.

The dolls he'd bought and salvaged and sneaked home. The dolls that completed the ritual he'd learned at five years old.

They were all wired to a pegboard, their smooth plastic bodies covering nearly every hole, and the pegboard was the whole wall, by now. This was the work of years. This was a lifetime.

To honor them, the blood and meat the dolls had been wrapped in to simulate the birth for Daniel, it had been left to dry on them.

I threw up, had to fall onto my hands to do it, it was so violent.

And then the scurrying again. In the hall.

I looked up just after *something* had crossed from one side of the doorway to the other. And where my ears told my eyes to look, it wasn't up at head-level, at person-level, but at knee-level.

Instead of a possum now, what I saw in my head was the doll my dad had bought for Janine. The one we'd buried. Only, it was crawling around on all fours, its elbows cocked higher than its back, its face turned up, to keep its eyes opened.

And when she talked, it was going to be that same language she'd taught Daniel. That same dead tongue.

I stood, fell back, dizzy, not used to this kind of exertion, and my hand splashed into the insides of the girl on the table, and I felt two things in the same instant. The first was the warmth of this girl's viscera, when I'd assumed she'd been dead for hours, long enough to have cooled down. The second thing I felt was what Daniel was always looking for: a hard plastic doll foot. From the doll inside each of us, if you know where to look. If you cut at the exact right instant, and reach in with confidence, with faith.

My hand closed on the smooth foot and the moment dilated, threatened to swallow me whole.

I brought my hand back gently, so as not to disturb. So as to pretend this hadn't just happened.

Whatever was in the hall had seen, though. Or heard the girl's insides, trying to suction my hand in place.

Save her, a hoarse voice whispered, from just past the doorway. *Don't let her drown.*

I stared at the wall of dolls, none of their lips able to move. I stared into the black abyss of the doorway. I studied the front- and backside of my gore-smeared hand.

"Daniel?" I said. Because I'd recognized the voice. Because who else could it be.

"Save her," the voice whispered again, from lower in the hallway than a person's head would be.

Unless *that person was* crawling. Unless, in the privacy of his own home, that person flashed around from room to room like that. Because that was who he was. That was *what* he was.

"Please," I said.

No answer.

I backed to the wall shaking my head no, shaking my head please, and, from this new angle, could see into the supply closet, the one Daniel had taken the door off of. Probably because his hands, in this room, didn't want to be touching doorknobs.

The doll our father had buried in our childhood, she was standing between two stacks of foggy plastic containers.

She'd been dressed, was just staring, her eyelashes black and perfect, her expression so innocent, so waiting.

Janine.

I wanted to fall to my knees—to give up or in thanks, I wasn't really sure. I put my hand to my face and didn't just smear my cheek and open eyes with the black insides of this dead girl, but my lips as well. My tongue darted out like for a crumb, just instinct, and the breathing in the hall got raspier. Less patient. Like this was building to something for him.

It made me cough that kind of cough that comes right before throwing up.

Out in the hall, Daniel sighed from deep in his mania, and then there was sound like he'd fallen over. From my wall, I could see one of his bare feet through the doorway, toes-up.

It was trembling. Like something was feeding on his face. Like the possum had come for him after all these years.

I crashed to the doorway to protect him, my little brother, to kick away whatever had him by the face.

It was just Daniel, though. He was spasming, his whole body, his eyes closed. It was a seizure. It was ecstasy.

"Daniel, Daniel," I said, on my knees now, taking his head in my lap.

He trembled and drew his arms in tight, his mouth frothing.

After a whole life of being alone with his task, with his compulsion, with his crusade, I'd finally joined him, I knew.

This wasn't a seizure, it was an orgasm. A culmination of all his dreams. I was the only one who could possibly understand what he'd become. What he was doing. And I was here.

His breath, it smelled like soap, and I had to picture him flaking a bar into a pile then lining his gums with it.

I sat down farther, to better cradle his head, and, when I had to angle him up to an almost sitting position, his eyes rolled open and he looked over to me, then down to my stomach as well, for the gift he'd been denied. The miracle he'd trained himself to sense.

My stomach. My digestion.

It wasn't nerves. What I was experiencing, what I was feeling, it was smoother than nerves. More plastic.

I unsnapped my shirt, looked down where Daniel was, and the vague outline of a tiny hand pressed against the backside of my skin when I breathed in, like it was stable, it was steady. It was me doing the moving.

I pushed away, into the hall wall, let Daniel's head fall to the carpet and bounce, his eyes closing mechanically, his right foot still trembling.

I was breathing too fast and I was breathing not at all.

And I could hear it now too, the whispering.

From the shop.

A whispering, but a gurgling, too.

The doll in the dead girl's still-warm entrails. The doll Daniel had wanted me to save.

The whole wall watched me cross the room on ghost feet. I looked to Janine for confirmation, and when she didn't say this was wrong, I plunged my hand back into the remains on the table, found the foot I'd felt earlier, and birthed this smooth plastic body up into the light, the body's corruption stringing off it.

When I turned the doll right-side up, its eyes rolled open to greet me, its lashes caked with blood.

I carried the doll by the leg to Daniel, and brought it up between us like a real fresh-born baby, but it only made him shake his head no, like I wasn't getting it. Like I didn't see.

"Over, over, over again," he said, turning sideways to reach down the hall. He tried to stand to go down there but wasn't recovered from his fit yet. He fell into the wall, slid down.

I looked where he'd meant to go, though.

The only light that way was the bathroom.

I drifted there, the doll upside-down by my leg again, its hard plastic fingers brushing my calf through my slacks.

The hair. The sedimentary tufts of hair.

That had to be what he meant. Over, over: *start* over. The traffic light goes red, then it cycles back to green again, and hovers on yellow, spilling back to red.

I carried the tufts of hair back, jewels of glass glittering on those dried strands.

When I knelt down by Daniel again, he opened his mouth like a baby bird and I knew I was right: this was part of his process. You save one doll from inside a woman, and you start over with hair from one of the other women. Like paying. Like trading. Like closing a thing you'd opened.

"Here, here," I said, fingering the hair from the jar, packing his mouth with it. His eyes watered, spilled over with what I took to be joy. "It'll be all right," I whispered. "We're saving her, Daniel. We're saving her."

He coughed once, hearing his name, then again from deeper, and, using two fingers, I shoved the wad of hair in deeper, so it could bathe in his stomach juice like a pearl. So it could become a soul for him again.

I kissed him once on the forehead when his body started jerking again, this time for air, and, when he bit the two fingers I was using to make him human again, I inserted the new doll's hand instead.

It held the hair in place until Daniel calmed. Until he went to sleep. Until there was no more breath.

I moved his right foot, to get his tremble going again, but there was nothing left.

My little brother was dead. His mission was over.

I kissed Daniel's closed eyes, my lips pressing into each thin eyelid for too long, like I could keep him here, at least until I removed my lips.

Behind those eyelids, though, the balls of his eyes were already turning hard like the yolks of boiled eggs.

This is how you say goodbye.

I stood, wiped that new doll's ankle clean—plastic holds prints—and stepped back into the shop, used a scalpel to remove the patch of carpet I'd thrown up into. I rolled that carpet up like a burrito.

Without looking up to them, I nodded to the open-eyed dolls then turned the light off with my wrist, stepped over what was left of Daniel, and made my way through the living room, out the front door.

"He ever show up?" the super or maintenance man asked, suddenly pruning something in the flower bed that didn't need pruning. Meaning he'd had second thoughts about letting me in. He was standing guard, now. He was on alert.

In one hand I was clutching a small patch of rolled carpet I'd never be able to explain.

On my other hip, her cool face in my neck, was Janine.

I looked back to the door I'd just locked.

"No, never did," I said, "but there's water on the floor in his kitchen."

The super or maintenance man stood, his brow furrowed.

"Sink?" he said.

"Refrigerator," I said back, and followed him back in, pulled the door shut behind us, twisting the deadbolt.

Ten minutes later I stepped out again, my breathing back to normal, almost.

"Well that was different," I said to Janine, and hitched her higher.

Walking along the side of the house back to the garage, to my car, I had to turn my head away from her to cough, and then place my hand on the wall to steady myself.

What is it? she asked

Her voice was perfect.

I spit a shiny conglomerate of segmented blackness up into my palm, and studied it.

"Nothing," I told her, and somewhere between there and the car, I left my soul behind me on the ground.

DANIEL'S THEORY ABOUT DOLLS

Dolls. I've been collecting three-faced dolls and doll parts—especially heads—for a number of years (I have no idea why). So what could be more natural than for me to edit *The Doll Collection* (thanks to Veronica Schanoes for the title). In addition to weird and dark stories, the book contains b&w photographs of dolls owned by me, Ellen Klages, and Richard Bowes. The masterful "Daniel's Theory About Dolls" by Stephen Graham Jones is one of the extraordinarily creepy stories in the book.

The Mysteries

by Livia Llewellyn

(From *Nightmare Carnival*, 2014)

1

It is that unnamable time of a late December morning, that nighttime hour that bleeds into tired dawn. My great-great-great-great grandmother sits in the living room, in the dark. I hear the rustling of her ancient newspaper as she turns each delicate page. The furnace has shut down after its daily muted roar, and a distant tick sounds through the walls as the metal ducts contract and cool. Other than the paper's whispers, it is the only sound in the house.

In the same dark, around the corner, past the foyer, I stand in the middle of the hallway, in my stained nightgown and robe, the ones I left behind some fifteen years ago when I left this place, my childhood home. My mother's house, so lovely and modern and clean—before The Grand moved in and took over, like she takes over everything. The outline of my overweight body hovers in the large black-stained mirror at the end of the hall, by the always-locked front door. A distorted Pierrette with a marshmallow body and mouthless face. I raise my hand. A second later, the creature in the mirror reluctantly moves. I can't blame it, I know why. The Grand can't see me, but she knows I'm there. She reads in the dark. She outlines her lips bright red in the pitch black of windowless closets. She embroiders tiny, perfect stitches in absolute gloom. Even during the day, the curtains in all the rooms are drawn, the lamps turned off. —This is how it used to be, she tells me over and over again. —When I was a child, we didn't have electric lamps. We didn't have radios. There were no televisions or computers; we weren't compulsed to entertain ourselves all day. We were self-contained. Everything we needed came out of ourselves, out of our own family. This is how it was in the world. This is how it will always be for me.

I open my robe and pull the nightgown up. If there is a demarcation between fabric and flesh, mercury and air, the creature and me, I cannot see it. I search for the familiar black triangle between my legs. Even that has vanished. I am no different than the bare, cream walls around me. Outside of us, nothing can be seen. Yet within—a carnelevare of the numinous, waiting for release. Everything I need will come out of me.

—What are you doing? the Grand calls out from the living room. —Are you up? As she speaks, I hear her sniffing me out, and my blood runs peppermint hot and cold. She likes it like that.

I let my nightgown drop, and shuffle and squint my way around the corner. Morning presses against the thick curtains, to no avail. Everything glows, but dimly so. Against the far corner of the couch she curls, a fragile mound of bones and skin dressed in soft, flowery clothes. The open newspaper obscures the upper half of her body. I see only legs and knife-sharp fingers, the leaves of dark print flapping back in between. Her feet are small and perfectly formed, with nails like mother-of-pearl. She hasn't walked in a hundred and fifty years. She hasn't needed to.

—Give your great grand a sweet breakfast kiss, she says, floating up from the cushions. The newspaper flutters to the floor.

2

—It's time, my sister said. Her voice poured out of the phone like poison.

—No. Not yet. No.

—The Grand is sending for you, she continued over me, as if she couldn't hear my voice.

—I don't want to go.

—You don't have a choice. Check your email—I sent the plane ticket to you already. You have a month to pack up and say goodbye.

—I have a life here.

The Mysteries

—I had a life, too. And now I get it back. But only if you come. You know what happens to me if you don't. She'll use me up until there's nothing left.

—You know I'd never let that happen. But why so soon?

—She's tired of me. I don't please her anymore, or so she says. At any rate, I've done my time. It's your turn now.

—This is wrong. You know that.

—It doesn't matter. We can't change it. This is why we were born.

It was late summer, back then, and my city was a volcano of bright life. I took her call at work, in an empty corner office. I gave an obfuscated answer that pleased us both and hung up. Outside, day was racing down into the shimmery fires of night. Twenty floors down, clogged streets were transforming into long-running strands of rubies and diamonds, winding around buildings slick with coruscated light. I pressed my hand against the glass. Hard and hot. When I took my hand away, a thin film of perspiration remained, outstretched against the avenue as though trying to grasp it. The ghost hand of a ghost girl. Within seconds, it disappeared.

I said my goodbyes at work without telling them I'd never return, and bought boxes on the way home, just enough to ship a few piles of books and clothes. My small room in the SRO building didn't hold that much, anyway. I'd always known this moment would come, and so my decisions had already been made, years ago, how I would live my life and how I would defend it. I was more prepared than my sister could imagine, and more ruthless than The Grand could ever be. Desperation made me so. In a way, I was no different than her.

The next morning I settled my account at the SRO, made a stop at the post office, then walked twenty blocks south, down through my beautiful city. Past blight-tinged gentrification, past markets and parks and coffee shops and wide bustling avenues; and then west, over to the edge of the river, to block after block of monolithic warehouses and factories, moldering in shadowed silence and brick dust until their moment in history came again. It was like I'd walked this path just yesterday, even though a decade had passed.

—When you've made your decision, be it tomorrow or a million tomorrows from now, you'll find us, he had said with his yellow-teethed smile as I looked over his exhibits and wares. —You won't ever need a map.

3

She leans into me in the queer morning light for her kiss, and my mouth slackens and my head lolls back. Every day is the same, and night no different than day. Darkness, rain needling against the rooftop and windows, wind thundering through distant trees. She never sleeps. Her need keeps her running hot and constant, a nuclear reactor of hunger that can never be shut down. —It's not so bad, my sister said, the few times I spoke with her until she stopped taking my calls. —She takes from you, but she gives you something back, in a way. It's almost an even exchange. —What does she do, what is she, how can she be? I asked over and over again. —Is she a vampire? A ghoul? An insect? Why do we submit?

—I don't know, my sister always replied. —Who can say?

Sometimes, at night, I awake in the dark and feel her hovering over me, a weight and emotion I sense but never feel or see. Paralyzed, I breathe all my damp terror and fear into the emptiness of my childhood room. Above, mote by mote she sucks it in. Sleep itself is no refuge. In my dreams I rise to the ceiling, my skin brushing against the faded outlines of spiraling galaxies my mother painted for me long ago. And then the ceiling, the stars, soften and yield—her arms are around me, mouth against mine, while in the waking world, my body moans and shivers, ten feet above my bed. The days are worse. I can't hide in my room forever, and so I venture out into the house, wandering like a restless ghost of myself through the still rooms. Everywhere, vestiges of the life I had before, of my sister and me as children, of my mother and the father I too briefly knew. Cobwebbed tableaus of toys and dishes. Photos of distant summers, succumbing to speckled mold. A faint scent of my mother's perfume rising from a dresser of musty clothes. Old folders of school homework, boxes of books my aching eyes could no longer read in the ever-dim light. And I, always never knowing where she is, in what room, squeezed into what tight corner or closet or crack. Never knowing when she will ooze out and ignore me, or play with me, or pounce.

—You're different, she says this morning, her vulpine face hovering just above my head. —I don't like it. I smell animals. I smell fire and sugar and rust. The words wash over my face like gasoline fumes, and tears dribble out of my eyes into my mouth. My flesh grows heavy and prickly-numb. Her face is an amorphous stain, a blur. I open my mouth to speak. All that comes forth is a burp, loud and wet. Bile dribbles down my lips and chin. It tastes like rotting grapes.

The Grand recoils. —You're sick, she hisses. She hates any hint of illness or disease.

—No, I'm not, I garble. Thin pine needles slide out of my running nose and onto my tongue. —It's the carnival.

—You're delirious.

—It's coming.

—What are you talking about?

A slow, long tremor erupts throughout my belly. My tearing eyes shut tight, and I smile. I am horrifying and new. She leans back into me, curious. Lips and breath against my cheek, mouth open, seeking, seeking. —Tell me everything, she whispers. —Fill me up with everything.

I lift my wet nightgown. —Stay with me, and you can take everything you need.

I drop to the floor, back arched, thighs apart. The second contraction rips through me, and I howl. The barker said there would be pain, and he didn't lie. He said it would be the eighth wonder of the world.

4

The barker stood where I had seen him a decade ago, as if he had never moved from the spot: on a wood-planked platform in the middle of a vast dirt and sawdust-covered warehouse floor, surrounded by rows and rows of broken and abandoned caravans and carousels and fair rides in fading pastels, painted canvases depicting creatures and humans of sublime beauty and deformity, statues and stuffed beasts, tanks and cages, carts and costume-choked trunks. It took an eternity of footsteps to walk to him. The musk of animal and tang of sea creature and the green of chipped wood filled my lungs—none of it had moved in ten years, none of it had changed. Bits of jewel-colored glitter floated through the smoky, popcorn-scented air. ANTIQUES, it said on the crumpled brochure I'd found blowing about on the street that spring day so long ago, and had carried in my purse ever since. RARE CIRCUS ITEMS CURATED FROM AMERICA'S GOLDEN AGE OF ENTERTAINMENT. POWERFUL CARNIVAL ARTIFACTS RESCUED FROM CIVILIZATIONS LOST FOREVER IN THE MISTS OF TIME. A VERITABLE CORNUCOPIA OF WONDERS, MESMERIZING AND TERRIFYING. THIS ONCE IN A LIFETIME OPPORTUNITY, ONLY FOR YOU.

—Are you ready? he called out, and his words echoed back and forth between the high walls before dying out in a faint burst of calliope music. —Have you made your choice? He lifted his cane and pointed down. Below the stage sat a massive flat-topped megalith, with five black marble boxes resting on its rough surface, each carved on the top with the name of an ancient carnival, culled from histories lost forever, as the brochure had said. Within each box, though, anything but dry history resided. Chaos, essence, power, folding in on itself in infinite spirals. Waiting for an incubator, a warm walking womb to carry it to its new home, to release. Unchecked primal appetite, that could consume anything, even a woman with an endless appetite of her own. I felt my breath shallow out, my heart beat fluttery and weak.

I reached out and touched the box labeled *KRONIA*. It vibrated slightly under my fingertips. After a pause, I pushed it back.

—Masks and merriment, as I recall. Too weak, I said. The barker nodded and smiled.

I picked up the boxed labeled *NAVIGIUM ISIDIS*, and immediately placed it on top of the *KRONIA* box. —Floats, processionals, parades. I think she'd be amused. I don't want to amuse her.

At the far edge of the floor, a chair moved. I felt the contents of the space shifting, as if rousing itself from a too-long dream. A low sigh wafted across the room, or perhaps it was only the wind, or the ghost of a dream of the wind.

Three boxes were left on the stone. —*BACCHANALIA*, I said, picking up the one to the left. I placed it on top of the stack. —Savage. She'd be disoriented, repulsed. But not incapacitated.

—Are you certain, madam? the barker said. —Wine-soaked madness and lust in the night? Nothing to stop you from partaking as well, if you desire. If you aren't dismembered, that is.

But I had moved on. SATURNALIA, said the next box. I lifted it up.

—What's this one again?

—Pageants. Very theatrical, said the barker.—I must warn you: there will be many, many clowns.

I added SATURNALIA to the stack. A single box remained. DIONYSIA, it said. I ran my fingertips over the carved letters. The barker smiled.

—Great festivities within, he said. —A carnelevare of god-frenzied transformation, which subsumes and liberates all.

—I don't want to transform her, I said, adding the box to the stack. —I don't want to liberate or destroy her.

For the first time, the barker looked unsure. —What is it that you want, then?

—I want something so wondrous and primal, she'll never be able to leave it. I want to fill her up, completely. I want her to fall in love.

The warehouse floor grew quiet. —There are no boxes left, the barker said. —There are no more choices.

I reached out, placing both hands flat on the megalith as I contemplated the stack. The stone was warm and smooth, except for spider-thin scratches. I moved my fingers over them. Back and forth. A sixth name, in a language I did not recognize, running across the surface. A secret, sixth carnelevare.

—No more choices, the barker repeated.

—There never was a choice. This is the one I've always wanted, I said. —The carnival with no name.

—The first. Do you know what it is you're asking for? The barker motioned to the dusty rides and ruins scattered across the warehouse floor. —It won't be like any of these. No sequins or carousels or quaint colored lights.

I pointed to the black boxes. —The other carnivals I considered were nothing like that.

The barker's cane came to rest on the pitted surface of the megalith. —
Nothing since the dawn of history has been like this.

I said nothing. There was nothing more to say. After a time, the
barker nodded.

—As you wish, he said. —The conception will be—complex. I will
need time.

—I have thirty days.

—Thirty days out there, you mean. He pointed to the pale blue sky outside the high windows. —In here, it will be as long as I need it to be.

—All right.

—I am compelled to caution you: your body will change. Your mind
will change. And there will be pain.

—I'm a woman. There always is.

5

Outside the house, days have come and gone. Months have bled away.
Within these walls, the universe pauses to watch.

In the undiscovered country of my torso, from out the limitless valleys of
my most intimate self, another monster emerges another child of the carnelevare, horns and hooves slicing through skin and muscle and bone and
capillaries. By my side, The Grand struggles, but I do not lessen my grip.
Massive clawed hands clutch at my slick thighs, hoisting its heavy furred
body up and out and into a room so spattered by my blood that I cannot tell
where my body ends and where the house begins, except there is no beginning and ending, it is all one and the same, an ouroboros of continual birth.
And the monster cleans its bull-shaped face against my stomach and licks
my breasts, and crawls away, far into the house, and something else begins to
emerge from my body, worse or better I cannot tell. This is the sixth carnelevare, the great removing and raising of the flesh, the coming of a god so old
it does not remember its name, and with it all its attendants beautiful and
hideous, bursting forth from every orifice of my flesh to celebrate the mystery
of all mysteries.

The floor beneath me shudders beneath my sudden burgeoning weight, and I hear the crackling of tree limbs, the cracking of bones. The dislocation of my jaw, the colossal clang of bells. Vastness pours out of me like an ocean. And the backwash of darkness rolls over my mind like a breaking wheel, and I float in the spirals of those faded painted galaxies of my childhood, holding my great-great-great-great grandmother's slender hand. Who lives around all those stars, can they see us, what are their names, my nine-year-old self asks her as the ghost of my mother daubs specks of gold and silver paint across the fathomless blue, and my grandmother replies, I am the only human in the world who will ever know.

Together we look up, and up, and up, and from our starry perch we see the deep woods of all the worlds, the labyrinths and groves, we see the satyrs and stags and bulls and the wolves and women and men. Masked and naked, they dance and contort around frightened fires, they chant their prayers and pleas into the shadowed cracks of the world, they laugh and crash together in god-fevered horror and cry out as the sparks of their devotion float up and wink out with their ecstasy. They gyre together and pull apart transformed, endless variations of monstrosities kaleidoscoping out of their frenzied couplings. And I am the night, and out of the night and the woods their god comes to them, into them, into her, in the strike of lightning and the shuddering of the earth, in the terminal vastation of his song.

—Close your eyes, I whisper.

—Never.

I sigh, and the fires wink out one by one, and I sink back down to the floor, to a room filled with clear light and the silk rattle of morning through the tree's wintery bones.

I force my sticky eyelids open. My body feels empty, still. I blink, and the ceiling swims in a thin wash of red. I can't tell if I'm dead or alive. I'm not breathing, and I cannot feel the beating of my heart. There is no pain, I realize in shock: the complete absence of such an all-consuming presence makes me light, free. I roll slightly, slowly, and sit up. I am covered head to toe in blood, and I am whole. My right hand holds the mangled, broken wrist of a woman's severed arm, the grip so tight and deep beneath her flesh that I cannot see my fingertips. Crimson-brown gobs of placenta and blood cover every inch of our joined skin. Under the drying gore, I recognize The Grand's flower-carved wedding ring. I leave the ring on the couch, with the arm.

Outside, gossamer trails of night-blue mist waft through the backyard like torn strands of the Milky Way, sparking with millions of little pinpricks of pure white light. They drift and catch on the sleeping faces of the women and men pulled from their neighboring homes in the carnelevare's orgiastic wake, settle into their hair and over their bare tangled limbs, crash and break apart against tall pine trees and dissipate with the rising sun. A thread of it trails against my bare leg, disappearing beneath the triangle of matted hair. The effluvium of a nameless carnival as it blew in and out of town. I gently pull it out and let it float away.

At the edge of the yard, legs tucked under thighs white and hard as marble, the small body of a woman with a missing left arm rests under a large tree. I walk over, and kneel before The Grand. She looks no older than me. Her pale green eyes are open, wide, blank. They stare through and beyond me, up into the sky. Her face is raised and lips are parted, as if being forced to drink from a bottomless cup. Or perhaps, as if about to speak a name.

6

A blood-orange sun was sinking slowly into the edges of my city's wide electric edges, and I raised my worshiping hands and face like a grateful Akhenaton into its early autumn heat. I had lost a month, and so much more. It was time to go home, all the way home. Behind me, just within the shadows of the open warehouse doors, behind the boundary he could not see or cross, the barker stood, hesitant.

—What does it feel like? he asked.

—This? I turned, hand on my stomach, already slightly curved.

—That. All of it, the god and the power and the mysteries, folded into something so small and insignificant as you. To be so full. And, the sun. The weight of the air on your body. The pleasure of bearing so much pain. Being a part of the world, while knowing you're not really a part of anything at all.

—I couldn't tell you. I don't have any answers.

He stared at me, waiting, disappointed yet still expectant; and then his eyes glazed. I could see him moving beyond me, his mind traveling to that invisible realm beyond the carnelevare's end, where all questions are answered, all hunger sated, where all the endless pleasurable and terrifying variations of the chase dwindle down to a dead and desiccated end.

—Do you really want to know?

He looked up into the sky, then smiled his yellow-teethed grin.

—No.

THE MYSTERIES

Nightmare Carnival published in 2014 by Dark Horse Books, was my third anthology for them.

I was then on my third in-house editor (each had left the company between my books). Never expert at selling books vs. their successful comic book line, they tried. I asked specifically for no killer clown on the cover, so instead I got a dead clown on a comic book-like cover. Oh well. Katherine Dunn, the late author of *Geek Love*, provided an Introduction.

Livia Llewellyn's writing is fearless and I love all of her short stories. "The Mysteries" is a good example.

Dancing Men

by Glen Hirshberg

(From *The Dark,* 2003)

"These are the last days of our lives so we give a signal maybe there still will be relatives or acquaintances of these persons… They were tortured and burnt goodbye…"

—Testimonial found at Chelmno

1

We'd been all afternoon in the Old Jewish Cemetery, where green light filters through the trees and lies atop the tumbled tombstones like algae. Mostly I think the kids were tired. The two-week Legacy of the Holocaust tour I had organized had taken us to Zeppelin Field in Nuremberg, where downed electrical wires slither through the brittle grass, and Bebelplatz in East Berlin, where ghost-shadows of burned books flutter in their chamber in the ground like white wings. We'd spent our nights not sleeping on sleeper trains east to Auschwitz and Birkenau and our days on public transport, traipsing through the fields of dead and the monuments to them, and all seven high school juniors in my care had had enough.

From my spot on a bench alongside the roped off stone path that meandered through the grounds and back out to the streets of Josefov, I watched six of my seven charges giggling and chattering around the final resting place of Rabbi Loew. I'd told them the story of the Rabbi and the clay man he'd supposedly created and then animated, and now they were running their hands over his tombstone, tracing Hebrew letters they couldn't read, chanting *"Amet,"* the word I'd taught them, in low voices and laughing. As of yet, nothing had risen from the dirt. The Tribe, they'd taken to calling themselves, after I told them that the Wandering Jews didn't really work, historically, since the essential characteristic of the Wanderer himself was his solitude.

There are teachers, I suppose, who would have been considered members of the Tribe by the Tribe, particularly on a summer trip, far from home and school and television and familiar language. But I had never been that sort of teacher.

Nor was I the only excluded member of our traveling party. Lurking not far from me, I spotted Penny Berry, the quietest member of our group and the only Goy, staring over the graves into the trees with her expressionless eyes half closed and her lipstickless lips curled into the barest hint of a smile. Her auburn hair sat cocked on the back of her head in a tight, precise ponytail. When she saw me watching, she wandered over, and I swallowed a sigh. It wasn't that I didn't like Penny, exactly. But she asked uncomfortable questions, and she knew how to wait for answers, and she made me nervous for no reason I could explain.

"Hey, Mr. Gadeuszki," she said, her enunciation studied, perfect. She'd made me teach her how to say it right, grind the s and z and k together into that single, Slavic snarl of sound. "What's with the stones?"

She gestured at the tiny gray pebbles placed across the tops of several nearby tombstones. Those on the slab nearest us glinted in the warm, green light like little eyes. "In memory," I said. I thought about sliding over on the bench to make room for her, then thought that would only make both of us even more awkward.

"Why not flowers?" Penny said.

I sat still, listening to the clamor of new-millennium Prague just beyond the stone wall that enclosed the cemetery. "Jews bring stones."

A few minutes later, when she realized I wasn't going to say anything else, Penny moved off in the general direction of the Tribe. I watched her go and allowed myself a few more peaceful seconds. Probably, I thought, it was time to move us along. We had the Astronomical Clock left to see today, puppet theatre tickets for tonight, the plane home to Cleveland in the morning. And just because the kids were tired didn't mean they would tolerate loitering here much longer. For seven summers in a row, I had taken students on some sort of exploring trip. "Because you've got nothing better to do," one member of the Tribe had cheerfully informed me one night the preceding week. Then he'd said, "Oh my God, I was just kidding, Mr. G."

And I'd had to reassure him that I knew he was, I always looked like that.

"That's true. You do," he'd said, and returned to his tripmates.

Now, I rubbed my hand over the stubble on my shaven scalp, stood, and blinked as my family name—in its original, Polish spelling—flashed behind my eyelids again, looking just the way it had this morning amongst all the other names etched into the Pinkas Synagogue wall. The ground went slippery underneath me, the tombstones slid sideways in the grass, and I teetered and sat down hard.

When I lifted my head and opened my eyes, the Tribe had swarmed around me, a whirl of backwards baseball caps and tanned legs and Nike symbols. "I'm fine," I said quickly, stood up, and to my relief I found I did feel fine. I had no idea what had just happened. "Slipped."

"Kind of," said Penny Berry from the edges of the group, and I avoided looking her way.

"Time to go, gang. Lots more to see."

It has always surprised me when they do what I say, because mostly, they do. It's not me, really. The social contract between teachers and students may be the oldest mutually accepted enacted ritual on this earth, and its power is stronger than most people imagine.

We passed between the last of the graves and through a low stone opening. The dizziness or whatever it had been was gone, and I felt only a faint tingling in my fingertips as I drew my last breath of that too-heavy air, thick with loam and grass springing from bodies stacked a dozen deep in the ground.

The side street beside the Old-New Synagogue was crammed with tourists, their purses and backpacks open like the mouths of grotesquely overgrown chicks. Into those open mouths went wooden puppets and embroidered kepot and Chamsa hands from the rows of stalls that lined the sidewalk; the walls, I thought, of an all new, much more ingenious sort of ghetto. In a way, this place had become exactly what Hitler had meant for it to be: the Museum of a Dead Race, only the paying customers were descendents of the Race, and they spent money in amounts he could never have dreamed. The ground had begun to roll under me again, and I closed my eyes. When I opened them, the tourists had cleared in front of me, and I saw the stall, a lopsided wooden hulk on bulky brass wheels. It tilted toward me, the puppets nailed to its side leering and chattering while the gypsy leaned out from between them, nose studded with a silver star, grinning.

He touched the toy nearest him, set it rocking on its terrible, thin wire. "*Loh-oot-kovay deevahd-low,*" he said, and then I was down, flat on my face in the street.

I don't know how I wound up on my back. Somehow, somebody had rolled me over. I couldn't breathe. My stomach felt squashed, as though there was something squatting on it, wooden and heavy, and I jerked, gagged, opened my eyes, and the light blinded me.

"I didn't," I said, blinking, brain flailing. I wasn't even sure I'd been all the way unconscious, couldn't have been out more than a few seconds. But the way the light affected my eyes, it was as though I'd been buried for a month.

"*Doh-bree den, doh-bree den,*" said a voice over me, and I squinted, teared up, blinked into the gypsy's face, the one from the stall, and almost screamed. Then he touched my forehead, and he was just a man, red Manchester United cap on his head, black eyes kind as they hovered around mine. The cool hand he laid against my brow had a wedding ring on it, and the silver star in his nose caught the afternoon light.

I meant to say I was okay, but what came out was "I didn't" again.

The gypsy said something else to me. The language could have been Czech or Slovakian or Romani. I didn't know enough to tell the difference, and my ears weren't working right. In them I could feel a painful, persistent pressure.

The gypsy stood, and I saw my students clustered behind him like a knot I'd drawn taut. When they saw me looking, they burst out babbling, and I shook my head, tried to calm them, and then I felt their hands on mine, pulling me to a sitting position. The world didn't spin. The ground stayed still. The puppet stall I would not look at kept its distance.

"Mr. G., are you all right?" one of them asked, her voice shrill, slipping toward panic.

Then Penny Berry knelt and looked straight into me, and I could see her formidable brain churning behind those placid eyes, the silvery color of Lake Erie when it's frozen.

"Didn't what?" she asked.

And I answered, because I had no choice. "Kill my grandfather."

2

They propped me at my desk in our *pension* not far from the Charles Bridge and brought me a glass of "nice water," which was one of our traveling jokes. It was what the too-thin waitress at Terezin—the *"town presented to the Jews by the Nazis,"* as the old propaganda film we saw at the museum proclaimed—thought we were saying when we asked for ice.

For a while, the Tribe sat on my bed and talked quietly to each other and refilled my glass for me. But after thirty minutes or so, when I hadn't keeled over again and wasn't babbling and seemed my usual sullen, solid, bald self, they started shuffling around, playing with my curtains, ignoring me. One of them threw a pencil at another. For a short while, I almost forgot about the nausea churning in my stomach, the trembling in my wrists, the puppets bobbing on their wires in my head.

"Hey," I said. I had to say it twice more to get their attention. I usually do.

Finally, Penny noticed and said, "Mr. Gadeuszki's trying to say something," and they slowly quieted down.

I put my quivering hands on my lap under the desk and left them there. "Why don't you kids get back on the metro and go see the Clock?"

The Tribe members looked at each other uncertainly. "Really," I told them. "I'm fine. When's the next time you're going to be in Prague?"

They were good kids, and they looked unsure for a few seconds longer. In the end, though, they started trickling toward the door, and I thought I'd gotten them out until Penny Berry stepped in front of me.

"You killed your grandfather," she said.

"Didn't," I snarled, and Penny blinked, and everyone whirled to stare at me. I took a breath, almost got control of my voice. "I said I didn't kill him."

"Oh," Penny said. She was on this trip not because of any familial or cultural heritage but because this was the most interesting experience she could find to devour this month. She was pressing me now because she suspected I had something more startling to share than Prague did at the moment. And she was always hungry.

Or maybe she was just lonely, confused about the kid she had never quite been and the world she didn't quite feel part of. Which would make her more than a little like me, and might explain why she had always annoyed me as much as she did.

"It's stupid," I said. "It's nothing."

Penny didn't move. In my memory, the little wooden man on his black pine branch quivered, twitched, and began to rock side to side.

"I need to write it down," I said, trying to sound gentle. Then I lied. "Maybe I'll show you when I'm done."

Five minutes later, I was alone in my room with a fresh glass of nice water, and there was sand on my tongue and desert sun on my neck and that horrid, gasping breathing like a snake rattle in my ears, and for the first time in many, many years, I was home.

3

In June, 1978, on the day after school let out, I was sitting in my bedroom in Albuquerque, New Mexico, thinking about absolutely nothing when my dad came in and sat down on my bed and said, "I want you to do something for me."

In my nine years of life, my father had almost never asked me to do anything for him. As far as I could tell, he had very few things that he wanted. He worked at an insurance firm and came home at exactly 5:30 every night and played an hour of catch with me before dinner or, sometimes, walked me to the ice cream shop. After dinner, he sat on the black couch in the den reading paperback mystery novels until 9:30. The paperbacks were all old with bright yellow or red covers featuring men in trench coats and women with black dresses sliding down the curves in their bodies like tar. It made me nervous, sometimes, just watching my father's hands on the covers. I asked him once why he liked those kinds of books, and he just shook his head. "All those people," he said, sounding, as usual, as though he were speaking to me through a tin can from a great distance. "Doing all those things." At exactly 9:30, every single night I can remember, my father clicked off the lamp next to the couch and touched me on the head if I was up and went to bed.

"What do you want me to do?" I asked that June morning, though I didn't much care. This was the first weekend of summer vacation, and I had months of free time in front of me, and I never knew quite what to do with it anyway.

"What I tell you, okay?" my father said.

Without even thinking, I said, "Sure."

And he said, "Good. I'll tell Grandpa you're coming." Then he left me gaping on the bed while he went into the kitchen to use the phone.

My grandfather lived seventeen miles from Albuquerque in a red adobe hut in the middle of the desert. The only sign of humanity anywhere around him was the ruins of a small pueblo maybe half a mile away. Even now, what I remember most about my grandfather's house is the desert rolling up to and through it in an endless red tide that never receded. From the back steps, I could see the pueblo honeycombed with caves like a giant beehive tipped on its side, empty of bees but buzzing as the wind whipped through it.

Four years before, my grandfather had told my parents to knock off the token visits. Then he'd had his phone shut off. As far as I knew, none of us had seen him since.

All my life, he'd been dying. He had emphysema and some kind of weird allergic condition that turned swatches of his skin pink. The last time I'd been with him, he'd just sat in a chair in a tank top, breathing through a tube. He'd looked like a piece of petrified wood.

Now, the day after somehow telling my grandfather I was coming, my father packed my green camp duffel bag with a box of new, unopened wax packs of baseball cards and the transistor radio my mother had given me for my birthday the year before, then loaded it and me into the grimy green Datsun he always meant to wash and never did. "Time to go," he told me in his mechanical voice, and I was still too baffled by what was happening to protest as he led me outside. Moments before, a morning thunderstorm had rocked the whole house, but now the sun was up, searing the whole sky orange. Our street smelled like creosote and green chili and adobe mud.

"I don't want to go," I said to my father.

"I wouldn't either, if I were you," he told me, and started the car.

"You don't even like him," I said.

My father just looked at me, and for an astonishing second, I thought he was going to hug me. But he looked away instead, dropped the car into gear, and drove us out of town.

All the way to my grandfather's house, we followed the thunderstorm. It must have been traveling at exactly our speed, because we never got any closer, and it never got further away. It just retreated before us, a big black wall of nothing, like a shadow the whole world cast, and every now and then streaks of lightning flew up the clouds like signal flares and illuminated the sand and mountains and rain.

"Why are we doing this?" I asked when my dad started slowing, studying the sand on his side of the car for the dirt track that lead to my grandfather's.

"Want to drive?" he answered, gesturing to me to slide across the seat into his lap.

Again, I was surprised. My dad always seemed willing enough to play catch with me. But he rarely generated ideas for things we could do together on his own. And the thought of sitting in his lap with his arms around me was too alien to fathom. I waited too long, and the moment passed. My father didn't ask again. Through the windshield, I looked at the wet road already drying in patches in the sun. The whole day felt distant, like someone else's dream.

"'You know he was in the war, right?' my father said, and despite our crawling speed he had to jam on the brakes to avoid passing the turnoff. No one, it seemed to me, could possibly have intended this to be a road. It wasn't dug or flattened or marked, just a rumple in the earth.

"Yeah," I said.

That he'd been in the war was pretty much the only thing I knew about my grandfather. Actually, he'd been in the camps. After the war, he'd been in other camps in Israel for almost five years while Red Cross workers searched for living relatives and found none and finally turned him loose to make his way as best he could.

As soon as we were off the highway, sand ghosts rose around the car, ticking against the trunk and hood as we passed. Thanks to the thunderstorm, they left a wet, red residue like bug smear on the hood and windshield.

"You know, now that I think about it," my father said, his voice flat as ever but the words clearer, somehow, and I found myself leaning closer to him to make sure I heard him over the churning wheels. "He was even less of a grandfather to you than a father to me." He rubbed a hand over the bald spot just beginning to spread over the top of his head like an egg yolk being squashed. I'd never seen him do that before. It made him look old.

My grandfather's house rose out of the desert like a druid mound. There was no shape to it. It had exactly one window, and that couldn't be seen from the road. No mailbox. Never in my life, I realized abruptly, had I had to sleep in there.

"Dad, please don't make me stay," I said as he stopped the car fifteen feet or so from the front door.

He looked at me, and his mouth turned down a little, and his shoulders tensed. Then he sighed. "Three days," he said, and got out.

"You stay," I said, but I got out, too.

When I was standing beside him, looking past the house at the distant pueblo, he said, "Your grandfather didn't ask for me, he asked for you. He won't hurt you. And he doesn't ask for much from us, or from anyone."

"Neither do you," I said.

After a while, and very slowly, as though remembering how, my father smiled. "And neither do you, Seth."

Neither the smile nor the statement reassured me.

"Just remember this, son. Your grandfather has had a very hard life, and not just because of the camps. He worked two jobs for twenty-five years to provide for my mother and me. He never called in sick. He never took vacations. And he was ecstatic when you were born."

That surprised me. "Really? How do you know?"

For the first time I could remember, my father blushed, and I thought maybe I'd caught him lying, and then I wasn't sure. He kept looking at me. "Well, he came to town, for one thing. Twice."

For a little longer, we stood together while the wind rolled over the rocks and sand. I couldn't smell the rain anymore, but I thought I could taste it, a little. Tall, leaning cacti prowled the waste around us like stick figures who'd escaped from one of my doodles. I was always doodling, then, trying to get the shapes of things.

Finally, the thin, wooden door to the adobe clicked open, and out stepped Lucy, and my father straightened and put his hand on his bald spot again and put it back down.

She didn't live there, as far as I knew. But I'd never been to my grandfather's house when she wasn't in it. I knew she worked for some foundation that provided care to Holocaust victims, though she was Navajo, not Jewish, and that she'd been coming out here all my life to make my grandfather's meals, bathe him, keep him company. I rarely saw them speak to each other. When I was little and my grandmother was still alive and we were still welcome, Lucy used to take me to the pueblo after she'd finished with my grandfather and watch me climb around on the stones and peer into the empty caves and listen to the wind chase 500 year-old echoes out of the walls.

There were gray streaks now in the black hair that poured down Lucy's shoulders, and I could see semi-circular lines like tree rings in her dark, weathered cheeks. But I was uncomfortably aware, this time, of the way her breasts pushed her plain, white denim shirt out of the top of her jeans while her eyes settled on mine, black and still.

"Thank you for coming," she said, as if I'd had a choice. When I didn't answer, she looked at my father. "Thank you for bringing him. We're set up out back."

I threw one last questioning glance at my father as Lucy started away, but he just looked bewildered or bored or whatever he generally was. And that made me angry. "Bye," I told him, and moved toward the house.

"Goodbye," I heard him say, and something in his tone unsettled me; it was too sad. I shivered, turned around, and my father said, "He want to see me?"

He looked thin, I thought, just another spindly cactus, holding my duffle bag out from his side. If he'd been speaking to me, I might have run to him. I wanted to. But he was watching Lucy, who had stopped at the edge of the square of patio cement outside the front door.

"I don't think so," she said, and came over to me and took my hand.

Without another word, my father tossed my duffle bag onto the miniature patio and climbed back in his car. For a moment, his eyes caught mine through the windshield, and I said, "Wait," but my father didn't hear me. I said it louder, and Lucy put her hand on my shoulder.

"This has to be done, Seth," she said.

"What does?"

"This way." She gestured toward the other side of the house, and I followed her there and stopped when I saw the hogan.

It sat next to the squat gray cactus I'd always considered the edge of my grandfather's yard. It looked surprisingly solid, its mud walls dry and gray and hard, its pocked, stumpy wooden pillars firm in the ground, almost as if they were real trees that had somehow taken root there.

"You live here now?" I blurted, and Lucy stared at me.

"Oh, yes, Seth. Me sleep-um ground. *How*." She pulled aside the hide curtain at the front of the hogan and ducked inside, and I followed.

I thought it would be cooler in there, but it wasn't. The wood and mud trapped the heat but blocked the light. I didn't like it. It reminded me of an oven, of Hansel and Gretel. And it reeked of the desert: burnt sand, hot wind, nothingness.

"This is where you'll sleep," Lucy said. "It's also where we'll work." She knelt and lit a beeswax candle and placed it in the center of the dirt floor in a scratched glass drugstore candlestick. "We need to begin right now."

"Begin what?" I asked, fighting down another shudder as the candlelight played over the room. Against the far wall, tucked under a miniature canopy constructed of metal poles and a tarpaulin, were a sleeping bag and a pillow. My bed, I assumed. Beside it sat a low, rolling table, and on the table were another candlestick, a cracked ceramic bowl, some matches, and the Dancing Man.

In my room in the *pension* in the Czech Republic, five thousand miles and twenty years removed from that place, I put my pen down and swallowed the entire glass of lukewarm water my students had left me. Then I got up and went to the window, staring out at the trees and the street. I was hoping to see my kids returning like ducks to a familiar pond, flapping their arms and jostling each other and squawking and laughing. Instead, I saw my own face, faint and featureless, too white in the window glass. I went back to the desk and picked up the pen.

The Dancing Man's eyes were all pupil, carved in two perfect ovals in the knottiest wood I had ever seen. The nose was just a notch, but the mouth was enormous, a giant O, like the opening of a cave. I was terrified of the thing even before I noticed that it was moving.

Moving, I suppose, is too grand a description. It…*leaned*. First one way, then the other, on a bent black pine branch that ran straight through its belly. In a fit of panic, after a nightmare, I described it to my college roommate, a physics major, and he shrugged and said something about perfect balance and pendulums and gravity and the rotation of the earth. For the one and only time, right in that first moment, I lifted the branch off the table, and the Dancing Man leaned a little faster, weaving to the beat of my blood. I put the branch down fast.

"Take the drum," Lucy said behind me, and I ripped my eyes away from the Dancing Man.

"What?" I said.

She gestured at the table, and I realized she meant the ceramic bowl. I didn't understand, and I didn't want to go over there. But I didn't know what else to do, and I felt ridiculous under Lucy's stare.

The Dancing Man was at the far end of its branch, leaning, mouth open. Trying to be casual, I snatched the bowl from underneath it and retreated to where Lucy knelt. The water inside the bowl made a sloshing sound but didn't splash out, and I held it away from my chest in surprise and noticed the covering stitched over the top. It was hide of some kind, moist when I touched it.

"Like this," said Lucy, and she leaned close and tapped on the skin of the drum. The sound was deep and tuneful, like a voice. I sat down next to Lucy. She tapped again in a slow, repeating pattern. I put my hands where hers had been, and when she nodded at me, I began to play.

"'Okay?' I said.

"Harder," Lucy said, and she reached into her pocket and pulled out a long, wooden stick. The candlelight flickered across the stick, and I saw the carving. A pine tree, and underneath it, roots that bulged along the base of the stick like long, black veins.

"What is that?" I asked.

"A rattle stick. My grandmother made it. I'm going to rattle it while you play. So if you would. Like I showed you."

I beat on the drum, and the sound came out dead in that airless space.

"For God's sake," Lucy snapped. "Harder." She had never been exceptionally friendly to me. But she'd been friendlier than this.

I slammed my hands down harder, and after a few beats, Lucy leaned back and nodded and watched. Not long after, she lifted her hand, stared at me as though daring me to stop her, and shook the stick. The sound it made was less rattle than buzz, as though it had wasps inside it. Lucy shook it a few more times, always at the same half-pause in my rhythm. Then her eyes rolled back in her head, and her spine arched, and my hand froze over the drum and Lucy snarled, "Don't stop."

After that, she began to chant. There was no tune to it, but a pattern, the pitch sliding up a little, down some, up a little more. When Lucy reached the top note, the ground under my crossed legs seemed to tingle, as though there were scorpions sliding out of the sand, but I didn't look down. I thought of the wooden figure behind me, but I didn't turn around. I played the drum, and I watched Lucy, and I kept my mouth shut.

We went on for a long, long time. After that first flush of fear, I was too mesmerized to think. My bones were tingling, too, and the air in the hogan was heavy. I couldn't get enough of it in my lungs. Tiny tidepools of sweat had formed in the hollow of Lucy's neck and under her ears and at the throat of her shirt. Under my palms, the drum was sweating, too, and the skin got slippery and warm. Not until Lucy stopped chanting did I realize that I was rocking side to side. Leaning.

"Want lunch?" Lucy said, standing and brushing the earth off her jeans.

I put my hands out perpendicular, felt the skin prickle and realized my wrists had gone to sleep even as they pounded out the rhythm Lucy had taught me. When I stood, the floor of the hogan seemed unstable, like the bottom of one of those balloon-tents my classmates sometimes had at birthday parties. I didn't want to look behind me, and then I did. The Dancing Man rocked slowly in no wind.

I turned around again, but Lucy had left the hogan. I didn't want to be alone in there, so I leapt through the hide curtain and winced against the sudden blast of sunlight and saw my grandfather.

He was propped up in his wheelchair, positioned halfway between the hogan and the back of his house. He must have been there the whole time, I thought, and somehow I'd managed not to notice him when I came in, because unless he'd gotten a whole lot better in the years since I'd seen him last, he couldn't have wheeled himself out. And he looked worse.

For one thing, his skin was falling off. At every exposed place on him, I saw flappy folds of yellow-pink. What was underneath was uglier still, not red or bleeding, just not skin. Too dry. Too colorless. He looked like a corn husk. An empty one.

Next to him, propped on a rusty blue dolly, was a cylindrical silver oxygen tank. A clear tube ran from the nozzle at the top of the tank to the blue mask over my grandfather's nose and mouth. Above the mask, my grandfather's heavy-lidded eyes watched me, though they didn't seem capable of movement, either. Leave him out here, I thought, and those eyes would simply fill up with sand.

"Come in, Seth," Lucy told me, without any word to my grandfather or acknowledgment that he was there.

I had my hand on the screen door, was halfway into the house when I realized I'd heard him speak. I stopped. It had to have been him, I thought, and couldn't have been. I turned around and saw the back of his head tilting toward the top of the chair. Retracing my steps—I'd given him a wide berth—I returned to face him. The eyes stayed still, and the oxygen tank was silent. But the mask fogged, and I heard the whisper again.

"*Ruach,*" he said. It was what he always called me, when he called me anything.

In spite of the heat, I felt goosebumps spring from my skin, all along my legs and arms. I couldn't move. I couldn't answer. I should say hello, I thought. Say something.

I waited instead. A few seconds later, the oxygen mask fogged again. "*Trees,*" said the whisper-voice. "*Screaming. In the trees.*" One of my grandfather's hands raised an inch or so off the arm of the chair and fell back into place.

"Patience," Lucy said from the doorway. "Come on, Seth." This time, my grandfather said nothing as I slipped past him into the house.

Lucy slid a bologna sandwich and a bag of Fritos and a plastic glass of apple juice in front of me. I lifted the sandwich, found that I couldn't imagine putting it in my mouth, and dropped it on the plate.

"Better eat," Lucy said. "We have a long day yet."

I ate a little. Eventually, Lucy sat down across from me, but she didn't say anything else. She just gnawed a celery stick and watched the sand outside change color as the sun crawled west. The house was silent, the countertops and walls bare.

"Can I ask you something?" I finally asked.

Lucy was washing my plate in the sink. She didn't turn around, but she didn't say no.

"What are we doing? Out there, I mean."

No answer. Through the kitchen doorway, I could see my grandfather's living room, the stained wood floor and the single brown armchair lodged against a wall across from the tv. My grandfather had spent every waking minute of his life in this place for fifteen years or more, and there was no trace of him in it.

"It's a Way, isn't it?" I said, and Lucy shut off the water.

When she turned, her expression was the same as it had been all day, a little mocking, a little angry. She took a step toward the table.

"We learned about them at school," I said.

"Did you."

"We're studying lots of Indian things."

The smile that spread over Lucy's face was cruel. Or maybe just tired. "Good for you," she said. "Come on. We don't have much time."

"Is this to make my grandfather better?"

"Nothing's going to make your grandfather better." Without waiting for me, she pushed through the screen door into the heat.

This time, I made myself stop beside my grandfather's chair. I could just hear the hiss of the oxygen tank, like steam escaping from the boiling ground. When no fog appeared in the blue mask and no words emerged from the hiss, I followed Lucy into the hogan and let the hide curtain fall shut.

All afternoon and into the evening, I played the water drum while Lucy chanted. By the time the air began to cool outside, the whole hogan was vibrating, and the ground, too. Whatever we were doing, I could feel the power in it. I was the beating heart of a living thing, and Lucy was its voice. Once, I found myself wondering just what we were setting loose or summoning here, and I stopped for a single beat. But the silence was worse. The silence was like being dead. And I thought I could hear the Dancing Man behind me. If I inclined my head, stopped playing for too long, I almost believed I'd hear him whispering.

When Lucy finally rocked to her feet and left without speaking to me, it was evening, and the desert was alive. I sat shaking as the rhythm spilled out of me and the sand soaked it up. Then I stood, and that unsteady feeling came over me again, stronger this time, as if the air were wobbling, too, threatening to slide right off the surface of the Earth. When I emerged from the hogan, I saw black spiders on the wall of my grandfather's house, and I heard wind and rabbits and the first coyotes yipping somewhere to the west. My grandfather sat slumped in the same position he had been in hours and hours ago, which meant he had been baking out here all afternoon. Lucy was on the patio, watching the sun melt into the horizon's open mouth. Her skin was slick, and her hair was wet where it touched her ear and neck.

"Your grandfather's going to tell you a story," she said, sounding exhausted. "And you're going to listen."

My grandfather's head rolled upright, and I wished we were back in the hogan, doing whatever it was we'd been doing. At least there, I was moving, pounding hard enough to drown sound out. Maybe. The screen door slapped shut, and my grandfather looked at me. His eyes were deep, deep brown, almost black, and horribly familiar. Did my eyes look like that?

"*Ruach,*" he whispered, and I wasn't sure, but his whisper seemed stronger than it had before. The oxygen mask fogged and stayed fogged. The whisper kept coming, as though Lucy had spun a spigot and left it open. "*You will know... Now... Then the world...won't be yours...anymore.*" My grandfather shifted like some sort of giant, bloated sand-spider in the center of its web, and I heard his ruined skin rustle. Overhead, the whole sky went red.

"*At war's end...*" my grandfather hissed. "*Do you...understand?*"

I nodded, transfixed. I could hear his breathing, now, the ribs rising, parting, collapsing. The tank machinery had gone strangely silent. Was he breathing on his own, I wondered? Could he, still?

"*A few days. Do you understand? Before the Red Army came...*" He coughed. Even his cough sounded stronger. "*The Nazis took...me. And the Gypsies. From...our camp. To Chelmno.*"

I'd never heard the word before. I've almost never heard it since. But as my grandfather said it, another cough roared out of his throat, and when it was gone, the tank was hissing again. Still, my grandfather continued to whisper.

"*To die. Do you understand?*" Gasp. Hiss. Silence. "*To die. But not yet. Not...right away.*" Gasp. "*We came...by train, but open train. Not cattle car. Wasteland. Farmland. Nothing. And then trees.*" Under the mask, the lips twitched, and above it, the eyes closed completely. *"That first time. Ruach. All those...giant...green...trees. Unimaginable. To think anything...on the Earth we knew...could live that long."*

His voice continued to fade, faster than the daylight. A few minutes more, I thought, and he'd be silent again, just machine and breath, and I could sit out here in the yard and let the evening wind roll over me.

"When they took...us off the train," my grandfather said, *"for one moment... I swear I smelled...leaves. Fat, green leaves...the new green...in them. Then the old smell... The only smell. Blood in dirt. The stink...of us. Piss. Shit. Open... sores. Skin on fire. Hnnn."*

His voice trailed away, hardly-there air over barely-moving mouth, and still he kept talking. *"Prayed for...some people...to die. They smelled...better. Dead. That was one prayer...always answered.*

"They took us...into the woods. Not to barracks. So few of them. Ten. Maybe twenty. Faces like...possums. Stupid. Blank. No thoughts. We came to...ditches. Deep. Like wells. Half full, already. They told us 'Stand still'... 'Breathe in.'"

At first, I thought the ensuing silence was for effect. He was letting me smell it. And I *could* smell it, the earth and the dead people, and there were German soldiers all around us, floating up out of the sand with black uniforms and white, blank faces. Then my grandfather crumpled forward, and I screamed for Lucy.

She came fast but not running and put a hand on my grandfather's back and another on his neck. After a few seconds, she straightened. "He's asleep," she told me. "Stay here." She wheeled my grandfather into the house, and she was gone a long time.

Sliding to a sitting position, I closed my eyes and tried not to hear my grandfather's voice. After a while I thought I could hear bugs and snakes and something larger padding out beyond the cacti. I could feel the moonlight, too, white and cool on my skin. The screen door banged, and I opened my eyes to find Lucy moving toward me, past me, carrying a picnic basket into the hogan.

"I want to eat out here," I said quickly, and Lucy turned with the hide curtain in her hand.

"Why don't we go in?" she said, and the note of coaxing in her voice made me nervous. So did the way she glanced over her shoulder into the hogan, as though something in there had spoken.

I stayed where I was, and eventually Lucy shrugged and let the curtain fall and dropped the basket at my feet. From the way she was acting, I thought she might leave me alone out there, but she sat down instead and looked at the sand and the cacti and the stars.

Inside the basket, I found warmed canned chili in a plastic Tupperware container and fry bread with cinnamon-sugar and two cellophane-wrapped broccoli stalks that reminded me of uprooted miniature trees. In my ears, my grandfather's voice murmured, and to drown out the sound, I began to eat.

As soon as I was finished, Lucy began to stack the containers inside the basket, but she stopped when I spoke. "Please. Just talk to me a little."

She looked at me. The same look. As though we'd never even met. "Get some sleep. Tomorrow…well, let's just say tomorrow's a big day."

"For who?"

Lucy pursed her lips, and all at once, inexplicably, she seemed on the verge of tears. "Go to sleep."

"I'm not sleeping in the hogan," I told her.

"Suit yourself."

She was standing, and her back was to me now. I said, "Just tell me what kind of Way we're doing."

"An Enemy Way."

"What does it do?"

"It's nothing, Seth. God's sake. It's silly. Your grandfather thinks it will help him talk. He thinks it will sustain him while he tells you what he needs to tell you. Don't worry about the Goddamn Way. Worry about your grandfather, for once."

My mouth flew open, and my skin stung as though she'd slapped me. I started to protest, then found I couldn't, and didn't want to. All my life, I'd built my grandfather into a figure of fear, a gasping, grotesque monster in a wheelchair. And my father had let me. I started to cry.

"I'm sorry," I said.

"Don't apologize to me." Lucy walked to the screen door.

"Isn't it a little late?" I called after her, furious at myself, at my father, at Lucy. Sad for my grandfather. Scared and sad.

One more time, Lucy turned around, and the moonlight poured down the white streaks in her hair like wax through a mold. Soon, I thought, she'd be made of it.

"I mean for my grandfather's Enemies," I said. "The Way can't really do anything to the Nazis. Right?"

"His Enemies are inside him," Lucy said, and left me.

For hours, it seemed, I sat in the sand, watching constellations explode like firecrackers out of the blackness, one after another. In the ground, I heard night creatures stirring. I thought about the tube in my grandfather's mouth and the unspeakable hurt in his eyes—because that's what it was, I thought now, not boredom, not hatred—and the enemies inside him. And then, slowly, exhaustion overtook me. The taste of fry bread lingered in my mouth, and the starlight got brighter still. I leaned back on my elbows. And finally, at God knows what hour, I crawled into the hogan, under the tarpaulin canopy Lucy had made me, and fell asleep.

When I awoke, the Dancing Man was leaning over me on its branch, and I knew, all at once, where I'd seen eyes like my grandfather's, and the old fear exploded through me all over again. How had he done it, I wondered? The carving on the wooden man's face was basic, the features crude. But the eyes were his. They had the same singular, almost oval shape, with identical little notches right near the tear-ducts. The same too-heavy lids. Same expression, or lack of any.

I was transfixed, and I stopped breathing. All I could see were those eyes dancing above me. When the Dancing Man was perfectly perpendicular, it seemed to stop momentarily, as though studying me, and I remembered something my dad had told me about wolves. "They're not trial-and-error animals," he'd said. "They wait and watch, wait and watch, until they're sure they know how the thing is done. And then they do it."

The Dancing Man went on weaving. First to one side, then the other, then back. Slower and slower. If it gets itself completely still, I thought—I *knew*—I would die. Or I would change. That was why Lucy was ignoring me. She had lied to me about what we were doing here. That was the reason they hadn't let my father stay. Leaping to my feet, I grabbed the Dancing Man around its clunky wooden base, and it came off the table with the faintest little suck, as though I'd yanked a weed out of the ground. I wanted to throw it, but I didn't dare. Instead, bent double, not looking at my clenched fist, I crab-walked to the entrance of the hogan, brushed back the hide curtain, slammed the Dancing Man down in the sand outside, and flung the curtain closed again. Then I squatted in the shadows, panting. Listening.

I crouched there a long time, watching the bottom of the curtain, expecting to see the Dancing Man slithering beneath it. But the hide stayed motionless, the hogan shadowy but still. I let myself sit back, and eventually, I slid into my sleeping bag again. I didn't expect to sleep anymore, but I did.

The smell of fresh fry bread woke me, and when I opened my eyes, Lucy was laying a tray of breads and sausage and juice on a red, woven blanket on the floor of the hogan. My lips tasted sandy, and I could feel grit in my clothes and between my teeth and under my eyelids, as though I'd been buried overnight and dug up again.

"Hurry," Lucy told me, in the same chilly voice as yesterday.

I threw back the sleeping bag and started to sit up and saw the Dancing Man tilting on its branch, watching me. My whole body clenched, and I glared at Lucy and shouted, "How did that get back here?" Even as I said it, I realized that wasn't what I wanted to ask. More than how, I needed to know *when*. Exactly how long had it been hovering there without my knowing?

Without raising an eyebrow or even looking at me, Lucy shrugged and sat back. "Your grandfather wants you to have it," she said.

"I don't want it."

"Grow up."

Edging as far from the nightstand as possible, I shed the sleeping bag and sat down on the blanket and ate. Everything tasted sweet and sandy. My skin prickled with the intensifying heat. I still had a piece of fry bread and half a sausage left when I put my plastic fork down and looked at Lucy, who was arranging a new candle, settling the water-drum near me, tying her hair back with a red rubber-band.

"Where did it come from?" I asked.

For the first time that day, Lucy looked at me, and this time, there really were tears in her eyes. "I don't understand your family," she said.

I shook my head. "Neither do I."

"Your grandfather's been saving that for you, Seth."

"Since when?"

"Since before you were born. Before your father was born. Before he ever imagined there could be a you."

This time, when the guilt came for me, it mixed with my fear rather than chasing it away, and I broke out sweating. I thought I might be sick.

"You have to eat. Damn you," said Lucy.

I picked up my fork and squashed a piece of sausage into the fry-bread and put it in my mouth. My stomach convulsed but accepted what I gave it.

I managed a few more bites. As soon as I pushed the plate back, Lucy shoved the drum onto my lap. I played while she chanted, and the sides of the hogan seemed to breathe in and out, very slowly. I felt drugged. Then I wondered if I had been. Had they sprinkled something over the bread? Was that the next step? And toward what? Erasing me, I thought, almost chanted. Erasing me, and my hands flew off the drum, and Lucy stopped.

"Alright," she said. "That's probably enough." Then, to my surprise, she actually reached out and tucked some of my hair behind my ear. She even touched my face for a second as she took the drum from me. "It's time for your Journey," she said.

I stared at her. The walls, I noticed, had stilled. I didn't feel any less strange, but a little more awake, at least. "Journey where?"

"You'll need water. And I've packed you a lunch." She slipped through the hide curtain, and I followed, dazed, and almost walked into my grandfather, parked right outside the hogan with a black towel on his head, so that his eyes and splitting skin were in shadow. He wore black leather gloves. His hands, I thought, must be on fire.

Right at the moment I noticed that Lucy was no longer with us, the hiss from the oxygen tank sharpened, and my grandfather's lips moved beneath the mask. "*Ruach.*" This morning, the nickname sounded almost affectionate.

I waited, unable to look away. But the oxygen hiss settled again, like leaves after a gust of wind, and my grandfather said nothing more. A few seconds later, Lucy came back carrying a red backpack, which she handed to me.

"Follow the signs," she said, and turned me around until I was facing straight out from the road into the empty desert.

Struggling to life, I shook her hand off my shoulder. "Signs of what? What am I supposed to be doing?"

"Finding. Bringing back."

"I won't go," I said.

"You'll go," said Lucy coldly. "The signs will be easily recognizable, and easy to locate. I have been assured of that. All you have to do is pay attention."

"'Assured by who?'"

"The first sign, I am told, will be left by the tall, flowering cactus."

She pointed, which was unnecessary. A hundred yards or so from my grandfather's house, a spiky green cactus poked out of the rock and sand, supported on either side by two miniature versions of itself. A little cactus family, staggering in out of the waste.

I glanced at my grandfather under his mock-cowl, Lucy with her ferocious black eyes trained on me. Tomorrow, I thought, my father would come for me, and with any luck, I would never have to come out here again.

Then, suddenly, I felt ridiculous, and sad, and guilty once more.

Without even realizing what I was doing, I stuck my hand out and touched my grandfather's arm. The skin under his thin, cotton shirt depressed beneath my fingers like the squishy center of a misshapen pillow. It wasn't hot. It didn't feel alive at all. I yanked my hand back, and Lucy glared at me. Tears sprang to my eyes.

"Get out of here," she said, and I stumbled away into the sand.

I don't really think the heat intensified as soon as I stepped away from my grandfather's house. But it seemed to. Along my bare arms and legs, I could feel the little hairs curling as though singed. The sun had scorched the sky white, and the only place to look that didn't hurt my eyes was down. Usually, when I walked in the desert, I was terrified of scorpions, but not that day. It was impossible to imagine anything scuttling or stinging or even breathing out there. Except me.

I don't know what I expected to find. Footprints, maybe, or animal scat, or something dead. Instead, stuck to the stem by a cactus needle, I found a yellow stick-em note. It said, "*Pueblo.*"

Gently, avoiding the rest of the spiny needles, I removed the note. The writing was black and blocky. I glanced toward my grandfather's house, but he and Lucy were gone. The ceremonial hogan looked silly from this distance, like a little kid's pup tent.

Unlike the pueblo, I thought. I didn't even want to look that way, let alone go there. Already I could hear it, calling for me in a whisper that sounded far too much like my grandfather's. I could head for the road, I thought. Start toward town instead of the pueblo, and wait for a passing truck to carry me home. There would have to be a truck, sooner or later.

I did go to the road. But when I got there, I turned in the direction of the pueblo. I don't know why. I didn't feel as if I had a choice.

The walk, if anything, was too short. No cars passed. No road signs sprang from the dirt to point the way back to the world I knew. I watched the asphalt rise out of itself and roll in the heat, and I thought of my grandfather in the woods of Chelmno, digging graves in long, green shadows. Lucy had put ice in the thermos she gave me, and the cubes clicked against my teeth when I drank.

I walked, and I watched the desert, trying to spot a bird or a lizard. Even a scorpion would have been welcome. What I saw was sand, distant, colorless mountains, and white sky, a world as empty of life and its echoes as the surface of Mars, and just as red.

Even the lone road sign pointing to the pueblo was rusted through, crusted with sand, the letters so scratched away that the name of the place was no longer legible. I'd never seen a tourist here, or another living soul. Even calling it a pueblo seemed grandiose.

It was two sets of caves dug into the side of a cliff-face, the top one longer than the bottom, so that together they formed a sort of gigantic, cracked harmonica for the desert wind to play. The roof and walls of the top set of caves had fallen in. The whole structure seemed more monument than ruin, a marker of a people who no longer existed rather than a place they had lived.

The bottom stretch of caves was largely intact, and as I stumbled toward them along the cracking macadam, I could feel their pull in my ankles. They seemed to be sucking the desert inside them, bit by bit. I stopped in front and listened.

I couldn't hear anything. I looked at the cracked, nearly square window openings, the doorless entryways leading into what had once been living spaces, the low, shadowed caves of dirt and rock. The whole pueblo just squatted there, inhaling sand through its dozens of dead mouths in a mockery of breath. I waited a while longer, but the open air didn't feel any safer, just hotter. If my grandfather's Enemies were inside him, I suddenly wondered, and if we were calling them out, then where were they going? Finally, I ducked through the nearest entryway and stood in the gloom.

After a few seconds, my eyes adjusted. But there was nothing to see. Along the window openings, blown sand lay in waves and mounds, like miniature relief maps of the desert outside. At my feet lay tiny stones, too small to hide scorpions, and a few animal bones, none of them larger than my pinky, distinguishable primarily by the curve of them, their stubborn whiteness.

Then, as though my entry had triggered some sort of mechanical magic show, sound coursed into my ears. In the walls, tiny feet and bellies slithered and scuttled. Nothing rattled a warning. Nothing hissed. And the footsteps, when they came, came so softly that at first I mistook them for sand shifting along the sills and the cool, clay floor.

I didn't scream, but I stumbled backwards, lost my footing, slipped down. I had the thermos raised and ready to swing when my father stepped out of the shadows and sat down cross-legged across the room from me.

"What…" I said, tears flying down my face, heart thudding.

My father said nothing. From the pocket of his plain, yellow, button-up shirt, he pulled a packet of cigarette paper and a pouch of tobacco, then rolled a cigarette in a series of quick, expert motions.

"You don't smoke," I said, and my father lit the cigarette and dragged air down his lungs with a rasp.

"Far as you know," he answered. The orange glow from the tip looked like an open sore on his lips. Around us, the pueblo lifted, settled.

"Why does grandpa call me 'Ruach?'" I snapped. And still, my father only sat and smoked. The smell tickled unpleasantly in my nostrils. "God, Dad. What's going on? What are you doing here, and—"

"Do you know what *ruach* means?" he said.

I shook my head.

"It's a Hebrew word. It means ghost."

Hearing that was like being slammed to the ground. I couldn't get my lungs to work.

My father went on. "Sometimes, that's what it means. It depends what you use it with, you see? Sometimes, it means spirit, as in the spirit of God. Spirit of life. What God gave to his creations." He stubbed his cigarette in the sand, and the orange glow winked out like an eye blinking shut. "And sometimes, it just means wind."

By my sides, I could feel my hands clutch as breath returned to my body. The sand felt cool and soft against my palms. "You don't know Hebrew, either," I said.

"I made a point of knowing that."

"Why?"

"Because that's what he called me, too," my father said, and rolled a second cigarette but didn't light it. For a while, we sat. Then my father said, "Lucy called me two weeks ago. She told me it was time, and she said she needed a partner for your...ceremony. Someone to hide this, then help you find it. She said it was essential to the ritual." Reaching behind him, he produced a brown paper grocery bag with the top rolled down and tossed it to me. "I didn't kill it," he said.

I stared at him, and more tears stung my eyes. Sand licked along the skin of my legs and arms and crawled up my shorts and sleeves as though seeking pores, points of entry. Nothing about my father's presence here was reassuring. Nothing about him had ever been reassuring, or anything else, I thought furiously, and the fury felt good. It helped me move. I yanked the bag to me.

The first thing I saw when I ripped it open was an eye. It was yellow-going-grey, almost dry. Not quite, though. Then I saw the folded, black, ridged wings. A furry, broken body, twisted into a J. Except for the smell and the eye, it could have been a Halloween decoration.

"Is that a bat?" I whispered. Then I shoved the bag away and gagged.

My father glanced around at the walls, back at me. He made no move toward me. He was part of it, I thought wildly, he knew what they were doing, and then I pushed the thought away. It couldn't be true. "Dad, I don't understand," I pleaded.

"I know you're young," my father said. "He didn't do this to me until I left for college. But there's no more time, is there? You've seen him. He doesn't have long."

"Why do I have to do this at all?"

At that, my father's gaze swung down on me. He cocked his head and pursed his lips, as though I'd asked something completely incomprehensible. "It's your birthright," he said, and stood up.

We drove back to my grandfather's adobe in silence. The trip lasted less than five minutes. I couldn't even figure out what else to ask, let alone what I might do. I glanced at my father, wanting to scream at him, pound on him until he told me why he was acting this way.

Except that I wasn't sure he was acting anything but normal, for him. He didn't generally speak during our afternoon walks to the ice cream shop, either. When we arrived at the adobe, he leaned across me to push my door open, and I grabbed his hand.

"Dad. At least tell me what the bat is for."

My father sat up, moved the air-conditioning lever right, then hard back to the left, as though he could surprise it into working. He always did this. It never worked. My father and his routines. "Nothing," he said. "It's a symbol."

"For what?"

"Lucy will tell you."

"But you know." I was almost snarling at him now.

"Only what Lucy told me. It stands for the skin at the tip of the tongue. It's the Talking God. Or associated with it. Or something. It goes where nothing else can go. Or helps someone else go there. I think. I'm sorry."

Gently, hand on my shoulder, he eased me out of the car before it occurred to me to wonder what he was apologizing for. "I promise you this, Seth," he murmured. "This is the last time in your life that you'll have to come here. Shut the door."

Too stunned and confused and scared to do anything else, I shut it, then watched as my father's car disintegrated into the first, far-off shadows of twilight. Already, too soon, I felt the change in the air, the night chill seeping through the gauze-dry day like blood through a bandage.

My grandfather and Lucy were waiting on the patio. She had her hand on his shoulder, her long hair gathered on her head, and without its dark frame, her face looked much older. And his—fully exposed now, without its protective shawl—looked like a rubber mask on a hook, with no bones inside to support it.

Slowly, my grandfather's wheelchair squeaked over the patio onto the hard sand as Lucy propelled it. I could do nothing but watch. The wheelchair stopped, and my grandfather studied me.

"*Ruach*," he said. There was still no tone in his voice. But there were no holes in it, either, no gaps where last night his breath had failed him. "*Bring it to me.*"

It was my imagination, surely, or the first hint of breeze, that made the bag seem to squirm in my hands. This would be the last time, my father had said. I stumbled forward and dropped the paper bag in my grandfather's lap.

Faster than I'd ever seen him move, but still not fast, my grandfather crushed the bag against his chest. His head tilted forward, and I had the insane idea that he was about to sing to it, like a baby. But all he did was close his eyes and hold it.

"Alright, that's enough, I told you it doesn't work like that," Lucy said, and took the bag from him. She touched him gently on the back but didn't look at me.

"What did he just do?" I asked, challenging her. "What did the bat do?"

Once more, Lucy smiled her slow, nasty smile. "Wait and see."

Then she was gone, and my grandfather and I were alone in the yard. The dark came drifting down the distant mountainsides like a fog bank, but faster. When it reached us, I closed my eyes and felt nothing except an instantaneous chill. I opened my eyes, and my grandfather was still watching me, head cocked a little on his neck.

"Digging," he said. *"All we did, at first. Making pits deeper. The dirt so black. So soft. Like sticking your hands…inside an animal. All those trees leaning over us. Pines. Great white birches. Bark, smooth as baby skin. The Nazis gave…nothing to drink. Nothing to eat. But they paid…no attention, either. I sat next to the gypsy I had slept beside all…through the war. On a single slab of rotted wood. We had shared body heat. Blood from…each other's wounds. Infections. Lice.*

"I never…even knew his name. Four years six inches from each other…never knew it. Couldn't understand each other. Never really tried. He'd saved—" a cough rattled my grandfather's entire body, and his eyes got wilder, began to bulge, and I thought he wasn't breathing and almost yelled for Lucy again, but he gathered himself and went on. *"Buttons,"* he said. *"You understand? From somewhere. Rubbed their edges on rocks. Posts. Anything handy. Until they were… sharp. Not to kill. Not as a weapon."* More coughing. *"As a tool. To whittle."*

"Whittle," I said automatically, as though talking in my sleep.

"When he was starving. When he…woke up screaming. When we had to watch children's…bodies dangle from gallows…until the first crows came for their eyes. When it was snowing, and…we had to march…barefoot…or stand outside all night. The gypsy whittled."

Again, my grandfather's eyes ballooned in their sockets as though they would burst. Again came the cough, shaking him so hard that he almost fell from the chair. And again, he fought his body to stillness.

"Wait," he gasped. *"You will wait. You must."*

I waited. What else could I do?

A long while later, he said, *"Two little girls."*

I stared at him. His words wrapped me like strands of a cocoon. "What?"

"Listen. Two girls. The same ones, over and over. That's what…the gypsy…whittled."

Dimly, in the part of my brain that still felt alert, I wondered how anyone could tell if two figures carved in God knows what with the sharpened edge of a button were the same girls.

But my grandfather just nodded. "*Even at the end. Even at Chelmno. In the woods. In the moments…when we weren't digging, and the rest of us…sat. He went straight for the trees. Put his hands on them like they were warm. Wept. First time, all war. Despite everything we saw. Everything we knew…no tears from him, until then. When he came back, he had…strips of pine bark in his hands. And while everyone else slept…or froze…or died…he worked. All night. Under the trees.*"

"*Every few hours…shipments came. Of people, you understand? Jews. We heard trains. Then, later, we saw creatures…between tree trunks. Thin. Awful. Like dead saplings walking. When the Nazis…began shooting…they fell with no sound. Poppoppop from the guns. Then silence. Things lying in leaves. In the wet.*

"*The killing wasn't…enough fun…for the Nazis, of course. They made us roll bodies…into the pits, with our hands. Then bury them. With our hands. Or our mouths. Sometimes our mouths. Dirt and blood. Bits of person in your teeth. A few of us lay down. Died on the ground. The Nazis didn't have…to tell us. We just…pushed anything dead…into the nearest pit. No prayers. No last look to see who it was. It was no one. Do you see? No one. Burying. Or buried. No difference.*

"*And still, all night, the gypsy whittled.*

"*For the dawn…shipment…the Nazis tried…something new. Stripped the newcomers…then lined them up…on the lip of a pit…twenty, thirty at a time. Then they played…perforation games. Shoot up the body…down it…see if you could get it…to flap apart…before it fell. Open up, like a flower.*

"*All through the next day. And all the next night. Digging. Waiting. Whittling. Killing. Burying. Over and over. Sometime…late second day, maybe…I got angry. Not at the Nazis. For what? Being angry at human beings…for killing…for cruelty…like being mad at ice for freezing. It's just…what to expect. So I got angry…at the trees. For standing there. For being green, and alive. For not falling when bullets hit them.*

"I started…screaming. Trying to. In Hebrew. In Polish. The Nazis looked up, and I thought they would shoot me. They laughed instead. One began to clap. A rhythm. See?"

Somehow, my grandfather lifted his limp hands from the arms of the wheelchair and brought them together. They met with a sort of crackle, like dry twigs crumbling.

"The gypsy…just watched. Still weeping. But also…after a while…nodding."

All this time, my grandfather's eyes had seemed to swell, as though there was too much air being pumped into his body. But now the air went out of him in a rush, and the eyes went dark, and the lids came down. I thought maybe he'd fallen asleep again, the way he had last night. But I still couldn't move. Dimly, I realized that the sweat from my long day's walking had cooled on my skin, and that I was freezing.

My grandfather's lids opened, a little. He seemed to be peering at me from inside a trunk, or a coffin.

"I don't know how the gypsy knew…that it was ending. That it was time. Maybe just because…it had been hours…half a day…between shipments. The world had gone…quiet. Us. Nazis. Trees. Corpses. There had been worse places…I thought…to stop living. Despite the smell.

"Probably, I was sleeping. I must have been, because the gypsy shook me…by the shoulder. Then held out…what he'd made. He had it…balanced…on a stick he'd bent. So the carving moved. Back and forth. Up and down."

My mouth opened and then hung there. I was rock, sand, and the air moved through me and left me nothing.

"'Life,' the gypsy said to me, in Polish. First Polish I ever heard him speak. 'Life. You see?'

"I shook…my head. He said it again. 'Life.' And then…I don't know how… but I did…see.

"I asked him… 'Why not you?' He took…from his pocket…one of his old carvings. The two girls. Holding hands. I hadn't noticed…the hands before. And I understood.

"'My girls,' he said. Polish, again. 'Smoke. No more. Five years ago.' I understood that, too.

"I took the carving from him. We waited. We slept, side by side. One last time. Then the Nazis came.

"They made us stand. Hardly any of them, now. The rest gone. Fifteen of us. Maybe less. They said something. German. None of us knew German. But to me…at least…the word meant…run.

"The gypsy…just stood there. Died where he was. Under the trees. The rest…I don't know. The Nazi who caught me…laughing…a boy. Not much…older than you. Laughing. Awkward with his gun. Too big for him. I looked at my hand. Holding…the carving. The wooden man. 'Life,' I found myself chanting…instead of Shma. 'Life.' Then the Nazi shot me in the head. Bang."

And with that single word, my grandfather clicked off, as though a switch had been thrown. He slumped in his chair. My paralysis lasted a few more seconds, and then I started waving my hands in front of me, as if I could ward off what he'd told me, and I was so busy doing that that I didn't notice, at first, the way my grandfather's torso heaved and rattled. Whimpering, I lowered my hands, but by then, my grandfather wasn't heaving anymore, and he'd slumped forward further, and nothing on him was moving.

"LUCY!" I screamed, but she was already out of the house, wrestling my grandfather out of his chair to the ground. Her head dove down on my grandfather's as she shoved the mask up his face, but before their mouths even met, my grandfather coughed, and Lucy fell back, sobbing, tugging the mask back into place.

My grandfather lay where he'd been thrown, a scatter of bones in the dirt. He didn't open his eyes. The oxygen tank hissed, and the blue tube stretching to his mask filled with wet mist.

"How?" I whispered

Lucy swept tears from her eyes. "What?"

"He said he got shot in the head." And even as I said that, I felt it for the first time, that cold slithering up my intestines into my stomach, then my throat.

"Stop it," I said. But Lucy slid forward so that her knees were under my grandfather's head and ignored me. Overhead, I saw the moon half-embedded in the ridged black of the sky like the lidded eye of a gila monster.

I stumbled around the side of the house and, without thinking about it, slipped into the hogan.

Once inside, I jerked the curtain down to block out the sight of Lucy and my grandfather and that moon, then drew my knees tight against my chest to pin that freezing feeling where it was. I stayed that way a long while, but whenever I closed my eyes, I saw people splitting open like peeled bananas, limbs strewn across bare, black ground like tree branches after a lightning storm, pits full of naked dead people.

I'd wished him dead, I realized. At the moment he tumbled forward in his chair, I'd hoped he was dead. And for what, exactly? For being in the camps? For telling me about it? For getting sick and making me confront it?

But with astonishing, disturbing speed, the guilt over those thoughts passed. And when it was gone, I realized that the cold had seeped down my legs and up to my neck. It clogged my ears, coated my tongue like a paste, sealing the world out. All I could hear was my grandfather's voice, like blown sand against the inside of my skull. *Life.* He was inside me, I thought. He had absorbed me, taken my place. He was becoming me.

I threw my hands over my ears, which had no effect. My thoughts flashed through the last two days, the drumming and chanting, the dead Talking God-bat in the paper bag, my father's goodbye, while that voice beat in my ears, attaching itself to my pulse. *Life.* And finally, I realized that I'd trapped myself. I was alone in the hogan in the dark. When I turned around, I would see the Dancing Man. It would be floating over me with its mouth wide open. And then it would be over, too late. It might already be.

Flinging my hands behind me, I grabbed the Dancing Man around its thin, black neck. I could feel it bob on its branch, and I half-expected it to squirm as I fought to my feet. It didn't, but its wooden skin gave where I pressed it, like real skin. Inside my head, the new voice kept beating.

At my feet on the floor lay the matches Lucy had used to light her ceremonial candles. I snatched up the matchbook, then threw the carved thing to the ground, where it smacked on its base and tipped over, face up, staring at me. I broke a match against the matchbox, then another. The third match lit.

For one moment, I held the flame over the Dancing Man. The heat felt wonderful crawling toward my fingers, a blazing, living thing, chasing back the cold inside me. I dropped the match, and the Dancing Man disintegrated in a spasm of white-orange flame.

And then, abruptly, there was nothing to be done. The hogan was a dirt and wood shelter, the night outside the plain old desert night, the Dancing Man a puddle of red and black ash I scattered with my foot. Still cold, but mostly tired, I staggered back outside and sat down hard against the side of the hogan and closed my eyes.

Footsteps woke me, and I sat up and found, to my amazement, that it was daylight. I waited, tense, afraid to look up, and then I did.

My father was kneeling beside me on the ground.

"You're here already?" I asked.

"Your grandpa died, Seth," he said. In his zombie-Dad voice, though he touched my hand the way a real father would. "I've come to take you home."

4

The familiar commotion in the hallway of the *pension* alerted me to my students' return. One of them, but only one, stopped outside my door. I waited, holding my breath, wishing I'd snapped out the light. But Penny didn't knock, and after a few seconds, I heard her careful, precise footfall continuing toward her room. And so I was alone with my puppets and my memories and my horrible suspicions, the way I have always been.

The way I am now, one month later, in my plain, posterless Ohio apartment with its cable-less television and nearly bare cupboards and single shelf stacked with textbooks, on the eve of the new school year. I'm remembering rousing myself out of the malaise I couldn't quite seem to shake—have never, for one instant, shaken since—during that last ride home from my grandfather's. "I killed him," I told my father, and when he glanced at me, expressionless, I told him all of it, my grandfather's gypsy and the Dancing Man and the Way and the thoughts I'd had.

My father didn't laugh. He also didn't touch me. All he said was, "That's silly, Seth" And for a while, I thought it was.

But today, I am thinking of Rabbi Loew and his golem, the creature he infected with a sort of life. A creature that walked, talked, thought, saw, but couldn't taste. Couldn't feel. I'm thinking of my father, the way he always was. If I'm right, then of course it had been done to him, too. And I'm thinking of the way I only seem all the way real, even to me, when I see myself in the vividly reflective faces of my students.

It's possible, I realize, that nothing happened to me during those last days at my grandfather's. It could have happened years before I was born. The gypsy had offered what he offered, and my grandfather had accepted, and as a result became what he was. Might have been. If that was true, then my father and I were unexceptional, in a way. Natural progeny. We'd simply inherited our natures, and our limitations, the way all earthly creatures do.

But I can't help thinking about the graves I saw on this summer's trip, and the millions of people in them. And the millions more without graves. The ones who are smoke.

And I find that I can feel it, at last. Or that I've always felt it, without knowing what it was: the Holocaust, roaring down the generations like a wave of radiation, eradicating in everyone it touches the ability to trust people, experience joy, fall in love, believe in love when you see it in others.

And I wonder what difference it makes, in the end, whether it really was my grandfather, or the golem-grandfather that the gypsy made, who finally crawled out of the woods of Chelmno.

DANCING MEN

The Dark, published in 2003, was the first ghost story anthology I edited. In the early 2000s I realized that some of my favorite stories were extraordinarily moving, excellent ghost stories such as "Dust Motes" by P. D. Cacek,

"Things I Didn't Know My Father Knew" by Peter Crowther, and "Each Night, Every Year" by Kathryn Ptacek, to name just a few. So in my contrary fashion, I decided I wanted to edit a new ghost story anthology that was filled exclusively with ghost stories that would create a sense of unease. Nothing heart-warming.

I freely admit that Glen Hirshberg's multi-layered "Dancing Men," is one of my all time favorite stories. Both it and the anthology won the International Horror Guild Award.

The Office of Doom

by Richard Bowes

(From *Lovecraft Unbound,* 2009)

The view from the University Science Reference Desk is all about dark and light. It looks out over a balcony into an illuminated twelve story atrium. The front of the library building has ranks of tall windows. Outside are the dark trees of New York's Washington Square and beyond them the lights of the brownstones and skyscrapers on the far side of the park.

My thoughts ran to the past on a night when I sat behind that desk waiting with curiosity and a bit of dread for an old acquaintance to reappear. I was in the last months before my retirement from this University where I'd been employed for most of my adult life. Until the day before, I'd enjoyed the freedom that came from no one knowing what to do with me.

Once I announced I was leaving after thirty-five years, I was kind of beyond the law. I could sit at the Information Desk—I'd been a library reference assistant for most of those years—making notes for stories I was writing and neither the librarians nor the public could quite bring themselves to bother me.

Then my boss asked me to see if there was anything of archival interest in the Office of Doom before it got renovated. She was very polite about it and I couldn't really refuse. Also I did feel some desire to tie up all my affairs, including some troublesome ones, before I left.

She didn't call it the Office of Doom, of course. She referred to it as Room 975, which is the number on the door. I was among the last ones who remembered the nickname.

The office is in a far corner of our floor and for many years it had been used for nothing but the storage of boxes of old university records. Those had been moved out but the dust remained. There were roach motels in the corners, a glue trap under the desk and strange stains on the rug. An old wooden hat rack was missing two of its hooks. The only thing on it was a gnarly woolen scarf in a rusty orange shade. The lock on one of the desk's side drawers had been broken open at some time in the past.

Even for a building designed by a former admirer of Hitler and financed by the man who put Richard Nixon in the White House, the room had always been especially creepy. I'd brought a rolling plastic trash bin with me and used it to keep the door propped open so as not to get shut in. Then I dusted off the swivel chair and sat at the desk.

Room 975 got its nickname among the lower echelon library staff because when the place first opened in the early 1970's, this windowless ten foot by six foot hole was where they stuck people who had fallen from grace and were on their way out.

Pulling up the creaking chair, I went through the desk drawers not expecting to find anything much after all these years but wanting to make sure. It was mundane stuff at first: jotted notes, a photo of an office party from a couple of decades back with some people who almost looked familiar, pamphlets, and outdated fire evacuation instructions. Everything went into the trash.

Then way in the back of a bottom drawer, I found a small plastic nail manicure kit with the words '50th Annual Convention of the Financial Officers of New York State' in gold lettering.

The first occupant of the Office of Doom was a pale weasel of a man named Siddons. He had been the chief financial officer to the president of the University; William (Dollar Bill) Bradshaw who built this very library and brought the school nearly to bankruptcy doing it. When Bradshaw was abruptly axed by the board of trustees, Siddons found himself in this office. He spent his days whispering into the phone and doing his nails (which I must admit were quite immaculate and trim). Then one day he was gone to a place where apparently his reputation had not yet traveled.

I tossed the manicure kit into the bin.

That set me looking for signs of the Office of Doom's next occupant, Dr. Harold Kassin. Known to us all as 'Kassin the Assassin' he had been the hatchet man for a very aggressive Dean of Libraries. The Dean and Dr. Kassin wanted to fire everybody. But one morning the Dean was called into the office of the University President who succeeded Bradshaw and summarily dismissed for forging documents. He was escorted off the premises by security guards as we all cheered. Kassin was in this office the very next day.

He had a face like an ax. At one time or another he'd confronted just about everyone in the library and told them he was watching them and they'd better straighten up. We practically ran group tours for all the people who wanted to look in and see his disgrace. He too was gone without any forewarning one fine day. Word was that he'd taken a job as head of a small library in New Jersey. I pitied the staff.

The desk yielded no traces of Kassin, which didn't really surprise me. He was careful in the way of professional killers. I stood up and riffled through the file cabinet. Old folders full of invoices got tossed with scarcely a second glance. If anyone had been seriously interested in evaluating this stuff they wouldn't have given this assignment to me.

Then I found a stack of menus for long gone pizza parlors, announcements of music acts at the Bottom Line and CBGB's, flyers from Comic Book stores on Bleecker Street and horror film festivals at the Waverly theater.

After they ran out of disgraced administrators, the office got returned to library use. For a few years it was where our student assistants got stashed.

Among the artifacts were a few scribbled notes and I recognized the handwriting. Chris McLaren was a film major who worked for us in the early '80's, a skinny kid who wore black clothes and spiked hair and had an intense interest in Alistair Crowley, Roman Polanski, the Illuminati, and role playing games. Even when you were face to face with him he seemed to be staring at you slightly askance from around some corner only he could see.

Chris and I got along OK. We shared a certain detachment and interest in the strange. I'd told him about the nickname we'd given the room and he loved it.

As I riffled through the next layer of folders I realized the material I was tossing in the trash had been left behind by Frances Hooker, a librarian and the last occupant of this office. With that name, her life in junior high school must have been a living hell. I felt not an iota of sympathy for her.

Miss Hooker was youngish but wore dresses that fell below the knee and blouses that came up to her chin. She never smiled and only discussed business.

The student employees lost their office when she arrived. For that and for reasons of temperament, she and Chris hated each other from the start. I hadn't been entirely sad about this. She and I didn't get along either and Chris kept her distracted. I don't feel proud about not having tried to protect him.

Then, as if remembering those two had evoked it, I spotted an old Interlibrary Loan shipping envelope addressed to Chris. Scrawled in black marker was Necronom/Miskaton.

Careful not to disturb it in any way, I quickly shut the drawer and got outside. Then I locked the office and told everyone I was going to lunch.

What I actually did was to visit the strega, the witch who worked among us.

Her office was on the east side of Washington Square Park. Back before the University became an academic high-roller, this was a gritty urban campus with a bunch of old commercial buildings converted to classrooms. I went in the side entrance of one of these, took a turn just inside the door, walked down a short corridor, descended spiral metal stairs and found myself in Central Supply.

Years ago the place had hummed. Anyone who wanted anything had to get a requisition order and bring it here. Normally there was a line and three or four clerks behind a tall counter handling requests, making sure everything was filled out correctly and properly signed and dated and then piling office supplies on the counter. If there was a problem Ambrose was the man you saw first, a black guy built like a walking bunker who was always a little too busy to listen.

Central Supply was almost deserted now. Piles of dusty, broken furniture—tables, desks, chairs sat where lines once formed. Ambrose was still at the counter but no one else was. He sat, older, bigger but somehow frail, absorbed in whatever was on his computer screen. I had to say, "Hello," twice before he looked up.

"Is Mrs. Rossi, here?" Once upon a time only unusual requests from the highest University echelon or esoteric problems that defied clear definition got referred to Teresa Rossi.

Now Ambrose nodded without looking up and called out, "Teresa, someone for you."

"I know," was the answer like, somehow, she expected me. "Send him in."

With no more formality than that, I lifted a hinged section of the counter and walked back to her office.

The University locksmith many years ago was a tiny man with a large head and a beautiful face—like the ones on shepherds in Renaissance nativity paintings. He had come from Palermo and lived in Greenwich Village. Once he said that back when he first arrived here, Teresa Rossi's mother had been the neighborhood strega. He mentioned that her mother was a witch with great respect and added as an afterthought that her father had a hardware shop on Mercer Street.

All else had changed but Teresa Rossi at first glance was just the same, dark hair with little highlights, nice but anonymous at-work dress and jewelry that caught the eye (Was that a minute owl's face staring out from that earring?) but when you looked closely seemed perfectly mundane.

"You're still here," she said expressing no surprise. Part of her shtick was that she was never surprised.

"For a little while longer," I said. "You too."

She shrugged. "Each department orders everything online from Staples now. What we do is receive broken furniture and call for carting companies to come and haul it away."

"But you're still in business?" She nodded and waited for me to speak. "There was a kid working for us years ago who pulled a stupid prank with Interlibrary Loan."

"Chris McLaren," Teresa Rossi said like it happened earlier in the week and not twenty-five years before. "That went way beyond being a prank. I thought all that had been taken care of." She showed a flash of irritation. At moments she could be chilling.

"Something connected to that turned up today." I told her what I'd found.

"You didn't touch it."

"No."

"It will have to be dealt with when there's nobody around."

"I work late tomorrow night."

"That will be good." And the session was over.

Many years before, I had brought Chris with me to help carry stuff back to our department. We were waiting in line when Teresa emerged from her office with the University Counsel and escorted him out as he babbled his gratitude. "Don't know how you found those letters. The secretary swore she'd discarded them years ago." The strega nodded as if this was nothing.

Chris was fascinated by Teresa Rossi. Something made her notice him too. I stepped up to place my order and she motioned him over and spoke to him. Later I asked what she'd had to say.

"She wanted to know who I was. Said not to trust you too far but I think she was kidding."

I told him what the locksmith told me and about the stories of how she had certain control over lost objects and future events.

"People like her and you are like the limbic system of this place," he said. "You know how in our brains behind all the recent flashy developments that gave us stuff like emotions and aesthetics and cosmic awareness there's this lizard brain. It's what makes the heart beat and what stays alert to odd noises and sudden movements in the dark while we sleep. Don't wonder where the dinosaurs went, there's a bit of one inside each of us."

"So Mrs. Rossi and I are ancient lizards?"

"Yeah man. You're The Old Ones and it's cool."

Thinking back, I can remember Chris talking about H. P. Lovecraft and the evil book the *Necronomicon* and Miskatonic University, the accursed New England institution of higher learning that shows up in Lovecraft stories.

We joked about accursed universities not being that far fetched. I remember him talking about doing an Interlibrary Loan request for the *Necronomicon*. I even showed him how to search the huge print tomes of library holdings as one did in those pre-internet years and as part of the gag I approved the ILL request for him.

He told me, months, maybe a year later that the book had arrived. I said, "It's probably some kind of cheap reprint."

"It's close enough," he said peaking around the invisible corner and I assumed he was joking.

By the time Chris got the book, Frances Hooker had been hired. She apparently never slept, never went home and had no interest in life except library science. Even other librarians didn't like her but they agreed that she was excellent at her work and shut themselves in their offices when she was round.

I had to deal with her and found she hated me because I didn't have a library degree. I believe she hated everyone who was not a librarian. She thought that librarians should be addressed as 'Curator' in the same way as medical people are called Doctor. No one went along with this.

Mad librarians were no novelty. The first one I worked for at the University was Alice Marlow. She had dyed blond hair and, though somewhat pudgy, wore leather mini-skirts and mesh stockings. It was 1970 and stuff like that did get worn but not by any other librarians that I can recall.

The main library hadn't yet been built and departments and collections were stuck in odd places around campus. We had been installed in a small office on the floor above the Gates of Eden Beer Hall, a student hangout on Waverly Place. There was a men's hat manufacturer on the floor above us in those dusty, far gone days.

Alice was erratic, sweet and zaftig one minute, insanely suspicious the next. I was no prize either, always slipping down to the Gates of Eden to get drunk or over to Washington Square to cop drugs. She threatened to fire me for being habitually late to work.

She'd usually forget about that but I made it a point to come in early the next day. She never showed up and wasn't there the day after that either. I began to wonder what had happened. That afternoon two people from administration came and took all her personal effects. It seemed she'd gone berserk in the West Fourth Street subway station two days before, screaming that people were putting LSD in her coffee, and her family had her committed.

Hooker was unpleasant to me but she was hell on Chris, who was used to easy-going supervision. I assumed that was what made him increasingly twitchy. I tried telling him not to let her get to him. He stopped speaking to anyone and then stopped coming to work. I made inquiries and got nowhere.

His roommates said he'd gotten very moody and had taken off suddenly. "He talked about needing to go somewhere up in New England, man," one of them said.

Later I was told to go through his locker. There was the *Necronomicon* with leather binding and gold lettering that looked not at all cheap or new. I won't say that it exuded evil, but I'd read enough Lovecraft not to touch it. While I stood wondering what to do, Frances Hooker walked by. I thought it was Fate.

"This looks like a rare book," I said, "It's from Inter-Library Loan and I don't know how to handle something like this." I didn't even have to say that was because I wasn't a librarian. She glared at me, gathered up the volume and stalked off to the Office of Doom.

Ms. Hooker's behavior over the next year or so grew stranger than Marlow's ever had been. The cleaning people heard her shrieking in her office late at night. On one occasion she stood up at a faculty meeting and spoke in tongues. The rare books librarian said that once when she spoke to him, a tongue long and forked like a snake's lolled out of her mouth. But he drank and nobody but me believed him. Then she disappeared, leaving a disjointed note about mountains and madness and needing to travel.

Even at the time I felt a certain amount of guilt about having knowingly let Frances Hooker have the *Necronomicon*. When I was ordered to clear out her office, the book was in the top drawer of her desk. I went to Central Supply and told Teresa Rossi what had happened. She was not pleased. "Chris brought the *Necronomicon* to this place. He's young but not a child and will pay a price." The witch looked me in the eye, "You're a disappointment." She shrugged. "Stay at work late and someone will be there."

That someone appeared just before closing time. It was early fall and not that cold but he wore an overcoat; a wide brimmed hat and dark glasses and carried a leather satchel. Chris had barely been gone twelve months but from what I could see he looked twenty years older, gaunt, and stone faced.

Without a word he went into the Office of Doom and came out with something in his satchel. "Chris, I'm sorry…" I said.

"It's OK." The voice was faint and from far away. Then he was gone.

I was the one who suggested that the now vacant Office of Doom be used as a storage space. Everyone thought it was a good idea.

Twenty-five years later in the digital age, students and faculty no longer come into the libraries. And yet the surroundings are pleasant enough and the computer facilities are excellent. So just before eleven o'clock on the night I sat waiting once again, the place was full of foreign doctors from around the world studying to pass their U.S. equivalency exams.

Busy, conspiratorial, they would jump up and dash downstairs to smoke foul smelling cigarettes outdoors. And as always, they watched me from the corners of their eyes convinced that I worked for the secret police and was going to turn them in.

Their names; Visascia, Yadaminia sounded like obscure 19th century diseases. The one thing they all wanted was to pass their exams and go work in American emergency rooms.

They barely looked up when Chris McLaren appeared. In fact nothing about him would have attracted their attention. Things apparently had gotten easier for him. Except for a certain wariness, he looked like a guy you'd see in any suburban mall, balding, a bit overweight, a little pressed for time. He carried a satchel.

"You're still here." The voice was a breath, a whisper. He showed no surprise.

I let him into The Office of Doom, showed him where I'd found the envelope and left. They announced closing time over the loud speakers as he came back to the desk.

He peered at me from around his corner. "Some kind of errata sheet," he said. "Must have missed it the last time. I've gotten better over the years."

"Chris, what happened to you?"

"Awful stuff at first. Mrs. Rossi, though, told me who to talk to, how to throw myself on their mercy. She said they always need someone to clean up little mistakes."

"What happened with Frances Hooker bothers me…" I trailed off.

Chris gave what might have been the ghost of a smile. Then he turned and was gone.

Everyone thought my retirement party was quite a success: a large crowd, a couple of my young relatives in attendance, plenty of sentimental and funny gifts.

Teresa Rossi showed up unexpectedly. People asked her when she was going to call it quits and she said, "Soon, maybe." At one point when we were alone, she told me, "An old friend wants you to know the case is closed and nobody holds any grudge against you." When I started to thank her she added, "It's not strictly justice. But ones like us don't always want that."

THE OFFICE OF DOOM

Lovecraft Unbound, my first Lovecraftian anthology, came about from a reunion with Rob Simpson, a former editor at DC Comics who had moved to the Pacific Northwest for a job with Dark Horse. DH was starting a book line and he asked if I'd be interested in editing an anthology for them. I don't recall who thought about me doing a Lovecraftian anthology, but I was game. However, loathing Lovecraftian pastiches, I told him I didn't want to edit an anthology of them. On the spot, I came up with the title *Lovecraft Unbound*, riffing off Brian Aldiss's novel *Frankenstein Unbound*, feeling it perfectly expressed what I wanted to do with H.P. Lovecraft. My only direction in my guidelines was: "no ichor, no tentacles." I mentioned the theme to Rick Bowes, someone who started writing for me at SCIFICTION, and he thought he might come up with something—although he professed to hate Lovecraft's writings. Most of Rick's fiction is based on his life, in one way or another, and this, "The Office of Doom," is influenced by Rick's manning the reference desk at the NYU Library for a couple of decades until retiring a few years ago.

Black Nightgown

by K. W. Jeter

(From *Little Deaths,* 1994)

Everyone knew.

Everyone knows, he murmured to himself. His lips brushed across the white skin of her neck, the soft region between her throat and ear, when he spoke aloud, a whisper, her name. His lips brushed across the delicate strands of hair that trembled with the exhalation of his breath. He breathed in her scent that wasn't roses but just as sweet. He murmured her name, he couldn't stop himself, and she shifted in his arms but didn't wake.

They all knew, but he didn't care. Not here in this world that he wrapped his arms around and was held by at the same time. A world bound by her scent and their mingled warmth, caught by the tunneled sheets and the white-tasseled covers. Her breasts encircled by his arm…

Outside, in that other world, the streetlamp's blue merged with the faint shadows of the moon. The thin light slid around the edges of the curtain, made empty shapes of her bedroom dresser and the door that led to the rest of the empty, silent house. She moved in his embrace, eyes closed, her mouth parting slightly, her breath a sigh.

"They all know."

Another's whisper. His sweat felt cold upon his naked shoulders. He turned his face away from hers and looked up at the figure standing beside the bed.

Her dead husband could see through the drawn curtain and through the walls of all the houses lining the street, the lights left on in kitchens and sleeping hallways shining through the red bricks as though through glass. "Your mother…your sisters…even your father." The dead man looked away from the window and everything beyond, turning toward his sleeping wife. "They all know."

Of course his mother and sisters would know. He brought his face back down to hers. They had known before any of this had ever come about. He closed his eyes, lashes brushing the curve of her cheekbone. His father would never speak of what he knew. He kissed the corner of her mouth.

They all know…

And now he did as well. He knew; he knew something.

He held her fast in the night of their small world. Held her, and felt her dead husband watching them. Watching them in the great night's world.

The women spoke the old world's language. The mothers less than the grandmothers, and the daughters only a few words. But they all knew, and understood. The grey-haired poked their tree-root fingers through the shelled peas, the bowls held in their laps as they sat gossiping to each other or murmuring to themselves; the youngest turned their dark-eyed gaze at him as he stepped into the street to pass by their jump ropes slapping the cracked sidewalk. Whisper into each other's ears, laugh and run away, their white anklets flashing like the teeth of an ocean's waves.

He asked his father what women talked about.

"Christ in his fucking Heaven—who knows?" Sweating through his undershirt as a cleaver snapped free the ribs of a dangling carcass, the knotted spine turned naked as a row of babies' fists. In the store's glass-fronted cabinets, the mounds of beef liver glistened like soft, wet rubies. "Ask them and get told what a fool you are." Drops of blood spattered the sawdust and the broken leather of his father's boots.

Outside the door, with the slow overhead fan trying to keep the flies away, the little girls' ropes had been left behind like shed snakeskins. He rang open the cash register and sorted out the dollar bills that the neighborhood housewives had paid him for their deliveries. His hands still smelled like raw sausages and the red water that had leaked through the wrapping paper.

Later, he took a beer from the case kept just inside the door of the meat locker, a privilege he'd earned when he'd started shaving, and sat in the alley doorway. He tossed his stained white apron across a hook on the rail that the slaughterhouse trucks backed up to, and tilted his head to drink the bottle half-empty. He could watch, undetected as an evening ghost, as the married women walked by the alley's mouth, flat summer sandals and arms shining from the tarry pavement's heat. The shy, pretty one who had married last autumn bent her head over her newborn. All their voices were like the sounds of nesting birds, too soft to tell what they were saying.

He rolled the bottle between his wet hands. He knew that they were probably talking, among other things, about him and the widow.

"She oughta wax that upper lip of hers." That was what his oldest sister had said, not because the woman had a moustache, but because she was so dark and wore hollow gold bracelets on her wrists like a gypsy. She looked like their grandmother's wedding photograph, the framed sepia oval in the hallway. His other sisters had giggled behind their hands, though the widow wasn't any darker than any of them.

She hadn't been a widow then. Her husband was a Cracow dandy and still alive. That was what his mother called a man who wore a pinstripe suit with a waist nipped in like a woman's. A hat and a red silk tie that turned black around the knot, like a hummingbird's throat. It must have been winter when he'd heard his mother call the man that, because he remembered the kitchen window being covered with steam from the pots upon the stove. His father had sat at the table eating, his suspenders hanging loose from his waist, his big-knuckled fists swallowing the knife and fork. She'd glanced back at his father, her husband, then leaned across the sink to look out the part of the window she'd wiped transparent with her hand, looking out at the men talking under the streetlight, the shoulders of their thin jackets hunched up against the cold, their breath silver mingled plumes.

"A Cracow dandy," she'd said again, her voice filled with the same terrible empty longing it held when she spoke of her dead father. It must have been something she'd heard from her dead mother; she'd been born here. What did she know of the old world? Nothing but the old language, and less of that than her mother and her grandmother had known.

The last of the beer had warmed between his hands; on his tongue, it tasted sour and flat. He leaned forward, elbows against his knees, and watched the little girls run past the alley, called to set the tables for their fathers and older brothers who would be coming home from work soon.

He had wondered if the widow still set a place for her dead husband. And then he had found out.

Before that, he could have asked his mother—he would have, regardless of his father's warning—if it was something women do. Were supposed to do, an empty plate in front of an empty chair. He would have, except that he knew his mother and all his sisters were on the other side of the blood feud that had broken out in the parish church. It was doubtful if his mother would say anything now, good or bad, about any of that tribe, the widow included.

Something about the altar flowers; those were all women's doing, their world, so he could never be sure of the exact details. The priest had told the women to make room in the flower rotation for the newcomers, the ones who'd come to live in the parish only a few years ago, arriving with all their children and husbands and sons, bringing with them the air of the old world, the one that had been left a generation before. The newcomers' presence could be endured in silence, but the priest's order had caused grumbling among the women.

He took another sip of the beer's dregs and wondered how many languages the priest spoke. Not the languages that changed from place to place, but the others, the secret ones. The priest was like some black, slightly threadbare angel, neither man nor woman, occupying a barren holy ground between them. Perhaps he knew what women talked about, understood what they said; perhaps he had talked about the altar flowers in their own tongue.

Grumbling, then bad words in a language anyone could understand. He remembered his own mother muttering something under her breath as she'd passed by one of the newcomer women in the street—not the yet-to-be widow, but one of her cousins—her eyes narrowing as though the bell-like rattle of the other woman's gold bracelets made the fillings in her teeth ache. It could only get worse, and did. Especially after the toad crawled from the chalice at the altar rail.

He heard his father calling him from inside the shop. The last of the evening's customers would have come and gone by now; it would be time to close up and make their own way home.

Everything in its appointed time. The gears of this world's machinery meshed with the other's.

He would have to eat something of what his mother put on the table, or pretend to, pushing things around on the plate with his fork, knowing all the while that he wasn't fooling anyone. Just as he wouldn't be fooling them later, when the summer night was finally dark, and he would walk past his mother and father in the living room, pulling on a thin sweater as he stepped toward the front door without saying a word. As though he were going to do nothing more than sit out on the stoop, to catch a cooling breeze. At his back he would be able to feel, as he did every night, his mother looking up from the sewing basket on her lap, his father's glance over the top of the newspaper. Everybody knew—why he didn't eat, where he was going, even when he would be back, in the cold pearl light before dawn.

He could hear his father rummaging through the cash register, scooping the coins out of the little trays, bundling up the dollar bills with a rubber band, dumping everything into the little drawstring bag that he'd carry home inside his coat. One night a week—not this night, but another—he'd sit at the bare kitchen table and sort out the bit that would be placed inside a simple white envelope, to be left on top of the shop's counter. The widow's husband used to come in to pick it up, with a smile and a nod and a few overly polite words that the butcher had acknowledged with a simmering anger in his eyes. Now one of the other Cracow dandies came in every week to pick up the money.

His father called his name again, louder. He drained the last weak taste of beer and pitched the empty bottle in among the waste bin's red bones. He pulled the apron down from the hook and walked inside with it in his hand.

"You were thinking about that silly animal, weren't you? That toad." She sat on the other side of the table from him, her bare elbows on the white cloth, holding a glass of wine in her hands, rubbing the corner of her brow with it. Her face was shining, the loose curls of her tied-up hair dampened against her neck and by her ears, from the steam off the pots on the stove. "That was stupid, it spoils your appetite." The widow smiled, eyes half-lidded, as though there were some indefinable pleasure in watching him eat. "Think about things like that, a frog will grow in your belly and your eyes will bulge out. All the time." She lowered the glass and sipped from it.

He looked up from the plate, not sure—never sure—if she was joking or not. They knew so many things, all women did; maybe that was one of them, a true thing. How would he know? Then he caught the lifting of one corner of her mouth. "Bullshit."

"Bullshit, he says." She gazed up at the ceiling. "I fix him dinner, he picks at it like I'm trying to poison him, then he says *bullshit* to me." Her gaze, still smiling, settled back upon him. "What would your mother say if she heard you talking like that?"

He had to wonder. Not about what his mother would say, but about the possibility of some conspiracy between her and the widow, a dealing in confidences that ran beneath the little feuds and hushed glares on the ordinary world's surface.

"I don't know." No man did. He laid down his fork, a garlic clove and a bite of mutton—it hadn't come from his father's shop, he knew that at least—speared upon it. What they told each other, what all women shared amongst themselves, even the little girls with their jump ropes and knowing laughter. "I mean, I don't know what she'd say."

He looked down at the plate, at the speckled grease congealing, a scrap of bread as white as the underside of her breasts. As dark as she was, how shining black her hair and eyes…he'd laid his hand upon skin as pale as glass, beneath which the trembling of her veins could be seen, blue ink written on milk. He'd been rendered wordless by how that soft curve had fitted its cloudlike weight into his palm, an event foreordained by dreaming prophets.

Now he bit and chewed, laying the emptied fork back down, the motion of his jaws massaging the brain. To thoughts unbidden, still the blasphemous toad. He hadn't even been in the church that day, but he'd heard—everyone had; they all knew—and he could imagine the woman's cry as she'd fainted from the rail, the chalice rolling through the blood of Christ spilled upon the floor, as clearly as though he'd been in one of the pews. One of the altar boys had scooped up the toad to keep it from being trampled upon in the uproar or beaten to death with a broom-handle by the verger who saw Satan in every unusual thing. The toad was let go by the boys, with a degree of fearful reverence—it did, after all, count as some kind of miracle—in the tangled weeds behind the rectory. Nothing that had happened had been the toad's fault; everyone knew the ones responsible. The newcomer women had sat together, a long row of them wearing the old-fashioned black clothing in which they came to church, bits of their gold ornaments gleaming out through the stiff black lace at their wrists and throats. Through all the crying and shouting, they had passed a smile both secret and public amongst themselves. He knew that the widow-to-be had been there with her sisters and cousins, the grandmother with gold in her mouth as well, all of them; because they had known what was going to happen. All this over the altar flowers.

"Such a little thing," she said. The widow gazed into her wineglass as though a mirror were there. "What a thing to worry about. And let it spoil your appetite."

He swallowed, the lamb sticking in his throat for a moment. He hadn't come here for dinner; he never had. He closed his eyes to see better, just what he was thinking of.

"You're so stupid." She said it with great affection, the way she might have said it to her husband when he was alive. She laid her hand on top of his beside the plate. "A toad—what's that?"

He shook his head. That she could tell what he was thinking of, he couldn't doubt. But never exactly; always a little shifted in focus, the circle around the bull's-eye. He supposed that was another difference between men and women, one that made all the other differences bearable.

Not *that* toad, but the other. A story that was not even whispered about, but which everybody knew somehow. That the men knew something of, enough to keep their silence, and the women, even the little girls, knew everything. Because it dealt with the business of women, even more than the altar flowers had.

Eyes closed, he felt the soft weight of her hand upon his. The widow must have leaned closer to him, across the table; he could smell her scent, both her perfume of ancient roses and the other, that would taste of salt when he kissed her brow.

"You're so pretty."

He opened his eyes. "No, I'm not."

"Don't be mad. I just meant I like to look at you. That's all."

Her eyes were so dark, he could have fallen inside them. That was a scary enough thought—scary that he would want to—he had to turn his face away from hers.

"Why do you think about these things?" Her scolding voice touched his ear. "If they make you feel so strange?" Then softer: "Better you should think about me." Her fingers closed around his wrist. "Here." She had undone the buttons of her throat. She pressed his palm against the skin; he could feel her pulse echoing among the small bones of his hand.

He looked round and saw the whiteness caught beneath his fingertips. His skin was already chafed and hardened, like his father's, from the knives and icy flesh of the butcher shop.

"Nobody was hurt." She whispered to him now; he could feel the words move inside the widow's throat. "What happened had to be done. And the girl's fine now. Isn't she?"

He nodded. Everything she said was true. The war that had started with the altar flowers had come to an end, not by the parish women admitting defeat, but by their recognizing that the dark-eyed newcomers hadn't left their skills and secrets in the old world. That, in fact, what they knew was a worthy match for those who had come over generations before them. For everyone to know that was enough.

And the girl, the one who had taken the newcomers' flowers, roses dark and red, and dumped them in the battered trashcans behind the church hall's kitchen—she was just fine now. Or as well as could be expected. She was actually some second or third cousin of his, in those ways that could only be figured out by his grandmother or one of her sisters poring, mumbling, over a sepia photograph album, was just fine now. Or as well as could be expected. The girl had come back, tanned and loud-voiced, from a long vacation with her aunt and her uncle who ran a construction business in far-off Tempe, Arizona. The girl had only stayed around long enough to show how healthy she was now, that none of what had happened to her really mattered, that everything, her brief marriage and pregnancy and what had happened in the delivery room, that had all been something like a dream. From which she had wakened with a Reno divorce certificate and a cantaloupe webbing of stretch marks across her stomach, that just meant she couldn't wear two-piece bathing suits any more. Then the girl had gone with her barking, brittle laugh into the city, to work as a secretary in another uncle's import-export company and sleep with negro musicians. There were enough of her friends left behind who envied her, that the widow could say now that no one had been hurt and it would be true enough.

It was only the men who knew, and the older boys who knew, and those like himself who were caught between those estates, who dreamed and let their waking thoughts be troubled by such things, that were women's business and none of their own. They all knew, even though they had seen nothing of what had happened to the girl. Fool that he was, fool that both he and the widow knew him to be, as all women know all men are; he could close his eyes, like the point of his tongue unable to resist prodding an aching tooth, and see a chrome and white-tiled room, the girl's feet up in the stirrups, a hospital-green sheet over her enormous belly. And then another tongue poke, and he would see more of what he didn't want to see and couldn't keep from seeing: the doctor's sweat soaking through his mask as he shouted at the nurses and anesthesiologist to get out, to get out of the delivery room and leave him alone here. Then the doctor had turned back to his task, lifting the sheet above the girl's spread-apart knees with one gloved hand, while the sharpest scalpel from the tray glittered in his other hand. Bringing the metal close enough to reflect the idiot round eyes peering from the small darkness, the webbed claws braced to keep it inside the wet sling of flesh it was so reluctant to leave.

How did these pictures get inside their heads, if they were of things the men had never seen, never been told about? But they all knew, after a night of bad dreams they could see it in each other's eyes; he had seen it in the way his father had bent over the broom, sweeping off the sidewalk in front of the store, counting the money into the till to get ready for the morning's first customer. And silence, the silence that lay behind the words even when someone spoke, silence that had looked at and then turned away from the cruel necessities of women's business. All the men, the priest included, had been grateful that the war of the altar flowers had ended, that this truce both grudgeful and admiring had been achieved.

And he, the butcher's son, had been grateful, because by that time he had already begun sleeping with the dark-eyed widow.

In her kitchen, the night velvet behind the steamy windows, he sat leaning across the table toward her. She loosened another button at the front of her dress, and his hand fell of its own weight, almost without will, to cup her breast.

"You're so stupid," she murmured and smiled, her own eyes half-lidded now. He knew she meant not just him, but all of them.

There was one more picture inside his head, that he turned his face down toward his plate to see, as though ashamed of this weakness. But he had to, so he could forget for a while, or long enough. Her heartbeat rocked inside his palm even louder now. His arm felt hollow into his chest, where his own pulse caught in time with hers.

Inside his head, in that other night, the doctor still wore his surgical scrubs from the delivery room. As he walked across the field behind the hospital's parking lot, the high grass silvered by the moon. Carrying something wadded up inside the green sheet, something that leaked through red upon his bare hands. Until the doctor flung open the sheet from where he stood upon the high bank of a creek, and heard a second later the pieces drop into the water. He threw in the red-edged scalpel as well, and it disappeared among the soft weeds like the bright flash of a minnow. In that picture, the doctor looked over his shoulder at the hospital's lights, face hardened against what he'd come to know about the business of women. The doctor and the priest were brothers apart from other men, and the same as all men. They all knew, but could not speak of these things.

He felt the widow kiss him on the side of his face. He looked up and saw her, and nothing else. Nothing at all.

She wore a black nightgown to bed, or what would have been black if her skin hadn't shone so luminous through it. To him it looked like smoke in her bedroom's darkness, smoke across a city of a thousand doors, the shadow across the crypt deep in the white stone where Our Redeemer was both born and buried.

The black nightgown felt like smoke as well, if smoke could have been gathered into his hands. He lay with her in his arms, her eyes closed now, the sheets molded with sweat to his ribs.

"She likes it very much that way." Her husband's awkward English came from above them, from the side of the bed. "To be held, and held just so."

He turned his head and looked up at the dead man. The Cracow dandy. Half of the man's face was gone, from the first bullet that had struck him in the eye, then the rest that his murderer had poured like water from an outstretched hand, feet spread to either side of the man's shoulders upon the pavement. Not murder really, but a business disagreement between the Cracow dandy and his dark-eyed brothers; it was the business of men to know the difference. Just as it had been the business of the butcher, every other Friday, to ring **NO SALE** on the cash register and count again the thin sheaf of fives and tens in the plain white envelope that he set beside the Saint Vincent de Paul charity jar. So that the Cracow dandy, when he'd been alive, or one of his elegantly tailored associates, could come in, smile and talk to the butcher, and buy nothing and leave, the envelope somehow magically transported into the dandy's coat pocket without his ever having shown his soft, manicured hands. Then nodding to the butcher's son with the pushbroom and smiling, all of them knowing that this was how the business of men was done. So much so, knowledge passed from one generation to the next, from the old world to this, that he had known what to do without being told, to wait upon the rest of the day's customers, to wrap chops and stew bones, and make change and finally lock the shop up, turning the sign in the door from **OPEN** to **CLOSED**, all while his father sat on the alley stoop and knocked back thimbles of schnapps with a heavy, brooding scowl on his face.

"I know," he told the dead man. "I know what to do next. You don't have to tell me."

"You know…"

But that wasn't the dead man who spoke, who whispered, it was the widow with the dark eyes and the black nightgown, the stuff of smoke and silk, pushed above her hips. His hand passed from there to the curve of her thigh, and it felt like laying his palm upon his mother's stove, if anything in the world could be both that soft and yet as hot as heated iron. Hot enough to burn the tongue in his mouth until he was as mute as dead men should be.

"Like this…"

He knew that her dead husband stood by the bed, an angel in an elegant suit. A Cracow dandy, a rose with splinters of bone for white thorns where his right eye and cheekbone had been. He felt the dead man's fingers curve around his hand, the way his father's had when he had first been shown how to bring the cleaver between the compliant ribs. Now he let the dead man cup his palm around the widow's breast.

I'm not such a fool, he thought. *I know all this. I was born knowing.*

But he let the dead man show him anyway. Because that was what she wanted. He knew that as well.

"Kiss her." The dead man whispered in his ear. "While you hold her. Press tight and don't be afraid. Be a man…"

I'm not afraid. He hadn't been afraid the first time he had been in her bed—their bed—and he had looked over his shoulder and seen her dead husband with the ruined face. How could anyone lying in bed with a woman ever be afraid? And with her clad only in a nightgown of black smoke and silk…

That was what women didn't know. For all their mysteries and secrets, for even the youngest girls' knowing smiles—they didn't know that when men trembled in this place, in the grave of desire, it was not from fear.

He opened his eyes and looked down. Looked down and saw what the dead man above him saw. He saw her with her eyes closed, lips slightly parted, her naked arms reaching…

For her husband.

His face burning with shame, he looked over his shoulder to the one who the dark-eyed widow loved, who she would always love.

"Don't feel bad." The Cracow dandy's voice was the kindness of one man to another. "It's not that she doesn't care for you. She might even have loved you, or someone like you, if she hadn't loved me first."

"I know. I know that," he said. "It doesn't matter."

Here…

He no longer knew whose voice it was, that told him what to do. It could have been his own.

Like this…

Or hers. He watched his hand, or that of her dead husband, stroke her dark hair upon the pillow. She turned her face toward that touch.

And smiled.

"You see?" said the dead man. "Just like that. Just like that. Just like that."

He closed his own eyes. And kissed her. The tear between his lashes and her cheek burned like fire, if fire were salt.

As he knew would happen—as none of them told him, but he knew anyway—a year passed, from the time a sealed coffin was lain in earth, to the time when he knocked upon her door, his hands smelling of blood from his father's shop, no matter how much he scrubbed them with soap and vinegar. A year passed from the Cracow dandy's death, he knew it had, but he still came and knocked at her door.

The dark-eyed widow opened the door just wide enough that he could see the others inside, the bottles of wine upon the table, and hear their bright laughter. She looked out upon him, standing there in the darkness that came so early in the winter. She smiled with enough sadness to break his heart, then shook her head and silently closed the door. He could still hear the laughter and singing on the other side.

He turned away and saw the cardboard box at the curb, the box of her old clothes, for the trash collectors to pick up and carry away. All the black dresses that she had worn for the last year. The black with which she had mourned her dead husband. A year had passed and she didn't need them anymore.

He knelt down and pushed his hands through the contents of the box. Until he found, at the bottom, something of silk and smoke. He drew it out and held it against his face, breathing in the scent that was part her and part the perfume of ancient roses that she had used.

He knew. He had always known. A year would pass, and she would forget about both of them, the butcher's son and the Cracow dandy. She was still young, and a year had passed.

He heard steps running on the sidewalk. They halted, and he looked up and saw one of the youngest girls watching him without smiling, a coil of jump rope in her hand. It got dark so early, this time of year.

The little girl ran past him, toward her home and supper. He let the nightgown slip from his hands, drifting across his knee and a corner of the box like smoke, if smoke could fall.

BLACK NIGHTGOWN

Little Deaths was commissioned by Deborah Beale for Millennium in the UK and it's a big one: 464 pages of twenty-four stories, almost all of them new. It won the World Fantasy Award. Then Millennium sold "foreign" rights to a U.S. publisher, whose editor insisted on cutting nine stories, and adding one "name" reprint.

In 1988, K.W. Jeter wrote what I later discovered was his first short story, for one of my commissioned themed groupings of "short-shorts" (now called flash fiction) in *Omni*. If you've read his 1994 classic *Dr. Adder*, you know how over the top and twisted his fiction can be. "Black Nightgown" is relatively subtle but still—of course—twisted.

A Delicate Architecture

by Catherynne M. Valente

(From *Troll's Eye View: A Book of Villainess Tales,* 2009)

My father was a confectioner. I slept on pillows of spun sugar; when I woke, the sweat and tears of my dreams had melted it all to nothing, and my cheek rested on the crisp sheets of red linen. Many things in my father's house were made of candy, for he was a prodigy, having at the age of five invented a chocolate trifle so dark and rich that the new emperor's chocolatier sat down upon the steps of his great golden kitchen and wept into his truffle-dusted mustache. So it was that when my father found himself in possession of a daughter, he cut her corners and measured her sweetness with no less precision than he used in his candies.

My breakfast plate was clear, hard butterscotch, full of oven-bubbles. I ate my soft-boiled marzipan egg gingerly, tapping its little cap with a toffee-hammer. The yolk within was a lemony syrup that dribbled out into my egg-cup. I drank chocolate in a black vanilla-bean mug. But I ate sugared plums with a fork of sparrow bones; the marrow left salt in the fruit and the strange, thick taste of a thing once alive in all that sugar. When I asked my father why I should taste these bones along with the sweetness of the candied plums, he told me very seriously that I must always remember that sugar was once alive. It grew tall and green and hard as my own knuckles in a far-away place, under a red sun that burned on the face of the sea. I must always remember that children just like me cut it down and crushed it up with tan and strong hands, and that their sweat, which gave me my sugar, tasted also of salt.

"If you forget that red sun and those long, green stalks, then you are not truly a confectioner, you understand nothing about candy but that it tastes good and is colorful—and these things a pig can tell, too. We are the angels of the cane, we are oven-magicians, but if you would rather be a pig snuffling in the leaves—"

"No, Papa."

"Well then, eat your plums, magician of my heart."

And so I did, and the tang of marrow in the sugar-meat was rich and disturbing and sweet.

Often I would ask my father where my mother had gone, if she had not liked her fork of sparrow bones, or if she had not wanted to eat marzipan eggs every day. These were the only complaints I could think of. My father ruffled my hair with his sticky hand and said:

"One morning, fine as milk, when I lived in Vienna and reclined on turquoise cushions with the empress licking my fingers for one taste of my sweets, I went walking past the city shops, my golden cane cracking on the cobbles, peering into their frosted windows and listening to the silver bells strung from the doors. In the window of a competitor who hardly deserved the name, being but a poor maker of trifles which would hardly satisfy a duchess, I saw the loveliest little crystal jar. It was as intricately cut as a diamond and full of the purest sugar I have ever seen. The little shopkeeper, bent with decades of hunching over trays of chocolate, smiled at me with few enough teeth and cried:

'Alonzo! I see you have cast your discerning gaze upon my little vial of sugar! I assure you it is the finest of all the sugars ever made, rendered from the tallest cane in the isles by a fortunate virgin snatched at the last moment from the frothing red mouth of her volcano! It was then blanched to the snowy shade you see in a bath of lion's milk and ground to sweetest dust with a pearl pestle, and finally poured into a jar made from the glass of three church windows. I am no emperor's darling, but in this I exceed you at last!'

The little man did a shambling dance of joy, to my disgust. But I poured out coins onto his scale until his eyes gleamed wet with longing, and took that little jar away with me." My father pinched my chin affectionately. "I hurried back home, boiled the sugar with costly dyes and other secret things, and poured it into a Constanze-shaped mold, slid it into the oven, and out you came in an hour or two, eyes shining like caramels!"

My father laughed when I pulled his ear and told him not to tease me, that every girl has a mother, and an oven is no proper mother! He gave me a slice of honeycomb, and shooed me into the garden, where raspberries grew along the white gate.

And thus I grew up. I ate my egg every morning, and licked the yolk from my lips. I ate my plums with my bone fork, and thought very carefully about the tall cane under the red sun. I scrubbed my pillow from my cheeks until they were quite pink. Every old woman in the village remarked on how much I resembled the little ivory cameos of the emperor, the same delicate nose, high brow, thick red hair. I begged my father to let me go to Vienna, as he had done when he was a boy. After all, I was far from a dense child. I had my suspicions—I wanted to see the emperor. I wanted to hear the violas playing in white halls with green and rose checkered floors. I wanted to ride a horse with long brown reins. I wanted to taste radishes and carrots and potatoes, even a chicken, even a fish on a plate of real porcelain, with no oven-bubbles in it.

"Why did we leave Vienna, Papa?" I cried, over our supper of marshmallow crèmes and caramel cakes. "I could have learned to play the flute there; I could have worn a wig like spun sugar. You learned these things—why may I not?"

My father's face reddened and darkened all at once, and he gripped the sides of the butcher's board where he cut caramel into bricks. "I learned to prefer sugar to white curls," he growled, "and peppermints to piccolos, and cherry creams to the emperor. You will learn this, too, Constanze." He cleared his throat. "It is an important thing to know."

I bent myself to the lesson. I learned how to test my father's syrups by dropping them into silver pots of cold water. By the time I was sixteen I hardly needed to do it, I could sense the hard crack of finished candy, feel the brittle snap prickling the hairs of my neck. My fingers were red with so many crushed berries; my palms were dry and crackling with the pale and scratchy wrapping papers we used for penny sweets. I was a good girl. By the time my father gave me the dress, I was a better confectioner than he, though he would never admit it. It was almost like magic, the way candies would form, glistening and impossibly colorful, under my hands.

It was very bright that morning. The light came through the window panes like butterscotch plates. When I came into the kitchen, there was no egg on the table, no toffee-hammer, no chocolate in a sweet black cup. Instead, lying over the cold oven like a cake waiting to be iced, was a dress. It was the color of ink, tiered and layered like the ones Viennese ladies wore in my dreams, floating blue to the floor, dusted with diamonds that caught the morning light and flashed cheerfully.

"Oh, Papa! Where would I wear a thing like that?"

My father smiled broadly, but the corners of his smile were wilted and sad.

"Vienna," he said. "The court. I thought you wanted to go, to wear a wig, to hear a flute?"

He helped me on with the dress, and as he cinched in my waist and lifted my red hair from bare shoulders, I realized that the dress was made of hard blue sugar and thousands of blueberry skins stitched together with syrupy thread. The diamonds were lumps of crystal candy, still a bit sticky, and at the waist were icing flowers in a white cascade. Nothing of that dress was not sweet, was not sugar, was not my father's trade and mine.

Vienna looked like a Christmas cake we had once made for a baroness: all hard, white curls and creases and carvings, like someone had draped the city in vanilla cream. There were brown horses, and brown carriages attached to them. In the emperor's palace, where my father walked as though he had built it, there were green and rose checkered floors, and violas playing somewhere far off. My father took my hand and led me to a room which was harder and whiter than all the rest, where the emperor and the empress sat frowning on terrible silver thrones of sharpened filigree, like two demons on their wedding day. I gasped, and shrank behind my father, the indigo train of my dress showing so dark against the floor. I could not hope to hide from those awful royal eyes.

"Why have you brought us this thing, Alonzo?" barked the emperor, who had a short blond mustache and copper buttons running down his chest. "This thing which bears such a resemblance to our wife? Do you insult us by dragging this reminder of your crimes and hers across our floor like a dust broom?"

The empress blushed deeply, her skin going the same shade as her hair, the same shade as my hair. My father clenched his teeth.

"I told you then, when you loved my chocolates above all things, that I did not touch her, that I loved her as a man loves God, not as he loves a woman."

"Yet you come back, begging to return to my grace, towing a child who is a mirror of her! This is obscene, Alonzo!"

My father's face broke open, pleading. It was terrible to see him so. I clutched my icing flowers, confused and frightened.

"But she is not my child! She is not the empress' child! She is the greatest thing I have ever created, the greatest of all things I have baked in my oven. I have brought her to show you what I may do in your name, for your grace, if you will look on me with love again, if you will give me your favor once more. If you will let me come back to the city, to my home."

I gaped, and tears filled my eyes. My father drew a little silver icing-spade from his belt and started toward me. I cried out and my voice echoed in the hard, white hall like a sparrow cut into a fork. I cringed, but my father gripped my arms tight as a tureen's handles, and his eyes were wide and wet. He pushed me to my knees on the emperor's polished floor, and the two monarchs watched impassively as I wept in my beautiful blue dress, though the empress let a pale hand flutter to her throat. My father put the spade to my neck and scraped it up, across my skin, like a barber giving a young man his first shave.

A shower of sugar fell glittering across my chest.

"I never lied to you, Constanze," he murmured in my ear.

He pierced my cheek with the tip of the spade, and blood trickled down my chin, over my lips. It tasted like raspberries.

"Look at her, your majesty. She is nothing but sugar, nothing but candy, through and through. I made her in my own oven. I raised her up. Now she is grown—and so beautiful! Look at her cinnamon hair, her marzipan skin, her tears of sugar and salt! And you may have her, you may have the greatest confection made on this earth, if you will but let me come home, and make you chocolates as I used to, and put your hand to my shoulder in friendship again."

The empress rose from her throne and walked toward me, like a mirror gliding on a hidden track, so like me she was, though her gown was golden, and its train longer than the hall. She looked at me, her gaze pointed and deep, but did not seem to hear my sobbing, or see my tears. She put her hand to my bleeding cheek, and tasted the blood on her palm, daintily, with the tip of her tongue.

"She looks so much like me, Alonzo. It is a strange thing to see."

My father flushed. "I was lonely," he whispered. "And perhaps a man may be forgiven for casting a doll's face in the image of God."

I was kept in the kitchens, hung up on the wall like a copper pot, or a length of garlic. Every day a cook would clip my fingernails to sweeten the emperor's coffee, or cut off a curl of my scarlet hair to spice the Easter cakes of the emperor's first child—a boy with brown eyes like my father's. Sometimes, the head cook would lance my cheek carefully and collect the scarlet syrup in a hard white cup. Once, they plucked my eyelashes, ever so gently, for a licorice comfit the empress' new daughter craved. They were kind enough to ice my lids between plucking.

They tried not to cause me any pain. Cooks and confectioners are not wicked creatures by nature, and the younger kitchen girls were disturbed by the shape of me hanging there, toes pointed at the oven. Eventually, they grew accustomed to it, and I was no more strange to them than a shaker of salt or a pepper-mill. My dress sagged and browned, as blueberry skins will do, and fell away. A kind little boy who scrubbed the floors brought me a coarse black dress from his mother's closet. It was made of wool, real wool, from a sheep and not an oven. They fed me radishes and carrots and potatoes, and sometimes chicken, sometimes even fish, on a plate of real porcelain, with no heat-bubbles in it, none at all.

I grew old on that wall, my marzipan-skin withered and wrinkled no less than flesh, helped along by lancings and scrapings and trimmings. My hair turned white and fell out, eagerly collected. As I grew old, I was told that the emperor liked the taste of my hair better and better, and soon I was bald.

But emperors die, and so do fathers. Both of these occurred in their way, and when at last the emperor died, there was no one to remember that the source of the palace sugar was not a far off isle, under a red sun that burned on the face of the sea. On the wall, I thought of that red sun often, and the children cutting cane, and the taste of the bird's marrow deep in my plum. That same kind floor-scrubber, grown up and promoted to butler, cut me down when my bones were brittle, and touched my shorn hair gently. But he did not apologize. How could he? How many cakes and teas had he tasted which were sweetened by me?

I ran from the palace in the night, as much as I could run, an old, scraped-out crone, a witch in a black dress stumbling across the city and through, across and out. I kept running and running, my sugar-body burning and shrieking with disuse. I ran past the hard white streets and past the villages where I had been a child who knew nothing of Vienna, into the woods, into the black forest with the creeping loam and nothing sweet for miles. Only there did I stop, panting, my spiced breath fogging in the air. There were great dark green boughs arching over me, pine and larch and oak. I sank down to the earth, wrung dry of weeping, safe and far from anything hard, anything white, anything with accusing eyes and a throne like a demon's wedding. No one would scrape me for teatime again. No one would touch me again. I put my hands to my head and stared up at the stars though the leaves. It was quiet, at last, quiet, and dark. I curled up on the leaves and slept.

When I woke, I was cold. I shivered. I needed more than a black dress to cover me. I would not go back, not to any place which had known me, not to Vienna, not to a village without a candy-maker. I would not hang a sign over a door and feed sweets to children. I would stay, in the dark, under the green. And so I needed a house. But I knew nothing of houses. I was not a bricklayer or a thatcher. I did not know how to make a chimney. I did not know how to make a door-hinge. I did not know how to stitch curtains.

But I knew how to make candy.

I went begging in the villages, a harmless old crone—was it odd that she asked for sugar and not for coins? Certainly. Did they think it mad that she begged for berries and liquors and cocoa, but never alms? Of course. But the elderly are strange and their ways inexplicable to the young. I collected, just as they had done from me all my years on the wall, and my hair grew. I went to my place in the forest, under the black and the boughs, and I poured a foundation of caramel. I raised up thick, brown gingerbread walls, with cinnamon for wattle and marshmallow for daub. Hard-crack windows clear as the morning air, a smoking licorice chimney, stairs of peanut brittle and carpets of red taffy, a peppermint bathtub. And a great black oven, all of blackened, burnt sugar, with a yellow flame within. Gumdrops studded my house like jewels, and a little path of molasses ran liquid and dark from my door. And when my hair had grown long enough, I thatched my roof with cinnamon strands.

It had such a delicate architecture, my house, that I baked and built. It was as delicately made as I had been. I thought of my father all the while, and the red sun on waving green cane. I thought of him while I built my pastry-table, and I thought of him while I built my gingerbread floors. I hated and loved him in turns, as witches will do, for our hearts are strange and inexplicable. He had never come to see me on the wall, even once. I could not understand it. But I made my caramel bricks and I rolled out sheets of toffee onto my bed, and I told his ghost that I was a good girl, I had always been a good girl, even on the wall.

I made a pillow of spun sugar. I made plates of butterscotch. Each morning I tapped a marzipan egg with a little toffee-hammer. But I never caught a sparrow for my plums. They are so very quick. I was always hungry for them, for something living, and salty, and sweet amid all my sugar. I longed for something alive in my crystalline house, something to remind me of the children crushing up cane with tan, strong hands. There was no marrow in my plums. I could not remember the red sun and the long, green stalks, and so I bent low in my lollipop rocking-chair, weeping and whispering to my father that I was sorry, I was sorry, I was no more than a pig snuffling in the leaves, after all.

❦

And one morning, when it was very bright, and the light came through the window like a viola playing something very sweet and sad, I heard footsteps coming up my molasses-path. Children: a boy and a girl. They laughed, and over their heads blackbirds cawed hungrily.

I was hungry, too.

❦

A DELICATE ARCHITECTURE

Terri Windling and I were for a middle-grade fairy tale anthology. Neither of us had worked with middle grade material at the time, but we hit up some of the adult writers we'd used for our adult fairy tale anthologies in addition to some young adult writers we knew. Thus was *A Wolf at the Door* born in 2000. It did remarkably well and we were asked for another. We were surprised that so may adults seemed to enjoy the book.

Our editor left as we were finishing the book and we were assigned another editor to shepherd the book through production and publication. We turned in *Swan Sister*, got cover art we and the B&N sales rep hated, but the publisher refused to change it. The book did okay, but not as well as *A Wolf at the Door*. Oh yeah, and we subsequently found out that the editor who took the book over wasn't into fantasy.

I believe it was Terri's idea to pitch another middle grade fairy tale anthology, this one from the villain's point of view. We sold it to Sharyn November, the YA editor of our "mythic" series books. It was *Troll's Eye View: A Book of Villainess Tales*, and Catherynne M. Valente's "A Delicate Architecture" is one of the wonderful tales from it.

The Goosle

by Margo Lanagan

(From *The Del Rey Book of Science Fiction and Fantasy,* 2008)

"There," said Grinnan as we cleared the trees. "Now, you keep your counsel, Hanny-boy."

Why, that is the mudwife's house, I thought. Dread thudded in me. Since two days ago among the older trees when I knew we were in my father's forest, I'd feared this.

The house looked just as it did in my memory: the crumbling, glittery yellow walls, the dreadful roof sealed with drippy white mud. My tongue rubbed the roof of my mouth just looking. It is crisp as wafer-biscuit on the outside, that mud. You bite through to a sweetish sand inside. You are frightened it will choke you, but you cannot stop eating.

The mudwife might be dead, I thought hopefully. So many are dead, after all, of the black.

But then came a convulsion in the house. A face passed the window-hole, and there she was at the door. Same squat body with a big face snarling above. Same clothing, even, after all these years, the dress trying for bluishness and the pinafore for brown through all the dirt. She looked just as strong. However much bigger *I'd* grown, it took all my strength to hold my bowels together.

"Don't come a step nearer." She held a red fire-banger in her hand, but it was so dusty—if I'd not known her I'd have laughed.

"Madam, I pray you," said Grinnan. "We are clean as clean—there's not a speck on us, not a blister. Humble travellers in need only of a pig-hut or a chicken-shed to shelter the night."

"Touch my stock and I'll have you," she says to all his smoothness. "I'll roast your head in a pot."

I tugged Grinnan's sleeve. It was all too sudden—one moment walking wondering, the next on the doorstep with the witch right there, talking heads in pots.

"We have pretties to trade," said Grinnan.

"You can put your pretties up your poink-hole where they belong."

"We have all the news of long travel. Are you not at all curious about the world and its woes?"

"Why would I live here, tuffet-head?" And she went inside and slammed her door and banged the shutter across her window.

"She is softening," said Grinnan. "She is curious. She can't help herself."

"I don't think so."

"You watch me. Get us a fire going, boy. There on that bit of bare ground."

"She will come and throw her bunger in it. She'll blind us, and then—"

"Just make and shut. I tell you, this one is as good as married to me. I have her heart in my hand like a rabbit-kitten."

I was sure he was mistaken, but I went to, because fire meant food and just the sight of the house had made me hungry. While I fed the fire its kindling I dug up a little stone from the flattened ground and sucked the dirt off it.

Grinnan had me make a smelly soup. Salt-fish, it had in it, and sea-celery and the yellow spice.

When the smell was strong, the door whumped open and there she was again. Ooh, she was so like in my dreams, with her suddenness and her ugly intentions that you can't guess. But it was me and Grinnan this time, not me and Kirtle. Grinnan was big and smart, and he had his own purposes. And I knew there was no magic in the world, just trickery on the innocent. Grinnan would never let anyone else trick me; he wanted that privilege all for himself.

"Take your smelly smells from my garden this instant!" the mudwife shouted.

Grinnan bowed as if she'd greeted him most civilly. "Madam, if you'd join us? There is plenty of this lovely bull-a-bess for you as well."

"I'd not touch my lips to such mess. What kind of foreign muck—"

Even I could hear the longing in her voice, that she was trying to shout down.

There before her he ladled out a bowlful—yellow, splashy, full of delicious lumps. Very humbly—he does humbleness well when he needs to, for such a big man—he took it to her. When she recoiled he placed it on the little table by the door, the one that I ran against in my clumsiness when escaping, so hard I still sometimes feel the bruise in my rib. I remember, I knocked it skittering out the door, and I flung it back meaning to trip up the mudwife. But instead I tripped up Kirtle, and the wife came out and plucked her up and bellowed after me and kicked the table onto the path, and ran out herself with Kirtle like a tortoise swimming from her fist and kicked the table aside again—

Bang! went the cottage door.

Grinnan came laughing quietly back to me.

"She is ours. Once they've et your food, Hanny, you're free to eat theirs. Fish and onion pie tonight, I'd say."

"Eugh."

"Jealous, are we? Don't like old Grinnan supping at other pots, hnh?"

"It's *not* that!" I glared at his laughing face. "She's so ugly, that's all. So old. I don't know how you can even think of—"

"Well, I am no primrose myself, golden boy," he says. "And I'm grateful for any flower that lets me pluck her."

I was not old and desperate enough to laugh at that joke. I pushed his soup-bowl at him.

"Ah, bull-a-bess," he said into the steam. "Food of gods and seducers."

When the mudwife let us in, I looked straight to the corner, and the cage *was still there!* It had been repaired in places with fresh plaited withes, but it was still of the same pattern. Now there was an animal in it, but the cottage was so dim...a very thin cat, maybe, or a ferret. It rippled slowly around its borders, and flashed little eyes at us, and smelled as if its own piss were combed through its fur for pomade. I never smelled that bad when I lived in that cage. I ate well, I remember; I fattened. She took away my leavings in a little cup, on a little dish, but there was still plenty of me left.

So that when Kirtle freed me I *lumbered* away. As soon as I was out of sight of the mud-house I stopped in the forest and just stood there blowing from the effort of propelling myself, after all those weeks of sloth.

So that Grinnan when he first saw me said, *Here's a jubbly one. Here's a cheese cake. Wherever did you get the makings of those round cheeks?* And he fell on me like a starving man on a roasted mutton-leg. Before too long he had used me thin again, and thin I stayed thereafter.

He was busy at work on the mudwife now.

"Oh my, what an array of herbs! You must be a very knowledgeable woman. And hasn't she a lot of pots, Hansel! A pot for every occasion, I think."

Oh yes, I nearly said, *including head-boiling, remember?*

"Well, you are very comfortably set up here indeed, Madam." He looked about him as if he's found himself inside some kind of enchanted palace, instead of in a stinking hovel with a witch in the middle of it. "Now, I'm sure you told me your name—"

"I did not. My name's not for such as you to know." Her mouth was all pruny and she strutted around and banged things and shot him sharp looks, but I'd seen it. We were in here, weren't we? We'd made it this far.

"Ah, a guessing game!" says Grinnan delightedly. "Now, you'd have a good strong name, I'm sure. Bridda, maybe, or Gert. Or else something fiery and passionate, such as Rossavita, eh?"

He can afford to play her awhile. If the worst comes to the worst, he has the liquor, after all. The liquor has worked on me when nothing else would, when I've been ready to run, to some town's wilds where I could hide—to such as that farm-wife with the worried face who beat off Grinnan with a broom. The liquor had softened me and made me sleepy, made me give in to the old bugger's blandishments; next day it had stopped me thinking with its head-pain, further than to obey Grinnan's grunts and gestures.

How does yours like it? said Gadfly's red-haired boy viciously. *I've heard him call you "honey", like a girl-wife; does he do you like a girl, face to face and lots of kissing? Like your boy-bits, which they is so small, ain't even there, so squashed and ground in?*

He calls me Hanny, because Hanny is my name. Hansel.

Honey is your name, eh? said the black boy—a boy of black skin from naturalness, not illness. *After your honey hair?*

Which they commenced patting and pulling and then held me down and chopped all away with Gadfly's good knife. When Grinnan saw me he went pale, but I'm pretty sure he was trying to cut some kind of deal with Gadfly to swap me for the red-hair (with the *skin like milk, like freckled milk,* he said), so the only thing it changed, he did not come after me for several nights until the hair had settled and I did not give off such an air of humiliation.

Then he whispered, *You were quite handsome under that thatch, weren't you? All along.* And things were bad as ever, and the next day he tidied off the stragglier strands, as I sat on a stump with my poink-hole thumping and the other boys idled this way and that, watching, warping their faces at each other and snorting.

The first time Grinnan did me, I could imagine that it didn't happen. I thought, I had that big dump full of so much nervous earth and stones and some of them must have had sharp corners and cut me as I passed them, and the throbbing of the cuts gave me the dream, that the old man had done that to me. Because I was so fearful, you know, frightened of everything coming straight from the mudwife, and I put fear and pain together and made it up in my sleep. The first time I could trick myself, because it was so terrible and mortifying a thing, it could not be real. It could not.

I have watched Grinnan a long time now, in success and failure, in private and on show. At first I thought he was too smart for me, that I was trapped by his cleverness. And this is true. But I have seen others laugh at him, or walk away from his efforts easily, shaking their heads. Others are cleverer.

What he does to me, he waits till I am weak. Half-asleep, he waits till. I never have much fight in me, but dozing off I have even less.

Then what he does—it's so simple I'm ashamed. He bares the flesh of my back. He strokes my back as if that is all he is going to do. He goes straight to the very oldest memory I have—which, me never having told him, how does he know it?—of being sickly, of my first mother bringing me through the night, singing and stroking my back, the oldest and safest piece of my mind, and he puts me there, so that I am sodden with sweetness and longing and nearly-being-back-to-a-baby.

And then he proceeds. It often hurts—it *mostly* hurts. I often weep. But there is a kind of bargain goes on between us, you see. I pay for the first part with the second. The price of the journey to that safe, sweet-sodden place is being spiked in the arse and dragged kicking and biting my blanket back to the real and dangerous one.

Show me your boy-thing, the mudwife would say. *Put it through the bars.*

I won't.

Why not?

You will bite it off. You will cut it off with one of your knives. You will chop it with your axe.

Put it out. I will do no such thing. I only want to wash it.

Wash it when Kirtle is awake, if you so want me clean.

It will be nice, I promise you. I will give you a nice feeling, so warm, so wet. You'll feel good.

But when I put it out, she exclaimed, *What am I supposed to do with that?*

Wash it, like you said.

There's not enough of it even to wash! How would one get that little peepette dirty?

I put it away, little shred, little scrap I was ashamed of.

And she flung around the room awhile, and then she sat, her face all red crags in the last little light of the banked-up fire. *I am going to have to keep you forever!* she said. *For* years *before you are any use to me. And you are expensive! You eat like a pig! I should just cook you up now and enjoy you while you are tender.*

I was all wounded pride and stupid. I didn't know what she was talking about. *I can do anything my sister can do, if you just let me out of this cage. And I'm a better wood-chopper.*

Wood-chopper! she said disgustedly. *As if I needed a wood-chopper!* And she went to the door and took the axe off the wall there, and tested the edge with one of her horny fingertips, and looked at me in a very *thoughtful* way that I did not much like.

Sometimes he speaks as he strokes. *My Hanny*, he says, very gentle and loving like my mother, *my goosle, my gosling, sweet as apple, salt as sea.* And it feels as if we are united in yearning for my mother and her touch and voice.

She cannot have gone forever, can she, if I can remember this feeling so clearly? But, ah, to get back to her, so much would have to be undone! So much would have to un-happen: all of Grinnan's and my wanderings, all the witch-time, all the time of our second mother. That last night of our first mother, our real mother, and her awful writhing and the noises and our father begging, and Kirtle weeping and needing to be taken away—that would have to become a nightmare, from which my father would shake me awake with the news that the baby came out just as Kirtle and I did, just as easily. And our mother would rise from her bed with the baby; we would all rise into the baby's first morning, and begin.

It is very deep in the night. I have done my best to be invisible, to make no noise, but now the mudwife pants, *He's not asleep.*

Of course he's asleep. Listen to his breathing.

I do the asleep-breathing.

Come, says Grinnan. *I've done with these, bounteous as they are. I want to go below.* He has his ardent voice on now. He makes you think he is barely in control of himself, and somehow that makes you, somehow that flatters you enough to let him do what he wants.

After some uffing and puffing, *No,* she says, very firm, and there's a slap. *I want that boy out of here.*

What, wake him so he can go and listen at the window?

Get him out, she says. *Send him beyond the pigs and tell him to stay.*

You're a nuisance, he says. *You're a sexy nuisance. Look at this! I'm all mis-shapen and you want me herding children.*

You do it, she says, rearranging her clothing, *or you'll stay that shape.*

So he comes to me and I affect to be woken up and to resist being hauled out the door, but really it's a relief of course. I don't want to hear or see or know. None of that stuff I understand, why people want to sweat and pant and poke bits of themselves into each other, why anyone would want to do more than hold each other for comfort and stroke each other's back.

Moonlight. Pigs like slabs of moon, like long, fat fruit fallen off a moon-vine. The trees tall and brainy all around and above—*they* never sweat and pork; the most they do is sway in a breeze, or crash to the ground to make useful wood. The damp smell of night forest. My friends in the firmament, telling me where I am: two and a half days north of the ford with the knotty rope; four and a half days north and a bit west of "Devilstown", which Grinnan called it because someone made off in the night with all the spoils *we'd* made off with the night before.

I'd thought we were the only ones not black in their beds! he'd stormed on the road.

They must have come very quiet, I said. *They must have been accom-plished thieves.*

They must have been sprites or devils, he spat, *that I didn't hear them, with* my *ears.*

We were seven and a half days north and very very west of Gadfly's camp, where we had, as Grinnan put it, *tried the cooperative life for a while.*

But those boys, *they were a gang of no-goods,* Grinnan says now. Whatever deal he had tried to make for Freckled-Milk, they laughed him off, and Grinnan could not stand it there having been laughed at. He took me away before dawn one morning, and when we stopped by a stream in the first light he showed me the brass candlesticks that Gadfly had kept in a sack and been so proud of.

And what'll you use those for? I said foolishly, for we had managed up until then with moon and stars and our own wee fire.

I did not take them to use them, Hanny-pot, he said with glee. *I took them because he loved and polished them so.* And he flung them into the stream, and I gasped—and Grinnan laughed to hear me gasp—at the sight of them cutting through the foam and then gone into the dark cold irretrievable.

Anyway, it was new for me still, there beyond the mudwife's pigs, this knowing where we were—though I had lost count of the days since Ardblarthen when it had come to me how Grinnan looked *up* to find his way, not down among a million tree-roots that all looked the same, among twenty million grass-stalks, among twenty million million stones or sand-grains. It was even newer how the star-pattern and the moon movements had steadied out of their meaningless whirling and begun to tell me whereabouts I was in the wide world. All my life I had been stupid, trying to mark the things around me on the ground, leaving myself trails to get home by because every tree looked the same to me, every knoll and declivity, when all the time the directions were hammered hard into their system up there, pointing and changing-but-never-completely-changing.

So if we came at the cottage from this angle, whereas Kirtle and I came from the front, that means...but Kirtle and I wandered so many days, didn't we? I filled my stomach with earths, but Kirtle was piteous weeping all the way, so hungry. She would not touch the earth; she watched me eating it and wept. I remember, I told her, *No wonder you are thirsty! Look how much water you're wasting on those tears!* She had brown hair, I remember. I remember her pushing it out of her eyes so that she could see to sweep in the dark cottage—the cottage where the mudwife's voice is rising, like a saw through wood.

The house stands glittering and the sound comes out of it. My mouth waters; they wouldn't hear me over that noise, would they?

I creep in past the pigs to where the blobby roof-edge comes low. I break off a blob bigger than my hand; the wooden shingle it was holding slides off, and my other hand catches it soundlessly and leans it against the house. The mudwife howls; something is knocked over in there; she howls again and Grinnan is grunting with the effort of something. I run away from all those noises, the white mud in my hand like a hunk of cake. I run back to the trees where Grinnan told me to stay, where the woman's howls are like mouse-squeaks and I can't hear Grinnan, and I sit between two high roots and I bite in.

Once I've eaten the mud I'm ready to sleep. I try dozing, but it's not comfortable among the roots there, and there is still noise from the cottage—now it is Grinnan working himself up, calling her all the things he calls me, all the insults. *You love it,* he says, with such deep disgust. *You filth, you filthy cunt.* And she *oh's* below, not at all like me, but as if she really does love it. I lie quiet, thinking, Is it true, that she loves it? That I do? And if it's true, how is it that Grinnan knows, but I don't? She makes noise, she agrees with whatever he says. *Harder, harder,* she says. *Bang me till I burst. Harder!* On and on they go, until I give up waiting—they will never finish!

I get up and go around the pigsty and behind the chicken house. There is a poor field there, pumpkins gone wild in it, blackberry bushes foaming dark around the edges. At least the earth might be softer here. If I pile up enough of this floppy vine, if I gather enough pumpkins around me—

And then I am holding, not a pale baby pumpkin in my hand but a pale baby skull.

Grinnan and the mudwife bellow together in the house, and something else crashes broken.

The skull is the colour of white-mud, but hard, inedible—although when I turn it in the moonlight I find tooth-marks where someone has tried.

The shouts go up high—the witch's loud, Grinnan's whimpering.

I grab up a handful of earth to eat, but a bone comes with it, long, white, dry. I let the earth fall away from it.

I crouch there looking at the skull and the bone, as those two finish themselves off in the cottage.

They will sleep now—but I'm not sleepy any more. The stars in their map are nailed to the inside of my skull; my head is filled with dark clarity. When I am sure they are asleep, I scoop up a mouthful of earth, and start digging.

Let me go *and get the mudwife,* our father murmured. *Just for this once.*

I've done it twice and I'll do it again. Don't you bring that woman here! Our mother's voice was all constricted, as if the baby were trying to come up her throat, not out her nethers.

But this is not like *the others!* he said, desperate after the following pain. *They say she knows all about children. Delivers them all the time.*

Delivers them? She eats them! said our mother. *It's not just this one. I've two others might catch her eye, while I feed and doze. I'd rather die than have her near my house, that filthy hag.*

So die she did, and our new brother or sister died as well, still inside her. We didn't know whichever it was. *Will it be another little Kirtle-child?* our father had asked us, bright-eyed by the fire at night. *Or another baby wood-cutter, like our Hans?* It had seemed so important to know. Even when the baby was dead, I wanted to know.

But the whole reason! our father sobbed. *Is that it could not come out, for us to see!* Which had shamed me quiet.

And then later, going into blackened towns where the only way you could tell man from woman was by the style of a cap, or a hair-ribbon draggling into the dirt beneath them, or a rotted pinafore, or worst by the amount of shrunken scrag between an unclothed person's legs—why, then I could see how small a thing it was not to know the little one's sex. I could see that it was not important at all.

When I wake up, they are at it again with their sexing. My teeth are stuck to the inside of my cheeks and lips by two ridges of earth. I have to break the dirt away with my finger.

What was I thinking, last night? I sit up. The bones are in a pile beside me; the skulls are in a separate pile—for counting, I remember. What I thought was: Where did she *find* all these children? Kirtle and I walked for days, I'm sure. There was nothing in the world but trees and owls and foxes and that one deer. Kirtle was afraid of bats at night, but I never saw even one. And we never saw people—which was what we were looking for, which was why we were so unwise when we came upon the mudwife's house.

But what am I going to do? What was I planning, piling these up? I thought I was only looking for all Kirtle's bits. But then another skull turned up and I thought, Well, maybe this one is more Kirtle's size, and then skull after skull—I dug on, crunching earth and drooling and breathing through my nose, and the bones seemed to rise out of the earth at me, seeking out the moon the way a tree reaches for the light, pushing up thinly among the other trees until it finds light enough to spread into, seeking out *me*, as if they were thinking, Here, finally, is someone who can do something for us.

I pick up the nearest skull. Which of these is my sister's? Even if there were just a way to tell girls' skulls from boys'! Is hers even here? Maybe she's still buried, under the blackberries where I couldn't go for thorns.

Now I have a skull in either hand, like someone at a market weighing one cabbage against another. And the thought comes to me: Something is different. Listen.

The pigs. The mudwife, her noises very like the pigs'. There is no rhythm to them; they are random grunting and gasping. And I—

Silently I replace the skulls on the pile.

I haven't heard Grinnan this morning. Not a word, not a groan. Just the woman. The woman and the pigs.

The sunshine shows the cottage as the hovel it is, its saggy sides propped, its sloppy roofing patched with mud-splats simply thrown from the ground. The back door stands wide, and I creep up and stand right next to it, my back to the wall.

Wet slaps and stirrings sound inside. The mudwife grunts—she sounds muffled, desperate. Has he tied her up? Is he strangling her? There's not a gasp or word from him. That *thing* in the cage gives off a noise, though, a kind of low baying. It never stops to breathe. There is a strong smell of shit. Dawn is warming everything up; flies zoom in and out the doorway.

I press myself to the wall. There is a dip in the doorstep. Were I brave enough to walk in, that's where I would put my foot. And right at that place appears a drop of blood, running from inside. It slides into the dip, pauses modestly at being seen, then shyly hurries across the step and dives into hiding in the weeds below.

How long do I stand there, looking out over the pigsty and the chicken house to the forest, wishing I were there among the trees instead of here clamped to the house wall like one of those gargoyles on the monks' house in Devilstown, with each sound opening a new pocket of fear in my bowels? A fly flies into my gaping mouth and out again. A pebble in the wall digs a little chink in the back of my head, I'm pressed so hard there.

Finally, I have to know. I have to take one look before I run, otherwise I'll dream all the possibilities for nights to come. She's not a witch; she can't spell me back; I'm thin now and nimble; I can easily get away from her.

So I loosen my head, and the rest of me, from the wall. I bend one knee and straighten the other, pushing my big head, my popping eyes, around the doorpost.

I only meant to glimpse and run. So ready am I for the running, I tip outward even when I see there's no need. I put out my foot to catch myself, and I stare.

She has her back to me, her bare, dirty white back, her baggy arse and thighs. If she weren't doing what she's doing, that would be horror enough, how everything is wet and withered and hung with hair, how everything shakes.

Grinnan is dead on the table. She has opened his legs wide and eaten a hole in him, in through his soft parts. She has pulled all his innards out onto the floor, and her bare bloody feet are trampling the shit out of them, her bare shaking legs are trying to brace themselves on the slippery carpet of them. I can smell the salt-fish in the shit; I can smell the yellow spice.

That devilish moan, up and down it wavers, somewhere between purr and battle-yowl. I thought it was me, but it's that shadow in the cage, curling over and over itself like a ruffle of black water, its eyes fixed on the mess, hungry, hungry.

The witch pulls her head out of Grinnan for air. Her head and shoulders are shiny red; her soaked hair drips; her purple-brown nipples point down into two hanging rubies. She snatches some air between her red teeth and plunges in again, her head inside Grinnan like the bulge of a dead baby, but higher, forcing higher, pummelling up inside him, *fighting* to be un-born.

In my travels I have seen many wrongnesses done, and heard many others told of with laughter or with awe around a fire. I have come upon horrors of all kinds, for these are horrible times. But never has a thing been laid out so obvious and ongoing in its evil before my eyes and under my nose and with the flies feasting even as it happens. And never has the means to end it hung as clearly in front of me as it hangs now, on the wall, in the smile of the mudwife's axe-edge, fine as the finest nail-paring, bright as the dawn sky, the only clean thing in this foul cottage.

I reach my father's house late in the afternoon. How I knew the way, when years ago you could put me twenty paces into the trees and I'd wander lost all day, I don't know; it just came to me. All the loops I took, all the mistakes I made, all laid themselves down in their places on the world, and I took the right way past them and came here straight, one sack on my back, the other in my arms.

When I dreamed of this house it was big and full of comforts; it hummed with safety; the spirit of my mother lit it from inside like a sacred candle. Kirtle was always here, running out to greet me all delight.

Now I can see the poor place for what it is, a plague-ruin like so many that Grinnan and I have found and plundered. And tiny—not even as big as the witch's cottage. It sits in its weedy quiet and the forest chirps around it. The only thing remarkable about it is that I am the first here; no one has touched the place. I note it on my star map—there *is* safety here, the safety of a distance greater than most robbers will venture.

A blackened boy-child sits on the step, his head against the doorpost as if only very tired. Inside, a second child lies in a cradle. My father and second-mother are in their bed, side by side just like that lord and lady on the stone tomb in Ardblarthen, only not so neatly carved or richly dressed. Everything else is exactly the same as Kirtle and I left it. So sparse and spare! There is nothing of value here. Grinnan would be angry. *Burn these bodies and beds, boy!* he'd say. *We'll take their rotten roof if that's all they have.*

'But Grinnan is not here, is he?' I say to the boy on the step, carrying the mattock out past him. 'Grinnan is in the ground with his lady-love, under the pumpkins. And with a great big pumpkin inside him, too. And Mrs Pumpkin-Head in his arms, so that they can sex there underground forever.'

I take a stick and mark out the graves: Father, Second-Mother, Brother, Sister—and a last big one for the two sacks of Kirtle-bones. There's plenty of time before sundown, and the moon is bright these nights, don't I know it. I can work all night if I have to; I am strong enough, and full enough still of disgust. I will dig and dig until this is done.

I tear off my shirt.

I spit in my hands and rub them together.

The mattock bites into the earth.

THE GOOSLE

Shortly after the Sci-Fi Channel (now Syfy) eliminated most of the original content (including fiction) from their website, Chris Schluep, at Del Rey Books, took me for lunch and expressed interest in having me edit an original anthology of sf/f/h in the vein of what I published for six years at SCIFICTION.

Of course I said you bet, and that anthology became *The Del Rey Book of Science Fiction and Fantasy*. The lack of theme enabled me to publish a wide variety of stories, including "The Goosle" by Margo Lanagan, a powerful story that attracted a lot of attention. One reviewer was so offended by it that he accused the author, me, and the publisher of promoting child abuse, hence missing the entire point of the story. It won Australia's Ditmar Award for Best Short Story.

Eaten
(Scenes from a Moving Picture)

by Neil Gaiman

(From *Off Limits: Tales of Alien Sex,* 1996)

INT. WEBSTER'S OFFICE. DAY
As WEBSTER sits
reading the LA Times, MCBRIDE walks in
and tells in

FLASHBACK
how his SISTER came
to Hollywood eleven months ago
to make her fortune, and to meet the stars.
Of how he'd heard from friends that she'd "gone strange."
Imagining the needle, or far worse,
he travels out to Hollywood himself
and finds her standing underneath a bridge.
Her skin is pale. She screams at him "Get lost!"
and sobs and runs. A TALL MAN DRESSED IN BLACK
grabs hold his sleeve, tells him to let it drop
"Forget your sister," but of course he can't…

(IN SEPIA
we see the two as teens,
a YOUNG MCBRIDE and SISTER way back when,
giggles beneath the porch, "I'll show you mine,"
closer perhaps than siblings ought to be…
PAN UP

to watch a passing butterfly.
We hear them breathe and fumble in the dark:
IN CLOSE-UP now he spurts into her hand,
she licks her palm: first makes a face, then smiles…
HOLD on her lips and teeth and on her tongue).

END FLASHBACK
WEBSTER says he'll take the case,
says something flip and hard about LA,
like how it eats young girls and spits them out,
and takes a hundred dollars on account.

CUT TO

THE PURPLE PUSSY. INT. A DIVE,
THREE NAKED WOMEN dance for dollar bills.
WEBSTER comes in, and talks to one of them,
slips her a twenty, shows a photograph,
the stripper—standing close enough that he
could touch her (but they've bouncers on patrol,
weird steroid cases who will break your wrists)—
admits she thinks she knows the girl he means.
Then WEBSTER leaves.

INT. WEBSTER'S CONDO. NIGHT.
A video awaits him at his home.
It shows A WOMAN lovelier than life
Shot from the rib cage up (her breasts exposed)
Advising him to "let this whole thing drop,
forget it," promising she'll see him soon…

DISSOLVE TO

INT. MCBRIDE'S HOTEL ROOM. NIGHT.
MCBRIDE'S alone and lying on the bed,

He's watching soft-core porn on pay-per-view.
Naked. He rubs his cock with vaseline,
lazy and slow, he doesn't want to come.
A BANG upon the window. He sits up,
flaccid and scared (he's on the second floor)
and opens up the window of his room.
HIS SISTER enters, looking almost dead,
implores him to forget her. He says no.
THE SISTER shambles over to the door.
A WOMAN DRESSED IN BLACK waits in the hall.
Brunette in leather, kinky as all hell,
who steps over the threshold with a smile.
And they have sex.

                      THE SISTER stands alone.
She watches as THE BRUNETTE takes MCBRIDE
(her skin's necrotic blue. She's fully dressed).
THE BRUNETTE gestures curtly with her hand,
off come THE SISTER'S clothes. She looks a mess.
Her skin's all scarred and scored; one nipple's gone.
She takes her gloves off and we see her hands:
Her fingers look like ribs, or chicken wings,
well chewed, and rescued from a garbage can—
dry bones with scraps of flesh and cartilage.
She puts her fingers in THE BRUNETTE'S mouth…
AND FADE TO BLACK.

INT. WEBSTER'S OFFICE. DAY.
THE PHONE RINGS. It's MCBRIDE. "Just drop the case.
I've found my sister, and I'm going home.
You've got five hundred dollars, and my thanks."
PULL BACK on WEBSTER, puzzled and confused.

MONTAGE of WEBSTER here. A week goes by,
we see him eating, pissing, drinking, drunk.
We watch him throw HIS GIRLFRIEND out of bed.
We see him play the video again…
The VIDEO GIRL stares at him and says
she'll see him soon. "I promise, Webster, soon."

CUT TO

THE PLACE OF EATERS, UNDERGROUND.
Pale people stand like cattle in a pen.
We see MCBRIDE. The flesh is off his chest.
White meat is good. We're looking through his ribs:
his heart is still. His lungs, however, breathe,
inflate, deflate. And tears of pus run down
his sunken cheeks. He pisses in the muck.
It doesn't steam. He wishes he were dead.

A DREAM:
As WEBSTER tosses in his bed.
He sees MCBRIDE, a corpse beneath a bridge,
all INTERCUT with lots of shots of food,
to make our theme explicit: this is art.

EXT. LA. DAY.
WEBSTER'S become obsessed.
He has to find the woman from the screen.
He beats somebody up, fucks someone else,
fixated on "I'll see you, Webster, soon."

He's thrown in prison. And they come for him,
THE MAN IN BLACK attending THE BRUNETTE.
Open his cell with keys, escort him out,
and leave the prison building. Through a door.

Eaten (Scenes from a Moving Picture)

They walk him to the car park. They go down,
below the car park, deep beneath the town,
past shadowed writhing things that suck and hiss
and glossy things that laugh, and things that scream.
Now other feeder-folk are walking past…
They handcuff WEBSTER to A TINY MAN
who's covered with vaginas and with teeth,
and escorts WEBSTER to

THE QUEEN'S SALON.

(An interjection here: my wife awoke,
scared by an evil dream. "You hated me.
You brought these women home I didn't know,
but they knew me, and then we had a fight,
and after we had shouted you stormed out.
You said you'd find a girl to fuck and eat."

This scares me just a little. As we write
we summon little demons. So I shrug.)

The handcuffs are removed. He's left alone.
The hangings are red velvet, then they lift,
reveal THE QUEEN. We recognize her face,
the woman we saw on the VCR.
"The world divides so sweetly, neatly up
into the feeder-folk, into their prey."
That's what she says. Her voice is soft and sweet.
Imagine honey ants: the tiny head,
the chest, the tiny arms, the tiny hands,
and after that the bloat of honey-swell,
the abdomen enormous as it hangs
translucent, made of honey, sweet as lust.

THE QUEEN has quite a perfect little face,
her breasts are pale, blue-veined; her nipples pink;
her hands are white. But then, below her breasts
the whole swells like a whale or like a shrine,
a human honey ant, she's huge as rooms,
as elephants, as dinosaurs, as love.
Her flesh is opalescent, and she calls
poor WEBSTER to her. And he nods and comes.
(She must be over twenty-five feet long.)
She orders him to take off all his clothes.
His cock is hard. He shivers. He looks lost.
He moans "I'm harder than I've ever been."
Then, with her mouth, she licks and tongues his cock…

We linger here. The language of the eye
becomes a bland, unflinching, blow-job porn,
(her lips are glossy, and her tongue is red)
HOLD on her face. We hear him gasping "Oh.
Oh, baby. Yes. Oh. Take it in your mouth."
And then she opens up her mouth, and grins,
and bites his cock off.
                    Spurting blood pumps out
into her mouth. She hardly spills a drop.
We never do pan up to see his face,
just her. It's what they call the money shot.

Then, when his cock's gone down, and blood's congealed,
we see his face. He looks all dazed and healed.
Some feeders come and take him out of there.
Down in the pens he's chained beside MCBRIDE.
Deep in the mud lie carcasses picked clean
who grin at them and dream of being soup.

Poor things.

We're almost done.

We'll leave them there.

CUT to some lonely doorway, where A TRAMP
has three cold fingers up ANOTHER TRAMP,
they're starving but they fingerfuck like hell,
and underneath the layers of old clothes
beneath the cardboard, newspaper and cloth,
their genders are impossible to tell.

PAN UP

to watch a butterfly go past.

(ENDS)

EATEN (SCENES FROM A MOVING PICTURE)

Off Limits: Tales of Alien Sex was my follow-up to *Alien Sex*, and was published in 1996. The theme, as was the first volume, is gender relations, with the "aliens" sometimes human, sometimes not. Four of the stories are reprints.

All I will say about Neil's little "screenplay," is that someone needs to actually make it into a film.

Teratisms

by Kathe Koja

(From *A Whisper of Blood,* 1991)

"**B**eaumont." Dreamy, Alex's voice. Sitting in the circle of the heat, curtains drawn in the living room: laddered magenta scenes of birds and dripping trees. "Delcambre. Thibodaux." Slow-drying dribble like rusty water on the bathroom floor. "Abbeville," car door slam, "Chinchuba," screen door slam. Triumphant through its echo, "Baton Rouge!"

Tense hoarse holler almost childish with rage: "Will you shut the fuck *up?*"

From the kitchen, woman's voice, Randle's voice, drawl like cooling blood: "Mitch's home."

"You're damn right Mitch is home." Flat slap of his unread newspaper against the cracked laminate of the kitchen table, the whole set from the Goodwill for thirty dollars. None of the chairs matched. Randle sat in the cane-bottomed one, leg swinging back and forth, shapely metronome, making sure the ragged gape of her tank top gave Mitch a good look. Fanning herself with four slow fingers.

"Bad day, big brother?"

Too tired to sit, propping himself jackknife against the counter. "They're all bad, Francey."

"Mmmm, forgetful. My name's Randle now."

"Doesn't matter what your name is, you're still a bitch."

Soft as dust, from the living room: "De Quincy. Longville." Tenderly, "Bewelcome."

Mitch's sigh. "Numbnuts in there still at it?"

"All day."

Another sigh, he bent to prowl the squat refrigerator, let the door fall shut. Half-angry again, "There's nothing in here to eat, Fran—Randle."

"So what?"

"So what'd you eat?"

More than a laugh, bubbling under. "I don't think you really want to know." Deliberately exposing half a breast, palm lolling beneath like a sideshow, like a street-corner card trick. Presto. "Big brother."

His third sigh, lips closed in decision. "I don't need this," passing close to the wall, warding the barest brush against her, her legs in the chair as deliberate, a sluttish spraddle but all of it understood: an old, unfunny family joke; like calling names; nicknames.

The door slamming, out as in, and in the settling silence of departure: "Is he gone?"

Stiff back, Randle rubbing too hard the itchy tickle of sweat. Pushing at the table to move the chair away. "You heard the car yourself, Alex. You know he's gone."

Pause, then plaintive, "Come sit with me." Sweet; but there are nicknames and nicknames, jokes and jokes; a million ways to say I love you. Through the raddled arch into the living room, Randle's back tighter still, into the smell, and Alex's voice, bright.

"Let's talk," he said.

Mitch, so much later, pausing at the screenless front door, and on the porch Randle's cigarette, drawing lines in the dark like a child with a sparkler.

"Took your time," she said.

Defensively, "It's not that late."

"I know what time it is."

He sat down, not beside her but close enough to speak softly and be heard. "You got another cigarette?"

She took the pack from somewhere, flipped it listless to his lap. "Keep 'em. They're yours anyway."

He lit the cigarette with gold foil matches, JUDY'S DROP-IN. An impulse, shaming, to do as he used to, light a match and hold it to her fingertips to see how long it took to blister. No wonder she hated him. "Do you hate me?"

"Not as much as I hate him." He could feel her motion, half a head-shake. "Do you know what he did?"

"The cities."

"Besides the cities." He did not see her fingers, startled twitch as he felt the pack of cigarettes leave the balance of his thigh. "He was down by the grocery store, the dumpster. Playing. It took me almost an hour just to talk him home." A black sigh. "He's getting worse."

"You keep saying that."

"It keeps being true, Mitch, whether you want to think so or not. Something really bad's going to happen if we don't get him—"

"Get him what?" Sour. No, bitter. "A doctor? A *shrink?* How about a one-way ticket back to Shitsburg so he—"

"Fine, that's fine. But when the cops come knocking I'll let you answer the door," and her quick feet bare on the step, into the house. Tense unconscious rise of his shoulders: Don't slam the door. Don't wake him up.

Mitch slept, weak brittle doze in the kitchen, head pillowed on the Yellow Pages. Movement, the practiced calm of desire. Stealth, until denouement, a waking startle to Alex's soft growls and tweaks of laughter, his giggle and spit. All over the floor. All over the floor and his hands, oh God Alex your *hands*—

Showing them off the way a child would, elbows turned, palms up. Showing them in the jittery bug-light of the kitchen in the last half hour before morning, Mitch bent almost at the waist, then sinking back, nausea subsiding but unbanished before the immensity, the drip and stutter, there was some on his mouth too. His chin, Mitch had to look away from what was stuck there.

"Go on," he said. "Go get your sister."

And waited there, eyes closed, hands spread like a medium on the Yellow Pages. While Alex woke his sister. While Randle used the washcloth. Again.

Oxbow lakes. Flat country. Randle sleeping in the back seat, curled and curiously hot, her skin ablush with sweat in the sweet cool air. Big creamy Buick with all the windows open. Mitch was driving, slim black sunglasses like a cop in a movie, while Alex sat playing beside him. Old wrapping paper today, folding in his fingers, disappearing between his palms. Always paper. Newsprint ink under his nails. Glossy foilwrap from some party, caught between the laces of his sneakers. Or tied there. Randle might have done that, it was her style. Grim droll jokery. Despite himself he looked behind, into the back seat, into the stare of her open eyes, so asphalt blank that for one second fear rose like a giant waiting to be born and he thought, Oh no, oh not her too.

Beside him Alex made a playful sound.

Randle's gaze snapped true into her real smile; bared her teeth in burlesque before she rolled over, pleased.

"Fucking bitch," with dry relief. With feeling.

Alex said, "I'm hungry."

Mitch saw he had begun to eat the paper. "We'll find a drive-through somewhere," he said, and for a moment dreamed of flinging the wheel sideways, of fast and greasy death. Let someone else clean up for a change.

There was a McDonald's coming up, garish beside the blacktop; he got into the right lane just a little too fast. "Randle," coldly, "put your shirt on."

Chasing the end of the drive-through line, lunchtime and busy and suddenly Alex was out of the car, leaned smiling through the window to say, "I want to eat inside." And gone, trotting across the parking lot, birthday paper forgotten on the seat beside.

"Oh God," Mitch craning, tracking his progress, "go after him, Randle," and Randle's snarl, the bright slap of her sandals as she ran. Parking, he considered driving off. Alone. Leaving them there. Don't you ever leave them, swear me. You have to swear me, Michie. Had she ever really said that? Squeezed out a promise like a dry log of shit? I hope there is a hell, he thought, turning off the car, I hope it's big and hot and eternal and that she's in it.

They were almost to the counter, holding hands. When Randle saw him enter, she looked away; he saw her fingers squeeze Alex's, twice and slow. What was it like for her? Middleman. Alex was staring at the wall menu as if he could read. "I'll get a booth," Mitch said.

A table, instead; there were no empty booths. One by one Alex crumbled the chocolate-chip cookies, licked his fingers to dab up the crumbs. Mitch drank coffee.

"That's making me sick," he said to Randle.

Her quick sideways look at Alex. "What?" through half a mouthful, a tiny glob of tartar sauce rich beside her lower lip.

"That smell," nodding at her sandwich. "Fish."

Mouth abruptly stretched, chewed fish and half-smeared sauce, he really was going to be sick. Goddamned *bitch.* Nudging him under the table with one bare foot. Laughing into her Coke.

"Do you always have to make it worse?"

Through another mouthful, "It can't get any worse." To Alex, "Eat your cookies."

Mitch drank more coffee; it tasted bitter, boiled. Randle stared over his head as she ate: watching the patrons? staring at the wall? Alex coughed on cookie crumbs, soft dry cough. Gagged a little. Coughed harder.

"Alex?" Randle put down her sandwich. "You okay? Slap his back," commandingly to Mitch, and he did, harder as Alex kept coughing, almost a barking sound now and heads turned, a little, at the surrounding tables, the briefest bit of notice that grew more avid as Alex's distress increased, louder whoops and Randle suddenly on her feet, trying to raise him up as Mitch saw the first flecks of blood.

"Oh *shit,*" but it was too late, Alex spitting blood now, spraying it, coughing it out in half-digested clots as Randle, frantic, working to haul him upright as Mitch in some stupid reflex swabbed with napkins at the mess. Tables emptied around them. Kids crying, loud and scared, McDonald's employees surrounding them but not too close, Randle shouting, "*Help* me, you asshole!" and Mitch in dumb paralysis watched as a tiny finger, red but recognizable, flew from Alex's mouth to lie wetly on the seat.

Hammerlock, no time to care if it hurts him, Randle already slamming her back against the door to hold it open and Alex's staining gurgle hot as piss against his shoulder, Randle screaming, "Give me the keys! Give me the keys!" Her hand digging hard into his pocket as he swung Alex, white-faced, into the back seat, lost his balance as the car jerked into gear and fell with the force of motion to hit his temple, dull and cool, against the lever of the seat release.

And lay there, smelling must and the faint flavor of motor oil, Alex above collapsed into silence, lay a long time before he finally thought to ask, "Where're we going?" He had to ask it twice to cut the blare of the radio.

Randle didn't turn around. "Hope there's nothing in that house you wanted."

Night, and the golden arches again. This time they ate in the car, taking turns to go inside to pee, to wash, the rest rooms small as closets. Gritty green soap from the dispenser. Alex ate nothing. Alex was still asleep.

Randle's lolling glance, too weary to sit up straight anymore. "You drive for a while," she said. "Keep on I-10 till you get—"

"I know," louder than he meant; he was tired too. It was a chore just to keep raising his hand to his mouth. Randle was feeling for something, rooting slowly under the seat, in her purse. When he raised his eyebrows at her she said, "You got any cigarettes?"

"Didn't you just buy a pack?"

Silence, then, "I left them at the house. On the back of the toilet," and without fuller warning began to weep, one hand loose against her mouth. Mitch turned his head, stared at the parking lot around them, the fluttering jerk of headlights like big fat clumsy birds. "I'm sick of leaving stuff places," she said. Her hand muffled her voice, made it sound like she spoke from underwater, some calm green place where voices could never go. "Do you know how long I've been wearing this shirt?" and before he could think if it was right to give any answer, "Five days. That's how long. Five fucking days in this same fucking shirt."

From the back seat Alex said, "Breaux Bridge," in a tone trusting and tender as a child's. Without turning, without bothering to look, Randle pistoned her arm in a backhand punch so hard Mitch flinched watching it.

Flat-voiced, "You just shut up," still without turning, as if the back seat had become impossible for her. "That's all you have to do. Just shut up."

Mitch started the car. Alex began to moan, a pale whimper that undercut the engine noise. Randle said, "I don't care what happens, don't wake me up." She pulled her T-shirt over her head and threw it out the window.

"Randle, for God's sake! At least wait till we get going."

"Let them look." Her breasts were spotted in places, a rashy speckle strange in the greenish dashlight, like some intricate tattoo the details of which became visible only in hard daylight. She lay with her head on his thigh, the flesh beneath her area of touch asleep before she was. He drove for almost an hour before he lightly pushed her off.

And in the back seat the endless sound of Alex, his rustling paper, the marshy odor of his tears. To Mitch it was as if the envelope of night had closed around them not forever but for so long there was no difference to be charted or discerned. Like the good old days. Like Alex staggering around and around, newspaper carpets and the funnies especially, vomiting blood that eclipsed the paler smell of pigeon shit from the old pigeon coop. Pigeonnier. Black dirt, alluvial crumble and sprayed like tarot dust across the blue-tiled kitchen floor. Wasn't it strange that he could still remember that tile, its gaudy Romanesque patterns? Remember it as he recalled his own nervous shiver, hidden like treasure behind the mahogany boards. And Randle's terrified laughter. Momma. Promises, his hands between her dusty palms; they were so small then, his hands. Alex wiping uselessly at the scabby drip of his actions, even then you had to watch him all the time. Broken glasses, one after another. Willow bonfires. The crying cicadas, no, that was happening now, wasn't it? Through the Buick's open windows. Through the hours and hours of driving until the air went humid with daylight and the reeking shimmer of exhaust, and Randle stirring closed-eyed on the front seat beside him and murmuring, anxious in her sleep, "Alex?"

He lay one hand on her neck, damp skin, clammy. "Shhhh, he's all right. It's still my turn. He's all right."

And kept driving. The rustle of paper in the back seat. Alex's soft sulky hum, like some rare unwanted engine that no lack of fuel could hamper, that no one could finally turn off.

And his hands on the wheel as silent as Randle's calmed breathing, as stealthy as Alex's cities, the litany begun anew: Florien, Samtown, Echo, Lecomte, drifting forward like smoke from a secret fire, always burning, like the fires on the levees, like the fire that took their home. Remember that? Mouth open, catching flies his mother would have said. Blue flame like a gas burner. What color does blood burn?

And his head hanging down as if shamefaced, as if dunned and stropped by the blunt hammer of anger, old anger like the fires that never burned out. And his eyes closing, sleeping, though he woke to think, Pull over, had to, sliding heedless as a drunken man over to the shoulder to let himself fall, forehead striking gentle against the steering wheel as if victim of the mildest of accidents. Randle still asleep on the seat beside. Alex, was he still saying his cities? Alex? Paper to play with? "Alex," but he spoke the word without authority, in dreams against a landscape not welcome but necessary: in which the rustle of Alex's paper mingled with the slower dribble of his desires, the whole an endless pavane danced through the cities of Louisiana, the smaller, the hotter, the better. And he, and Randle too, were somehow children again, kids at the old house where the old mantle of protection fell new upon them, and they unaware and helpless of the burden, ignorant of the loss they had already and irrevocably sustained, loss of life while living it. You have to swear me, Michie. And Randle, not Randle then, not Francey but Marie-Claire, that was her name, Marie-Claire promising as he did, little sister with her hands outstretched.

The car baked slow and thorough in the shadeless morning, too far from the trees. Alex, grave as a gargoyle chipped cunningly free, rose, in silence the back door handle and through the open windows his open palms, let the brownish flakes cascade down upon Mitch and Randle both, swirling like the glitter-snow in a paperweight, speckles, freckles, changing to a darker rain, so lightly they never felt it, so quiet they never heard. And gone.

The slap of consciousness, Randle's cry, disgust, her hands grubby with it, scratching at the skin of her forearms so new blood rose beneath the dry. Scabbed with blood, painted with it. Mitch beside her, similarly scabbed, brushing with a detached dismay, not quite fastidious, as if he were used to waking covered with the spoor of his brother's predilections.

"I'm not his mother!" Screaming. She was losing it, maybe already had. Understandable. Less so his own lucidity, back calm against the seat; shock-free? Maybe he was crazier than she was. Crazier than Alex, though that would be pushing it. She was still screaming, waves of it that shook her breasts. He was getting an erection. Wasn't that something.

"I'm sick of him being a monster. I can't—"

"We have to look for him."

"You look! You look! I'm tired of looking!" Snot on her lips. He grabbed her by the breasts, distant relish, and shoved her very hard against the door. She stopped screaming and started crying, a dry drone that did not indicate if she had actually given in or merely cracked. Huh-huh-huh. "Put your shirt on," he said, and remembered she didn't have one, she had thrown it away. Stupid bitch. He gave her his shirt, rolled his window all the way down. Should they drive, or go on foot? How far? How long had they slept? He remembered telling her it was his turn to watch Alex. Staring out the window. Willows. Floodplain. Spanish moss. He had always hated Spanish moss. So *hot,* and Randle's sudden screech, he hated that too, hated the way her lips stretched through mucus and old blood and new blood and her pointing finger, pointing at Alex. Walking toward them.

Waving, extravagant, exuberant, carrying something, something it took both hands to hold. Even from this distance Mitch could see that Alex's shirt was soaked. Saturated. Beside him Randle's screech had shrunk to a blubber that he was certain, this time, would not cease. Maybe ever. Nerves, it got on his nerves, mosquito with a dentist's drill digging at your ear. At your brain.

At his fingers on the car keys or maybe it was just the itch of blood as he started the car, started out slow, driving straight down the middle of the road to where he, and Randle, and Alex, slick and sticky to the hairline, would intersect. His foot on the gas pedal was gentle, and Alex's gait rocked like a chair on the porch as he waved his arms again, his arms and the thing within.

Randle spoke, dull through a mouthful of snot. "Slow down," and he shook his head without looking at her, he didn't really want to see her at this particular moment.

"I don't think so," he said as his foot dipped, elegant, like the last step in a dance. Behind Alex, the diagonal shadows of willow trees, old ones; sturdy? Surely. There was hardly any gas left in the car, but he had just enough momentum for all of them.

TERATISMS

"Teratisms," a short, sharp shock by Kathe Koja, is the second story reprinted from *A Whisper of Blood*.

The Monsters of Heaven

by Nathan Ballingrud

(From *Inferno,* 2007)

"Who invented the human heart, I wonder? Tell me,
then show me the place where he was hanged."

—Lawrence Durrell, *Justine*

For a long time, Brian imagined reunions with his son. In the early days, these fantasies were defined by spectacular violence. He would find the man who stole him and open his head with a claw hammer. The more blood he spilled, the further removed he became from his own guilt. The location would often change: a roach-haunted tenement building; an abandoned warehouse along the Tchoupitoulas wharf; a pre-fab bungalow with an American flag out front and a two-door hatchback parked in the driveway.

Sometimes the man lived alone, sometimes he had his own family. On these latter occasions Brian would cast himself as a moral executioner, spraying the walls with the kidnapper's blood but sparing his wife and child—freeing them, he imagined, from his tyranny. No matter the scenario, Toby was always there, always intact; Brian would feel his face pressed into his shoulders as he carried him away, feel the heat of his tears bleed into his shirt. You're safe now, he would say. Daddy's got you. Daddy's here.

After some months passed, he deferred the heroics to the police. This marked his first concession to reality. He spent his time beached in the living room, drinking more, working less, until the owner of the auto shop told him to take time off, a lot of time off, as much as he needed. Brian barely noticed. He waited for the red and blue disco lights of a police cruiser to illuminate the darkness outside, to give some shape and measure to the night. He waited for the phone to ring with a glad summons to the station. He played out scenarios, tried on different outcomes, guessed at his own reactions. He gained weight and lost time.

Sometimes he would get out of bed in the middle of the night, careful not to wake his wife, and get into the car. He would drive at dangerous speeds through the city, staring into the empty sockets of unlighted windows. He would get out of the car and stand in front of some of these houses, looking and listening for signs. Often, the police were called. When the officers realized who he was, they were usually as courteous as they were adamant. He'd wonder if it had been the kidnapper who called the police. He would imagine returning to those houses with a gun.

This was in the early days of what became known as the Lamentation. At this stage, most people did not know anything unusual was happening. What they heard, if they heard anything, was larded with rumor and embellishment. Fogs of gossip in the barrooms and churches. This was before the bloodshed. Before their pleas to Christ clotted in their throats.

Amy never told Brian that she blamed him. She elected, rather, to avoid the topic of the actual abduction, and any question of her husband's negligence. Once the police abandoned them as suspects, the matter of their own involvement ceased to be a subject of discussion. Brian was unconsciously grateful, because it allowed him to focus instead on the maintenance of grief. Silence spread between them like a glacier. In a few months, entire days passed with nothing said between them.

It was on such a night that Amy rolled up against him and kissed the back of his neck. It froze Brian, filling him with a blast of terror and bewilderment; he felt the guilt move inside of him, huge but seemingly distant, like a whale passing beneath a boat. Her lips felt hot against his skin, sending warm waves rolling from his neck and shoulders all the way down to his legs, as though she had injected something lovely into him. She grew more ardent, nipping him with her teeth, breaking through his reservations. He turned and kissed her. He experienced a leaping arc of energy, a terrifying, violent impulse; he threw his weight onto her and crushed his mouth into hers, scraping his teeth against hers. But there immediately followed a cascade of unwelcome thought: Toby whimpering somewhere in the dark, waiting for his father to save him; Amy, dressed in her bedclothes in the middle of the day, staring like a corpse into the sunlight coming through the windows; the playground, and the receding line of kindergarteners. When she reached under the sheets she found him limp and unready. He opened his mouth to apologize but she shoved her tongue into it, her hand working at him with a rough urgency, as though more depended on this than he knew. Later he would learn that it did. Her teeth sliced his lip and blood eeled into his mouth. She was pulling at him too hard, and it was starting to hurt. He wrenched himself away.

"Jesus," he said, wiping his lip. The blood felt like an oil slick in the back of his throat.

She turned her back to him and put her face into the pillow. For a moment he thought she was crying. But only for a moment.

"Honey," he said. "Hey." He put his fingers on her shoulder; she rolled it away from him.

"Go to sleep," she said.

He stared at the landscape of her naked back, pale in the streetlight leaking through the blinds, feeling furious and ruined.

The next morning, when he came into the kitchen, Amy was already up. Coffee was made, filling the room with a fine toasted smell, and she was leaning against the counter with a cup in her hand, wearing her pink terry-cloth robe. Her dark hair was still wet from the shower. She smiled and said, "Good morning."

"Hey," he said, feeling for a sense of her mood.

Dodger, Toby's dog, cast him a devastated glance from his customary place beneath the kitchen table. Amy had wanted to get rid of him—she couldn't bear the sight of him anymore, she'd said—but Brian wouldn't allow it. When Toby comes back, he reasoned, he'll wonder why we did it. What awful thing guided us. So Dodger remained, and his slumping, sorrowful presence tore into them both like a hungry animal.

"Hey boy," Brian said, and rubbed his neck with his toe.

"I'm going out today," Amy said.

"Okay. Where to?"

She shrugged. "I don't know. The hardware store. Maybe a nursery. I want to find myself a project."

Brian looked at her. The sunlight made a corona around her body. This new resolve, coupled with her overture of the night before, struck him as a positive sign. "Okay," he said.

He seated himself at the table. The newspaper had been placed there for him, still bound by a rubberband. He snapped it off and unfurled the front page. Already he felt the gravitational pull of the Jack Daniels in the cabinet, but when Amy leaned over his shoulder and placed a coffee cup in front of him, he managed to resist the whiskey's call with an ease that surprised and gratified him. He ran his hand up her forearm, pushing back the soft pink sleeve, and he kissed the inside of her wrist. He felt a wild and incomprehensible hope. He breathed in the clean, scented smell of her. She stayed there for a moment, and then gently pulled away.

They remained that way in silence for some time—maybe fifteen minutes or more—until Brian found something in the paper he wanted to share with her. Something being described as "angelic"—"apparently not quite a human man," as the writer put it—had been found down by the Gulf Coast, in Morgan City; it had been shedding a faint light from under two feet of water; whatever it was had died shortly after being taken into custody, under confusing circumstances. He turned in his chair to speak, a word already gathering on his tongue, and he caught her staring at him. She wore a cadaverous, empty look, as though she had seen the worst thing in the world and died in the act. It occurred to him that she had been looking at him that way for whole minutes. He turned back to the table, his insides sliding, and stared at the suddenly indecipherable glyphs of the newspaper. After a moment he felt her hand on the back of his neck, rubbing him gently. She left the kitchen without a word.

This is how it happened:

They were taking Dodger for a walk. Toby liked to hold the leash—he was four years old, and gravely occupied with establishing his independence—and more often than not Brian would sort of half-trot behind them, one hand held indecisively aloft should Dodger suddenly decide to break into a run, dragging his boy behind him like a string of tin cans. He probably bit off more profanities during those walks than he ever did changing a tire. He carried, as was their custom on Mondays, a blanket and a picnic lunch. He would lie back in the sun while Toby and the dog played, and enjoy not being hunched over an engine block. At some point they would have lunch. Brian believed these afternoons of easy camaraderie would be remembered by them both for years to come. They'd done it a hundred times.

A hundred times.

On that day a kindergarten class arrived shortly after they did. Toby ran up to his father and wrapped his arms around his neck, frightened by the sudden bright surge of humanity; the kids were a loud, brawling tumult, crashing over the swings and monkey bars in a gabbling surf. Brian pried Toby's arms free and pointed at them.

"Look, screwball, they're just kids. See? They're just like you. Go on and play. Have some fun."

Dodger galloped out to greet them and was received as a hero, with joyful cries and grasping fingers. Toby observed this gambit for his dog's affections and at last decided to intervene. He ran toward them, shouting, "That's my dog! That's my dog!" Brian watched him go, made eye contact with the teacher and nodded hello. She smiled at him—he remembered thinking she was kind of cute, wondering how old she was—and she returned her attention to her kids, gamboling like lunatics all over the park. Brian reclined on the blanket and watched the clouds skim the atmosphere, listened to the sound of children. It was a hot, windless day.

He didn't realize he had dozed until the kindergarteners had been rounded up and were halfway down the block, taking their noise with them. The silence stirred him.

He sat up abruptly and looked around. The playground was empty. "Toby? Hey, Toby?"

Dodger stood out in the middle of the road, his leash spooled at his feet. He watched Brian eagerly, offered a tentative wag.

"Where's Toby?" he asked the dog, and climbed to his feet. He felt a sudden sickening lurch in his gut. He turned in a quick circle, a half-smile on his face, utterly sure that this was an impossible situation, that children didn't disappear in broad daylight while their parents were *right fucking there.* So he was still here. Of course he was still here. Dodger trotted up to him and sat down at his feet, waiting for him to produce the boy, as though he were a hidden tennis ball.

"Toby?"

The park was empty. He jogged after the receding line of kids. "Hey. *Hey!* Is my son with you? *Where's my son?*"

One morning, about a week after the experience in the kitchen, Brian was awakened by the phone. Every time this happened he felt a thrill of hope, though by now it had become muted, even dreadful in its predictability. He hauled himself up from the couch, nearly overturning a bottle of Jack Daniels stationed on the floor. He crossed the living room and picked up the phone.

"Yes?" he said.

"Let me talk to Amy." It was not a voice he recognized. A male voice, with a thick rural accent. It was the kind of voice that inspired immediate prejudice: the voice of an idiot; of a man without any right to make demands of him.

"Who is this?"

"Just let me talk to Amy."

"How about you go fuck yourself."

There was a pause as the man on the phone seemed to assess the obstacle. Then he said, with a trace of amusement in his voice, "Are you Brian?"

"That's right."

"Look, dude. Go get your wife. Put her on the phone. Do it now, and I won't have to come down there and break your fucking face."

Brian slammed down the receiver. Feeling suddenly lightheaded, he put his hand on the wall to steady himself, to reassure himself that it was still solid, and that he was still real. From somewhere outside, through an open window, came the distant sound of children shouting.

It was obvious that Amy was sleeping with another man. When confronted with the call, she did not admit to anything, but made no special effort to explain it away, either. His name was Tommy, she said. She'd met him once when she was out. He sounded rough, but he wasn't a bad guy. She chose not to elaborate, and Brian, to his amazement, found a kind of forlorn comfort in his wife's affair. He'd lost his son; why not lose it all?

On television the news was filling with the creatures, more of which were being discovered all the time. The press had taken to calling them angels. Some were being found alive, though all of them appeared to have suffered from some violent experience.

At least one family had become notorious by refusing to let anyone see the angel they'd found, or even let it out of their home. They boarded their windows and warned away visitors with a shotgun.

Brian was stationed on the couch, staring at the television with the sound turned down to barely a murmur. He listened to the familiar muted clatter from the medicine cabinet as Amy applied her make-up in the bathroom. A news program was on, and a handheld camera followed a street reporter into someone's house. The JD bottle was empty at his feet, and the knowledge that he had no more in the house smoldered in him.

Amy emerged from the kitchen with her purse slung over her arm and made her way to the door. "I'm going out," she said.

"Where?"

She paused, one hand on the doorknob. She wavered there, in her careful make-up and her push-up bra. He tried to remember the last time he'd seen her look like this and failed dismally. Something inside her seemed to collapse—a force of will, perhaps, or a habit of deception. Maybe she was just too tired to invent another lie.

"I'm going to see Tommy," she said.

"The redneck."

"Sure. The redneck, if that's how you want it."

"Does it matter how I want it?"

She paused. "No," she said. "I guess not."

"Well well. The truth. Look out."

She left the door, walked into the living room. Brian felt a sudden trepidation; this is not what he imagined would happen. He wanted to get a few weak barbs in before she walked out, that was all. He did not actually want to talk.

She sat on the rocking chair across from the couch. Beside her, on the television, the camera focused on an obese man wearing overalls smiling triumphantly and holding aloft an angel's severed head.

Amy shut it off.

"Do you want to know about him?" she said.

"Let's see. He's stupid and violent. He called my home and threatened me. He's sleeping with my wife. What else is there to know?"

She appraised him for a moment, weighing consequences. "There's a little more to know," she said. "For example, he's very kind to me. He thinks I'm beautiful." He must have made some sort of sound then, because she said, "I know it must be very hard for you to believe, but some men still find me attractive. And that's important to me, Brian. Can you understand that?"

He turned away from her, shielding his eyes with a hand, although without the TV on there was very little light in the room. Each breath was laced with pain.

"When I go to see him, he talks to me. Actually talks. I know he might not be very smart, according to your standards, but you'd be surprised how much he and I have to talk about. You'd be surprised how much more there is to life—to my life—than your car magazines, and your tv, and your bottles of booze."

"Stop it," I said.

"He's also a very considerate lover. He paces himself. For my sake. For me. Did you ever do that, Brian? In all the times we made love?"

He felt tears crawling down his face. Christ. When did that start?

"I can forget things when I sleep with him. I can forget about… I can forget about everything. He lets me do that."

"You cold bitch," he rasped.

"You passive little shit," she bit back, with a venom that surprised him. "You let it happen, do you know that? You let it all happen. Every awful thing."

She stood abruptly and walked out the door, slamming it behind her. The force of it rattled the windows. After a while—he had no idea how long—he picked up the remote and turned the TV back on. A girl pointed to moving clouds on a map.

Eventually Dodger came by and curled up at his feet. Brian slid off the couch and lay down beside him, hugging him close. Dodger smelled the way dogs do, musky and of the earth, and he sighed with the abiding patience of his kind.

Violence filled his dreams. In them he rent bodies, spilled blood, painted the walls using severed limbs as gruesome brushes. In them he went back to the park and ate the children while the teacher looked on. Once he awoke after these dreams with blood filling his mouth; he realized he had chewed his tongue during the night. It was raw and painful for days afterward. A rage was building inside him and he could not find an outlet for it. One night Amy told him she thought she was falling in love with Tommy. He only nodded stupidly and watched her walk out the door again. That same night he kicked Dodger out of the house. He just opened the door to the night and told him to go. When he wouldn't—trying instead to slink around his legs and go back inside—he planted his foot on the dog's chest and physically pushed him back outside, sliding him backwards on his butt. *"Go find him!"* he yelled. *"Go find him! Go and find him!"* He shut the door and listened to Dodger whimper and scratch at it for nearly an hour. At some point he gave up and Brian fell asleep. When he awoke it was raining. He opened the door and called for him. The rain swallowed his voice.

"Oh no," he said quietly, his voice a whimper. "Come back! I'm sorry! Please, I'm so sorry!"

When Dodger did eventually return, wet and miserable, Brian hugged him tight, buried his face in his fur, and wept for joy.

Brian liked to do his drinking alone. When he drank in public, especially at his old bar, people tried to talk to him. They saw his presence as an invitation to share sympathy, or a request for a friendly ear. It got to be too much. But tonight he made his way back there, endured the stares and the weird silence, took the beers sent his way, although he wanted none of it. What he wanted tonight was Fire Engine, and she didn't disappoint.

Everybody knew Fire Engine, of course; if she thought you didn't know her, she'd introduce herself to you post haste. One hand on your shoulder, the other on your thigh. Where her hands went after that depended on a quick negotiation. She was a redhead with an easy personality, and was popular with the regular clientele, including the ones that would never buy her services. She claimed to be twenty-eight but looked closer to forty. At some unfortunate juncture in her life she had contrived to lose most of her front teeth, either to decay or to someone's balled fist; either way common wisdom held she gave the best blowjob in downtown New Orleans.

Brian used to be amused by that kind of talk. Although he'd never had an interest in her he'd certainly enjoyed listening to her sales pitch; she'd become a sort of bar pet, and the unselfconscious way she went about her life was both endearing and appalling. Her lack of teeth was too perfect, and too ridiculous. Now, however, the information had acquired a new kind of value to him. He pressed his gaze onto her until she finally felt it and looked back. She smiled coquettishly, with gruesome effect. He told the bartender to send her a drink.

"You sure? She ain't gonna leave you alone all night."

"Fuck yeah, I'm sure."

All night didn't concern him. What concerned him were the next ten minutes, which was what he figured ten dollars would buy him. After the necessary negotiations and bullshit they left the bar together, trailing cat-calls; she took his hand and led him around back, into the alley.

The smell of rotting garbage came at him like an attack, like a pillowcase thrown over his head. She steered him into the alley's dark mouth, with its grime-smeared pavement and furtive skittering sounds, and its dumpster so stuffed with straining garbage bags that it looked like some fearsome monster choking on its dinner. "Now you know I'm a lady," she said, "but sometimes you just got to make do with what's available."

That she could laugh at herself this way touched Brian, and he felt a wash of sympathy for her. He considered what it would be like to run away with her, to rescue her from the wet pull of her life; to save her.

She unzipped his pants and pulled his dick out. "There we go, honey, that's what I'm talking about. Ain't you something."

After a couple of minutes she released him and stood up. He tucked himself back in and zipped his pants, afraid to make eye contact with her.

"Maybe you just had too much to drink," she said.

"Yeah."

"It ain't nothing."

"I know it isn't," he said harshly.

When she made no move to leave, he said, "Will you just get the fuck away from me? Please?"

Her voice lost its sympathy. "Honey, I still got to get paid."

He opened his wallet and fished out a ten dollar bill. She plucked it from his fingers and walked out of the alley, back toward the bar. "Don't get all bent out of shape about it," she called. "Shit happens, you know?"

He slid down the wall until his ass hit the ground. He brought his hand to his mouth and choked out a sob, his eyes squeezed shut. He banged his head once against the brick wall behind him and then thought better of it. Down here the stench was a steaming blanket, almost soothing in its awfulness. He felt like he deserved to be there, that it was right that he should sleep in shit and grime. He listened to the gentle ticking of the roaches in the dark. He wondered if Toby was in a place like this.

Something glinted further down the alley.

He strained to see it. It was too bright to be merely a reflection.

It moved.

"Son of a," he said, and pushed himself to his feet.

It lay mostly hidden; it had pulled some stray garbage bags atop itself in an effort to remain concealed, but its dim luminescence worked against it. Brian loped over to it, wrenched the bags away; its clawed hands clutched at them and tore them open, spilling a clatter of beer and liquor bottles all over the ground. They caromed with hollow music through the alley, coming at last to silent rest, until all Brian could hear was the thin, high-pitched noise the creature made through the tiny O-shaped orifice he supposed passed for a mouth. Its eyes were black little stones. The creature—*angel*, he thought, *they're calling these things angels*—was tall and thin, abundantly male, and it shed a thin light that illuminated exactly nothing around it. *If you put some clothes on it*, Brian thought, *hide its face, gave it some gloves, it might pass for a human.*

Exposed, it held up a long-fingered hand, as if to ward him off. It had clearly been hurt: its legs looked badly broken, and it breathed in short, shallow gasps. A dark bruise spread like a mold over the right side of its chest.

"Look at you, huh? You're all messed up." He felt a strange glee as he said this; he could not justify the feeling and quickly buried it. "Yeah, yeah, somebody worked you over pretty good."

It managed to roll onto its belly and it scrabbled along the pavement in a pathetic attempt at escape. It loosed that thin, reedy cry. Calling for help? Begging for its life?

The sight of it trying to flee from him catalyzed some deep predatory impulse, and he pressed his foot onto the angel's ankle, holding it easily in place. "No you don't." He hooked the thing beneath its shoulders and lifted it from the ground; it was astonishingly light. It mewled weakly at him. "Shut up, I'm trying to help you." He adjusted it in his arms so that he held it like a lover, or a fainted woman. He carried it back to his car, listening for the sound of the barroom door opening behind him, of laughter or a challenge chasing him down the sidewalk. But the door stayed shut. He walked in silence.

Amy was awake when he got home, silhouetted in the doorway. Brian pulled the angel from the passenger seat, cradled it against his chest. He watched her face alter subtly, watched as some dark hope crawled across it like an insect, and he squashed it before it could do any real harm.

"It's not him," he said. "It's something else."

She stood away from the door and let him come in.

Dodger, who had been dozing in the hallway, lurched to his feet with a sliding and skittering of claws and growled fiercely at it, his lips curled away from his teeth.

"Get away, you," Brian said. He eased past him, bearing his load down the hall.

He laid it in Toby's bed. Together he and Amy stood over it, watching as it stared back at them with dark flat eyes, its body twisting away from them as if it could fold itself into another place altogether. Its fingers plucked at the train-spangled bedsheets, wrapping them around its nakedness. Amy leaned over and helped to tuck she sheets around it.

"He's hurt," she said.

"I know. I guess a lot of them are found that way."

"Should we call somebody?"

"You want camera crews in here? Fuck no."

"Well. He's really hurt. We need to do something."

"Yeah. I don't know. We can at least clean him up I guess."

Amy sat on the mattress beside it; it stared at her with its expressionless face. Brian couldn't tell if there were thoughts passing behind those eyes, or just a series of brute reflex arcs. After a moment it reached out with one long dark fingernail and brushed her arm. She jumped as though shocked.

"Jesus! Be careful," said Brian.

"What if it's him?"

"What?" It took him a moment to understand her. "Oh my god. Amy. It's not him, okay? It's *not him.*"

"But what if it is?"

"It's *not.* We've seen them on the news, okay? It's a, it's a *thing.*"

"You shouldn't call it an 'it.'"

"How do I know what the fuck to call it?"

She touched her fingers to its cheek. It pressed its face into them, making some small sound.

"Why did you leave me?" she said. "You were everything I had."

Brian swooned beneath a tide of vertigo. Something was moving inside him, something too large to stay where it was. "It's an angel," he said. "Nothing more. Just an angel. It's probably going to die on us, since that's what they seem to do." He put his hand against the wall until the dizziness passed. It was replaced by a low, percolating anger. "Instead of thinking of it as Toby, why don't you ask it where Toby *is.* Why don't you make it explain to us why it happened."

She looked at him. "It happened because you let it," she said.

Dodger asked to be let outside. Brian opened the door for him to let him run around the front yard. There was a leash law here, but Dodger was well known by the neighbors and generally tolerated. He walked out of the house with considerably less than his usual enthusiasm. He lifted his leg desultorily against a shrub, then walked down to the road and followed the sidewalk further into the neighborhood. He did not come back.

Over the next few days it put its hooks into them, and drew them in tight. They found it difficult to leave it alone. Its flesh seemed to pump out some kind of soporific, like an invisible spoor, and it was better than the booze—better than anything they'd previously known. Its pull seemed to grow stronger as the days passed. For Amy, especially. She stopped going out, and for all practical purposes moved into Toby's room with it. When Brian joined her in there, she seemed to barely tolerate his presence. If he sat beside it she watched him with naked trepidation, as though she feared he might damage it somehow.

It was not, he realized, an unfounded fear. Something inside him became turbulent in its presence, something he couldn't identify but which sparked flashes of violent thought, of the kind he had not had since just after Toby vanished. This feeling came in sharp relief to the easy lethargy the angel normally inspired, and he was reminded of a time when he was younger, sniffing heroin laced with cocaine. So he did not object to Amy's efforts at excluding him.

Finally, though, her vigilance slipped. He went into the bathroom and found her sleeping on the toilet, her robe hiked up around her waist, her head resting against the sink. He left her there and crept into the angel's room.

It was awake, and its eyes tracked him as he crossed the room and sat beside it on the bed. Its breath wheezed lightly as it drew air through its puckered mouth. Its body was still bruised and bent, though it did seem to be improving.

Brian touched its chest where the bruise seemed to be diminishing. *Why does it bruise?* he wondered. *Why does it bleed the same way I do? Shouldn't it be made of something better?* Also, it didn't have wings. Not even vestigial ones. Why were they called angels? Because of how they made people feel? It looked more like an alien than a divine being. *It has a cock, for Christ's sake. What's that all about? Do angels fuck?*

He leaned over it, so his face was inches away, almost touching its nose. He stared into its black, irisless eyes, searching for some sign of intelligence, some evidence of intent or emotion. From this distance he could smell its breath; he drew it into his own lungs, and it warmed him like a shot of whiskey. The angel lifted its head and pressed its face into his. Brian jerked back and felt something brush his elbow. He looked behind him and discovered the angel had an erection.

He lurched out of bed, tripping over himself as he rushed to the door, dashed through it and slammed it shut. His blood sang. It rose in him like the sea and filled him with tumultuous music. He dropped to his knees and vomited all over the carpet.

Later, he stepped into its doorway, watching Amy trace her hands down its face. Through the window he could see that night was gathering in little pockets outside, lifting itself toward the sky. At the sight of the angel his heart jumped in his chest as though it had come unmoored. "Amy, I have to talk to you," he said. He had some difficulty making his voice sound calm.

She didn't look at him. "I know it's not really him," she said. "Not really."

"No."

"But don't you think he is, kind of? In a way?"

"No."

She laid her head on the pillow beside it, staring into its face. Brian was left looking at the back of her head, the unwashed hair, tangled and brittle. He remembered cupping the back of her head in his hand, its weight and its warmth. He remembered her body.

"Amy. Where does he live?"

"Who."

"Tommy. Where does he live?"

She turned and looked at him, a little crease of worry on her brow. "Why do you want to know?"

"Just tell me. Please."

"Brian, don't."

He slammed his fist into the wall, startling himself. He screamed at her. *"Tell me where he lives! God damn it!"*

Tommy opened the door of his shotgun house, clad only in boxer shorts, and Brian greeted him with a blow to the face. Tommy staggered back into his house, due more to surprise than the force of the punch; his foot slipped on a throw rug and he crashed to the floor. The small house reverberated with the impact. Brian had a moment to take in Tommy's hard physique and imagine his wife's hands moving over it. He stepped forward and kicked him in the groin.

Tommy grunted and seemed to absorb it. He rolled over and pushed himself quickly to his feet. Tommy's fist swung at him and he had time to experience a quick flaring terror before his head exploded with pain. He found himself on his knees, staring at the dust collecting in the crevices of the hardwood floor. Somewhere in the background a television chattered urgently.

A kick to the ribs sent Brian down again. Tommy straddled him, grabbed a fistful of hair, and slammed Brian's face into the floor several times. Brian felt something in his face break and blood poured onto the floor. He wanted to cry but it was impossible, he couldn't get enough air. *I'm going to die,* he thought. He felt himself hauled up and thrown against a wall. Darkness crowded his vision; he began to lose his purchase on events.

Someone was yelling at him. There was a face in front of him, skin peeled back from its teeth in a smile or a grimace of rage. It looked like something from hell.

He awoke to the feel of cold grass, cold night air. The right side of his face burned like a signal flare; his left eye refused to open. It hurt to breathe. He pushed himself to his elbows and spit blood from his mouth; it immediately filled again. Something wrong in there. He rolled onto his back and laid there for a while, waiting for the pain to subside to a tolerable level. The night was high and dark. At one point he felt sure that he was rising from the ground, that something up there was pulling him into its empty hollows.

Somehow he managed the drive home. He remembered nothing of it except occasional stabs of pain as opposing headlights washed across his windshield; he would later consider his safe arrival a kind of miracle. He pulled into the driveway and honked the horn a few times until Amy came out and found him there. She looked at him with horror, and with something else.

"Oh, baby. What did you do. What did you do."

She steered him toward the angel's room. He stopped himself in the doorway, his heart pounding again, and he tried to catch his breath. It occurred to him, on a dim level, that his nose was broken. She tugged at his hand, but he resisted. Her face was limned by moonlight, streaming through the window like some mystical tide, and by the faint luminescence of the angel tucked into their son's bed. She'd grown heavy over the years, and the past year had taken a harsh toll: the flesh on her face sagged, and was scored by grief. And yet he was stunned by her beauty.

Had she always looked like this?

"Come on," she said. "Please."

The left side of his face pulsed with hard beats of pain; it sang like a war drum. His working eye settled on the thing in the bed: its flat black eyes, its wickedly curved talons. Amy sat beside it and put her hand on its chest. It arched its back, seeming to coil beneath her.

"Come lay down," she said. "He's here for us. He's come home for us."

Brian took a step into Toby's room, and then another. He knew she was wrong; that the angel was not home, that it had wandered here from somewhere far away.

Is heaven a dark place?

The angel extended a hand, its talons flexing. The sheets over its belly stirred as Brian drew closer. Amy took her husband's hands, easing him onto the bed. He gripped her shoulders, squeezing them too tightly. "I'm sorry," he said suddenly, surprising himself. "I'm sorry! I'm sorry!" Once he began he couldn't stop. He said it over and over again, so many times it just became a sound, a sobbing plaint, and Amy pressed her hand against his mouth, entwined her fingers into his hair, saying, "Shhhh, shhhhh," and finally she silenced him with a kiss. As they embraced each other the angel played its hands over their faces and their shoulders, its strange reedy breath and its narcotic musk drawing them down to it. They caressed each other, and they caressed the angel, and when they touched their lips to its skin the taste of it shot spikes of joy through their bodies. Brian felt her teeth on his neck and he bit into the angel, the sudden dark spurt of blood filling his mouth, the soft pale flesh tearing easily, sliding down his throat. He kissed his wife furiously and when she tasted the blood she nearly tore his tongue out; he pushed her face toward the angel's body, and watched the blood blossom from beneath her. The angel's eyes were frozen, staring at the ceiling; it extended a shaking hand toward a wall decorated with a Spider-Man poster, its fingers twisted and bent.

They ate until they were full.

That night, heavy with the sludge of bliss, Brian and Amy made love again for the first time in nearly a year. It was wordless and slow, a synchronicity of pressures and tender familiarities. They were like rare creatures of a dying species, amazed by the sight of each other.

Brian drifts in and out of sleep. He has what will be the last dream about his son. It is morning in this dream, by the side of a small country road. It must have rained during the night, because the world shines with a wet glow. Droplets of water cling, dazzling, to the muzzle of a dog as it rests beside the road, unmenaced by traffic, languorous and dull-witted in the rising heat. It might even be Dodger. His snout is heavy with blood. Some distance away from him Toby rests on the street, a small pile of bones and torn flesh, glittering with dew, catching and throwing sunlight like a scattered pile of rubies and diamonds.

By the time he wakes, he has already forgotten it.

THE MONSTERS OF HEAVEN

"The Monsters of Heaven" by Nathan Ballingrud was published in *Inferno*, and won the first Shirley Jackson award for Best Short Story.

That Old School Tie

by Jack Womack

(From *Little Deaths,* 1994)

Charles spun webs of charm and guilt around his friends, entwining them tighter if they tried to wander, loosing them once they drew near. The resulting networks were so complex that it was impossible for onlookers, or even participants, to discern who might be spider and who, fly.

We met at college and grew closer over the years, as people do when they have nothing in common but the length of time they've known one another. He taught English at NYU and wrote several books about lesser figures of the Romantic period, who seemed all the lesser once he was through with them. I'd been in pre-med until discovering how readily I weakened at the sight of real blood, and so I edited medico-legal textbooks instead; forensic pathology was my *métier*. Call it slumming amid the stews of human behavior, if you like; Charles once did. The manuscripts arrived in my office exclusive of their photographs—cake without frosting, as it were.

Charles and his wife Elaine, a divorce lawyer, lived on Riverside Drive, in a long-hall apartment overlooking the shadier side of 99th Street; their six-year old daughter, Cecily, attended a good school, although one unblessed with alumni of more than moderate renown. I lived alone, on 95th Street. They rented a house in Springs every other August; he invited me out one weekend, the summer before his final semester. On Saturday we went to the beach, smothering sand fleas beneath our towels as we roasted ourselves. Cecily begged her mother to put away the phone she'd brought along.

"Charles," Elaine said. "Put some sunblock on me, please. I'm burning already." While she consulted with her client, Charles rubbed oil into his wife's shoulders until they shone. His own were as muscular as they'd been in college, when he was on the crew; I was never one for sports, myself. Rubbing his hands dry against his plaid swim trunks, he reached into Elaine's bag, extracted a cigarette and lit it.

"He's got nothing to go on, believe me," she told her client. "Give him enough rope, they always use it."

"*Mommy*—!" Cecily said; Elaine lifted a finger, shushing her. She shook her father's arm as if to break it off, and whispered into his ear. "You take me swimming."

"Mom's a better swimmer," Charles said, gently pushing her aside. "She was on the team at Vassar. Want to go to Vassar?"

"Take me now."

"Shouldn't complain until you have something to complain about, honey."

"*Now!*"

He looked at his daughter, appearing to love her. Charles' parents held old Yankee notions of appropriate behavior, and drummed into him the belief that revealing one's emotions to a feckless world is a shameful act. While young, he perfected an impenetrable facade—bland half-smile, eyes lowered but alert—that served him in every situation, however pleasant or grotesque. The structure was unimportant to the facing; the person, superfluous to the mask.

"*Cecily!*" She quieted.

"The writ's in order. Don't worry, I said. Call you Monday."

Elaine put away her phone and stood, dropping her towel. "I hope the water's not too cold still."

Her bathing suit, a white maillot, sheathed her torso in condom smoothness. Her suit rode up with every step as she led Cecily to the sea. Charles stared at his wife, evincing no more evident emotion than when he'd watched her talking on the phone.

"Doesn't she look good in that?" Charles asked, assuring me he'd served as fashion advisor. He snuffed his cigarette in a tuffet of sand, and lit another.

"She looks uncomfortable."

"First thing she said to me was take it back. Too old, she said. Got her to reconsider. Told her to give it a spin. You never can predict when she gets insecure."

Elaine and Charles were married twenty years. They had a competition, rather than a relationship, throughout. I declined to sit as judge however often he passed me the gavel.

"When's class start?" I asked.

"Two weeks."

"Anticipating or dreading?"

"A challenge, either way. Finding the one who stands out. I anticipate finding them. I dread not finding them."

"You got freshman courses this year?"

He shivered, as if the breeze were chilly. "One. The rest, juniors and seniors."

"Better informed?"

"School's out when it's in, these days." He eyed Cecily, digging her way across the beach as Elaine rode the ocean.

"What've you been working on?"

"*The Pathology of Trauma.*"

His eyelids crinkled as he confronted the sun. "The usual?"

"Mostly. Couple of new ones on me," I said. "Suicide by dynamite." He looked at me. "Used as cigar."

"Don't see how you keep your head on straight, editing this material."

"I like what I'm doing, Charlie."

"You ever want to change, I know people. I could call around."

"That's fine."

Charles' sense of *noblesse oblige* was as genuine as it was selectively fulsome. Yet, little disgruntled him more than having his proffered altruism declined—save when his help was accepted, and the gratitude resulting struck him as incommensurate with his beneficence.

"You don't get out enough," he said. "Haven't I always told you that? You're not getting younger, you know."

Charles was my age. For a minute he said nothing more. He was accomplished at drawing out the guilt in others for having felt its frisson so keenly, so often, himself. "Remember Gail Hamilton?"

"Yes. Why?"

"Ran into her on Lexington. Held up pretty well. Told me I held up pretty well too."

Had his hair still been brown he would have looked two, or even three years younger than he was. "I didn't know she lived here."

"Moved back from San Francisco in April. Divorced. Lives at Second and 68th. Told her we should have lunch one day."

"Going to?"

He shook his head. "Been so long. So many questions. What's she been doing? Why'd she get divorced? Like I said, looks great but who's to know inside?"

"Why'd you suggest lunch then?"

Charles put on his sunglasses. "Have to be polite."

Elaine, treading water a short way beyond the breakers, called to Cecily, who then ran to us, stopping in front of her father. "Mommy wants her towel," she told Charles. "She wants *you* to bring it to her."

"Why me?"

"Mommy says just bring it."

He stood, hoisting his trunks up to approach his waistline. Retrieving Elaine's towel, he followed his daughter to the water and walked into the surf. Elaine came inland, practically leaping to take the towel from him. It was just possible to see that her suit's fabric, once wet, became translucent. Cloaking herself while still coming out of the water, she walked to and picked up her bag. "I have to put something else on. Charles, watch Ceese."

Charles called after her as she ascended the dunes. "Wear it at home in the bathtub."

"Give it to one of your students."

His smile flattened. Cecily slapped his knee with a plastic bucket, then wandered a few feet away and started filling it with sand. While waiting for Elaine to return we watched a speedboat scarring the waves. He said something I didn't catch.

"Pardon?"

Charles examined his knee, as if fearful his daughter had damaged it. "Beautiful day, don't you think?"

Two or three times a month Charles and I met for drinks and, sometimes, drinks after work. At some point during every evening our conversation inevitably began revolving around our old college days. If our memories differed, it was expected that I support his version, which he felt suffered less from time's limitless rewrites. Often—more often, of late—we'd speak of obits of one-time friends from school who'd died of coronaries, or cancer, or mortal error, and mourn them as we remembered them, their collegiate portraits hazy with thirty years' distance. Charles always grew uncomfortable considering the oft wayward course of many undergraduate lives.

For example, once I was sure that a remarkable case study I'd edited was one of our housemates during our sophomore year.

"Wasn't him," said Charles, with uninflected voice. "If he was going to die, he wouldn't have gone that way. Too public."

After a while I avoided trifling with my friend's preferred realities, and so concurred in his opinions without going so far as to believe them. Change didn't disturb him so much as unpredictability. One of many talents of his on which he prided himself was his ability to foresee situations early enough to benefit from their results; in truth, he rarely did. The first time we got together that semester Charles raised an unanticipated subject, however. He told me he'd already encountered the student who stood out.

"A brilliant young woman," he said, intoning his new mantra repeatedly as the fettucine cooled. "Brilliant. Audited my poetry class on the second day. By the end of the hour she was the only active participant. She is a student, so I had her assigned to the class. Brilliant."

"How so?"

His face was indecipherable; his unchangingly cheerful expression was as if he'd molded it that morning and didn't want it to shatter. "What's her name?"

"Valerie," he said. "We spoke further after class. She's formulating her own critical theory. Non-traditional, willfully so at times, perhaps, but that's the pleasure of it. And as near as I can tell it works. You only meet students like her once in a lifetime."

"She's a junior? Senior?" A dish broke in the kitchen. "I didn't hear you."

"Freshman. She went to Swarthmore last year but transferred." He shook his head in wonder, and chuckled. "They didn't get the concept of chaos philology at all."

"I'm sorry?"

"Her critical theory," Charles said. "Takes semiotics one step beyond."

"How?"

His smile broke loose of its moorings. "Ask her," he said, rising. "Valerie, I'd like you to meet—"

"Charmed," she said, taking my hand before I offered it. Charles expropriated another table's chair so that she could sit.

Valerie wore a gray cashmere turtleneck, striped leggings, and yellow running shoes. She looked slender enough to slip through mail slots. Her pale skin possessed the matte finish older women sometimes obtain when their features are updated. She had a child's smile, a doll's eyes, hair black as the wing of a carrion crow. She was beautiful, though seemingly through compulsion. Taking a roll from his plate, she bit into it.

"Charles was starting to tell me about your theory—"

"Which?" Seizing a knife, she smeared butter over the remains of the roll, and crammed it into her mouth.

"Chaos philology," Charles said. Valerie grinned, and snatched the fork from his plate, wreathing its tines in chilled fettuccini.

"Did he explain it? The bottom line is that unraveling always works, even when deconstruction doesn't."

Valerie reached for another forkful, overturning my glass, baptizing the table with barely sipped bourbon.

"Unraveling?"

"Unraveling whatever's communicated," she said. "Whether written or verbal narratives. One: unravel the text as presented. Two: reweave into a turbulent pattern of discourse. Three: examine the new design. Chaos philology allows the deepest penetration into the author's auctorial intent."

Charles slid his plate in front of her so that she could reload her fork with less collateral damage. "Maybe if you give me an example I'll—"

"Sure. Let's stick to the Romantics. His favorite." Charles smiled. "Take a typical passage from Shelley's *Adonais* such as 'Peace, peace, he is not dead, he doth not sleep.'" From her backpack she took a pen and notebook and began to write, dripping strands of pasta onto the paper. "Start simple, finish big," she said, presenting it to me. "The turbulent pattern as obtained."

I read:

He he sleep doth not peace dead not peace is he he

Each word was harnessed to its mates by curves, lines and arrows, singly, in pairs, and as *ménages à trois*. I examined the fetishistic intricacy of the lacings. I'd never seen a sentence so parsed.

"Very subtle patterns," I said.

"They leap out at you, after a while," said Charles.

"If you desire, you can defer the critical climax indefinitely," Valerie continued, "and if not, bang and run. Strip sense from nonsense. See what fantastical conceits the author is trying to hide. Here, it's so obvious that what Shelley is doing in that particular line is laughing at the prospect of his own predictable death."

"But, uh, the poem, Keats—"

"No, Shelley. Keats was already dead I think."

Charles gave Valerie a look that gave me a toothache. "Well," I said. "Must have taken the wrong Lit courses."

"Wouldn't have helped," she said. As she lay down her fork I thought I glimpsed a tattoo of a green butterfly on her left wrist.

"Authors never mean what you think they're saying. You have to find a quick way to get them to confess. Chaos philology may seem violent, assaulting the author as it does, but how else do you get to know what's really there? Nothing wrong with that. Nothing wrong with anything as long as it doesn't hurt someone you don't know."

She slumped, and looked over at Charles.

"Method broadens the range of readings," he said. "Makes what's obvious to me obvious to anyone tying themselves into the network. The Romantics always lied about what they were up to. We all know that."

"Downright morbid, most of them. If you hadn't had Romantics, you wouldn't have had Hitler."

"Chaos philology is usable in unravelling any fantasy in any field, the more I think about it," said Charles.

"I'm lost," I admitted.

"No. You're unravelling!" she said, bouncing up and down in her chair.

"Not everybody gets it first time around," said Charles, his smile resetting itself into a shallow, upturned arc. "We'll try again sometime." He looked at my glass, never refilled. "When we're more sober, perhaps."

Valerie rested her chin in her palms. Her sleeves drew up as she moved her arms. Seeing her wrist more plainly, I realized that the greenish blotch wasn't a butterfly, but a bruise. "You and Charles went to school together?" she asked. "Nothing like an Ivy League man." She caressed my silk tie with her fingers, oiling it nicely. "*These* aren't the school colors."

"Chaos haberdashery," I said.

She laughed again, and then jumped to her feet. "I've got to go pee. Be back."

Charles tapped the table with his fingers as he watched her walk away. I straightened my tie. "She's a corker, isn't she? Overexuberant sometimes, sure."

"Genius knows its own etiquette," I said. "How's the family?"

"Fine," he said, staring at the ladies' room as if ready to lunge for it. "Fine, fine."

I suppose his deeper involvement with Valerie began about a month into the semester. I was sure that one night they'd forged bonds that were other than intellectual, but he didn't say, and I didn't ask. He'd had an affair once before while married to Elaine, alluding to it only after it was long broken off, and only to me. Afterward, having confessed, he could live the rest of his life pretending it had never happened. Years later, I'd asked him her name, but by then the affair had never happened and she had never had one.

Throughout that fall Valerie came with him nearly every time we met. They sat on either side of me at the table, rambling about her unorthodox theories, the elaborate projects they'd dreamed of shortly undertaking, the officials at Barnard they'd contacted, using whatever pull he actually had. At no time would it have appeared to anyone who didn't know Charles (or, know him as well as I did) that anything was ongoing between him and his new associate but a mutual fondness for the miraculous workings of the mind, the interest they most deeply shared so long as theirs were the minds involved.

One afternoon in late October he called me at work. "Meet me in the public area in my building instead of at the restaurant tonight, would you? Something I want to talk to you about."

Possibly he intended a fresh confession, but that as it happened that was a moot concern. When I arrived, the secretary in the reception area had gone home, and no one else was around. I strolled down the hall to his office, whose door was shut. As I prepared to knock, Valerie's voice came from within, rising over the building's white noise. She sounded as if she'd been running. No; hyperventilating. She spoke.

"How's that? How? How?"

I returned to the reception area without finding out how. Ten minutes later, he and Valerie emerged from his office, looking no more disheveled than if they'd been unravelling one of the thornier passages of Byron. "Look who's here," Charles exclaimed, as if it were a surprise. "Hungry?" I nodded. When I looked at Valerie she turned her eyes away, and nodded a quiet Hello. "Let's go."

We went. Once in public, she was happy enough to announce "I've got to go facilitate," before stepping away from our table. I asked Charles why he'd asked me to meet him at the school, and what he wanted to talk to me about.

"Why do you say I wanted to talk to you about something?"

"That's what you said. This afternoon. Don't you remember?"

"Oh, I think you just misunderstood me." His smile slid firmly into place. "Meant that if you met us there, we'd have more time to talk on the way over here. Weren't waiting long, were you?"

"No," I said. "We didn't talk the whole way over from the school to the restaurant."

"We're talking now, aren't we?" Charles said. Valerie returned. She scoured her chin with a tissue, studying it as if fearful she'd drawn blood.

"You haven't said anything about Charles' tie," she said, pitching the tissue on the table. Hooking his repp, she reeled him in. "School colors."

"Out of the closet," he explained. "Pop made me buy one first day we went up. Told me to wear it once a week. Bought it at the Co-op first day." He laughed. "Never wore it again. Till now."

"But I'm the one telling you to wear it now," she said. "Not him." Letting go, she opened her pill container and took out a couple. Earlier I'd asked Charles what she was on, and he said an assortment of the milder antidepressants and such. "I have to tie it for him. He's all thumbs."

"Bit more conservative than what you hang around your neck," I said. He blanched, as if nauseated by memories of required high school accoutrements from Brooks, J.Press, or Chipp. Valerie, I saw, could really tie a tie. The dimple in the knot appeared mathematically centered, and the knot itself fit against his Adam's apple so closely it might have been glued there. "Isn't that awfully tight?"

"You'd be surprised," he said, pulling his collar away from his neck.

"Cocteau used to tie his neckties as tight as he could, to lessen the flow of blood to his brain," said Valerie. "He claimed it inspired."

"Penny for your thoughts," I said to Charles.

"Thinking about our work," he said. "Going to do a book detailing her theories. Should turn a few heads. An amazing number of my ideas tally perfectly with Valerie's as it happens."

"We're two of a kind, in our own ways."

Soon after, tiring of their camaraderie as it grew ever more exclusive as time passed, I excused myself and went home. It wasn't long after I got there that Elaine called.

"I have to ask you something," she said. "When do you think you'll finish up this project you and Charles are working on?"

"Project."

"I'm only asking because I'm rarely in before ten during the week and I'm going to advertise for a full-time nanny if you think it'll be much longer. I've asked Charles but he's so vague about everything."

"Better look for a nanny," I said.

"Just what I thought."

By morning I'd almost convinced myself I hadn't lied to her.

Several evenings later Charles called me, sounding considerably more frantic than usual. "I'm at Valerie's apartment. Get over here, fast."

"Where? What's the matter?"

"Broadway and 86th, southwest. Buzz 5E. Hurry."

In ten minutes I reached the building and rushed upstairs. Charles opened the door as I rang the bell. A lone ribbon of gauze was wrapped around his right hand, a dab of blood marring its whiteness. "It's okay now," he said, his smile flickering. "Come on in."

Valerie's studio was the size of my living room. Rain blew in the open windows. Notebooks and papers were stacked upon the kitchenette's table, near two uncleared dinner plates. A pair of wire clippers lay atop an unpacked box of dishes. Six hanging baskets brimming with unwatered ivy dangled from hooks in the ceiling, swaying as if they were pendulums. Clothing and linens blanketed two file cabinets. In the bathroom was a metal wastepaper can split open along the side seam. Hundreds of books, their titles facing inward, were shoved onto the shelves of three bookcases. Chaotique Moderne, you could have called the decor.

"Hi," Valerie said. She lay on her futon. "Thanks for coming by." A thin quilt covered her from neck to knees; her bare calves appeared more muscular than they did in the leggings she usually wore. She breathed heavily, as if she'd been running. The room's single lamp shadowed her face, making her eyes appear more deep-set than usual. The tip of her nose and her forehead bore fresh abrasions, as if she'd fallen and scraped them on the sidewalk. She'd smeared Vaseline or another soothing ointment on her cheeks and beneath her jaw.

"You have an accident?" I asked. "What happened?"

"Damnest thing," Charles said. "Valerie asked if I'd take the garbage down the hall to the compactor. Sliced my hand open on the can, came apart while I was holding it. Closed up fast enough, though."

"Are you all right?" I asked Valerie, who smiled.

"Sorry to make you run over like this. Tell you what, I've got to be going. Walk you back home?"

"Sure," I said, recalling the panic earlier in his voice. I suspected any higher authority whom he might have contacted might notify his wife to where he'd been found. It was possible they'd been working; Charles always looked most guilty when there was least reason.

Valerie watched him take his raincoat from the closet.

"You can't stay?" she asked, rolling over. Her quilt fell away for a moment. She trimmed her pubic hair into a tuft. Thin dark bruises resembling calligraphy laced her ribcage. "Get home safe."

While walking to the elevator I looked for the trash compactor, but perhaps it was at the other end of the floor.

"I didn't know she lived in the neighborhood," I said as we descended.

"Close to Barnard," he said, though Valerie was presently going to NYU.

"Elaine called me the night we all went out," I said. "She said something about a project we were working on?"

He wore his school tie; he must have knotted it himself, as its four-in-hand seemed tied by one unused to opposable thumbs. "We're busy putting Valerie's ideas into shape for publication. Get together sometimes to work on it."

"I think she was talking about a project you and I were working on," I said. "What project?"

"You know how Elaine gets sometimes," he said. "She's that age, you know."

"She's a year older than us."

"Well," he said, "one evening last week I got back later than I expected. Had to improvise an excuse."

"Which was?"

"That you're helping me edit my new book as I'm writing it. Kills two birds with one stone. Improves my text, helps you out."

"You know," I said, "you should have at least warned me. And I don't know why I was such a good excuse in the first place. And excuse for—"

"My intention, my intention. Didn't have the chance. I don't doubt you were upset." A pause. "Look, Valerie doesn't have to be involved with this."

"No?"

"She's young but hasn't had an easy life, however it may seem."

"You two are getting along," I asked.

"We mesh. Same channel, great minds. She did gymnastics in high school. First rate, I'm sure. Had to give it up. Balance beam accident. Made the best of it." He unexpectedly snatched at air with such intensity that I thought for a moment he might be having a convulsion. "It's impossible to say where she could go if she gets the opportunities. I'm just trying to make sure she gets them."

"If she only had some redeeming fault," I said, hoping to lighten the mood.

"Valerie'll do anything." He spoke so softly that I wouldn't have heard him had I not seen his lips as they let the words loose; he seemed as much terrified as excited. "Could do anything, with the right opportunities. Elaine's imagining a rival where none exists."

"No?" I asked. "Any school gossip?"

"Intellectual envy," he said. "Nothing more."

"Is anything they're saying true?"

He didn't immediately respond. "Troubles me that you'd feel the need to ask that." We reached 99th Street. "I'll give you the benefit of the doubt.'"

"That's big of you."

"People will think what they want to think, whatever the truth is. Let 'em."

"It upset me when Elaine called, Charlie. I'm not as good at lying as some people."

"You're not lying," he called back to me over my shoulder, as he headed toward Riverside. "Remember that."

In the third week of November he left me a message, asking if I wanted to get together with him before Thanksgiving. When I phoned, Elaine answered.

"Charles isn't here at the moment."

"I can call back—"

"How late are you two working tonight?"

No matter how quickly I reacted, it wouldn't have been quickly enough. "That's why I was calling, to double check." The silence following lasted longer than I should have preferred.

"Should I tell him you were looking for him?" she said, before hanging up.

The next morning Charles called me from his office, asking if I was available to see him later that day. "Don't worry about Elaine," he assured me.

"What did you tell her this time?"

He gave no indication of having heard me. Deafness at command was an ability he admired so long as he was the one conveniently handicapped. By five that afternoon I was at our chosen rendezvous, a coffee shop on 86th at Columbus. Charles had a filled cloth bag slung over his shoulder. His eyes were pouched; his face appeared to have more new wrinkles than a floater's. He'd lost weight, but not where it mattered. Although he usually avoided artificial stimuli, save for a pack of cigarettes filtered daily through his lungs, his ravaged look warned of a dilatory concern for the more mundane aspects of life, as when what was once thought a pleasant distraction proves addictive unto death.

"What's in there?" I asked, pointing to his bag. He flashed his demi-smile.

"The cat."

"What'd Elaine say when you got home? Charles, I—"

"All taken care of," he replied, his gaze drifting to a mirror behind the counter, perhaps suspecting his wife of lurking beyond the glass and the cereal.

"You knew I talked to her—"

"Misunderstanding, that's all. Told her an emergency department meeting came up."

"That worked?"

He looked puzzled. "Why wouldn't it?"

"I wish you'd tell me what your plans are if I'm involved with them."

"You're right," he said. The waiter brought our coffee. I had no appetite, and also declined a menu. Charles ran his fingers through his hair, as if surprised to find it still there. "You're absolutely right."

"If you've got nothing to hide, why are you hiding?"

"Is that what you'd call it?"

"If all you're doing with Valerie is working, why do you tell Elaine and God knows who else that you're out with me?"

"You're assuming I was with Valerie last night."

"Weren't you?" I half-shouted. "Is it that hard to say?"

Charles lifted his cup to his mouth. His hand shook; he splashed coffee on his sleeve. "No need to be hostile," he said. "Your work getting to you? Only a matter of time—"

"She knew I was lying and I didn't want to lie to her."

"But you did," he said. "Your decision."

"I've had it, Charlie," I said, tossing my napkin on the table and standing up. He scanned the restaurant to see if anyone was watching. "You've got me involved in this and I hardly know what I'm involved in."

He took hold of my arm and gestured that I should sit back down. "Get control over yourself. I hadn't realized you were so angry."

"Give me a straight answer and I won't be."

"I can understand transference," he said. "Let me try to explain."

"Fine. Why so much secrecy about something so obvious—"

"It's a private matter, but I'll share it with you if you insist," he said. "You know Elaine's not the easiest person to get along with. Going through a difficult time of life now. Up some days, down the rest. We've had more than our share of disagreements since Cecily was born."

"I'd not noticed and you never said."

"Nothing to say. Cecily's a beautiful child, we love her dearly, but she was an accident, after all. Didn't expect to have one so late. Bad timing. Knocked Elaine right off the fast track at her old firm. Now she's got her own office, has to work twice as hard. Not many women want to be new mothers at her age." Charles shook his head as if to reshuffle its contents, to see what settled where. "Elaine didn't." While speaking he began straightening his old tie's knot, aligning it precisely between his shirt's frayed collar lapels. "Didn't please her. Started transferring. Thank God she takes it out on me and not Cecily. Came to an arrangement after, mind you. Upper and lower bunks in the marriage bed since. But you have to get along."

"Both of you always seemed happy."

"Essential precept of chaos philology, remember."

"What is?"

"Nothing is ever as it seems," he said, seemingly in awe. "Situations like that don't make anyone feel secure. And she's always been a worrywart. Insecure. Won't surprise you to hear she's never thought much of my students. Early on I introduced her to Valerie. It was the right thing to do, and it wasn't."

"They must not have much in common."

"Both need my time." He watched the entrance as if expecting, or fearing, them to arrive simultaneously. "That's my excuse, take it or leave it. Something about her sets Elaine off. If she knew I was working with Valerie and not you, she'd eat us alive."

"Valerie knows this?"

"She's perceptive. Call me overprotective but I haven't seen the need to involve her in the problems of Elaine and myself."

"How is that possible?"

Charles sighed, as if accepting that he'd again have to explain the difference between noun and verb before the class could understand the syllabus. "Questions like that complicate a simple situation. I try to help her, and she helps me." Forcing his fingers between skin and cloth, he scratched his throat. "Valerie comes on strong because she's insecure in her own ways. At this point she's not going to be able to polish her theories on her own and I'm able to provide discipline and guidance."

Between sentences he drifted, at moments appearing unaware of my presence even as he spoke to me. His explanation was more straightforward than any he'd given me before: he'd revealed nominal truths shorn of convenient tangents. I saw no reason to do more than partially believe him. "Charlie, if you were having another affair, what would you want out of it at this point?"

"Why do you say another affair?"

He tapped his spoon rapidly against his saucer, seeming either to send code or trying to break it. I had neither energy nor desire to hurdle another set of circumlocutions, and reworded my question. "An affair, I meant to say. What would you want out of it—"

"What if you ever *had* a relationship?" he asked. "What would you want out of it?"

"I've had relationships and you know it. That's not the point, Charlie—"

"I've known women. Have a good marriage. A few problems, not many. Young women like Valerie want to work with me. Why would I have an affair?"

"Never mind," I said "Forget it."

"Average person has to have an affair to have sex, I think," he said, staring into his coffee, looking up at me when he found the answer sought. "And having sex's a given with most people, don't you think?"

"Charlie, I—"

"Ever imagine you're back in school again?" he asked, eyes half-shut. "Remember what that was like?" I stopped trying to interrupt. "Imagine you're twenty, and you're with her," he said. "She says do what you want, she can't get away." His voice never rose above a stage whisper. "She screams your name. Why does this make you uncomfortable? You're the one who brought it up."

I got ready to go.

"Have to be careful applying chaos philology to anything other than the text," he said. "Finding out what's what can be as hard on the one unraveling as it is on what's being unraveled."

"What's the matter with you, Charlie?"

"Why do you distance yourself so fast whenever something takes a sexual turn? You always have. Don't people live up to your fantasies? Afraid somebody else is doing better than you? Like always?"

"Yeah, let's just leave it at that," I said, putting on my jacket. As I stood up I kept my eyes directed to the floor. I noticed he only wore one sock. A furrowed black bruise encircled the exposed ankle.

"That's right. My business is my business, and what yours is, is yours."

"If I don't talk to you before Thanksgiving give my love to the family."

An avuncular superiority reappeared on his features. His smile remained embedded in his face. "Thanks for helping with Elaine," he said. "I mean it."

"Stop telling her you're with me when you're not," I said. His expression remained the same. Some texts defy unraveling. Upon reaching my home I checked and found a message from Elaine.

Is Charles there?

Two weeks before Christmas they had their annual party. For days I debated whether or not I should go, finally deciding that I should, briefly. The day of the party I worked late, editing manuscripts. By the time I arrived, everyone else was there. Half of those attending were Charles' friends, half Elaine's; there was little commingling of subcultures.

"Good to see you," Elaine said, greeting me by kissing the air in the vicinity of my cheek. "Charles is in the kitchen. I told him to bring in more eggnog if he thought he could handle it."

"How are you?"

She glared. "Have the man fix you a drink. I know you're usually thirsty."

The caterers had the setups in their library, and performed their duties with the enthusiasm of rowers on a Roman galley. Cecily wore a red velvet party dress and spent the night entertaining the guests to some degree or the other. An eight-foot Norwegian pine bedizened with white lights and blue balls was in the living room. The soundtrack from *A Charlie Brown Christmas* played mercilessly. The press of the crowd was great enough that had it not been for those yuletide touches I should have thought a reenactment of the Black Hole was underway. I shoehorned myself in near a group that appeared as lawful as they did academic, and eavesdropped.

"Is she here?" asked a man with caterpillar eyebrows. "Tell me no."

"She is," said an older woman of forbidding mien.

"I hope it's more than just physical," said a woman my age, with black-rimmed glasses.

"Or intellectual," said caterpillar man. "There's Columbine and Pantaloon now."

They ploughed separate furrows through through the crowd, so intent on ignoring each other as to be unignorable. Charles wore a black turtleneck. Valerie came as a party favor, enshrouded in green ruffles with a red silk scarf around her neck. She carried a tureen of eggnog.

"Match made in heaven," said the woman with glasses.

With deliberate steps Charles inched into the dining room, schmoozing with those he passed. Reaching the breakfast table he commandeered two empty chairs, sitting in one and placing his drink in another. A sheet draped over the table reaching to the floor was imprinted with the legend BAH HUMBUG! several thousand times.

Valerie materialized so immediately at Charles' side that she might have teleported. Academics from departments other than their own hovered buzzard-like around them.

Charles and I hadn't seen each other since our contretemps. We'd been in touch once or twice but the memory of his assault remained, and I wasn't anxious to talk to him for long during the short time I expected to be here. I squeezed down the hall toward the library as a clot squeezes through an artery. Having gotten a fresh drink I encountered Elaine on the way back. She stood at the doorway of the dining room, watching her husband and his comely protege.

"You're not leaving yet, are you?" she asked me. "Say you're not."

"Not yet," I said, smiling. I remembered how much trouble she had quitting smoking while pregnant with Cecily, and I hadn't expected her to backslide. Her gown sagged slightly around her waist; I estimated she'd lost twenty pounds, by design or accident, since August.

"You've said hello to Charles?"

"Hard to get his eye."

"Depends." She smiled. "Go talk to him, why not? I'll be there shortly."

Valerie waved briskly as I approached. "You've got a school tie too," she said, recognizing my cravat, having seen its mate often enough around Charles' neck.

"I wasn't sure if you were coming or not," he said, flashing those teeth. "You know the chairman of the English Department? Doctor Bubenhofer? I didn't expect him but here he is."

The doctor, bald and dusty, lounged in a chair across the table, looking at me from beyond the eggnog, grunting in my direction as if to be polite.

"Doctor, let me tell you something," Valerie suddenly said. The doctor appeared somewhat more interested than he had earlier. "Charles and I are developing a new critical approach."

"Charles, is it? So I've heard."

"Would you like to hear it from people who know what they're talking about?"

"No one works at a party," Charles said. "Some other time."

"This isn't work—"

"Valerie!" he said, speaking to her as if to Cecily. Tapping me on the arm once he was sure she appeared distracted, he gestured that I should lower my head to hear something he had to say. She scooted her chair forward, closer, and reclined. She took his left hand in hers and pulled it off the table.

"I'm sorry about the other day," he said. "Lots of pressure."

"That's all right."

"We should talk. We should." He looked toward the ceiling. "Not here. Later."

Valerie stared arid, transfixed by the candelabra's electric flames. With an idle hand she fondled her scarf. I looked up and stared away when Elaine appeared at tableside.

"Charles," she said, "I need to ask you something."

"Maybe not here, dear,"

"It won't take a minute."

"After the party, Elaine," he said. "Please."

Suddenly bending down, she seized the tablecloth's hem in her hands. With effortless motions she whipped it away. Glassware, crockery, and tureen shattered against the floor. Eggnog drenched the doctor's tweed. Through the glass-topped table we all saw Valerie's panties draped around her right ankle, and Charles' left hand still trapped between her legs. Just then he managed to free himself, and when he did his arm jerked up and his class ring rapped sharply against the glass, calling the company to complete attention as if to announce a retirement toast.

"Are you moving in with her before or after Christmas?" Elaine asked. She left the room. Her supporters hastened after her. Charles' associates glanced at one another before filing into the hall, refusing to look at what they left behind. Valerie pulled up her underwear with the aplomb of a bather preparing to leave the beach. Charles clasped his hands before him as if to say grace.

"Honey?" he called out. "It's not what it seems."

In February I ran into Valerie as she came out of a drugstore on Columbus. "Got a few minutes?" she asked, entwining her arm with mine. We went to the coffee shop at 86th. She left her muffler on when we sat down. The bright glare inside illuminated a dime-size bruise on her forehead.

"Charles misses you," she said. "He'd never say, but I can tell. Half a dozen times I've tried getting him to call you, but it's like talking to a wall."

"We'd had an argument a while back."

"He's been himself more than he's not been himself, lately." As I watched she dumped seven packs of sugar into her coffee and stirred it into a whirl-pool. "You may have just misread each other's texts."

"The longer we were friends, the less I knew him."

"The first time I met you I thought you two had once been lovers." She slipped off her shoes and lifted her legs onto the booth's seat, contorting her-self into a variorum lotus position, and began rocking back and forth. "Then I re-theorized and realized it was only body language. Why have you stayed friends so long?"

"We went to school together."

"And?"

When called upon, I couldn't think of any other reasons. "Do you like me?" she asked. "I mean, you don't dislike me, do you?"

"I don't know you," I said. "Why do you ask?"

"Most of his friends think I'm bad for him. And, Elaine."

"You're surprised?"

"We've had an equal relationship," she said. "I was sure you liked me. I'm glad you admit it. Men your age usually don't talk at all. Ones my age never shut up. Not that most of them have nothing to say in the first place. Are you as close-mouthed about yourself as Charles?"

"Probably. Different reasons."

"Well. Ask me anything, I'll talk about it. He talks about you."

"What does he say?"

"You care?" she asked. "You disappointed him. He thought you'd understand."

"I didn't know what there was to understand, and didn't know I should have understood."

"Charles said the situation is something you should have understood," she said, brushing her hair from her face. "He told me he wanted to be closer to you but you wouldn't let him. He said that when you think somebody's getting too close to you, you run." She suddenly drank her coffee in three swallows and signaled the waiter for more. "What got you so upset?"

"He did something that reminded me of something he did before. Doesn't bear repeating."

"That's what he'd say. You two are more alike than you'd ever admit."

"How is he, anyway?" I asked.

"Could be better. NYU will let him return for the summer semester. He's told Elaine she can have everything, but that's not enough for her. She won't let him see Cecily. Elaine is so insecure. I think *they* stayed together because each of them reminded the other of their least intimidating parent."

"What's he doing?"

"Hangs around the apartment. Rewrites our notes. My ideas are generally easy to understand until he improves them. I write a sentence, he rewrites a chapter. He puts masks on while I try to take them off."

"You and Charles have been having an affair, haven't you?" I asked. "Not that I need to know."

"He wouldn't call it that," she said, rocking more slowly. "He never expected to have this kind of relationship, so he thinks of it as being something apart. If you asked, do we fuck each other, there's no denying. How did we seem when you first saw us together?"

"Isolated."

"I asked him why the folderol around you. He said it would make you uncomfortable if we didn't, and you'd run."

"No," I said. "He hurts everybody around him, starting with himself. It's masochistic."

"It's as deliberate as it could be needless," she said. "Masochists love the sin, they don't hate the sinners. Charles knows you can't be happy without pain, but that might be his background. Do you know anything about his childhood?"

"His parents were old guard. That's all he's said."

"Whatever happened to him then isn't something he won't let me unravel," she said. "It might not have been anything major at the time. You never know what'll affect you most, years later." She returned one of her feet to the floor, resting it beside mine. "I don't have any trouble, myself. I could tell you a horrible thing that happened to me."

"Is it something you need to tell me?"

"In high school. Late gymnastics practice. I came out of the shower and two boys jumped me. They shoved a can over my head so I couldn't see them. They dragged me out and bent me over a horse."

Valerie told me what had happened to her as if recounting the plot of a movie she'd seen long ago, nonetheless weaving the narrative with such precision that I would never attempt an unraveling. The flat manner in which she told me assured me of its truth; its detailing led me to think she'd retold the story many times, to herself, and if it were smooth it was only the act of continual revision enabled to tell it at all.

"I passed out. My coach was still there. He untied me but couldn't get the can off my head at first and that's when I started screaming. It came off and he was looking at me and I was still naked."

"And—?"

"You want to know how it ends, don't you?" She smiled. "He wrapped me up and made a couple of calls. He didn't do anything, himself," she said. "In any way. I never knew for certain but I supposed the boys were on the team, and that's why anything I said afterward didn't go anywhere. So." She studied the surface of the table in our booth. "I dealt with it. Stare at a wound long enough and it doesn't hurt anymore. You might even see its beauty, eventually. Do you think I'm beautiful?"

Caught unaware as I was, I can only imagine what my face showed. Charles once told me mine was as readable as a cheap novel. "I'm so sorry," I said. "Yes. And you have a remarkable—"

"Mind?" I nodded. "Were you and Charles ever in love with the same woman?"

I understood the nature of his attraction to Valerie that afternoon. Those oncoming lights transfixed so. "It's much more complicated than that."

"What was her name?"

"Gail," I said. "We were together during our junior year. College. College juniors."

"What happened?"

"I don't like to think about it."

"Except when you do," she said. "We'll keep each other's secrets."

"We'd had an argument," I told her. "I don't even remember what about. Charles told me he could tell I was upset and he'd go smooth things out. Next night he went to her apartment. She lived off campus." I stopped. "Valerie, I don't think—"

"Go on."

"He was still asleep when I woke up. I called Gail. She hung up. Wouldn't let me in when I went to her apartment. Stood at her door, asked her what happened. She just said go ask your friend. When I got back to the house Charles was having breakfast."

"What did he tell you?"

"He said she was drunk when he got there. Things got weird, was all he said. Then he left."

"You didn't believe him."

"She thought I'd sent him over to do that," I said. "A friend of hers told me that, after she left."

"She didn't report it?"

"It was years ago," I told Valerie. "She transferred to Berkeley."

"And you stayed friends with Charles after that." She reached over to pat the side of my head, and ran her tongue along her lips as if they were dry. "Maybe you understand masochism more than I thought. Maybe you don't."

"I'd better—"

"Run?"

"Get home safe," I said.

"I will. He's at my place or I'd say walk me there. I keep telling him he should get out more. We should all start hooking up more often."

"Yes—"

"Charles gave me a lot of new material," Valerie said, smiling. "I could use a good editor."

FORWARD TO: **Editorial** Production
Legault & Van Gelder/Adv Forens Comp/JANUARY

The following account appears to be the only case in the literature involving joint participants in what has recently (Hazelwood, Dietz, Burgess, 1983) termed Kotzwarraism, [FLAG 32] or hypoxyphilia. The diagnostic criteria for these paraphilia include the acting out of masochistic fantasies involving torture, abuse, or execution and a desire for sexual arousal through risk-inherent situations, being generally in these cases the employment of a preferred mode of self-induced (or, induced through the employment of agency of others: *op. cit.* Asa and Burroughs, 1978) sexual excitement by means of mechanical or chemical asphyxiation. This case should be considered *sui generis* but the patterns are unmistakable.

129. The victims were a fifty-year-old Caucasian male and a twenty-two-year old Caucasian female. A good state of preservation was observed, the temperature within the female deceased's studio apartment being forty-six degrees Fahrenheit [FLAG 33].

Both victims were nude, obliquely reclined back to back in arched positions, touching only at the head and heels. An electrical cord was attached at one end to the female deceased's neck by a slip knot, and tied at the other end around the male deceased's ankles. Another cord interconnected her ankles to his neck in like manner. Both victims were also tied together at the neck with a blue and white repp necktie looped and knotted around the throats of the victims [FLAG 34]. Commercial lubrication cream was detected in the rectums of the deceased. A small pink bow was tied in a bow on the male deceased's penis. No indications of struggle were noted. Neither a suicide note nor any writings indicative of depressive states were found.

The positioning of the victims assured that the leg movements of one would exert increasing pressure upon the neck of the other, compressing the carotid baroreceptors, slowing the heart rate and within a short time causing unconsciousness. The male deceased died of asphyxia due to laryngeal ligature. The female deceased died concurrently through vagal inhibition. Examination of the slip knots, in these cases often serving as a self-rescue mechanism, revealed that the female deceased's hair had become entangled in her cord's knot, precluding release. It was not evident that such release was attempted.

Six metal hooks had been installed in the ceiling to facilitate evident bondage activity. A dented metal wastepaper can showed signs of having been recently worn on the head by the female deceased as an entrapment device. Thirty-nine standard paper school notebooks kept in file cabinets were found to contain variant texts of a masochistic fantasy written in the hand of the female deceased.

Prescriptions for Stelazine and Tofranil in the name of the female deceased had been recently refilled. The male deceased evident possessions consisted of a worn cloth travel bag and leather toiletry case. Among the female's possessions were a braided leather whip of the type known as a cat o'nine tails, lengths of 3/8" diameter hemp rope, three spools of cloth twine, two children's red jump ropes, twenty feet of clothesline, a roll of piano wire, a pair of wire clippers, battery cables, seventy-three printed color photographs depicting the female deceased in earlier asphyxial episodes, battery-operated vibrating devices of assorted sizes including one capable of ejecting fluids, a sculler's oar, two wooden paddles of a model used frequently in fraternity/sorority initiations, scrotum weights, a penis vice, and a leather belt studded along its inner length with tacks [FLAG 35].

Smiles noted on the faces of both deceased were ascribed to rigor mortis until investigators ascertained the estimated time of death [FLAG 36].

32. Correct? Not in Stedman's
OK
33 Dangling
Not unexpected in these accounts. Fix
34 Hard to picture as described
Photo en route to Art Dept should clarify
35 Authors as obsessional as victims. Cut?
Coroner's list already trimmed by half
36 Necessary?
Stet.

THAT OLD SCHOOL TIE

"That Old School Tie," a vicious little story by Jack Womack, is the second reprint from *Little Deaths*, my 1994 anthology of sexual horror. Jack's a fabulous novelist, but every story of his I've published had to be pried out of him.

Love and Sex Among the Invertebrates

by Pat Murphy

(From *Alien Sex,* 1990)

This is not science. This has nothing to do with science. Yesterday, when the bombs fell and the world ended, I gave up scientific thinking. At this distance from the blast site of the bomb that took out San Jose, I figure I received a medium-sized dose of radiation. Not enough for instant death, but too much for survival. I have only a few days left, and I've decided to spend this time constructing the future. Someone must do it.

It's what I was trained for, really. My undergraduate studies were in biology—structural anatomy, the construction of body and bone. My graduate studies were in engineering. For the past five years, I have been designing and constructing robots for use in industrial processing. The need for such industrial creations is over now. But it seems a pity to waste the equipment and materials that remain in the lab that my colleagues have abandoned.

I will put robots together and make them work. But I will not try to understand them. I will not take them apart and consider their inner workings and poke and pry and analyze. The time for science is over.

The pseudoscorpion, *Lasiochernes pilosus*, is a secretive scorpion-like insect that makes its home in the nests of moles. Before pseudoscorpions mate, they dance—a private underground minuet, observed only by moles and voyeuristic entomologists. When a male finds a receptive female, he grasps her claws in his and pulls her toward him. If she resists, he circles, clinging to her claws and pulling her after him, refusing to take no for an answer. He tries again, stepping forward and pulling the female toward him with trembling claws. If she continues to resist, he steps back and continues the dance: circling, pausing to tug on his reluctant partner, then circling again.

After an hour or more of dancing, the female inevitably succumbs, convinced by the dance steps that her companion's species matches her own. The male deposits a packet of sperm on the ground that has been cleared of debris by their dancing feet. His claws quiver as he draws her forward, positioning her over the package of sperm. Willing at last, she presses her genital pore to the ground and takes the sperm into her body.

Biology texts note that the male scorpion's claws tremble as he dances, but they do not say why. They do not speculate on his emotions, his motives, his desires. That would not be scientific.

I theorize that the male pseudoscorpion is eager. Among the everyday aromas of mole shit and rotting vegetation, he smells the female, and the perfume of her fills him with lust. But he is fearful and confused: a solitary insect, unaccustomed to socializing, he is disturbed by the presence of another of his kind. He is caught by conflicting emotions: his all-encompassing need, his fear, and the strangeness of the social situation.

I have given up the pretense of science. I speculate about the motives of the pseudoscorpion, the conflict and desire embodied in his dance.

I put the penis on my first robot as a kind of joke, a private joke, a joke about evolution. I suppose I don't really need to say it was a private joke—all my jokes are private now. I am the last one left, near as I can tell. My colleagues fled—to find their families, to seek refuge in the hills, to spend their last days running around, here and there. I don't expect to see anyone else around anytime soon. And if I do, they probably won't be interested in my jokes. I'm sure that most people think the time for joking is past. They don't see that the bomb and the war are the biggest jokes of all. Death is the biggest joke. Evolution is the biggest joke.

I remember learning about Darwin's theory of evolution in high school biology. Even back then, I thought it was kind of strange, the way people talked about it. The teacher presented evolution as a *fait accompli*, over and done with. She muddled her way through the complex speculations regarding human evolution, talking about *Ramapithecus, Australopithecus, Homo erectus, Homo neanderthalensis* and *Homo sapiens*. At *Homo sapiens* she stopped, and that was it. The way the teacher looked at the situation, we were the last word, the top of the heap, the end of the line.

I'm sure the dinosaurs thought the same, if they thought at all. How could anything get better than armor plating and a spiked tail. Who could ask for more?

Thinking about the dinosaurs, I build my first creation on a reptilian model, a lizard-like creature constructed from bits and pieces that I scavenge from the industrial prototypes that fill the lab and the storeroom. I give my creature a stocky body, as long as I am tall; four legs, extending to the side of the body then bending at the knee to reach the ground; a tail as long as the body, spiked with decorative metal studs; a crocodilian mouth with great curving teeth.

The mouth is only for decoration and protection; this creature will not eat. I equip him with an array of solar panels, fixed to a sail-like crest on his back. The warmth of sunlight will cause the creature to extend his sail and gather electrical energy to recharge his batteries. In the cool of the night, he will fold his sail close to his back, becoming sleek and streamlined.

I decorate my creature with stuff from around the lab. From the trash beside the soda machine, I salvage aluminum cans. I cut them into a colorful fringe that I attach beneath the creature's chin, like the dewlap of an iguana. When I am done, the words on the soda cans have been sliced to nonsense: Coke, Fanta, Sprite, and Dr. Pepper mingle in a collision of bright colors. At the very end, when the rest of the creature is complete and functional, I make a cock of copper tubing and pipe fittings. It dangles beneath his belly, copper bright and obscene-looking. Around the bright copper, I weave a rat's nest of my own hair, which is falling out by the handful. I like the look of that: bright copper peeking from a clump of wiry black curls.

Sometimes, the sickness overwhelms me. I spend part of one day in the ladies room off the lab, lying on the cool tile floor and rousing myself only to vomit into the toilet. The sickness is nothing that I didn't expect. I'm dying, after all. I lie on the floor and think about the peculiarities of biology.

For many male spiders, mating is a dangerous process. This is especially true in the spider species that weave intricate orb-shaped webs, the kind that catch the morning dew and sparkle so nicely for nature photographers. In these species, the female is larger than the male. She is, I must confess, rather a bitch; she'll attack anything that touches her web.

At mating time, the male proceeds cautiously. He lingers at the edge of the web, gently tugging on a thread of spider silk to get her attention. He plucks in a very specific rhythm, signaling to his would-be lover, whispering softly with his tugs: "I love you. I love you."

After a time, he believes that she has received his message. He feels confident that he has been understood. Still proceeding with caution, he attaches a mating line to the female's web. He plucks the mating line to encourage the female to move onto it. "Only you, baby," he signals. "You are the only one."

She climbs onto the mating line—fierce and passionate, but temporarily soothed by his promises. In that moment, he rushes to her, delivers his sperm, then quickly, before she can change her mind, takes a hike. A dangerous business, making love.

Before the world went away, I was a cautious person. I took great care in my choice of friends. I fled at the first sign of a misunderstanding. At the time, it seemed the right course.

I was a smart woman, a dangerous mate. (Odd—I find myself writing and thinking of myself in the past tense. So close to death that I consider myself already dead.) Men would approach with caution, delicately signaling from a distance: "I'm interested. Are you?" I didn't respond. I didn't really know how.

An only child, I was always wary of others. My mother and I lived together. When I was just a child, my father had left to pick up a pack of cigarettes and had never returned. My mother, protective and cautious by nature, warned me that men could not be trusted. People could not be trusted. She could trust me and I could trust her, and that was all.

When I was in college, my mother died of cancer. She had known of the tumor for more than a year; she had endured surgery and chemotherapy, while writing me cheery letters about her gardening. Her minister told me that my mother was a saint—she hadn't told me because she hadn't wanted to disturb my studies. I realized then that she had been wrong. I couldn't really trust her after all.

I think perhaps I missed some narrow window of opportunity. If, at some point along the way, I had had a friend or a lover who had made the effort to coax me from hiding, I could have been a different person. But it never happened. In high school, I sought the safety of my books. In college, I studied alone on Friday nights. By the time I reached graduate school, I was, like the pseudoscorpion, accustomed to a solitary life.

I work alone in the laboratory, building the female. She is larger than the male. Her teeth are longer and more numerous. I am welding the hip joints into place when my mother comes to visit me in the laboratory.

"Katie," she says, "Why didn't you ever fall in love? Why didn't you ever have children?"

I keep on welding, despite the trembling of my hands. I know she isn't there. Delirium is one symptom of radiation poisoning. But she keeps watching me as I work.

"You're not really here," I tell her, and realize immediately that talking to her is a mistake. I have acknowledged her presence and given her more power.

"Answer my questions, Katie," she says. "Why didn't you?"

I do not answer. I am busy and it will take too long to tell her about betrayal, to explain the confusion of a solitary insect confronted with a social situation, to describe the balance between fear and love. I ignore her just as

I ignore the trembling of my hands and the pain in my belly, and I keep on working. Eventually, she goes away.

I use the rest of the soda cans to give the female brightly colored scales: Coca-Cola red, Sprite green, Fanta orange. From soda cans, I make an oviduct, lined with metal. It is just large enough to accommodate the male's cock.

The male bowerbird attracts a mate by constructing a sort of art piece. From sticks and grasses, he builds two close-set parallel walls that join together to make an arch. He decorates this structure and the area around it with gaudy trinkets: bits of bone, green leaves, flowers, bright stones, and feathers cast off by gaudier birds. In areas where people have left their trash, he uses bottle caps and coins and fragments of broken glass.

He sits in his bower and sings, proclaiming his love for any and all females in the vicinity. At last, a female admires his bower, accepts his invitation, and they mate.

The bowerbird uses discrimination in decorating his bower. He chooses his trinkets with care—selecting a bit of glass for its glitter, a shiny leaf for its natural elegance, a cobalt-blue feather for a touch of color. What does he think about as he builds and decorates? What passes through his mind as he sits and sings, advertising his availability to the world?

I have released the male and I am working on the female when I hear rattling and crashing outside the building. Something is happening in the alley between the laboratory and the nearby office building. I go down to investigate. From the mouth of the alley, I peer inside, and the male creature runs at me, startling me so that I step back. He shakes his head and rattles his teeth threateningly.

I retreat to the far side of the street and watch him from there. He ventures from the alley, scuttling along the street, then pauses by a BMW that is parked at the curb. I hear his claws rattling against metal. A hubcap clangs as it hits the pavement. The creature carries the shiny piece of metal to the mouth of the alley and then returns for the other three, removing them one by one. When I move, he rushes toward the alley, blocking any attempt to invade his territory. When I stand still, he returns to his work, collecting the hubcaps, carrying them to the alley, and arranging them so that they catch the light of the sun.

As I watch, he scavenges in the gutter and collects things he finds appealing: a beer bottle, some colorful plastic wrappers from candy bars, a length of bright yellow plastic rope. He takes each find and disappears into the alley with it.

I wait, watching. When he has exhausted the gutter near the mouth of the alley, he ventures around the corner and I make my move, running to the alley entrance and looking inside. The alley floor is covered with colored bits of paper and plastic; I can see wrappers from candy bars and paper bags from Burger King and McDonalds. The yellow plastic rope is tied to a pipe running up one wall and a protruding hook on the other. Dangling from it, like clean clothes on the clothesline, are colorful pieces of fabric: a burgundy-colored bathtowel, a paisley-print bedspread, a blue satin bedsheet.

I see all this in a glance. Before I can examine the bower further, I hear the rattle of claws on pavement. The creature is running at me, furious at my intrusion. I turn and flee into the laboratory, slamming the door behind me. But once I am away from the alley, the creature does not pursue me.

From the second-story window, I watch him return to the alley and I suspect that he is checking to see if I have tampered with anything. After a time, he reappears in the alley mouth and crouches there, the sunlight glittering on his metal carapace.

In the laboratory, I build the future. Oh, maybe not—but there's no one here to contradict me, so I will say that it is so. I complete the female and release her.

The sickness takes over then. While I still have the strength, I drag a cot from a backroom and position it by the window, where I can look out and watch my creations.

What is it that I want from them? I don't know exactly.

I want to know that I have left something behind. I want to be sure that the world does not end with me. I want the feeling, the understanding, the certainty that the world will go on.

I wonder if the dying dinosaurs were glad to see the mammals, tiny rat-like creatures that rustled secretively in the underbrush.

When I was in seventh grade, all the girls had to watch a special presentation during gym class one spring afternoon. We dressed in our gym clothes, then sat in the auditorium and watched a film called "Becoming a Woman." The film talked about puberty and menstruation. The accompanying pictures showed the outline of a young girl. As the film progressed, she changed into a woman, developing breasts. The animation showed her uterus as it grew a lining, then shed it, then grew another. I remember watching with awe as the pictures showed the ovaries releasing an egg that united with a sperm, and then lodged in the uterus and grew into a baby.

The film must have delicately skirted any discussion of the source of the sperm, because I remember asking my mother where the sperm came from and how it got inside the woman. The question made her very uncomfortable. She muttered something about a man and woman being in love—as if love were somehow all that was needed for the sperm to find its way into the woman's body.

After that discussion, it seems to me that I was always a little confused about love and sex—even after I learned about the mechanics of sex and what goes where. The penis slips neatly into the vagina—but where does the love come in? Where does biology leave off and the higher emotions begin.

Does the female pseudoscorpion love the male when their dance is done? Does the male spider love his mate as he scurries away, running for his life? Is there love among the bowerbirds as they copulate in their bower? The textbooks fail to say. I speculate, but I have no way to get the answers.

My creatures engage in a long, slow courtship. I am getting sicker. Sometimes, my mother comes to ask me questions that I will not answer. Sometimes, men sit by my bed—but they are less real than my mother. These are men I cared about—men I thought I might love, though I never got beyond the thought. Through their translucent bodies, I can see the laboratory walls. They never were real, I think now.

Sometimes, in my delirium, I remember things. A dance back at college; I was slow-dancing, with someone's body pressed close to mine. The room was hot and stuffy and we went outside for some air. I remember he kissed me, while one hand stroked my breast and the other fumbled with the buttons of my blouse. I kept wondering if this was love—this fumbling in the shadows.

In my delirium, things change. I remember dancing in a circle with someone's hands clasping mine. My feet ache, and I try to stop, but my partner pulls me along, refusing to release me. My feet move instinctively in time with my partner's, though there is no music to help us keep the beat. The air smells of dampness and mold; I have lived my life underground and I am accustomed to these smells.

Is this love?

I spend my days lying by the window, watching through the dirty glass. From the mouth of the alley, he calls to her. I did not give him a voice, but he calls in his own way, rubbing his two front legs together so that metal rasps against metal, creaking like a cricket the size of a Buick.

She strolls past the alley mouth, ignoring him as he charges toward her, rattling his teeth. He backs away, as if inviting her to follow. She walks by. But then, a moment later, she strolls past again and the scene repeats itself. I understand that she is not really oblivious to his attention. She is simply taking her time, considering her situation. The male intensifies his efforts, tossing his head as he backs away, doing his best to call attention to the fine home he has created.

I listen to them at night. I cannot see them—the electricity failed two days ago and the streetlights are out. So I listen in the darkness, imagining. Metal legs rub together to make a high creaking noise. The sail on the male's back rattles as he unfolds it, then folds it, then unfolds it again, in what must be a sexual display. I hear a spiked tail rasping over a spiny back in a kind of caress. Teeth chatter against metal—love bites, perhaps. (The lion bites the lioness on the neck when they mate, an act of aggression that she accepts as affection.) Claws scrape against metal hide, clatter over metal scales. This, I think, is love. My creatures understand love.

I imagine a cock made of copper tubing and pipe fittings sliding into a canal lined with sheet metal from a soda can. I hear metal sliding over metal. And then my imagination fails. My construction made no provision for the stuff of reproduction: the sperm, the egg. Science failed me there. That part is up to the creatures themselves.

My body is giving out on me. I do not sleep at night; pain keeps me awake. I hurt everywhere, in my belly, in my breasts, in my bones. I have given up food. When I eat, the pains increase for a while, and then I vomit. I cannot keep anything down, and so I have stopped trying.

When the morning light comes, it is gray, filtering through the haze that covers the sky. I stare out the window, but I can't see the male. He has abandoned his post at the mouth of the alley. I watch for an hour or so, but the female does not stroll by. Have they finished with each other?

I watch from my bed for a few hours, the blanket wrapped around my shoulders. Sometimes, fever comes and I soak the blanket with my sweat. Sometimes, chills come, and I shiver under the blankets. Still, there is no movement in the alley.

It takes me more than an hour to make my way down the stairs. I can't trust my legs to support me, so I crawl on my knees, making my way across the room like a baby too young to stand upright. I carry the blanket with me, wrapped around my shoulders like a cape. At the top of the stairs, I rest, then I go down slowly, one step at a time.

The alley is deserted. The array of hubcaps glitters in the dim sunlight. The litter of bright papers looks forlorn and abandoned. I step cautiously into the entrance. If the male were to rush me now, I would not be able to run away. I have used all my reserves to travel this far.

The alley is quiet. I manage to get to my feet and shuffle forward through the papers. My eyes are clouded, and I can just make out the dangling bedspread halfway down the alley. I make my way to it. I don't know why I've come here. I suppose I want to see. I want to know what has happened. That's all.

I duck beneath the dangling bedspread. In the dim light, I can see a doorway in the brick wall. Something is hanging from the lintel of the door.

I approach cautiously. The object is gray, like the door behind it. It has a peculiar, spiraling shape. When I touch it, I can feel a faint vibration inside, like the humming of distant equipment. I lay my cheek against it and I can hear a low-pitched song, steady and even.

When I was a child, my family visited the beach and I spent hours exploring the tide pools. Among the clumps of blue-black mussels and the black turban snails, I found the egg casing of a horn shark in a tide pool. It was spiral-shaped, like this egg, and when I held it to the light, I could see a tiny embryo inside. As I watched, the embryo twitched, moving even though it was not yet truly alive.

I crouch at the back of the alley with my blanket wrapped around me. I see no reason to move—I can die here as well as I can die anywhere. I am watching over the egg, keeping it safe.

Sometimes, I dream of my past life. Perhaps I should have handled it differently. Perhaps I should have been less cautious, hurried out on the mating line, answered the song when a male called from his bower. But it doesn't matter now. All that is gone, behind us now.

My time is over. The dinosaurs and the humans—our time is over. New times are coming. New types of love. I dream of the future, and my dreams are filled with the rattle of metal claws.

LOVE AND SEX AMONG THE INVERTEBRATES

Alien Sex was the second half reprint/half original anthology I ever edited. It was one of the themes I came up for that ill-fated pitch. My agent started sending the proposal out and we both informally called it the "alien sex" anthology. She sent it to a young mainstream editor who was excited about it. The original title I had planned for the book was *Off Limits* but the editor loved loved loved *Alien Sex*, so that's what we went with.

There have been several foreign sales, but my favorite is the crazy-looking Italian version with cover and illustrations by cartoonist Milo Manaro.

"Love and Sex Among the Invertebrates" by Pat Murphy is an uplifting sf story about the end of the world. Really.

Overlooking

by Carol Emshwiller

(From *The Green Man: Tales From the Mythic Forest,* 2002)

If you want to hug a tree, here's the perfect place for it. They all belong to us, and we wouldn't bother, but we don't mind if *you* do it. There's no better ones than these to hug, stunted, weathered, half dead. They're more used to hardships than any of us so, good to hug them.

We're crepuscular. And grayish, which makes us hard to see. We're wide awake when you're tired.

You bring dogs to sniff us out, but we outwit them. If caught, which is rare, we lie about ourselves. We pretend we're *you.*

When it's cool we wear squirrel hats and jackets. From a distance, you think we're those wild furry people you keep talking about, but those wild people are of another sort entirely. But if you think we're them, all the better.

In certain spots, way up here, there are more of us than of you. You come in small groups or alone. It's *us* you're looking for. Sightings? If we want you to have them, then you'll have them.

But we watch *you*—follow you, here and there; set up blinds you think are piles of brush. We use your own field glasses. (You often lose them. When we come out to clean up after you, there they are. Sometimes cameras, too. We don't use those. How would we get film developed way out here? Though sometimes we play a joke on you and take pictures of each other and then leave the camera back where one of your kind will find it, develop it, and wonder: Who are these odd people making funny faces?)

We giggle when we see you, crunch, crunching around, your big feet on dry leaves, or slipping on wet moss. We giggle when you think you've caught a glimpse of us. *That's* not us.

Lately the woods are full of you—*and* tin cans *and* plastic water bottles, sunglasses… There's hardly a place to sit alone and contemplate anymore. And God forbid (your God) that we should stand, anymore, at the top of anything, silhouetted against the sky!

Don't think we don't have weapons. Silent ones, unlike yours. You don't know you're hit till you're hit, and you never know which direction it came from. Crossbow with darts. So silent, we can shoot and miss more times than several and *you* don't know you're being shot at until you're shot.

As to *your* weapons, we make sure our babies' first words are, "DON'T SHOOT."

I'm the mother. I don't mean really. I mean I'm the oldest and wisest. I lead my group around at an arthritic limp and everybody calls me Maaaaaaaah. I haven't had any other name since… I can't remember when. If I approve of something, then that's what happens.

When one of us gets hurt it's me they call. They know, by now, that I know about all there is to know around here.

In order to avoid *you*, we have nothing to do with the highest and therefore most popular mountains. What difference does it make, high or a little bit less high?

But we've captured one of you.

I was sitting here reading from your manuals about us. Most of the books insist we *do* exist. A few say maybe. Some say we don't. There are many of you who swear you've seen us and have pictures to prove it. They're lying and the pictures are fakes. Others write about how those people are crazy. We're like flying saucers, maybe yes, maybe no. Except it's not exactly us they write about. It's those others who live farther back. It's said those others are so cold they sleep with rattlesnakes to keep them warm. We don't believe that, anymore than we believe *we* don't exist.

You say we're seven feet tall and fuzzy. *That's* not us.

So I was sitting here in my favorite shady spot reading when they brought one of *you* in. An old man almost as old as my own old man got to be. I wondered why they'd bring a grown man up home this time of year. Our women are running around as if it was mating time. All because of this poor old man. It's the gang caught him. They'll do anything just to be different or to shake their elders up.

I like the old man's looks. Gray haired like us and nice and bony. Younger men are too baby-faced for my taste. I never liked that look even when I had a baby face myself. Such faces are all right for the young but softness of that sort is scary in a man when one must trust one's life to him. Mostly it's our men who keep *you* from us. They will sacrifice themselves if need be.

You can see on his face that this man can't figure out if we're us or his kind? I suppose we look odd. (*You* never look odd to us. We've seen you much too often.)

This man has the usual paraphernalia: camera, backpack, field glasses, big notebook full of notes and maps. He must be here on purpose. In his backpack, food, including three little easy-open cans of apricots. I sample one right away. Since I'm the maaaaaah, I have the right.

I ask the gang, "Why have you brought this one up here among us. If you don't know that's got to be the end of him, you should go down with the fathers and stay there."

"He knew."

"He didn't, but now he does."

"He did, too."

"There's nothing to know."

But then I see he's hurt. His arm hangs in an odd way and he's holding on to it.

"We didn't do that. He had that already."

I don't trust those young ones. They're at a bad age. Well, but they usually tell the truth.

"Bring him here and hold him down."

(Up this close those young ones smell bad. It's a sign of maturing.)

I put my foot in the man's armpit, grab his wrist and pull and twist and pop his shoulder back in place. I bandage him so it won't move.

If he didn't look good to me, I wouldn't have... Well, yes, good looking or not I would have. Would I do less for a wounded turkey vulture than for this man? I nursed a vulture all spring. Everybody knows that.

I give this man broth. I don't tell him what's in it. We know *you* better than you know us. Best he not know. To him it'll taste as buttery as snails.

"I'm Maaaaah," I say.

Right after, when he says his name, I don't listen. Why know a thing like that when...well...

I've been inside your cabins lots of times—even when you were there. Sometimes, as I walked right past you, I could hardly keep from laughing out loud at how you didn't even know I was in your shadows. I made myself peanut butter sandwiches. I drank your milk. There was one particular cabin—large for a summer house. It was all woody inside. Smelled of cedar and pine. Big wood pile outside... (You never miss what wood we take.) Usually your cabins have chandeliers made from wagon wheels and horse shoes, but here there was a cut glass chandelier, small though, in the cabinet, tea cups with gold on them, on the table, silver candlestick holders. I really did want one of those. Each held three candles and had silver leaves all up and down it. I went up to our home and thought about it for a couple of days, and then I came back down and took one. After all, there were four. After all I'm the maaaah.

I could have made this man soup from *your* supplies because, once your campers get started, you don't realize how heavy your packs are and how tired you'll be, and how you'll lose your appetite because of altitude. You hide things along the trail that you think to pick up on the way home. We watch from our watching spots, thinking: Ha, ha, you'll search and search and wonder how you could have forgotten so soon and only a couple of days later. You even wrote where you hid it in your little book on flowers or the little one on birds or the little book where you write about this trip you're taking right now, and you still can't find that food.

(Why do you leave your food so as to cut down on the weight and not your books? More often we find glasses and cameras than we find those little nature books or your note books.)

By now this man will be wondering, where are those furry ones? You're *always* getting us mixed up with them.

I say, "I can take you where you want to go."

But he has to rest up a bit first so I can still sit here in my shade listening to the ravens. It's the stone that doesn't roll, that sits as I do, that gathers moss. That accounts for my greenish tinge.

I say, "You can catch a glimpse of them."

Now look at this. Already he's clumping around, snooping, peering but seeing nothing, standing right on our vegetables. Of course our gardens don't look like gardens to *you*, they just look like the normal forest floor. (Our walls look like just more greenery or random piles of sticks. You walk right through them. This man already has done it several times.)

But our rattlesnake is waiting there, in the garden.

I should have listened when that man said his name. I hadn't thought there'd be any need to call him.

I say, "I'll go with you and lead the way."

(I'll go with him even though the gang thinks he's theirs.)

This year those young ones won't wear hats. Even in the rain. (They chew your used up gum. Smoke your cigarette butts. They want to try everything.)

I do love that gang. I love the overgrown, the clumsy and wild and insecure and smelly. Or, on the other hand, I love the stunted, the dry, the half dead. This old man has eyes as gray as shadowy water.

What attracted me right away were his stringy muscles, the hair on his arm, that wispy mustache, mostly white. What attracted me was how he laughed when he tried on our hats.

There has to be a reason why he came. What if he's tired of being one of *you* all the time and would rather be *us?*

Helicopters come, flying low. They keep searching back and forth. They're noisy. Even the noisy gang doesn't like it. Even this man doesn't like it. If he wanted to, he could show himself and get himself rescued. I couldn't stop him.

The gang goes out and cavorts around in plain sight. We're as pale as the slate-like fragments of limestone we sit on. We wear cobwebs. They make us wispy and dim. We can disappear right before your eyes.

Since the man isn't showing himself, he might as well look out over those fuzzy others in their habitat.

"In situ," I say. "Just look over, don't go down. You have to promise not to."

I give him a lesson for the journey as I've already done, and many times, to the gang. "Some mosses you can eat, and some pine needles. You can eat the roots of Solomon seal if you don't mind a little—quite a bit, that is, of grit. You can eat ants. You can roll in dust as a sun screen or plaster on mud."

He's taking more notes. (I *do* love the way all of you cling to your notes and your bird books.)

Overlooking

When I was young I once showed myself right in the middle of the trail. I just stood there, all greenish and gray. It was to one of you about my own age, climbing up, geologist's hammer hanging on his belt. I liked his looks though I couldn't see much under his hat. Well, I liked his *legs*, strong and brown and covered with curly golden hairs.

I stood in a spot where the sun streamed, one of those shiny golden streaks, down, just on me. I wanted to be his vision of a forest nymph of some sort, and that he'd never forget me, but he looked at me, staring so, that I got scared and and skipped away, not as gracefully as I'd hoped. It turns out I'm the one has the memory forever. That man might have been this man right here.

✲

There was an episode in a cabin, I the succubus. It was dark but not completely. There was a moon, gibbous of course. I'm not sure who the man was but it might have been this one. (I caught a glimpse of legs with curly hair.) I was no more than a shadow in a shadow, but I was hoping there was a glistening around my edges.

At first he didn't want to but I don't think he was frightened. He resisted. Just in case, I had feathers in my hair-do and a bag of wild strawberries. I whispered things. I sucked.

Then after twisting about a bit, one position and another, I lay under, as a succubus should.

Once he got started, I lost count of how many times. After all, he was a mountain climber and in perfect shape as all those who come here usually are. I felt he loved me. Too bad I hadn't seen his face, neither then nor on the trail in the shadow of his hat.

Misty or Dandy, I forget which, could be his own son.

✲

We begin the journey to the looking-over site.

I flit and flutter, slither and slide. My old man used to say I was like a humming bird or a butterfly. I wonder if this old man can see that? We always think of you as not noticing much.

He takes my picture.

He says, "I've always believed in you creatures. When I looked out the windows of my cabin, I saw shapes dancing. I locked my doors, even so I saw, in the corners, shadows that seemed on top of shadows. Now and then I missed a package of frozen green beans." (Maybe *I* took those beans.)

Flit and flutter, skip and slide and so forth... I wanted to be, "shrouded in mystery," as you always say we are, but I was thinking too much about how I looked flitting. I'm the one who stumbles. I had not thought such a thing would ever happen. *You're* usually the ones who fall. I scrape myself, top to bottom. I hurt my good leg. I tear my grays.

That man picks me up. His arm, my leg... We'll have to help each other. At least it's *my* forest.

So, and with many hardships along the way, including the aforementioned, having climbed up and over from one valley to the next, having slept in a hollow with leaves over us, having chewed on wintergreen, having eaten whole meals of nothing but chanterelles, we arrive at the looking over point.

I dress him in a stick hat and a few vines. He'll look like that candelabra of mine (or perhaps it's his), leaves all up and down him. He gets his camera ready and we enter the blind. I push a peep hole for him and one for myself, and we look down on the fuzzy ones' habitat.

Cottages of stone and wood, gardens with little flags to label the vegetables, bird baths, goldfish ponds, here and there a ceramic rabbit. There's an iron deer.

I say, "There's a deer," and, "Here they are, the furry ones. Don't they look nice, all glittery in their golden coats?"

Except they're not there. He'll think I made this all up.

I say, "Their little ones are *so* cute."

He's got his field glasses out now. He says, "Where? Where?"

"You can't see it from here, but their eyes are green."

Why am I saying all this, *I'm* the romantic notion. *I'm* the hope. *I'm* the story. He's been writing me down everyday. We're the wish-you-existed-after-all people.

I think he's going to go on down even though he promised not to. I don't think I'm strong enough to keep him from it.

I say, "We're as important to the forest as these fuzzy ones. If we weren't here some other creature would have to take our place. Put that in your notebook."

But he's going on down.

Of course the gang has followed us. There's not a place they don't roam (or anybody they don't follow), outskirts of towns, back yards, mountain tops… Those young ones not only won't wear hats. This year they expose their navels. They cut cute little three inch holes in their shirts. Where did that idea come from? As if it has to come from anywhere. Those young ones think all sorts of things. But it could be worse.

We try to keep them out of danger, but they don't listen. I used to be that way myself. They're at an age when they're easily mortified. Just as I used to be, and they never apologize.

However it's when your little kids get lost in the woods, that our young ones show their best side. First they take them by the hand and lead them to a place full of flowers. Then they feed them berries. After that they take them to where *you* can find them and they sit with them until you do. Or, if you don't come, they bring them home to us.

He says, "Well, where are they?"

I say, "But it's *you*, the mysterious ones and don't even realize it. Perhaps it's even *you*, the ones important to the trees. You hug them and kiss them. You sit in the tops to protect them. Sit sometimes for *months*. What could be more like us than what *you* do?"

But he's crawled out of the blind. He's standing up in plain sight, field glasses at his eyes, camera dangling.

"Why don't you sit and contemplate for a few minutes. Give them time to manifest themselves. There's one now. Over to the right, half way behind the rose bush." (There isn't.)

I could have sneaked away and gone down there myself in one of our fur suits, but I forgot to bring one.

I have my cross bow and a dozen darts. I told him the dangers are few, but one never knows. I said, "No harm in being ready."

We always aim for the lower leg.

Then, there they are at last, the fuzzies! A dozen. Of course it's our young ones. I can practically see who's which by the way they cavort. Dandy, the thinnest and oldest, doing his usual leaps over hedges. They're doing everything right, climbing fruit trees, digging in the marigolds…

Except my finger's on the release already. There'll be just a little swishing sound. I let go right where I aimed, into the big muscle of the lower leg. Those darts are small and sharp. At first he doesn't know what happened and then he's on the ground. Not so much because of pain. *Yet.* But because his leg gave way. He thinks it collapsed by itself.

It's too bad, but I don't think he even had a chance to take one single picture of the furry ones. (Nobody would have believed the pictures anyway.)

Does he realize I'm the one who shot him?

I throw the bow into the brush. Best to pretend I don't know he's shot.

There's no blood. There never is.

He's examining his calf. He's going to pull the dart out.

"Don't do that!…till I get my bandages ready."

He won't be able to go much of anywhere, especially not in a hurry.

Overlooking

Those young ones finally realize what's happened. They come up to us, still wearing their fur suits. Dandy is the first to get up here. He's more or less the leader. I suppose exposed belly buttons was his idea.

Oh, for Heaven's sake, they've even done that to their fur suits—cut little holes. They love to take chances.

I say, "He got shot."

"We didn't do that." They all say it, practically in unison.

"Well… I suppose not."

It's *so* easy to put the blame on them. They expect it, too. All I have to do is keep my mouth shut.

"Make one of those little stick stools. Four of you to carry him and two can help me. Then, when we get to the edge, you know what to do."

And they do it. Showing their navels and all. And with clicks and clucks and lots of giggling. They don't even realize, but when have young ones ever?

There's this longing in you. *All* of you. Even if you were sure we didn't exist you'd still hope. We intend to live so as to fullfull *your* dreams and expectations—be of some worth to those of *your* ilk. Who would there be to sneak and follow? Come upon you suddenly. Who would live at the corners of your lives? Who would there be to be us if not us?

You stop and listen. *All* of you do. Every snap and rustle has a meaning. You look. You turn around fast to see what's behind you.

You want to believe in us and we… *I*, especially, want to be believed in. It's always been my main goal.

That man went over with his field glasses and camera and notes and birding book and tree book, even one left-over can of apricots.

I wish I knew which cabin used to be his.

I wish I knew his name. I should have listened when he said it.

I wanted to keep him but of course that was never possible.

Well, at least we didn't break any of our own rules. At least I don't have to know what happened. I mean, not *exactly*.

OVERLOOKING

The Green Man: Tales From the Mythic Forest, published in 2002, was the first of Terri Windling and my "mythic tale" young adult anthology series (although we didn't know it would be a series at the time). Charles Vess did the cover and provided spot illustrations for each story, creating a gorgeous package.

It won the World Fantasy Award.

Carol Emshwiller's agent sent me a few of Carol's stories when I was at *Omni*, but the first few weren't fantastical enough so I turned them down. Finally, in 1987 I bought one, "The Circular Library of Stones," bought three more for *Omni*, several for SCIFICTION, and more for the "mythic" series. One of those stories is "Overlooking," from *The Green Man*.

Sonny Liston Takes the Fall

by Elizabeth Bear

(From *The Del Rey Book of Science Fiction and Fantasy,* 2008)

1.

66 **I** **gotta** tell you, Jackie," Sonny Liston said, "I lied to my wife about that. I gotta tell you, I took that fall."

It was Christmas eve, 1970, and Sonny Liston was about the furthest thing you could imagine from a handsome man. He had a furrowed brow and downcast hound dog prisoner eyes that wouldn't meet mine, and the matching furrows on either side of his broad, flat nose ran down to a broad, flat mouth under a pencil thin moustache that was already out of fashion six years ago, when he was still King of the World.

"We all lie sometimes, Sonny," I said, pouring him another scotch. We don't mind if you drink too much in Vegas. We don't mind much of anything at all. "It doesn't signify."

He had what you call a tremendous physical presence, Sonny Liston. He filled up a room so you couldn't take your eyes off him—didn't *want* to take your eyes off him, and if he was smiling you were smiling, and if he was scowling you were shivering—even when he was sitting quietly, the way he was now, turned away from his kitchen table and his elbows on his knees, one hand big enough for a man twice his size wrapped around the glass I handed him and the other hanging between his legs, limp across the back of the wrist as if the tendons'd been cut. His suit wasn't long enough for the length of his arms. The coat sleeves and the shirt sleeves with their French cuffs and discreet cufflinks were ridden halfway up his forearms, showing wrists I couldn't have wrapped my fingers around. Tall as he was, he wasn't tall enough for that frame—as if he didn't get enough to eat as a kid—but he was that wide.

Sonny Liston, he was from Arkansas. And you would hear it in his voice, even now. He drank that J&B scotch like knocking back a blender full of raw eggs and held the squat glass out for more. "I could of beat Cassius Clay if it weren't for the fucking Mob," he said, while I filled it up again. "I could of beat that goddamn flashy pansy."

"I know you could, Sonny," I told him, and it wasn't a lie. "I know you could."

His hands were like mallets, like mauls, like the paws of the bear they styled him. It didn't matter.

He was a broken man, Sonny Liston. He wouldn't meet your eyes, not that he ever would have. You learn that in prison. You learn that from a father who beats you. You learn that when you're black in America.

You keep your eyes down, and maybe there won't be trouble this time.

2.

It's the same thing with fighters as with horses. Race horses, I mean, thoroughbreds, which I know a lot about. I'm the genius of Las Vegas, you see. The One-Eyed Jack, the guardian and the warden of Sin City.

It's a bit like being a magician who works with tigers—the city is my life, and I take care of it. But that means it's my job to make damned sure it doesn't get out and eat anybody.

And because of that, I also know a little about magic and sport and sacrifice, and the real, old blood truth of the laurel crown and what it means to be King for a Day.

The thing about race horses, is that the trick with the good ones isn't getting them to run. It's getting them to *stop*.

They'll kill themselves running, the good ones. They'll run on broken hearts, broken legs, broken wind. Legend says Black Gold finished his last race with nothing but a shipping bandage holding his flopping hoof to his leg. They shot him on the track, Black Gold, the way they did in those days. And it was mercy when they did it.

He was King, and he was claimed. He went to pay the tithe that only greatness pays.

Ruffian, perhaps the best filly that ever ran, shattered herself in a match race that was meant to prove she could have won the Kentucky Derby if she'd raced in it. The great colt Swale ran with a hole in his heart, and no one ever knew until it killed him in the paddock one fine summer day in the third year of his life.

And then there's Charismatic.

Charismatic was a Triple Crown contender until he finished his Belmont third, running on a collapsed leg, with his jockey Chris Antley all but kneeling on the reins, doing anything to drag him down.

Antley left the saddle as soon as his mount saw the wire and could be slowed. He dove over Charismatic's shoulder and got underneath him before the horse had stopped moving; he held the broken Charismatic up with his shoulders and his own two hands until the veterinarians arrived. Between Antley and the surgeons, they saved the colt. Because Antley took that fall.

Nobody could save Antley, who was dead himself within two years from a drug overdose. He died so hard that investigators first called it a homicide.

When you run with all God gave you, you run out of track goddamned fast.

3.

Sonny was just like that. Just like a race horse. Just like every other goddamned fighter. A little bit crazy, a little bit fierce, a little bit desperate, and ignorant of the concept of defeat under any circumstances.

Until he met Cassius Clay in the ring.

They fought twice. First time was in 1964, and I watched that fight live in a movie theatre. We didn't have pay-per-view then, and the fight happened in Florida, not here at home in Vegas.

I remember it real well, though.

Liston was a monster, you have to understand. He wasn't real big for a fighter, only six foot one, but he *hulked*. He *loomed*. His opponents would flinch away before he ever pulled back a punch.

I've met Mike Tyson too, who gets compared to Liston. And I don't think it's just because they're both hard men, or that Liston also was accused of sexual assault. It's because Tyson has that same thing, the power of personal gravity that bends the available light and every eye down to him, even when he's walking quietly through a crowded room, wearing a warm-up jacket and a smile.

So that was Liston. He was a stone golem, a thing out of legend, the fucking bogeyman. He was going to walk through Clay like the Kool-Aid pitcher walking through a paper wall.

And we were all in our seats, waiting to see this insolent prince beat down by the barbarian king.

And there was a moment when Clay stepped up to Liston, and they touched gloves, and the whole theatre went still.

Because Clay was just as big as Liston. And Clay wasn't looking down.

Liston retired in the seventh round. Maybe he had a dislocated shoulder, and maybe he didn't, and maybe the Mob told him to throw the fight so they could bet on the underdog Clay and Liston just couldn't quite make himself fall over and play dead.

And Cassius Clay, you see, he grew up to be Muhammad Ali.

4.

Sonny didn't tell me about *that* fight. He told me about the other one.

Phil Ochs wrote a song about it, and so did Mark Knopfler: that legendary fight in 1965, the one where, in the very first minute of the very first round, Sonny Liston took a fall.

Popular poets, Ochs and Knopfler, and what do you think the bards were? That kind of magic, the old dark magic that soaks down the roots of the world and keeps it rich, it's a transformative magic. It never goes away.

However you spill it, it's blood that makes the cactus grow.

Ochs, just to interject a little more irony here, paid for his power in *his* own blood as well.

5.

Twenty-fifth child of twenty-six, Sonny Liston. A tenant farmer's son, whose father beat him bloody. He never would meet my eye, even there in his room, *this* close to Christmas, near the cold bent stub end of 1970.

He never would meet a white man's eyes. Even the eye of the One-Eyed Jack, patron saint of Las Vegas, when Jackie was pouring him J&B. Not a grown man's eye, anyway, though he loved kids—and kids loved him. The bear was a teddy bear when you got him around children.

But he told me all about that fight. How the Mob told him to throw it or they'd kill him and his Momma and a selection of his brothers and sisters too. How he did what they told him in the most defiant manner possible. So the whole fucking world would know he took that fall.

The thing is, I didn't believe him.

I sat there and nodded and listened, and I thought, Sonny Liston didn't throw that fight. That famous "Phantom Punch"? Mohammad Ali got lucky. Hit a nerve cluster or something. Sonny Liston, the unstoppable Sonny Liston, the man with a heart of piston steel and a hand like John Henry's hammer—Sonny Liston, he went down. It was a fluke, a freak thing, some kind of an accident.

I thought going down like that shamed him, so he told his wife he gave up because he knew Ali was better and he didn't feel like fighting just to get beat. But he told *me* that other story, about the mob, and he drank another scotch and he toasted Muhammad Ali, though Sonny'd kind of hated him. Ali had been barred from fighting from 1967 until just that last year, and was facing a jail term because he wouldn't go and die in Vietnam.

Sensible man, if you happen to ask me.

But I knew Sonny didn't throw that fight for the Mob. I knew because I also knew this other thing about that fight, because I am the soul of Las Vegas, and in 1965, the Mob *was* Las Vegas.

And I knew they'd had a few words with Sonny before he went into the ring.

Sonny Liston was supposed to win. And Muhammad Ali was supposed to die.

6.

The one thing in his life that Sonny Liston could never hit back against was his daddy. Sonny, whose given name was Charles, but who called himself Sonny all his adult life.

Sonny had learned the hard way that you never look a white man in the eye. That you never look *any* man in the eye unless you mean to beat him down. That you never look *the Man* in the eye, because if you do *he's* gonna beat *you* down.

He did his time in jail, Sonny Liston. He went in a boy and he came out a prize fighter, and when he came out he was owned by the Mob.

You can see it in the photos and you could see it in his face, when you met him, when you reached out to touch his hand; he almost never smiled, and his eyes always held this kind of deep sonorous seriousness over his black, flat, damaged nose.

Sonny Liston was a jailbird. Sonny Liston belonged to the Mob the same way his daddy belonged to the land.

Cassius Clay, God bless him, changed his slave name two days after that first bout with Sonny, as if winning it freed up something in him. Muhammad Ali, God bless him, never learned that lesson about looking down.

7.

Boxing is called the sweet science. And horse racing is the sport of kings.

When Clay beat Liston, he bounced up on his stool and shouted that he was King of the World. Corn king, summer king, America's most beautiful young man. An angel in the boxing ring. A new and powerful image of black manhood.

He stepped up on that stool in 1964 and he put a noose around his neck.

The thing about magic is that it happens in spite of everything you can do to stop it.

And the wild old Gods will have their sacrifice.

No excuses.

If they can't have Charismatic, they'll take the man that saved him.

So it goes.

8.

Sometimes it's easier to tell yourself you quit than to admit that they beat you. Sometimes it's easier to look down.

The civil rights movement in the early 1960s found Liston a thug and an embarrassment. He was a jailbird, an illiterate, a dark unstoppable monster. The rumor was that he had a second career as a standover man—a mob enforcer. The NAACP protested when Floyd Patterson agreed to fight him in 1962.

9.

Sonny didn't know his own birthday or maybe he lied about his age. Forty's old for a fighter, and Sonny said he was born in '32 when he was might have been born as early as '27. There's a big damned difference between thirty-two and thirty-seven in the boxing ring.

And there's another thing, something about prize fighters you might not know. In Liston's day, they shot the fighters' hands full of anesthetic before they wrapped them for the fight. So a guy who was a hitter—a *puncher* rather than a *boxer*, in the parlance—he could pound away on his opponent and never notice he'd broken all the goddamned bones in his goddamned hands.

Sonny Liston was a puncher. Muhammad Ali was a boxer.

Neither one of them, as it happens, could abide the needles. So when they went swinging into the ring, they earned every punch they threw.

Smack a sheetrock wall a couple of dozen times with your shoulder behind it if you want to build up a concept of what that means, in terms of endurance and of pain. Me? I would have taken the needle over *feeling* the bones I was breaking. Taken it in a heartbeat.

But Charismatic finished his race on a shattered leg, and so did Black Gold. What the hell were a few broken bones to Sonny Liston?

10.

You know when I said Sonny was not a handsome man? Well, I also said Muhammad Ali was an angel. He was a black man's angel, an avenging angel, a messenger from a better future. He was the *way* and the *path*, man, and they marked him for sacrifice, because he was a warrior god, a Black Muslim Moses come to lead his people out of Egypt land.

And the people in power like to stay that way, and they have their ways of making it happen. Of making sure the sacrifice gets chosen.

Go ahead and curl your lip. White man born in the nineteenth century, reborn in 1905 as the Genius of the Mississippi of the West. What do I know about the black experience?

I am my city, and I contain multitudes. I'm the African-American airmen at Nellis Air Force Base, and I'm the black neighborhoods near D Street that can't keep a supermarket, and I'm Cartier Street and I'm Northtown and I'm Las Vegas, baby, and it doesn't matter a bit what you see when you look at my face.

Because Sonny Liston died here, and he's buried here in the palm of my hand. And I'm Sonny Liston too, wronged and wronging; he's in here, boiling and bubbling away.

11.

I filled his glass one more time and splashed what was left into my own, and that was the end of the bottle. I twisted it to make the last drop fall. Sonny watched my hands instead of my eyes, and folded his own enormous fists around his glass so it vanished. "You're here on business, Jackie," he said, and dropped his eyes to his knuckles. "Nobody wants to listen to me talk."

"I want to listen, Sonny." The scotch didn't taste so good, but I rolled it over my tongue anyway. I'd drunk enough that the roof of my mouth was getting dry, and the liquor helped a little. "I'm here to listen as long as you want to talk."

His shoulders always had a hunch. He didn't stand up tall. They hunched a bit more as he turned the glass in his hands. "I guess I run out of things to say. So you might as well tell me what you came for."

At Christmastime in 1970, Muhammad Ali—recently allowed back in the ring, pending his appeal of a draft evasion conviction—was preparing for a title bout against Joe Frazier in March. He was also preparing for a more wide-reaching conflict; in April of that year, his appeal, his demand to be granted status as a conscientious objector, was to go before the United States Supreme Court.

He faced a five-year prison sentence.

In jail, he'd come up against everything Sonny Liston had. And maybe Ali was the stronger man. And maybe the young king wouldn't break where the old one fell. Or maybe he wouldn't make it out of prison alive, or free.

"Ali needs your help," I said.

"Fuck Cassius Clay," he said.

Sonny finished his drink and spent a while staring at the bottom of his glass. I waited until he turned his head, skimming his eyes along the floor, and tried to sip again from the empty glass. Then I cleared my throat and said, "It isn't just for him."

Sonny flinched. See, the thing about Sonny—that he never learned to read, that doesn't mean he was *dumb*. "The NAACP don't want me. The Nation of Islam don't want me. They didn't even want Clay to box me. I'm *an embarrassment to the black man.*"

He dropped his glass on the table and held his breath for a moment before he shrugged and said, "Well, they got their nigger now."

Some of them know up front; they listen to the whispers, and they know the price they might have to pay if it's their number that comes up. Some just kind of know in the back of their heads. About the corn king, and the laurel wreath, and the price that sometimes has to be paid.

Sonny Liston, like I said, he wasn't dumb.

"Ali can do something you can't, Sonny." *Ali can be a symbol.*

"I can't have it," he drawled. "But I can buy it? Is that what you're telling me, Jack?"

I finished my glass too, already drunk enough that it didn't make my sinuses sting. "Sonny," I said, with that last bit of Dutch courage in me, "you're gonna have to take another fall."

12.

When his wife—returning from a holiday visit to her relatives—found his body on January fifth, eleven days after I poured him that drink, maybe a week or so after he died, Sonny had needle marks in the crook of his arm, though the coroner's report said *heart failure.*

Can you think of a worse way to kill the man?

13.

On March 8, 1971, a publicly reviled Muhammad Ali was defeated by Joe Frazier at Madison Square Garden in New York City in a boxing match billed as the "Fight of the Century." Ali had been vilified in the press as a Black Muslim, a religious and political radical, a black man who wouldn't look down.

Three months later, the United States Supreme Court overturned the conviction, allowing Muhammad Ali's conscientious objector status to stand.

He was a free man.

Ali fought Frazier twice more. He won both times, and went on to become the most respected fighter in the history of the sport. A beautiful avenging outspoken angel.

Almost thirty-five years after Sonny Liston died, in November of 2005, President George W. Bush awarded America's highest civilian honor, the Presidential Medal of Freedom, to the draft-dodging, politically activist lay preacher Muhammad Ali.

14.

Sonny Liston never looked a man in the eye unless he meant to beat him down. Until he looked upon Cassius Clay and hated him. And looked past that hate and saw a dawning angel, and he saw the future, and he wanted it that bad.

Wanted it bad, Sonny Liston, illiterate jailbird and fighter and standover man. Sonny Liston the drunk, the sex offender. Broken, brutal Sonny Liston with the scars on his face from St. Louis cops beating a confession from him, with the scars on his back from his daddy beating him down on the farm.

Sonny Liston, who loved children. He wanted that thing, and he knew it could never be his.

Wanted it and saw a way to make it happen for somebody else.

15.

And so he takes that fall, Sonny Liston. Again and again and again, like John Henry driving steel until his heart burst, like a jockey rolling over the shoulder of a running, broken horse. He takes the fall, and he saves the King.

And Muhammad Ali? He never once looks down.

SONNY LISTON TAKES THE FALL

Elizabeth Bear wrote the marvelous "Sonny Liston Takes the Fall" for *The Del Rey Book of Science Fiction and Fantasy*. It's unlike anything else I had read, or have read by her.

Technicolor

by John Langan

(From Poe: *19 New Tales of Suspense, Dark Fantasy and Horror,* 2009)

Come on, say it out loud with me: "And Darkness and Decay and the Red Death held illimitable dominion over all." Look at that sentence. Who says Edgar Allan Poe was a lousy stylist? Thirteen words—good number for a horror story, right? Although it's not so much a story as a masque. Yes, it's about a masque, but it is a masque, too. Of course, you all know what a masque is. If you didn't, you looked it up in your dictionaries, because that's what you do in a senior seminar. Anyone?

No, not a play, not exactly. Yes? Good, okay, "masquerade" is one sense of the word, a ball whose guests attend in costume. Anyone else?

Yes, very nice, nicely put. The masque does begin in the sixteenth century. It's the entertainment of the elite, and originally, it's a combination of pantomime and dance. Pantomime? Right—think "mime." The idea is to perform without words, gesturally, to let the movements of your body tell the story. You do that, and you dance, and there's your show. Later on, there's dialogue and other additions, but I think it's this older sense of the word the story intends. Remember that tall, silent figure at the end.

I'm sorry? Yes, good point. The two kinds of masque converge.

Back to that sentence, though. Twenty-two syllables that break almost perfectly in half, ten and twelve, "And Darkness and Decay and the Red Death" and "held illimitable dominion over all." A group of short words, one and two syllables each, takes you through the first part of the sentence, then they give way to these long, almost luxurious words, "illimitable dominion." The rhythm—you see how complex it is? You ride along on these short words, bouncing up and down, alliterating from one "d" to the next, and suddenly you're mired in those Latinate polysyllables. All the momentum goes out of your reading; there's just enough time for the final pair of words, which are short, which is good, and you're done.

Wait, just let me—no, all right, what was it you wanted to say?

Exactly, yes, you took the words out of my mouth. The sentence does what the story does, carries you along through the revelry until you run smack-dab into that tall figure in the funeral clothes. Great job.

One more observation about the sentence, then I promise it's on to the story itself. I know you want to talk about Prospero's castle, all those colored rooms. Before we do, however, the four "d"'s. We've mentioned already, there are a lot of "d" sounds in these thirteen words. They thread through the line, help tie it together. They also draw our attention to four words in particular. The first three are easy to recognize: they're capitalized, as well. Darkness, Decay, Death. The fourth? Right, dominion. Anyone want to take a stab at why they're capitalized?

Yes? Well…okay, sure it makes them into proper nouns. Can you take that a step farther? What kind of proper nouns does it make them? What's happened to the Red Death in the story? It's gone from an infection you can't see to a tall figure wandering around the party. Personification, good. Darkness, Decay, (the Red) Death: the sentence personifies them; they're its trinity, its unholy trinity, so to speak. And this godhead holds dominion, what the dictionary defines as "sovereign authority" over all. Not only the prince's castle, not only the world of the story, but all, you and me.

In fact, in a weird sort of way, this is the story of the incarnation of one of the persons of this awful trinity.

All right, moving on, now. How about those rooms? Actually, how about the building those rooms are in, first? I've been calling it a castle, but it isn't, is it? It's "castellated," which is to say, castle-like, but it's an abbey, a monastery. I suppose it makes sense to want to wait out the Red Death in a place like an abbey. After all, it's both removed from the rest of society and well-fortified. And we shouldn't be too hard on the prince and his followers for retreating there. It's not the first time this has happened, in literature or life. Anyone read *The Decameron?* Boccaccio? It's a collection of one hundred stories told by ten people, five women and five men, who have sequestered themselves in, I'm pretty sure it's a convent, to wait out the plague ravaging Florence. The Black Death, that one.

If you consider that the place in which we find the seven rooms is a monastery, a place where men are supposed to withdraw from this world to meditate on the next, its rooms appear even stranger. What's the set-up? Seven rooms, yes, thank you, I believe I just said that. Running east to west, good. In a straight line? No. There's a sharp turn every twenty or thirty yards, so that you can see only one room at a time. So long as they follow that east to west course, you can lay the rooms out in any form you like. I favor steps, like the ones that lead the condemned man to the chopping block, but that's just me.

Hang on, hang on, we'll get to the colors in a second. We need to stay with the design of the rooms for a little longer. Not everybody gets this the first time through. There are a pair of windows, Gothic windows, which means what? That they're long and pointed at the top. The windows are opposite one another, and they look out on, anybody? Not exactly: a chandelier hangs down from the ceiling. It is a kind of light, though. No, a candelabra holds candles. Anyone else? A brazier, yes, there's a brazier sitting on a tripod outside either window. They're, how would you describe a brazier? Like a big metal cup, a bowl, that you fill with some kind of fuel and ignite. Wood, charcoal, oil. To be honest, I'm not as interested in the braziers as I am in where they're located. Outside the windows, right, but where outside the windows? Maybe I should say, What is outside the windows? Corridors, yes, there are corridors to either side of the rooms, and it's along these that the braziers are stationed. Just like our classroom. Not the tripods, of course, and I guess what's outside our windows is more a gallery than a corridor, since it's open to the parking lot on the other side. All right, all right, so I'm stretching a bit, here, but have you noticed, the room has seven windows? One for each color in Prospero's Abbey. Go ahead, count them.

So here we are in this strange abbey, one that has a crazy zig-zag suite of rooms with corridors running beside them. You could chalk the location's details up to anti-Catholic sentiment; there are critics who have argued that anti-Catholic prejudice is the secret engine driving Gothic literature. No, I don't buy it, not in this case. Sure, there are stained-glass windows, but they're basically tinted glass. There's none of the iconography you'd expect if this were anti-Catholic propaganda, no statues or paintings. All we have is that enormous clock in the last room, the mother of all grandfather clocks. Wait a minute…

What about those colors, then? Each of the seven rooms is decorated in a single color that matches the stained glass of its windows. From east to west, we go from blue to purple to green to orange to white to violet to—to the last room, where there's a slight change. The windows are red, but the room itself is done in black. There seems to be some significance to the color sequence, but what that is—well, this is why we have literature professors, right? (No snickering.) Not to mention, literature students. I've read through your responses to the homework assignment, and there were a few interesting ideas as to what those colors might mean. Of course, most of you connected them to times of the day, blue as dawn, black as night, the colors in between morning, noon, early afternoon, that kind of thing. Given the east-west layout, it makes a certain amount of sense. A few more of you picked up on that connection to time in a slightly different way, and related the colors to times of the year, or the stages in a person's life. In the process, some clever arguments were made. Clever, but not, I'm afraid, too convincing.

What! What's wrong! What is it! Are you all—oh, them. Oh for God's sake. When you screamed like that, I thought—I don't know what I thought. I thought I'd need a new pair of trousers. Those are a couple of graduate students I've enlisted to help me with a little presentation I'll be putting up shortly. Yes, I can understand how the masks could startle you. They're just generic white masks; I think they found them downtown somewhere. It was their idea: once I told them what story we would be discussing, they immediately hit on wearing the masks. To tell the truth, I half-expected they'd show up sporting the heads of enormous fanged monsters. Those are relatively benign.

Yes, I suppose they do resemble the face the Red Death assumes for its costume. No blood splattered on them, though.

If I could have your attention up here, again. Pay no attention to that man behind the curtain. Where was I? Your homework, yes, thank you. Right, right. Let's see…oh—I know. A couple of you read the colors in more original ways. I made a note of them somewhere—here they are. One person interpreted the colors as different states of mind, beginning with blue as tranquil and ending with black as despair, with stops for jealousy—green, naturally—and passion—white, as in white-hot—along the way. Someone else made the case for the colors as, let me make sure I have the phrasing right, "phases of being."

Actually, that last one's not bad. Although the writer could be less obtuse; clarity, people, academic writing needs to be clear. Anyway, the gist of the writer's argument is that each color is supposed to take you through a different state of existence, blue at one end of the spectrum representing innocence, black at the other representing death. Death as a state of being, that's…provocative. Which is not to say it's correct, but it's headed in the right direction.

I know, I know: Which is? The answer requires some explanation. Scratch that. It requires a boatload of explanation. That's why I have Tweedledee and Tweedledum setting up outside. (Don't look! They're almost done.) It's also why I lowered the screen behind me for the first time this semester. There are some images I want to show you, and they're best seen in as much detail as possible. If I can remember what the Media Center people told me…click this…then this…

Voila!

Matthew Brady's *Portrait* of Edgar, taken 1848, his last full year alive. It's the best-known picture of him; were I to ask you to visualize him, this is what your minds' eyes would see. That forehead, that marble expanse—yes, his hair does make the top of his head look misshapen, truncated. As far as I know, it wasn't. The eyes—I suppose everyone comments on the eyes, slightly shadowed under those brows, the lids lowered just enough to suggest a certain detachment, even dreaminess. It's the mouth I notice, how it tilts up ever-so-slightly at the right corner. It's hard to see; you have to look closely. A strange mixture of arrogance, even contempt, and something else, something that might be humor, albeit of the bitter variety. It wouldn't be that much of a challenge to suggest colors for the picture, but somehow, black and white is more fitting, isn't it? Odd, considering how much color there is in the fiction. I've often thought all those old Roger Corman adaptations, the ones Vincent Price starred in—whatever their other faults, one thing they got exactly right was Technicolor, which was the perfect way to film these stories, just saturate the screen with the most vibrant colors you could find.

I begin with the *Portrait* as a reminder. This is the man. His hand scraped the pen across the paper, brought the story we've been discussing into existence word by word. Not creation *ex nihilo*, out of nothing, creation…if my Latin were better, or existent, I'd have a fancier way to say out of the self, or out of the depths of the self, or—hey—out of the depth that is the self.

Moving on to our next portrait… Anyone?

I'm impressed. Not many people know this picture. Look closely, though. See it?

That's right: it isn't a painting. It's a photograph that's been tweaked to resemble a painting. The portrait it imitates is a posthumous representation of Virginia Clemm, Edgar's sweetheart and child bride. The girl in the photo? She'll be happy you called her a girl. That's my wife, Anna. Yes, I'm married. Why is that so hard to believe? We met many years ago, in a kingdom by the sea. From? "Annabel Lee," good. No, just Anna; although we did meet in the King of the Sea Arcade, on the Jersey shore. Seriously. She is slightly younger than I am. Four years, thank you very much. You people. For Halloween one year, we dressed up as Edgar and Virginia—pretty much from the start, it's been a running joke between us. In her case, the resemblance is striking.

As it so happened, yes we did attend a masquerade as the happy couple. That was where this photo was taken. One of the other guests was a professional photographer. I arranged the shot; he took it, then used a program on his computer to transform it into a painting. The guy was quite pleased with it; apparently it's on his website. I'm showing it to you because…well, because I want to. There's probably a connection I could draws between masquerade, the suppression of one identity in order to invoke and inhabit another, that displacement, and the events of our story, but that's putting the car about a mile before the horse. She'll like that you thought she was a girl, though; that'll make her night. Those were her cookies, by the way. Are there any left? Not even the sugar cookies? Figures.

Okay, image number three. If you can name this one, you get an "A" for the class and an autographed picture of the Pope. Put your hand down, you don't know. How about the rest of you?

Just us crickets…

It's just as well; I don't have that picture of the Pope anymore. This gentleman is Prosper Vauglais. Or so he claimed. There's a lot about this guy no one's exactly sure of, like when he was born, or where, or when and where he died. He showed up in Paris in the late eighteen-teens and caused something of a stir. For one winter, he appeared at several of the less reputable *salons* and a couple of the, I wouldn't go so far as to say more reputable—maybe less disreputable ones.

His "deal?" His deal, as you put it, was that he claimed to have been among the quarter of a million soldiers under Napoleon Bonaparte's personal command when, in June of 1812, the Emperor decided to invade Russia. Some of you may remember from your European history classes, this was a very bad idea. The worst. Roughly a tenth of Napoleon's forces survived the campaign; I want to say the number who limped back into France was something like twenty-two thousand. In and of itself, being a member of that group is nothing to sneeze at. For Vauglais, though, it was only the beginning. During the more-or-less running battles the French army fought as it retreated from what had been Moscow, Vauglais was separated from his fellows, struck on the head by a Cossack's sword and left for dead in a snow bank. When he came to, he was alone, and a storm had blown up. Prosper had no idea where he was; he assumed still Russia, which wasn't too encouraging. Any Russian peasants or what have you who came across French soldiers, even those trying to surrender, tended to hack them to death with farm implements first and ask questions later. So when Prosper strikes out in what he hopes is the approximate direction of France, he isn't what you'd call terribly optimistic.

Nor is his pessimism misplaced. Within a day, he's lost, frozen and starving, wandering around the inside of a blizzard like you read about, white-out conditions, shrieking wind, unbearable cold. The blow to his head isn't helping matters, either. His vision keeps going in and out of focus. Sometimes he feels so nauseated he can barely stand, let alone continue walking. Once in a while, he'll see a light shining in the window of a farmhouse, but he gives these a wide berth. Another day, and he'll be closer to death than he was even at the worst battles he saw—than he was when that saber connected with his skull. His skin, which has been numb since not long after he started his trek, has gone from pale to white to this kind of blue-gray, and it's hardened, as if there's a crust of ice on it. He can't feel his pulse through it. His breath, which had been venting from his nose and mouth in long white clouds, seems to have slowed to a trickle, if that. He can't see anything; although, with the storm continuing around him, maybe that isn't so strange. He's not cold anymore—or, it's not that he isn't cold so much as it is that the cold isn't torturing him the way it was. At some point, the cold moved inside him, took up residence just beneath his heart, and once that happened, that transition was accomplished, the temperature outside became of much less concern.

There's a moment—while Vauglais is staggering around like you do when you're trying to walk in knee-high snow without snowshoes, pulling each foot free, swiveling it forward, crashing it through the snow in front of you, then repeating the process with your other foot—there's a moment when he realizes he's dead. He isn't sure when it happened. Some time in the last day or so. It isn't that he thinks he's in some kind of afterlife, that he's wandering around a frozen hell. No, he knows he's still stuck somewhere in western Russia. It's just that, now he's dead. He isn't sure why he's stopped moving. He considers doing so, giving his body a chance to catch up to his apprehension of it, but decides against it. For one thing, he isn't sure it would work, and suppose while he's standing in place, waiting to fall over, someone finds him, one of those peasants, or a group of Russian soldiers? Granted, if he's already dead, they can't hurt him, but the prospect of being cut to pieces while still conscious is rather horrifying. And for another thing, Prosper isn't ready to quit walking. So he keeps moving forward. Dimly, the way you might hear a noise when you're fast asleep, he's aware that he isn't particularly upset at finding himself dead and yet moving, but after recent events, maybe that isn't so surprising.

Time passes; how much, he can't say. The blizzard doesn't lift, but it thins, enough for Vauglais to make out trees, evergreens. He's in a forest, a pretty dense one, from what he can see, which may explain why the storm has lessened. The trees are—there's something odd about the trees. For as close together as they are, they seem to be in almost perfect rows, running away into the snow on either side of him. In and of itself, maybe that isn't strange. Could be, he's wandered into some kind of huge formal garden. But there's more to it. When he looks at any particular tree, he sees, not so much bark and needles as black, black lines like the strokes of a paintbrush, or the scratches of a pen, forming the approximation of an evergreen. It's as if he's seeing a sketch of a tree, an artist's estimate. The black lines appear to be moving, almost too quickly for him to notice; it's as if he's witnessing them being drawn and re-drawn. Prosper has a sudden vision of himself from high above, a small, dark spot in the midst of long rows of black on white, a stray bit of punctuation loose among the lines of an unimaginable text.

Eventually, Vauglais reaches the edge of the forest. Ahead, there's a building, the title to this page he's been traversing. The blizzard has kicked up again, so he can't see much, but he has the impression of a long, low structure, possibly stone. It could be a stable, could be something else. Although there are no religious symbols evident, Prosper has an intuition the place is a monastery. He should turn right or left, avoid the building—the Russian clergy haven't taken any more kindly to the French invaders than the Russian people—instead, he raises one stiff leg and strikes off towards it. It isn't that he's compelled to do so, that he's in the grip of a power that he can't resist, or that he's decided to embrace the inevitable, surrender to death. He isn't even especially curious about the stone structure. Forward is just a way to go, and he does.

As he draws closer, Vauglais notices that the building isn't becoming any easier to distinguish. If anything, it's more indistinct, harder to make out. If the trees behind him were rough drawing, this place is little more than a scribble, a jumble of lines whose form is as much in the eye of the beholder as anything. When a figure in a heavy coat and hat separates from the structure and begins to trudge in his direction, it's as if a piece of the place has broken off. Prosper can't see the man's face, all of which except the eyes is hidden by the folds of a heavy scarf, but he lifts one mittened hand and gestures for Vauglais to follow him inside, which the Frenchman does.

And...no one knows what happens next.

What do I mean? I'm sorry: wasn't I speaking English? No one knows what happened inside the stone monastery. Prosper writes a fairly detailed account of the events leading up to that point, which is where the story I'm telling you comes from, but when the narrative reaches this moment, it breaks off with Vauglais's declaration that he's told us as much as he can. End of story.

All right, yes, there are hints of what took place during the five years he was at the Abbey. That was what he called the building, the Abbey. Every so often, Prosper would allude to his experiences in it, and sometimes, someone would note his remarks in a letter or diary. From combing through these kinds of documents, it's possible to assemble and collate Vauglais's comments into a glimpse of his life with the Fraternity. Again, his name. There were maybe seven of them, or seven after he arrived, or there were supposed to be seven. He referred to "Brother Red," once; to "The White Brother" at another time. Were the others named Blue, Purple, Green, Orange, and Violet? We can't say; although, as an assumption, it isn't completely unreasonable. They spent their days in pursuit of something Vauglais called The Great Work; he also referred to it as The Transumption. This seems to have involved generous amounts of quiet meditation combined with the study of certain religious texts—Prosper doesn't name them, but they may have included some Gnostic writings.

The Gnostics? I don't suppose you would have heard of them. How many of you actually got to church? As I feared. What would Sr. Mary Mary say? The Gnostics were a religious sect who sprang up around the same time as the early Christians. I guess they would have described themselves as the true Christians, the ones who understood what Jesus' teachings were really about. They shared sacred writings with the more orthodox Christians, but they had their own books, too. They were all about *gnosis*, knowledge, especially of the self. For them, the secret to what lay outside the self was what lay inside the self. The physical world was evil, a wellspring of illusions and delusions. Gnostics tended to retreat to the desert, lead lives of contemplation. Unlike the mainstream Christians, they weren't much on formal organization; that, and the fact that those Christians did everything in their power to shunt the Gnostics and their teachings to the margins and beyond, branding some of their ideas as heretical, helps explain why they pretty much vanished from the religious scene.

"Pretty much," though, isn't the same thing as "completely." (I know: such precise, scientific terminology.) Once in a while, Gnostic ideas would resurface, usually in the writings of some fringe figure or another. Rumors persist of Gnostic secret societies, occasionally as part of established groups like the Jesuits or the Masons. Which begs the question, Was Vauglais's Fraternity one of these societies, a kind of order of Gnostic monks? The answer to which is—

Right: no one knows. There's no record of any official, which is to say, Russian Orthodox religious establishment: no monastery, no church, in the general vicinity of where we think Prosper was. Of course, a bunch of Gnostic monastics would hardly constitute anything resembling an official body, and so might very well fly under the radar. That said, the lack of proof against something does not count as evidence for it.

That's true. He could have been making the whole thing up.

Transumption? It's a term from classical rhetoric. It refers to the elision of a chain of associations. Sorry—sometimes I like to watch your heads explode. Let's say you're writing your epic poem about the fall of Troy, and you describe one of the Trojans being felled by an arrow. Let's say that arrow was made from the wood of a tree in a sacred grove; let's say, too, that that grove was planted by Hercules, who scattered some acorns there by accident. Now let's say that, when your Trojan hero sinks to the ground, drowning in his own blood, one of his friends shouts, "Curse the careless hand of Hercules!" That statement is an example of transumption. You've jumped from one link in a chain of associations back several. Make sense?

Yes, well, what does a figure of speech have to do with what was going on inside that Abbey?

Oh wait—hold on for a moment. My two assistants are done with their set up. Let me give them a signal… Five more minutes? All right, good, yes. I have no idea if they understood me. Graduate students.

Don't worry about what's on the windows. Yes, yes, those are lamps. Can I have your attention up here, please? Thank you. Let me worry about Campus Security. Or my masked friends out there will.

Okay—let's skip ahead a little. We were talking about The Transumption, a.k.a. The Great Work. There's nothing in his other references to the Abbey that offers any clue as to what he may have meant by it. However, there is an event that may shed some light on things.

It occurs in Paris, towards the end of February. An especially fierce winter scours the streets, sends people scurrying from the shelter of one building to another. Snow piles on top of snow, all of it turning dirty gray. Where there isn't snow, there's ice, inches thick in places. The sky is gray, the sun a pale blur that puts in a token appearance for a few hours a day. Out into this glacial landscape, Prosper leads half a dozen men and women from one of the city's less-disreputable *salons*. Their destination, the catacombs, the long tunnels that run under Paris. They're quite old, the catacombs. In some places, the walls are stacked with bones, from when they were used as a huge ossuary. (That's a place to hold the bones of the dead.) They're also fairly crowded, full of beggars, the poor, searching for shelter from the ravages of the season. Vauglais has to take his party deep underground before they can find a location that's suitably empty. It's a kind of side-chamber, roughly circular, lined with shelves full of skull piled on skull. The skulls make a clicking sound, from the rats shuffling through them. Oh yes, there are plenty of rats down here.

Prosper fetches seven skulls off the shelves and piles them in the center of the room. He opens a large flask he's carried with him, and pours its contents over the bones. It's lamp oil, which he immediately ignites with his torch. He sets the torch down, and gathers the members of the *salon* around the skulls. They join hands.

It does sound as if he's leading a séance, doesn't it? The only difference is, he isn't asking the men and women with him to think of a beloved one who's passed beyond. Nor does he request they focus on a famous ghost. Instead, Vauglais tells them to look at the flames licking the bones in front of them. Study those flames, he says, watch them as they trace the contours of the skulls. Follow the flames over the cheeks, around the eyes, up the brows. Gaze into those eyes, into the emptiness inside the fire. Fall through the flames; fall into that blackness.

He's hypnotizing them, of course—Mesmerizing would be the more historically-accurate term. Under the sway of his voice, the members of the *salon* enter a kind of vacancy. They're still conscious—well, they're still perceiving, still aware of that heap of bones burning in front of them, the heavy odor of the oil, the quiet roar of the flames—but their sense of their selves, the accumulation of memory and inclination that defines each from the other, is gone.

Now Prosper is telling them to think of something new. Picture the flesh that used to clothe these skulls, he says. Warm and smooth, flushed with life. Look closely—it glows, doesn't it? It shines with its living. Watch! Watch—it's dying. It's growing cold, pale. The glow, that dim light floating at the very limit of the skin—it's changing, drifting up, losing its radiance. See—there!—ah, it's dead. Cool as a cut of meat. Gray. The light is gone. Or is it? Is that another light? Yes, yes it is; but it is not the one we have watched dissipate. This is a darker glow. Indigo, that most elusive of the rainbow's hues. It curls over the dull skin like fog, and the flesh opens for it, first in little cracks, then in long windows, and then in wide doorways. As the skin peels away, the light thickens, until it is as if the bone is submerged in a bath of indigo. The light is not done moving; it pours into the air above the skull, over all the skulls. Dark light is rising from them, twisting up in thick streams that seek each other, that wrap around one another, that braid a shape. It is the form of a man, a tall man dressed in black robes, his face void as a corpse's, his head crowned with black flame—

Afterwards, when the half-dozen members of the *salon* compare notes, none of them can agree on what, if anything, they saw while under Vauglais's sway. One of them insists that nothing appeared. Three admit to what might have been a cloud of smoke, or a trick of the light. Of the remaining pair, one states flat-out that she saw the Devil. The other balks at any statement more elaborate than, "Monsieur Vauglais has shown me terrible joy." Whatever they do or don't see, it doesn't last very long. The oil Prosper doused the skulls with has been consumed. The fire dies away; darkness rushes in to fill the gap. The trance in which Vauglais has held the *salon* breaks. There's a sound like wind rushing, then quiet.

A month after that expedition, Prosper disappeared from Paris. He had attempted to lead that same *salon* back into the catacombs for a second—well, whatever you'd call what he'd done. A summoning? (But what was he summoning?) Not surprisingly, the men and women of the *salon* declined his request. In a huff, Vauglais left them and tried to insert himself into a couple of even-less-disreputable *salons*, attempting to use gossip about his former associates as his price of admission. But either the secrets he knew weren't juicy enough—possible, but I suspect unlikely—or those other *salons* had heard about his underground investigations and decided they preferred the comfort of their drawing rooms. Then one of the men from that original *salon* raised questions about Prosper's military service—he claimed to have found a sailor who swore that he and Vauglais had been on an extended debauch in Morocco at the very time he was supposed to have been marching towards Moscow. That's the problem with being the flavor of the month: before you know it, the calendar's turned, and no one can remember what they found so appealing about you in the first place. In short order, there's talk about an official inquiry into Prosper's service record—probably more rumor than fact, but it's enough for Vauglais, and he departs Paris for parts unknown. No one sees him leave, just as no one saw him arrive. In the weeks that follow, there are reports of Prosper in Libya, Madagascar, but they don't disturb a single eyebrow. Years—decades later, when Gauguin's in Tahiti, he'll hear a story about a strange white man who came to the island a long time ago and vanished into its interior, and Vauglais's name will occur to him, but you can't even call that a legend. It's…a momentary association. Prosper Vauglais vanishes.

Well, not all of him. That's right: there's the account he wrote of his discovery of the Abbey.

I beg your pardon? Dead? Oh, right, yes. It's interesting—apparently, Prosper permitted a physician connected to the first *salon* he frequented to conduct a pretty thorough examination of him. According to Dr. Zumachin, Vauglais's skin was stubbornly pallid. No matter how much the doctor pinched or slapped it, Prosper's flesh remained the same gray-white. Not only that, it was cold, cold and hard, as if it were packed with ice. Although Vauglais had to inhale in order to speak, his regular respiration was so slight as to be undetectable. It wouldn't fog the doctor's pocket mirror. And try as Zumachin might, he could not locate a pulse.

Sure, Prosper could have paid him off; aside from his part in this story, there isn't that much information on the good doctor. For what it's worth, most of the people who met Vauglais commented on his skin, its pallor, and, if they touched it, its coldness. No one else noted his breathing, or lack thereof, but a couple of the members of that last *salon* described him as extraordinarily still.

Okay, back to that book. Actually, wait. Before we do, let me bring this up on the screen…

I know—talk about something completely different. No, it's not a Rorschach test. It does look like it, though, doesn't it? Now if my friends outside will oblige me…and there we go. Amazing what a sheet of blue plastic and a high-power lamp can do. We might as well be in the east room of Prospero's Abbey.

Yes, the blue light makes it appear deeper—it transforms it from ink-spill to opening. Prosper calls it *"La Bouche,"* the Mouth. Some mouth, eh?

That's where the design comes from, Vauglais's book. The year after his disappearance, a small Parisian press whose biggest claim to fame was its unauthorized edition of the Marquis de Sade's *Justine* publishes Prosper's *L'Histoire de Mes Aventures dans L'Etendu Russe*, which translates something like, "The History of My Adventures in the Russian," either "Wilderness" or "Vastness." Not that anyone calls it by its title. The publisher, one Denis Prebend, binds Vauglais's essay between covers the color of a bruise after three or four days. Yes, that sickly, yellowy-green. Of course that's what catches everyone's attention, not the less-than-inspired title, and it isn't long before customers are asking for "*le livre verte*," the green book. It's funny—it's one of those books that no one will admit to reading, but that goes through ten printings the first year after its appears.

Some of those copies do find their way across the Atlantic, very good. In fact, within a couple of months of its publication, there are at least three pirated translations of the green book circulating the booksellers of London, and a month after that, they're available in Boston, New York, and Baltimore.

To return to the book itself for a moment—after that frustrating ending, there's a blank page, which is followed by seven more pages, each showing a separate design. What's above me on the screen is the first of them. The rest—well, let's not get ahead of ourselves. Suffice it to say, the initial verdict was that something had gone awry in the printing process, with the result that the *bouche* had become *bouché*, cloudy. A few scholars have even gone so far as to attempt to reconstruct what Prosper's original images must have been. Prebend, though—the publisher—swore that he'd presented the book exactly as he had been instructed.

For those of us familiar with abstract art, I doubt there's any great difficulty in seeing the black blot on the screen as a mouth. The effect—there used to be these books; they were full of what looked like random designs. If you held them the right distance from your face and let your eyes relax, almost to the point of going cross-eyed, all of sudden, a picture would leap out of the page at you. You know what I'm talking about? Good. I don't know what the name for that effect is, but it's the nearest analogue I can come up with for what happens when you look at the Mouth under blue light—except that the image doesn't jump forward so much as sink back. The way it recedes—it's as if it extends, not just through the screen, or the wall behind it, but beyond all that, to the very substratum of things.

To tell the truth, I have no idea what's responsible for the effect. If you find this impressive, however…

Look at that: a new image and a fresh color. How's that for coordination? Good work, nameless minions. Vauglais named this "*Le Gardien*," the Guardian. What's that? I suppose you could make an octopus out of it; although aren't there a few too many tentacles? True, it's close enough; it's certainly more octopus than squid. Do you notice…right. The tentacles, loops, whatever we call them, appear to be moving. Focus on any one in particular, and it stands still—but you can see movement out of the corner of your eye, can't you? Try to take in the whole, and you swear its arms are performing an intricate dance.

So the Mouth leads to the Guardian, which is waving its appendages in front of…

That green is bright after the purple, isn't it? Voila *"Le Récif,"* the Reef. Makes sense, a cuttlefish protecting a reef. I don't know: it's angular enough. Personally, I suspect this one is based on some kind of pun or word play. *"Récif"* is one letter away from *"récit,"* story, and this reef comes to us as the result of a story; in some weird way, the reef may be the story. I realize that doesn't make any sense; I'm still working through it.

This image is a bit different from the previous two. Anyone notice how?

Exactly: instead of the picture appearing to move, the light itself seems to—I like your word, "shimmer." You could believe we're gazing through water. It's—not hypnotic, that's too strong, but it is soothing. Don't you think?

I'll take your yawn as a "yes." Very nice. What a way to preface a question. All right, all right. What is it that's keeping you awake?

Isn't it obvious? Apparently not.

Yes! Edgar read Prosper's book!

When. The best evidence is sometime in the early eighteen thirties, after he'd relocated to Baltimore. He mentions hearing about the green book from one of his fellow cadets at West Point, but he doesn't secure his own copy until he literally stumbles upon one in a bookshop near Baltimore's inner harbor. He wrote a fairly amusing account of it in a letter to Virginia. The store was this long, narrow space located halfway down an alley; its shelves were stuffed past capacity with all sizes of books jammed together with no regard for their subject. Occasionally, one of the shelves would disgorge its contents without warning. If you were underneath or to the side of it, you ran the risk of substantial injury. Not to mention, the single aisle snaking into the shop's recesses was occupied at irregular intervals by stacks of books that looked as if a strong sneeze would send them tumbling down.

It's as he's attempting to maneuver around an especially tall tower of books, simultaneously trying to avoid jostling a nearby shelf, that Edgar's foot catches on a single volume he hadn't seen, sending him—and all books in the immediate vicinity—to the floor. There's a huge puff of dust; half a dozen books essentially disintegrate. Edgar's sense of humor is such that he appreciates the comic aspect of a poet—as he styled himself—buried beneath a deluge of books. However, he insists on excavating the book that undid him.

The copy of Vauglais's essay he found was a fourth translation that had been done by a Boston publisher hoping to cash in on the popularity of the other editions. Unfortunately for him, the edition took longer to prepare than he'd anticipated—his translator was a Harvard professor who insisted on translating Prosper as accurately as he could. This meant an English version of Vauglais's essay that was a model of fidelity to the original French, but that wasn't ready until Prosper's story was last week's news. The publisher went ahead with what he titled *The Green Book of M. Prosper Vauglais* anyway, but he pretty much lost his shirt over the whole thing.

Edgar was so struck at having fallen over this book that he bought it on the spot. He spent the next couple of days reading and re-reading it, puzzling over its contents. As we've seen in "The Gold Bug" and "The Purloined Letter," this was a guy who liked a puzzle. He spent a good deal of time on the seven designs at the back of the book, convinced that their significance was right in front of him.

Speaking of those pictures, let's have another one. Assistants, if you please—

Hey, it's Halloween! Isn't that what you associate orange with? And especially an orange like this—this is the sun spilling the last of its late light, right before all the gaudier colors, the violets and pinks, splash out. You don't think of orange as dark, do you? I know I don't. Yet it is, isn't it? Is it the darkest of the bright colors? To be sure, it's difficult to distinguish the design at its center; the orange is filmy, translucent. There are a few too many curves for it to be the symbol for infinity; at least, I think there are. I want to say I see a pair of snakes wrapped around one another, but the coils don't connect in quite the right way. Vauglais's name for this was *"Le Coeur,"* the Heart, and also the Core, as well as the Height or the Depth, depending on usage. Obviously, we're cycling through the seven rooms from "The Masque of the Red Death;" obviously, too, I'm arguing that Edgar takes their colors from Prosper's book. In that schema, orange is at the center, three colors to either side of it; in that sense, we have reached the heart, the core, the height or the depth. Of course, that core obscures the other one—or maybe not.

While you try to decide, let's return to Edgar. It's an overstatement to say that Vauglais obsesses him. When his initial attempt at deciphering the designs fails, he puts the book aside. Remember, he's a working writer at a time when the American economy really won't support one—especially one with Edgar's predilections—so there are always more things to be written in the effort to keep the wolf a safe distance from the door. Not to mention, he's falling in love with the girl who will become his wife. At odd moments over the next decade, though, he retrieves Prosper's essay and spends a few hours poring over it. He stares at its images until they're grooved into the folds of his brain. During one long afternoon in 1840, he's sitting with the book open to the Mouth, a glass of water on the table to his right. The sunlight streaming in the windows splinters on the water glass, throwing a rainbow across the page in front of him. The arc of the images that's under the blue strip of the bow looks different; it's as if that portion of the paper has sunk into the book—behind the book. A missing and apparently lost piece of the puzzle snaps into place, and Edgar starts up from the table, knocking over his chair in the process. He races through the house, searching for a piece of blue glass. The best he can do is a heavy blue jug, which he almost drops in his excitement. He returns to the book, angles the jug to catch the light, and watches as the Mouth opens. He doesn't waste any time staring at it; shifting the jug to his right hand, he flips to the next image with his left, positions the glass jug over the Guardian, and…nothing. For a moment, he's afraid he's imagined the whole thing, had an especially vivid waking dream. But when he pages back to the Mouth and directs the blue light onto it, it clearly recedes. Edgar wonders if the effect he's observed is unique to the first image, then his eye lights on the glass of water, still casting its rainbow. He sets the jug on the floor, turns the page, and slides the book closer to the glass.

That's how Edgar spends the rest of the afternoon, matching the designs in the back of Vauglais's book to the colors that activate them. The first four come relatively quickly; the last three take longer. Once he has all seven, Edgar re-reads Prosper's essay and reproaches himself as a dunce for not having hit on the colors sooner. It's all there in Vauglais's prose, he declares, plain as day. (He's being much too hard on himself. I've read the green book a dozen times and I have yet to find the passage where Prosper hints at the colors.)

How about a look at the most difficult designs? Gentlemen, if you please...

There's nothing there. I know—that's what I said, the first time I saw the fifth image. "*Le Silence*," the Silence. Compared to the designs that precede it, this one is so faint as to be barely detectable. And when you shine a bright, white light onto it, it practically disappears. There is something in there, though; you have to stare at it for a while. Moreso than with the previous images, what you see here varies dramatically from viewer to viewer.

Edgar never records his response to the Silence, which is a pity. Having cracked the secret of Vauglais's designs, he studies the essay more carefully, attempting to discern the use to which the images were to be put, the nature of Prosper's Great Work, his Transumption. (There's that word again. I never clarified its meaning vis à vis Vauglais's ideas, did I?) The following year, when Edgar sits down to write "The Masque of the Red Death," it is no small part as an answer to the question of what Prosper was up to. That answer shares features with some of the stories he had written prior to his 1840 revelation; although, interestingly, they came after he had obtained his copy of the green book.

From the looks on your faces, I'd say you've seen what the Silence contains. I don't suppose anyone wants to share?

I'll take that as a, "No." It's all right: what you find there can be rather...disconcerting.

We're almost at the end of our little display. What do you say we proceed to number six? Here we go...

Violet's such a nice color, isn't it? You have to admit, some of those other colors are pretty intense. Not this one, though; even the image—"*L'Arbre,*" the Tree—looks more or less like a collection of lines trying to be a tree. Granted, if you study the design, you'll notice that each individual line seems to fade and then re-inscribe itself, but compared to the effect of the previous image, this is fairly benign. Does it remind you of anything? Anything we were discussing, say, in the last hour or so?

Oh never mind, I'll just tell you. Remember those trees Vauglais saw outside the Abbey? Remember the way that, when he tried to focus on any of them, he saw a mass of black lines? Hmmm. Maybe there's more to this pleasant design than we'd thought. Maybe it's, not the key to all this, but the key trope, or figure.

I know: which means what, exactly? Let's return to Edgar's story. You have a group of people who are sequestered together, made to disguise their outer identities, encouraged to debauch themselves, to abandon their inner identities, all the while passing from one end of this color schema to the other. They put their selves aside, become a massive blank, a kind of psychic space. That opening allows what is otherwise an abstraction, a personification, to change states, to manifest itself physically. Of course, the Red Death doesn't appear of its own volition; it's called into being by Prince Prospero, who can't stop thinking about the reason he's retreated into his abbey.

This is what happened—what started to happen to the members of the *salon* Prosper took into the Parisian catacombs. He attempted to implement what he'd learned during his years at the Abbey, what he first had perceived through the snow twirling in front of his eyes in that Russian forest. To manipulate—to mold—to…

Suppose that the real—what we take to be the real—imagine that world outside the self, all this out here, is like a kind of writing. We write it together; we're continuously writing it together, onto the surface of things, the paper, as it were. It isn't something we do consciously, or that we exercise any conscious control over. We might glimpse it in moments of extremity, as Vauglais did, but that's about as close to it as most of us will come. What if, though, what if it were possible to do something more than simply look?

What if you could clear a space on that paper and write something *else?* What might you bring into being?

Edgar tries to find out. Long after "The Masque," which is as much caution as it is field guide, he decides to apply Prosper's ideas for real. He does so during that famous lost week at the end of his life, that gap in the biographical record that has prompted so much speculation. Since Virginia succumbed to tuberculosis some two years prior, Edgar's been on a long downward slide, a protracted effort at joining his beloved wife. You know, extensive forests have been harvested for the production of critical studies of Edgar's "bizarre" relationship with Virginia; rarely, if ever, does it occur to anyone that Edgar and Virginia might honestly have been in love, and that the difference in their ages might have been incidental. Yet what is that final couple of years but a man grieving himself to death? Yes, Edgar approaches other women about possible marriage, but why do you think none of those proposals work out?

Not only is Edgar actively chasing his death, paddling furiously towards it on a river of alcohol; little known to him, death has noticed his pursuit, and responded by planting a black seed deep within his brain, a gift that is blossoming into a tumor. Most biographers have remained ignorant of this disease, but years after his death, Edgar's body is exhumed—it doesn't matter why; given who Edgar was, of course this was going to happen to him. During the examination of his remains, it's noted that his brain is shrunken and hard. Anyone who knows about these things will tell you that the brain is one of the first organs to decay, which means that what those investigators found rattling around old Edgar's cranium would not have been petrified gray matter. Cancer, however, is a much more durable beast; long after it's killed you, a tumor hangs around to testify to its crime. Your guess is as good as mine when it comes to how long he'd had it, but by the time I'm talking about, Edgar is in a pretty bad way. He's having trouble controlling the movements of his body, his speech; half the time he seems drunk, he's stone cold sober.

There's something else. Increasingly, wherever he turns his gaze, whatever he looks at flickers, and instead of, say, an orange resting on a plate, he sees a jumble of black lines approximating a sphere on a circle. It takes him longer to recall Vauglais's experience in that Russian forest than you'd expect; the cancer, no doubt, devouring his memory. Sometimes the confusion of lines that's replaced the streetlamp in front of him is itself replaced by blankness, by an absence that registers as a dull white space in the middle of things. It's as if a painter took a palette knife and scraped the oils from a portion of their picture until all that remained was the canvas, slightly stained. At first, Edgar thinks there's something wrong with his vision; when he understands what he's experiencing, he speculates that the blank might be the result of his eyes' inability to endure their own perception, that he might be undergoing some degree of what we would call hysterical blindness. As he's continued to see that whiteness, though, he's realized that he isn't seeing less, but more. He's seeing through to the surface those black lines are written on.

In the days immediately prior to his disappearance, Edgar's perception undergoes one final change. For the slightest instant after that space has uncovered itself to him, something appears on it, a figure—a woman. Virginia, yes, as he saw her last, ravaged by tuberculosis, skeletally thin, dark hair in disarray, mouth and chin scarlet with the blood she'd hacked out of her lungs. She appears barefoot, wrapped in a shroud stained with dirt. Almost before he sees her, she's gone, her place taken by whatever he'd been looking at to begin with.

Is it any surprise that, presented with this dull white surface, Edgar should fill it with Virginia? Her death has polarized him; she's the lodestone that draws his thoughts irresistibly in her direction. With each glimpse of her he has, Edgar apprehends that he's standing at the threshold of what could be an extraordinary chance. Although he's discovered the secret of Prosper's designs, discerned the nature of the Great Work, never once has it occurred to him that he might put that knowledge to use. Maybe he hasn't really believed in it; maybe he's suspected that, underneath it all, the effect of the various colors on Vauglais's designs is some type of clever optical illusion. Now, though, now that there's the possibility of gaining his beloved back—

Edgar spends that last week sequestered in a room in a boarding house a few streets up from that alley where he tripped over Prosper's book. He's arranged for his meals to be left outside his door; half the time, however, he leaves them untouched, and even when he takes the dishes into his room, he eats the bare minimum to sustain him. About midway through his stay, the landlady, a Mrs. Foster, catches sight of him as he withdraws into his room. His face is flushed, his skin slick with sweat, his clothes disheveled; he might be in the grip of a fever whose fingers are tightening around him with each degree it climbs. As his door closes, Mrs. Foster considers running up to it and demanding to speak to this man. The last thing she wants is for her boarding house to be known as a den of sickness. She has taken two steps forward when she stops, turns, and bolts downstairs as if the Devil himself were tugging her apron strings. For the remainder of the time this lodger is in his room, she will send one of the serving girls to deliver his meals, no matter their protests. Once the room stands unoccupied, she will direct a pair of those same girls to remove its contents—including the cheap bed—carry them out back, and burn them until nothing remains but a heap of ashes. The empty room is closed, locked, and removed from use for the rest of her time running that house, some twenty-two years.

I know: what did she see? What could she have seen, with the door shut? Perhaps it wasn't what she saw; perhaps it was what she felt: the surface of things yielding, peeling away to what was beneath, beyond—the strain of a will struggling to score its vision onto that surface—the waver of the brick and mortar, of the very air around her, as it strained against this newness coming into being. How would the body respond to what could only register as a profound wrongness? Panic, you have to imagine, maybe accompanied by sudden nausea, a fear so intense as to guarantee a lifetime's aversion to anything associated with its cause.

Had she opened that door, though, what sight would have confronted her? What would we see?

Nothing much—at least, that's likely to have been our initial response. Edgar seated on the narrow bed, staring at the wall opposite him. Depending on which day it was, we would have noticed his shirt and pants looking more or less clean. Like Mrs. Foster, we would have remarked his flushed face, the sweat soaking his shirt; we would have heard his breathing, deep and hoarse.

We might have caught his lips moving, might have guessed he was repeating Virginia's name over and over again, but been unable to say for sure. Were we to guess he was in a trance, caught in an opium dream, aside from the complete and total lack of opium-related paraphernalia, we could be forgiven.

If we were to remain in that room with him—if we could stand the same sensation that sent Mrs. Foster running—it wouldn't take us long to turn our eyes in the direction of Edgar's stare. His first day there, we wouldn't have noticed much if anything out of the ordinary. Maybe we would have wondered if the patch of bricks he was so focused on didn't look just the slightest shade paler than its surroundings, before dismissing it as a trick of the light. Return two, three days later, and we would find that what we had attributed to mid-afternoon light blanching already-faded masonry is a phenomenon of an entirely different order. Those bricks are blinking in and out of sight. One moment, there's a worn red rectangle, the next, there isn't. What takes its place is difficult to say, because it's back almost as fast as it was gone; although, after its return, the brick looks a bit less solid...less certain, you might say. Ragged around the edges, though not in any way you could put words to. All over that stretch of wall, bricks are going and coming and going. It almost looks as if some kind of code is spelling itself out using the stuff of Edgar's wall as its pen and paper.

Were we to find ourselves in that same room, studying that same spot, a day later, we would be startled to discover a small area of the wall, four bricks up, four down, vanished. Where it was—let's call what's there—or what isn't there—white. To tell the truth, it's difficult to look at that spot—the eye glances away automatically, the way it does from a bright light. Should you try to force the issue, tears dilute your vision.

Return to Edgar's room over the next twenty-four hours, and you would find that gap exponentially larger—from four bricks by four bricks to sixteen by sixteen, then from sixteen by sixteen to—basically, the entire wall. Standing in the doorway, you would have to raise your hand, shield your eyes from the dull whiteness in front of you. Blink furiously, squint, and you might distinguish Edgar in his familiar position, staring straight into that blank. Strain your gaze through the narrowest opening your fingers can make, and for the half a second until your head jerks to the side, you see a figure, deep within the white. Later, at a safe remove from Edgar's room, you may attempt to reconstruct that form, make sense of your less-than-momentary vision. All you'll be able to retrieve, however, is a pair of impressions, the one of something coalescing, like smoke filling up a jar, the other of thinness, like a child's stick-drawing grown life-sized. For the next several months, not only your dreams, but your waking hours will be plagued by what you saw between your fingers. Working late at night, you will be overwhelmed by the sense that whatever you saw in that room is standing just outside the cone of light your lamp throws. Unable to help yourself, you'll reach for the shade, tilt it back, and find...nothing, your bookcases. Yet the sensation won't pass; although you can read the spines of the hardcovers ranked on your bookshelves, your skin won't stop bristling at what you can't see there.

What about Edgar, though? What image do his eyes find at the heart of that space? I suppose we should ask, What image of Virginia?

It—she changes. She's thirteen, wearing the modest dress she married him in. She's nine, wide-eyed as she listens to him reciting his poetry to her mother and her. She's dead, wrapped in a white shroud. So much concentration is required to pierce through to the undersurface in the first place—and then there's the matter of maintaining the aperture—that it's difficult to find, let alone summon, the energy necessary to focus on a single image of Virginia. So the figure in front of him brushes a lock of dark hair out of her eyes, then giggles in a child's high-pitched tones, then coughs and sprays scarlet blood over her lips and chin. Her mouth is pursed in thought; she turns to a knock on the front door; she thrashes in the heat of the disease that is consuming her. The more time that passes, the more Edgar struggles to keep his memories of his late wife separate from one another. She's nine, standing beside her mother, wound in her burial cloth. She's in her coffin, laughing merrily. She's saying she takes him as her lawful husband, her mouth smeared with blood.

Edgar can't help himself—he's written, and read, too many stories about exactly this kind of situation for him not to be aware of all the ways it could go hideously wrong. Of course, the moment such a possibility occurs to him, it's manifest in front of him. You know how it is: the harder you try to keep a pink elephant out of your thoughts, the more that animal cavorts center-stage. Virginia is obscured by white linen smeared with mud; where her mouth is, the shroud is red. Virginia is naked, her skin drawn to her skeleton, her hair loose and floating around her head as if she's under water. Virginia is wearing the dress she was buried in, the garment and the pale flesh beneath it opened by rats. Her eyes—or the sockets that used to cradle them—are full of her death, of all she has seen as she was dragged out of the light down into the dark.

With each new monstrous image of his wife, Edgar strives not to panic. He bends what is left of his will toward summoning Virginia as she was at sixteen, when they held a second, public wedding. For an instant, she's there, holding out her hand to him with that simple grace she's displayed as long as he's known her—and then she's gone, replaced by a figure whose black eyes have seen the silent halls of the dead, whose ruined mouth has tasted delicacies unknown this side of the grave. This image does not flicker; it does not yield to other, happier pictures. Instead, it grows more solid, more definite. It takes a step towards Edgar, who is frantic, his heart thudding in his chest, his mouth dry. He's trying to stop the process, trying to close the door he's spent so much time and effort prying open, to erase what he's written on that blankness. The figure takes another step forward, and already, is at the edge of the opening. His attempts at stopping it are useless—what he's started has accrued sufficient momentum for it to continue regardless of him. His lips are still repeating, "Virginia."

When the—we might as well say, when Virginia places one gray foot onto the floor of Edgar's room, a kind of ripple runs through the entire room, as if every last bit of it is registering the intrusion. How Edgar wishes he could look away as she crosses the floor to him. In a far corner of his brain that is capable of such judgments, he knows that this is the price for his *hubris*—really, it's almost depressingly formulaic. He could almost accept the irony if he did not have to watch those hands dragging their nails back and forth over one another, leaving the skin hanging in pale strips; if he could avoid the sight of whatever is seething in the folds of the bosom of her dress; if he could shut his eyes to that mouth and its dark contents as they descend to his. But he can't; he cannot turn away from his Proserpine as she rejoins him at last.

Four days prior to his death, Edgar is found on the street, delirious, barely-conscious. He never recovers. Right at the end, he rallies long enough to dictate a highly-abbreviated version of the story I've told you to a Methodist minister, who finds what he records so disturbing he sews it into the binding of the family Bible, where it will remain concealed for a century and a half.

As for what Edgar called forth—she walks out of our narrative and is not seen again.

It's a crazy story. It makes the events of Vauglais's life seem almost reasonable in comparison. If you were so inclined, I suppose you could ascribe Edgar's experience in that rented room to an extreme form of auto-hypnosis which, combined with the stress on his body from his drinking and the brain tumor, precipitates a fatal collapse. In which case, the story I've told you is little more than an elaborate symptom. It's the kind of reading a literary critic prefers; it keeps the more...*outré* elements safely quarantined within the writer's psyche.

Suppose, though, suppose. Suppose that all this insanity I've been feeding you isn't a quaint example of early-nineteenth-century pseudoscience. Suppose that its interest extends well beyond any insights it might offer in interpreting "The Masque of the Red Death." Suppose—let's say the catastrophe that overtakes Edgar is the result of—we could call it poor planning. Had he paid closer attention to the details of Prosper's history, especially to that sojourn in the catacombs, he would have recognized the difficulty—to the point of impossibility—of making his attempt alone. Granted, he was desperate. But there was a reason Vauglais took the members of his *salon* underground with him—to use as a source of power, a battery, as it were. They provided the energy; he directed it. Edgar's story is a testament to what must have been a tremendous—an almost unearthly will. In the end, though, it wasn't enough.

Of course, how could he have brought together a sufficient number of individuals, and where? By the close of his life, he wasn't the most popular of fellows. Not to mention, he would have needed to expose the members of this hypothetical group to Prosper's designs and their corresponding colors.

Speaking of which: pleasant as this violet has been, what do you say we proceed to the *pièce de résistance?* Faceless lackeys, on my mark—

Ahh. I don't usually talk about these things, but you have no idea how much trouble this final color combination gave me. I mean, red and black gives you dark red, right? Right, except that for the design to achieve its full effect, putting up a dark red light won't do. You need red layered over black—and a true black light, not ultraviolet. The result, though—I'm sure you'll agree, it was worth sweating over. It's like a picture painted in red on a black canvas, wouldn't you say? And look what it does for the final image. It seems to be reaching right out of the screen for you, doesn't it? Strictly speaking, Vauglais's name for it, *"Le Dessous,"* the Underneath, isn't quite grammatical French, but we needn't worry ourselves over such details. There are times I think another name would be more appropriate: the Maw, perhaps, and then there are moments I find the Underneath perfect. You can see why I might lean towards calling it a mouth—the Cave would do, as well—except that the perspective's all wrong. If this is a mouth, or a cave, we aren't looking into it; we're already inside, looking out.

Back to Edgar. As we've said, even had he succeeded in gathering a group to assist him in his pursuit, he would have had to find a way to introduce them to Prosper's images and their colors. If he could have, he would have... reoriented them, their minds, the channels of their thoughts. Vauglais's designs would have brought them closer to where they needed to be; they would have made available certain dormant faculties within his associates.

Even that would have left him with challenges, to be sure. Mesmerism, hypnosis, as Prosper himself discovered, is a delicate affair, one subject to such external variables as running out of lamp oil too soon. It would have been better if he could have employed some type of pharmacological agent, something that would have deposited them into a more useful state, something sufficiently concentrated to be delivered via a few bites of an innocuous food—a cookie, say, whose sweetness would mask any unpleasant taste, and which he could cajole his assistants to sample by claiming that his wife had baked them.

Then, if Edgar had been able to keep this group distracted while the cookies did their work—perhaps by talking to them about his writing—about the genesis of one of his stories, say, "The Masque of the Red Death"—if he had managed this far, he might have been in a position to make something happen, to perform the Great Work.

There's just one more thing, and that's the object for which Edgar would have put himself to all this supposed trouble: Virginia. I like to think I'm as romantic as the next guy, but honestly—you have the opportunity to rescript reality, and the best you can come up with is returning your dead wife to you? Talk about a failure to grasp the possibilities...

What's strange—and frustrating—is that it's all right there in "The Masque," in Edgar's own words. The whole idea of the Great Work, of Transumption, is to draw one of the powers that our constant, collective writing of the real consigns to abstraction across the barrier into physicality. Ideally, one of the members of that trinity Edgar named so well, Darkness and Decay and the Red Death, those who hold illimitable dominion over all. The goal is to accomplish something momentous, to shake the world to its foundations, not play out some hackneyed romantic fantasy. That was what Vauglais was up to, trying to draw into form the force that strips the flesh from our bones, that crumbles those bones to dust.

No matter. Edgar's mistake still has its uses as a distraction, and a lesson. Not that it'll do any of you much good. By now, I suspect few of you can hear what I'm saying, let alone understand it. I'd like to tell you the name of what I stirred into that cookie dough, but it's rather lengthy and wouldn't do you much good, anyway. I'd also like to tell you it won't leave you permanently impaired, but that wouldn't exactly be true. One of the consequences of its efficacy, I fear. If it's any consolation, I doubt most of you will survive what's about to follow. By my reckoning, the power I'm about to bring into our midst will require a good deal of...sustenance in order to establish a more permanent foothold here. I suspect this is of even less consolation, but I do regret this aspect of the plan I'm enacting. It's just—once you come into possession of such knowledge, how can you not make use—full use of it?

You see, I'm starting at the top. Or at the beginning—before the beginning, really, before light burst across the perfect formlessness that was everything. I'm starting with Darkness, with something that was already so old at that moment of creation that it had long forgotten its identity. I plan to restore it. I will give myself to it for a guide, let it envelop me and consume you and run out from here in a flood that will wash this world away. I will give to Darkness a dominion more complete than it has known since it was split asunder.

Look—in the air—can you see it?

For Fiona

TECHNICOLOR

Poe: 19 New Tales of Suspense, Dark Fantasy and Horror, was commissioned by the UK publisher, and published in honor of the 200th anniversary of Edgar Allan Poe's birth in 2009. It won the Shirley Jackson Award. It's one of the few anthologies for which I've asked potential contributors to alert me in advance as to what story/poem/nonfiction piece they're riffing on. I did this, even though I knew that the writers I commissioned each had distinct voices, so that if there was overlap (and there was) the treatments would be quite different (and they were).

John Langan (whose stories are always late and usually lengthy) contributed the weird and wonderful story "Technicolor," reprinted here.

The Sawing Boys

by Howard Waldrop

(From *Black Thorn, White Rose*, 1994)

There was a place in the woods where three paths came together and turned into one big path heading south.

A bearded man in a large straw hat and patched bib overalls came down one. Over his shoulder was a tow sack, and out of it stuck the handle of a saw. The man had a long wide face and large thin ears.

Down the path to his left came a short man in butternut pants and a red checkerboard shirt that said *Ralston-Purina Net Wt. 20 lbs.* on it. He had on a bright red cloth cap that stood up on the top of his head. Slung over his back was a leather strap; hanging from it was a big ripsaw.

On the third path were two people, one of whom wore a yellow-and-black-striped shirt, and had a mustache that stood straight out from the sides of his nose. The other man was dressed in a dark brown barn coat. He had a wrinkled face, and wore a brown Mackenzie cap down from which the ear-flaps hung, even though it was a warm morning. The man with the mustache carried a narrow folding ladder; the other carried a two-man bucksaw.

The first man stopped.

"Hi yew!" he said in the general direction of the other two paths.

"Howdee!" said the short man in the red cap.

"Well, well, well!" said the man with the floppy-eared hat, putting down his big saw.

"Weow!" said the man with the wiry mustache.

They looked each other over, keeping their distance, eyeing each others' clothing and saws.

"Well, I guess we know where we're all headed," said the man with the brown Mackenzie cap.

"I reckon," said the man in the straw hat. "I'm Luke Apuleus, from over Cornfield County way. I play the crosscut."

"I'm Rooster Joe Banty," said the second. "I'm a ripsaw bender myself."

"I'm Felix Horbliss," said the man in stripes with the ladder. "That thar's Cave Canem. We play this here big bucksaw."

They looked at each other some more.

"I'm to wonderin'," said Luke, bringing his tow sack around in front of him. "I'm wonderin' if'n we know the same tunes. Seems to me it'd be a shame to have to play agin' each other if'n we could help it."

"You-all know 'Trottin' Gertie Home'?" asked Felix.

Luke and Rooster Joe nodded.

"How about 'When the Shine comes Out'n the Dripper'?" asked Rooster Joe.

The others nodded.

"How are you on 'Snake Handler's Two-Step'?" asked Luke Apuleus.

More nods.

"Well, that's a start on it," said Cave Canem. "We can talk about it on the way there. I bet we'd sound right purty together."

So side by side by bucksaw and ladder, they set out down the big path south.

What we are doing is, we are walking down this unpaved road. How we have come to be walking down this unpaved road is a very long and tiresome story that I should not bore you with.

We are being Chris the Shoemaker, who is the brains of this operation, and a very known guy back where we come from, which is south of Long Island, and Large Jake and Little Willie, who are being the brawn, and Miss Millie Dee Chantpie, who is Chris the Shoemaker's doll, and who is always dressed to the nines, and myself, Charlie Perro, whose job it is to remind everyone what their job is being.

"I am astounded as all get-out," says Little Willie, "that there are so many places with no persons in them nowise," looking around at the trees and bushes and such. "We have seen two toolsheds which looked as if they once housed families of fourteen, but of real-for-true homes, I am not seeing any."

"Use your glims for something besides keeping your nose from sliding into your eyebrows," says Chris the Shoemaker. "You will have seen the sign that said one of the toolcribs is the town of Podunk, and the other shed is the burg of Shtetl. I am believing the next one we will encounter is called Pratt Falls. I am assuming it contains some sort of trickle of fluid, a stunning and precipitous descent in elevation, established by someone with the aforementioned surname."

He is called Chris the Shoemaker because that is now his moniker, and he once hung around shoestores. At that time the cobbler shops was the place where the policy action was hot, and before you can be saying Hey Presto! there is Chris the Shoemaker in a new loud suit looking like a comet, and he is the middle guy between the shoemakers and the elves that rig the policy.

"Who would have thought it?" asked Little Willie, "both balonies on the rear blowing at the same time, and bending up the frammus, and all the push and pull running out? I mean, what are the chances?"

Little Willie is called that because he is the smaller of the two brothers. Large Jake is called that because, oh my goodness, is he large. He is so large that people have confused him for nightfall—they are standing on the corner shooting the breeze with some guys, and suddenly all the light goes away, and so do the other guys. There are all these cigarettes dropping to the pavement where guys used to be, and the person looks around and Whoa! it is not night at all, it is only Large Jake.

For two brothers they do not look a thing alike. Little Willie looks, you should excuse the expression, like something from the family Rodentia, whereas Large Jake is a very pleasant-looking individual, only the pleasant is spread across about three feet of mook.

Miss Millie Dee Chantpie is hubba-hubba stuff (only Chris the Shoemaker best not see you give her more than one Long Island peek) and the talk is she used to be a roving debutante. Chris has the goo-goo eyes for her, and she is just about a whiz at the new crossword puzzles, which always give Little Willie a headache when he tries to do one.

Where we are is somewhere in the state of Kentucky, which I had not been able to imagine had I not seen it yesterday from the train. Why we were here was for a meet with this known guy who runs a used furniture business on South Wabash Street in Chi City. The meet was to involve lots of known guys, and to be at some hunting lodge in these hills outside Frankfort, where we should not be bothered by prying eyes. Only first the train is late, and the jalopy we bought stalled on us in the dark, and there must have been this wrong turn somewhere, and the next thing you are knowing the balonies blow and we are playing in the ditch and gunk and goo are all over the place.

So here we are walking down this (pardon the expression) road, and we are looking for a phone and a mechanically inclined individual, and we are not having such a hot time of it.

"You will notice the absence of wires," said Chris the Shoemaker, "which leads me to believe we will not find no blower at this watery paradise of Pratt Falls."

"Christ Almighty, I'm gettin' hungry!" says Miss Millie Dee Chantpie of a sudden. She is in this real flapper outfit, with a bandeau top and fringes, and is wearing pearls that must have come out of oysters the size of freight trucks.

"If we do not soon find the object of our quest," says Chris the Shoemaker, "I shall have Large Jake blow you the head off a moose, or whatever they have in place of cows out here."

It being a meet, we are pretty well rodded up, all except for Chris, who had to put on his Fall Togs last year on Bargain Day at the courthouse and do a minute standing on his head, so of course he can no longer have an oscar anywhere within a block of his person, so Miss Millie Dee Chantpie carries his cannon in one of her enchanting little reticules.

Large Jake is under an even more stringent set of behavioral codes, but he just plain does not care, and I do not personally know any cops or even the Sammys who are so gauche as to try to frisk him without first calling out the militia. Large Jake usually carries a powder wagon—it is the kind of thing they use on mad elephants or to stop runaway locomotives only it is sawed off on both ends to be only about a foot long.

Little Willie usually carries a sissy rod, only it is a dumb gat so there is not much commotion when he uses it—just the sound of air coming out of it, and then the sound of air coming out of whomsoever he uses it on. Little Willie has had a date to Ride Old Sparky before, only he was let out on a technical. The technical was that the judge had not noticed the big shoe box full of geetas on the corner of his desk before he brought the gavel down.

I am packing my usual complement of calibers which (I am prouder than anything to say) I have never used. They are only there for the bulges for people to ogle at while Chris the Shoemaker is speaking.

Pratt Falls is another couple of broken boards and a sign saying Feed and Seed. There was this dry ditch with a hole with a couple of rocks in it.

"It was sure no Niagara," says Little Willie, "that's for certain."

At the end of the place was a sign, all weathered out except for the part that said 2 MILES.

We are making this two miles in something less than three-quarters of an hour because it is mostly uphill and our dogs are barking, and Miss Millie Dee Chantpie, who has left her high heels in the flivver, is falling off the sides of her flats very often.

We are looking down into what passes for a real live town in these parts.

"This is the kind of place," says Little Willie, "where when you are in the paper business, and you mess up your double sawbuck plates, and print a twenty-one-dollar bill, you bring it here and ask for change. And the guy at the store will look in the drawer and ask you if two nines and a three will do."

"Ah, but look, gentlemen and lady," says Chris the Shoemaker, "there are at least two wires coming down over the mountain into this metropolis, and my guess is that they are attached to civilization at the other end."

"I do not spy no filling station," I says. "But there does seem to be great activity for so early of a morning." I am counting houses. "More people are already in town than live here."

"Perhaps the large gaudy sign up ahead will explain it," says Little Willie. The sign is being at an angle where another larger dirt path comes into town.

From all around on the mountains I can see people coming in in wagons and on horses and on foot.

We get to the sign. This is what it says, I kid you not:

BIG HARMONY CONTEST!
BRIMMYTOWN SQUARE SAT MAY 16
$50 FIRST PRIZE
Brought to you by Watkins Products
and CARDUI, Makers of BLACK DRAUGHT
Extra! Sacred Harp Singing
Rev. Shapenote and the Mt. Sinai Choir.

"Well, well," says Chris. "Looks like there'll be plenty of *étrangers* in this burg. We get in there, make the call on the meet, get someone to fix the jalopy, and be on our way. We should fit right in."

While Chris the Shoemaker is saying this, he is adjusting his orange-and-pink tie and shooting the cuffs on his purple-and-white pinstripe suit. Little Willie is straightening his pumpkin-colored, double-breasted suit and brushing the dust off his yellow spats. Large Jake is dressed in a pure white suit with a black shirt and white tie, and has on a white fedora with a thin black band. Miss Millie Dee Chantpie swirls her fringes and rearranges the ostrich feather in her cloche. I feel pretty much like a sparrow among peacocks.

"Yeah," I says, looking over the town, "they'll probably never notice we been here."

They made their way into town and went into a store. They bought themselves some items, and went out onto the long, columned verandah of the place, and sat down on some nail kegs, resting their saws and ladders against the porch railings.

Cave Canem had a big five-cent RC Cola and a bag of Tom's Nickel Peanuts. He took a long drink of the cola, tore the top off the celluloid bag, and poured the salted peanuts into the neck of the bottle. The liquid instantly turned to foam and overflowed the top, which Canem put into his mouth. When it settled down, he drank from the bottle and chewed on the peanuts that came up the neck.

Rooster Joe took off his red cap. He had a five-cent Moon Pie the size of a dinner plate and took bites off that.

Horbliss had a ten-cent can of King Oscar Sardines. The key attached to the bottom broke off at the wrong place. Rather than tearing his thumb up, he took out his pocketknife and cut the top of the can off and peeled the ragged edge back. He drank off the oil, smacking his lips, then took out the sardines between his thumb and the knife blade and ate them.

Luke had bought a two-foot length of sugarcane and was sucking on it, spitting out the fine slivers which came away in his mouth.

They ate in silence and watched the crowds go by, clumps of people breaking away and eddying into the stores and shops. At one end of town, farmers stopped their wagons and began selling the produce. From the other end, at the big open place where the courthouse would be if Brimmytown were the county seat, music started up.

They had rarely seen so many men in white shirts, even on Sunday, and women and kids in their finest clothes, even if they were only patched and faded coveralls, they were starched and clean.

Then a bunch of city flatlanders came by—the men all had on hats and bright suits and ties, and the woman—a goddess—was the first flapper they had ever seen—the eyes of the flatlanders were moving everywhere. Heads turned to watch them all along their route. They were moving toward the general mercantile, and they looked tired and dusty for all their fancy duds.

"Well, boys," said Luke. "That were a right smart breakfast. I reckon us-all better be gettin' on down towards the musical place and see what the otherns look like."

They gathered up their saws and ladders and walked toward the sweetest sounds this side of Big Bone Lick.

"So," says Little Willie to a citizen, "tell us where we can score a couple of motorman's gloves?"

The man is looking at him like he has just stepped off one of the outermost colder planets. This is fitting, for the citizen looks to us vice versa.

"What my friend of limited vocabulary means," says Chris the Shoemaker to the astounding and astounded individual, "is where might we purchase a mess of fried pork chops?"

The man keeps looking at us with his wide eyes the size of doorknobs.

"Eats?" I volunteers.

Nothing is happening.

Large Jake makes eating motions with his mitt and goozle.

Still nothing.

"Say, fellers," says this other resident, "you won't be gettin' nothing useful out'n him. He's one of the simpler folks hereabouts, what them Victorian painter fellers used to call 'naturals.' What you want's Ma Gooser's place, straight down this yere street."

"Much obliged," says Chris.

"It's about time, too," says Miss Millie Dee Chantpie. "I'm so hungry I could eat the ass off a pigeon through a park bench!"

I am still staring at the individual who has given us directions, who is knocking the ashes out of his corncob pipe against a rain barrel.

"Such a collection of spungs and feebs I personally have never seen," says Chris the Shoemaker, who is all the time looking at the wire that comes down the hill into town.

"I must admit you are right," says Little Willie. And indeed it seems every living thing for three counties is here—there are nags and wagons, preggo dolls with stair-step children born nine months and fifteen minutes apart, guys wearing only a hat and one blue garment, a couple of men with what's left of Great War uniforms with the dago dazzlers still pinned to the chests—yes indeedy, a motley and hilarity-making group.

The streets are being full of wagons with melons and the lesser legumes and things which for a fact I know grow in the ground. The indigenous peoples are selling everything what moves. And from far away you can hear the beginnings of music.

"I spy," says Chris the Shoemaker.

"Whazzat?" asks Little Willie.

"I spy the blacksmith shop, and I spy the general mercantile establishment to which the blower wire runs. Here is what we are doing. William and I will saunter over to the smithy and forge, where we will inquire of aid for the vehicle. Charlie Perro, you will go make the call which will tender our apologies as being late for the meet, and get some further instructions. Jacob, you will take the love of my life, Miss Millie, to this venerable Ma Gooser's eatatorium where we will soon join you in a prodigious repast."

The general mercantile is in the way of selling everything on god's green earth, and the aroma is very mouth-watering—it is a mixture of apple candy and nag tack, coal oil and licorice and flour, roasted coffee and big burlap sacks of nothing in particular. There is ladies' dresses and guy hats and weapons of all kinds.

There is one phone; it is on the back wall; it is the kind Alexander Graham Bell made himself.

"Good person," I says to the man behind the counter, who is wearing specs and a vest and has a tape measure draped over his shoulder, "might I use your telephonic equipment to make a collect long-distance call?"

"Everthin's long-distance from here," he opines. "Collect, you say?"

"That is being correct."

He goes to the wall and twists a crank and makes bell sounds. "Hello, Gertie. This is Spoon. How's things in Grinder Switch?... You don't say? Well, there's a city feller here needs to make a collect call. Right. You fix him up." He hands me the long earpiece, and puts me in the fishwife care of this Gertie, and parks himself nearby and begins to count some bright glittery objects.

I tells Gertie the number I want. There are these sounds like the towers are falling. "And what's your name," asks this Gertie.

I gives her the name of this known newspaper guy who hangs out at Chases' and who writes about life in the Roaring Forties back in the Big City. The party on the other end will be wise that that is not who it is, but will know I know he knows.

I hear this voice and Gertie gives them my name and they say okay.

"Go ahead," says Gertie.

"We are missing the meet," I says.

"Bleaso!" says the voice. "Eetmay alledoffcay. Ammysays Iseway! Izzyoway and Oemay erehay."

Itshay I am thinking to myself. To him I says: "Elltay usoway atwhay otay ooday?"

"Ogay Omehay!"

He gets off the blower.

"I used to have a cousin that could talk Mex," says Spoon at the counter. I thank him for the use of the phone. "Proud as a peach of it," he says, wiping at it with a cloth.

"Well, you should be," I tell him. Then I buy two cents worth of candy and put it in a couple of pockets, and then I ease on down this town's Great White Way.

This Ma Gooser's is some hopping joint. I don't think the griddle here's been allowed to cool off since the McKinley Administration. Large Jake and Miss Millie Dee Chantpie are already tucking in. The place is as busy as a chophouse on Chinese New Year.

There are these indistinguishable shapes on the platters.

A woman the size of Large Jake comes by with six full plates along each arm, headed towards a table of what looks like two oxdrivers in flannel shirts. These two oxdrivers are as alike as all get-out. The woman puts three plates in front of each guy and they fall into them mouth first.

The woman comes back. She has wild hair, and it does not look like she has breasts; it looks like she has a solid shelf across her chest under her work shirt. "Yeah?" she says, wiping sweat from her brow.

"I'd like a steak and some eggs," I says, "over easy on the eggs, steak well-done, some juice on the side."

"You'll get the breakfast, if'n you get anything," she says. "Same's everybody else." She follows my eyes back to the two giants at the next table. Large Jake can put away the groceries, but he is a piker next to these two. A couple of the plates in front of them are already shining clean and they are reaching for a pile of biscuits on the next table as they work on their third plates.

"Them's the Famous Singin' Eesup Twins, Bert and Mert," says Ma Gooser. "If'n everybody could pile it in like them, I'd be a rich woman." She turns to the kitchen.

"Hey, Jughead," she yells, "where's them six dozen biscuits?"

"Comin', Ma Gooser!" yells a voice from back in the hell there.

"More blackstrap 'lasses over here, Ma!" yells a corncob from another table.

"Hold your water!" yells Ma. "I only got six hands!" She runs back towards the kitchen.

Chris the Shoemaker and Little Willie comes in and settles down.

"Well, we are set in some departments. The blacksmith is gathering up the tools of his trade and Little William will accompany him in his wagon to the site of the vehicular happenstance. I will swear to you, he picks up his anvil and puts into his wagon, just like that. The thing must have dropped the wagon bed two foot. What is it they are feeding the locals around here?" He looks down at the plates in front of Large Jake and Miss Millie. "What is *dat?*"

"I got no idea, sweetie," says Miss Millie, putting another forkful in, "but it sure is good!"

"And what's the news from our friends across the ways?"

"Zex," I says.

He looks at me. "*You* are telling *me* zex in this oomray full of oobrays?"

"No, Chris," I says, "the *word* is zex."

"Oh," he says, "and for why?"

"Izzy and Moe," I says.

"Izzy and Moe?! How did Izzy and Moe get wise to this deal?"

"How do Izzy and Moe get wise to anything," I says, keeping my voice low and not moving my goozle. "Hell, if someone could get *them* to come over, this umray unningray biz would be a snap. If they can dress like women shipwrecks and get picked up by runners' ships, they can get wind of a meet somewhere."

"So what are our options being?" asks Chris the Shoemaker.

"That is why we have all these round-trip tickets," I says.

He is quiet. Ma Gooser slaps down these plates in front of us, and coffee all round, and takes two more piles of biscuits over to the Famous Singing Eesup Twins.

"Well, that puts the damper on my portion of the Era of Coolidge Prosperity," says Chris the Shoemaker. "I am beginning to think this decade is going to be a more problematical thing than first imagined. In fact, I am getting in one rotten mood." He takes a drink of coffee. His beezer lights up. "Say, the flit in the *Knowledge Box* got *nothing* on this." He drains the cup dry. He digs at his plate, then wolfs it all down. "Suddenly my mood is changing. Suddenlike, I am in a working mood."

I drops my fork.

"Nix?" I asks nice, looking at him like I am a tired halibut.

"No, not no nix at all. It is of a sudden very clear why we have come to be in this place through these unlikely circumstances. I had just not realized it till now."

Large Jake has finished his second plate. He pushes it away and looks at Chris the Shoemaker.

"Later," says Chris. "Outside."

Jake nods.

Of a sudden-like, I am not enjoying Ma Gooser's groaning board as much as I should wish.

For when Chris is in a working mood, things happen.

They had drawn spot #24 down at the judging stand. Each contestant could sing three songs, and the Black Draught people had a big gong they could ring if anyone was too bad.

"I don't know 'bout the ones from 'round here," said Cave Canem, "but they won't need that there gong for the people we know about. We came in third to some of 'em last year in Sweet Tater City."

"Me neither," said Rooster Joe. "The folks I seen can sure play and sing. Why even the Famous Eesup Twins, Bert and Mert, is here. You ever hear them do 'Land Where No Cabins Fall'?"

"Nope," said Luke, "but I have heard of 'em. It seems we'll just have to outplay them all."

They were under a tree pretty far away from the rest of the crowd, who were waiting for the contest to begin.

"Let's rosin up, boys," said Luke, taking his crosscut saw out of his tow sack.

Felix unfolded the ladder and climbed up. Cave pulled out a big willow bow strung with braided muletail hair.

Rooster Joe took out an eight-ounce ball peen hammer and sat back against a tree root.

Luke rosined up his fiddle bow.

"Okay, let's give 'er about two pounds o' press and bend."

He nodded his head. They bowed, Felix pressing down on the big bucksaw handle from above, Rooster Joe striking his ripsaw, Luke pulling at the back of his crosscut.

The same note, three octaves apart, floated on the air.

"Well, that's enough rehearsin'," said Luke. "Now all we got to do is stay in this shady spot and wait till our turn."

They put their instruments and ladder against the tree, and took naps.

When Chris the Shoemaker starts to working, usually someone ends up with cackle fruit on their mug.

When Little Willie and Chris first teamed up when they were oh so very young, they did all the usual grifts. They worked the cherry-colored cat and the old hydrophoby lay, and once or twice even pulled off the glim drop, which is a wonder since neither of them has a glass peeper. They quit the grift when it turns out that Little Willie is always off nugging when Chris needs him, or is piping some doll's stems when he should be laying zex. So they went into various other forms of getting the mazuma.

The ramadoola Chris has come up with is a simple one. We are to get the lizzie going, or barring that are to Hooverize another one; then we cut the lines of communication; immobilize the town clown, glom the loot, and give them the old razoo.

"But Chris," says I, "it is so simple and easy there must be something wrong with your brainstorm. And besides, it is what? Maybe a hundred simoleons in all? I have seen you lose that betting on which raindrop will run down a windowpane first."

"We have been placed here to do this thing," says Chris the Shoemaker. We are all standing on the porch of Ma Gooser's. "We cut the phone," says Chris, "no one can call out. Any other jalopies, Large Jake makes inoperable. That leaves horses, which even we can go faster than. We make the local yokel do a Brodie so there is no Cicero lightning or Illinois thunder. We are gone, and the news takes till next week to get over the ridge yonder."

Miss Millie Dee Chantpie has one of her shoes off and is rubbing her well-turned foot. "My corns is killing me," she says, "and Chris, I think this is the dumbest thing you have ever thought about!"

"I will note and file that," says Chris. "Meantimes, that is the plan. Little William here will start a rumor that will make our presence acceptable before he goes off with the man with the thews of iron. We will only bleaso this caper should the flivver not be fixable or we cannot kipe another one. So it is written. So it shall be done."

Ten minutes later, just before Little Willie leaves in the wagon, I hear two people talking close by, pointing to Miss Millie Dee Chantpie and swearing she is a famous chanteuse, and that Chris the Shoemaker is a talent scout from Okeh Records.

"The town clown," says Chris to me in a while, "will be no problem. He is that gent you see over there sucking on the yamsicle, with the tin star pinned to his long johns with the Civil War cannon tucked in his belt."

I nod.

"Charlie Perro," he says to me, "now let us make like we are mesmerized by this screeching and hollering that is beginning."

The contest is under way. It was like this carnival freak show had of a sudden gone into a production of *No, No Nanette* while you were trying to get a good peek at the India Rubber Woman.

I am not sure whether to be laughing or crying, so I just puts on the look a steer gets just after the hammer comes down, and pretends to watch. What I am really thinking, even I don't know.

There had been sister harmony groups, and guitar and mandolin ensembles, three guys on one big harmonica, a couple of twelve-year-olds playing ocarinas and washboards, a woman on gutbucket broom bass, a handbell choir from a church, three one-man bands, and a guy who could tear newspapers to the tune of "Hold That Tiger!"

Every eight acts or so, Reverend Shapenote and the Mt. Sinai Choir got up and sang sacred harp music, singing the notes only, with no words because their church believed you went straight to Hell if you sang words to a hymn; you could only lift your voice in song.

Luke lay with his hat over his eyes through two more acts. It was well into the afternoon. People were getting hot and cranky all over the town.

As the next act started, Luke sat up. He looked toward the stage. Two giants in coveralls and flannel shirts got up. Even from this far away, their voices carried clear and loud, not strained: deep bass and baritone.

The words of "Eight More Miles To Home" and then "You Are My Sunshine" came back, and for their last song, they went into the old hymn, "Absalom, Absalom":

> *Day-Vid The King—He-Wept—and Wept Saying—*
> *Oh My Son—Oh my son…*

and a chill went up Luke's back.

"That's them," said Rooster Joe, seeing Luke awake.

"Well," said Luke Apuleus, pulling his hat back down over his eyes as the crowd went crazy, "them is the ones we really have to beat. Call me when they gets to the Cowbell Quintet so we can be moseying up there."

I am being very relieved when Little Willie comes driving into town in the flivver; it is looking much the worse for wear but seems to be running fine. He parks it on Main Street at the far edge of the crowd and comes walking over to me and Chris the Shoemaker.

"How are you standing this?" he asks.

"Why do you not get up there, William?" asks Chris. "I know for a fact you warbled for the cheese up at the River Academy, before they let you out on the technical."

"It was just to keep from driving an Irish buggy," says Little Willie. "The Lizzie will go wherever you want it to. Tires patched. Gassed and lubered up. Say the syllable."

Chris nods to Large Jake over at the edge of the crowd. Jake saunters back towards the only two trucks in town, besides the Cardui vehicle, which, being too gaudy even for us, Jake has already fixed while it is parked right in front of the stage, for Jake is a very clever fellow for someone with such big mitts.

"Charlie Perro," says Chris, reaching in Miss Millie Dee Chantpie's purse, "how's about taking these nippers here," handing me a pair of wire cutters, "and go see if that blower wire back of the general mercantile isn't too long by about six feet when I give you the nod. Then you should come back and help us." He also takes his howitzer out of Miss Millie's bag.

"Little William," he says, turning. "Take Miss Millie Dee Chantpie to the car and start it up. I shall go see what the Cardui Black Draught people are doing."

So it was we sets out to pull the biggest caper in the history of Brimmytown.

"That's them," said Rooster Joe. "The cowbells afore us."

"Well, boys," said Luke, "it's do-or-die time."

They gathered up their saws and sacks and ladder, and started for the stage.

Miss Millie Dee Chantpie is in the car, looking cool as a cucumber. Little Willie is at one side of the crowd, standing out like a sore thumb; he has his hand under his jacket on The Old Crowd Pleaser.

Large Jake is back, shading three or four people from the hot afternoon sun. I am at the corner of the general mercantile, one eye on Chris the Shoemaker and one on the wire coming down the back of the store.

The prize moolah is in this big glass cracker jar on the table with the judges so everybody can see it. It is in greenbacks.

I am seeing Large Jake move up behind the John Law figure, who is sucking at a jug of corn liquor—you would not think the Prohib was the rule of the land here.

I am seeing these guys climb onto the stage, and I cannot believe my peepers, because they are pulling saws and ladders out of their backs. Are these carpenters or what? There is a guy in a straw hat, and one with a bristle mustache, and one with a redchecked shirt and red hat, and one with a cap with big floppy earflaps. One is climbing on a ladder. They are having tools everywhere. What the dingdong is going on?

And they begin to play, a corny song, but it is high and sweet, and then I am thinking of birds and rivers and running water and so forth. So I shakes myself, and keeps my glims on Chris the Shoemaker.

The guys with the saws are finishing their song, and people are going ga-ga over them.

And then I see that Chris is in position.

"Thank yew, thank yew," said Luke. "We-all is the Sawing Boys and we are pleased as butter to be here. I got a cousin over to Cornfield County what has one uh them new cat-whisker crystal *raddio* devices, and you should hear the things that comes right over the air from it. Well, I learned a few of them, and me and the boys talked about them, and now we'll do a couple for yew. Here we're gonna do one by the Molokoi Hotel Royal Hawaiian Serenaders called 'Ule Uhi Umekoi Hwa Hwa.' Take it away, Sawing Boys!" He tapped his foot.

He bent his saw and bowed the first high, swelling notes, then Rooster Joe came down on the harmony rhythm on the ripsaw. Felix bent down on the ladder on the handle of the bucksaw, and Cave pulled the big willow bow and they were off into a fast, swinging song that was about lagoons and fish and food. People were jumping and yelling all over town, and Luke, whose voice was nothing special, started singing:

> *"Ume hoi uli koi hwa hwa*
> *Wa haweaee omi oi lui lui…"*

And the applause began before Rooster Joe finished alone with a dying struck high note that held for ten or fifteen seconds. People were yelling and screaming and the Cardui people didn't know what to do with themselves.

"Thank yew, thank yew!" said Luke Apuleus, wiping his brow with his arm while holding his big straw hat in his hand. "Now, here's another one I heerd. We hope you-all like it. It's from the Abe Schwartz Orchestra and it's called 'Beym Rebn in Palestine.' Take it away, Sawing Boys."

They hit halting, fluttering notes, punctuated by Rooster Joe's hammered ripsaw, and then the bucksaw went rolling behind it, Felix pumping up and down on the handle, Cave Canem bowing away. It sounded like flutes and violins and clarinets and mandolins. It sounded a thousand years old, but not like moonshine mountain music; it was from another time and another land.

Something is wrong, for Chris is standing very still, like he is already in the old oak kimono, and I can see he is not going to be giving me the High Sign.

I see that Little Willie, who never does anything on his own, is motioning to me and Large Jake to come over. So over I trot, and the music really washes over me. I know it in my bones, for it is the music of the old neighborhood where all of us but Miss Millie grew up.

I am coming up on Chris the Shoemaker and I see he has turned on the waterworks. He is transfixed, for here, one thousand miles from home he is being caught up in the mighty coils of memory and transfiguration.

I am hearing with his ears, and what the saws are making is not the Abe Schwartz Orchestra but Itzikel Kramtweiss of Philadelphia, or perhaps Naftalie Brandwein, who used to play bar mitzvahs and weddings with his back to the audience so rival clarinet players couldn't see his hands and how he made those notes.

There is maybe ten thousand years behind that noise, and it is calling all the way across the Kentucky hills from the Land of Gaza.

And while they are still playing, we walk with Chris the Shoemaker back to the jalopy, and pile in around Miss Millie Dee Chantpie, who, when she sees Chris crying, begins herself, and I confess I, too, am a little blurry-eyed at the poignance of the moment.

And we pull out of Brimmytown, the saws still whining and screeching their jazzy ancient tune, and as it is fading and we are going up the hill, Chris the Shoemaker speaks for us all, and what he says is:

"God Damn. You cannot be going anywhere these days without you run into a bunch of half-assed *klezmorim.*"

For Arthur Hunnicutt and the late Sheldon Leonard.

Glossary to "The Sawing Boys"

Balonies—tires

Bargain Day—court time set aside for sentencing plea-bargain cases

Beezer—the face, sometimes especially the nose

Bleaso!—1. an interjection—Careful! You are being overheard! Some chump is wise to the deal! 2. verb—to forgo something, change plans, etc.

The Cherry-colored Cat—an old con game

Cicero Lightning and Illinois Thunder—the muzzle flashes from machine guns and the sound of hand grenades going off

Do a minute—thirty days

Dogs are barking—feet are hurting

Fall Togs—the suit you wear going into, and coming out of, jail

Flit—prison coffee, from its resemblance to the popular fly spray of the time

Flivver—a jalopy

Frammus—a thingamajig or doohickey

Geetas—money, of any kind or amount

Glim Drop—con game involving leaving a glass eye as security for an amount of money; *at least* one of the con men should have a glass eye…

Glims—eyes

Goozle—mouth

Hooverize—(pre-Depression)—Hoover had been Allied Food Commissioner during the Great War, and was responsible for people getting the most use out of whatever foods they had; the standard command from parents was "Hooverize that plate!"; possibly a secondary reference to vacuum cleaners of the time.

Irish buggy (also Irish surrey)—a wheelbarrow

Jalopy—a flivver

Lizzie—a flivver

Mazuma—money, of any kind or amount

Mook—face

Motorman's gloves—any especially large cut of meat

Nugging—porking

The Old Hydrophoby Lay—con game involving pretending to be bitten by someone's (possibly mad) dog

Piping Some Doll's Stems—looking at some woman's legs

Push and Pull—gas and oil

Sammys—the Feds

Zex—Quiet (as in bleaso), cut it out, jiggies! Beat it!

Laying zex—keeping lookout

Rules of pig Latin: initial consonants are moved to the end of the word and -ay is added to the consonant; initial vowels are moved to the end of the word and -way is added to the vowel

Afterword

Ellen Datlow and Terri Windling did a series of anthologies of retold fairy tales in the mid and late '90s, and they wanted me in them.

I said "I'll do the Brementown Musicians" without thinking much about what I was saying.

Well, now. Go read "The Brementown Musicians": I'll wait.

Back already? Tell me what happens in the tale.

Not much, you say. Well, that's what struck me, too, on rereading it for the first time in 40-some-odd years.

A bunch of animals who want to be musicians go to Brementown, meet up with a bunch of robbers, make a lot of noise, and scare them off. The end.

Now tell me that's not what happens in "The Sawing Boys"?

Writing like Damon Runyan is not as easy as it looks; present tense for one thing is counter to how we think; we tell stories in the past tense—they've already happened as they're being told. Runyan wrote as if the story hadn't happened yet, was taking place as he wrote it. What you have to do is, you write a part for the late Sheldon Leonard to say out of the side of his mouth. The other part—the Sawing Boys part—I wanted to write for the late Denver Pyle to speak in his role as the father of the band (played by the Dillards) on the old Andy Griffith Show set in Mayberry RFD.

I think I did a swell job on both counts.

There are some philology/fairy-tale collecting references here, but pretty subtle (not as many as in my later contribution to the series—"Our Mortal Span"—which came from an epiphanic moment as the Middle Billy-Goat-Gruff in a second-grade play.)

When I tell people what this story is really about—the spread of mass communications (radio and gramophone records) in the early 20th Century, they don't believe me.

THE SAWING BOYS

Black Thorn, White Rose was the second of Terri and my adult re-told fairy tale anthologies. It came out in 1994.

Howard Waldrop has one of the most fertile minds in the field of sf/f, deftly weaving his knowledge of history with the present, reality and fantasy. If you haven't read his work, you must. You can either guess what tale he's retelling in "The Sawing Boys" or jump to the back of this story (which also has a glossary).

Shay Corsham Worsted

by Garth Nix

(From *Fearful Symmetries,* 2014)

The young man came in one of the windows, because the back door had proved surprisingly tough. He'd kicked it a few times, without effect, before looking for an easier way to get in. The windows were barred, but the bars were rusted almost through, so he had no difficulty pulling them away. The window was locked as well, but he just smashed the glass with a half brick pried out of the garden wall. He didn't care about the noise. He knew there was only the old man in the house, the garden was large and screened by trees, and the evening traffic was streaming past on the road out front. That was plenty loud enough to cloak any noise he might make.

Or any quavering cries for help from the old man, thought the intruder, as he climbed through. He went to the back door first, intending to open it for a quick getaway, but it was deadlocked. More afraid of getting robbed than dying in a fire, thought the young man. That made it easier. He liked the frightened old people, the power he had over them with his youth and strength and anger.

When he turned around, the old man was standing behind him. Just standing there, not doing a thing. It was dim in the corridor, the only light a weak bulb hanging from the ceiling, its pallid glow falling on the bald head of the little man, the ancient slight figure in his brown cardigan and brown corduroy trousers and brown slippers, just a little old man that could be picked up and broken like a stick and then whatever pathetic treasures were in the house could be—

A little old man whose eyes were silver.

And what was in his hands?

Those gnarled hands had been empty, the intruder was sure of it, but now the old bloke held long blades, though he wasn't exactly holding the blades… they were growing, growing from his fingers, the flesh fusing together and turning silver…silver as those eyes!

The young man had turned half an inch towards the window and escape when the first of those silvery blades penetrated his throat, destroying his voice box, changing the scream that rose there to a dull, choking cough. The second blade went straight through his heart, back out, and through again.

Pock! Pock!

Blood geysered, but not on the old man's brown cardigan. He had moved back almost in the same instant as he struck and was now ten feet away, watching with those silver eyes as the young man fell writhing on the floor, his feet drumming for eighteen seconds before he became still.

The blades retreated, became fingers once again. The old man considered the body, the pooling blood, the mess.

"Shay Marazion Velvet," he said to himself, and walked to the spray of blood farthest from the body, head-high on the peeling wallpaper of green lilies. He poked out his tongue, which grew longer and became as silver as the blades.

He began to lick, tongue moving rhythmically, head tilted as required. There was no expression on his face, no sign of physical excitement. This was not some fetish.

He was simply cleaning up.

"You'll never guess who I saw walking up and down outside, Father," said Mary Shires, as she bustled in with her ludicrously enormous basket filled with the weekly tribute of home-made foods and little luxuries that were generally unwanted and wholly unappreciated by her father, Sir David Shires.

"Who?" grunted Sir David. He was sitting at his kitchen table, scrawling notes on the front page of the *Times*, below the big headlines with the latest from the war with Argentina over the Falklands, and enjoying the sun that was briefly flooding the whole room through the open doors to the garden.

"That funny little Mister Shea," said Mary, putting the basket down on the table.

Sir David's pencil broke. He let it fall and concentrated on keeping his hand still, on making his voice sound normal. He shouldn't be surprised, he told himself. It was why he was here, after all. But after so many years, even though every day he told himself this could be *the* day, it was a terrible, shocking surprise.

"Really, dear?" he said. He thought his voice sounded mild enough. "Going down to the supermarket like he normally does, I suppose? Getting his bread and milk?"

"No, that's just the thing," said Mary. She took out a packet of some kind of biscuit and put it in front of her father. "These are very good. Oatmeal and some kind of North African citrus. You'll like them."

"Mister Shea," prompted Sir David.

"Oh, yes. He's just walking backwards and forwards along the footpath from his house to the corner. Backwards and forwards! I suppose he's gone ga-ga. He's old enough. He must be ninety if he's a day, surely?"

She looked at him, without guile, both of them knowing he was eighty himself. But not going ga-ga, thank god, even if his knees were weak reeds and he couldn't sleep at night, remembering things that he had forced himself to forget in his younger days.

But Shay was much older than ninety, thought Sir David. Shay was much, much older than that.

He pushed his chair back and stood up.

"I might go and…and have a word with the old chap," he said carefully. "You stay here, Mary."

"Perhaps I should come—"

"No!"

He grimaced, acknowledging he had spoken with too much emphasis. He didn't want to alarm Mary. But then again, in the worst case…no, not the worst case, but in a quite plausible minor escalation…

"In fact, I think you should go out the back way and get home," said Sir David.

"Really, Father, why on—"

"Because I am ordering you to," snapped Sir David. He still had the voice, the tone that expected to be obeyed, deployed very rarely with the family, but quite often to the many who had served under him, first in the Navy and then for considerably longer in the Department, where he had ended up as the Deputy Chief. Almost fifteen years gone, but it wasn't the sort of job where you ever completely left, and the command voice was the least of the things that had stayed with him.

Mary sniffed, but she obeyed, slamming the garden gate on her way out. It would be a few years yet, he thought, before she began to question everything he did, perhaps start bringing brochures for retirement homes along with her special biscuits and herbal teas she believed to be good for reducing the chance of dementia.

Dementia. There was an apposite word. He'd spent some time thinking he might be suffering from dementia or some close cousin of it, thirty years ago, in direct connection to "funny old Mister Shea." Who was not at all funny, not in any sense of the word. They had all wondered if they were demented, for a time.

He paused near his front door, wondering for a moment if he should make the call first, or even press his hand against the wood paneling just so, and flip it open to take out the .38 Colt Police revolver cached there. He had a 9mm Browning automatic upstairs, but a revolver was better for a cached weapon. You wouldn't want to bet your life on magazine springs in a weapon that had sat too long. He checked all his armament every month, but still…a revolver was more certain.

But automatic or revolver, neither would be any use. He'd learned that before, from direct observation, and had been lucky to survive. Very lucky, because the other two members of the team hadn't had the fortune to slip in the mud and hit themselves on the head and be forced to lie still. They'd gone in shooting, and kept shooting, unable to believe the evidence of their eyes, until it was too late…

Sir David grimaced. This was one of the memories he'd managed to push aside for a long, long time. But like all the others, it wasn't far below the surface. It didn't take much to bring it up, that afternoon in 1953, the Department's secure storage on the fringe of RAF Bicester...

He did take a walking stick out of the stand. A solid bog oak stick, with a pommel of bronze worked in the shape of a spaniel's head. Not for use as a weapon, but simply because he didn't walk as well as he once did. He couldn't afford a fall now. Or at any time really, but particularly not now.

The sun was still shining outside. It was a beautiful day, the sky as blue as a bird's egg, with hardly a cloud in sight. It was the kind of day you only saw in films, evoking some fabulous summer time that never really existed, or not for more than half an hour at a time.

It was a good day to die, if it came to that, if you were eighty and getting tired of the necessary props to a continued existence. The medicines and interventions, the careful calculation of probabilities before anything resembling activity, calculations that Sir David would never have undertaken at a younger age.

He swung out on to the footpath, a military stride, necessarily adjusted by age and a back that would no longer entirely straighten. He paused by the kerb and looked left and right, surveying the street, head back, shoulders close to straight, sandy eyebrows raised, hair no longer quite so regulation short, catching a little of the breeze, the soft breeze that added to the day's delights.

Shay was there, as Mary had said. It was wearing the same clothes as always, the brown cardigan and corduroy. They'd put fifty pairs in the safe house, at the beginning, uncertain whether Shay would buy more or not, though its daily purchase of bread, milk and other basics was well established. It could mimic human behavior very well.

It looked like a little old man, a bald little man of some great age. Wrinkled skin, hooded eyes, head bent as if the neck could no longer entirely support the weight of years. But Sir David knew it didn't always move like an old man. It could move fluidly, like an insect, faster than you ever thought at first sighting.

Right now Shay was walking along the footpath, away from Sir David. Halfway to the corner, it turned back. It must have seen him, but as usual, it gave no outward sign of recognition or reception. There would be no such sign, until it decided to do whatever it was going to do next.

Sir David shuffled forward. Best to get it over with. His hand was already sweating, slippery on the bronze dog handle of his stick, his heart hammering in a fashion bound to be at odds with a cardio-pulmonary system past its best. He knew the feeling well, though it had been an age since he'd felt it more than fleetingly.

Fear. Unalloyed fear, that must be conquered, or he could do nothing, and that was not an option. Shay had broken free of its programming. It could be about to do anything, anything at all, perhaps reliving some of its more minor exploits like the Whitechapel murders of 1888, or a major one like the massacre at Slapton Sands in 1944.

Or something greater still.

Not that Sir David was sure he *could* do anything. He'd only ever been told two of the command phrases, and lesser ones at that, a pair of two word groups. They were embossed on his mind, bright as new brass. But it was never known exactly what they meant, or how Shay understood them.

There was also the question of which command to use. Or to try and use both command phrases, though that might somehow have the effect of one of the four word command groups. An unknown effect, very likely fatal to Sir David and everyone for miles, perhaps more.

It was not inconceivable that whatever he said in the next two minutes might doom everyone in London, or even the United Kingdom.

Perhaps even the world.

The first command would be best, Sir David thought, watching Shay approach. They were out in public, the second would attract attention, besides its other significant drawback. Public attention was anathema to Sir David, even in such dire circumstances. He straightened his tie unconsciously as he thought about publicity. It was a plain green tie, as his suit was an inconspicuous grey flannel, off the rack. No club or regimental ties for Sir David, no identifying signet rings, no ring, no earring, no tattoos, no unusual facial hair. He worked to look a type that had once been excellent camouflage, the retired military officer. It still worked, though less well, there being fewer of the type to hide amongst. Perhaps the Falklands War would help in this regard.

Shay was drawing nearer, walking steadily, perfectly straight. Sir David peered at it. Were its eyes silver? If they were, it would be too late. All bets off, end of story. But the sun was too bright, Sir David's own sight was not what it once was. He couldn't tell if Shay's eyes were silver.

"Shay Risborough Gabardine," whispered Sir David. Ludicrous words, but proven by trial and error, trial by combat, death by error. The name it apparently gave itself, a station on the Great Western Line, and a type of fabric. Not words you'd ever expect to find together, there was its safety, the cleverness of Isambard Kingdom Brunel showing through. Though not as clever as how IKB had got Shay to respond to the words in the first place. So clever that no one else had worked out how it had been done, not in the three different attempts over more than a hundred years. Attempts to try to change or expand the creature's lexicon, each attempt another litany of mistakes and many deaths. And after each such trial, the fear that had led to it being shut away. Locked underground the last time, and then the chance rediscovery in 1953 and the foolishness that had led it to being put away here, parked and forgotten.

Except by Sir David.

Shay was getting very close now. Its face looked innocuous enough. A little vacant, a man not too bright perhaps, or very short of sleep. Its skin was pale today, matching Sir David's own, but he knew it could change that in an instant. Skin colour, height, apparent age, gender…all of these could be changed by Shay, though it mostly appeared as it was right now.

Small and innocuous, old and tired. Excellent camouflage among humans.

Ten paces, nine paces, eight paces…the timing had to be right. The command had to be said in front of its face, without error, clear and precise—

"Shay Risborough Gabardine," barked Sir David, shivering in place, his whole body tensed to receive a killing blow.

Shay's eyes flashed silver. He took half a step forward, putting him inches away from Sir David, and stopped. There was a terrible stillness, the world perched on the brink. Then it turned on its heel, crossed the road and went back into its house. The old house, opposite Sir David's, that no one but Shay had set foot in for thirty years.

Sir David stood where he was for several minutes, shaking. Finally he quelled his shivering enough to march back inside his own house, where he ignored the phone on the hall table, choosing instead to open a drawer in his study to lift out a chunkier, older thing that had no dial of any kind, push-button or rotary. He held the handset to his head and waited.

There were a series of clicks and whines and beeps, the sound of disparate connections working out how they might after all get together. Finally a sharp, quick male voice answered on the other end.

"Yes."

"Case Shay Zulu," said Sir David. There was a pause. He could hear the flipping of pages, as the operator searched through the ready book.

"Is there more?" asked the operator.

"What!" exploded Sir David. "Case Shay Zulu!"

"How do you spell it?"

Sir David's lip curled almost up to his nose, but he pulled it back.

"S-H-A-Y," he spelled out. "Z-U-L-U."

"I can spell Zulu," said the operator, affronted. "There's still nothing."

"Look up my workname," said Sir David. "Arthur Brooks."

There was tapping now, the sound of a keyboard. He'd heard they were using computers more and more throughout the Department, not just for the boffins in the back rooms.

"Ah, I see… I've got you now, sir," said the operator. At least there was a "sir," now.

"Get someone competent to look up Shay Zulu and report my communication at once to the duty officer with instruction to relay it to the Chief," ordered Sir David. "I want a call back in five minutes."

The call came in ten minutes, ten minutes Sir David spent looking out his study window, watching the house across the road. It was eleven a.m., too late for Shay to go to the supermarket like it had done every day for the last thirty years. Sir David wouldn't know if it had returned to its previous safe routine until 10:30am tomorrow. Or earlier, if Shay was departing on some different course...

The insistent ringing recalled him to the phone.

"Yes."

"Sir David? My name is Angela Terris, I'm the duty officer at present. We're a bit at sea here. We can't find Shay Zulu in the system at all—what was that?"

Sir David had let out a muffled cry, his knuckles jammed against his mouth.

"Nothing, nothing," he said, trying to think. "The paper files, the old records to 1977, you can look there. But the important thing is the book, we... I must have the notebook from the Chief's safe, a small green leather book embossed on the cover with the gold initials IKB."

"The Chief's not here right now," said Angela brightly. "This Falklands thing, you know. He's briefing the cabinet. Is it urgent?"

"Of course it's urgent!" barked Sir David, regretting it even as he spoke, remembering when old Admiral Puller had called up long after retirement, concerned about a suspicious new postman, and how they had laughed on the Seventh Floor. "Look, find Case Shay Zulu and you'll see what I mean."

"Is it something to do with the Soviets, Sir David? Because we're really getting on reasonably well with them at the moment—"

"No, no, it's nothing to do with the Soviets," said Sir David. He could hear the tone in her voice, he remembered using it himself when he had taken Admiral Fuller's call. It was the calming voice that meant no immediate action, a routine request to some functionary to investigate further in days, or even weeks, purely as a courtesy to the old man. He had to do something that would make her act, there had to some lever.

"I'm afraid it's something to do with the Service itself," he said. "Could be very, very embarrassing. Even now. I need that book to deal with it."

"Embarrassing as in likely to be of media interest, Sir David?" asked Angela.

"Very much so," said Sir David heavily.

"I'll see what I can do," said Angela.

"**We were really** rather surprised to find the Department owns a safe house that isn't on the register," said the young, nattily dressed and border-line rude young man who came that afternoon. His name, or at least the one he had supplied, was Redmond. "Finance were absolutely delighted, it must be worth close to half a million pounds now, a huge place like that. Fill a few black holes with that once we sell it. On the quiet, of course, as you say it would be very embarrassing if the media get hold of this little real estate venture."

"Sell it?" asked Sir David. "Sell it! Did you only find the imprest accounts, not the actual file? Don't you understand? The only thing that stops Shay from running amok is routine, a routine that is firmly embedded in and around that house! Sell the house and you unleash the…the beast!"

"Beast, Sir David?" asked Redmond. He suppressed a yawn and added, "Sounds rather Biblical. I expect we can find a place for this Shea up at Exile House. I daresay they'll dig his file up eventually, qualify him as a former employee."

They could find a place for Sir David too, were the unspoken words. Exile House, last stop for those with total disability suffered on active service, crippled by torture, driven insane from stress, shot through both knees and elbows. There were many ways to arrive at Exile House.

"Did you talk to the Chief?" asked Sir David. "Did you ask about the book marked 'IKB'?"

"Chief's very busy," said Redmond. "There's a war on you know. Even if it is only a little one. Look, why don't I go over and have a chat to old Shea, get a feel for the place, see if there's anything else that might need sorting?"

"If you go over there you introduce another variable," said Sir David, as patiently as he could. "Right now, I've got Shay to return to its last state, which may or may not last until ten thirty tomorrow morning, when it goes and gets its bread and milk, as it has done for the last thirty years. But if you disrupt it again, then who knows what will happen."

"I see, I see," said Redmond. He nodded as if he had completely understood. "Bit of a mental case, hey? Well, I did bring a couple of the boys in blue along just in case."

"Boys in blue!"

Sir David was almost apoplectic. He clutched at Redmond's sleeve, but the young man effortlessly withdrew himself and sauntered away.

"Back in half a 'mo," he called out cheerfully.

Sir David tried to chase him down, but by the time he got to the front door it was shut in his face. He scrabbled at the weapon cache, pushing hard on a panel till he realized it was the wrong one. By the time he had the revolver in his hand and had wrestled the door open, Redmond was already across the road, waving to the two policemen in the panda car to follow him. They got out quickly, large men in blue, putting their hats on as they strode after the young agent.

"Not even Special Branch," muttered Sir David. He let the revolver hang by his side. What could he do with it anyway? He couldn't shoot Redmond, or the policemen.

Perhaps, he thought bleakly, he could shoot himself. That would bring them back, delay the knock on the door opposite...but it would only be a delay. And if he was killed, and if they couldn't find Brunel's book, then the other command words would be lost.

Redmond went up the front steps two at a time, past the faded sign that said, "Hawkers and Salesmen Not Welcome. Beware of the Vicious Dog" and the one underneath it that had been added a year after the first, "No Liability for Injury or Death, You Have Been Warned."

Sir David blinked, narrowing his eyes against the sunshine that was still streaming down, flooding the street. It was just like the afternoon, that afternoon in '43 when the sun had broken through after days of fog and ice, but even though it washed across him on the bridge of his frigate he couldn't feel it, he could only see the light, he was so frozen from the cold Atlantic days the sunshine couldn't touch him, there was no warmth that could reach him...

He felt colder now. Redmond was knocking on the door. Hammering on the door. Sir David choked a little on his own spit, apprehension rising. There was a chance Shay wouldn't answer, and the door was very heavy, those two policemen couldn't kick it down, there would be more delay—

The door opened. There was the flash of silver, and Redmond fell down the steps, blood geysering from his neck as if some newfangled watering system had suddenly switched on beside him, drawing water from a rusted tank.

A blur of movement followed. The closer policeman spun about, as if suddenly inspired to dance, only his head was tumbling from his shoulders to dance apart from him. The surviving policeman, that is the policeman who had survived the first three seconds of contact with Shay, staggered backwards and started to turn around to run.

He took one step before he too was pierced through with a silver spike, his feet taking him only to the gutter where he lay down to die.

Sir David went back inside, leaving the door open. He went to his phone in the hall and called his daughter. She answered on the fourth ring. Sir David's hand was so sweaty he had to grip the plastic tightly, so the phone didn't slip from his grip.

"Mary? I want you to call Peter and your girls and tell them to get across the Channel now. France, Belgium, doesn't matter. No, wait, Terence is in Newcastle, isn't he? Tell him...listen to me...he can get the ferry to Stavanger. Listen! There is going to be a disaster here. It doesn't matter what kind! I haven't gone crazy, you know who I know. They have to get out of the country and across the water! Just go!"

Sir David hung up. He wasn't sure Mary would do as he said. He wasn't even sure that the sea would stop Shay. That was one of the theories, never tested, that it wouldn't or couldn't cross a large body of water. Brunel almost certainly knew, but his more detailed papers had been lost. Only the code book had survived. At least until recently.

He went to the picture window in his study. It had been installed on his retirement, when he'd moved here to keep an eye on Shay. It was a big window, taking up the place of two old Georgian multi-paned affairs, and it had an excellent view of the street.

There were four bodies in full view now. The latest addition was a very young man. Had been a young man. The proverbial innocent bystander, in the wrong place at the wrong time. A car sped by, jerking suddenly into the other lane as the driver saw the corpses and the blood.

Shay walked into the street and looked up at Sir David's window.

Its eyes were silver.

The secure phone behind Sir David rang. He retreated, still watching Shay, and picked it up.

"Yes."

"Sir David? Angela Terris here. The police are reporting multiple 999 calls, apparently there are people—"

"Yes. Redmond and the two officers are dead. I told him not to go, but he did. Shay is active now. I tried to tell you."

Shay was moving, crossing the road.

"Sir David!"

"Find the book," said Sir David wearily. "That's the only thing that can help you now. Find the leather book marked "IKB." It's in the Chief's safe."

Shay was on Sir David's side of the street, moving left, out of sight.

"The Chief's office was remodeled last year," said Angela Terris. "The old safe… I don't know—"

Sir David laughed bitter laughter and dropped the phone.

There was the sound of footsteps in the hall.

Footsteps that didn't sound quite right.

Sir David stood at attention and straightened his tie. Time to find out if the other command did what it was supposed to do. It would be out of his hands then. If it worked, Shay would kill him and then await further instructions for twenty-four hours. Either they'd find the book or they wouldn't, but he would have done his best.

As always.

Shay came into the room. It didn't look much like an old man now. It was taller, and straighter, and its head was bigger. So was its mouth.

"Shay Corsham Worsted," said Sir David.

SHAY CORSHAM WORSTED

Fearful Symmetries is an un-themed anthology kickstarted in partnership with the publisher. As I've said previously, unthemed anthologies are a hard sell. Some of the stories in this 2014 book have become my favorites, including the one reprinted here: "Shay Corsham Worsted" by Garth Nix. The story was a finalist for the Aurealis Award and the Shirley Jackson Award. The book itself won the Bram Stoker and Shirley Jackson awards.

Seventy-Two Letters

by Ted Chiang

(From *Vanishing Acts,* 2002)

When he was a child, Robert's favorite toy was a simple one, a clay doll that could do nothing but walk forward. While his parents entertained their guests in the garden outside, discussing Victoria's ascension to the throne or the Chartist reforms, Robert would follow the doll as it marched down the corridors of the family home, turning it around corners or back where it came from. The doll didn't obey commands or exhibit any sense at all; if it met a wall, the diminutive clay figure would keep marching until it gradually mashed its arms and legs into misshapen flippers. Sometimes Robert would let it do that, strictly for his own amusement. Once the doll's limbs were thoroughly distorted, he'd pick the toy up and pull the name out, stopping its motion in mid-stride. Then he'd knead the body back into a smooth lump, flatten it out into a plank, and cut out a different figure: a body with one leg crooked, or longer than the other. He would stick the name back into it, and the doll would promptly topple over and push itself around in a little circle.

It wasn't the sculpting that Robert enjoyed; it was mapping out the limits of the name. He liked to see how much variation he could impart to the body before the name could no longer animate it. To save time with the sculpting, he rarely added decorative details; he refined the bodies only as was needed to test the name.

Another of his dolls walked on four legs. The body was a nice one, a finely detailed porcelain horse, but Robert was more interested in experimenting with its name. This name obeyed commands to start and stop and knew enough to avoid obstacles, and Robert tried inserting it into bodies of his own making. But this name had more exacting body requirements, and he was never able to form a clay body it could animate. He formed the legs separately and then attached them to the body, but he wasn't able to erase the seams fully; the name didn't recognize the body as a single continuous piece.

He scrutinized the names themselves, looking for some simple substitutions that might distinguish two-leggedness from four-leggedness, or make the body obey simple commands. But the names looked entirely different; on each scrap of parchment were inscribed seventy-two tiny Hebrew letters, arranged in twelve rows of six, and so far as he could tell, the order of the letters was utterly random.

Robert Stratton and his fourth-form classmates sat quietly as Master Trevelyan paced between the rows of desks.

"Langdale, what is the doctrine of names?"

"All things are reflections of God, and, um, all—"

"Spare us your bumbling. Thorburn, can *you* tell us the doctrine of names?"

"As all things are reflections of God, so are all names reflections of the divine name."

"And what is an object's true name?"

"That name which reflects the divine name in the same manner as the object reflects God."

"And what is the action of a true name?"

"To endow its object with a reflection of divine power."

"Correct. Halliwell, what is the doctrine of signatures?"

The natural philosophy lesson continued until noon, but because it was a Saturday, there was no instruction for the rest of the day. Master Trevelyan dismissed the class, and the boys of Cheltenham school dispersed.

After stopping at the dormitory, Robert met his friend Lionel at the border of school grounds. "So the wait's over? Today's the day?" Robert asked.

"I said it was, didn't I?"

"Let's go, then." The pair set off to walk the mile and a half to Lionel's home.

During his first year at Cheltenham, Robert had known Lionel hardly at all; Lionel was one of the day boys, and Robert, like all the boarders, regarded them with suspicion. Then, purely by chance, Robert ran into him while on holiday, during a visit to the British Museum. Robert loved the museum: the frail mummies and immense sarcophagi; the stuffed platypus and pickled mermaid; the wall bristling with elephant tusks and moose antlers and unicorn horns. That particular day he was at the display of elemental sprites: he was reading the card explaining the salamander's absence when he suddenly recognized Lionel, standing right next to him, peering at the undine in its jar. Conversation revealed their shared interest in the sciences, and the two became fast friends.

As they walked down the road, they kicked a large pebble back and forth between them. Lionel gave the pebble a kick, and laughed as it skittered between Robert's ankles. "I couldn't wait to get out of there," he said. "I think one more doctrine would have been more than I could bear."

"Why do they even bother calling it natural philosophy?" said Robert. "Just admit it's another theology lesson and be done with it." The two of them had recently purchased *A Boy's Guide to Nomenclature*, which informed them that nomenclators no longer spoke in terms of God or the divine name. Instead, current thinking held that there was a lexical universe as well as a physical one, and bringing an object together with a compatible name caused the latent potentialities of both to be realized. Nor was there a single "true name" for a given object: depending on its precise shape, a body might be compatible with several names, known as its "euonyms," and conversely a simple name might tolerate significant variations in body shape, as his childhood marching doll had demonstrated.

When they reached Lionel's home, they promised the cook they would be in for dinner shortly and headed to the garden out back. Lionel had converted a toolshed in his family's garden into a laboratory, which he used to conduct experiments. Normally Robert came by on a regular basis, but recently Lionel had been working on an experiment that he was keeping secret. Only now was he ready to show Robert his results. Lionel had Robert wait outside while he entered first, and then let him enter.

A long shelf ran along every wall of the shed, crowded with racks of vials, stoppered bottles of green glass, and assorted rocks and mineral specimens. A table decorated with stains and scorch marks dominated the cramped space, and it supported the apparatus for Lionel's latest experiment: a cucurbit clamped in a stand so that its bottom rested in a basin full of water, which in turn sat on a tripod above a lit oil lamp. A mercury thermometer was also fixed in the basin.

"Take a look," said Lionel.

Robert leaned over to inspect the cucurbit's contents. At first it appeared to be nothing more than foam, a dollop of suds that might have dripped off a pint of stout. But as he looked closer, he realized that what he thought were bubbles were actually the interstices of a glistening latticework. The froth consisted of *homunculi*: tiny seminal foetuses. Their bodies were transparent individually, but collectively their bulbous heads and strandlike limbs adhered to form a pale, dense foam.

"So you wanked off into a jar and kept the spunk warm?" he asked, and Lionel shoved him. Robert laughed and raised his hands in a placating gesture. "No, honestly, it's a wonder. How'd you do it?"

Mollified, Lionel said, "It's a real balancing act. You have to keep the temperature just right, of course, but if you want them to grow, you also have to keep just the right mix of nutrients. Too thin a mix, and they starve. Too rich, and they get over lively and start fighting with each other."

"You're having me on."

"It's the truth; look it up if you don't believe me. Battles amongst sperm are what cause monstrosities to be born. If an injured foetus is the one that makes it to the egg, the baby that's born is deformed."

"I thought that was because of a fright the mother had when she was carrying." Robert could just make out the minuscule squirmings of the individual foetuses. He realized that the froth was ever so slowly roiling as a result of their collective motions.

"That's only for some kinds, like ones that are all hairy or covered in blotches. Babies that don't have arms or legs, or have misshapen ones, they're the ones that got caught in a fight back when they were sperm. That's why you can't provide too rich a broth, especially if they haven't any place to go: they get in a frenzy. You can lose all of them pretty quick that way."

"How long can you keep them growing?"

"Probably not much longer," said Lionel. "It's hard to keep them alive if they haven't reached an egg. I read about one in France that was grown till it was the size of a fist, and they had the best equipment available. I just wanted to see if I could do it at all."

Robert stared at the foam, remembering the doctrine of preformation that Master Trevelyan had drilled into them: all living things had been created at the same time, long ago, and births today were merely enlargements of the previously imperceptible. Although they appeared newly created, these *homunculi* were countless years old; for all of human history they had lain nested within generations of their ancestors, waiting for their turn to be born.

In fact, it wasn't just them who had waited; he himself must have done the same thing prior to his birth. If his father were to do this experiment, the tiny figures Robert saw would be his unborn brothers and sisters. He knew they were insensible until reaching an egg, but he wondered what thoughts they'd have if they weren't. He imagined the sensation of his body, every bone and organ soft and clear as gelatin, sticking to those of myriad identical siblings. What would it be like, looking through transparent eyelids, realizing the mountain in the distance was actually a person, recognizing it as his brother? What if he knew he'd become as massive and solid as that colossus, if only he could reach an egg? It was no wonder they fought.

Robert Stratton went on to read nomenclature at Cambridge's Trinity College. There he studied kabbalistic texts written centuries before, when nomenclators were still called *ba'alei shem* and automata were called *golem*, texts that laid the foundation for the science of names: the *Sefer Yezirah*, Eleazar of Worms' *Sodei Razayya*, Abulafia's *Hayyei ha-Olam ha-Ba*. Then he studied the alchemical treatises that placed the techniques of alphabetic manipulation in a broader philosophical and mathematical context: Llull's *Ars Magna*, Agrippa's *De Occulta Philosophia*, Dee's *Monas Hieroglyphica*.

He learned that every name was a combination of several epithets, each designating a specific trait or capability. Epithets were generated by compiling all the words that described the desired trait: cognates and etymons, from languages both living and extinct. By selectively substituting and permuting letters, one could distill from those words their common essence, which was the epithet for that trait. In certain instances, epithets could be used as the bases for triangulation, allowing one to derive epithets for traits undescribed in any language. The entire process relied on intuition as much as formulae; the ability to choose the best letter permutations was an unteachable skill.

He studied the modern techniques of nominal integration and factorization, the former being the means by which a set of epithets—pithy and evocative—were commingled into the seemingly random string of letters that made up a name, the latter by which a name was decomposed into its constituent epithets. Not every method of integration had a matching factorization technique: a powerful name might be refactored to yield a set of epithets different from those used to generate it, and those epithets were often useful for that reason. Some names resisted refactorization, and nomenclators strove to develop new techniques to penetrate their secrets.

Nomenclature was undergoing something of a revolution during this time. There had long been two classes of names: those for animating a body, and those functioning as amulets. Health amulets were worn as protection from injury or illness, while others rendered a house resistant to fire or a ship less likely to founder at sea. Of late, however, the distinction between these categories of names was becoming blurred, with exciting results.

The nascent science of thermodynamics, which established the interconvertibility of heat and work, had recently explained how automata gained their motive power by absorbing heat from their surroundings. Using this improved understanding of heat, a *Namenmeister* in Berlin had developed a new class of amulet that caused a body to absorb heat from one location and release it in another. Refrigeration employing such amulets was simpler and more efficient than that based on the evaporation of a volatile fluid, and had immense commercial application. Amulets were likewise facilitating the improvement of automata: an Edinburgh nomenclator's research into the amulets that prevented objects from becoming lost had led him to patent a household automaton able to return objects to their proper places.

Upon graduation, Stratton took up residence in London and secured a position as a nomenclator at Coade Manufactory, one of the leading makers of automata in England.

Stratton's most recent automaton, cast from plaster of Paris, followed a few paces behind him as he entered the factory building. It was an immense brick structure with skylights for its roof; half of the building was devoted to casting metal, the other half to ceramics. In either section, a meandering path connected the various rooms, each one housing the next step in transforming raw materials into finished automata. Stratton and his automaton entered the ceramics portion.

They walked past a row of low vats in which the clay was mixed. Different vats contained different grades of clay, ranging from common red clay to fine white kaolin, resembling enormous mugs abrim with liquid chocolate or heavy cream; only the strong mineral smell broke the illusion. The paddles stirring the clay were connected by gears to a drive shaft, mounted just beneath the skylights, that ran the length of the room. At the end of the room stood an automatous engine: a cast-iron giant that cranked the drive wheel tirelessly. Walking past, Stratton could detect a faint coolness in the air as the engine drew heat from its surroundings.

The next room held the molds for casting. Chalky white shells bearing the inverted contours of various automata were stacked along the walls. In the central portion of the room, apron-clad journeymen sculptors worked singly and in pairs, tending the cocoons from which automata were hatched.

The sculptor nearest him was assembling the mold for a putter, a broad-headed quadruped employed in the mines for pushing trolleys of ore. The young man looked up from his work. "Were you looking for someone, sir?" he asked.

"I'm to meet Master Willoughby here," replied Stratton.

"Pardon, I didn't realize. I'm sure he'll be here shortly." The journeyman returned to his task. Harold Willoughby was a Master Sculptor First-Degree; Stratton was consulting him on the design of a reusable mold for casting his automaton. While he waited, Stratton strolled idly amongst the molds. His automaton stood motionless, ready for its next command.

Willoughby entered from the door to the metalworks, his face flushed from the heat of the foundry. "My apologies for being late, Mr. Stratton," he said. "We've been working toward a large bronze for some weeks now, and today was the pour. You don't want to leave the lads alone at a time like that."

"I understand completely," replied Stratton.

Wasting no time, Willoughby strode over to the new automaton. "Is this what you've had Moore doing all these months?" Moore was the journeyman assisting Stratton on his project.

Stratton nodded. "The boy does good work." Following Stratton's requests, Moore had fashioned countless bodies, all variations on a single basic theme, by applying modeling clay to an armature, and then used them to create plaster casts on which Stratton could test his names.

Willoughby inspected the body. "Some nice detail; looks straightforward enough—hold on now." He pointed to the automaton's hands: rather than the traditional paddle or mitten design, with fingers suggested by grooves in the surface, these were fully formed, each one having a thumb and four distinct and separate fingers. "You don't mean to tell me those are functional?"

"That's correct."

Willoughby's skepticism was plain. "Show me."

Stratton addressed the automaton. "Flex your fingers." The automaton extended both hands, flexed and straightened each pair of fingers in turn, and then returned its arms to its sides.

"I congratulate you, Mr. Stratton," said the sculptor. He squatted to examine the automaton's fingers more closely. "The fingers need to be bent at each joint for the name to take?"

"That's right. Can you design a piece mold for such a form?"

Willoughby clicked his tongue several times. "That'll be a tricky bit of business," he said. "We might have to use a waste mold for each casting. Even with a piece mold, these'd be very expensive for ceramic."

"I think they will be worth the expense. Permit me to demonstrate." Stratton addressed the automaton. "Cast a body; use that mold over there."

The automaton trudged over to a nearby wall and picked up the pieces of the mold Stratton had indicated: it was the mold for a small porcelain messenger. Several journeymen stopped what they were doing to watch the automaton carry the pieces over to a work area. There it fitted the various sections together and bound them tightly with twine. The sculptors' wonderment was apparent as they watched the automaton's fingers work, looping and threading the loose ends of the twine into a knot. Then the automaton stood the assembled mold upright and headed off to get a pitcher of clay slip.

"That's enough," said Willoughby. The automaton stopped its work and resumed its original standing posture. Examining the mold, Willoughby asked, "Did you train it yourself?"

"I did. I hope to have Moore train it in metal casting."

"Do you have names that can learn other tasks?"

"Not as yet. However, there's every reason to believe that an entire class of similar names exists, one for every sort of skill needing manual dexterity."

"Indeed?" Willoughby noticed the other sculptors watching, and called out, "If you've nothing to do, there's plenty I can assign to you." The journeymen promptly resumed their work, and Willoughby turned back to Stratton. "Let us go to your office to speak about this further."

"Very well." Stratton had the automaton follow the two of them back to the frontmost of the complex of connected buildings that was Coade Manufactory. They first entered Stratton's studio, which was situated behind his office proper. Once inside, Stratton addressed the sculptor. "Do you have an objection to my automaton?"

Willoughby looked over a pair of clay hands mounted on a worktable. On the wall behind the table were pinned a series of schematic drawings showing hands in a variety of positions. "You've done an admirable job of emulating the human hand. I am concerned, however, that the first skill in which you trained your new automaton is sculpture."

"If you're worried that I am trying to replace sculptors, you needn't be. That is absolutely not my goal."

"I'm relieved to hear it," said Willoughby. "Why did you choose sculpture, then?"

"It is the first step of a rather indirect path. My ultimate goal is to allow automatous engines to be manufactured inexpensively enough so that most families could purchase one."

Willoughby's confusion was apparent. "How, pray tell, would a family make use of an engine?"

"To drive a powered loom, for example."

"What are you going on about?"

"Have you ever seen children who are employed at a textile mill? They are worked to exhaustion; their lungs are clogged with cotton dust; they are so sickly that you can hardly conceive of their reaching adulthood. Cheap cloth is bought at the price of our workers' health; weavers were far better off when textile production was a cottage industry."

"Powered looms were what took weavers out of cottages. How could they put them back in?"

Stratton had not spoken of this before, and welcomed the opportunity to explain. "The cost of automatous engines has always been high, and so we have mills in which scores of looms are driven by an immense coal-heated Goliath. But an automaton like mine could cast engines very cheaply. If a small automatous engine, suitable for driving a few machines, becomes affordable to a weaver and his family, then they can produce cloth from their home as they did once before. People could earn a decent income without being subjected to the conditions of the factory."

"You forget the cost of the loom itself," said Willoughby gently, as if humoring him. "Powered looms are considerably more expensive than the hand looms of old."

"My automata could also assist in the production of cast-iron parts, which would reduce the price of powered looms and other machines. This is no panacea, I know, but I am nonetheless convinced that inexpensive engines offer the chance of a better life for the individual craftsman."

"Your desire for reform does you credit. Let me suggest, however, that there are simpler cures for the social ills you cite: a reduction in working hours, or the improvement of conditions. You do not need to disrupt our entire system of manufacturing."

"I think what I propose is more accurately described as a restoration than a disruption."

Now Willoughby became exasperated. "This talk of returning to a family economy is all well and good, but what would happen to sculptors? Your intentions notwithstanding, these automata of yours would put sculptors out of work. These are men who have undergone years of apprenticeship and training. How would they feed their families?"

Stratton was unprepared for the sharpness in his tone. "You overestimate my skills as a nomenclator," he said, trying to make light. The sculptor remained dour. He continued. "The learning capabilities of these automata are extremely limited. They can manipulate molds, but they could never design them; the real craft of sculpture can be performed only by sculptors. Before our meeting, you had just finished directing several journeymen in the pouring of a large bronze; automata could never work together in such a coordinated fashion. They will perform only rote tasks."

"What kind of sculptors would we produce if they spend their apprenticeship watching automata do their jobs for them? I will not have a venerable profession reduced to a performance by marionettes."

"That is not what would happen," said Stratton, becoming exasperated himself now. "But examine what you yourself are saying: the status that you wish your profession to retain is precisely that which weavers have been made to forfeit. I believe these automata can help restore dignity to other professions, and without great cost to yours."

Willoughby seemed not to hear him. "The very notion that automata would make automata! Not only is the suggestion insulting, it seems ripe for calamity. What of that ballad, the one where the broomsticks carry water buckets and run amuck?"

"You mean 'Der Zauberlehrling'?" said Stratton. "The comparison is absurd. These automata are so far removed from being in a position to reproduce themselves without human participation that I scarcely know where to begin listing the objections. A dancing bear would sooner perform in the London Ballet."

"If you'd care to develop an automaton that can dance the ballet, I would fully support such an enterprise. However, you cannot continue with these dexterous automata."

"Pardon me, sir, but I am not bound by your decisions."

"You'll find it difficult to work without sculptors' cooperation. I shall recall Moore and forbid all the other journeymen from assisting you in any way with this project."

Stratton was momentarily taken aback. "Your reaction is completely unwarranted."

"I think it entirely appropriate."

"In that case, I will work with sculptors at another manufactory."

Willoughby frowned. "I will speak with the head of the Brotherhood of Sculptors, and recommend that he forbid all of our members from casting your automata."

Stratton could feel his blood rising. "I will not be bullied," he said. "Do what you will, but you cannot prevent me from pursuing this."

"I think our discussion is at an end." Willoughby strode to the door. "Good day to you, Mr. Stratton."

"Good day to you," replied Stratton heatedly.

It was the following day, and Stratton was taking his midday stroll through the district of Lambeth, where Coade Manufactory was located. After a few blocks he stopped at a local market; sometimes among the baskets of writhing eels and blankets spread with cheap watchs were automatous dolls, and Stratton retained his boyhood fondness for seeing the latest designs. Today he noticed a new pair of boxing dolls, painted to look like an explorer and a savage. As he looked them over awhile, he could hear nostrum peddlers competing for the attention of a passerby with a runny nose.

"I see your health amulet failed you, sir," said one man whose table was arrayed with small square tins. "Your remedy lies in the curative powers of magnetism, concentrated in Doctor Sedgewick's Polarising Tablets!"

"Nonsense!" retorted an old woman. "What you need is tincture of mandrake, tried and true!" She held out a vial of clear liquid. "The dog wasn't cold yet when this extract was prepared! There's nothing more potent."

Seeing no other new dolls, Stratton left the market and walked on, his thoughts returning to what Willoughby had said yesterday. Without the cooperation of the sculptors' trade union, he'd have to resort to hiring independent sculptors. He hadn't worked with such individuals before, and some investigation would be required: ostensibly they cast bodies only for use with public-domain names, but for certain individuals these activities disguised patent infringement and piracy, and any association with them could permanently blacken his reputation.

"Mr. Stratton."

Stratton looked up. A small, wiry man, plainly dressed, stood before him. "Yes; do I know you, sir?"

"No, sir. My name is Davies. I'm in the employ of Lord Fieldhurst." He handed Stratton a card bearing the Fieldhurst crest.

Edward Maitland, third earl of Fieldhurst and a noted zoologist and comparative anatomist, was president of the Royal Society. Stratton had heard him speak during sessions of the Royal Society, but they had never been introduced. "What can I do for you?"

"Lord Fieldhurst would like to speak with you, at your earliest convenience, regarding your recent work."

Stratton wondered how the earl had learned of his work. "Why did you not call on me at my office?"

"Lord Fieldhurst prefers privacy in this matter." Stratton raised his eyebrows, but Davies didn't explain further. "Are you available this evening?"

It was an unusual invitation, but an honor nonetheless. "Certainly. Please inform Lord Fieldhurst that I would be delighted."

"A carriage will be outside your building at eight tonight." Davies touched his hat and was off.

At the promised hour, Davies arrived with the carriage. It was a luxurious vehicle, with an interior of lacquered mahogany and polished brass and brushed velvet. The tractor that drew it was an expensive one as well, a steed cast of bronze and needing no driver for familiar destinations.

Davies politely declined to answer any questions while they rode. He was obviously not a manservant, nor a secretary, but Stratton could not decide what sort of employee he was. The carriage carried them out of London into the countryside, until they reached Darrington Hall, one of the residences owned by the Fieldhurst lineage.

Once inside the home, Davies led Stratton through the foyer and then ushered him into an elegantly appointed study; he closed the doors without entering himself.

Seated at the desk within the study was a barrel-chested man wearing a silk coat and cravat; his broad, deeply creased cheeks were framed by woolly gray muttonchops. Stratton recognized him at once.

"Lord Fieldhurst, it is an honor."

"A pleasure to meet you, Mr. Stratton. You've been doing some excellent work recently."

"You are most kind. I did not realize that my work had become known."

"I make an effort to keep track of such things. Please, tell me what motivated you to develop such automata."

Stratton explained his plans for manufacturing affordable engines. Fieldhurst listened with interest, occasionally offering cogent suggestions.

"It is an admirable goal," he said, nodding his approval. "I'm pleased to find that you have such philanthropic motives, because I would ask your assistance in a project I'm directing."

"It would be my privilege to help in any way I could."

"Thank you." Fieldhurst's expression became solemn. "This is a matter of grave import. Before I speak further, I must first have your word that you will retain everything I reveal to you in the utmost confidence."

Stratton met the earl's gaze directly. "Upon my honor as a gentleman, sir, I shall not divulge anything you relate to me."

"Thank you, Mr. Stratton. Please come this way." Fieldhurst opened a door in the rear wall of the study and they walked down a short hallway. At the end of the hallway was a laboratory; a long, scrupulously clean worktable held a number of stations, each consisting of a microscope and an articulated brass framework of some sort, equipped with three mutually perpendicular knurled wheels for performing fine adjustments. An elderly man was peering into the microscope at the furthest station; he looked up from his work as they entered.

"Mr. Stratton, I believe you know Dr. Ashbourne."

Stratton, caught off guard, was momentarily speechless. Nicholas Ashbourne had been a lecturer at Trinity when Stratton was studying there, but had left years ago to pursue studies of, it was said, an unorthodox nature. Stratton remembered him as one of his most enthusiastic instructors. Age had narrowed his face somewhat, making his high forehead seem even higher, but his eyes were as bright and alert as ever. He walked over with the help of a carved ivory walking stick.

"Stratton, good to see you again."

"And you, sir. I was truly not expecting to see you here."

"This will be an evening full of surprises, my boy. Prepare yourself." He turned to Fieldhurst. "Would you care to begin?"

They followed Fieldhurst to the far end of the laboratory, where he opened another door and led them down a flight of stairs. "Only a small number of individuals—either Fellows of the Royal Society or Members of Parliament, or both—are privy to this matter. Five years ago, I was contacted confidentially by the Académie des Sciences in Paris. They wished for English scientists to confirm certain experimental findings of theirs."

"Indeed?"

"You can imagine their reluctance. However, they felt the matter outweighed national rivalries, and once I understood the situation, I agreed."

The three of them descended to a cellar. Gas brackets along the walls provided illumination, revealing the cellar's considerable size; its interior was punctuated by an array of stone pillars that rose to form groined vaults. The long cellar contained row upon row of stout wooden tables, each one supporting a tank roughly the size of a bathtub. The tanks were made of zinc and fitted with plate-glass windows on all four sides, revealing their contents as a clear, faintly straw-colored fluid.

Stratton looked at the nearest tank. There was a distortion floating in the center of the tank, as if some of the liquid had congealed into a mass of jelly. It was difficult to distinguish the mass's features from the mottled shadows cast on the bottom of the tank, so he moved to another side of the tank and squatted down low to view the mass directly against a flame of a gas lamp. It was then that the coagulum resolved itself into the ghostly figure of a man, clear as aspic, curled up in foetal position.

"Incredible," Stratton whispered.

"We call it a megafoetus," explained Fieldhurst.

"This was grown from a spermatozoon? This must have required decades."

"It did not, more's the wonder. Several years ago, two Parisian naturalists named Dubuisson and Gille developed a method of inducing hypertrophic growth in a seminal foetus. The rapid infusion of nutrients allows such a foetus to reach this size within a fortnight."

By shifting his head back and forth, he saw slight differences in the way the gaslight was refracted, indicating the boundaries of the megafoetus's internal organs. "Is this creature...alive?"

"Only in an insensate manner, like a spermatozoon. No artificial process can replace gestation; it is the vital principle within the ovum which quickens the foetus, and the maternal influence which transforms it into a person. All we've done is effect a maturation in size and scale." Fieldhurst gestured toward the megafoetus. "The maternal influence also provides a foetus with pigmentation and all distinguishing physical characteristics. Our megafoetuses have no features beyond their sex. Every male bears the generic appearance you see here, and all the females are likewise identical. Within each sex, it is impossible to distinguish one from another by physical examination, no matter how dissimilar the original fathers might have been; only rigorous record keeping allows us to identify each megafoetus."

Stratton stood up again. "So what was the intention of the experiment if not to develop an artificial womb?"

"To test the notion of the fixity of species." Realizing that Stratton was not a zoologist, the earl explained further. "Were lens grinders able to construct microscopes of unlimited magnifying power, biologists could examine the future generations nested in the spermatozoa of any species and see whether their appearance remains fixed, or changes to give rise to a new species. In the latter case, they could also determine if the transition occurs gradually or abruptly.

"However, chromatic aberration imposes an upper limit on the magnifying power of any optical instrument. Messieurs Dubuisson and Gille hit upon the idea of artificially increasing the size of the foetuses themselves. Once a foetus reaches its adult size, one can extract a spermatozoon from it and enlarge a foetus from the next generation in the same manner." Fieldhurst stepped over to the next table in the row and indicated the tank it supported. "Repetition of the process lets us examine the unborn generations of any given species."

Stratton looked around the room. The rows of tanks took on a new significance. "So they compressed the intervals between 'births' to gain a preliminary view of our genealogical future."

"Precisely."

"Audacious! And what were the results?"

"They tested many animal species, but never observed any changes in form. However, they obtained a peculiar result when working with the seminal foetuses of humans. After no more than five generations, the male foetuses held no more spermatozoa, and the females held no more ova. The line terminated in a sterile generation."

"I imagine that wasn't entirely unexpected," Stratton said, glancing at the jellied form. "Each repetition must further attenuate some essence in the organisms. It's only logical that at some point the offspring would be so feeble that the process would fail."

"That was Dubuisson and Gille's initial assumption as well," agreed Fieldhurst, "so they sought to improve their technique. However, they could find no difference between megafoetuses of succeeding generations in terms of size or vitality. Nor was there any decline in the number of spermatozoa or ova; the penultimate generation was fully as fertile as the first. The transition to sterility was an abrupt one.

"They found another anomaly as well: while some spermatozoa yielded only four or fewer generations, variation occurred only across samples, never within a single sample. They evaluated samples from father and son donors, and in such instances, the father's spermatozoa produced exactly one more generation than the son's. And from what I understand, some of the donors were aged individuals indeed. While their samples held very few spermatozoa, they nonetheless held one more generation than those from sons in the prime of their lives. The progenitive power of the sperm bore no correlation with the health or vigor of the donor; instead, it correlated with the generation to which the donor belonged."

Fieldhurst paused and looked at Stratton gravely. "It was at this point that the Académie contacted me to see if the Royal Society could duplicate their findings. Together we have obtained the same result using samples collected from peoples as varied as the Lapps and the Hottentots. We are in agreement as to the implication of these findings: that the human species has the potential to exist for only a fixed number of generations, and we are within five generations of the final one."

Stratton turned to Ashbourne, half expecting him to confess that it was all an elaborate hoax, but the elder nomenclator looked entirely solemn. Stratton looked at the megafoetus again and frowned, absorbing what he had heard. "If your interpretation is correct, other species must be subject to a similar limitation. Yet from what I know, the extinction of a species has never been observed."

Fieldhurst nodded. "That is true. However, we do have the evidence of the fossil record, which suggests that species remain unchanged for a period of time, and then are abruptly replaced by new forms. The Catastrophists hold that violent upheavals caused species to become extinct. Based on what we've discovered regarding preformation, it now appears that extinctions are merely the result of a species reaching the end of its lifetime. They are natural rather than accidental deaths, in a manner of speaking." He gestured to the doorway from which they had entered. "Shall we return upstairs?"

Following the two other men, Stratton asked, "And what of the origination of new species? If they're not born from existing species, do they arise spontaneously?"

"That is as yet uncertain. Normally only the simplest animals arise by spontaneous generation: maggots and other vermiform creatures, typically under the influence of heat. The events postulated by Catastrophists—floods, volcanic eruptions, cometary impacts—would entail the release of great energies. Perhaps such energies affect matter so profoundly as to cause the spontaneous generation of an entire race of organisms, nested within a few progenitors. If so, cataclysms are not responsible for mass extinctions, but rather generate new species in their wake."

Back in the laboratory, the two elder men seated themselves in the chairs present. Too agitated to follow suit, Stratton remained standing. "If any animal species were created by the same cataclysm as the human species, they should likewise be nearing the end of their life spans. Have you found another species that evinces a final generation?"

Fieldhurst shook his head. "Not as yet. We believe that other species have different dates of extinction, correlated with the biological complexity of the animal; humans are presumably the most complex organism, and perhaps fewer generations of such complex organisms can be nested inside a spermatozoon."

"By the same token," countered Stratton, "perhaps the complexity of the human organism makes it unsuitable for the process of artificially accelerated growth. Perhaps it is the process whose limits have been discovered, not the species."

"An astute observation, Mr. Stratton. Experiments are continuing with species that more closely resemble humans, such as chimpanzees and ourang-outangs. However, the unequivocal answer to this question may require years, and if our current interpretation is correct, we can ill afford the time spent waiting for confirmation. We must ready a course of action immediately."

"But five generations could be over a century—" He caught himself, embarrassed at having overlooked the obvious: not all persons became parents at the same age.

Fieldhurst read his expression. "You realize why not all the sperm samples from donors of the same age produced the same number of generations: some lineages are approaching their end faster than others. For a lineage in which the men consistently father children late in life, five generations might mean over two centuries of fertility, but there are undoubtedly lineages that have reached their end already."

Stratton imagined the consequences. "The loss of fertility will become increasingly apparent to the general populace as time passes. Panic may arise well before the end is reached."

"Precisely, and rioting could extinguish our species as effectively as the exhaustion of generations. That is why time is of the essence."

"What is the solution you propose?"

"I shall defer to Dr. Ashbourne to explain further," said the earl.

Ashbourne rose and instinctively adopted the stance of a lecturing professor. "Do you recall why it was that all attempts to make automata out of wood were abandoned?"

Stratton was caught off guard by the question. "It was believed that the natural grain of wood implies a form in conflict with whatever we try to carve upon it. Currently there are efforts to use rubber as a casting material, but none have met with success."

"Indeed. But if the native form of wood were the only obstacle, shouldn't it be possible to animate an animal's corpse with a name? There the form of the body should be ideal."

"It's a macabre notion; I couldn't guess at such an experiment's likelihood of success. Has it ever been attempted?"

"In fact it has: also unsuccessfully. So these two entirely different avenues of research proved fruitless. Does that mean there is no way to animate organic matter using names? This was the question I left Trinity in order to pursue."

"And what did you discover?"

Ashbourne deflected the question with a wave of his hand. "First let us discuss thermodynamics. Have you kept up with recent developments? Then you know the dissipation of heat reflects an increase in disorder at the thermal level. Conversely, when an automaton condenses heat from its environment to perform work, it increases order. This confirms a long-held belief of mine that lexical order induces thermodynamic order. The lexical order of an amulet reinforces the order a body already possesses, thus providing protection against damage. The lexical order of an animating name increases the order of a body, thus providing motive power for an automaton.

"The next question was, how would an increase in order be reflected in organic matter? Since names don't animate dead tissue, obviously organic matter doesn't respond at the thermal level; but perhaps it can be ordered at another level. Consider: a steer can be reduced to a vat of gelatinous broth. The broth comprises the same material as the steer, but which embodies a higher amount of order?"

"The steer, obviously," said Stratton, bewildered.

"Obviously. An organism, by virtue of its physical structure, embodies order; the more complex the organism, the greater the amount of order. It was my hypothesis that increasing the order in organic matter would be evidenced by imparting form to it. However, most living matter has already assumed its ideal form. The question is, what has life but not form?"

The elder nomenclator did not wait for a response. "The answer is, an unfertilized ovum. The ovum contains the vital principle that animates the creature it ultimately gives rise to, but it has no form itself. Ordinarily, the ovum incorporates the form of the foetus compressed within the spermatozoon that fertilizes it. The next step was obvious." Here Ashbourne waited, looking at Stratton expectantly.

Stratton was at a loss. Ashbourne seemed disappointed, and continued. "The next step was to artificially induce the growth of an embryo from an ovum, by application of a name."

"But if the ovum is unfertilized," objected Stratton, "there is no preexisting structure to enlarge."

"Precisely."

"You mean structure would arise out of a homogenous medium? Impossible."

"Nonetheless, it was my goal for several years to confirm this hypothesis. My first experiments consisted of applying a name to unfertilized frog eggs."

"How did you embed the name into a frog's egg?"

"The name is not actually embedded, but rather impressed by means of a specially manufactured needle." Ashbourne opened a cabinet that sat on the worktable between two of the microscope stations. Inside was a wooden rack filled with small instruments arranged in pairs. Each was tipped with a long glass needle; in some pairs they were nearly as thick as those used for knitting, in others as slender as a hypodermic. He withdrew one from the largest pair and handed it to Stratton to examine. The glass needle was not clear, but instead seemed to contain some sort of dappled core.

Ashbourne explained. "While that may appear to be some sort of medical implement, it is in fact a vehicle for a name, just as the more conventional slip of parchment is. Alas, it requires far more effort to make than taking pen to parchment. To create such a needle, one must first arrange fine strands of black glass within a bundle of clear glass strands so that the name is legible when they are viewed end-on. The strands are then fused into a solid rod, and the rod is drawn out into an ever thinner strand. A skilled glassmaker can retain every detail of the name no matter how thin the strand becomes. Eventually one obtains a needle containing the name in its cross section."

"How did you generate the name that you used?"

"We can discuss that at length later. For the purposes of our current discussion, the only relevant information is that I incorporated the sexual epithet. Are you familiar with it?"

"I know of it." It was one of the few epithets that was dimorphic, having male and female variants.

"I needed two versions of the name, obviously, to induce the generation of both males and females." He indicated the paired arrangement of needles in the cabinet.

Stratton saw that the needle could be clamped into the brass framework with its tip approaching the slide beneath the microscope; the knurled wheels presumably were used to bring the needle into contact with an ovum. He returned the instrument. "You said the name is not embedded, but impressed. Do you mean to tell me that touching the frog's egg with this needle is all that's needed? Removing the name doesn't end its influence?"

"Precisely. The name activates a process in the egg that cannot be reversed. Prolonged contact of the name had no different effect."

"And the egg hatched a tadpole?"

"Not with the names initially tried; the only result was that symmetrical involutions appeared in the surface of the egg. But by incorporating different epithets, I was able to induce the egg to adopt different forms, some of which had every appearance of embryonic frogs. Eventually I found a name that caused the egg not only to assume the form of a tadpole, but also to mature and hatch. The tadpole thus hatched grew into a frog indistinguishable from any other member of the species."

"You had found a euonym for that species of frog," said Stratton.

Ashbourne smiled. "As this method of reproduction does not involve sexual congress, I have termed it 'parthenogenesis.'"

Stratton looked at both him and Fieldhurst. "It's clear what your proposed solution is. The logical conclusion of this research is to discover a euonym for the human species. You wish for mankind to perpetuate itself through nomenclature."

"You find the prospect troubling," said Fieldhurst. "That is to be expected: Dr. Ashbourne and myself initially felt the same way, as has everyone who has considered this. No one relishes the prospect of humans being conceived artificially. But can you offer an alternative?" Stratton was silent, and Fieldhurst went on. "All who are aware of both Dr. Ashbourne's and Dubuisson and Gille's work agree: there is no other solution."

Stratton reminded himself to maintain the dispassionate attitude of a scientist. "Precisely how do you envision this name being used?" he asked.

Ashbourne answered. "When a husband is unable to impregnate his wife, they will seek the services of a physician. The physician will collect the woman's menses, separate out the ovum, impress the name upon it, and then reintroduce it into her womb."

"A child born of this method would have no biological father."

"True, but the father's biological contribution is of minimal importance here. The mother will think of her husband as the child's father, so her imagination will impart a combination of her own and her husband's appearance and character to the foetus. That will not change. And I hardly need mention that name impression would not be made available to unmarried women."

"Are you confident this will result in well-formed children?" asked Stratton. "I'm sure you know to what I refer." They all knew of the disastrous attempt in the previous century to create improved children by mesmerizing women during their pregnancies.

Ashbourne nodded. "We are fortunate in that the ovum is very specific in what it will accept. The set of euonyms for any species of organism is very small; if the lexical order of the impressed name does not closely match the structural order of that species, the resulting foetus does not quicken. This does not remove the need for the mother to maintain a tranquil mind during her pregnancy; name impression cannot guard against maternal agitation. But the ovum's selectivity provides us assurance that any foetus induced will be well formed in every aspect, except the one anticipated."

Stratton was alarmed. "What aspect is that?"

"Can you not guess? The only incapacity of frogs created by name impression was in the males; they were sterile, for their spermatozoa bore no preformed foetuses inside. By comparison, the female frogs created were fertile: their eggs could be fertilized in either the conventional manner, or by repeating the impression with the name."

Stratton's relief was considerable. "So the male variant of the name was imperfect. Presumably there needs to be further differences between the male and female variants than simply the sexual epithet."

"Only if one considers the male variant imperfect," said Ashbourne, "which I do not. Consider: while a fertile male and a fertile female might seem equivalent, they differ radically in the degree of complexity exemplified. A female with viable ova remains a single organism, while a male with viable spermatozoa is actually many organisms: a father and all his potential children. In this light, the two variants of the name are well matched in their actions: each induces a single organism, but only in the female sex can a single organism be fertile."

"I see what you mean." Stratton realized he would need practice in thinking about nomenclature in the organic domain. "Have you developed euonyms for other species?"

"Just over a score, of various types; our progress has been rapid. We have only just begun work on a name for the human species, and it has proved far more difficult than our previous names."

"How many nomenclators are engaged in this endeavor?"

"Only a handful," Fieldhurst replied. "We have asked a few Royal Society members, and the Académie has some of France's leading designateurs working on it. You will understand if I do not mention any names at this point, but be assured that we have some of the most distinguished nomenclators in England assisting us."

"Forgive me for asking, but why are you approaching me? I am hardly in that category."

"You have not yet had a long career," said Ashbourne, "but the genus of names you have developed is unique. Automata have always been specialized in form and function, rather like animals: some are good at climbing, others at digging, but none at both. Yet yours can control human hands, which are uniquely versatile instruments: what else can manipulate everything from a wrench to a piano? The hand's dexterity is the physical manifestation of the mind's ingenuity, and these traits are essential to the name we seek."

"We have been discreetly surveying current nomenclatoral research for any names that demonstrate marked dexterity," said Fieldhurst. "When we learned of what you had accomplished, we sought you out immediately."

"In fact," Ashbourne continued, "the very reason your names are worrisome to sculptors is the reason we are interested in them: they endow automata with a more humanlike manner than any before. So now we ask, will you join us?"

Stratton considered it. This was perhaps the most important task a nomenclator could undertake, and under ordinary circumstances he would have leapt at the opportunity to participate. But before he could embark upon this enterprise in good conscience, there was another matter he had to resolve.

"You honor me with your invitation, but what of my work with dexterous automata? I still firmly believe that inexpensive engines can improve the lives of the labouring class."

"It is a worthy goal," said Fieldhurst, "and I would not ask you to give it up. Indeed, the first thing we wish you to do is to perfect the epithets for dexterity. But your efforts at social reform would be for naught unless we first ensure the survival of our species."

"Obviously, but I do not want the potential for reform that is offered by dexterous names to be neglected. There may never be a better opportunity for restoring dignity to common workers. What kind of victory would we achieve if the continuation of life meant ignoring this opportunity?"

"Well said," acknowledged the earl. "Let me make a proposal. So that you can best make use of your time, the Royal Society will provide support for your development of dexterous automata as needed: securing investors and so forth. I trust you will divide your time between the two projects wisely. Your work on biological nomenclature must remain confidential, obviously. Is that satisfactory?"

"It is. Very well then, gentlemen: I accept." They shook hands.

Some weeks had passed since Stratton last spoke with Willoughby, beyond a chilly exchange of greetings in passing. In fact, he had little interaction with any of the union sculptors, instead spending his time working on letter permutations in his office, trying to refine his epithets for dexterity.

He entered the manufactory through the front gallery, where customers normally perused the catalogue. Today it was crowded with domestic automata, all the same model char-engine. Stratton saw the clerk ensuring they were properly tagged.

"Good morning, Pierce," he said. "What are all these doing here?"

"An improved name is just out for the 'Regent'," said the clerk. "Everyone's eager to get the latest."

"You're going to be busy this afternoon." The keys for unlocking the automata's name slots were themselves stored in a safe that required two of Coade's managers to open. The managers were reluctant to keep the safe open for more than a brief period each afternoon.

"I'm certain I can finish these in time."

"You couldn't bear to tell a pretty housemaid that her char-engine wouldn't be ready by tomorrow."

The clerk smiled. "Can you blame me, sir?"

"No, I cannot," said Stratton, chuckling. He turned toward the business offices behind the gallery, when he found himself confronted by Willoughby.

"Perhaps you ought to prop open the safe," said the sculptor, "so that housemaids might not be inconvenienced. Seeing how destroying our institutions seems to be your intent."

"Good morning, Master Willoughby," said Stratton stiffly. He tried to walk past, but the other man stood in his way.

"I've been informed that Coade will be allowing nonunion sculptors onto the premises to assist you."

"Yes, but I assure you, only the most reputable independent sculptors are involved."

"As if such persons exist," said Willoughby scornfully. "You should know that I recommended that our trade union launch a strike against Coade in protest."

"Surely you're not serious." It had been decades since the last strike launched by the sculptors, and that one had ended in rioting.

"I am. Were the matter put to a vote of the membership, I'm certain it would pass: other sculptors with whom I've discussed your work agree with me about the threat it poses. However, the union leadership will not put it to a vote."

"Ah, so they disagreed with your assessment."

Here Willoughby frowned. "Apparently the Royal Society intervened on your behalf and persuaded the Brotherhood to refrain for the time being. You've found yourself some powerful supporters, Mr. Stratton."

Uncomfortably, Stratton replied, "The Royal Society considers my research worthwhile."

"Perhaps, but do not believe that this matter is ended."

"Your animosity is unwarranted, I tell you," Stratton insisted. "Once you have seen how sculptors can use these automata, you will realize that there is no threat to your profession."

Willoughby merely glowered in response and left.

The next time he saw Lord Fieldhurst, Stratton asked him about the Royal Society's involvement. They were in Fieldhurst's study, and the earl was pouring himself a whiskey.

"Ah yes," he said. "While the Brotherhood of Sculptors as a whole is quite formidable, it is composed of individuals who individually are more amenable to persuasion."

"What manner of persuasion?"

"The Royal Society is aware that members of the trade union's leadership were party to an as-yet-unresolved case of name piracy to the Continent. To avoid any scandal, they've agreed to postpone any decision about strikes until after you've given a demonstration of your system of manufacturing."

"I'm grateful for your assistance, Lord Fieldhurst," said Stratton, astonished. "I must admit, I had no idea that the Royal Society employed such tactics."

"Obviously, these are not proper topics for discussion at the general sessions." Lord Fieldhurst smiled in an avuncular manner. "The advancement of Science is not always a straightforward affair, Mr. Stratton, and the Royal Society is sometimes required to use both official and unofficial channels."

"I'm beginning to appreciate that."

"Similarly, although the Brotherhood of Sculptors won't initiate a formal strike, they might employ more indirect tactics; for example, the anonymous distribution of pamphlets that arouse public opposition to your automata." He sipped at his whiskey. "Hmm. Perhaps I should have someone keep a watchful eye on Master Willoughby."

Stratton was given accommodations in the guest wing of Darrington Hall, as were the other nomenclators working under Lord Fieldhurst's direction. They were indeed some of the leading members of the profession, including Holcombe, Milburn, and Parker; Stratton felt honored to be working with them, although he could contribute little while he was still learning Ashbourne's techniques for biological nomenclature.

Names for the organic domain employed many of the same epithets as names for automata, but Ashbourne had developed an entirely different system of integration and factorization, which entailed many novel methods of permutation. For Stratton it was almost like returning to university and learning nomenclature all over again. However, it was apparent how these techniques allowed names for species to be developed rapidly; by exploiting similarities suggested by the Linnaean system of classification, one could work from one species to another.

Stratton also learned more about the sexual epithet, traditionally used to confer either male or female qualities to an automaton. He knew of only one such epithet, and was surprised to learn it was the simplest of many extant versions. The topic went undiscussed by nomenclatoral societies, but this epithet was one of the most fully researched in existence; in fact its earliest use was claimed to have occurred in biblical times, when Joseph's brothers created a female *golem* they could share sexually without violating the prohibition against such behavior with a woman. Development of the epithet had continued for centuries in secrecy, primarily in Constantinople, and now the current versions of automatous courtesans were offered by specialized brothels right here in London. Carved from soapstone and polished to a high gloss, heated to blood temperature and sprinkled with scented oils, the automata commanded prices exceeded only by those for incubi and succubi.

It was from such ignoble soil that their research grew. The names animating the courtesans incorporated powerful epithets for human sexuality in its male and female forms. By factoring out the carnality common to both versions, the nomenclators had isolated epithets for generic human mascu-linity and femininity, ones far more refined than those used when generating animals. Such epithets were the nuclei around which they formed, by accre-tion, the names they sought.

Gradually Stratton absorbed sufficient information to begin participat-ing in the tests of prospective human names. He worked in collaboration with the other nomenclators in the group, and between them they divided up the vast tree of nominal possibilities, assigning branches for investigation, pruning away those that proved unfruitful, cultivating those that seemed most productive.

The nomenclators paid women—typically young housemaids in good health—for their menses as a source of human ova, which they then impressed with their experimental names and scrutinized under microscopes, looking for forms that resembled human foetuses. Stratton inquired about the possi-bility of harvesting ova from female megafoetuses, but Ashbourne reminded him that ova were viable only when taken from a living woman. It was a basic dictum of biology: females were the source of the vital principle that gave the offspring life, while males provided the basic form. Because of this division, neither sex could reproduce by itself.

Of course, that restriction had been lifted by Ashbourne's discov-ery: the male's participation was no longer necessary since form could be induced lexically. Once a name was found that could generate human foe-tuses, women could reproduce purely by themselves. Stratton realized that such a discovery might be welcomed by women exhibiting sexual inver-sion, feeling love for persons of the same rather than the opposite sex. If the name were to become available to such women, they might establish a commune of some sort that reproduced via parthenogenesis. Would such a society flourish by magnifying the finer sensibilities of the gentle sex, or would it collapse under the unrestrained pathology of its membership? It was impossible to guess.

Before Stratton's enlistment, the nomenclators had developed names capable of generating vaguely homuncular forms in an ovum. Using Dubuisson and Gille's methods, they enlarged the forms to a size that allowed detailed examination; the forms resembled automata more than humans, their limbs ending in paddles of fused digits. By incorporating his epithets for dexterity, Stratton was able to separate the digits and refine the overall appearance of the forms. All the while, Ashbourne emphasized the need for an unconventional approach.

"Consider the thermodynamics of what most automata do," said Ashbourne during one of their frequent discussions. "The mining engines dig ore, the reaping engines harvest wheat, the woodcutting engines fell timber; yet none of these tasks, no matter how useful we find them to be, can be said to create order. While all their names create order at the thermal level, by converting heat into motion, in the vast majority the resulting work is applied at the visible level to create disorder."

"This is an interesting perspective," said Stratton thoughtfully. "Many long-standing deficits in the capabilities of automata become intelligible in this light: the fact that automata are unable to stack crates more neatly than they find them; their inability to sort pieces of crushed ore based on their composition. You believe that the known classes of industrial names are not powerful enough in thermodynamic terms."

"Precisely!" Ashbourne displayed the excitement of a tutor finding an unexpectedly apt pupil. "This is another feature that distinguishes your class of dexterous names. By enabling an automaton to perform skilled labour, your names not only create order at the thermal level, they use it to create order at the visible level as well."

"I see a commonality with Milburn's discoveries," said Stratton. Milburn had developed the household automata able to return objects to their proper places. "His work likewise involves the creation of order at the visible level."

"Indeed it does, and this commonality suggests a hypothesis." Ashbourne leaned forward. "Suppose we were able to factor out an epithet common to the names developed by you and Milburn: an epithet expressing the creation of two levels of order. Further suppose that we discover a euonym for the human species, and were able to incorporate this epithet into the name. What do you imagine would be generated by impressing the name? And if you say 'twins' I shall clout you on the head."

Stratton laughed. "I daresay I understand you better than that. You are suggesting that if an epithet is capable of inducing two levels of thermodynamic order in the inorganic domain, it might create two generations in the organic domain. Such a name might create males whose spermatozoa would contain preformed foetuses. Those males would be fertile, although any sons they produced would again be sterile."

His instructor clapped his hands together. "Precisely: order that begets order! An interesting speculation, wouldn't you agree? It would halve the number of medical interventions required for our race to sustain itself."

"And what about inducing the formation of more than two generations of foetuses? What kind of capabilities would an automaton have to possess, for its name to contain such an epithet?"

"The science of thermodynamics has not progressed enough to answer that question, I'm afraid. What would constitute a still-higher level of order in the inorganic domain? Automata working cooperatively, perhaps? We do not yet know, but perhaps in time we will."

Stratton gave voice to a question that had posed itself to him some time ago. "Dr. Ashbourne, when I was initiated into our group, Lord Fieldhurst spoke of the possibility that species are born in the wake of catastrophic events. Is it possible that entire species were created by use of nomenclature?"

"Ah, now we tread in the realm of theology. A new species requires progenitors containing vast numbers of descendants nested within their reproductive organs; such forms embody the highest degree of order imaginable. Can a purely physical process create such vast amounts of order? No naturalist has suggested a mechanism by which this could occur. On the other hand, while we do know that a lexical process can create order, the creation of an entire new species would require a name of incalculable power. Such mastery of nomenclature could very well require the capabilities of God; perhaps it is even part of the definition.

"This is a question, Stratton, to which we may never know the answer, but we cannot allow that to affect our current actions. Whether or not a name was responsible for the creation of our species, I believe a name is the best chance for its continuation."

"Agreed," said Stratton. After a pause, he added, "I must confess, much of the time when I am working, I occupy myself solely with the details of permutation and combination, and lose sight of the sheer magnitude of our endeavor. It is sobering to think of what we will have achieved if we are successful."

"I can think of little else," replied Ashbourne.

Seated at his desk in the manufactory, Stratton squinted to read the pamphlet he'd been given on the street. The text was crudely printed, the letters blurred.

"Shall Men be the Masters of NAMES, or shall Names be the masters of MEN? For too long the Capitalists have hoarded Names within their coffers, guarded by Patent and Lock and Key, amassing fortunes by mere possession of LETTERS, while the Common Man must labour for every shilling. They will wring the ALPHABET until they have extracted every last penny from it, and only then discard it for us to use. How long will We allow this to continue?"

Stratton scanned the entire pamphlet, but found nothing new in it. For the past two months he'd been reading them, and encountered only the usual anarchist rants; there was as yet no evidence for Lord Fieldhurst's theory that the sculptors would use them to target Stratton's work. His public demonstration of the dexterous automata was scheduled for next week, and by now Willoughby had largely missed his opportunity to generate public opposition. In fact, it occurred to Stratton that he might distribute pamphlets himself to generate public support. He could explain his goal of bringing the advantages of automata to everyone, and his intention to keep close control over his names' patents, granting licenses only to manufacturers who would use them conscientiously. He could even have a slogan: "Autonomy through Automata," perhaps?

There was a knock at his office door. Stratton tossed the pamphlet into his wastebasket. "Yes?"

A man entered, somberly dressed, and with a long beard. "Mr. Stratton?" he asked. "Please allow me to introduce myself: my name is Benjamin Roth. I am a kabbalist."

Stratton was momentarily speechless. Typically such mystics were offended by the modern view of nomenclature as a science, considering it a secularization of a sacred ritual. He never expected one to visit the manufactory. "A pleasure to meet you. How may I be of assistance?"

"I've heard that you have achieved a great advance in the permutation of letters."

"Why, thank you. I didn't realize it would be of interest to a person like yourself."

Roth smiled awkwardly. "My interest is not in its practical applications. The goal of kabbalists is to better know God. The best means by which to do that is to study the art by which He creates. We meditate upon different names to enter an ecstatic state of consciousness; the more powerful the name, the more closely we approach the Divine."

"I see." Stratton wondered what the kabbalist's reaction would be if he learned about the creation being attempted in the biological nomenclature project. "Please continue."

"Your epithets for dexterity enable a *golem* to sculpt another, thereby reproducing itself. A name capable of creating a being that is, in turn, capable of creation would bring us closer to God than we have ever been before."

"I'm afraid you're mistaken about my work, although you aren't the first to fall under this misapprehension. The ability to manipulate molds does not render an automaton able to reproduce itself. There would be many other skills required."

The kabbalist nodded. "I am well aware of that. I myself, in the course of my studies, have developed an epithet designating certain other skills necessary."

Stratton leaned forward with sudden interest. After casting a body, the next step would be to animate the body with a name. "Your epithet endows an automaton with the ability to write?" His own automaton could grasp a pencil easily enough, but it couldn't inscribe even the simplest mark. "How is it that your automata possess the dexterity required for scrivening, but not that for manipulating molds?"

Roth shook his head modestly. "My epithet does not endow writing ability, or general manual dexterity. It simply enables a *golem* to write out the name that animates it, and nothing else."

"Ah, I see." So it didn't provide an aptitude for learning a category of skills; it granted a single innate skill. Stratton tried to imagine the nomenclatoral contortions needed to make an automaton instinctively write out a particular sequence of letters. "Very interesting, but I imagine it doesn't have broad application, does it?"

Roth gave a pained smile; Stratton realized he had committed a *faux pas*, and the man was trying to meet it with good humor. "That is one way to view it," admitted Roth, "but we have a different perspective. To us the value of this epithet, like any other, lies not in the usefulness it imparts to a *golem*, but in the ecstatic state it allows us to achieve."

"Of course, of course. And your interest in my epithets for dexterity is the same?"

"Yes. I am hoping that you will share your epithets with us."

Stratton had never heard of a kabbalist making such a request before, and clearly Roth did not relish being the first. He paused to consider. "Must a kabbalist reach a certain rank in order to meditate upon the most powerful ones?"

"Yes, very definitely."

"So you restrict the availability of the names."

"Oh no; my apologies for misunderstanding you. The ecstatic state offered by a name is achievable only after one has mastered the necessary meditative techniques, and it's these techniques that are closely guarded. Without the proper training, attempts to use these techniques could result in madness. But the names themselves, even the most powerful ones, have no ecstatic value to a novice; they can animate clay, nothing more."

"Nothing more," agreed Stratton, thinking how truly different their perspectives were. "In that case, I'm afraid I cannot grant you use of my names."

Roth nodded glumly, as if he'd been expecting that answer. "You desire payment of royalties."

Now it was Stratton who had to overlook the other man's *faux pas*. "Money is not my objective. However, I have specific intentions for my dexterous automata which require that I retain control over the patent. I cannot jeopardize those plans by releasing the names indiscriminately." Granted, he had shared them with the nomenclators working under Lord Fieldhurst, but they were all gentlemen sworn to an even greater secrecy. He was less confident about mystics.

"I can assure you that we would not use your name for anything other than ecstatic practices."

"I apologize; I believe you are sincere, but the risk is too great. The most I can do is remind you that the patent has a limited duration; once it has expired, you'll be free to use the name however you like."

"But that will take years!"

"Surely you appreciate that there are others whose interests must be taken into account."

"What I see is that commercial considerations are posing an obstacle to spiritual awakening. The error was mine in expecting anything different."

"You are hardly being fair," protested Stratton.

"Fair?" Roth made a visible effort to restrain his anger. "You 'nomenclators' steal techniques meant to honor God and use them to aggrandize yourselves. Your entire industry prostitutes the techniques of *yezirah*. You are in no position to speak of fairness."

"Now see here—"

"Thank you for speaking with me." With that, Roth took his leave.

Stratton sighed.

Peering through the eyepiece of the microscope, Stratton turned the manipulator's adjustment wheel until the needle pressed against the side of the ovum. There was a sudden enfolding, like the retraction of a mollusc's foot when prodded, transforming the sphere into a tiny foetus. Stratton withdrew the needle from the slide, unclamped it from the framework, and inserted a new one. Next he transferred the slide into the warmth of the incubator and placed another slide, bearing an untouched human ovum, beneath the microscope. Once again he leaned toward the microscope to repeat the process of impression.

Recently, the nomenclators had developed a name capable of inducing a form indistinguishable from a human foetus. The forms did not quicken, however: they remained immobile and unresponsive to stimuli. The consensus was that the name did not accurately describe the non-physical traits of a human being. Accordingly, Stratton and his colleagues had been diligently compiling descriptions of human uniqueness, trying to distill a set of epithets both expressive enough to denote these qualities, and succinct enough to be integrated with the physical epithets into a seventy-two-letter name.

Stratton transferred the final slide to the incubator and made the appropriate notations in the logbook. At the moment he had no more names drawn in needle form, and it would be a day before the new foetuses were mature enough to test for quickening. He decided to pass the rest of the evening in the drawing room upstairs.

Upon entering the walnut-paneled room, he found Fieldhurst and Ashbourne seated in its leather chairs, smoking cigars and sipping brandy. "Ah, Stratton," said Ashbourne. "Do join us."

"I believe I will," said Stratton, heading for the liquor cabinet. He poured himself some brandy from a crystal decanter and seated himself with the others.

"Just up from the laboratory, Stratton?" inquired Fieldhurst.

Stratton nodded. "A few minutes ago I made impressions with my most recent set of names. I feel that my latest permutations are leading in the right direction."

"You are not alone in feeling optimistic; Dr. Ashbourne and I were just discussing how much the outlook has improved since this endeavor began. It now appears that we will have a euonym comfortably in advance of the final generation." Fieldhurst puffed on his cigar and leaned back in his chair until his head rested against the antimacassar. "This disaster may ultimately turn out to be a boon."

"A boon? How so?"

"Why, once we have human reproduction under our control, we will have a means of preventing the poor from having such large families as so many of them persist in having right now."

Stratton was startled, but tried not to show it. "I had not considered that," he said carefully.

Ashbourne also seemed mildly surprised. "I wasn't aware that you intended such a policy."

"I considered it premature to mention it earlier," said Fieldhurst. "Counting one's chickens before they're hatched, as they say."

"Of course."

"You must agree that the potential is enormous. By exercising some judgment when choosing who may bear children or not, our government could preserve the nation's racial stock."

"Is our racial stock under some threat?" asked Stratton.

"Perhaps you have not noticed that the lower classes are reproducing at a rate exceeding that of the nobility and gentry. While commoners are not without virtues, they are lacking in refinement and intellect. These forms of mental impoverishment beget the same: a woman born into low circumstances cannot help but gestate a child destined for the same. Consequent to the great fecundity of the lower classes, our nation would eventually drown in coarse dullards."

"So name impressing will be withheld from the lower classes?"

"Not entirely, and certainly not initially: when the truth about declining fertility is known, it would be an invitation to riot if the lower classes were denied access to name impressing. And of course, the lower classes do have their role to play in our society, as long as their numbers are kept in check. I envision that the policy will go in effect only after some years have passed, by which time people will have grown accustomed to name impression as the method of fertilization. At that point, perhaps in conjunction with the census process, we can impose limits on the number of children a given couple would be permitted to have. The government would regulate the growth and composition of the population thereafter."

"Is this the most appropriate use of such a name?" asked Ashbourne. "Our goal was the survival of the species, not the implementation of partisan politics."

"On the contrary, this is purely scientific. Just as it's our duty to ensure the species survives, it's also our duty to guarantee its health by keeping a proper balance in its population. Politics doesn't enter into it; were the situation reversed and there existed a paucity of labourers, the opposite policy would be called for."

Stratton ventured a suggestion. "I wonder if improvement in conditions for the poor might eventually cause them to gestate more refined children?"

"You are thinking about changes brought about by your cheap engines, aren't you?" asked Fieldhurst with a smile, and Stratton nodded. "Your intended reforms and mine may reinforce each other. Moderating the numbers of the lower classes should make it easier for them to raise their living conditions. However, do not expect that a mere increase in economic comfort will improve the mentality of the lower classes."

"But why not?"

"You forget the self-perpetuating nature of culture," said Fieldhurst. "We have seen that all megafoetuses are identical, yet no one can deny the differences between the populaces of nations, in both physical appearance and temperament. This can only be the result of the maternal influence: the mother's womb is a vessel in which the social environment is incarnated. For example, a woman who has lived her life among Prussians naturally gives birth to a child with Prussian traits; in this manner the national character of that populace has sustained itself for centuries, despite many changes in fortune. It would be unrealistic to think the poor are any different."

"As a zoologist, you are undoubtedly wiser in these matters than we," said Ashbourne, silencing Stratton with a glance. "We will defer to your judgment."

For the remainder of the evening the conversation turned to other topics, and Stratton did his best to conceal his discomfort and maintain a facade of bonhomie. Finally, after Fieldhurst had retired for the evening, Stratton and Ashbourne descended to the laboratory to confer.

"What manner of man have we agreed to help?" exclaimed Stratton as soon as the door was closed. "One who would breed people like livestock?"

"Perhaps we should not be so shocked," said Ashbourne with a sigh. He seated himself upon one of the laboratory stools. "Our group's goal has been to duplicate for humans a procedure that was intended only for animals."

"But not at the expense of individual liberty! I cannot be a party to this."

"Do not be hasty. What would be accomplished by your resigning from the group? To the extent that your efforts contribute to our group's endeavor, your resignation would serve only to endanger the future of the human species. Conversely, if the group attains its goal without your assistance, Lord Fieldhurst's policies will be implemented anyway."

Stratton tried to regain his composure. Ashbourne was right; he could see that. After a moment, he said, "So what course of action should we take? Are there others whom we could contact, members of Parliament who would oppose the policy that Lord Fieldhurst proposes?"

"I expect that most of the nobility and gentry would share Lord Fieldhurst's opinion on this matter." Ashbourne rested his forehead on the fingertips of one hand, suddenly looking very old. "I should have anticipated this. My error was in viewing humanity purely as a single species. Having seen England and France working toward a common goal, I forgot that nations are not the only factions that oppose one another."

"What if we surreptitiously distributed the name to the labouring classes? They could draw their own needles and impress the name themselves, in secret."

"They could, but name impression is a delicate procedure best performed in a laboratory. I'm dubious that the operation could be carried out on the scale necessary without attracting governmental attention, and then falling under its control."

"Is there an alternative?"

There was silence for a long moment while they considered. Then Ashbourne said, "Do you recall our speculation about a name that would induce two generations of foetuses?"

"Certainly."

"Suppose we develop such a name but do not reveal this property when we present it to Lord Fieldhurst."

"That's a wily suggestion," said Stratton, surprised. "All the children born of such a name would be fertile, so they would be able to reproduce without governmental restriction."

Ashbourne nodded. "In the period before population control measures go into effect, such a name might be very widely distributed."

"But what of the following generation? Sterility would recur, and the labouring classes would again be dependent upon the government to reproduce."

"True," said Ashbourne, "it would be a short-lived victory. Perhaps the only permanent solution would be a more liberal Parliament, but it is beyond my expertise to suggest how we might bring that about."

Again Stratton thought about the changes that cheap engines might bring; if the situation of the working classes was improved in the manner he hoped, that might demonstrate to the nobility that poverty was not innate. But even if the most favorable sequence of events obtained, it would require years to sway Parliament. "What if we could induce multiple generations with the initial name impression? A longer period before sterility recurs would increase the chances that more liberal social policies would take hold."

"You're indulging a fancy," replied Ashbourne. "The technical difficulty of inducing multiple generations is such that I'd sooner wager on our successfully sprouting wings and taking flight. Inducing two generations would be ambitious enough."

The two men discussed strategies late into the night. If they were to conceal the true name of any name they presented to Lord Fieldhurst, they would have to forge a lengthy trail of research results. Even without the additional burden of secrecy, they would be engaged in an unequal race, pursuing a highly sophisticated name while the other nomenclators sought a comparatively straightforward euonym. To make the odds less unfavorable, Ashbourne and Stratton would need to recruit others to their cause; with such assistance, it might even be possible to subtly impede the research of others.

"Who in the group do you think shares our political views?" asked Ashbourne.

"I feel confident that Milburn does. I'm not so certain about any of the others."

"Take no chances. We must employ even more caution when approaching prospective members than Lord Fieldhurst did when establishing this group originally."

"Agreed," said Stratton. Then he shook his head in disbelief. "Here we are forming a secret organization nested within a secret organization. If only foetuses were so easily induced."

It was the evening of the following, the sun was setting, and Stratton was strolling across Westminster Bridge as the last remaining costermongers were wheeling their barrows of fruit away. He had just had supper at a club he favored, and was walking back to Coade Manufactory. The previous evening at Darrington Hall had disquieted him, and he had returned to London earlier today to minimize his interaction with Lord Fieldhurst until he was certain his face would not betray his true feelings.

He thought back to the conversation where he and Ashbourne had first entertained the conjecture of factoring out an epithet for creating two levels of order. At the time he had made some efforts to find such an epithet, but they were casual attempts given the superfluous nature of the goal, and they hadn't borne fruit. Now their gauge of achievement had been revised upward: their previous goal was inadequate, two generations seemed the minimum acceptable, and any additional ones would be invaluable.

He again pondered the thermodynamic behavior induced by his dexterous names: order at the thermal level animated the automata, allowing them to create order at the visible level. Order begetting order. Ashbourne had suggested that the next level of order might be automata working together in a coordinated fashion. Was that possible? They would have to communicate in order to work together effectively, but automata were intrinsically mute. What other means were there by which automata could engage in complex behavior?

He suddenly realized he had reached Coade Manufactory. By now it was dark, but he knew the way to his office well enough. Stratton unlocked the building's front door and proceeded through the gallery and past the business offices.

As he reached the hallway fronting the nomenclators' offices, he saw light emanating from the frosted-glass window of his office door. Surely he hadn't left the gas on? He unlocked his door to enter, and was shocked by what he saw.

A man lay facedown on the floor in front of the desk, hands tied behind his back. Stratton immediately approached to check on the man. It was Benjamin Roth, the kabbalist, and he was dead. Stratton realized several of the man's fingers were broken; he'd been tortured before he was killed.

Pale and trembling, Stratton rose to his feet, and saw that his office was in utter disarray. The shelves of his bookcases were bare; his books lay strewn facedown across the oak floor. His desk had been swept clear; next to it was a stack of its brass-handled drawers, emptied and overturned. A trail of stray papers led to the open door to his studio; in a daze, Stratton stepped forward to see what had been done there.

His dexterous automaton had been destroyed; the lower half of it lay on the floor, the rest of it scattered as plaster fragments and dust. On the worktable, the clay models of the hands were pounded flat, and his sketches of their design torn from the walls. The tubs for mixing plaster were overflowing with the papers from his office. Stratton took a closer look, and saw that they had been doused with lamp oil.

He heard a sound behind him and turned back to face the office. The front door to the office swung closed and a broad-shouldered man stepped out from behind it; he'd been standing there ever since Stratton had entered. "Good of you to come," the man said. He scrutinized Stratton with the predatory gaze of a raptor, an assassin.

Stratton bolted out the back door of the studio and down the rear hallway. He could hear the man give chase.

He fled through the darkened building, crossing workrooms filled with coke and iron bars, crucibles and molds, all illuminated by the moonlight entering through skylights overhead; he had entered the metalworks portion of the factory. In the next room he paused for breath, and realized how loudly his footsteps had been echoing; skulking would offer a better chance at escape than running. He distantly heard his pursuer's footsteps stop; the assassin had likewise opted for stealth.

Stratton looked around for a promising hiding place. All around him were cast-iron automata in various stages of near-completion; he was in the finishing room, where the runners left over from casting were sawed off and the surfaces chased. There was no place to hide, and he was about to move on when he noticed what looked like a bundle of rifles mounted on legs. He looked more closely, and recognized it as a military engine.

These automata were built for the War Office: gun carriages that aimed their own cannon, and rapid-fire rifles, like this one, that cranked their own barrel-clusters. Nasty things, but they'd proven invaluable in the Crimea; their inventor had been granted a peerage. Stratton didn't know any names to animate the weapon—they were military secrets—but only the body on which the rifle was mounted was automatous; the rifle's firing mechanism was strictly mechanical. If he could point the body in the right direction, he might be able to fire the rifle manually.

He cursed himself for his stupidity. There was no ammunition here. He stole into the next room.

It was the packing room, filled with pine crates and loose straw. Staying low between crates, he moved to the far wall. Through the windows he saw the courtyard behind the factory, where finished automata were carted away. He couldn't get out that way; the courtyard gates were locked at night. His only exit was through the factory's front door, but he risked encountering the assassin if he headed back the way he'd come. He needed to cross over to the ceramicworks and double back through that side of the factory.

From the front of the packing room came the sound of footsteps. Stratton ducked behind a row of crates, and then saw a side door only a few feet away. As stealthily as he could, he opened the door, entered, and closed the door behind him. Had his pursuer heard him? He peered through a small grille set in the door; he couldn't see the man, but felt he'd gone unnoticed. The assassin was probably searching the packing room.

Stratton turned around, and immediately realized his mistake. The door to the ceramicworks was in the opposite wall. He had entered a storeroom, filled with ranks of finished automata, but with no other exits. There was no way to lock the door. He had cornered himself.

Was there anything in the room he could use as a weapon? The menagerie of automata included some squat mining engines, whose forelimbs terminated in enormous pickaxes, but the axheads were bolted to their limbs. There was no way he could remove one.

Stratton could hear the assassin opening side doors and searching other storerooms. Then he noticed an automaton standing off to the side: a porter used for moving the inventory about. It was anthropomorphic in form, the only automaton in the room of that type. An idea came to him.

Stratton checked the back of the porter's head. Porters' names had entered the public domain long ago, so there were no locks protecting its name slot; a tab of parchment protruded from the horizontal slot in the iron. He reached into his coat pocket for the notebook and pencil he always carried and tore out a small portion of a blank leaf. In the darkness he quickly wrote seventy-two letters in a familiar combination, and then folded the paper into a tight square.

To the porter, he whispered, "Go stand as close to the door as you can." The cast-iron figure stepped forward and headed for the door. Its gait was very smooth, but not rapid, and the assassin would reach this storeroom any moment now. "Faster," hissed Stratton, and the porter obeyed.

Just as it reached the door, Stratton saw through the grille that his pursuer had arrived on the other side. "Get out of the way," barked the man.

Ever obedient, the automaton shifted to take a step back when Stratton yanked out its name. The assassin began pushing against the door, but Stratton was able to insert the new name, cramming the square of paper into the slot as deeply as he could.

The porter resumed walking forward, this time with a fast, stiff gait: his childhood doll, now life-size. It immediately ran into the door and, unperturbed, kept it shut with the force of its marching, its iron hands leaving fresh dents in the door's oaken surface with every swing of its arms, its rubber-shod feet chafing heavily against the brick floor. Stratton retreated to the back of the storeroom.

"Stop," the assassin ordered. "Stop walking, you! Stop!"

The automaton continued marching, oblivious to all commands. The man pushed on the door, but to no avail. He then tried slamming into it with his shoulder, each impact causing the automaton to slide back slightly, but its rapid strides brought it forward again before the man could squeeze inside. There was a brief pause, and then something poked through the grille in the door; the man was prying it off with a crowbar. The grille abruptly popped free, leaving an open window. The man stretched his arm through and reached around to the back of the automaton's head, his fingers searching for the name each time its head bobbed forward, but there was nothing for them to grasp; the paper was wedged too deeply in the slot.

The arm withdrew. The assassin's face appeared in the window. "Fancy yourself clever, don't you?" he called out. Then he disappeared.

Stratton relaxed slightly. Had the man given up? A minute passed, and Stratton began to think about his next move. He could wait here until the factory opened; there would be too many people about for the assassin to remain.

Suddenly the man's arm came through the window again, this time carrying a jar of fluid. He poured it over the automaton's head, the liquid splattering and dripping down its back. The man's arm withdrew, and then Stratton heard the sound of a match being struck and then flaring alight. The man's arm reappeared bearing the match, and touched it to the automaton.

The room was flooded with light as the automaton's head and upper back burst into flames. The man had doused it with lamp oil. Stratton squinted at the spectacle: light and shadow danced across the floor and walls, transforming the storeroom into the site of some druidic ceremony. The heat caused the automaton to hasten its vague assault on the door, like a salamandrine priest dancing with increasing frenzy, until it abruptly froze: its name had caught fire, and the letters were being consumed.

The flames gradually died out, and to Stratton's newly light-adapted eyes the room seemed almost completely black. More by sound than by sight, he realized the man was pushing at the door again, this time forcing the automaton back enough for him to gain entrance.

"Enough of that, then."

Stratton tried to run past him, but the assassin easily grabbed him and knocked him down with a clout to the head.

His senses returned almost immediately, but by then the assassin had him facedown on the floor, one knee pressed into his back. The man tore the health amulet from Stratton's wrist and then tied his hands together behind his back, drawing the rope tightly enough that the hemp fibers scraped the skin of his wrists.

"What kind of man are you, to do things like this?" Stratton gasped, his cheek flattened against the brick floor.

The assassin chuckled. "Men are no different from your automata; slip a bloke a piece of paper with the proper figures on it, and he'll do your bidding." The room grew light as the man lit an oil lamp.

"What if I paid you more to leave me alone?"

"Can't do it. Have to think about my reputation, haven't I? Now let's get to business." He grasped the smallest finger of Stratton's left hand and abruptly broke it.

The pain was shocking, so intense that for a moment Stratton was insensible to all else. He was distantly aware that he had cried out. Then he heard the man speaking again. "Answer my questions straight now. Do you keep copies of your work at home?"

"Yes." He could only get a few words out at a time. "At my desk. In the study."

"No other copies hidden anywhere? Under the floor, perhaps?"

"No."

"Your friend upstairs didn't have copies. But perhaps someone else does?"

He couldn't direct the man to Darrington Hall. "No one."

The man pulled the notebook out of Stratton's coat pocket. Stratton could hear him leisurely flipping through the pages. "Didn't post any letters? Corresponding with colleagues, that sort of thing?"

"Nothing that anyone could use to reconstruct my work."

"You're lying to me." The man grasped Stratton's ring finger.

"No! It's the truth!" He couldn't keep the hysteria from his voice.

Then Stratton heard a sharp thud, and the pressure in his back eased. Cautiously, he raised his head and looked around. His assailant lay unconscious on the floor next to him. Standing next to him was Davies, holding a leather blackjack.

Davies pocketed his weapon and crouched to unknot the rope that bound Stratton. "Are you badly hurt, sir?"

"He's broken one of my fingers. Davies, how did you—?"

"Lord Fieldhurst sent me the moment he learned whom Willoughby had contacted."

"Thank God you arrived when you did." Stratton saw the irony of the situation—his rescue ordered by the very man he was plotting against—but he was too grateful to care.

Davies helped Stratton to his feet and handed him his notebook. Then he used the rope to tie up the assassin. "I went to your office first. Who's the fellow there?"

"His name is—was Benjamin Roth." Stratton managed to recount his previous meeting with the kabbalist. "I don't know what he was doing there."

"Many religious types have a bit of the fanatic in them," said Davies, checking the assassin's bonds. "As you wouldn't give him your work, he likely felt justified in taking it himself. He came to your office to look for it, and had the bad luck to be there when this fellow arrived."

Stratton felt a flood of remorse. "I should have given Roth what he asked."

"You couldn't have known."

"It's an outrageous injustice that he was the one to die. He'd nothing to do with this affair."

"It's always that way, sir. Come on, let's tend to that hand of yours."

Davies bandaged Stratton's finger to a splint, assuring him that the Royal Society would discreetly handle any consequences of the night's events.

They gathered the oil-stained papers from Stratton's office into a trunk so that Stratton could sift through them at his leisure, away from the manufactory. By the time they were finished, a carriage had arrived to take Stratton back to Darrington Hall; it had set out at the same time as Davies, who had ridden into London on a racing-engine. Stratton boarded the carriage with the trunk of papers, while Davies stayed behind to deal with the assassin and make arrangements for the kabbalist's body.

Stratton spent the carriage ride sipping from a flask of brandy, trying to steady his nerves. He felt a sense of relief when he arrived back at Darrington Hall; although it held its own variety of threats, Stratton knew he'd be safe from assassination there. By the time he reached his room, his panic had largely been converted into exhaustion, and he slept deeply.

He felt much more composed the next morning, and ready to begin sorting through his trunkful of papers. As he was arranging them into stacks approximating their original organization, Stratton found a notebook he didn't recognize. Its pages contained Hebrew letters arranged in the familiar patterns of nominal integration and factorization, but all the notes were in Hebrew as well. With a renewed pang of guilt, he realized it must have belonged to Roth; the assassin must have found it on his person and tossed it in with Stratton's papers to be burned.

He was about to set it aside, but his curiosity bested him: he'd never seen a kabbalist's notebook before. Much of the terminology was archaic, but he could understand it well enough; among the incantations and sephirotic diagrams, he found the epithet enabling an automaton to write its own name. As he read, Stratton realized that Roth's achievement was more elegant than he'd previously thought.

The epithet didn't describe a specific set of physical actions, but instead the general notion of reflexivity. A name incorporating the epithet became an autonym: a self-designating name. The notes indicated that such a name would express its lexical nature through whatever means the body allowed. The animated body wouldn't even need hands to write out its name; if the epithet were incorporated properly, a porcelain horse could likely accomplish the task by dragging a hoof in the dirt.

Combined with one of Stratton's epithets for dexterity, Roth's epithet would indeed let an automaton do most of what was needed to reproduce. An automaton could cast a body identical to its own, write out its own name, and insert it to animate the body. It couldn't train the new one in sculpture, though, since automata couldn't speak. An automaton that could truly reproduce itself without human assistance remained out of reach, but coming this close would undoubtedly have delighted the kabbalists.

It seemed unfair that automata were so much easier to reproduce than humans. It was as if the problem of reproducing automata need be solved only once, while that of reproducing humans was a Sisyphean task, with every additional generation increasing the complexity of the name required.

And abruptly Stratton realized that he didn't need a name that redoubled physical complexity, but one than enabled lexical duplication.

The solution was to impress the ovum with an autonym, and thus induce a foetus that bore its own name.

The name would have two versions, as originally proposed: one used to induce male foetuses, another for female foetuses. The women conceived this way would be fertile as always. The men conceived this way would also be fertile, but not in the typical manner: their spermatozoa would not contain preformed foetuses, but would instead bear either of two names on their surfaces, the self-expression of the names originally born by the glass needles. And when such a spermatozoon reached an ovum, the name would induce the creation of a new foetus. The species would be able to reproduce itself without medical intervention, because it would carry the name within itself.

He and Dr. Ashbourne had assumed that creating animals capable of reproducing meant giving them preformed foetuses, because that was the method employed by nature. As a result they had overlooked another possibility: that if a creature could be expressed in a name, reproducing that creature was equivalent to transcribing the name. An organism could contain, instead of a tiny analogue of its body, a lexical representation instead.

Humanity would become a vehicle for the name as well as a product of it. Each generation would be both content and vessel, an echo in a self-sustaining reverberation.

Stratton envisioned a day when the human species could survive as long as its own behavior allowed, when it could stand or fall based purely on its own actions, and not simply vanish once some predetermined life span had elapsed. Other species might bloom and wither like flowers over seasons of geologic time, but humans would endure for as long as they determined.

Nor would any group of people control the fecundity of another; in the procreative domain, at least, liberty would be restored to the individual. This was not the application Roth had intended for his epithet, but Stratton hoped the kabbalist would consider it worthwhile. By the time the autonym's true power became apparent, an entire generation consisting of millions of people worldwide would have been born of the name, and there would be no way any government could control their reproduction. Lord Fieldhurst—or his successors—would be outraged, and there would eventually be a price to be paid, but Stratton found he could accept that.

He hastened to his desk, where he opened his own notebook and Roth's side by side. On a blank page, he began writing down ideas on how Roth's epithet might be incorporated into a human euonym. Already in his mind Stratton was transposing the letters, searching for a permutation that denoted both the human body and itself, an ontogenic encoding for the species.

SEVENTY-TWO LETTERS

Vanishing Acts, an anthology about endangered species, was published in 2000, and was inspired by my having read Avram Davidson's classic, heartbreaking story about genocide, "Now Let Us Sleep" in the reprint anthology *Time of Passage*, edited by Martin H. Greenberg and Joseph D. Olander. My anthology reprinted Avram's story and three stories I originally published in *Omni* plus ten new stories and a poem. "Seventy-Two Letters" by Ted Chiang won the Sidewise Award for Short Form Alternate History.

Interview with Ellen Datlow

by Gwenda Bond

GB: I realized that even though we've known each other for a long time, I don't know much about how you fell in love with fiction in the first place. Since this anthology gathers stories from the many, many anthologies you've edited over the course of your career, let's start at the beginning. What kind of a child reader were you? Did your family have books around?

ED: We had books around the house, but I don't even know why we had many of the books we had. But whatever my parents had on the bookshelves, I would read. Everything from cartoon books of risque cartoons to the little popular library hardcover collections of Nathaniel Hawthorne and Guy de Maupassant. When my mom went back to college, she took an art class, so lots of art books. And my aunt, one of my father's sisters, gave me a series of books for young adults in hardcover—and I actually hated those books. Like Captains Courageous. No, I don't want to read this shit. But I had those around the house. I was the kind of kid who read the Rice Krispies box while I was eating and then Bullfinch's Mythology.

I grew up in the Bronx until I was 8 and then moved to Yonkers, and I was always in the public library. I didn't read a lot of classics, no Winnie the Pooh, no Mary Poppins. I did read all the Nancy Drew books and I loved them. I went to the library and my mom let me take out whatever I wanted.

And my father had a luncheonette and he brought home soft porn. I have said this before, and he's dead so it doesn't matter. He can't be offended. The luncheonette was a little diner plus books and magazines and comic books. He didn't have science fiction magazines, and I didn't realize until decades later, most of luncheonettes did. But he had those revolving spinner racks of soft core porn, men's adventure books. He always had a few in his drawer. I read them when he wasn't home.

GB: My dad reads pulp westerns, which were basically the same thing. And I used to sneak them.

ED: My dad would go to the bookstore and skim the historical novels with sex in them—some of them anyway. He loved reading about history, though he didn't finish college.

There were these kind of magazines with covers of men carrying women over crocodile infested water—my father always had those. And Playboy. I was interested in that. The weird thing about those books, the soft core novels, is every few pages there was a sex scene. Not graphic, so I didn't really know what was going on. But I remember thinking, how do these people make a living? I was maybe 12 or 13 years old and I couldn't understand how they never worked. Even then, I was editing.

I read every comic book that existed. Always at the luncheonette—I wasn't allowed to take them home. The classics illustrated, and of course illustrated Bible stories. I loved those and read them over and over. If you don't take them literally, they're all fantasy.

GB: When did your tastes start to drift toward SFF and horror, if you can remember?

ED: I always loved the grotesque, but I'm not sure when I got hooked on it. Bullfinch's maybe, and the *Odyssey*—but I *hated* the *Illiad*. I thought the *Iliad* was boring. The fantastical started invading my interests fairly early on. At a certain point in my life, I read historical potboilers, all the Irving Stone novels. And I discovered more fantastical mainstream fiction, like John Fowles' *The Magus* and Herman Hesse's *Steppenwolf,* which had a wolf in it in my mind whether it did in reality or not. I was in my late teens or early 20s, and I became very interested in these stories of transformation.

I realized I didn't like realistic fiction as much as stories that had weird things in them. I read a lot of Lovecraft, and had all his paperback short stories.

It was such a conglomeration of influences on me, but a lot of individual ones I don't recall. I don't remember how I discovered Lovecraft. But I loved science fiction. I started reading Bradbury. I loved *The Golden Apples of the Sun*, many of his collections. Obviously now I can see that much of it was fantasy, not science fiction, but the Mars stories are supposedly science fiction. Reading those at the same time as reading Lovecraft, I remember thinking, even then, about the difference between SF and horror. Science fiction has a sense of wonder, which I probably first read about in books by Harlan Ellison. Anyway, I remember thinking SF is the sense of wonder and horror is the opposite of science fiction, terror of the unknown.

GB: That brings up an interesting question. How did you go from being a reader to an editor—how did you figure out this is a job you might be able to do?

ED: The weird thing is I'm not really sure. I grew up in the era when I thought I'd grow up, go to college, get married, and have kids. That's just what everyone around me did. I knew I wanted to work, and I knew I loved reading. So I remember thinking, what kind of job can you do as a reader? I could work at a bookstore or a library or I could go into publishing.

What I've never been able to replicate in my mind is that jump—I didn't know what a publisher did, other than published books, or what an editor did.

I graduated with an English lit degree, and I took two independent studies. As I said, I expected I would go to college, get married, and have kids, but I took a one on one independent study on what you could call women's studies. I had a male teacher and he assigned all these books to me that basically turned me into a feminist. Which is weird—I mean, it's only weird because I visited him at Bennington years later and he made a pass at me.

But he was a good teacher. I also took a science fiction independent study with a few other students. During that class, I read many of the classic SF novels. Before that, I still read mostly short fiction.

So I graduated college, I went to Europe for a year, and then I came home and had to figure out what to do. I lived with my parents for about six months and had a bunch of boring temp jobs—office work of various types. I knew I didn't want to work in a bookstore. My mom always wanted me to teach, but I didn't want to do that. I realized okay, maybe I should try to get into magazine publishing. I sent out my resume to every magazine and book publisher I'd ever heard of, getting their addresses from the phone book. I had no literary marketplace or any other reference like that.

GB: And did it work?

ED: Little, Brown and Company had a New York office and they called me in for an interview as sales secretary, and I was hired. The reason I was hired was because the person who had been sales secretary had been promoted to full time slush reader. Amazing, right? I worked for several months in that job and there were all these people who went on to prominent careers. They were hot shit then, but they became hotter shit.

Nine months in, someone suggested I apply for an opening in editorial at an imprint called Charterhouse. There was a clique of powerful publishing women in the '80s and I was helped to get a job through that. Unfortunately, the imprint was dying. I don't think the person who hired me knew. It only lasted a few months.

GB: Where'd you go from there?

ED: The first long-term job I had in publishing was at Holt, Rinehart, and Winston and I was able to take a publishing course through that. Initially, (before getting to HRW) I didn't actually know what editing was. At one time I worked for a well-known monster. I worked for him for six months when I was desperate for a job. I edited a novel there, and I did some publicity, because it was such a small office. It was unhealthy. He was horrible. Twice a year, the building manager would get complaints from neighboring offices that they couldn't work because of his screaming. I was one of the few people who actually resigned—gave two weeks notice—instead of quitting.

I didn't know what I was going to do but within a couple of weeks I became an editorial assistant at Holt, Rinehart, and Winston, which was very Ivy League. I resigned after three years because I wasn't getting anywhere. Then, I was hired at Crown to be assistant editor. The Editor-in-Chief I worked for was passive aggressively horrible and fired me after a few months of mutual misery and he got kicked upstairs. I asked his replacement if I could stay, but because she was just hired she said that politically she couldn't do it. The next job I got was at *Omni*.

GB: How did you end up there?

ED: What happened is that while I was at Holt, I'd started doing some freelance reading for the Science Fiction Book, the Book of the Month Club, Dell and Ace Books, and even Twentieth Century Fox. The Executive Editor at Holt, Don Hutter, who was publishing Robert Sheckley and reprinting J.G. Ballard in the US, had a non-fiction author who had just been hired as Editor of this new magazine named *Omni*. After I was fired from Crown, Don knew I was looking for a job. He said, 'Why don't you talk to the *Omni* people?' So I went in and talked to them, but they had no openings. Ben Bova was the fiction editor at the time. There was someone before him, but only for a week or two. He was essentially the fiction editor at *Omni* from close to the beginning. He had a secretary and not an assistant, and the secretary didn't read or know anything about SF.

So I talked to Ben and he said there were no openings. I had temporary work over the summer, but I would haunt him and the Editor, calling them every few weeks. Finally, Ben said he was going to the Brighton World Con in '79 and I was going to California for a few weeks. I was going to get home a week before he would. I told him I would read his slush—and he didn't know me from a hole in the wall, other than that I was an avid reader and I wanted to work for him—so I told him I could read his whole slush pile, which was three feet tall, before he got back. First he said no, but then he called back and said okay. I honestly don't know what possessed him to hire me.

GB: He probably just had this glorious vision of no slush pile!

ED: Yup (laughing). I did it, and he got back, and he was happy. For all I know, I rejected things I shouldnt've but I'd never read a magazine slush pile before. He said, 'Okay, hang around and you can help out.' So…everyone else at *Omni* is doing nonfiction, and here I am wandering around this very small office offering to do…anything. What I think Ben knew was that he was going to be promoted to Editor of the magazine. They brought in Bob Sheckley who had no office experience as far as I could tell. He had a huge expense account and only had to come in three days a week. It was like the blind leading the blind. Neither of us knew what the hierarchy was in magazine editing. I read all the manuscripts, whether they were agented or not, well known or not. I didn't know I wasn't supposed to. I read everything and handed a story to him or not.

I basically learned on the job. When Ben hired me I told him I wanted the title of Associate Fiction Editor because I'd already been in publishing several years. Bob and I worked together for about a year and a half. Part of the reason Sheckley got the job was because he was blocked as writer. He eventually got past that block, and asked Ben for two months off during the summer to write and he did. I was acting fiction editor during that period. He requested another month, Ben said no, and Bob left.

Omni was owned by Penthouse and for the first few years they were really struggling for respectability. Ben had been the respected editor of *Analog*, bringing that prestige to *Omni*. Ben and then Bob only worked for three days a week. *Omni* started publishing October 1978. When they hired Bob, he was a relatively well-known writer. After he left, I told Ben I'll work five days a week and we've already gained enough respectability so the Fiction Editor no longer has to be a well-known writer.' So Ben (and the Gucciones) said we'll see. Finally, I was made fiction editor.

GB: So what happened when you became editor?

ED: When I took over, the first story I wanted to buy was "Petra" by Greg Bear, about gargoyles coming to life, a really weird horror story. I think I somehow justified it as weird science fiction, I don't remember. At first, Ben had to approve all my acquisitions. Ben initially didn't like "Petra," but I somehow persuaded him to let me buy it anyway. The next one was Dan Simmons' "Eyes I Dare Not Meet in Dreams," which later was expanded into a novel. Again, Ben didn't like that, but I said, 'I'll get him to rewrite it,' which I did, and Ben let me buy it.

When I started as Fiction Editor I was told that I couldn't buy horror. So I couldn't buy "The Monkey Treatment" by George RR Martin or "Down Among the Dead Men" by Gardner Dozois and Jack Dann, a novelette about a vampire in the concentration camp. There were also wonderful downbeat, utterly depressing stories by Gardner solo ("Dinner Party"—turned down) and one with Jay (Jack C.) Haldeman—that I bought ("Executive Clemency")—but Ben was not a fan of all this downbeat stuff.

Eventually I remember talking to Dick Teresi, a non-fiction editor at *Omni* who I considered a friend. I told him I was really frustrated that I couldn't buy what I want, and he said, 'Just take the power.' And I said, 'What do you mean?' He said, 'Don't show him the contracts.' I said, 'What?' He said, 'Just take the power.' Ooookay. It was such a weird thing to say. What I think was happening—and obviously Dick knew this—was that Ben was on his way out and Dick was being made the Editor. We never had a top editor who lasted more than two or three years at most because they were either fired or walked out.

Dick took over and he knew nothing about science fiction. He pretty much would let me buy whatever I wanted. Initially I was very nervous about it. There are stories that I didn't take.

But stories I loved that I rejected for *Omni*, I often used for reprint anthologies like the year's bests, or for half origin/half reprint anthologies like Alien Sex and Blood Is Not Enough. "All My Darling Daughters," "Down Among the Dead Men," are good examples.

GB: What was your first anthology?

ED: My very first were the reprint anthologies consisting of *Omni* stories. My first original one was Blood Is Not Enough. The way that happened is when I was at *Omni*, I was friendly with this guy who worked at Penthouse, an editor there, and he aproached me and said, 'I may have a deal with a book publisher to do a series of science fiction, fantasy, and horror anthologies. Can you come up with some themes and you could edit for them?' So I came up with four or five themes. One was alien sex, about gender relations. One about vampires/vampirism, one dubbed monkey tales, because there were a lot of stories about monkeys that I turned down and a few I'd taken. And a couple of other ideas. But the deal didn't happen. Agent Merrilee Heiffetz was a friend, and suggested that she take me on as a client and try to sell them to publishers.

Blood Is Not Enough sold to David Hartwell at William Morrow. What I did to show proof of concept was give him several already published stories on the theme that I loved, so he'd have an idea of what I wanted to do. For the vampirism anthology, I immediately thought of the Dozois/Dann story I had to turn down for *Omni*: "Down Among the Dead Men," and others that just weren't approrpiate for *Omni* but that I liked. I decided I'd publish half reprints and half originals, so that's what I actually did. The same thing with Alien Sex.

Originally, I thought it would be a conflict with *Omni* to edit a straight science fiction anthology-which is why I started with horror and with stories about sexuality that I couldn't publish in *Omni*. Initially *Omni* was publishing four or five stories a month but later on the amount became fewer and fewer, until it was only one or two- because of the mix of advertising. I wanted to edit more. No one cared that I was doing this other work. No one questioned it.

So that's how I got into creating anthologies: I wanted to do more editing.

GB: What makes for a successful anthology in your view?

ED: It depends on what you mean by successful!

First of all, trying to find a theme that is general enough—broad enough—so you can acquire stories that push against the boundaries. I especially appreciate stories that push the limit of the theme without crashing through it. If I can justify a story going into an anthology to myself, I figure that's fine.

I try to avoid narrow themes. If I could publish all non-themed anthologies, I would, but they're much harder to sell. I understand that, because there's nothing for people to hang onto. The reader doesn't know what they're going to get. So it's always difficult for the publisher to sell such an anthology. I find that readers say they want them, but not enough buy them to make them profitable. I'd love to edit more non-themed anthologies. It hasn't anything to do with quality.

Terri Windling and I co-edited *Salon Fantastique*, an anthology of all original fantasy stories, for instance, and it didn't sell well. It might have been the cover. It might have been the fact that the publishing imprint was dissolved around the publication date. But you don't know. You have no idea why one book does well and another doesn't. If anyone knew why books were bestsellers… You might think a big author will ensure an anthology sells like hotcakes—someone like Neil Gaiman—but it doesn't. Terri and I co-edited a YA vampire anthology—*Teeth* and it sold okay, but considering our advance, the sales were not good enough. *Naked City*, my urban fantasy anthology, is another book that sold a lot of copies, but not enough considering the advance.

GB: What was putting this book together like?

ED: What was interesting—and fun—putting together *Edited By* is that I had to look over all of my anthologies. I remembered most of the stories. But doing this made me realize which anthologies have the most stories that I really like. *Supernatural Noir* is one of my favorites. I took Laird Barron's story, which I love. But I could've easily taken five different stories from that book. *Inferno*, an un-themed horror anthology is another like that. I tried not to take more than one story from any one anthology.

I couldn't get all the contributors I wanted to include into the book. There just wasn't enough room for everyone.

Some decisions weren't difficult, but others were very hard. I didn't want to repeat stories from other recent reprint anthologies of mine. You don't want to edit the same book over and over.

ISFDB is great because I can see how many times stories have been reprinted and where. There were a couple I wasn't sure about that have been reprinted a lot, and ended up not taking. But then there's something like the Garth Nix that I took anyway.

Other things I had to consider: How long since a story was reprinted and, of course, the word count of each story. I had a specific amount of space.

Did I take my favorite stories by some people? No, because they might have been overused or they were too long. Lucius Shepherd's best stories are very long and many of my favorites I published in magazines or webzine, not anthologies. It was a juggling act. It always is with a reprint anthology.

GB: What makes a short story exceptional?

ED: Oh boy.

GB: Sorry.

ED: It's hitting everything. It's hitting on every cylinder. It's a combination. The perfect storm of elements. The plot may be interesting, the characters are intersting, the tone, the writing might be really great but it doesn't have to be. I love beautiful writing, but it's not necessary to all great stories. But the writing has to be at least competent. You have to at least not notice it, and if you do notice it then it must be beautiful. So…either I don't want to notice the writing at all, or I want to notice it in the "Oh my god, what a great sentence" kind of way.

You don't want it to interfere with the telling of the story. That's also an issue with some writers who are wonderful line by line writers. It depends on the story. If it's a novella or a leisurely told story, you can let beautiful writing distract a little bit. It's a combination of all the elements that make up a story. I'm always looking for what's new within the story. It might be the setting. There are only limited themes, so that's not important—it's how the story is told. It's always how the story is told. From what point of view, what time and place, the tone, the characters.

What I consider a great story may not be what someone else considers a great story. Some people find what I buy boring. Amazon reviews may say something isn't horror and I just have to say, 'I say it's horror and I don't care what you say. I'm sorry you didn't like the book, but fuck you.'

Any time an editor publishes a writer a lot, it means that editor likes their writing. We have writers who we know will write fabulous stories each year. We publish so many writers, and we don't want the same people in every anthology and I couldn't fit them anyway. I have to pick and choose.

GB: How do you look for new writers?

ED: I read so much for the *Year's Best* and I don't read only horror for it. I have an eye out for new writers whose work I like. If I like it a lot, I'll solicit them to write a story. Sometimes I solicit and the story doesn't work for me. It's heartbreaking for me (but hopefully not for them) when that happens, because I worry they'll never send me anything again. But when you're working with professionals, they don't take rejection personally.

GB: It feels like short fiction in the field is in a robust place right now.

ED: Yes. Absolutely. I have to say I don't think a lot of what is being called science fiction today is science fiction. I've always liked the term speculative fiction. It's useful for the type of fiction that isn't quite fantasy but deals more with current concerns. Fewer writers are writing what I consider to be science fiction, that is, fiction set in the future (near or far) and extrapolating from current scientific ideas (soft or hard). Science fiction is hard to write-much of it requires research that many writers have no interest in pursuing.

GB: What trends in short fiction are you seeing?

ED: First of all, the influx of non-US-based voices. I've published a lot of Canadians, Australian, and UK writers, and I don't think the US used to do that. So that's one thing that started happening, 15-20 years ago. Then in the last five years, there are even more voices-from China, Japan, India, Pakistan, Malaysia, Mexico. Not such a Western-centric point of view.

An explosion of new voices. It's great. This influences what everyone is doing.

GB: Thanks so much for talking to me, Ellen.

About the Contributors

Nathan Ballingrud is the author of *North American Lake Monsters*, *The Visible Filth*, and the forthcoming *The Atlas of Hell*. Several of his stories are in development for film and TV. He has twice won the Shirley Jackson Award. He lives somewhere in the mountains of North Carolina.

Laird Barron spent his early years in Alaska. He is the author of several books, including *The Beautiful Thing That Awaits Us All*, and *Swift to Chase*, and *Blood Standard*. His work has also appeared in many magazines and anthologies. Barron currently resides in the Rondout Valley writing stories about the evil that men do.

Elizabeth Bear was born on the same day as Frodo and Bilbo Baggins, but in a different year. She is the Hugo, Sturgeon, Locus, and Campbell Award winning author of 30 novels and over a hundred short stories. Her most recent novels are *Ancestral Night* and *The Red-Stained Wing*.

Richard Bowes has, over the last thirty-five years, published six novels, four short story collections, and eighty-plus stories. He has won two World Fantasy Awards, and the Lambda, Million Writers and International Horror Guild awards for his work.

Pat Cadigan has won the Arthur C. Clarke Award, the Hugo Award, and the Seiun Award, and is hoping to live long enough to see this book come out. It's not a sure thing but she thinks it would be foolish to bet against her.

Ted Chiang is the author of the collections *Stories of Your Life and Others* and *Exhalation*, and has won four Hugo, four Nebula, and four Locus awards.

His work has been translated into twenty-one languages. He was born in Port Jefferson, New York, and currently lives near Seattle, Washington.

Carol Emshwiller grew up in Michigan and in France and for many years divided her time between New York and California. Her stories appeared in literary and science fiction magazines for over forty years, and published in a number of critically acclaimed collections including *The Collected Stories of Carol Emshwiller* and *In Time Of War & Master Of the Road To Nowhere*. Carol's work has been honored with two Nebula Awards and the Lifetime Achievement Award from the World Fantasy Convention. She was also the recipient of a National Endowment for the Arts grant and two literary grants from New York state. She died in 2019.

Jeffrey Ford is the author of the novels *The Physiognomy, Memoranda, The Beyond, The Portrait of Mrs. Charbuque, The Girl in the Glass, The Cosmology of the Wider World, The Shadow Year, Ahab's Return*. His short story collections are *The Fantasy Writer's Assistant, The Empire of Ice Cream, The Drowned Life, Crackpot Palace, and A Natural History of Hell*.

Neil Gaiman is the Newbery Medal-winning author of *The Graveyard Book* and a *New York Times* bestselling author. Several of his books, including *Coraline*, have been made into major motion pictures. *American Gods* has been made into a mini-series for television. He is also famous for writing the *Sandman* graphic novel series and numerous other books and comics for adult, young adult, and younger readers. He has won the Hugo, Nebula, Mythopoeic, and World Fantasy awards, among others. He is also the author of many short stories and poems. For more information: www.neilgaiman.com/

Elizabeth Hand is the author of fifteen multiple-award-winning novels and collections of short fiction including *Curious Toys, Wylding Hall*, and *Generation Loss. The Book of Lamps and Banners*, her fourth noir novel featuring punk provocateur and photographer Cass Neary, will be out this year. She divides her time between the Maine coast and North London.

Glen Hirshberg is the author of five novels, including the recently completed *Motherless Children* trilogy, and four story collections. His work has earned him the Shirley Jackson Award and three International Horror Guild Awards (including two for Outstanding Collection). With Peter Atkins and Dennis Etchison, he co-founded the Rolling Darkness Revue, a long-running ghost story performance tour. He lives with his family in the Los Angeles area, where he also teaches.

Award-winning Jamaican author Nalo Hopkinson lived in Jamaica, Guyana, the US and Trinidad before moving to Canada as a teenager. She has published six novels and numerous short stories. She is currently a professor of Creative Writing at the University of California, Riverside. She is the author of *The House of Whispers*, a serialized comic in Neil Gaiman's "Sandman" Universe.

K. W. Jeter is the author of *Dr. Adder*, *Farewell Horizontal*, and other novels. His most recent publication is *Real Dangerous Place*, the third book in his Kim Oh thriller series.

Kij Johnson's short fiction has won the Hugo, Nebula, World Fantasy, and Sturgeon Awards, as well as the Grand Prix de l'Imaginaire. She is the associate director for the Gunn Center for the Study of Science Fiction at the University of Kansas, where she is also an associate professor.

Stephen Graham Jones is the author of seventeen novels and six story collections. Coming next is *Elk Head Woman* from Saga Press. Stephen lives and teaches in Boulder, Colorado.

Caitlín R. Kiernan sold her first short story in 1993, and since then her short fiction has been collected in numerous volumes, beginning with *Tales of Pain and Wonder*, and including the World Fantasy Award-winning *The Ape's Wife and Other Stories*, and most recently *The Very Best of Caitlín R. Kiernan*. Her novels include *The Red Tree* and the Bram Stoker Award-winning *The Drowning Girl: A Memoir*. She lives in Birmingham, Alabama.

Kathe Koja writes award-winning novels and short fiction. *Velocities*, a new collection, and *The Cipher*, a reprint of her seminal first novel, are out in 2020. She creates immersive performance events, solo and in collaboration, with Loudermilk Productions.

Margo Lanagan has published eight collections of shorter works, two novels (*Tender Morsels* and *The Brides of Rollrock Island*) and numerous anthologized stories. She is a four-time winner of the World Fantasy Award. She lives in Sydney, Australia.

John Langan is the author of two novels and three collections of stories. He lives in the Mid-Hudson Valley with his wife and younger son.

Kelly Link is the author of four collections, including *Get in Trouble*, a Pulitzer finalist. With Gavin J. Grant, she cofounded Small Beer Press and continues to edit the zine *Lady Churchill's Rosebud Wristlet*. Together they edited the fantasy half of *The Year's Best Fantasy and Horror* for several years, as well as the anthologies *Monstrous Affections* and *Steampunk!* She lives with her family in Northampton, Massachusetts.

Livia Llewellyn's fiction has appeared in over forty anthologies and magazines and has been reprinted in multiple best-of anthologies, including *The Best Horror of the Year*, *Year's Best Weird Fiction*, and *The Mammoth Book of Best New Erotica*. Her short story collections *Engines of Desire: Tales of Love & Other Horrors* and *Furnace* were both nominated for the Shirley Jackson Award for Best Collection. You can find her online at liviallewellyn.com.

Ian McDonald is an SFF writer living in Northern Ireland, just outside Belfast. He's been nominated for all the major SF awards—and even won a few. His first novel was *Desolation Road* in 1988, his most recent is *Luna: Moon Rising*, the conclusion of the Luna trilogy, from Tor and Gollancz. His next project is *Hopeland*, a novel.

As a writer, a scientist, an educator, and a toy maker, Pat Murphy invents new futures. Her fiction has won the Nebula Award, the World Fantasy Award, the Philip K. Dick Award, the Christopher Award, and the Theodore Sturgeon Memorial Award. Currently she works as Activity Guru at Mystery. org, a company that inspires children to love science.

New York Times bestselling author Garth Nix has been a full-time writer since 2001, but has also worked in various roles in publishing and marketing, and as a part-time soldier in the Australian Army Reserve. Garth's books include the Old Kingdom series beginning with *Sabriel*; The Seventh Tower sequence; The Keys to the Kingdom series beginning with *Mister Monday*, and many more. His next book is a fantasy novel, *Angel Mage*, out late 2019. His work has been translated into 42 languages.

Priya Sharma's fiction has appeared in venues such as *Interzone, Black Static, Nightmare, The Dark* and *Tor* and has been anthologized in many *Best ofs*. Her story "Fabulous Beasts" was a Shirley Jackson Award finalist and won a British Fantasy Award for Short Fiction. *All the Fabulous Beasts* is a collection of some of her work published by Undertow Publications in 2018. www. priyasharmafiction.wordpress.com

Lucius Shepard was born in Lynchburg Virginia, grew up in Daytona Beach, Florida, and lived the last years of his life in Portland, Oregon. His short fiction won the Nebula Award, the Hugo Award, The International Horror Writers Award, The National Magazine Award, the Locus Award, The Theodore Sturgeon Award, and the World Fantasy Award.

His strongest suit might have been his novellas, the last collection of which was *Five Autobiographies and a Fiction*. He died in 2014.

Catherynne M. Valente is the *New York Times* and *USA Today* bestselling author of many fantasy and science fiction novels, short stories, and poetry, including the *Fairyland* novels, *Deathless, Palimpsest, The Refrigerator*

Monologues, and *Space Opera*. She lives on a small island off the coast of Maine with her partner, animals, and son.

Howard Waldrop was born in Mississippi and currently lives in Austin, Texas. He is the author of multiple collections of his work including *Howard Who? Night of the Cooters, Strange Monsters of the Distant Past*, and *Horse of a Different Color: Stories*. His novella "The Ugly Chickens" won the Nebula and World Fantasy Award.

Jack Womack, born in Lexington, KY, lives in NYC with his family. He has published seven novels and one non-fiction catalog, and is best known for the novel, *Random Acts of Senseless Violence*.

Jane Yolen has more than 376 books out as she writes this, more by the time you read it. Her books and stories have won two Nebulas, three World Fantasy awards, three Mythopoeic Awards, Two Christopher Medals, the Jewish Books Award, a National Book Award nomination, the Regina Medal from the Catholic Library Association, and more citations for a body of work than she can count. One of her awards set her good coat on fire.

About the Editor

Ellen Datlow has been editing science fiction, fantasy, and horror short fiction for over thirty-five years as fiction editor of *Omni Magazine* and editor of *Event Horizon* and SCIFICTION. She currently acquires short stories and novellas for Tor.com. In addition, she has edited about one hundred science fiction, fantasy, and horror anthologies, including the annual *The Best Horror of the Year* series, *The Doll Collection*, *Children of Lovecraft*, *Nightmares: A New Decade of Modern Horror*, *Black Feathers*, *Mad Hatters and March Hares*, *The Devil and the Deep: Horror Stories of the Sea*, *Echoes: The Saga Anthology of Ghost Stories*, and *The Best of the Best Horror of the Year*. Forthcoming is *Final Cuts*-all new horror stories about movies and movie-making (Blumhouse/Anchor).

She's won multiple World Fantasy Awards, Locus Awards, Hugo Awards, Bram Stoker Awards, International Horror Guild Awards, Shirley Jackson Awards, and the 2012 Il Posto Nero Black Spot Award for Excellence as Best Foreign Editor. Datlow was named recipient of the 2007 Karl Edward Wagner Award, given at the British Fantasy Convention for "outstanding contribution to the genre," was honored with the Life Achievement Award by the Horror Writers Association, in acknowledgment of superior achievement over an entire career, and honored with the World Fantasy Life Achievement Award at the 2014 World Fantasy Convention.

She lives in New York and co-hosts the monthly Fantastic Fiction Reading Series at KGB Bar. More information can be found at www.datlow.com, on Facebook, and on twitter as @EllenDatlow. She's owned by two cats.

Copyrights

Copyrights

"Black Nightgown" by K. W. Jeter. Copyright © 1994. First published in *Little Deaths* edited by Ellen Datlow, Millennium. Reprinted with permission of the author.

"A Delicate Architecture" by Catherynne M. Valente. Copyright © 2009. First published in *Troll's Eye View: A Book of Villainess Tales* edited by Ellen Datlow and Terri Windling, Viking Books for Young Readers. Reprinted with permission of the author.

"The Goosle" by Margo Lanagan. Copyright © 2008. First published in *The Del Rey Anthology of Science Fiction and Fantasy* edited by Ellen Datlow, Del Rey Books. Reprinted with permission of the author.

"Eaten (Scenes from a Moving Picture)" by Neil Gaiman. Copyright © 1996. First published in *Off Limits* edited by Ellen Datlow, St. Martin's Press. Reprinted by permission of the author.

"Teratisms" by Kathe Koja. Copyright © 1991. First published in *A Whisper of Blood* edited by Ellen Datlow, William Morrow. Reprinted with permission of the author.

"The Monsters of Heaven" by Nathan Ballingrud. Copyright © 2007. First published in *Inferno* edited by Ellen Datlow, Tor Books. Reprinted with permission of the author.

"That Old School Tie" by Jack Womack. Copyright © 1994. First published in *Little Deaths: Twenty-Four Tales of Sex and Horror* edited by Ellen Datlow, Millennium. Reprinted with permission of the author.

"Love and Sex Among the Invertebrates" by Pat Murphy. Copyright © 1990. First published in *Alien Sex* edited by Ellen Datlow, E.P. Dutton. Reprinted with permission of the author.

"Overlooking" by Carol Emshwiller. Copyright © 2002. First published in *The Green Man: Tales From the Mythic Forest* edited by Ellen Datlow and Terri Windling, Viking. Reprinted with permission of the author's estate.